WYLDER'S HAND

WYLDER'S HAND

J. SHERIDAN LEFANU

DOVER PUBLICATIONS, INC.
NEW YORK

Published in Canada by General Publishing Company, Ltd., 30 Lesmill Road, Don Mills, Toronto, Ontario.

Published in the United Kingdom by Constable and Company, Ltd., 10 Orange Street, London WC2H 7EG.

This Dover edition, first published in 1978, is an unabridged republication of the 1898 edition, published by Downey & Co., Ltd., London, of the work originally published in 1864.

International Standard Book Number: 0-486-23570-X
Library of Congress Catalog Card Number: 77-84059

Manufactured in the United States of America
Dover Publications, Inc.
180 Varick Street
New York, N.Y. 10014

CONTENTS.

WYLDER'S HAND.

CHAPTER I.

RELATING HOW I DROVE THROUGH THE VILLAGE OF GYLING-DEN WITH MARK WYLDER'S LETTER IN MY VALISE.

T was late in the autumn, and I was skimming along, through a rich English county, in a postchaise, among tall hedgerows gilded, like all the landscape, with the slanting beams of sunset. The road makes a long and easy descent into the little town of Gylingden, and down this we were going at an exhilarating pace, and the jingle of the vehicle sounded like sledge-bells in my ears, and its swaying and jerking were pleasant and life-like. I fancy I was in one of those moods which, under similar circumstances, I sometimes experience still—a semi-narcotic excitement, silent but delightful.

An undulating landscape, with a homely farmstead here and there, and plenty of old English timber scattered grandly over it, extended mistily to my right ; on the left the road is overtopped by masses of noble forest. The old park of Brandon lies there, more than four miles from end to end. These masses of solemn and discoloured verdure, the faint but splendid lights, and long filmy shadows, the slopes and hollows—my eyes wandered over them all with that strange sense of unreality, and that mingling of sweet and bitter fancy, with which we revisit a scene familiar in very remote and early childhood, and which has haunted a long interval of maturity and absence, like a romantic reverie.

As I looked through the chaise-windows, every moment presented some group, or outline, or homely object, for years forgotten ; and now, with a strange surprise how vividly remembered and how affectionately greeted ! We drove by the small old house at the left, with its double gable and pretty grass garden, and trim yews and modern lilacs and laburnums, backed by the grand timber of the park. It was the parsonage, and old bachelor Doctor Crewe, the rector, in my nonage, still stood, in memory, at the door, in his black shorts and gaiters, with his hands in his pockets, and a puckered smile on his hard ruddy countenance, as I approached. He smiled little on others I believe, but always kindly upon me. This general liking for children and instinct of smiling on them is one source of the delightful illusions which make the remembrance of early days so like a dream of Paradise, and give us, at starting, such false notions of our value.

There was a little fair-haired child playing on the ground before the steps as I whirled by. The old rector had long passed away; the shorts, gaiters, and smile—a phantom; and nature, who had gathered in the past, was providing for the future.

The pretty mill-road, running up through Redman's Dell, dank and dark with tall romantic trees, was left behind in another moment; and we were now traversing the homely and antique street of the little town, with its queer shops and solid steep-roofed residences. Up Church-street I contrived a peep at the old gray tower where the chimes hung; and as we turned the corner a glance at the 'Brandon Arms.' How very small and low that palatial hostelry of my earlier recollections had grown! There were new faces at the door. It was only two-and-twenty years ago, and I was then but eleven years old. A retrospect of a score of years or so, at three-and-thirty, is a much vaster affair than a much longer one at fifty.

The whole thing seemed like yesterday; and as I write, I open my eyes and start and cry, 'can it be twenty, five-and-twenty, aye, by Jove! five-and-thirty, years since then?' How my days have flown! And I think when another such yesterday shall have arrived, where shall I be?

The first ten years of my life were longer than all the rest put together, and I think would continue to be so were my future extended to an ante-Noachian span. It is the first ten that emerge from nothing, and commencing in a point, it is during them that consciousness, memory—all the faculties grow, and the experience of sense is so novel, crowded, and astounding. It is this beginning at a point, and expanding to the immense disk of our present range of sensuous experience, that gives to them so prodigious an illusory perspective, and makes us in childhood, measuring futurity by them, form so wild and exaggerated an estimate of the duration of human life. But, I beg your pardon.

My journey was from London. When I had reached my lodgings, after my little excursion up the Rhine, upon my table there lay, among the rest, one letter—there generally *is* in an overdue bundle—which I viewed with suspicion. I could not in the least tell why. It was a broad-faced letter, of bluish complexion, and had made inquisition after me in the country—had asked for me at Queen's Folkstone; and, *vised* by my cousin, had presented itself at the Friars, in Shropshire, and thence proceeded by Sir Harry's direction (there was the autograph) to Nolton Hall; thence again to Ilchester, whence my fiery and decisive old aunt sent it straight back to my cousin, with a whisk of her pen which seemed to say, 'How the plague can I tell where the puppy is ?—'tis your business, Sir, not mine, to find him out!' And so my cousin despatched it to my head-quarters in town, where from the table it looked up in my face, with a broad red seal, and a countenance scarred and marred all over with various post-marks, erasures, and transverse directions, the scars and furrows of disappointment and adventure.

It had not a good countenance, somehow. The original lines were not prepossessing. The handwriting I knew as one sometimes knows a face, without being able to remember who the plague it belongs to; but, still, with an unpleasant association about it. I examined it carefully, and laid it down unopened. I went through half-a-dozen others, and recurred to it, and puzzled over its exterior again, and again postponed what I fancied would prove a disagreeable discovery; and this happened every now and again, until I had quite exhausted my budget, and then I did open it, and looked straight to the signature.

'Pooh! Mark Wylder,' I exclaimed, a good deal relieved.

Mark Wylder! Yes, Master Mark could not hurt *me*. There was nothing about him to excite the least uneasiness; on the contrary, I believe he liked me as well as he was capable of liking anybody, and it was now seven years since we had met.

I have often since thought upon the odd sensation with which I hesitated over his unopened letter; and now, remembering how the breaking of that seal resembled, in my life, the breaking open of a portal through which I entered a labyrinth, or rather a catacomb, where for many days I groped and stumbled, looking for light, and was, in a manner, lost, hearing strange sounds, witnessing imperfectly strange sights, and, at last, arriving at a dreadful chamber—a sad sort of superstition steals over me.

I had then been his working junior in the cause of Wylder *v.* Trustees of Brandon, minor—Dorcas Brandon, his own cousin. There was a complicated cousinship among these Brandons, Wylders, and Lakes—inextricable intermarriages, which, five years ago, before I renounced the bar, I had at my fingers' ends, but which had now relapsed into haze. There must have been some damnable taint in the blood of the common ancestor—a spice of the insane and the diabolical. They were an ill-conditioned race—that is to say, every now and then there emerged a miscreant, with a pretty evident vein of madness. There was Sir Jonathan Brandon, for instance, who ran his own nephew through the lungs in a duel fought in a paroxysm of Cencian jealousy; and afterwards shot his coachman dead upon the box through his coach-window, and finally died in Vienna, whither he had absconded, of a pike-thrust received from a sentry in a brawl.

The Wylders had not much to boast of, even in contrast with that wicked line. They had produced their madmen and villains, too; and there had been frequent intermarriages—not very often happy. There had been many lawsuits, frequent disinheritings, and even worse doings. The Wylders of Brandon appear very early in history; and the Wylder arms, with their legend, 'resurgam,' stands in bold relief over the great door of Brandon Hall. So there were Wylders of Brandon, and Brandons of Brandon. In one generation, a Wylder ill-using his wife and hating his children, would cut them all off, and send the estate bounding back again to the Brandons. The next generation or two would amuse themselves with a lawsuit, until the old Brandon type reappeared in some bachelor brother or uncle, with a Jezebel on his left hand, and an attorney on his right, and, presto! the estates were back again with the Wylders.

A 'statement of title' is usually a dry affair. But that of the dynasty of Brandon Hall was a truculent romance. Their very 'wills' were spiced with the devilment of the 'testators,' and abounded in insinuations and even language which were scandalous.

Here is Mark Wylder's letter:—

'DEAR CHARLES—Of course you have heard of my good luck, and how kind poor Dickie—from whom I never expected anything—proved at last. It was a great windfall for a poor devil like me; but, after all, it was only right, for it ought never to have been his at all. I went down and took possession on the 4th, the tenants very glad, and so they might well be; for, between ourselves, Dickie, poor fellow, was not always pleasant to deal with. He let the roof all out of repair, and committed waste beside in timber he had no right to in life, as I am told; but that don't signify much, only the house will cost me a pretty penny to get it into order and furnish. The rental is five thousand a-year and some hundreds, and the rents can be got up a bit—so Larkin tells me. Do you know anything of him? He says he did business for your uncle once. He seems a clever fellow—a bit too clever, perhaps—and was too much master here, I suspect, in poor Dickie's reign. Tell me all you can make out about him. It is a long time since I saw you, Charles; I'm grown brown, and great whiskers. I met poor Dominick—what an ass that chap is—but he did not know me till I introduced myself, so I must be a good deal changed. Our ship was at Malta when I got the letter. I was sick of the service, and no wonder: a lieutenant—and there likely to stick all my days.

Six months, last year, on the African coast, watching slavers—think of that! I had a long yarn from the viscount—advice, and that sort of thing. I do not think he is a year older than I, but takes airs because he's a trustee. But I only laugh at trifles that would have riled me once. So I wrote him a yarn in return, and drew it uncommon mild. And he has been useful to me; and I think matters are pretty well arranged to disappoint the kind intention of good Uncle Wylder—the brute; he hated my father, but that was no reason to persecute me, and I but an infant, almost, when he died, d— him. Well, you know he left Brandon with some charges to my Cousin Dorcas. She is a superbly fine girl. Our ship was at Naples when she was there two years ago; and I saw a good deal of her. Of course it was not to be thought of then; but matters are quite different, you know, now, and the viscount, who is a very sensible fellow in the main, saw it at once. You see, the old brute meant to leave her a life estate; but it does not amount to that, though it won't benefit me, for he settled that when I die it shall go to his right heirs—that will be to my son, if I ever have one. So Miss Dorcas must pack, and turn out whenever I die, that is, if I slip my cable first. Larkin told me this—and I took an opinion—and found it is so; and the viscount seeing it, agreed the best thing for her as well as me would be, we should marry. She is a wide-awake young lady, and nothing the worse for that: I'm a bit that way myself. And so very little courtship has sufficed. She is a splendid beauty, and when you see her you'll say any fellow might be proud of such a bride; and so I am. And now, dear Charlie, you have it all. It will take place somewhere about the twenty-fourth of next month; and you must come down by the first, if you can. Don't disappoint. I want you for best man, maybe; and besides, I would like to talk to you about some things they want me to do in the settlements, and you were always a long-headed fellow: so pray don't refuse.

'Dear Charlie, ever most sincerely,

'Your old Friend,

'MARK WYLDER.

'P.S.—I stay at the Brandon Arms in the town, until after the marriage; and then you can have a room at the Hall, and capital shooting when we return, which will be in a fortnight after.'

I can't say that Wylder was an old *friend*. But he was certainly one of the oldest and most intimate acquaintances I had. We had been for nearly three years at school together; and when his ship came to England, met frequently; and twice, when he was on leave, we had been for months together under the same roof; and had for some years kept up a regular correspondence, which first grew desultory, and finally, as manhood supervened, died out. The plain truth is, I did not *very* much like him.

Then there was that beautiful apathetic Dorcas Brandon. Where is the laggard so dull as to experience no pleasing flutter at his heart in anticipation of meeting a perfect beauty in a country house. I was romantic, like every other youngish fellow who is not a premature curmudgeon ; and there was something indefinitely pleasant in the consciousness that, although a betrothed bride, the young lady still was fancy free : not a bit in love. It was but a marriage of convenience, with mitigations. And so there hovered in my curiosity some little flicker of egotistic romance, which helped to rouse my spirits, and spur me on to action.

CHAPTER II.

IN WHICH I ENTER THE DRAWING-ROOM.

I WAS now approaching Brandon Hall ; less than ten minutes more would set me down at its door-steps. The stiff figure of Mrs. Marston, the old housekeeper, pale and austere, in rustling black silk (she was accounted a miser, and estimated to have saved I dare not say how much money in the Wylder family—kind to me with the bread-and-jam and Naples-biscuit-kindness of her species, in old times)—stood in fancy at the doorway. She, too, was a dream, and, I dare say, her money spent by this time. And that other dream, to which she often led me, with the large hazel eyes, and clear delicate tints—so sweet, so *riante*, yet so sad ; poor Lady Mary Brandon, dying there—so unhappily mated—a young mother, and her baby sleeping in long 'Broderie Anglaise' attire upon the pillow on the sofa, and whom she used to show me with a peeping mystery, and her finger to her smiling lip, and a gaiety and fondness in her pretty face. That little helpless, groping, wailing creature was now the Dorcas Brandon, the mistress of the grand old mansion and all its surroundings, who was the heroine of the splendid matrimonial compromise which was about to reconcile a feud, and avert a possible lawsuit, and, for one generation, at least, to tranquillise the troubled annals of the Brandons and Wylders.

And now the ancient gray chapel, with its stained window, and store of old Brandon and Wylder monuments among its solemn clump of elm-trees, flitted by on my right ; and in a moment more we drew up at the great gate on the left, not a hundred yards removed from it, and with an eager recognition, I gazed on the noble front of the old manorial house.

Up the broad straight avenue with its solemn files of gigantic timber towering at the right and the left hand, the chaise rolled smoothly, and through the fantastic iron gate of the courtyard, and with a fine swinging sweep and a jerk, we drew up handsomely before the door-steps, with the Wylder arms in bold and florid projection carved above it.

The sun had just gone down. The blue shadows of twilight overcast the landscape, and the mists of night were already stealing like thin smoke among the trunks and roots of the trees. Through the stone mullions of the projecting window at the right, a flush of fire-light looked pleasant and hospitable, and on the threshold were standing Lord Chelford and my old friend Mark Wylder; a faint perfume of the mildest cheroot declared how they had been employed.

So I jumped to the ground and was greeted very kindly by the smokers.

' I'm here, you know, *in loco parentis;*—my mother and I keep watch and ward. We allow Wylder, you see, to come every day to his devotions. But you are not to go to the Brandon Arms—you got my note, didn't you ?'

I had, and had come direct to the Hall in consequence.

I looked over the door. Yes, my memory had served me right. There were the Brandon arms, and the Brandon quartered with the Wylder ; but the Wylder coat in the centre, with the grinning griffins for supporters, and flaunting scrolls all round, and the ominous word ' resurgam' underneath, proclaimed itself sadly and vauntingly over the great entrance. I often wonder how the Wylder coat came in the centre ; who built the old house—a Brandon or a Wylder ; and if a Wylder, why was it Brandon Hall ?

Dusty and seedy somewhat, as men are after a journey, I chatted with Mark and the noble peer for a few minutes at the door, while my valise and *et ceteras* were lifted in and hurried up the stairs to my room, whither I followed them.

While I was at my toilet, in came Mark Wylder laughing, as was his wont, and very unceremoniously he took possession of my easy-chair, and threw his leg over the arm of it.

' I'm glad you're come, Charlie ; you were always a good fellow, and I really want a hand here confoundedly. I think it will all do very nicely ; but, of course, there's a lot of things to be arranged—settlements, you know—and I can't make head or tail of their lingo, and a fellow don't like to sign and seal hand over head—*you* would not advise that, you know ; and Chelford is a very good fellow, of course, and all that—but he's taking care of Dorcas, you see ; and I might be left in the lurch.'

It is a better way, at all events, Mark, than Wylder *versus* Trustees of Brandon, minor,' said I.

'Well, things do turn out very oddly ; don't they ?' said Mark with a sly glance of complacency, and his hands in his pockets. ' But I know you'll hold the tiller till I get through ; hang me if I know the soundings, or where I'm going ; and you have the chart by heart, Charlie.'

' I'm afraid you'll find me by no means so well up now as six years ago in "Wylder and Brandon ;" but surely you have your lawyer, Mr. Larkin, haven't you ?'

' To be sure—that's exactly it—he's Dorcas's agent. I don't know anything about him, and I do know you—don't you see ? A fellow doesn't want to put himself into the hands of a stranger altogether, especially a lawyer, ha, ha ! it wouldn't pay.'

I did not half like the equivocal office which my friend Mark had prepared for me. If family squabbles were to arise, I had no fancy to mix in them ; and I did not want a collision with Mr. Larkin either ; and, on the whole, notwithstanding his modesty, I thought Wylder very well able to take care of himself. There was time enough, however, to settle the point. So by this time, being splendid in French boots and white vest, and altogether perfect and refreshed, I emerged from my dressing-room, Wylder by my side.

We had to get along a dim oak-panelled passage, and into a sort of *œil-de-bœuf*, with a lantern light above, from which diverged two other solemn corridors, and a short puzzling turn or two brought us to the head of the upper stairs. For I being a bachelor, and treated accordingly, was airily perched on the third storey.

To my mind, there is something indescribably satisfactory in the intense solidity of those old stairs and floors—no spring in the planks, not a creak ; you walk as over strata of stone. What clumsy grandeur ! What Cyclopean carpenters ! What a prodigality of oak !

It was dark by this time, and the drawing-room, a vast and grand chamber, with no light but the fire and a pair of dim soft lamps near the sofas and ottomans, lofty, and glowing with rich tapestry curtains and pictures, and mirrors, and carved oak, and marble—was already tenanted by the ladies.

Old Lady Chelford, stiff and rich, a Vandyke dowager, with a general effect of deep lace, funereal velvet, and pearls ; and pale, with dreary eyes, and thin high nose, sat in a high-backed carved oak throne, with red cushions. To her I was first presented, and cursorily scrutinised with a stately old-fashioned insolence, as if I were a candidate footman, and so dismissed. On a low seat, chatting to her as I came up, was a very handsome and rather singular-looking girl, fair, with a light golden-tinted hair ; and a countenance, though then grave enough, instinc•

with a certain promise of animation and spirit not to be mistaken. Could this be the heroine of the pending alliance? No; I was mistaken. A third lady, at what would have been an ordinary room's length away, half reclining on an ottoman, was now approached by Wylder, who presented me to Miss Brandon.

'Dorcas, this is my old friend, Charles de Cresseron. You have often heard me speak of him; and I want you to shake hands and make his acquaintance, and draw him out—do you see; for he's a shy youth, and must be encouraged.'

He gave me a cheerful slap on the shoulder as he uttered this agreeable bit of banter, and altogether disconcerted me confoundedly. Wylder's dress-coats always smelt of tobacco, and his talk of tar. I was quietly incensed and disgusted; for in those days I *was* a little shy.

The lady rose, in a soft floating way; tall, black-haired—but a blackness with a dull rich shadow through it. I had only a general impression of large dusky eyes and very exquisite features—more delicate than the Grecian models, and with a wonderful transparency, like tinted marble; and a superb haughtiness, quite unaffected. She held forth her hand, which I did little more than touch. There was a peculiarity in her greeting, which I felt a little overawing, without exactly discovering in what it consisted; and it was I think that she did not smile. She never took that trouble for form's sake, like other women.

So, as Wylder had set a chair for me I could not avoid sitting upon it, though I should much have preferred standing, after the manner of men, and retaining my liberty.

CHAPTER III.

OUR DINNER PARTY AT BRANDON.

I WAS curious. I had heard a great deal of her beauty, and it had exceeded all I heard ; so I talked my sublimest and brightest chit-chat, in my most musical tones, and was rather engaging and amusing, I ventured to hope. But the best man cannot manage a dialogue alone. Miss Brandon was plainly not a person to make any sort of exertion towards what is termed keeping up a conversation ; at all events she did not, and after a while the present one got into a decidedly sinking condition. An acquiescence, a faint expression of surprise, a fainter smile—she contributed little more, after the first few questions of courtesy had been asked, in her low silvery tones, and answered by me. To me the natural demise of a *tête-à-tête* discourse has always seemed a disgrace. But this apathetic beauty had either more moral courage or more stupidity than I, and was plainly terribly indifferent about the catastrophe. I've sometimes thought my struggles and sinkings amused her cruel serenity.

Bella ma stupida !—I experienced, at last, the sort of pique with which George Sand's hero apostrophises *la derniere Aldini.* Yet I could not think her stupid. The universal instinct honours beauty. It is so difficult to believe it either dull or base. In virtue of some mysterious harmonies it is ' the image of God,' and must, we feel, enclose the God-like ; so I suppose I felt, for though I wished to think her stupid, I could not. She was not exactly languid, but a grave and listless beauty, and a splendid beauty for all that.

I told her my early recollections of Brandon and Gylingden, and how I remembered her a baby, and said some graceful trifles on that theme, which I fancied were likely to please. But they were only received, and led to nothing. In a little while in comes Lord Chelford, always natural and pleasant, and quite unconscious of his peerage—he was above it, I think—and chatted away merrily with that handsome animated blonde—who on earth, could she be ?—and did not seem the least chilled in the stiff and frosted presence of his mother, but was genial and playful even with that Spirit of the Frozen Ocean, who received his affectionate trifling with a sort of smiling, though wintry pride and complacency, reflecting back from her icy aspects something of the rosy tints of that kindly sunshine.

I thought I heard him call the young lady Miss Lake, and

there rose before me an image of an old General Lake, and a dim recollection of some reverse of fortune. He was—I was sure of that—connected with the Brandon family ; and was, with the usual fatality, a bit of a *mauvais sujet.* He had made away with his children's money, or squandered his own ; or somehow or another impoverished his family not creditably. So I glanced at her, and Miss Brandon divined, it seemed, what was passing in my mind, for she said :—

' That is my cousin, Miss Lake, and I think her very beautiful —don't you ? '

' Yes, she certainly is very handsome, and I was going to say something about her animation and spirit, but remembered just in time, that that line of eulogy would hardly have involved a compliment to Miss Brandon. I know her brother, a little—that is, Captain Lake—Stanley Lake ; he's her brother, I fancy ? '

' *Oh ?* ' said the young lady, in that tone which is pointed with an unknown accent, between a note of enquiry and of surprise. ' Yes ; he's her brother.'

And she paused ; as if something more were expected. But at that moment the bland tones of Larcom, the solemn butler, announced the Rev. William Wylder and Mrs. Wylder, and I said—

" William is an old college friend of mine ; ' and I observed him, as he entered with an affectionate and sad sort of interest. Eight years had passed since we met last, and that is something at any time. It had thinned my simple friend's hair a little, and his face, too, was more careworn than I liked, but his earnest, sweet smile was there still. Slight, gentle, with something of a pale and studious refinement in his face. The same gentle voice, with that slight, occasional hesitation, which somehow I liked. There is always a little shock after an absence of some years before identities adjust themselves, and then we find the change is not, after all, so very great. I suspect it is, rather, that something of the old picture is obliterated, in that little interval, to return no more. And so William Wylder was vicar now instead of that straight wiry cleric of the mulberry face and black leggings.

And who was this little Mrs. William Wylder who came in, so homely of feature, so radiant of goodhumour, so eager and simple, in a very plain dress—a Brandon housemaid would not have been seen in it, leaning so pleasantly on his lean, long, clerical arm—made for reaching books down from high shelves, a lank, scholarlike limb, with a somewhat threadbare cuff—and who looked round with that anticipation of pleasure, and that simple confidence in a real welcome, which are so likely to insure it ? Was she an helpmeet for a black-letter man, who talked with the Fathers in his daily walks, could extemporise Latin hexameters, and dream in Greek. Was she very wise, or at all learned ?

I think her knowledge lay chiefly in the matters of poultry, and puddings, and latterly, of the nursery, where one treasure lay— that golden-haired little boy, four years old, whom I had seen playing among the roses before the parsonage door, asleep by this time—half-past seven, 'precise,' as old Lady Chelford loved to write on her summons to dinner.

When the vicar, I dare say, in a very odd, quaint way, made his proposal of marriage, moved thereto assuredly, neither by fortune, nor by beauty, to good, merry, little Miss Dorothy Chubley, whom nobody was supposed to be looking after, and the town had, somehow, set down from the first as a natural-born old maid—there was a very general amazement; some disappointment here and there, with customary sneers and compassion, and a good deal of genuine amusement not ill-natured.

Miss Chubley, all the shopkeepers in the town knew and liked, and, in a way, respected her, as 'Miss Dolly.' Old Reverend John Chubley, D.D., who had been in love with his wife from the period of his boyhood; and yet so grudging was Fate, had to undergo an engagement of nigh thirty years before Hymen rewarded their constancy; being at length made Vicar of Huddelston, and master of church revenues to the amount of three hundred pounds a year—had, at forty-five, married his early love, now forty-two.

They had never grown old in one another's fond eyes. Their fidelity was of the days of chivalry, and their simplicity comical and beautiful. Twenty years of happy and loving life were allotted them and one pledge—poor Miss Dorothy—was left alone, when little more than nineteen years old. This good old couple, having loved early and waited long, and lived together with wonderful tenderness and gaiety of heart their allotted span, bid farewell for a little while—the gentle little lady going first, and, in about two years more, the good rector following.

I remembered him, but more dimly than his merry little wife, though she went first. She made raisin-wine, and those curious biscuits that tasted of Windsor soap.

And this Mrs. William Wylder just announced by soft-toned Larcom, is the daughter (there is no mistaking the jolly smile and lumpy odd little features, and radiance of amiability) of the good doctor and Mrs. Chubley, so curiously blended in her loving face. And last comes in old Major Jackson, smiling largely, squaring himself, and doing his courtesies in a firm but florid military style, and plainly pleased to find himself in good company and on the eve of a good dinner. And so our dinner-list is full.

The party were just nine—and it is wonderful what a row nine well-behaved people will contrive to make at a dinner-table. The inferior animals—as we see them caged and cared for, and fed at one o'clock, 'precise,' in those public institutions provided for their maintenance—confine their uproar to the period immediately antecedent to their meal, and perform the actual process of deglutition with silent attention, and only such suckings, lappings, and crunchings, as illustrate their industry and content. It is the distinctive privilege of man to exert his voice during his repast, and to indulge also in those specially human cachinnations which no lower creature, except that disreputable Australian biped known as the 'laughing jackass,' presumes to imitate ; and to these vocal exercises of the feasters respond the endless ring and tinkle of knife and fork on china plate, and the ministering angels in white chokers behind the chairs, those murmured solicitations which hum round and round the ears of the revellers.

Of course, when great guns are present, and people talk *pro bono publico*, one at a time, with parliamentary regularity, things are different; but at an ordinary symposium, when the garrulous and diffident make merry together, and people break into twos or threes and talk across the table, or into their neighbours' ears, and all together, the noise is not only exhilarating and peculiar, but sometimes perfectly unaccountable.

The talk, of course, has its paroxysms and its subsidences. I have once or twice found myself on a sudden in total silence in the middle of a somewhat prolix, though humorous story, commenced in an uproar for the sole recreation of my pretty neighbour, and ended — patched up, *renounced* — a faltering failure, under the converging gaze of a sternly attentive audience.

On the other hand, there are moments when the uproar whirls up in a crescendo to a pitch and volume perfectly amazing ; and at such times, I believe that anyone might say anything to the reveller at his elbow, without the smallest risk of being overheard by mortal. You may plan with young Cæsar Borgia, on your left, the poisoning of your host ; or ask pretty Mrs. Fusible, on your right, to elope with you from her grinning and gabbling lord, whose bald head flashes red with champagne only at the other side of the table. There is no privacy like it ; you may plot your wickedness, or make your confession, or pop the question, and not a soul but your confidant be a bit the wiser—provided only you command your countenance.

I don't know how it happened, but Wylder sat beside Miss Lake. I fancied he ought to have been differently placed, but Miss Brandon did not seem conscious of his absence, and it seemed to me that the handsome blonde would have been as well pleased if he had been anywhere but where he was. There was no look of liking, though some faint glimmerings both of annoyance and embarrassment in her face. But in Wylder's I saw a sort of conceited consciousness, and a certain eagerness, too, while he talked ; though a shrewd fellow in many ways, he had a secret conviction that no woman could resist him.

'I suppose the world thinks me a very happy fellow, Miss Lake?' he said, with a rather pensive glance of enquiry into that young lady's eyes, as he set down his hock-glass.

'I'm afraid it's a selfish world, Mr. Wylder, and thinks very little of what does not concern it.'

'Now, *you*, I dare say,' continued Wylder, not caring to perceive the *soupçon* of sarcasm that modulated her answer so musically, 'look upon me as a very fortunate fellow?'

'You *are* a very fortunate person, Mr. Wylder; a gentleman of very moderate abilities, with no prospects, and without fortune, who finds himself, without any deservings of his own, on a sudden, possessed of an estate, and about to be united to the most beautiful heiress in England, *is*, I think, rather a fortunate person.'

'You did not always think me so stupid, Miss Lake,' said Mr. Wylder, showing something of the hectic of vexation.

'Stupid! did I say? Well, you know, we learn by experience, Mr. Wylder. One's judgment matures, and we are harder to please—don't you think so?—as we grow older.'

'Aye, so we are, I dare say; at any rate, some things don't please us as we calculated. I remember when this bit of luck would have made me a devilish happy fellow—*twice* as happy; but, you see, if a fellow hasn't his liberty, where's the good of money? I don't know how I got into it, but I can't get away now; and the lawyer fellows, and trustees, and all that sort of prudent people, get about one, and persuade, and exhort, and they bully you, by Jove! into what they call a marriage of convenience—I forget the French word—you know; and then, you see, your feelings may be very different, and all that; and where's the good of money, I say, if you can't enjoy it?'

And Mr. Wylder looked poetically unhappy, and trundled over a little bit of fricandeau on his plate with his fork, desolately, as though earthly things had lost their relish.

'Yes; I think I know the feeling,' said Miss Lake, quietly. 'That ballad, you know, expresses it very prettily:—"Oh, thou hast been the cause of this anguish, my mother?"'

It was not then as old a song as it is now.

Wylder looked sharply at her, but she did not smile, and seemed to speak in good faith; and being somewhat thick in some matters, though a cunning fellow, he said—

'Yes; that is the sort of thing, you know—of course, with a difference—a girl is supposed to speak there; but men suffer that way, too—though, of course, very likely it's more their own fault.'

'It is very sad,' said Miss Lake, who was busy with a *pâté*.

'She has no life in her; she's a mere figurehead; she's

awfully slow ; I don't like black hair ; I'm taken by conversation —and all that. There are some men that can only really love once in their lives, and never forget their first love, I assure you.'

Wylder murmured all this, and looked as plaintive as he could without exciting the attention of the people over-the-way.

Mark Wylder had, as you perceive, rather vague notions of decency, and not much experience of ladies ; and thought he was making just the interesting impression he meditated. He was a good deal surprised, then, when Miss Lake said, and with quite a cheerful countenance, and very quickly, but so that her words stung his ear like the prick of a bodkin.

'Your way of speaking of my cousin, Sir, is in the highest degree discreditable to you and offensive to me, and should you venture to repeat it, I will certainly mention it to Lady Chelford.'

And so she turned to old Major Jackson at her right, who had been expounding a point of the battle of Vittoria to Lord Chelford ; and she led him again into action, and acquired during the next ten minutes a great deal of curious lore about Spanish muleteers and French prisoners, together with some particulars about the nature of picket duty, and 'that scoundrel, Castanos.'

CHAPTER IV.

IN WHICH WE GO TO THE DRAWING-ROOM AND THE PARTY BREAKS UP.

WYLDER was surprised, puzzled, and a good deal incensed—that saucy craft had fired her shot so unexpectedly across his bows. He looked a little flushed, and darted a stealthy glance across the table, but no one he thought had observed the manoeuvre. He would have talked to ugly Mrs. W. Wylder, his sister-in-law, at his left, but she was entertaining Lord Chelford now. He had nothing for it but to perform *cavalier seul* with his slice of mutton—a sensual sort of isolation, while all the world was chatting so agreeably and noisily around him. He would have liked, at that moment, a walk upon the quarter-deck, with a good head-wind blowing, and liberty to curse and swear a bit over the bulwark. Women are so full of caprice and hypocrisy, and 'humbugging impudence !'

Wylder was rather surly after the ladies had floated away from the scene, and he drank his liquor doggedly. It was his fancy, I suppose, to revive certain sentimental relations which had, it may be, once existed between him and Miss Lake ; and he was a person of that combative temperament that magnifies an object in proportion as its pursuit is thwarted.

In the drawing-room he watched Miss Lake over his cup of coffee, and after a few words to his *fiancée* he lounged toward the table at which she was turning over some prints.

' Do come here, Dorothy,' she exclaimed, not raising her eyes, I have found the very thing.'

' What thing? my dear Miss Lake,' said that good little woman, skipping to her side.

' The story of " Fridolin," and Retzch's pretty outlines. Sit down beside me, and I'll tell you the story.'

' Oh !' said the vicar's wife, taking her seat, and the inspection and exposition began ; and Mark Wylder, who had intended renewing his talk with Miss Lake, saw that she had foiled him, and stood with a heightened colour and his hands in his pockets, looking confoundedly cross and very like an outcast, in the shadow behind.

After a while, in a pet, he walked away. Lord Chelford had joined the two ladies, and had something to say about German art, and some pleasant lights to throw from foreign travel, and devious reading, and was as usual intelligent and agreeable ; and Mark was still more sore and angry, and strutted away to another table, a long way off, and tossed over the leaves of a folio of Wouverman's works, and did not see one of the plates he stared at so savagely.

I don't think Mark was very clear as to what he wanted, or, even if he had had a cool half-hour to define his wishes, that he would seriously have modified existing arrangements. But he had a passionate sort of obstinacy, and his whims took a violent character when they were crossed, and he was angry and jealous and unintelligible, reminding one of Carlyle's description of Philip Egalité—a chaos.

Then he joined a conversation going on between Dorcas Brandon and the vicar, his brother. He assisted at it, but took no part, and in fact was listening to that other conversation which sounded, with its pleasant gabble and laughter, like a little musical tinkle of bells in the distance. His gall rose, and that distant talk rang in his ears like a cool but intangible insult.

It was dull work. He looked at his watch—the brougham would be at the door to take Miss Lake home in a quarter of an hour; so he glided by old Lady Chelford, who was dozing stiffly through her spectacles on a French novel, and through a second drawing-room, and into the hall, where he saw Larcom's expansive white waistcoat, and disregarded his advance and respectful inclination, and strode into the outer hall or vestibule, where were hat-stands, walking-sticks, great coats, umbrellas, and the exuviæ of gentlemen.

Mark clapped on his hat, and rifled the pocket of his paletot of his cigar-case and matches, and spluttered a curse or two, according to old Nollekins' receipt for easing the mind, and on the door-steps lighted his cheroot, and became gradually more philosophical.

In due time the brougham came round with its lamps lighted, and Mark, who was by this time placid, greeted Price on the box familiarly, after his wont, and asked him whom he was going to drive, as if he did not know, cunning fellow ; and actually went so far as to give Price one of those cheap and nasty weeds, of which he kept a supply apart in his case for such occasions of good fellowship.

So Mark waited to put the lady into the carriage, and he meditated walking a little way by the window and making his peace, and there was perhaps some vague vision of jumping in afterwards ; I know not. Mark's ideas of ladies and of propriety were low, and he was little better than a sailor ashore, and not a good specimen of that class of monster.

He walked about the courtyard smoking, looking sometimes on the solemn front of the old palatial mansion, and sometimes breathing a white film up to the stars, impatient, like the enamoured Aladdin, watching in ambuscade for the emergence of the Princess Badroulbadour. But honest Mark forgot that young ladies do not always come out quite alone, and jump unassisted into their vehicles. And in fact not only did Lord Chelford assist the fair lady, cloaked and hooded, into the carriage, but the vicar's goodhumoured little wife was handed in also, the good vicar looking on, and as the gay good-night and leave-taking took place by the door-steps, Mark drew back, like a guilty thing, in silence, and showed no sign but the red top of his cigar, glowing like the eye of a Cyclops in the dark ; and away rolled the brougham, with the two ladies, and Chelford and the vicar went in, and Mark hurled the stump of his cheroot at Fortune, and delivered a fragmentary soliloquy through his teeth ; and so, in a sulk, without making his adieux, he marched off to his crib at the Brandon Arms

CHAPTER V.

IN WHICH MY SLUMBER IS DISTURBED.

THE ladies had accomplished their ascension to the upper regions. The good vicar had marched off with the major, who was by this time unbuckling in his lodgings ; and Chelford and I, *tête-à-tête*, had a glass of sherry and water together in the drawing-room before parting. And over this temperate beverage I told him frankly the nature of the service which Mark Wylder wished me to render him ; and he as frankly approved, and said he would ask Larkin, the family lawyer, to come up in the morning to assist.

The more I saw of this modest, refined, and manly peer, the more I liked him. There was a certain courteous frankness, and a fine old English sense of duty perceptible in all his serious talk. So I felt no longer like a conspirator, and was to offer such advice as might seem expedient, with the clear approbation of Miss Brandon's trustee. And this point clearly settled, I avowed myself a little tired ; and lighting our candles at the foot of the stairs, we scaled that long ascent together, and he conducted me through the intricacies of the devious lobbies up stairs to my chamber-door, where he bid me good-night, shook hands, and descended to his own quarters.

My room was large and old-fashioned, but snug ; and I, beginning to grow very drowsy, was not long in getting to bed, where I fell asleep indescribably quickly.

In all old houses one is, of course, liable to adventures. Where is the marvellous to find refuge, if not among the chambers, the intricacies, which have seen the vicissitudes, the crimes, and the deaths of generations of such men as had occupied these ?

There was a picture in the outer hall—one of those full-length gentlemen of George II.'s time, with a dark peruke flowing on his shoulders, a cut velvet coat, and lace cravat and ruffles. This picture was pale, and had a long chin, and somehow had impressed my boyhood with a singular sense of fear. The foot of my bed lay towards the window, distant at least five-and-twenty-feet ; and before the window stood my dressing-table, and on it a large looking-glass.

I dreamed that I was arranging my toilet before this glass—just as I had done that evening—when on a sudden the face of the portrait I have mentioned was presented on its surface, confronting me like a real countenance, and advancing towards me with a look of fury ; and at the instant I felt myself seized by the throat and unable to stir or to breathe. After a struggle with this infernal garotter, I succeeded in awaking myself; and as I did so, I felt a rather cold hand really resting on my throat, and quietly passed up over my chin and face. I jumped out of bed with a roar, and challenged the owner of the hand, but received no answer, and heard no sound. I poked up my fire and lighted my candle. Everything was as I had left it except the door, which was the least bit open.

In my shirt, candle in hand, I looked out into the passage. There was nothing there in human shape, but in the direction of the stairs the green eyes of a large cat were shining. I was so confoundedly nervous that even 'a harmless, necessary cat' appalled me, and I clapped my door, as if against an evil spirit.

In about half an hour's time, however, I had quite worked off the effect of this night-mare, and reasoned myself into the natural solution that the creature had got on my bed, and lay, as I have been told they will, upon my throat, and so, all the rest had followed.

Not being given to the fear of *larvæ* and *lemures*, and also knowing that a mistake is easily committed in a great house like that, and that my visitor might have made one, I grew drowsy in a little while, and soon fell asleep again. But knowing all I now do, I hold a different conclusion—and so, I think, will you.

In the morning Mark Wylder was early upon the ground. He had quite slept off what he would have called the nonsense of last night, and was very keen upon settlements, consols, mortgages, jointures, and all that dry but momentous lore.

I find a note in my diary of that day :—' From half-past ten o'clock until two with Mark Wylder and Mr. Larkin, the lawyer, in the study—dull work—over papers and title—Lord Chelford with us now and then to lend a helping hand.'

Lawyer Larkin, though he made our work lighter—for he was clear, quick, and orderly, and could lay his hand on any paper in those tin walls of legal manuscripts that built up two sides of his office—did not make our business, to me at least, any pleasanter. Wylder thought him a clever man (and so perhaps, in a certain sense, he was); Lord Chelford, a most honourable one; yet there came to me by instinct an unpleasant feeling about him. It was not in any defined way—I did not fancy that he was machinating, for instance, any sort of mischief in the business before us—but I had a notion that he was not quite what he pretended.

Perhaps his *personnel* prejudiced me—though I could not quite say why. He was a tall, lank man— rather long of limb, long of head, and gaunt of face. He wanted teeth at both sides, and there was rather a skull-like cavity when he smiled—which was pretty often. His eyes were small and reddish, as if accustomed to cry ; and when everything went smoothly were dull and dove-like, out when things crossed or excited him, which occurred when his own pocket or plans were concerned, they grew singularly unpleasant, and greatly resembled those of some not amiable animal—was it a rat, or a serpent? It was a peculiar concentrated vigilance and rapine that I have seen there. But that was long afterwards. Now, indeed, they were meek, and sad, and pink.

He had an ambition, too, to pass for a high-bred gentleman, and thought it might be done by a somewhat lofty and drawling way of talking, and distributing his length of limb in what he fancied were easy attitudes. If the tender mercies of the wicked are cruel, so are the elegances of a vulgar man ; and his made me wince.

I might be all in the wrong—and was, no doubt, unreasonable —for he bore a high character, and passed for a very gentle-manlike man among the villagers. He was also something of a religious light, and had for a time conformed to Methodism, but returned to the Church. He had a liking for long sermons, and a sad abhorrence of amusements, and sat out the morning and the evening services regularly—and kept up his dissenting connection too, and gave them money—and appeared in print, in all charitable lists—and mourned over other men's backslidings and calamities in a lofty and Christian way, shaking his tall bald head, and turning up his pink eyes mildly.

Notwithstanding all which he was somehow unlovely in my eyes, and in an indistinct way, formidable. It was not a pleasant misgiving about a gentleman of Larkin's species, the family lawyer, who become *viscera magnorum domuum.*

My duties were lighter, as adviser, than I at first apprehended. Wylder's crotchets were chiefly 'mare's nests.' We had read the draft of the settlement, preparatory to its being sent to senior counsel to be approved. Wylder's attorney had done his devoir, and Mr. Larkin avowed a sort of parental interest in both parties to the indentures, and made, at closing, a little speech, very high in morality, and flavoured in a manly way with religion, and congratulated Mark on his honour and plain dealing, which he gave us to understand were the secrets of all success in life, as they had been, in an humble way of his own.

CHAPTER VI.

IN WHICH DORCAS BRANDON SPEAKS.

IN answer to 'the roaring shiver of the gong' we all trooped away together to luncheon. Lady Chelford and Dorcas and Chelford had nearly ended that irregular repast when we entered. My chair was beside Miss Brandon; she had breakfasted with old Lady Chelford that morning, and this was my first meeting that day. It was not very encouraging.

People complained that acquaintance made little way with her. That you were, perhaps, well satisfied with your first day's progress, but the next made no head-way; you found yourself this morning exactly at the point from which you commenced yesterday, and to-morrow would recommence where you started the day before. This is very disappointing, but may sometimes be accounted for by there being nothing really to discover. It seemed to me, however, that the distance had positively increased since yesterday, and that the oftener she met me the more strange she became. As we went out, Wylder enquired, with his usual good taste : 'Well, what do you think of her?' Then he looked slily at me, laughing, with his hands in his pockets. 'A little bit slow, eh?' he whispered, and laughed again, and lounged into the hall. If Dorcas Brandon had been a plain woman, I think she would have been voted an impertinent bore ; but she was so beautiful that she became an enigma. I looked at her as she stood gravely gazing from the window. Is it Lady Macbeth? No; she never would have had energy to plan her husband's career and manage that affair of Duncan. A sultana rather—sublimely egotistical, without reverence—a voluptuous and haughty embodiment of indifference. I paused, looking at a picture, but thinking of her, and was surprised by her voice very near me.

'Will you give me just a minute, Mr. De Cresseron, in the drawing-room, while I show you a miniature? I want your opinion.'

So she floated on and I accompanied her.

'I think,' she said, 'you mentioned yesterday, that you remembered me when an infant. You remember my poor mamma, don't you, very well?'

This was the first time she had yet shown any tendency, so far as I had seen, to be interested in anything, or to talk to me. I seized the occasion, and gave her, as well as I could, the sad and pretty picture that remained, and always will, in the vacant air, when I think of her, on the mysterious retina of memory.

How filmy they are! the moonlight shines through them, as through the phantom Dane in Retzch's outlines—colour without substance. How they come, wearing for ever the sweetest and pleasantest look of their earthly days. Their sweetest and merriest tones hover musically in the distance; how far away, how near to silence, yet how clear! And so it is with our remembrance of the immortal part. It is the loveliest traits that remain with us perennially; all that was noblest and most beautiful is there, in a changeless and celestial shadow; and this is the resurrection of the memory, the foretaste and image which the 'Faithful Creator' accords us of the resurrection and glory to come—the body redeemed, the spirit made perfect.

On a cabinet near to where she stood was a casket of ormolu, which she unlocked, and took out a miniature, opened, and looked at it for a long time. I knew very well whose it was, and watched her countenance; for, as I have said, she interested me strangely. I suppose she knew I was looking at her; but she showed always a queenlike indifference about what people might think or observe. There was no sentimental softening; but her gaze was such as I once saw the same proud and handsome face turn upon the dead—pale, exquisite, perhaps a little stern. What she read there—what procession of thoughts and images passed by—threw neither light nor shadow on her face. Its apathy interested me inscrutably.

At last she placed the picture in my hand, and asked—

'Is this really very like her?'

'It is, and it is *not*,' I said, after a little pause. 'The features are true: it is what I call an accurate portrait, but that is all. I dare say, exact as it is, it would give to one who had not seen her a false, as it must an inadequate, idea, of the original. There was something *naïve* and *spirituel*, and very tender in her face, which he has not caught—perhaps it could hardly be fixed in colours.'

'Yes, I always heard her expression and intelligence were very beautiful. It was the beauty of mobility—true beauty.'

'There is a beauty of another stamp, equally exquisite, Miss Brandon, and perhaps more overpowering.' I said this in nearly a whisper, and in a very marked way, almost tender, and the next moment was amazed at my own audacity. She looked on me for a second or two, with her dark drowsy glance, and then it returned to the picture, which was again in her hand. There was a total want of interest in the careless sort of surprise she vouchsafed my little sally; neither was there the slightest resentment. If a wafer had been stuck upon my forehead, and she had observed it, there might have been just that look and no more. I was ridiculously annoyed with myself. I was betrayed,

I don't know how, into this little venture, and it was a flat failure. The position of a shy man, who has just made an unintelligible joke at a dinner-table, was not more pregnant with self-reproach and embarrassment.

Upon my honour, I don't think there was anything of the *roué* in me. I own I did feel towards this lady, who either was, or seemed to me, so singular, a mysterious interest just beginning —of that peculiar kind which becomes at last terribly absorbing.

I was more elated by her trifling notice of me than I can quite account for. It was a distinction. She was so indescribably handsome—so passively disdainful. I think if she had listened to me with even the faintest intimation of caring whether I spoke in this tone or not, with even a flash of momentary resentment, I might have rushed into a most reprehensible and ridiculous rigmarole.

In this, the subtlest and most perilous of all intoxications, it needs immense presence of mind to conduct ourselves always with decorum. But she was looking, just as before, at the miniature, as it seemed to me, in fancy infusing some of the spirit I had described into the artist's record, and she said, only in soliloquy, as it were, 'Yes, I see—I *think* I see.'

So there was a pause ; and then she said, without, however, removing her eyes from the miniature, 'You are, I believe, Mr. De Cresseron, a very old friend of Mr. Wylder's. Is it not so?'

So soon after my little escapade, I did not like the question ; but it was answered. There was not the faintest trace of a satirical meaning, however, in her face ; and after another very considerable interval, at the end of which she shut the miniature in its case, she said, 'It was a peculiar face, and very beautiful. It is odd how many of our family married for love—wild love-matches. My poor mother was the last. I could point you out many pictures, and tell you stories—my cousin, Rachel, knows them all. You know Rachel Lake?'

'I've not the honour of knowing Miss Lake. I had not an opportunity of making her acquaintance yesterday ; but I know her brother—so does Wylder.'

'What's that?' said Mark, who had just come in, and was tumbling over a volume of 'Punch' at the window.

'I was telling Miss Brandon that we both know Stanley Lake.' On hearing which, Wylder seemed to discover something uncommonly interesting or clever in the illustration before him ; for he approached his face very near to it, in a scrutinising way, and only said, 'Oh?'

'That marrying for love was a fatality in our family,' she continued in the same low tone—too faint I think to reach Mark. 'They were all the most beautiful who sacrificed themselves so— they were all unhappy marriages. So the beauty of our family never availed it, any more than its talents and its courage ; for

there were clever and witty men, as well as very brave ones, in
it. Meaner houses have grown up into dukedoms; ours never
prospers. I wonder what it is.'

'Many families have disappeared altogether, Miss Brandon.
It is no small thing, through so many centuries, to have retained
your ancestral estates, and your pre-eminent position, and even
this splendid residence of so many generations of your lineage.'

I thought that Miss Brandon, having broken the ice, was
henceforth to be a conversable young lady. But this sudden
expansion was not to last. Ovid tells us, in his 'Fasti,' how
statues sometimes surprised people by speaking more frankly
and to the purpose even than Miss Brandon, and straight were
cold chiselled marble again; and so it was with that proud, cold
chef d'œuvre of tinted statuary.

Yet I thought I could, even in that dim glimpse, discern how
the silent subterranean current of her thoughts was flowing; like
other representatives of a dynasty, she had studied the history
of her race to profit by its errors and misfortunes. There was
to be no weakness or passion in her reign.

The princess by this time was seated on the ottoman, and
chose to read a letter, thus intimating, I suppose, that my audience was at an end; so I took up a book, put it down, and then
went and looked over Wylder's shoulder, and made my criti-
cisms—not very novel, I fear—upon the pages he turned over;
and I am sorry to say I don't think he heard much of what I
was saying, for he suddenly came out with—

'And where is Stanley Lake now, do you know?'

'I saw him in town—only for a moment though—about a fortnight ago; he was arranging, he said, about selling out.'

'Oh! retiring; and what does he propose doing then?' asked
Wylder, without raising his eyes from his book. He spoke in a
sort of undertone, like a man who does not want to be overheard,
and the room was quite large enough to make that sort of secrecy
easy without the appearance of seeking it.

'I have not an idea. I don't think he's fit for many things.
He knows something of horses, I believe, and something of
play.'

'But he'll hardly make out a living that way,' said Wylder,
with a sort of sneer or laugh. I thought he seemed put out, and
a little flushed.

'I fancy he has enough to live upon, without adding to it,
however,' I said.

Wylder leaned back in his low chair, with his hands stuffed
in his pockets, and the air of a man trying to look unconcerned,
but both annoyed and disconcerted nevertheless.

'I tell you what, Charlie, between you and me, that fellow,
Stanley, is a d——d bad lot. I may be mistaken, of course;
he's always been very civil to me, but we don't like one another;

and I don't think I ever heard him say a good word of any one ;
I dare say he abuses you and me, as he does everyone else.'

'Does he ?' I said. ' I was not aware he had that failing.'

' Oh, yes. He does not stick at trifles, Master Stanley. He's
about the greatest liar, I think, I ever met with,' and he laughed
angrily.

I happened at that moment to raise my eyes, and I saw Dorcas's face reflected in the mirror ; her back was towards us, and
she held the letter in her hand as if reading it, but her large eyes
were looking over it, and on us, in the glass, with a gaze of
strange curiosity. Our glances met in the mirror ; but hers remained serenely undisturbed, and mine dropped and turned
away hastily. I wonder whether she heard us. I do not know.
Some people are miraculously sharp of hearing.

' I dare say,' said Wylder, with a sneer, ' he was asking affectionately for me, eh ?'

' No ; not that I recollect—in fact there was not time ; but I
suppose he does not like you less for what has happened ; you're
worth cultivating now, you know.'

Wylder was leaning on his elbow, with just the tip of his thumb
to his teeth, with a vicious character of biting it, which was peculiar to him when anything vexed him considerably, and glancing sharply this way and that—

' You know,' he said, suddenly, ' we are a sort of cousins ; his
mother was a Brandon—a second cousin of Dorcas's—no, of her
father's—I don't know exactly how. He's a pushing fellow, one
of the coolest hands I know ; but I don't see that I can be of
any use to him, or why the devil I should. I say, old fellow,
come out and have a weed, will you ?'

I raised my eyes. Miss Brandon had left the room. I don't
know that her presence would have prevented his invitation, for
Wylder's wooing was certainly of the coolest. So forth we sallied, and under the autumnal foliage, in the cool amber light of
the declining evening, we enjoyed our cheroots ; and with them,
Wylder his thoughts ; and I, the landscape, and the whistling
of the birds ; for we waxed Turkish and taciturn over our tobacco.

CHAPTER VII

RELATING HOW A LONDON GENTLEMAN APPEARED IN REDMAN'S DELL.

BELIEVE the best rule in telling a story is to follow events chronologically. So let me mention that just about the time when Wylder and I were filming the trunks of the old trees with wreaths of lingering perfume, Miss Rachel Lake had an unexpected visitor.

There is, near the Hall, a very pretty glen, called Redman's Dell, very steep, with a stream running at the bottom of it, but so thickly wooded that in summer time you can only now and then catch a glimpse of the water gliding beneath you. Deep in this picturesque ravine, buried among the thick shadows of tall old trees, runs the narrow mill-road, which lower down debouches on the end of the village street. There, in the transparent green shadow, stand the two mills—the old one with A.D. 1679, and the Wylder arms, and the eternal 'resurgam' projecting over its door ; and higher up, on a sort of platform, the steep bank rising high behind it, with its towering old wood overhanging and surrounding, upon a site where one of King Arthur's knights, of an autumn evening, as he rode solitary in quest of adventures, might have seen the peeping, gray gable of an anchorite's chapel dimly through the gilded stems, and heard the drowsy tinkle of his vesper-bell, stands an old and small two-storied brick and timber house ; and though the sun does not very often glimmer on its windows, it yet possesses an air of sad, old-world comfort—a little flower-garden lies in front with a paling round it. But not every kind of flowers will grow there, under the lordly shadow of the elms and chestnuts.

This sequestered tenement bears the name of Redman's Farm ; and its occupant was that Miss Lake whom I had met last night at Brandon Hall, and whose pleasure it was to live here in independent isolation.

There she is now, busy in her tiny garden, with the birds twittering about her, and the yellow leaves falling ; and her thick gauntlets on her slender hands. How fresh and pretty she looks in that sad, sylvan solitude, with the background of the dull crimson brick and the climbing roses. Bars of sunshine fall through the branches above, across the thick tapestry of blue, yellow, and crimson, that glow so richly upon their deep green ground.

There is not much to be done just now, I fancy, in the gardening way ; but work is found or invented—for sometimes the hour is dull, and that bright, spirited, and at heart, it may be, bitter exile, will make out life somehow. There is music, and drawing. There are flowers, as we see, and two or three correspondents, and walks into the village ; and her dark cousin, Dorcas, drives down sometimes in the pony-carriage, and is not always silent ; and indeed, they are a good deal together.

This young lady's little Eden, though overshadowed and encompassed with the solemn sylvan cloister of nature's building, and vocal with sounds of innocence—the songs of birds, and sometimes those of its young mistress—was no more proof than the Mesopotamian haunt of our first parents against the intrusion of darker spirits. So, as she worked, she lifted up her eyes, and beheld a rather handsome young man standing at the little wicket of her garden, with his gloved hand on the latch. A man of fashion—a town man—his dress bespoke him : smooth cheeks, light brown curling moustache, and eyes very peculiar both in shape and colour, and something of elegance of finish in his other features, and of general grace in the *coup d'œil*, struck one at a glance. He was smiling silently and slily on Rachel, who, with a little cry of surprise, said—

'Oh, Stanley ! is it you ?'

And before he could answer, she had thrown her arms about his neck and kissed him two or three times. Laughingly, half-resisting, the young man waited till her enthusiastic salutation was over, and with one gloved hand caressingly on her shoulder, and with the other smoothing his ruffled moustache, he laughed a little more, a quiet low laugh. He was not addicted to stormy greetings, and patted his sister's shoulder gently, his arm a little extended, like a man who tranquillises a frolicsome pony.

'Yes, Radie, you see I've found you out ;' and his eye wandered, still smiling oddly, over the front of her quaint habitation.

'And how have you been, Radie ?'

'Oh, very well. No life like a gardener's—early hours, work, air, and plenty of quiet.' And the young lady laughed.

'You are a wonderful lass, Radie.'

'Thank you, dear.'

'And what do you call this place ?'

'"The Happy Valley," *I* call it. Don't you remember "Rasselas ?"'

'No,' he said, looking round him ; 'I don't think I was ever there.'

'You horrid dunce !—it's a book, but a stupid one—so no matter,' laughed Miss Rachel, giving him a little slap on the shoulder with her slender fingers.

His reading, you see, lay more in circulating library lore, and he was not deep in Johnson—as few of us would be, I'm afraid, if it were not for Boswell.

'It's a confounded deal more like the "Valley of the Shadow of Death," in "Pilgrim's Progress"—you remember—that old Tamar used to read to us in the nursery,' replied Master Stanley, who had never enjoyed being quizzed by his sister, not being blessed with a remarkably sweet temper.

'If you don't like my scenery, come in, Stanley, and admire my decorations. You must tell me all the news, and I'll show you my house, and amaze you with my housekeeping. Dear me, how long it is since I've seen you.'

So she led him in by the arm to her tiny drawing-room ; and he laid his hat and stick, and gray paletot, on her little mar-queurie-table, and sat down, and looked languidly about him, with a sly smile, like a man amused.

'It is an odd fancy, living alone here.'

'An odd necessity, Stanley.'

'Aren't you afraid of being robbed and murdered, Radie?' he said, leaning forward to smell at the pretty bouquet in the little glass, and turning it listlessly round. 'There are lots of those burglar fellows going about, you know.'

'Thank you, dear, for reminding me. But, somehow, I'm not the least afraid. There hasn't been a robbery in this neighbour-hood, I believe, for eight hundred years. The people never think of shutting their doors here in summer time till they are going to bed, and then only for form's sake ; and, beside, there's nothing to rob, and I really don't much mind being murdered.'

He looked round, and smiled on, as before, like a man contemptuously amused, but sleepily withal.

'You are very oddly housed, Radie.'

'I like it,' she said quietly, also with a glance round her homely drawing-room.

'What do you call this, your boudoir or parlour?'

'I call it my drawing-room, but it's anything you please.'

'What very odd people our ancestors were,' he mused on. 'They lived, I suppose, out of doors like the cows, and only came into their sheds at night, when they could not see the absurd ugliness of the places they inhabited. I could not stand upright in this room with my hat on. Lots of rats, I fancy, Radie, behind that wainscoting? What's that horrid work of art against the wall?'

'A shell-work cabinet, dear. It is not beautiful, I allow. If I were strong enough, or poor old Tamar, I should have put it away ; and now that you're here, Stanley, I think I'll make you carry it out to the lobby for me.'

'I should not like to touch it, dear Radie. And pray how do you amuse yourself here? How on earth do you get over the day, and, worse still, the evenings?'

'Very well—well enough. I make a very good sort of a nun, and a capital housemaid. I work in the garden, I mend my dresses, I drink tea, and when I choose to be dissipated, I play and sing for old Tamar—why did not you ask how she is? I do believe, Stanley, you care for no one, but' (she was going to say yourself, she said instead, however, but) 'perhaps, the least in the world for me, and that not very wisely,' she continued, a little fiercely, 'for from the moment you saw me, you've done little else than try to disgust me more than I am with my penury and solitude. What do you mean? You always have a purpose —will you ever learn to be frank and straightforward, and speak plainly to those whom you ought to trust, if not to love? What are you driving at, Stanley?'

He looked up with a gentle start, like one recovering from a reverie, and said, with his yellow eyes fixed for a moment on his sister, before they dropped again to the carpet.

'You're miserably poor, Rachel: upon my word, I believe you haven't clear two hundred a year. I'll drink some tea, please, if you have got any, and it isn't too much trouble; and it strikes me as very curious you like living in this really very humiliating state.'

'I don't intend to go out for a governess, if that's what you mean; nor is there any privation in living as I do. Perhaps you think I ought to go and housekeep for you.'

'Why—ha, ha!—I really don't know, Radie, where I shall be. I'm not of any regiment now.'

'Why, you have not sold out?' She flushed and suddenly grew pale, for she was afraid something worse might have happened, having no great confidence in her brother.

But she was relieved.

'I *have* sold my commission.'

She looked straight at him with large eyes and compressed lips, and nodded her head two or three times, just murmuring, 'Well! well! well!'

'Women never understand these things. The army is awfully expensive—I mean, of course, a regiment like ours; and the interest of the money is better to me than my pay; and see, Rachel, there's no use in lecturing *me*—so don't let us quarrel. We're not very rich, you and I; and we each know our own affairs, you yours, and I mine, best.'

There was something by no means pleasant in his countenance when his temper was stirred, and a little thing sometimes sufficed to do so.

Rachel treated him with a sort of deference, a little contemptuous perhaps, such as spoiled children receive from indulgent elders; and she looked at him steadily, with a faint smile and arched brows, for a little while, and an undefinable expression of puzzle and curiosity.

'You are a very amusing brother—if not a very cheery or a very useful one, Stanley.'

She opened the door, and called across the little hall into the homely kitchen of the mansion.

'Tamar, dear, Master Stanley's here, and wishes to see you.'

'Oh! yes, poor dear old Tamar; ha, ha!' says the gentleman, with a gentle little laugh, 'I suppose she's as frightful as ever, that worthy woman. Certainly she *is* awfully like a ghost. I wonder, Radie, you're not afraid of her at night in this cheerful habitation. *I* should, I know.'

'A ghost *indeed*, the ghost of old times, an ugly ghost enough for many of us. Poor Tamar! she was always very kind to *you*, Stanley.'

And just then old Tamar opened the door. I must allow there was something very unpleasant about that worthy old woman; and not being under any personal obligations to her, I confess my acquiescence in the spirit of Captain Lake's remarks.

She was certainly perfectly neat and clean, but white predominated unpleasantly in her costume. Her cotton gown had once had a pale pattern over it, but wear and washing had destroyed its tints, till it was no better than white, with a mottling of gray. She had a large white kerchief pinned with a grisly precision across her breast, and a white linen cap tied under her chin, fitting close to her head, like a child's nightcap, such as they wore in my young days, and destitute of border or frilling about the face. It was a dress very odd and unpleasant to behold, and suggested the idea of an hospital, or a madhouse, or death, in an undefined way.

She was past sixty, with a mournful puckered and puffy face, tinted all over with a thin gamboge and burnt sienna glazing; and very blue under the eyes, which showed a great deal of their watery whites. This old woman had in her face and air, along with an expression of suspicion and anxiety, a certain character of decency and respectability, which made her altogether a puzzling and unpleasant apparition.

Being taciturn and undemonstrative, she stood at the door, looking with as pleased a countenance as so sad a portrait could wear upon the young gentleman.

He got up at his leisure and greeted 'old Tamar,' with his sleepy, amused sort of smile, and a few trite words of kindness. So Tamar withdrew to prepare tea; and he said, all at once, with a sudden accession of energy, and an unpleasant momentary glare in his eyes—

'You know, Rachel, this sort of thing is all nonsense. You cannot go on living like this; you must marry—you shall marry. Mark Wylder is down here, and he has got an estate and a house, and it is time he should marry you.'

'Mark Wylder is here to marry my cousin, Dorcas; and if he had no such intention, and were as free as you are, and again to urge his foolish suit upon his knees, Stanley, I would die rather than accept him.'

'It was not always so foolish a suit, Radie,' answered her brother, his eyes once more upon the carpet. 'Why should not *he* do as well as another? You liked him well enough once.'

The young lady coloured rather fiercely.

'I am not a girl of seventeen now, Stanley; and—and, besides, I *hate* him.'

'What d—d nonsense! I really beg your pardon, Radie, but it *is* precious stuff. You are, quite unreasonable; you've no cause to hate him; he dropped you because you dropped him. It was only prudent; he had not a guinea. But now it is different, and he *must* marry you.'

The young lady stared with a haughty amazement upon her brother.

'I've made up my mind to speak to him; and if he won't I promise you he shall leave the country,' said the young man gently, just lifting his yellow eyes for a second with another unpleasant glare.

'I almost think you're mad, Stanley; and if you do anything so insane, sure I am you'll rue it while you live; and wherever he is I'll find him out, and acquit myself, with the scorn I owe him, of any share in a plot so unspeakably mean and absurd.'

'Brava, brava! you're a heroine, Radie; and why the devil,' he continued, in a changed tone, 'do you apply those insolent terms to what I purpose doing?'

'I wish I could find words strong enough to express my horror of your plot—a plot every way disgusting. You plainly know something to Mark Wylder's discredit; and you mean, Stanley, to coerce him by fear into a marriage with your penniless sister, who *hates* him. Sir, do you pretend to be a gentleman?'

'I rather think so,' he said, with a quiet sneer.

'Give up every idea of it this moment. Has it not struck you that Mark Wylder may possibly know something of you, you would not have published?'

'I don't think he does. What do you mean?'

'On my life, Stanley, I'll acquaint Mr. Wylder this evening with what you meditate, and the atrocious liberty you presume —yes, Sir, though you are my brother, the *atrocious liberty* you dare to take with my name—unless you promise, upon your honour, now and here, to dismiss for ever the odious and utterly resultless scheme.'

Captain Lake looked very angry after his fashion, but said nothing. He could not at any time have very well defined his feelings toward his sister, but mingling in them, certainly, was a vein of unacknowledged dread, and, shall I say, respect. He knew she was resolute, fierce of will, and prompt in action, and not to be bullied.

'There's more in this, Stanley, than you care to tell me. You have not troubled yourself a great deal about me, you know : and I'm no worse off now than any time for the last three years. You've *not* come down here on *my* account—that is, altogether ; and be your plans what they may, you sha'n't mix my name in them. What you please—wise or foolish—you'll do in what concerns yourself ;—you always *have* —without consulting me ; but I tell you again, Stanley, unless you promise, upon your honour, to forbear all mention of my name, I will write this evening to Lady Chelford, apprising her of your plans, and of my own disgust and indignation ; and requesting her son's interference. *Do* you promise ?'

'There's no such *haste*, Radie. I only mentioned it. If you don't like it, of course it can lead to nothing, and there's no use in my speaking to Wylder, and so there's an end of it.'

'There *may* be some use, a purpose in which neither my feelings nor interests have any part. I venture to say, Stanley, your plans are all for *yourself*. You want to extort some advantage from Wylder ; and you think, in his present situation, about to marry Dorcas, you can use me for the purpose. Thank Heaven ! Sir, you committed for once the rare indiscretion of telling the truth ; and unless you make me the promise I require, I will take, before evening, such measures as will completely exculpate me. Once again, do you promise ?'

'Yes, Radie ; ha, ha ! of course I promise.'

Upon your honour ?'

'Upon my honour—*there*.'

' I believe, you gentlemen dragoons observe that oath—I hope so. If you choose to break it you may give me some trouble, but you sha'n't compromise me. And now, Stanley, one word more. I fancy Mr. Wylder is a resolute man—none of the Wylders wanted courage.'

Captain Lake was by this time smiling his sly, sleepy smile upon his French boots.

' If you have formed any plan which depends upon frightening him, it is a desperate one. All I can tell you, Stanley, is this, that if I were a man, and an attempt made to extort from me **any** sort of concession by terror, I would shoot the miscreant who made it through the head, like a highwayman.'

' What the devil are you talking about ?' said he.

' About *your danger*,' she answered. ' For once in your life listen to reason. Mark Wylder is as prompt as you, and has ten times your nerve and sense ; you are more likely to have committed yourself than he. Take care ; he may retaliate your *threat* by a counter move more dreadful. I know nothing of your doings, Stanley—Heaven forbid ! but be warned, or you'll rue it.'

'Why, Radie, you know nothing of the world. Do you sup

pose I'm quite demented? Ask a gentleman for his estate, or his watch, because I know something to his disadvantage! Why, ha, ha! dear Radie, every man who has ever been on terms of intimacy with another must know things to his disadvantage, but no one thinks of telling them. The world would not tolerate it. It would prejudice the betrayer at least as much as the betrayed. I don't affect to be angry, or talk romance and heroics, because you fancy such stuff; but I assure you—when will that old woman give me a cup of tea?—I assure you, Radie, there's nothing in it.'

Rachel made no reply, but she looked steadfastly and uneasily upon the enigmatical face and downcast eyes of the young man.

'Well, I hope so,' she said at last, with a sigh, and a slight sense of relief.

CHAPTER VIII.

IN WHICH CAPTAIN LAKE TAKES HIS HAT AND STICK.

SO the young people sitting in the little drawing-room of Redman's farm pursued their dialogue; Rachel Lake had spoken last, and it was the captain's turn to speak next.

'Do you remember Miss Beauchamp, Radie?' he asked, rather suddenly, after a very long pause.

'Miss Beauchamp? Oh! to be sure; you mean little Caroline; yes, she must be quite grown up by this time—five years—she promised to be pretty. What of her?'

Rachel, very flushed and agitated still, was now trying to speak as usual.

'She *is* good-looking—a little coarse some people think,' resumed the young man; 'but handsome; black eyes—black hair—rather on a large scale, but certainly handsome. A style I admire rather, though it is not very refined, nor at all classic. But I like her, and I wish you'd advise me.' He was talking, after his wont, to the carpet.

'Oh?' she exclaimed, with a gentle sort of derision.

'You mean,' he said, looking up for a moment, with a sudden stare, 'she has got money. Of course she has; I could not afford to admire her if she had not; but I see you are not just now in a mood to trouble yourself about my nonsense—we can talk about it to-morrow; and tell me now, how do you get on with the Brandon people?'

Rachel was curious, and would, if she could, have recalled

that sarcastic 'oh' which had postponed the story; but she was also a little angry, and with anger there was pride, which would not stoop to ask for the revelation which he chose to defer; so she said, 'Dorcas and I are very good friends; but I don't know very well what to make of her. Only I don't think she's quite so dull and apathetic as I at first supposed; but still I'm puzzled. She is either absolutely uninteresting, or very interesting indeed, and I can't say which.'

'Does she like you?' he asked.

'I really don't know. She tolerates me, like everything else; and I don't flatter her; and we see a good deal of one another upon those terms, and I have no complaint to make of her. She has some aversions, but no quarrels; and has a sort of laziness—mental, bodily, and moral—that is sublime, but provoking; and sometimes I admire her, and sometimes I despise her; and I do not yet know which feeling is the juster.'

'Surely she is woman enough to be fussed a little about her marriage?'

'Oh, dear, no! she takes the whole affair with a queenlike and supernatural indifference. She is either a fool or a very great philosopher, and there is something grand in the serene obscurity that envelopes her,' and Rachel laughed a very little.

'I must, I suppose, pay my respects; but to-morrow will be time enough. What pretty little tea-cups, Radie—quite charming—old cock china, isn't it? These were Aunt Jemima's, I think.'

'Yes; they used to stand on the little marble table between the windows.'

Old Tamar had glided in while they were talking, and placed the little tea equipage on the table unnoticed, and the captain was sipping his cup of tea, and inspecting the pattern, while his sister amused him.

'This place, I suppose, is confoundedly slow, is not it? Do they entertain the neighbours ever at Brandon?'

'Sometimes, when old Lady Chelford and her son are staying there.'

'But the neighbours can't entertain them, I fancy, or you. What a dreary thing a dinner party made up of such people must be—like "Æsop's Fables," where the cows and sheep converse.'

'And sometimes a wolf or a fox,' she said.

'Well, Radie, I know you mean me; but as you wish it, I'll carry my fangs elsewhere;—and what has become of Will Wylder?'

'Oh! he's in the Church!'

'Quite right—the only thing he was fit for;' and Captain Lake laughed like a man who enjoys a joke slily. 'And where is poor Billy quartered?'

'Not quite half a mile away; he has got the vicarage of Naunton Friars.'

'Oh, then, Will is not quite such a fool as we took him for.'

'It is worth just £180 a year! but he's very far from a fool.'

'Yes, of course, he knows Greek poets and Latin fathers, and all the rest of it. I don't mean he ever was plucked. I dare say he's the kind of fellow *you'd* like very well, Radie.' And his sly eyes had a twinkle in them which seemed to say, 'Perhaps I've divined your secret.'

'And so I do, and I like his wife, too, *very* much.'

'His wife! So William has married on £180 a year;' and the captain laughed quietly but very pleasantly again.

'On a very little more, at all events; and I think they are about the happiest, and I'm sure they are the best people in this part of the world.'

'Well, Radie, I'll see you to-morrow again. You preserve your good looks wonderfully. I wonder you haven't become an old woman here.'

And he kissed her, and went his way, with a slight wave of his hand, and his odd smile, as he closed the little garden gate after him.

He turned to his left, walking down towards the town, and the innocent green trees hid him quickly, and the gush and tinkle of the clear brook rose faint and pleasantly through the leaves, from the depths of the glen, and refreshed her ear after his unpleasant talk.

She was flushed, and felt oddly; a little stunned and strange, although she had talked lightly and easily enough.

'I forgot to ask him where he is staying: the Brandon Arms, I suppose. I don't at all like his coming down here after Mark Wylder; what *can* he mean? He certainly never would have taken the trouble for *me*. What *can* he want of Mark Wylder? I think *he* knew old Mr. Beauchamp. He may be a trustee, but that's not likely; Mark Wylder was not the person for any such office. I hope Stanley does not intend trying to extract money from him; anything rather than that degradation—than that *villainy*. Stanley was always impracticable, perverse, deceitful, and so foolish with all his cunning and suspicion—so *very* foolish. Poor Stanley. He's so unscrupulous; I don't know what to think. He said he could force Mark Wylder to leave the country. It must be some bad secret. If he tries and fails, I suppose he will be ruined. I don't know what to think; I never was so uneasy. He will blast himself, and disgrace all connected with him; and it is quite useless speaking to him.'

Perhaps if Rachel Lake had been in Belgravia, leading a town life, the matter would have taken no such dark colouring

and portentous proportions. But living in a small old house, in a
dark glen, with no companion, and little to occupy her, it was
different.

She looked down the silent way he had so lately taken, and
repeated, rather bitterly, ' My only brother ! my only brother !
my only brother !'

That young lady was not quite a pauper, though she may
have thought so. Comparatively, indeed, she was ; but not, I
venture to think, absolutely. She had just that symmetrical
three hundred pounds a year, which the famous Dean of St.
Patrick's tells us he so ' often wished that he had clear.' She
had had some money in the Funds besides, still more insigni-
cant but this her Brother Stanley had borrowed and begged
piecemeal, and the Consols were no more. But though something of a nun in her way of life, there was no germ of the old
maid in her, and money was not often in her thoughts. It was
not a bad *dot ;* and her Brother Stanley had about twice as
much, and therefore was much better off than many a younger
son of a duke. But these young people, after the manner of men
were spited with fortune ; and indeed they had some cause.
Old General Lake had once had more than ten thousand pounds
a year, and lived, until the crash came, in the style of a vicious
old prince. It was a great break up, and a worse fall for
Rachel than for her brother, when the plate, coaches, pictures,
and all the valuable effects' of old Tiberius went to the ham-
mer, and he himself vanished from his clubs and other haunts,
and lived only—a thin intermittent rumour—surmised to be in
gaol, or in Guernsey, and quite forgotten soon, and a little later
actually dead and buried.

CHAPTER IX.

I SEE THE RING OF THE PERSIAN MAGICIAN.

'THAT'S a devilish fine girl,' said Mark Wylder.

He was sitting at this moment on the billiard table, with his coat off and his cue in his hand, and had lighted a cigar. He and I had just had a game, and were tired of it.

'Who ?' I asked. He was looking on me from the corners of his eyes, and smiling in a sly, rakish way, that no man likes in another.

'Radie Lake—she's a splendid girl, by Jove ! Don't you think so ? and she liked me once devilish well, I can tell you. She was thin then, but she has plumped out a bit, and improved every way.'

Whatever else he was, Mark was certainly no beauty ; —a little short he was, and rather square—one shoulder a thought higher than the other—and a slight, energetic hitch in it when he walked. His features in profile had something of a Grecian character, but his face was too broad—very brown, rather a bloodless brown—and he had a pair of great, dense, vulgar, black whiskers. He was very vain of his teeth—his only really good point—for his eyes were a small, cunning, gray pair ; and this, perhaps, was the reason why he had contracted his habit of laughing and grinning a good deal more than the fun of the dialogue always warranted.

This sea-monster smoked here as unceremoniously as he would have done in 'Rees's Divan,' and I only wonder he did not call for brandy-and-water. He had either grown coarser a great deal, or I more decent, during our separation. He talked of his *fiancée* as he might of an opera-girl almost, and was now discussing Miss Lake in the same style.

'Yes, she is—she's very well ; but hang it, Wylder, you're a married man now, and must give up talking that way. People won't like it, you know ; they'll take it to mean more than it does, and you oughtn't. Let us have another game.'

'By-and-by ; what do you think of Larkin ?' asked Wylder, with a sly glance from the corners of his eyes. 'I think he prays rather more than is good for his clients ; mind I spell it with an 'a,' not with an 'e ;' but hang it, for an attorney, you know, and such a sharp chap, it does seem to me rather a—a joke, eh ?'

'He bears a good character among the townspeople, doesn't he?

And I don't see that it can do him any harm, remembering that he has a soul to be saved.'

'Or the other thing, eh?' laughed Wylder. 'But I think he comes it a little too strong—two sermons last Sunday, and a prayer-meeting at nine o'clock?'

'Well, it won't do him any harm,' I repeated.

'Harm! O, let Jos. Larkin alone for that. It gets him all the religious business of the county; and there are nice pickings among the charities, and endowments, and purchases of building sites, and trust deeds; I dare say it brings him in two or three hundred a year, eh?' And Wylder laughed again. 'It has broken up his hard, proud heart,' he says; 'but it left him a devilish hard head, I told him, and I think it sharpens his wits.'

'I rather think you'll find him a useful man ; and to be so in his line of business he must have his wits about him, I can tell you.'

'He amused me devilishly,' said Wylder, ' with a sort of exhortation he treated me to ; he's a delightfully impudent chap, and gave me to understand *I* was a limb of the Devil, and he a saint. I told him I was better than he, in my humble opinion, and so I am, by chalks. I know very well I'm a miserable sinner, but there's mercy above, and I don't hide my faults. I don't set up for a light or a saint ; I'm just what the Prayer-book says— neither more nor less—a miserable sinner. There's only one good thing I can safely say for myself—I am no Pharisee; that's all ; I am no religious prig, puffing myself, and trusting to forms, making long prayers in the market-place' (Mark's quotations were paraphrastic), 'and thinking of nothing but the uppermost seats in the synagogue, and broad borders, and the praise of men—hang them, I hate those fellows.'

So Mark, like other men we meet with, was proud of being a Publican ; and his prayer was—'I thank Thee that I am not as other men are, spiritually proud, formalists, hypocrites, or even as this Pharisee.'

'Do you wish another game?' I asked.

'Just now,' said Wylder, emitting first a thin stream of smoke, and watching its ascent. 'Dorcas is the belle of the county ; and she likes me, though she's odd, and don't show it the way other girls would. But a fellow knows pretty well when a girl likes him, and you know the marriage is a sensible sort of thing, and I'm determined, of course, to carry it through ; but, hang it, a fellow can't help thinking sometimes there are other things besides money, and Dorcas is not my style. Rachel's more that way ; she's a *tremendious* fine girl, by Jove ! and a spirited minx, too ; and I think,' he added, with an oath, having first taken two puffs at his cigar, ' if I had seen her first, I'd have thought twice before I'd have got myself into this business.'

I only smiled and shook my head. I did not believe a word of it. Yet, perhaps, I was wrong. He knew very well how to take care of his money ; in fact, compared with other young fellows, he was a bit of a screw. But he could do a handsome and generous thing for himself. His selfishness would expand nobly, and rise above his prudential considerations, and drown them sometimes ; and he was the sort of person, who, if the fancy were strong enough, might marry in haste, and repent— and make his wife, too, repent—at leisure.

'What do you laugh at, Charlie?' said Wylder, grinning himself.

'At your confounded grumbling, Mark. The luckiest dog in England ! Will nothing content you ?'

'Why, I grumble very little, I think, considering how well off I am,' rejoined he, with a laugh.

'Grumble ! If you had a particle of gratitude, you'd build a temple to Fortune—you're pagan enough for it, Mark.'

'Fortune has nothing to do with it,' says Mark, laughing again.

'Well, certainly, neither had you.'

'It was all the Devil. I'm not joking, Charlie, upon my word, though I'm laughing.' (Mark swore now and then, but I take leave to soften his oaths). 'It was the Persian Magician.'

'Come, Mark, say what you mean.'

'I mean what I say. When we were in the Persian Gulf, near six years ago, I was in command of the ship. The captain, you see, was below, with a hurt in his leg. We had very rough weather—a gale for two days and a night almost—and a heavy swell after. In the night time we picked up three poor devils in an open boat—. One was a Persian merchant, with a grand beard. We called him the magician, he was so like the pictures of Aladdin's uncle.'

'Why *he* was an African,' I interposed, my sense of accuracy offended.

'I don't care a curse what he was,' rejoined Mark ; 'he was exactly like the picture in the story-books. And as we were lying off—I forget the cursed name of it—he begged me to put him ashore. He could not speak a word of English, but one of the fellows with him interpreted, and they were all anxious to get ashore. Poor devils, they had a notion, I believe, we were going to sell them for slaves, and he made me a present of a ring, and told me a long yarn about it. It was a talisman, it seems, and no one who wore it could ever be lost. So I took it for a keepsake ; here it is,' and he extended his stumpy, brown little finger, and showed a thick, coarsely-made ring of gold, with an uncut red stone, of the size of a large cherry stone, set in it.

'The stone is a humbug,' said Wylder. 'It's not real. I

showed it to Platten and Foyle. It's some sort of glass. But I would not part with it. I got a fancy into my head that luck would come with it, and maybe that glass stuff was the thing that had the virtue in it. Now look at these Persian letters on the inside, for that's the oddest thing about it. Hang it, I can't pull it off—I'm growing as fat as a pig—but they are like a queer little string of flowers; and I showed it to a clever fellow at Malta—a missionary chap — and he read it off slick, and what do you think it means : " I will come up again ;"' and he swore a great oath. 'It's as true as you stand there—*our* motto. Is not it odd? So I got the " resurgam " you see there engraved round it, and by Jove ! it did bring me up. I was near lost, and did rise again. Eh?'

Well, it certainly was a curious accident. Mark had plenty of odd and not unamusing lore. Men who beat about the world in ships usually have ; and these 'yarns,' furnished, after the pattern of Othello's tales of Anthropophagites and men whose heads do grow beneath their shoulders, one of the many varieties of fascination which he practised on the fair sex. Only in justice to Mark, I must say that he was by no means so shameless a drawer of the long-bow as the Venetian gentleman and officer.

'When I got this ring, Charlie, three hundred a year and a London life would have been Peru and Paradise to poor Pill Garlick, and see what it has done for me.'

' Aye, and better than Aladdin's, for you need not rub it and bring up that confounded ugly genii ; the slave of your ring works unseen.'

' So he does,' laughed Wylder, in a state of elation, 'and he's not done working yet, I can tell you. When the estates are joined in one, they'll be good eleven thousand a year ; and Larkin says, with smart management, I shall have a rental of thirteen thousand before three years ! And that's only the beginning, by George ! Sir Henry Twisden can't hold his seat—ne's all but broke—as poor as Job, and the gentry hate him, and he lives abroad. He has had a hint or two already, and he'll never fight the next election. D'ye see—hey?'

And Wylder winked and grinned, with a wag of his head.

' M.P.—eh? You did not see that before. I look a-head a bit, eh ? and can take my turn at the wheel—eh ?'

And he laughed with cunning exultation.

' Miss Rachel will find I'm not quite such a lubber as she fancies. But even then it is only begun. Come, Charlie, you used to like a bet. What do you say ? I'll buy you that twenty-five guinea book of pictures—what's its name?—if you give me three hundred guineas one month after I'm a peer of Parliament. Hey? There's a sporting offer for you. Well! what do you say—eh ?'

' You mean to come out as an orator, then ?'

' Orator be diddled ! Do you take me for a fool ? No, Charlie ; but I'll come out strong as a *voter*—that's the stuff they like——at the right side, of course, and that is the way to manage it. Thirteen thousand a year—the oldest family in the county—and a steady thick and thin supporter of the minister. Strong points, eh, Charlie ? Well, do you take my offer ?'

I laughed and declined, to his great elation, and just then the gong sounded and we were away to our toilets.

While making my toilet for dinner, I amused myself by conjecturing whether there could be any foundation in fact for Mark's boast, that Miss Brandon liked him. Women are so enigmatical—some in everything—all in matters of the heart. Don't they sometimes actually admire what is repulsive ? Does not brutality in our sex, and even rascality, interest them sometimes ? Don't they often affect indifference, and occasionally even aversion, where there is a different sort of feeling ?

As I went down I heard Miss Lake chatting with her queen-like cousin near an open door on the lobby. Rachel Lake was, indeed, a very constant guest at the Hall, and the servants paid her much respect, which I look upon as a sign that the young heiress liked her and treated her with consideration ; and indeed there was an insubordinate and fiery spirit in that young lady which would have brooked nothing less and dreamed of nothing but equality.

CHAPTER X.

THE ACE OF HEARTS.

WHO should I find in the drawing-room, talking fluently and smiling, after his wont, to old Lady Chelford, who seemed to receive him very graciously, for her at least, but Captain Stanley Lake!

I can't quite describe to you the odd and unpleasant sort of surprise which that very gentlemanlike figure, standing among the Brandon household gods at this moment, communicated to me. I thought of the few odd words and looks that had dropped from Wylder about him with an ominous pang as I looked, and I felt somehow as if there were some occult relation between that confused prelude of Wylder's and the Mephistophelean image that had risen up almost upon the spot where it was spoken. I glanced round for Wylder, but he was not there.

'You know Captain Lake?' said Lord Chelford, addressing me.

And Lake turned round upon me, a little abruptly, his odd yellowish eyes, a little like those of the sea-eagle, and the ghost of his smile that flickered on his singularly pale face, with a stern and insidious look, confronted me. There was something evil and shrinking in his aspect, which I felt with a sort of chill, like the commencing fascination of a serpent. I often thought since that he had expected to see Wylder before him.

The church-yard meteor expired, there was nothing in a moment but his ordinary smile of recognition.

'You're surprised to see me here,' he said in his very pleasing low tones.

'I lighted on him in the village; and I knew Miss Brandon would not forgive me if I allowed him to go away without coming here. (He had his hand upon Lake's shoulder.) They are cousins, you know; we are all cousins. I'm bad at genealogies. My mother could tell us all about it — we, Brandons, Lakes, Wylders, and Chelfords.'

At this moment Miss Brandon entered, with her brilliant Cousin Rachel. The blonde and the dark, it was a dazzling contrast.

So Chelford led Stanley Lake before the lady of the castle. I thought of the 'Fair Brunnisende,' with the captive knight in the hands of her seneschal before her, and I fancied he said something of having found him trespassing in her town, and brought him up for judgment. Whatever Lord Chelford said, Miss Brandon received it very graciously, and even with a momentary smile. I wonder she did not smile oftener, it became her so.

But her greeting to Captain Lake was more than usually haughty and frozen, and her features, I fancied, particularly proud and pale. It seemed to me to indicate a great deal more than mere indifference—something of aversion, and nearer to a positive emotion than anything I had yet seen in that exquisitely apathetic face.

How was it that this man with the yellow eyes seemed to gleam from them an influence of pain or disturbance, wherever almost he looked.

'Shake hands with your cousin, my dear,' said old Lady Chelford, peremptorily. The little scene took place close to her chair ; and upon this stage direction the little piece of by-play took place, and the young lady coldly touched the captain's hand, and passed on.

Young as he was, Stanley Lake was an old man of the world, not to be disconcerted, and never saw more than exactly suited him. Waiting in the drawing-room, I had some entertaining talk with Miss Lake. Her conversation was lively, and rather bold, not at all in the coarse sense, but she struck me as having formed a system of ethics and views of life, both good-humoured and sarcastic, and had carried into her rustic sequestration the melancholy and precocious lore of her early London experience.

When Lord Chelford joined us, I perceived that Wylder was in the room, and saw a very cordial greeting between him and Lake. The captain appeared quite easy and cheerful ; but Mark, I thought, notwithstanding his laughter and general jollity, was uncomfortable ; and I saw him once or twice, when Stanley's eye was not upon him, glance sharply on the young man with an uneasy and not very friendly curiosity.

At dinner Lake was easy and amusing. That meal passed off rather pleasantly ; and when we joined the ladies in the drawing-room, the good vicar's enthusiastic little wife came to meet us, in one of her honest little raptures.

'Now, here's a thing worth your looking at ! Did you ever see anything so bee-utiful in your life? It is such a darling little thing ; and—look now—is not it magnificent?'

She arrested the file of gentlemen just by a large lamp, before whose effulgence she presented the subject of her eulogy—one of those costly trifles which announce the approach of Hymen, as flowers spring up before the rosy steps of May.

Well, it was pretty—French, I dare say—a little set of tablets —a toy—the cover of enamel, studded in small jewels, with a slender border of symbolic flowers, and with a heart in the centre, a mosaic of little carbuncles, rubies, and other red and crimson stones, placed with a view to light and shade.

'Exquisite, indeed !' said Lord Chelford. 'Is this yours, Mrs. Wylder?'

'Mine, indeed !' laughed poor little Mrs. Dorothy. 'Well,

dear me, no, indeed ;'—and in an earnest whisper close in his ear—'a present to Miss Brandon, and the donor is not a hundred miles away from your elbow, my lord !' and she winked slyly, and laughed, with a little nod at Wylder.

'Oh ! I see—to be sure—really, Wylder, it does your taste infinite credit.'

'I'm glad you like it,' says Wylder, chuckling benignantly on it, over his shoulder. 'I believe I *have* a little taste that way ; those are all real, you know, those jewels.'

'Oh, yes ! of course. Have you seen it, Captain Lake ?' And he placed it in that gentleman's fingers, who now took his turn at the lamp, and contemplated the little parallelogram with a gleam of sly amusement.

'What are you laughing at ?' asked Wylder, a little snappishly.

'I was thinking it's very like the ace of hearts,' answered the captain softly, smiling on.

'Fie, Lake, there's no poetry in you,' said Lord Chelford, laughing.

'Well, now, though, really it is funny ; it did not strike me before, but do you know, now, it *is*,' laughs out jolly Mrs. Dolly, 'isn't it. Look at it, do, Mr. Wylder—isn't it like the ace of hearts ?'

Wylder was laughing rather redly, with the upper part of his face very surly, I thought.

'Never mind, Wylder, it's the winning card,' said Lord Chelford, laying his hand on his shoulder.

Whereupon Lake laughed quietly, still looking on the ace of hearts with his sly eyes.

And Wylder laughed too, more suddenly and noisily than the humour of the joke seemed quite to call for, and glanced a grim look from the corners of his eyes on Lake, but the gallant captain did not seem to perceive it ; and after a few seconds more he handed it very innocently back to Mrs. Dorothy, only remarking—

'Seriously, it *is* very pretty, and *appropriate.*'

And Wylder, making no remark, helped himself to a cup of coffee, and then to a glass of Curaçoa, and then looked industriously at a Spanish quarto of Don Quixote, and lastly walked over to me on the hearthrug.

'What the d— has he come down here for ? It can't be for money, or balls, or play, and he has no honest business anywhere. Do you know ?'

'Lake ? Oh ! I really can't tell ; but he'll soon tire of country life. I don't think he's much of a sportsman.'

'Ha, isn't he ? I don't know anything about him almost ; but I hate him.'

'Why should you, though ? He's a very gentlemanlike fellow and your cousin.'

'My cousin—the Devil's cousin—everyone's cousin. I don't know who's my cousin, or who isn't ; nor you don't, who've been for ten years over those d—d papers ; but I think he's the nastiest dog I ever met. I took a dislike to him at first sight long ago, and that never happened me but I was right.'

Wylder looked confoundedly angry and flustered, standing with his heels on the edge of the rug, his hands in his pockets, jingling some silver there, and glancing from under his red forehead sternly and unsteadily across the room.

'He's not a man for country quarters ! he'll soon be back in town, or to Brighton,' I said.

'If *he* doesn't, *I* will. That's all.'

Just to get him off this unpleasant groove with a little jolt, I said—

'By-the-bye, Wylder, you know the pictures here ; who is the tall man, with the long pale face, and wild phosphoric eyes ? I was always afraid of him ; in a long peruke, and dark red velvet coat, facing the hall-door. I had a horrid dream about him last night.'

'That ? Oh, I know—that's Lorne Brandon. He was one of our family devils, he was. A devil in a family now and then is not such a bad thing, when there's work for him.' (All the time he was talking to me his angry little eyes were following Lake.) 'They say he killed his son, a blackguard, who was found shot, with his face in the tarn in the park. He was going to marry the gamekeeper's daughter, it was thought, and he and the old boy, who was for high blood, and all that, were at loggerheads about it. It was not proved, only thought likely, which showed what a nice character he was ; but he might have done worse. I suppose Miss Partridge would have had a precious lot of babbies ; and who knows where the estate would have been by this time.'

'I believe, Charlie,' he recommenced suddenly, 'there is not such an unnatural family on record as ours ; is there ? Ha, ha, ha ! It's well to be distinguished in any line. I forget all the other good things he did ; but he ended by shooting himself through the head in his bed-room, and that was not the worst thing ever he did.'

And Wylder laughed again, and began to whistle very low—not, I fancy, for want of thought, but as a sort of accompaniment thereto, for he suddenly said—

'And where is he staying ?'

'Who ?—Lake ?'

'Yes.'

'I don't know ; but I think he mentioned Larkins's house, didn't he ? I'm not quite sure.'

'I suppose he thinks I'm made of money. By Jove ! if he wants to borrow any I'll surprise him, the cur ; I'll talk to him ; ha, ha, ha !'

And Wylder chuckled angrily, and the small change in his pocket tinkled fiercely, as his eye glanced on the graceful captain, who was entertaining the ladies, no doubt, very agreeably in the distance.

———

CHAPTER XI.

IN WHICH LAKE UNDER THE TREES OF BRANDON, AND I IN MY CHAMBER, SMOKE OUR NOCTURNAL CIGARS.

ISS LAKE declined the carriage to-night. Her brother was to see her home, and there was a leave-taking, and the young ladies whispered a word or two, and kissed, after the manner of their kind. To Captain Lake, Miss Brandon's adieux were as cold and haughty as her greeting.

'Did you see that?' said Wylder in my ear, with a chuckle; and, wagging his head, he added, rather loftily for him, 'Miss Brandon, I reckon, has taken your measure, Master Stanley, as well as I. I wonder what the deuce the old dowager sees in him. Old women always like rascals.'

And he added something still less complimentary.

I suppose the balance of attraction and repulsion was overcome by Miss Lake, much as he disliked Stanley, for Wylder followed them out with Lord Chelford, to help the young lady into her cloak and goloshes, and I found myself near Miss Brandon for the first time that evening, and much to my surprise she was first to speak, and that rather strangely.

'You seem to be very sensible, Mr. De Cresseron; pray tell me, frankly, what do you think of all this?'

'I am not quite sure, Miss Brandon, that I understand your question,' I replied, enquiringly.

'I mean of the—the family arrangements, in which, as Mr. Wylder's friend, you seem to take an interest?' she said.

'There can hardly be a second opinion, Miss Brandon; I think it a very wise measure,' I replied, much surprised.

'Very wise—exactly. But don't these very wise things sometimes turn out very foolishly? Do you really think your friend, Mr. Wylder, cares about me?'

'I take that for granted: in the nature of things it can hardly be otherwise,' I replied, a good deal startled and perplexed by the curious audacity of her interrogatory.

'It was very foolish of me to expect from Mr. Wylder's friend any other answer; you are very loyal, Mr. De Cresseron.'

And without awaiting my reply she made some remark which

I forget to Lady Chelford, who sat at a little distance ; and, appearing quite absorbed in her new subject, she placed herself close beside the dowager, and continued to chat in a low tone.

I was vexed with myself for having managed with so little skill a conversation which, opened so oddly and frankly, might have placed me on relations so nearly confidential, with that singular and beautiful girl. I ought to have rejoiced—but we don't always see what most concerns our peace. In the meantime I had formed a new idea of her. She was so unreserved, it seemed, and yet in this directness there was something almost contemptuous.

By this time Lord Chelford and Wylder returned ; and, disgusted rather with myself, I ruminated on my want of generalship.

In the meantime, Miss Lake, with her hand on her brother's arm, was walking swiftly under the trees of the back avenue towards that footpath which, through wild copse and broken clumps near the park, emerges upon the still darker road which passes along the wooded glen by the mills, and skirts the little paling of the recluse lady's garden.

They had not walked far, when Lake suddenly said—

'What do you think of all this, Radie—this particular version, I mean, of marriage, *à-la-mode*, they are preparing up there ?' and he made a little dip of his cane towards Brandon Hall, over his shoulder. 'I really don't think Wylder cares twopence about her, or she about him,' and Stanley Lake laughed gently and sleepily.

'I don't think they pretend to like one another. It is quite understood. It was all, you know, old Lady Chelford's arrangement : and Dorcas is so supine, I believe she would allow herself to be given away by anyone, and to anyone, rather than be at the least trouble. She provokes me.'

'But I thought she liked Sir Harry Bracton : he's a good-looking fellow ; and Queen's Bracton is a very nice thing, you know.'

'Yes, so they said ; but that would, I think, have been worse. Something may be made of Mark Wylder. He has some sense and caution, has not he?—but Sir Harry is wickedness itself !'

'Why—what has Sir Harry done? That is the way you women run away with things ! If a fellow's been a little bit wild, he's Beelzebub at once. Bracton's a very good fellow, I can assure you.'

The fact is, Captain Lake, an accomplished player, made a pretty little revenue of Sir Harry's billiards, which were wild and noisy ; and liking his money, thought he liked himself—a confusion not uncommon.

'I don't know, and can't say, how you fine gentlemen define **wickedness** : only, as an obscure female, I speak according to my lights : and he is generally thought the wickedest man in this county.'

'Well, you know, Radie, women like wicked fellows : it is contrast, I suppose, but they do ; and I'm sure, from what Bracton has said to me—I know him intimately—that Dorcas likes him, and I can't conceive why they are not married.'

'It is very happy, for her at least, they are not,' said Rachel, and a long silence ensued.

Their walk continued silent for the greater part, neither was quite satisfied with the other. But Rachel at last said—

'Stanley, you meditate some injury to Mark Wylder.'

'I, Radie ?' he answered quietly, 'why on earth should you think so ?'

'I saw you twice watch him when you thought no one observed you—and I know your face too well, Stanley, to mistake.'

'Now that's impossible, Radie ; for I really don't think I once thought of him all this evening—except just while we were talking.'

'You keep your secret as usual, Stanley,' said the young lady.

'Really, Radie, you're quite mistaken. I assure you, upon my honour, I've no secret. You're a very odd girl—why won't you believe me ?'

Miss Rachel only glanced across her mufflers on his face. There was a bright moonlight, broken by the shadows of over-hanging boughs and withered leaves ; and the mottled lights and shadows glided oddly across his pale features. But she saw that he was smiling his sly, sleepy smile, and she said quietly—

'Well, Stanley, I ask no more — but you don't deceive me.'

'I don't try to. If your feelings indeed had been different, and that you had not made such a point—you know —'

'Don't insult me, Stanley, by talking again as you did this morning. What I say is altogether on your own account. Mark my words, you'll find him too strong for you ; aye, and too deep. I see very plainly that *he* suspects you as I do. You saw it, too, for nothing of that kind escapes you. Whatever you meditate, he probably anticipates it—you know best—and you will find him prepared. You have given him time enough. You were always the same, close, dark, and crooked, and wise in your own conceit. I am very uneasy about it, whatever it is. *I* can't help it. It will happen—and most ominously I feel that you are courting a dreadful retaliation, and that you will bring on yourself a great misfortune ; but it is quite vain, I know, speaking to you.'

'Really, Radie, you're enough to frighten a poor fellow ; you won't mind a word I say, and go on predicting all manner of mischief between me and Wylder, the very nature of which I can't surmise. Would you dislike my smoking a cigar, Radie?'

'Oh, no,' answered the young lady, with a little laugh and a heavy sigh, for she knew it meant silence, and her dark auguries grew darker.

To my mind there has always been something inexpressibly awful in family feuds. Mortal hatred seems to deepen and dilate into something diabolical in these perverted animosities. The mystery of their origin—their capacity for evolving latent faculties of crime—and the steady vitality with which they survive the hearse, and speak their deep-mouthed malignities in every new-born generation, have associated them somehow in my mind with a spell of life exceeding and distinct from human and a special Satanic action.

My chamber, as I have mentioned, was upon the third storey. It was one of many, opening upon the long gallery, which had been the scene, four generations back, of that unnatural and bloody midnight duel which had laid one scion of this ancient house in his shroud, and driven another a fugitive to the moral solitudes of a continental banishment.

Much of the day, as I told you, had been passed among the grisly records of these old family crimes and hatreds. They had been an ill-conditioned and not a happy race. When I heard the servant's step traversing that long gallery, as it seemed to me in haste to be gone, and when all grew quite silent, I began to feel a dismal sort of sensation, and lighted the pair of wax candles which I found upon the small writing table. How wonderful and mysterious is the influence of light! What sort of beings must those be who hate it?

The floor, more than anything else, showed the great age of the room. It was warped and arched all along by the wall between the door and the window. The portion of it which the carpet did not cover showed it to be oak, dark and rugged. My bed was unexceptionably comfortable, but, in my then mood, I could have wished it a great deal more modern. Its four posts were, like the rest of it, oak, well-nigh black, fantastically turned and carved, with a great urn-like capital and base, and shaped midway, like a gigantic lance-handle. Its curtains were of thick and faded tapestry. I was always a lover of such antiquities, but I confess at that moment I would have vastly preferred a sprightly modern chintz and a trumpery little French bed in a corner of the Brandon Arms. There was a great lowering press of oak, and some shelves, with withered green and gold leather borders. All the furniture belonged to other times.

I would have been glad to hear a step stirring, or a cough even, or the gabble of servants at a distance. But there was a silence and desertion in this part of the mansion which, somehow, made me feel that I was myself a solitary intruder **on this** level of the vast old house.

I sha'n't trouble you about my train of thoughts or fancies ; but I began to feel very like a gentleman in a ghost story, watching experimentally in a haunted chamber. My cigar case was a resource. I was not a bit afraid of being found out. I did not even take the precaution of smoking up the chimney. I boldly lighted my cheroot. I peeped through the dense window curtain : there were no shutters. A cold, bright moon was shining with clear sharp lights and shadows. Everything looked strangely cold and motionless outside. The sombre old trees, like gigantic hearse plumes, black and awful. The chapel lay full in view, where so many of the strange and equivocal race, under whose ancient roof-tree I then stood, were lying under their tombstones.

Somehow, I had grown nervous. A little bit of plaster tumbled down the chimney, and startled me confoundedly. Then some time after, I fancied I heard a creaking step on the lobby outside, and, candle in hand, opened the door, and looked out with an odd sort of expectation, and a rather agreeable disappointment, upon vacancy.

CHAPTER XII.

IN WHICH UNCLE LORNE TROUBLES ME.

WAS growing most uncomfortably like one of Mrs. Anne Radcliffe's heroes—a nervous race of demigods. I walked like a sentinel up and down my chamber, puffing leisurely the solemn incense, and trying to think of the Opera and my essay on ' Paradise Lost,' and other pleasant subjects. But it would not do. Every now and then, as I turned towards the door, I fancied I saw it softly close. I can't the least say whether it was altogether fancy. It was with the corner, or as the Italians have it, the ' tail ' of my eye that I saw, or imagined I saw, this trifling but unpleasant movement.

I called out once or twice sharply—' Come in !' ' Who's there ?' ' Who's that ?' and so forth, without any sort of effect, except that unpleasant reaction upon the nerves which follows the sound of one's own voice in a solitude of this kind.

The fact is I did not myself believe in that stealthy motion of my door, and set it down to one of those illusions which I have sometimes succeeded in analysing—a half-seen combination of objects which, rightly placed in the due relations of perspective, have no mutual connection whatever.

So I ceased to challenge the unearthly inquisitor, and allowed him, after a while, serenely enough, to peep as I turned my back, or to withdraw again as I made my regular right-about face.

I had now got half-way in my second cheroot, and the clock clanged ' one.' It was a very still night, and the prolonged boom vibrated strangely in my excited ears and brain. I had never been quite such an ass before ; but I do assure you I was now in an extremely unpleasant state. One o'clock was better, however, than twelve. Although, by Jove ! the bell was ' beating one,' as I remember, precisely as that king of ghosts, old Hamlet, revisited the glimpses of the moon, upon the famous platform of Elsinore.

I had pondered too long over the lore of this Satanic family, and drunk very strong tea, I suppose. I could not get my nerves into a comfortable state, and cheerful thoughts refused to inhabit the darkened chamber of my brain. As I stood in a sort of reverie, looking straight upon the door, I saw—and this time there could be no mistake whatsoever—the handle—the only modern thing about it—slowly turned, and the door itself as slowly pushed about a quarter open.

I do not know what exclamation I made. The door was **shut** instantly, and I found myself standing at it, and looking out upon the lobby, with a candle in my hand, and actually freezing with foolish horror.

I was looking towards the stair-head. The passage was empty and ended in utter darkness. I glanced the other way, and thought I saw—though not distinctly—in the distance a white figure, not gliding in the conventional way, but limping off, with a sort of jerky motion, and, in a second or two, quite lost in darkness.

I got into my room again, and shut the door with a clap that sounded loudly and unnaturally through the dismal quiet that surrounded me, and stood with my hand on the handle, with the instinct of resistance.

I felt uncomfortable ; and I would have secured the door, but there was no sort of fastening within. So I paused. I did not mind looking out again. To tell you the plain truth, I was just a little bit afraid. Then I grew angry at having been put into such remote, and, possibly, suspected quarters, and then my comfortable scepticism supervened. I was yet to learn a great deal about this visitation.

So, in due course having smoked my cheroot, I jerked the stump into the fire. Of course I could not think of depriving myself of candle-light ; and being already of a thoughtful, old-bachelor temperament, and averse from burning houses, I placed one of my tall wax-lights in a basin on the table by my bed—in which I soon effected a lodgment, and lay with a comparative sense of security.

Then I heard two o'clock strike ; but shortly after, as I suppose, sleep overtook me, and I have no distinct idea for how long my slumber lasted. The fire was very low when I awoke, and saw a figure—and a very odd one—seated by the embers, and stooping over the grate, with a pair of long hands expanded, as it seemed, to catch the warmth of the sinking fire.

It was that of a very tall old man, entirely dressed in white flannel—a very long spencer, and some sort of white swathing about his head. His back was toward me ; and he stooped without the slightest motion over the fire-place, in the attitude I have described.

As I looked, he suddenly turned toward me, and fixed upon me a cold, and as it seemed, a wrathful gaze, over his shoulder. It was a bleached and a long-chinned face—the countenance of Lorne's portrait—only more faded, sinister, and apathetic. And having, as it were, secured its awful command over me by a protracted gaze, he rose, supernaturally lean and tall, and drew near the side of my bed.

I continued to stare upon this apparition with the most dreadful fascination I ever experienced in my life. For two or three seconds I literally could not move. When I did, I am not ashamed to confess, it was to plunge my head under the bed-clothes, with the childish instinct of terror ; and there I lay breathless, for what seemed to me not far from ten minutes, during which there was no sound, nor other symptom of its presence.

On a sudden the bed-clothes were gently lifted at my feet, and I sprang backwards, sitting upright against the back of the bed, and once more under the gaze of that long-chinned old man.

A voice, as peculiar as the appearance of the figure, said :—

'You are in my bed—I died in it a great many years ago. I am Uncle Lorne ; and when I am not here, a devil goes up and down in the room. See ! he had his face to your ear when I came in. I came from Dorcas Brandon's bed-chamber door, where her evil angel told me a thing ;—and Mark Wylder must not seek to marry her, for he will be buried alive if he does, and he will, maybe, never get up again. Say your prayers when I go out, and come here no more.'

He paused, as if these incredible words were to sink into my memory ; and then, in the same tone, and with the same counte-nance, he asked—

'Is the blood on my forehead ?'

I don't know whether I answered.

'So soon as a calamity is within twelve hours, the blood comes upon my forehead, as they found me in the morning—it is a sign.'

The old man then drew back slowly, and disappeared behind the curtains at the foot of the bed, and I saw no more of him during the rest of that odious night.

So long as this apparition remained before me, I never doubted its being supernatural. I don't think mortal ever suf-fered horror more intense. My very hair was dripping with a cold moisture. For some seconds I hardly knew where I was. But soon a reaction came, and I felt convinced that the appari-tion was a living man. It was no process of reason or philo-sophy, but simply I became persuaded of it, and something like rage overcame my terrors.

CHAPTER XIII.

THE PONY CARRIAGE

SO soon as daylight came, I made a swift cold water toilet, and got out into the open air, with a solemn resolution to see the hated interior of that bed-room no more. When I met Lord Chelford in his early walk that morning, I'm sure I looked myself like a ghost—at all events, very wild and seedy—for he asked me, more seriously than usual, how I was ; and I think I would have told him the story of my adventure, despite the secret ridicule with which, I fancied, he would receive it, had it not been for a certain insurmountable disgust and horror which held me tongue-tied upon the affair.

I told him, however, that I had dreamed dreams, and was restless and uncomfortable in my present berth, and begged his interest with the housekeeper to have my quarters changed to the lower storey— quite resolved to remove to the 'Brandon Arms,' rather than encounter another such night as I had passed.

Stanley Lake did not appear that day ; Wylder was glowering and abstracted—worse company than usual ; and Rachel seemed to have quite passed from his recollection.

While Rachel Lake was, as usual, busy in her little garden that day, Lord Chelford, on his way to the town, by the pretty mill-road, took off his hat to her with a smiling salutation, and leaning on the paling, he said—

' I often wonder how you make your flowers grow here—you have so little sun among the trees—and yet, it is so pretty and flowery ; it remains in my memory as if the sun were always shining specially on this little garden.'

Miss Lake laughed.

' I am very proud of it. They try not to blow, but I never let them alone till they do. See all my watering-pots, and pruning-scissors, my sticks, and bass-mat, and glass covers. Skill and industry conquer churlish nature—and this is my Versailles.'

' I don't believe in those sticks, and scissors, and watering-pots. You won't tell your secret ; but I'm sure it's an influence —you smile and whisper to them.'

She smiled—without raising her eyes—on the flower she was tying up ; and, indeed, it was such a smile as must have made it happy—and she said, gaily—

' You forget that Lord Chelford passes this way sometimes, and shines upon them, too.'

'No, he's a dull, earthly dog ; and if he shines here, it is only in reflected light.'

'Margery, child, fetch me the scissors.'

And a hobble-de-hoy of a girl, with round eyes, and a long white apron, and bare arms, came down the little walk, and—eyeing the peer with an awful curiosity—presented the shears to the charming Atropos, who clipped off the withered blossoms that had bloomed their hour, and were to cumber the stalk no more.

'Now, you see what art may do ; how *passée* this creature was till I made her toilet, and how wonderfully the poor old beauty looks now,' and she glanced complacently at the plant she had just trimmed.

'Well, it is young again and beautiful ; but no—I have no faith in the scissors ; I still believe in the influence—from the tips of your fingers, your looks, and tones. Flowers, like fairies, have their favourites, whom they smile on and obey ; and I think this is a haunted glen—trees, flowers, all have an intelligence and a feeling—and I am sure you see wonderful things, by moonlight, from your window.'

With a strange meaning echo, those words returned to her afterwards—' I'm sure you see wonderful things, by moonlight, from your window.'

But no matter ; the winged words—making pleasant music—flew pleasantly away, now among transparent leaves and glimmering sun ; by-and-by, in moonlight, they will return to the casement piping the same tune, in ghostly tones.

And as they chatted in this strain, Rachel paused on a sudden, with upraised hand, listening pleasantly.

'I hear the pony-carriage ; Dorcas is coming,' she said.

And the tinkle of tiny wheels, coming down the road, was audible.

'There's a pleasant sense of adventure, too, in the midst of your seclusion. Sudden arrivals and passing pilgrims, like me, leaning over the paling, and refreshed by the glimpse the rogue steals of this charming oratory. Yes ; here comes the fair Brunnisende.'

And he made his salutation. Miss Brandon smiled from under her gipsy-hat very pleasantly for her.

'Will you come with me for a drive, Radie ?' she asked.

'Yes, dear—delighted. Margery, bring my gloves and cloak.'

And she unpinned the faded silk shawl that did duty in the garden, and drew off her gauntlets, and showed her pretty hands ; and Margery popped her cloak on her shoulders, and the young lady pulled on her gloves. All ready in a moment, like a young lady of energy ; and chatting merrily she sat down beside her cousin, who held the reins. As there were no more gates to open, Miss Brandon dismissed the servant, who stood at the ponies' heads, and who, touching his hat with his white glove, received his *congé*, and strode with willing steps up the road.

'Will you take me for your footman as far as the town?' asked Lord Chelford; so, with permission, up he jumped behind, and away they whirled, close over the ground, on toy wheels ringing merrily on the shingle, he leaning over the back and chatting pleasantly with the young ladies as they drove on.

They drew up at the Brandon Arms, and little girls courtesied at doors, and householders peeped from their windows, not standing close to the panes, but respectfully back, at the great lady and the nobleman, who was now taking his leave.

And next they pulled up at that official rendezvous, with white-washed front — and 'post-office,' in white letters on a brown board over its door, and its black, hinged window-pane, through which Mr. Driver—or, in his absence, Miss Anne Driver —answered questions, and transacted affairs officially.

In the rear of this establishment were kept some dogs of Lawyer Larkin's; and just as the ladies arrived, that person emerged, looking overpoweringly gentlemanlike, in a white hat, gray paletot, lavender trowsers, and white riding gloves. He was in a righteous and dignified way pleased to present himself in so becoming a costume, and moreover in good company, for Stanley Lake was going with him to Dutton for a day's sport, which neither of them cared for. But Stanley hoped to pump the attorney, and the attorney, I'm afraid, liked being associated with the fashionable captain; and so they were each pleased in the way that suited them.

The attorney, being long as well as lank, had to stoop under the doorway, but drew himself up handsomely on coming out, and assumed his easy, high-bred style, which, although he was not aware of it, was very nearly insupportable, and smiled very engagingly, and meant to talk a little about the weather; but Miss Brandon made him one of her gravest and slightest bows, and suddenly saw Mrs. Brown at her shop door on the other side, and had a word to say to her.

And now Stanley Lake drew up in the tax-cart, and greeted the ladies, and told them how he meant to pass the day; and the dogs being put in, and the attorney, I'm afraid a little spited at his reception, in possession of the reins, they drove down the little street at a great pace, and disappeared round the corner; and in a minute more the young ladies, in the opposite direction, resumed their drive. The ponies, being grave and trustworthy, and having the road quite to themselves, needed little looking after, and Miss Brandon was free to converse with her companion.

'I think, Rachel, you have a lover,' she said.

'Only a bachelor, I'm afraid, as my poor Margery calls the

young gentleman who takes her out for a walk on a Sunday, and
I fear means nothing more.'

'This is the second time I've found Chelford talking to you,
Rachel, at the door of your pretty little garden.'

Rachel laughed.

'Suppose, some fine day, he should put his hand over the
paling, and take yours, and make you a speech.'

'You romantic darling,' she said, 'don't you know that peers
and princes have quite given over marrying simple maidens of
low estate for love and liking, and understand match-making
better than you or I; though I could give a tolerable account of
myself, after the manner of the white cat in the story, which I
think is a pattern of frankness and modest dignity. I'd say with
a courtesy—"Think not, prince, that I have always been a cat,
and that my birth is obscure; my father was king of six king-
doms, and loved my mother tenderly," and so forth.'

'Rachel, I like you,' interrupted the dark beauty, fixing her
large eyes, from which not light, but, as it were, a rich shadow
fell softly on her companion. It was the first time she had made
any such confession. Rachel returned her look as frankly, with
an amused smile, and then said, with a comic little toss of her
head—

'Well, Dorcas, I don't see why you should not, though I don't
know why you say so.'

'You're not like other people; you don't complain, and you're
not bitter, although you have had great misfortunes, my poor
Rachel.'

There be ladies, young and old, who, the moment they are
pitied, though never so cheerful before, will forthwith dissolve in
tears. But that was not Rachel's way; she only looked at her
with a good-humoured but grave curiosity for a few seconds,
and then said, with rather a kindly smile—

'And now, Dorcas, I like you.'

Dorcas made no answer, but put her arm round Rachel's neck,
and kissed her; Dorcas made two kisses of it, and Rachel one,
but it was cousinly and kindly; and Rachel laughed a soft little
laugh after it, looking amused and very lovingly on her cousin;
but she was a bold lass, and not given in anywise to the melting
mood, and said gaily, with her open hand still caressingly on
Dorcas's waist—

'I make a very good nun, Dorcas, as I told Stanley the other
day. I sometimes, indeed, receive a male visitor, at the other
side of the paling, which is my grille; but to change my way of
life is a dream that does not trouble me. Happy the girl—and I
am one—who cannot like until she is first beloved. Don't you
remember poor, pale Winnie, the maid who used to take us on
our walks all the summer at Dawling; how she used to pluck
the leaves from the flowers, like Faust's Marguerite, saying, "He

loves me a littie—passionately, not at all." Now if I were loved passionately, I might love a little ; and if loved a little—it should be not at all.'

They had the road all to themselves, and were going at a walk up an ascent, so the reins lay loosely on the ponies' necks and Dorcas looked with an untold meaning in her proud face, on her cousin, and seemed on the point of speaking, but she changed her mind.

'And so Dorcas, as swains are seldom passionately in love with so small a pittance as mine, I think I shall mature into a queer old maid, and take all the little Wylders, masters and misses, with your leave, for their walks, and help to make their pinafores.' Whereupon Miss Dorcas put her ponies into a very quick trot, and became absorbed in her driving.

CHAPTER XIV.

IN WHICH VARIOUS PERSONS GIVE THEIR OPINIONS OF CAPTAIN STANLEY LAKE.

'STANLEY is an odd creature,' said Rachel, so soon as another slight incline brought them to a walk ; 'I can't conceive why he has come down here, or what he can possibly want of that disagreeable lawyer. They have got dogs and guns, and are going, of course, to shoot ; but he does not care for shooting, and I don't think Mr. Larkin's society can amuse him. Stanley is clever and cunning, I think, but he is neither wise nor frank. He never tells me his plans, though he must know—he *does* know—I love him ; yes, he's a strange mixture of suspicion and imprudence. He's wonderfully reserved. I am certain he trusts no one on earth, and at the same time, except in his confidences, he's the rashest man living. If he were like Lord Chelford, or even like our good vicar—not in piety, for poor Stanley's training, like my own, was sadly neglected there—I mean in a few manly points of character, I should be quite happy, I think, in my solitary nook.'

'Is he so very odd?' said Miss Brandon, coldly.

'I only know he makes me often very uncomfortable,' answered Rachel. 'I never mind what he tells me, for I think he likes to mislead everybody ; and I have been two often duped by him to trust what he says. I only know that his visit to Gylingden must have been made with some serious purpose, and his ideas are all so rash and violent.'

'He was at Donnyston for ten days, I think, when I was there, and seemed clever. They had charades and *proverbes drama-*

tiques. I'm no judge, but the people who understood it, said he was very good.'

'Oh! yes he is clever; I knew he was at Donnyston, but he did not mention he had seen you there; he only told me he had met you pretty often when you were at Lady Alton's last season.'

'Yes, in town,' she answered, a little drily.

While these young ladies are discussing Stanley Lake, I may be permitted to mention my own estimate of that agreeable young person.

Captain Lake was a gentleman and an officer, and of course an honourable man; but somehow I should not have liked to buy a horse from him. He was very gentlemanlike in appearance, and even elegant; but I never liked him, although he undoubtedly had a superficial fascination. I always thought, when in his company, of old Lord Holland's silk stocking with something unpleasant in it. I think, in fact, he was destitute of those fine moral instincts which are born with men, but never acquired; and in his way of estimating his fellow men, and the canons of honour, there was occasionally perceptible a faint flavour of the villainous, and an undefined savour, at times, of brimstone. I know also that when his temper, which was nothing very remarkable, was excited, he could be savage and brutal enough; and I believe he had often been violent and cowardly in his altercations with his sister—so, at least, two or three people, who were versed in the scandals of the family, affirmed. But it is a censorious world, and I can only speak positively of my own sensations in his company. His morality, however, I suppose, was quite good enough for the world, and he had never committed himself in any of those ways of which that respectable tribunal takes cognizance.

'So that d——d fellow Lake is down here still; and that stupid, scheming lubber, Larkin, driving him about in his tax-cart, instead of minding his business. I could not see him to-day. That sort of thing won't answer me; and he *is* staying at Larkin's house, I find.' Wylder was talking to me on the door steps after dinner, having in a rather sulky way swallowed more than his usual modicum of Madeira, and his remarks were delivered interruptedly—two or three puffs of his cigar interposed between each sentence.

'I suppose he expects to be asked to the wedding. He *may* expect—ha, ha, ha! You don't know that lad as I do.'

Then there came a second cigar, and some little time in lighting, and full twenty enjoyable puffs before he resumed.

'Now, you're a moral man, Charlie, tell me really what you think of a fellow marrying a girl he does not care that for,' and he snapt his fingers. 'Just for the sake of her estate—it's the way of the world, of course, and all that—but, is not it a little bit shabby, don't you think? Eh? Ha, ha, ha!'

'I'll not debate with you, Wylder, on that stupid old question. It's the way of the world, as you say, and there's an end of it.'

'They say she's such a beauty! Well, so I believe she is, but I can't fancy her. Now you must not be angry. I'm not a poet like you—book-learned, you know; and she's too solemn by half, and grand. I wish she was different. That other girl, Rachel— she's a devilish handsome craft. I wish almost she was not here at all, or I wish she was in Dorcas's shoes.'

'Nonsense, Wylder! stop this stuff; and it is growing cold: throw away that cigar, and come in.'

'In a minute. No, I assure you, I'm not joking. Hang it! I must talk to some one. I'm devilish uncomfortable about this grand match. I wish I had not been led into it. I don't think I'd make a good husband to any woman I did not fancy, and where's the good of making a girl unhappy, eh?'

'Tut, Wylder, you ought to have thought of all that before. I don't like your talking in this strain when you know it is too late to recede; besides, you are the luckiest fellow in creation. Upon my word, I don't know why the girl marries you; you can't sup-pose that she could not marry much better, and if you have not made up your mind to break off, of which the world would form but one opinion, you had better not speak in that way any more.'

'Why, it was only to you, Charlie, and to tell you the truth, I do believe it is the best thing for me; but I suppose every fellow feels a little queer when he is going to be spliced, a little bit nervous, eh? But you are right—and I'm right, and we are all right—it *is* the best thing for us both. It will make a deuced fine estate; but hang it! you know a fellow's never satisfied. And I suppose I'm a bit put out by that disreputable dog's being here—I mean Lake; not that I need care more than Dorcas, or anyone else; but he's no credit to the family, you see, and I never could abide him. I've half a mind, Charlie, to tell you a thing; but hang it! you're such a demure old maid of a chap. Will you have a cigar?'

'No.'

'Well, I believe two's enough for me,' and he looked up at the stars.

'I've a notion of running up to town, only for a day or two, before this business comes off, just on the sly; you'll not men-tion it, and I'll have a word with Lake, quite friendly, of course; but I'll shut him up, and that's all. I wonder he did not dine here to-day. Did you ever see so pushing a brute?'

So Wylder chucked away his cigar, and stood for a minute with his hands in his pockets looking up at the stars, as if reading fortunes there.

I had an unpleasant feeling that Mark Wylder was about some mischief—a suspicion that som game of mine and countermine was going on between him and Lake, to which I had no clue whatsoever.

Mark had the frankness of callosity, and could recount his evil deeds and confess his vices with hilarity and detail, and was prompt to take his part in a lark, and was a remarkably hard hitter, and never shrank from the brunt of the row ; and with these fine qualities, and a much superior knowledge of the ways of the flash world, had commanded my boyish reverence and a general popularity among strangers.   But, with all this, he could be as secret as the sea with which he was conversant, and as hard as a stonewall, when it answered his purpose.   He had no lack of cunning, and a convenient fund of cool cruelty when that stoical attribute was called for.   Years, I dare say, and a hard life and profligacy, and command, had not made him less selfish or more humane, or abated his craft and resolution.

If one could only see it, the manœuvring and the ultimate collision of two such generals as he and Lake would be worth observing.

I dare say my last night's adventure tended to make me more nervous and prone to evil anticipation.   And although my quarters had been changed to the lower storey, I grew uncomfortable as it waxed late, and half regretted that I had not migrated to the ' Brandon Arms.'

Uncle Lorne, however, made me no visit that night.   Once or twice I fancied something, and started up in my bed.   It was fancy, merely.   What state had I really been in, when I saw that long-chinned apparition of the pale portrait ?   Many a wiser man than I had been mystified by dyspepsia and melancholic vapours.

CHAPTER XV.

DORCAS SHOWS HER JEWELS TO MISS LAKE.

TANLEY LAKE and his sister dined next day at Brandon. Under the cold shadow of Lady Chelford, the proprieties flourished, and generally very little else. Awful she was, and prompt to lecture young people before their peers, and spoke her mind with fearful directness and precision. But sometimes she would talk, and treat her hearers to her recollections, and recount anecdotes with a sort of grim cleverness, not wholly unamusing.

She did not like Wylder, I thought, although she had been the inventor and constructor of the family alliance of which he was the hero. I did not venture to cultivate her ; and Miss Brandon had been, from the first, specially cold and repellent to Captain Lake. There was nothing very genial or promising, therefore, in the relations of our little party, and I did not expect a very agreeable evening.

Notwithstanding all this, however, our dinner was, on the whole, much pleasanter than I anticipated. Stanley Lake could be very amusing ; but I doubt if our talk would quite stand the test of print. I often thought if one of those artists who photograph language and thought—the quiet, clever 'reporters,' to whom England is obliged for so much of her daily entertainment, of her social knowledge, and her political safety, were, pencil in hand, to ensconce himself behind the arras, and present us, at the close of the agreeable banquet, with a literal transcript of the feast of reason, which we give and take with so much complacency—whether it would quite satisfy us upon reconsideration.

When I entered the drawing-room after dinner, Lord Chelford was plainly arguing a point with the young ladies, and by the time I drew near, it was Miss Lake's turn to speak.

'Flattering of mankind, I am sure, I have no talent for ; and without flattering and wheedling you'll never have conjugal obedience. Don't you remember Robin Hood? how—

'The mother of Robin said to her husband,
My honey, my love, and my dear '

And all this for leave to ride with her son to see her own brother at Gamwell.'

'I remember,' said Dorcas, with a smile. 'I wonder what has become of that old book, with its odd little woodcuts.

‘And he said, I grant thee thy boon, gentle Joan !
Take one of my horses straightway.’

‘Well, though the book is lost, we retain the moral, you see,’
said Rachel with a little laugh ; ‘and it has always seemed to
me that if it had not been necessary to say, “my honey, my
love, and my dear,” that good soul would not have said it, and
you may be pretty sure that if she had not, and with the suitable
by-play too, she might not have ridden to Gamwell that day.’

‘And you don’t think *you* could have persuaded yourself to
repeat that little charm, which obtained her boon and one of
his horses straightway?’ said Lord Chelford.

‘Well, I don’t know what a great temptation and a contuma-
cious husband might bring one to ; but I’m afraid I’m a stub-
born creature, and have not the feminine gift of flattery. If, indeed, he felt his inferiority and owned his dependence, I think I
might, perhaps, have called him “my honey, my love, and my
dear,” and encouraged and comforted him ; but to buy my
personal liberty, and the right to visit my brother at Gamwell—
never !’

And yet she looked, Lord Chelford thought, very good-
humoured and pleasant, and he fancied a smile from her might
do more with some men than all gentle Joan’s honeyed vocabulary.

‘I own,’ said Lord Chelford, laughing, ‘that, from prejudice,
I suppose, I am in favour of the apostolic method, and stand
up for the divine right of my sex ; but then, don’t you see, it is
your own fault, if you make it a question of right, when you may
make it altogether one of fascination?’

‘Who, pray, is disputing the husband’s right to rule?’ demanded old Lady Chelford unexpectedly.

‘I am very timidly defending it against very serious odds,’
answered her son.

‘Tut, tut ! my dears, what’s all this ; you *must* obey your
husbands,’ cried the dowager, who put down nonsense with a
high hand, and had ruled her lord with a rod of iron.

‘That’s no tradition of the Brandons,’ said Miss Dorcas,
quietly.

‘The Brandons—pooh ! my dear—it is time the Brandons
should grow like other people. Hitherto, the Brandon men
have all, without exception, been the wickedest in all England,
and the women the handsomest and the most self-willed. Of
course the men could not be obeyed in all things, nor the women
disobeyed. I’m a Brandon myself, Dorcas, so I’ve a right to
speak. But the words are precise—honour and obey—and obey
you *must ;* though, of course you may argue a point, if need be,
and let your husband hear reason.’

And, having ruled the point, old Lady Chelford leaned back
and resumed her doze.

There was no longer anything playful in Dorcas's look. On the contrary, something fierce and lurid, which I thought wonderfully becoming ; and after a little she said—

' I promised, Rachel, to show you my jewels. Come now—will you ?—and see them.'

And she placed Rachel's hand on her arm, and the two young ladies departed.

' Are you well, dear ?' asked Rachel when they reached her room.

Dorcas was very pale, and her gaze was stern, and something undefinably wild in her quietude.

' What day of the month is this ?' said Dorcas.

' The eighth—is not it ?—yes, the eighth,' answered Rachel.

' And our marriage is fixed for the twenty-second—just a fortnight hence. I am going to tell you, Rachel, what I have resolved on.'

' How really beautiful these diamonds are !—quite superb.'

' Yes,' said Dorcas, opening the jewel-cases, which she had taken from her cabinet, one after the other.

' And these pearls ! how very magnificent ! I had no idea Mark Wylder's taste was so exquisite.'

' Yes, very magnificent, I suppose.'

' How charming—quite regal—you will look, Dorcas !'

Dorcas smiled strangely, and her bosom heaved a little, Rachel thought. Was it elation, or was there not something wildly bitter gleaming in that smile ?

' I *must* look a little longer at these diamonds.'

' As long, dear, as you please. You are not likely, Rachel, to see them again.'

From the blue flash of the brilliants Rachel in honest amazement raised her eyes to her cousin's face. The same pale smile was there ; the look was oracular and painful. Had she overheard a part of that unworthy talk of Wylder's at the dinnertable, the day before, and mistaken Rachel's share in the dialogue ?

And Dorcas said—

' You have heard of the music on the waters that lures mariners to destruction. The pilot leaves the rudder, and leans over the prow, and listens. They steer no more, but drive before the wind ; and what care they for wreck or drowning ?'

I suppose it was the same smile ; but in Rachel's eyes, as pictures will, it changed its character with her own change of thought, and now it seemed the pale rapt smile of one who hears music far off, or sees a vision.

' Rachel, dear, I sometimes think there is an evil genius attendant on our family,' continued Dorcas in the same subdued tone, which, in its very sweetness, had so sinister a sound in Rachel's ear. ' From mother to child, from child to grandchild, the same influence continues, and, one after another, wrecks the daughters of our family—a wayward family, and full of misery. Here I stand, forewarned, with my eyes open, determinedly following in the funereal footsteps of those who have gone their way before me. These jewels all go back to Mr. Wylder. He never can be anything to me. I was, I thought, to build up our house. I am going, I think, to lay it in the dust. With the spirit of the insane, I feel the spirit of a prophetess, too, and I see the sorrow that awaits me. You will see.'

'Dorcas, darling, you are certainly ill. What is the matter?'

'No, dear Rachel, not ill, only maybe agitated a little. You must not touch the bell—listen to me; but first promise, so help you Heaven, you will keep my secret.'

'I do promise, indeed Dorcas, I swear I'll not repeat one word you tell me.'

'It has been a vain struggle. I know he's a bad man, a worthless man—selfish, cruel, maybe. Love is not blind with me, but quite insane. He does not know, nor you, nor anyone; and now, Rachel, I tell you what was unknown to all but myself and Heaven—looking neither for counsel, nor for pity, nor for sympathy, but because I must, and you have sworn to keep my secret. I love your brother. Rachel, you must try to like me.'

She threw her arms round her cousin's neck, and Rachel felt in her embrace the vibration of an agony.

She was herself so astonished that for a good while she could hardly collect her thoughts or believe her senses. Was it credible? Stanley! whom she had received with a coldness, if not aversion, so marked, that, if he had a spark of Rachel's spirit, he would never have approached her more! Then came the thought—perhaps they understood one another, and that was the meaning of Stanley's unexpected visit?

'Well, Dorcas, dear, I *am* utterly amazed. But does Stanley —he can hardly hope?'

Dorcas removed her arms from her cousin's neck; her face was pale, and her cheeks wet with tears, which she did not wipe away

'Sit down by me, Rachel. No, *he* does *not* like *me*—that is —I don't know; but, I am sure, he can't suspect that I like him. It was my determination it should not be. I resolved, Rachel, quite to extinguish the madness; but I could not. It was not his doing, nor mine, but something else. There are some families, I think, too wicked for Heaven to protect, and they are given over to the arts of those who hated them in life and pursue them after death; and this is the meaning of the curse that has always followed us. No good will ever happen us, and I must go like the rest.'

There was a short silence, and Rachel gazed on the carpet in troubled reflection, and then, with an anxious look, she took her cousin's hand, and said—

'Dorcas, you must think of this no more. I am speaking against my brother's interest. But you must not sacrifice yourself, your fortune, and your *happiness*, to a shadow ; whatever his means are, they hardly suffice for his personal expenses—indeed, they don't suffice, for I have had to help him. But that is all trifling compared with other considerations. I am his sister, and, though he has shown little love for me, I am not without affection—and strong affection—for him ; but I must and will speak frankly. You could not, I don't think anyone could be happy with Stanley for her husband. You don't know him : he's profligate ; he's ill-tempered ; he's cold ; he's selfish ; he's secret. He was a spoiled boy, totally without moral education ; he might, perhaps, have been very different, but he *is what* he is, and I don't think he'll ever change.'

'He may be what he will. It is vain reasoning with that which is not reason ; the battle is over ; possibly he may never know, and that might be best for both—but be it how it may, I will never marry anyone else.'

'Dorcas, dear, you must not speak to Lady Chelford, or to Mark Wylder, to-night. It is too serious a step to be taken in haste.'

'There has been no haste, Rachel, and there can be no change.'

'And what reason can you give ?'

'None ; no reason,' said Dorcas, slowly.

'Wylder would have been suitable in point of wealth. Not so well, I am sure, as you *might* have married ; but neither would *he* be a good husband, though not so bad as Stanley ; and I do not think that Mark Wylder will quietly submit to his disappointment.'

'It was to have been simply a marriage of two estates. It was old Lady Chelford's plan. I have now formed mine, and all that's over. Let him do what he will—I believe a lawsuit is his worst revenge—I'm indifferent.'

Just then a knock came to the chamber door.

'Come in,' said Miss Brandon : and her maid entered to say that the carriage, please Ma'am, was at the door to take Miss Lake home.

'I had no idea it was so late,' said Rachel.

'Stay, dear, don't go for a moment. Jones, bring Miss Lake's cloak and bonnet here. And now, dear,' she said, after a little pause, 'you'll remember your solemn promise ?'

'I never broke my word, dear Dorcas ; your secret is safe.'

'And, Rachel, try to like me.'

'I love you better, Dorcas, than I thought I ever could. Good-night, dear.'

'Good-night.'

And the young ladies parted with a kiss, and then another.

CHAPTER XVI.

'JENNY, PUT THE KETTLE ON.'

OLD Lady Chelford, having despatched a sharp and unceremonious message to her young kinswoman, absent without leave, warning her, in effect, that if she returned to the drawing-room it would be to preside, alone, over gentlemen, departed, somewhat to our secret relief.

Upon this, on Lord Chelford's motion, in our forlorn condition, we went to the billiard-room, and there, under the bright lights, and the gay influence of that wonderful game, we forgot our cares, and became excellent friends apparently—'cuts,' 'canons,' 'screws,' 'misses,' 'flukes'—Lord Chelford joked, Wylder 'chaffed,' even Lake seemed to enjoy himself; and the game proceeded with animation and no lack of laughter, beguiling the watches of the night; and we were all amazed, at length, to find how very late it was. So we laid down our cues, with the customary ejaculations of surprise.

We declined wine and water, and all other creature comforts. Wylder and Lake had a walk before them, and we bid Lord Chelford 'good-night' in the passage, and I walked with them through the deserted and nearly darkened rooms.

Our talk grew slow, and our spirits subsided in this changed and tenebrose scenery. The void and the darkness brought back, I suppose, my recollection of the dubious terms on which these young men stood, and a feeling of the hollowness and delusion of the genial hours just passed under the brilliant lights, together with an unpleasant sense of apprehension.

On coming out upon the door-steps we all grew silent.

The moon was low, and its yellow disk seemed, as it sometimes does, dilated to a wondrous breadth, as its edge touched the black outline of the distant woods. I half believe in presentiments, and I felt one now, in the chill air, the sudden silence, and the watchful gaze of the moon. I suspect that Wylder and Lake, too, felt something of the same ominous qualm, for I thought their faces looked gloomy in the light, as they stood together buttoning their loose wrappers and lighting their cigars.

With a 'good-night, good-night,' we parted, and I heard their retreating steps crunching along the walk that led to Redman's Hollow, and by Miss Rachel's quiet habitation. I heard no talking, such as comes between whiffs with friendly smokers, side by side; and, silent as mutes at a funeral, they walked on, and soon the fall of their footsteps was heard no more, and I re-entered the hall and shut the door. The level moonlight was shining through the stained heraldic window, and fell bright on the portrait of Uncle Lorne, at the other end, throwing a patch of red, like a stain, on one side of its pale forehead.

I had forgot, at the moment, that the ill-omened portrait hung there, and a sudden horror smote me. I thought of what my vision said of the 'blood upon my forehead,' and, by Jove! there it was!

At this moment the large white Marseilles waistcoat of grave Mr. Larcom appeared, followed by a tall powdered footman, and their candles and business-like proceedings frightened away the phantoms. So I withdrew to my chamber, where, I am glad to say, I saw nothing of Uncle Lorne.

Miss Lake, as she drove that night toward Gylingden, said little to the vicar's wife, whose good husband had been away to Friars, making a sick-call, and she prattled on very merrily about his frugal little tea awaiting his late return, and asked her twice on the way home whether it was half-past nine, for she did not boast a watch; and in the midst of her prattle was peeping at the landmarks of their progress.

'Oh, I'm so glad—here's the finger post, at last!' and then —'Well, here we are at the "Cat and Fiddle;" I thought we'd never pass it.'

And, at last, the brougham stopped at the little garden-gate, at the far end of the village; and the good little mamma called to her maid-of-all-work from the window—

'Has the master come yet, Becky?'

'No, Ma'am, please.'

And I think she offered up a little thanksgiving, she so longed to give him his tea herself; and then she asked—

'Is our precious mannikin asleep?' Which also being answered happily, as it should be, she bid her fussy adieux, with a merry smile, and hurried, gabbling amicably with her handmaid, across the little flower-garden; and Miss Lake was shut in and drove on alone, under the thick canopy of old trees, and up the mill-road, lighted by the flashing lamps, to her own little precincts, and was, in turn, at home—solitary, triste, but still her home.

'Get to your bed, Margery, child, you are sleepy,' said the young lady kindly to her queer little maid-of-honour. Rachel was one of those persons who, no matter what may be upon their minds, are quickly impressible by the scenes in which they find themselves. She stepped into her little kitchen—always a fairy kitchen, so tiny, so white, so raddled, and shining all over with that pleasantest of all effulgence—burnished tins, pewters, and the homely decorations of the dresser—and she looked

all round and smiled pleasantly, and kissed old Tamar, and
said—

'So, my dear old fairy, here's your Cinderella home again
from the ball, and I've seen nothing so pretty as this since I left
Redman's Farm. How white· your table is, how nice your
chairs; I wish you'd change with me and let me be cook week
about; and, really the fire is quite pleasant to-night. Come,
make a cup of tea, and tell us a story, and frighten me and
Margery before we go to our beds. Sit down, Margery, I'm
only here by permission. What do you mean by standing?'
And the young lady, with a laugh, sat down, looking so pleased,
and good-natured, and merry, that even old Tamar was fain to
smile a glimmering smile; and little Margery actively brought
the tea-caddy; and the kettle, being in a skittish singing state,
quickly went off in a boil, and Tamar actually made tea in
her brown tea-pot.

'Oh, no; the delf cups and saucers;—it will be twice as good
in them;' and as the handsome mistress of the mansion, sitting
in the deal chair, loosened her cloak and untied her bonnet, she
chatted away, to the edification of Margery and the amusement of both.

This little extemporised bivouac, as it were, with her domestics, delighted the young belle. Vanity of vanities, as Mr.
Thackeray and King Solomon cry out in turn. Silver trays and
powdered footmen, and Utrecht, velvet upholstery—miserable
comforters! What saloon was ever so cheery as this, or flashed
all over in so small a light so splendidly, or yielded such immortal nectar from chased teapot and urn, as this brewed in
brown crockery from the roaring kettle?

So Margery, sitting upon her stool in the background—for
the Queen had said it, and sit she must—and grinning from ear
to ear, in a great halo of glory, partook of tea.

'Well, Tamar, where's your story?' said the young lady.

'Story! La! bless you, dear Miss Radie, where should I
find a story? My old head's a poor one to remember,' whim-
pered white Tamar.

'Anything, no matter what—a ghost or a murder.'

Old Tamar shook her head.

'Or an elopement?'

Another shake of the head.

'Or a mystery—or even a dream?'

'Well—a dream! Sometimes I do dream. I dreamed how
Master Stanley was coming, the night before.'

'You did, did you? Selfish old thing! and you meant to
keep it all to yourself. What was it?'

Tamar looked anxiously and suspiciously in the kitchen fire,
and placed her puckered hand to the side of her white linen
cap.

'I dreamed, Ma'am, the night before he came, a great fellow was at the hall-door.'

'What ! here ?'

'Yes, Ma'am, this hall-door. So muffled up I could not see his face ; and he pulls out a letter all over red.'

'Red ?'

'Aye, Miss ; a red letter.'

'Red ink ?'

'No, Miss, red *paper*, written with black, and directed for you.'

'Oh !'

'And so, Miss, in my dream, I gave it you in the drawing-room ; and you opened it, and leaned your hand upon your head, sick-like, reading it. I never saw you read a letter so serious-like before. And says you to me, Miss, "It's all about Master Stanley ; he is coming." And sure enough, here he was quite unexpected, next morning.'

'And was there no more ?' asked Miss Lake.

'No more, Miss. I awoke just then.'

'It *is* odd,' said Miss Lake, with a little laugh. 'Had you been thinking of him lately ?'

'Not a bit, Ma'am. I don't know when.'

'Well, it certainly is *very* odd.'

At all events, it had glanced upon a sensitive recollection unexpectedly. The kitchen was only a kitchen now ; and the young lady, on a sudden, looked thoughtful—perhaps a little sad. She rose ; and old Tamar got up before her, with her scared, secret look, clothed in white—the witch, whose word had changed all, and summoned round her those shapes, which threw their indistinct shadows on the walls and faces around.

'Light the candles in the drawing-room, Margery, and then, child, go to your bed,' said the young lady, awakening from an abstraction. 'I don't mind dreams, Tamar, nor fortune-tellers —I've dreamed so many good dreams, and no good ever came of them. But talking of Stanley reminds me of trouble and follies that I can't help, or prevent. He has left the army, Tamar, and I don't know what his plans are.'

'Ah ! poor child ; he was always foolish and changeable, and a deal too innocent for them wicked officer-gentlemen ; and I'm glad he's not among them any longer to learn bad ways— I am.'

So, the drawing-room being prepared, Rachel bid Tamar and little Margery good-night, and the sleepy little handmaid stumped off to her bed ; and white old Tamar, who had not spoken so much for a month before, put on her solemn round spectacles, and by her dipt candle read her chapter in the pon-derous Bible she had thumbed so well, and her white lips told over the words as she read them in silence.

Old Tamar, I always thought, had seen many untold things in her day, and some of her recollections troubled her, I dare say ; and she held her tongue, and knitted her white worsteds when she could sit quiet—which was most hours of the day ; and now and then when evil remembrances, maybe, gathered round her solitude, she warned them off with that book of power—so that my recollection of her is always the same white-cad, cadaverous old woman, with a pair of barnacles on her nose, and her look of secrecy and suffering turned on the large print of that worn volume, or else on the fumbling-points of her knitting-needles.

It was a small house, this Redman's Farm, but very silent, for all that, when the day's work was over ; and very solemn, too, the look-out from the window among the colonnades of tall old trees, on the overshadowed earth, and through them into deepest darkness ; the complaining of the lonely stream far down is the only sound in the air.

There was but one imperfect vista, looking down the glen, and this afforded no distant view—only a downward slant in the near woodland, and a denser background of forest rising at the other side, and to-night mistily gilded by the yellow moon-beams, the moon herself unseen.

Rachel had opened her window-shutters, as was her wont when the moon was up, and with her small white hands on the window-sash, looked into the wooded solitudes, lost in haunted darkness in every direction but one, and there massed in vaporous and discoloured foliage, hardly more distinct, or less solemn.

' Poor old Tamar says her prayers, and reads her Bible ; I wish *I* could. How often I wish it. That good, simple vicar —how unlike his brother—is wiser, perhaps, than all the shrewd people that smile at him. He used to talk to me ; but I've lost that—yes—I let him understand I did not care for it, and so that good influence is gone from me—graceless creature. No one seemed to care, except poor old Tamar, whether I ever said a prayer, or heard any good thing ; and when I was no more than ten years old, I refused to say my prayers for her. My poor father. Well, Heaven help us all.'

So she stood in the same sad attitude, looking out upon the shadowy scene, in a forlorn reverie.

Her interview with Dorcas remained on her memory like an odd, clear, half-horrible dream. What a dazzling prospect it opened for Stanley ; what a dreadful one might it not prepare for Dorcas. What might not arise from such a situation between Stanley and Mark Wylder, each in his way a worthy representative of the ill-conditioned and terrible race whose blood he inherited ? Was this doomed house of Brandon never to know repose or fraternity ?

Was it credible? Had it actually occurred, that strange confession of Dorcas Brandon's? Could anything be imagined so mad—so unaccountable? She reviewed Stanley in her mind's eye. She was better acquainted, perhaps, with his defects than his fascinations, and too familiar with both to appreciate at all their effect upon a stranger.

'What can she see in him? There's nothing remarkable in Stanley, poor fellow, except his faults. There are much handsomer men than he, and many as amusing—and he with no estate.'

She had heard of charms and philtres. How could she account for this desperate hallucination?

Rachel was troubled by a sort of fear to-night, and the low fever of an undefined expectation was upon her. She turned from the window, intending to write two letters, which she had owed too long—young ladies' letters—for Miss Lake, like many of her sex, as I am told, had several little correspondences on her hands; and as she turned, with a start, she saw old Tamar standing in the door-way, looking at her.

'Tamar!'

'Yes, Miss Rachel.'

'Why do you come so softly, Tamar? Do you know, you frightened me?'

'I thought I'd look in, Miss, before I went to bed, just to see if you wanted anything.'

'No—nothing, thank you, dear Tamar.'

'And I don't think, Miss Rachel, you are quite well to-night, though you are so gay—you're pale, dear; and there's something on your mind. Don't be thinking about Master Stanley; he's out of the army now, and I'm thankful for it; and make your mind easy about him; and would not it be better, dear, you went to your bed, you rise so early.'

'Very true, good old Tamar, but to-night I must write a letter —not a long one, though—and I assure you, I'm quite well. Good-night, Tamar.'

Tamar stood for a moment with her odd weird look upon her, and then bidding her good-night, glided stiffly away, shutting the door.

So Rachel sat down to her desk and began to write; but she could not get into the spirit of her letter; on the contrary, her mind wandered away, and she found herself listening, every now and then, and at last she fancied that old Tamar, about whom that dream, and her unexpected appearance at the door, had given her a sort of spectral feeling that night, was up and watching her; and the idea of this white sentinel outside her door excited her so unpleasantly, that she opened it, but found no Tamar there; and then she revisited the kitchen, but that was empty too, and the fire taken down. And, finally, she passed into the old woman's bed-chamber, whom she saw, her white head upon her pillow, dreaming again, perhaps. And so, softly closing her door, she left her to her queer visions and deathlike slumber.

CHAPTER XVII.

RACHEL LAKE SEES WONDERFUL THINGS BY MOONLIGHT FROM HER WINDOW.

THOUGH Rachel was unfit for letter-writing, she was still more unfit for slumber. She leaned her temple on her hand, and her rich light hair half covered her fingers, and her amazing interview with Dorcas was again present with her, and the same feeling of bewilderment. The suddenness and the nature of the disclosures were dream-like and unreal, and the image of Dorcas remained impressed upon her sight ; not like Dorcas, though the same, but some-thing ghastly, wan, glittering, and terrible, like a priestess at a solitary sacrifice.

It was late now, not far from one o'clock, and around her the terrible silence of a still night. All those small sounds lost in the hum of midday life now came into relief—a ticking in the wainscot, a crack now and then in the joining of the furniture, and occasionally the tap of a moth against the window pane from outside, sounds sharp and odd, which made her wish the stillness of the night were not so intense.

As from her little table she looked listlessly through the window, she saw against the faint glow of the moonlight, the figure of a man who seized the paling and vaulted into the flower garden, and with a few swift, stumbling strides over the flower-beds, reached the window, and placing his pale face close to the glass, she saw his eyes glittering through it ; he tapped— or rather beat on the pane with his fingers—and at the same time he said, repeatedly : ' Let me in ; let me in.'

Her first impression, when she saw this person cross the little fence at the road-side was, that Mark Wylder was the man. But she was mistaken ; the face and figure were Stanley Lake's.

She would have screamed in the extremity of her terror, but that her voice for some seconds totally failed her ; and re-cognising her brother, though like Rhoda, in Holy Writ, she doubted whether it was not his angel, she rose up, and with an awful ejaculation, she approached the window.

' Let me in, Radie ; d— you, let me in,' he repeated, drum-ming incessantly on the glass. There was no trace now of his sleepy jeering way. Rachel saw that something was very wrong, and beckoned him toward the porch in silence, and having removed the slender fastenings of the door, it opened, and he entered in a rush of damp night air. She took him by the hand, and he shook hers mechanically, like a man rescued from shipwreck, and plainly not recollecting himself well.

'Stanley, dear, what's the matter, in Heaven's name?' she whispered, so soon as she had got him into her little drawing-room.

'He has done it; d— him, he has done it,' gasped Stanley Lake.

He looked in her face with a glazed and ashy stare. His hat remained on his head, overshadowing his face; and his boots were soiled with clay, and his wrapping coat marked, here and there, with the green of the stems and branches of trees, through which he had made his way.

'I see, Stanley, you've had a scene with Mark Wylder; I warned you of your danger—you have had the worst of it.'

'I spoke to him. He took a course I did not expect. I'm not well.'

'You've broken your promise. I see you have used *me*. How base; how stupid!'

'How could I tell he was such a *fiend?*'

'I told you how it would be. He has frightened you,' said Rachel, herself frightened.

'D— him; I wish I had done as you said. I wish I had never come here. Give me a glass of wine. He has ruined me.'

'You cruel, wretched creature!' said Rachel, now convinced that he had compromised her as he threatened.

'Yes, I was wrong; I'm sorry; things have turned out different. Who's that?' said Lake, grasping her wrist.

'Who—where—Mark Wylder?'

'No; it's nothing, I believe.'

'Where is he? Where have you left him?'

'Up there, at the pathway, near the stone steps.'

'Waiting there?'

'Well, yes; and I don't think I'll go back, Radie.'

'You *shall* go back, Sir, and carry my message; or, no, I could not trust you. I'll go with you and see him, and disabuse him. How could you—how *could* you, Stanley?'

'It was a mistake, altogether; I'm sorry, but I could not tell there was such a devil on the earth.'

'Yes, I told you so. *He* has frightened *you*,' said Rachel.

'He *has, maybe.* At any rate, I was a fool, and I think i'm ruined; and I'm afraid, Rachel, you'll be inconvenienced too.'

'Yes, you have made him savage and brutal; and between you, I shall be called in question, you wretched fool!'

Stanley was taking these hard terms very meekly for a savage young coxcomb like him. Perhaps they bore no very distinct meaning just then to his mind. Perhaps it was preoccupied with more exciting ideas ; or, it may be, his agitation and fear cried 'amen' to the reproach ; at all events, he only said, in a pettish but deprecatory sort of way—

'Well, where's the good of scolding? how can I help it now?'

'What's your quarrel? why does he wait for you there? why has he sent you here? It must concern *me*, Sir, and I insist on hearing it all.'

'So you shall, Radie ; only have patience just a minute—and give me a little wine or water—anything.'

'There is the key. There's some wine in the press, I think.'

He tried to open it, but his hand shook. He saw his sister look at him, and he flung the keys on the table rather savagely, with, I dare say, a curse between his teeth.

There was running all this time in Rachel's mind, and had been almost since the first menacing mention of Wylder's name by her brother, an indistinct remembrance of something unpleasant or horrible. It may have been mere fancy, or it may have referred to something long ago imperfectly heard. It was a spectre of mist, that evaporated before she could fix her eyes on it, but was always near her elbow.

Rachel took the key with a faint gleam of scorn on her face and brought out the wine in silence.

He took a tall-stemmed Venetian glass that stood upon th cabinet, an antique decoration, and filled it with sherry — a strange revival of old service ! How long was it since lips had touched its brim before, and whose? Lovers', maybe, and how How long since that cold crystal had glowed with the ripples of wine? This, at all events, was its last service. It is an old legend of the Venetian glass—its shivering at touch of poison ; and there are those of whom it is said, ' the poison of asps is under their lips.'

'What's that?' ejaculated Rachel, with a sudden shriek — that whispered shriek, so expressive and ghastly, that you, perhaps, have once heard in your life—and her very lips grew white.

'Hollo!' cried Lake. He was standing with his back to the window, and sprang forward, as pale as she, and grasped her, with a white leer that she never forgot, over his shoulder, and the Venice glass was shivered on the ground.

'Who's there?' he whispered.

And Rachel, in a whisper, ejaculated the awful name that must not be taken in vain.

She sat down. She was looking at him with a wild, stern stare, straight in the face, and he still holding her arm, and close to her.

'I see it all now,' she whispered.

'Who—what—what is it?' said he.

'I could not have fancied *that*,' she whispered with a gasp.

Stanley looked round him with pale and sharpened features.

'What the devil is it ! If that scoundrel had come to kill us you could not cry out louder,' he whispered, with an oath. 'Do you want to wake your people up?'

'Oh! Stanley,' she repeated, in a changed and horror-stricken way. 'What a fool I've been. I see it at last ; I see it all now,' and she waved her white hands together very slowly towards him, as mesmerisers move theirs.

There was a silence of some seconds, and his yellow ferine gaze met hers strangely.

'You were always a sharp girl, Radie, and I think you do see it,' he said at last, very quietly.

'The witness — the witness — the dreadful witness !' she repeated.

'I'll show you, though, it's not so bad as you fancy. I'm sorry I did not take your advice ; but how, I say, could I know he was such a devil? I must go back to him. I only came down to tell you, because Radie, you know you proposed it yourself ; *you* must come, too—you *must*, Radie.'

'Oh, Stanley, Stanley, Stanley !'

'Why, d— it, it can't be helped now ; can it?' said he, with a peevish malignity. But she was right ; there was something of the poltroon in him, and he was trembling.

'Why could you not leave me in peace, Stanley?'

'I can't go without you, Rachel. I won't ; and if we don't we're both ruined,' he said, with a bleak oath.

'Yes, Stanley, I knew you were a coward,' she replied, fiercely and wildly.

'You're always calling names, d— you ; do as you like. I care less than you think how it goes.'

'No, Stanley ; you know me too well. Ah ! No, you sha'n't be lost if I can help it.' Rachel shook her head as she spoke, with a bitter smile and a dreadful sigh.

Then they whispered together for three or four minutes, and Rachel clasped her jewelled fingers tight across her forehead, quite wildly, for a minute.

'You'll come then?' said Stanley.

She made no answer, and he repeated the question.

By this time she was standing ; and without answering, she began mechanically to get on her cloak and hat.

'You must drink some wine first ; he may frighten you, per-haps. You *must* take it, Rachel, or I'll not go.'

Stanley Lake was swearing, in his low tones, like a swell-mobsman to-night.

Rachel seemed to have made up her mind to submit pas-sively to whatever he required. Perhaps, indeed, she thought there was wisdom in his advice. At all events she drank some wine.

Rachel Lake was one of those women who never lose their presence of mind, even under violent agitation, for long, and who generally, even when highly excited, see, and do instinctively, and with decision, what is best to be done ; and now, with dilated eyes and white face, she walked noiselessly into the kitchen, listened there for a moment, then stole lightly to the servants' sleeping-room, and listened there at the door, and lastly looked in, and satisfied herself that both were still sleeping. Then as cautiously and swiftly she returned to her drawing-room, and closed the window-shutters and drew the curtain, and signalling to her brother they went stealthily forth into the night air, closing the hall-door, and through the little garden, at the outer gate of which they paused.

' I dont know, Rachel—I don't like it—I'm not fit for it. Go back again—go in and lock your door—we'll not go to him—*you* need not, you know. He may stay where he is—let him—I'll not return. I say, I'll see him no more. I'll get away. I'll consult Larkin—shall I ? Though that won't do—he's in Wylder's interest—curse him. What had I best do ? I'm not equal to it.'

' We *must* go, Stanley. You said right just now ; be resolute —we are both ruined unless we go. You have brought it to that —you *must* come.'

' I'm not fit for it, I tell you—I'm not. You were right, Radie —I think I'm not equal to a business of this sort, and I won't expose you to such a scene. *You're* not equal to it either, I think,' and Lake leaned on the paling.

'Don't mind me—you haven't much hitherto. Go or stay, I'm equally ruined now, but not equally disgraced ; and go we must, for it is *your only* chance of escape. Come, Stanley—for shame !'

In a few minutes more they were walking in deep darkness and silence, side by side, along the path, which diverging from the mill-road, penetrates the coppice of that sequestered gorge, along the bottom of which flows a tributary brook that finds its way a little lower down into the mill-stream. This deep gully in character a good deal resembles Redman's Glen, into which it passes, being fully as deep, and wooded to the summit at both sides, but much steeper and narrower, and therefore many shades darker.

They had now reached those rude stone steps, some ten or fifteen in number, which conduct the narrow footpath up a particularly steep acclivity, and here Lake lost courage again, for they distinctly heard the footsteps that paced the platform above

CHAPTER XVIII.

MARK WYLDER'S SLAVE.

NEARLY two hours had passed before they returned. As they did so, Rachel Lake went swiftly and silently before her brother. The moon had gone down, and the glen was darker than ever. Noiselessly they re-entered the little hall of Redman's Farm. The candles were still burning in the sitting-room, and the light was dazzling after the profound darkness in which they had been for so long.

Captain Lake did not look at all like a London dandy now. His dress was confoundedly draggled; the conventional countenance, too, was wanting. There was a very natural savagery and dejection there, and a wild leer in his yellow eyes.

Rachel sat down. No living woman ever showed a paler face, and she stared with a look that was sharp and stern upon the wainscot before her.

For some minutes they were silent; and suddenly, with an exceeding bitter cry, she stood up, close to him, seizing him in her tiny hands by the collar, and with wild eyes gazing into his, she said—

'See what you've brought me to—wretch, wretch, wretch!'

And she shook him with violence as she spoke. It was wonderful how that fair young face could look so terrible.

'There, Radie, there,' said Lake, disengaging her fingers. 'You're a little hysterical, that's all. It will be over in a minute; but don't make a row. You're a good girl, Radie. For Heaven's sake, don't spoil all by folly now.'

He was overawed and deprecatory.

'A slave! only think—a slave! Oh frightful, frightful! Is it a dream? Oh frightful, frightful! Stanley, Stanley, it would be *mercy* to kill me,' she broke out again.

'Now, Radie, listen to reason, and don't make a noise; you know we agreed, *you* must go, and *I can't* go with you.'

Lake was cooler by this time, and his sister more excited than before they went out.

'I used to be brave; my courage I think is gone; but who'd have imagined what's before me?'

Stanley walked to the window and opened the shutter a little. He forgot how dark it was. The moon had gone down. He looked at his watch and then at Rachel. She was sitting, and in no calmer state; serene enough in attitude, but the terribly wild look was unchanged. He looked at his watch again, and held it to his ear, and consulted it once more before he placed the tiny gold disk again in his pocket.

'This won't do,' he muttered.

With one of the candles in his hand he went out and made a hurried, peeping exploration, and soon, for the rooms were quickly counted in Redman's Farm, he found her chamber small, neat, *simplex munditiis.* Bright and natty were the chintz curtains, and the little toilet set out, not inelegantly, and her pet piping-goldfinch asleep on his perch, with his bit of sugar between the wires of his cage ; her pillow so white and unpressed, with its little edging of lace. Were slumbers sweet as of old ever to know it more ? What dreams were henceforward to haunt it ? Shadows were standing about that lonely bed already. I don't know whether Stanley Lake felt anything of this, being very decidedly of the earth earthy. But there are times when men are translated from their natures, and forced to be romantic and superstitious.

When he came back to the drawing-room, a toilet bottle of *eau de cologne* in his hand, with her lace handkerchief he bathed her temples and forehead. There was nothing very brotherly in his look as he peered into her pale, sharp features, during the process. It was the dark and pallid scrutiny of a familiar of the Holy Office, bringing a victim back to consciousness.

She was quickly better.

'There, don't mind me,' she said sharply ; and getting up she looked down at her dress and thin shoes, and seeming to recollect herself, she took the candle he had just set down, and went swiftly to her room.

Gliding without noise from place to place, she packed a small black leather bag with a few necessary articles. Then changed her dress quickly, put on her walking boots, a close bonnet and thick veil, and taking her purse, she counted over its contents, and then standing in the midst of the room looked round it with a great sigh, and a strange look, as if it was all new to her. And she threw back her veil, and going hurriedly to the toilet, mechanically surveyed herself in the glass. And she looked fixedly on the pale features presented to her, and said—

'Rachel Lake, Rachel Lake ! what are you now ?'

And so, with knitted brows and stern lips, a cadaveric gaze was returned on her from the mirror.

A few minutes later her brother, who had been busy down stairs, put his head in and asked—

'Will you come with me now, Radie, or do you prefer to wait here ?'

'I'll stay here—that is, in the drawing-room,' she answered, and the face was withdrawn.

In the little hall Stanley looked again at his watch, and getting quietly out. went swiftly through the tiny garden, and once upon the mill-road, ran at a rapid pace down towards the town.

The long street of Gylingden stretched dim and silent before him. Slumber brooded over the little town, and his steps sounded sharp and hollow among the houses. He slackened his pace, and tapped sharply at the little window of that modest post-office, at which the young ladies in the pony carriage had pulled up the day before, and within which Luke Waggot was wont to sleep in a sort of wooden box that folded up and appeared to be a chest of drawers all day. Luke took care of Mr. Larkin's dogs, and groomed Mr. Wylder's horse, and 'cleaned up' his dog-cart, for Mark being close about money, and finding that the thing was to be done more cheaply that way, put up his horse and dog-cart in the post-office premises, and so evaded the livery charges of the 'Brandon Arms.'

But Luke was not there; and Captain Lake recollecting his habits and his haunt, hurried on to the 'Silver Lion,' which has its gable towards the common, only about a hundred steps away, for distances are not great in Gylingden. Here were the flow of soul and of stout, long pipes, long yarns, and tolerably long credits; and the humble scapegraces of the town resorted thither for the pleasures of a club-life, and often revelled deep into the small hours of the morning.

So Luke came forth.

'D— it, where's the note?' said the captain, rummaging uneasily in his pockets.

'You know me—eh !'

'Captain Lake. Yes, Sir.'

'Well—oh ! here it is.'

It was a scrap pencilled on the back of a letter—

'LUKE WAGGOT,
　　'Put the horse to and drive the dog-cart to the "White House." Look out for me there. We must catch the up mail train at Dollington. Be lively. If Captain Lake chooses to drive you need not come.

'M. WYLDER.'

'I'll drive,' said Captain Lake. 'Lose no time and I'll give you half-a-crown.'

Luke stuck on his greasy wideawake, and in a few minutes more the dog-cart was trundled out into the lane, and the horse harnessed, went between the shafts with that wonderful cheerfulness with which they bear to be called up under startling circumstances at unseasonable hours.

'Easily earned, Luke,' said Captain Lake, in his soft tones.

The captain had buttoned the collar of his loose coat across his face, and it was dark beside. But Luke knew his peculiar smile, and presumed it; so he grinned facetiously as he put the coin in his breeches pocket and thanked him; and in another minute the captain, with a lighted cigar between his lips, mounted to the seat, took the reins, the horse bounded off, and away rattled the light conveyance, sparks flying from the road, at a devil of a pace, down the deserted street of Gylingden, and quickly melted in darkness.

That night a spectre stood by old Tamar's bedside, in shape of her young mistress, and shook her by the shoulder, and stooping, said sternly, close in her face—

' Tamar, I'm going away—only for a few days; and mind this —I'd rather be *dead* than any creature living should know it. Little Margery must not suspect—you'll manage that. Here's the key of my bed-room—say I'm sick—and you must go in and out, and bring tea and drinks, and talk and whisper a little, you understand, as you might with a sick person, and keep the shutters closed; and if Miss Brandon sends to ask me to the Hall, say I've a headache, and fear I can't go. You understand me clearly, Tamar?'

' Yes, Miss Radie,' answered old Tamar, wonder-stricken, with a strange expression of fear in her face.

' And listen,' she continued, ' you must go into my room, and bring the message back, as if from me, with *my love* to Miss Brandon; and if she or Mrs. William Wylder, the vicar's wife, should call to see me, always say I'm asleep and a little better. You see exactly what I mean?'

' Yes, Miss,' answered Tamar, whose eyes were fixed in a sort of fascination, full on those of her mistress.

' If Master Stanley should call, he is to do just as he pleases. You used to be accurate, Tamar; may I depend upon you?'

' Yes, Ma'am, certainly.'

' If I thought you'd fail me now, Tamar, I should *never* come back. Good-night, Tamar. There—don't bless me. Good-night.'

When the light wheels of the dog-cart gritted on the mill-road before the little garden gate of Redman's Farm, the tall slender figure of Rachel Lake was dimly visible, standing cloaked and waiting by it. Silently she handed her little black leather bag to her brother, and then there was a pause. He stretched his hand to help her up.

In a tone that was icy and bitter, she said—

To save myself I would not do it. You deserve no love from me—you've showed me none — *never*, Stanley; and yet I'm going to give the most desperate proof of love that ever sister gave—all for your sake; and it's guilt, guilt, but my *fate*, and I'll go, and you'll never thank me; that's all.'

In a moment more she sat beside him; and silent as the **dead** in Charon's boat, away they glided toward the 'White House which lay upon the high road to Dollington.

The sleepy clerk that night in the Dollington station stamped two first-class tickets for London, one of which was for a gentleman, and the other for a cloaked lady, with a very thick veil, who stood outside on the platform ; and almost immediately after the scream of the engine was heard piercing the deep cutting, the Cyclopean red lamps glared nearer and nearer, and the palpitating monster, so stupendous and so docile, came smoothly to a stand-still before the trelliswork and hollyhocks of that pretty station.

CHAPTER XIX.

THE TARN IN THE PARK.

NEXT morning Stanley Lake, at breakfast with the lawyer, said—

'A pretty room this is. That bow window is worth all the pictures in Brandon. To my eye there is no scenery so sweet as this, at least to breakfast by. I don't love your crags and peaks and sombre grandeur, nor yet the fat, flat luxuriance of our other counties. These undulations, and all that splendid timber, and the glorious ruins on that hillock over there ! How many beautiful ruins that picturesque old fellow Cromwell has left us.'

'You don't eat your breakfast, though,' said the attorney, with a charming smile of reproach.

'Ah, thank you ; I'm a bad breakfaster ; that is,' said Stanley, recollecting that he had made some very creditable meals at the same table, 'when I smoke so late as I did last night.'

'You drove Mr. Wylder to Dollington?'

'Yes ; he's gone to town, he says—yes, the mail train—to get some diamonds for Miss Brandon—a present—that ought to have come the day before yesterday. He says they'll never have them in time unless he goes and blows them up. Are you in his secrets at all?'

'Something in his confidence, I should hope,' said Mr. Larkin, in rather a lofty and reserved way.

'Oh, yes, of course, in serious matters ; but I meant other things. You know he has been a little bit wild ; and ladies, you know, ladies will be troublesome sometimes ; and to say truth, I don't think the diamonds have much to say to it.'

'Oh ?—hem !—well, you know, *I'm* not exactly the confidant

Mr. Wylder would choose, I suspect, in a case of that very painful, and, I will say, distressing character—I rather think—indeed,
I *hope* not.'

' No, of course—I dare say—but I just fancied he might want
a hint about the law of the matter.'

The gracious attorney glanced at his guest with a thoroughly
business-like and searching eye.

' You don't think there's any really serious annoyance—you
don't know the party ?' said he.

' *I ?*—Oh, dear, no. Wylder has always been very reserved
with me. He told me nothing. If he had, of course I should
not have mentioned it. I only conjecture, for he really did seem
to have a great deal more on his mind ; and he kept me
walking back and forward, near the mill-road, a precious long
time. And I really think once or twice he was going to tell me.'

' Oh ! you think then, Mr. Lake, there *may* be some serious—
a—a—well, I should hope not—I do most earnestly *trust* not.'
This was said with upturned eyes and much unction. ' But do
you happen, Captain Lake, to know of any of those unfortunate,
those miserable connections which young gentlemen of fashion
—eh ? It's very sad. Still it often needs, as you say, professional
advice to solve such difficulties—it is very sad—oh ! is not it
sad ?'

' Pray, don't let it affect your spirits,' said Lake, who was
leaning back in his chair, and looking on the carpet, about a
yard before his lacquered boots, in his usual sly way. ' I may
be quite mistaken, you know, but I wished you to understand—
having some little experience of the world, I'd be only too happy
to be of any use, if you thought my diplomacy could help poor
Wylder out of his trouble—that is, if there really is any. But
you don't know ?'

' *No,*' said Mr. Larkin, thoughtfully ; and thoughtful he continued for a minute or two, screwing his lips gently, as was his
wont, while ruminating, his long head motionless, the nails of his
long and somewhat large hand tapping on the arm of his chair,
with a sharp glance now and then at the unreadable visage of
the cavalry officer. It was evident his mind was working, and
nothing was heard in the room for a minute but the tapping of
his nails on the chair, like a death-watch.

' No,' said Mr. Larkin again, ' I'm not suspicious—naturally
too much the reverse, I fear ; but it certainly does look odd. Did
he tell the family at Brandon ?'

' Certainly not, that I heard. He may have mentioned it.
But I started with him, and we walked together, under the impression that he was going, as usual, to the inn, the—what d'ye
call it ?—" Brandon Arms ; " and it was a sudden thought—now
I think of it—for he took no luggage, though to be sure I dare
say he has got clothes and things in town.'

'And when does he return?'

'In a day or two, at furthest,' he said.

'I wonder what they'll think of it at Brandon?' said the attorney, with a cavernous grin of sly enquiry at his companion, which, recollecting his character, he softened into a sad sort of smile, and added, 'No harm, I dare say; and, after all, you know, why should there—any man may have business; and, indeed, it is very likely, after all, that he really went about the jewels. Men are too hasty to judge one another, my dear Sir; charity, let us remember, thinketh no evil.'

'By-the-bye,' said Lake, rather briskly for him, rummaging his pockets, 'I'm glad I remembered he gave me a little note to Chelford. Are any of your people going to Brandon this morning?'

'I'll send it,' said the lawyer, eyeing the little pencilled note wistfully, which Lake presented between two fingers.

'Yes, it is to Lord Chelford,' said the attorney, with a grand sort of suavity—he liked lords—placing it, after a scrutiny, in his waistcoat pocket.

'Don't you think it had best go at once?—there may be something requiring an answer, and your post leaves, doesn't it, at twelve?'

'Oh! an answer, is there?' said Mr. Larkin, drawing it from his pocket, and looking at it again with a perceptible curiosity.

'I really can't say, not having read it, but there *may*,' said Captain Lake, who was now and then a little impertinent, just to keep Mr. Larkin in his place, and perhaps to hint that he understood him.

'*Read* it! Oh, my *dear* Sir, my *dear* Captain Lake, how *could* you—but, oh! no—you *could* not suppose I meant such an idea—oh, dear—no, no. You and I have our notions about what's gentlemanlike and professional—a—and gentlemanlike, as I say—Heaven forbid.'

'Quite so!' said Captain Lake, gently.

'Though all the world does not think with us, *I* can tell you, things come before us in *our* profession. Oh, ho! ho!' and Mr. Larkin lifted up his pink eyes and long hands, and shook his long head, with a melancholy smile and a sigh like a shudder.

When at the later breakfast, up at Brandon, that irregular pencilled scroll reached Lord Chelford's hand, he said, as he glanced on the direction—

'This is Mark Wylder's; what does he say?'

'So Mark's gone to town,' he said; 'but he'll be back again on Saturday, and in the meantime desires me to lay his heart at your feet, Dorcas. Will you read the note?'

'No,' said Dorcas, quietly.

Lady Chelford extended her long, shrivelled fingers, on which glimmered sundry jewels, and made a little nod to her son, who

gave it to her, with a smile. Holding her glasses to her eyes, **the note** at a distance, and her head rather back, she said—

'It is not a pretty billet,' and she read in a slow and grim way :—

'DEAR CHELFORD,—I'm called up to London just for a day No lark, but honest business. I'll return on Saturday ; and tell Dorcas, with dozens of loves, I would write to her, but have not a minute for the train.

'Yours, &c.

'M. WYLDER.'

'No ; it is not pretty,' repeated the old lady ; and, indeed, in no sense was it. Before luncheon Captain Lake arrived.

'So Wylder has run up to town,' I said, so soon as we had shaken hands in the hall.

'Yes ; *I* drove him to Dollington last night ; we just caught the up train.'

'He says he'll be back again on Saturday,' I said.

'Saturday, is it ? He seemed to think—yes—it *would* be only a day or so. Some jewels, I think, for Dorcas. He did not say distinctly ; I only conjecture. Lady Chelford and Miss Brandon, I suppose, in the drawing-room ? '

So to the drawing-room he passed.

'How is Rachel ? how is your sister, Captain Lake, have you seen her to-day ? ' asked old Lady Chelford, rather benignantly. She chose to be gracious to the Lakes. 'Only, for a moment, thank you. She has one of her miserable headaches, poor thing ; but she'll be better, she says, in the afternoon, and hopes to come up here to see you, and Miss Brandon, this evening.'

Lord Chelford and I had a pleasant walk that day to the ruins of Willerton Castle. I find in my diary a note—'Chelford tells me it is written in old surveys, Wylderton, and was one of the houses of the Wylders. What considerable people those Wylders were, and what an antique stock.'

After this he wished to make a visit to the vicar, and so we parted company. I got into Brandon Park by the pretty gate near Latham.

It was a walk of nearly three miles across the park from this point to the Hall, and the slopes and hollows of this noble, undulating plain, came out grandly in the long shadows and slanting beams of evening. That yellow, level light has, in my mind, something undefinably glorious and melancholy, such as to make almost any scenery interesting, and my solitary walk was delightful.

People must love and sympathise very thoroughly, I think, to enjoy natural scenery together. Generally it is one of the few **spectacles** best seen alone. The silence that supervenes is indicative of the solitary character of the enjoyment. It is a poem and a reverie. I was quite happy striding in the amber light and soft, long shadows, among the ferns, the copsewood, and the grand old clumps of timber, exploring the undulations, and the wild nooks and hollows which have each their circumscribed and sylvan charm; a wonderful interest those little park-like broken dells have always had for me; dotted with straggling birch and oak, and here and there a hoary ash tree, with a grand and melancholy grace, dreaming among the songs of wild birds, in their native solitudes, and the brown leaves tipped with golden light, all breathing something of old-world romance—the poetry of bygone love and adventure—and stirring undefinable and delightful emotions that mingle unreality with sense, a music of the eye and spirit.

After many devious wanderings, I found, under shelter of a wonderful little hollow, in which lay, dim and still, a tarn, reflecting the stems of the trees that rose from its edge, in a way so clear and beautiful, that, with a smile and a sigh, I sat myself down upon a rock among the ferns, and fell into a reverie.

The image of Dorcas rose before me. There is a strange mystery and power in the apathetic, and in that unaffected carelessness, even defiance of opinion and criticism, which I had seen here for the first time, so beautifully embodied. I was quite sure she both thought and felt, and could talk, too, if she chose it. What tremendous self-reliance and disdain must form the basis of a female character, which accepted misapprehension and depreciation with an indifference so genuine as to scorn even the trifling exertion of disclosing its powers.

She could not possibly care for Wylder, any more than he cared for her. That odd look I detected in the mirror—what did it mean? and Wylder's confusion about Captain Lake—what was that? I could not comprehend the situation that was forming. I went over Wylder's history in my mind, and Captain Lake's—all I could recollect of it—but could find no clue, and that horrible visitation or vision! what was *it?*

This latter image had just glided in and taken its place in my waking dream, when I thought I saw reflected in the pool at my feet, the shape and face which I never could forget, of the white, long-chinned old man.

For a second I was unable, I think, to lift my eyes from the water which presented this cadaverous image.

But the figure began to move, and I raised my eyes, and saw it retreat, with a limping gait, into the thick copse before me, in the shadow of which it stopped and turned stiffly round, and directed on me a look of horror, and then withdrew.

It is all very fine laughing at me and my fancies. I do not think there are many men who in my situation would have felt very differently. I recovered myself; I shouted lustily after him to stay, and then in a sort of half-frightened rage, I pursued him ; but I had to get round the pool, a considerable circuit. I could not tell which way he had turned on getting into the thicket ; and it was now dusk, the sun having gone down during my reverie. So I stopped a little way in the copsewood, which was growing quite dark, and I shouted there again, peeping under the branches, and felt queer and much relieved that nothing answered or appeared.

Looking round me, in a sort of dream, I remembered suddenly what Wylder had told me of old Lorne Brandon, to whose portrait this inexplicable phantom bore so powerful a resemblance. He was suspected of having murdered his own son, at the edge of a tarn in the park. *This* tarn maybe—and with the thought the water looked blacker—and a deeper and colder shadow gathered over the ominous hollow in which I stood, and the rustling in the withered leaves sounded angrily.

I got up as quickly as might be to the higher grounds, and waited there for awhile, and watched for the emergence of the old man. But it did not appear ; and shade after shade was spreading solemnly over the landscape, and having a good way to walk, I began to stride briskly along the slopes and hollows, in the twilight, now and then looking into vacancy, over my shoulder.

The little adventure, and the deepening shades, helped to sadden my homeward walk ; and when at last the dusky outline of the Hall rose before me, it wore a sort of weird and haunted aspect.

CHAPTER XX.

CAPTAIN LAKE TAKES AN EVENING STROLL ABOUT GYLINGDEN.

GAIN I had serious thoughts of removing my person and effects to the Brandon Arms. I could not quite believe I had seen a ghost; but neither was I quite satisfied that the thing was altogether canny. The apparition, whatever it was, seemed to persecute me with a mysterious obstinacy; at all events, I was falling into a habit of seeing it; and I felt a natural desire to escape from the house which was plagued with its presence.

At the same time I had an odd sort of reluctance to mention the subject to my entertainers. The thing itself was a ghostly slur upon the house, and, to run away, a reproach to my manhood; and besides, writing now at a distance, and in the spirit of history, I suspect the interest which beauty always excites had a great deal to do with my resolve to hold my ground; and, I dare say, notwithstanding my other reasons, had the ladies at the Hall been all either old or ugly, I would have made good my retreat to the village hotel.

As it was, however, I was resolved to maintain my position. But that evening was streaked with a tinge of horror, and I more silent and *distrait* than usual.

The absence of an accustomed face, even though the owner be nothing very remarkable, is always felt; and Wylder was missed, though, sooth to say, not very much regretted. For the first time we were really a small party. Miss Lake was not there. The gallant captain, her brother, was also absent. The vicar, and his good little wife, were at Naunton that evening to hear a missionary recount his adventures and experiences in Japan, and none of the neighbours had been called in to fill the empty chairs.

Dorcas Brandon did not contribute much to the talk; neither, in truth, did I. Old Lady Chelford occasionally dozed and nodded sternly after tea, waking up and eyeing people grimly, as though enquiring whether anyone presumed to suspect her ladyship of having had a nap.

Chelford, I recollect, took a book, and read to us now and then, a snatch of poetry—I forget what. *My* book—except when I was thinking of the tarn and that old man I so hated—was Miss Brandon's exquisite and mysterious face.

That young lady was leaning back in her great oak chair, in

which she looked like the heroine of some sad and gorgeous romance of the old civil wars of England, and directing a gaze of contemplative and haughty curiosity upon the old lady, who was unconscious of the daring profanation.

All on a sudden Dorcas Brandon said—

'And pray what do you think of marriage, Lady Chelford?'

'What do I think of marriage?' repeated the dowager, throwing back her head and eyeing the beautiful heiress through her gold spectacles, with a stony surprise, for she was not accustomed to be catechised by young people. 'Marriage? —why 'tis a divine institution. What can the child mean?'

'Do you think, Lady Chelford, it may be safely contracted, solely to join two estates?' pursued the young lady.

'Do I think it may safely be contracted, solely to join two estates?' repeated the old lady, with a look and carriage that plainly showed how entirely she appreciated the amazing presumption of her interrogatrix.

There was a little pause.

'*Certainly,*' replied Lady Chelford; 'that is, of course, under proper conditions, and with a due sense of its sacred character and a—a—obligations.'

'The first of which is *love,*' continued Miss Brandon; 'the second *honour* — both involuntary; and the third *obedience,* which springs from them.'

Old Lady Chelford coughed, and then rallying, said—

'Very good, Miss!'

'And pray, Lady Chelford, what do you think of Mr. Mark Wylder?' pursued Miss Dorcas.

'I don't see, Miss Brandon, that my thoughts upon that subject can concern anyone but myself,' retorted the old lady, severely, and from an awful altitude. 'And I may say, considering who I am—and my years—and the manner in which I am usually treated, I am a little surprised at the tone in which you are pleased to question me.'

These last terrible remarks totally failed to overawe the serene temerity of the grave beauty.

'I assumed, Lady Chelford, as you had interested yourself in me so far as to originate the idea of my engagement to Mr. Wylder, that you had considered these to me very important questions a little, and could give me satisfactory answers upon points on which my mind has been employed for some days; and, indeed, I think I've a right to ask that assistance of you.'

'You seem to forget, young lady, that there are times and places for such discussions; and that to Mr.—a—a—your visitor (a glance at me), it can't be very interesting to listen to this kind of—of—conversation, which is neither very entertaining, nor very *wise.*'

'I am answerable only for *my* part of it; and I think my

questions very much to the purpose,' said the young lady, in her low, silvery tones.

'I don't question your good opinion, Miss Brandon, of your own discretion ; but *I* can't see any profit in now discussing an engagement of more than two months' standing, or a marriage, which is fixed to take place only ten days hence. And I think, Sir (glancing again at me), it must strike *you* a little oddly, that I should be invited, in your presence, to discuss family matters with Miss Dorcas Brandon ?'

Now, was it fair to call a peaceable inhabitant like me into the thick of a fray like this ? I paused long enough to allow Miss Brandon to speak, but she did not choose to do so, thinking, I suppose, it was my business.

'I believe I ought to have withdrawn a little,' I said, very humbly ; and old Lady Chelford at the word shot a gleam of contemptuous triumph at Miss Dorcas ; but I would not acquiesce in the dowager's abusing my concession to the prejudice of that beautiful and daring young lady—'I mean, Lady Chelford, in deference to you, who are not aware, as Miss Brandon is, that I am one of Mr. Wylder's oldest and most intimate friends ; and at his request, and with Lord Chelford's approval, have been advised with, in detail, upon all the arrangements connected with the approaching marriage.'

'I am not going, at present, to say any more upon these subjects, because Lady Chelford prefers deferring our conversation,' said this very odd young lady ; 'but there is nothing which either she or I may say, which I wish to conceal from any friend of Mr. Wylder's.'

The idea of Miss Brandon's seriously thinking of withdrawing from her engagement with Mark Wylder, I confess never entered my mind. Lady Chelford, perhaps, knew more of the capricious and daring character of the ladies of the Brandon line than I, and may have discovered some signs of a coming storm in the oracular questions which had fallen so harmoniously from those beautiful lips. As for me, I was puzzled. The old viscountess was flushed (she did not rouge), and very angry, and, I think, uncomfortable, though she affected her usual supremacy. But the young lady showed no sign of excitement, and lay back in her chair in her usual deep, cold calm.

Lake's late smoking with Wylder must have disagreed with him very much indeed, for he seemed more out of sorts as night approached. He stole away from Mr. Larkin's trellised porch, in the dusk. He marched into the town rather quickly, like a man who has business on his hands ; but he had none—for he walked by the 'Brandon Arms,' and halted, and stared at the post-office, as if he fancied he had something to say there. But no—there was no need to tap at the wooden window-pane.

Some idle boys were observing the dandy captain, and he turned down the short lane that opened on the common, and sauntered upon the short grass.

Two or three groups, and an invalid visitor or two—for Gylingden boasts a 'spa'—were lounging away the twilight half-hours there. He seated himself on one of the rustic seats, and his yellow eyes wandered restlessly and vaguely along the outline of the beautiful hills. Then for nearly ten minutes he smoked—an odd recreation for a man suffering from the cigars of last night—and after that, for nearly as long again, he seemed lost in deep thought, his eyes upon the misty grass before him, and his small French boot beating time to the music of his thoughts.

Several groups passed close by him, in their pleasant circuit. Some wondered what might be the disease of that pale, peevish-looking gentleman, who sat there so still, languid, and dejected. Others set him down as a gentleman in difficulties of some sort, who was using Gylingden for a temporary refuge.

Others, again, supposed he might be that Major Craddock who had lost thirty thousand pounds on Vanderdecken the other day. Others knew he was staying with Mr. Larkin, and supposed he was trying to raise money at disadvantage, and re-marked that some of Mr. Larkin's clients looked always unhappy, though they had so godly an attorney to deal with.

When Lake, with a little shudder, for it was growing chill, lifted up his yellow eyes suddenly, and recollected where he was, the common had grown dark, and was quite deserted. There were lights in the windows of the reading-room, and in the billiard-room beneath it ; and shadowy figures, with cues in their hands, gliding hither and thither, across its uncurtained windows.

With a shrug, and a stealthy glance round him, Captain Lake started up. The instinct of the lonely and gloomy man uncon-sciously drew him towards the light, and he approached. A bat, attracted thither like himself, was flitting and flickering, this way and that, across the casement.

Captain Lake, waiting, with his hand on the door-handle, for the stroke, heard the smack of the balls, and the score called by the marker, and entered the hot, glaring room. Old Major Jackson, with his glass in his eye, was contending in his shirt-sleeves heroically with a Manchester bag-man, who was pal-pably too much for him. The double-chinned and florid pro-prietor of the 'Brandon Arms,' with a brandy-and-water familiarity, offered Captain Lake two to one on the game in anything he liked, which the captain declined, and took his seat on the bench.

He was not interested by the struggle of the gallant major, who smiled like a prize-fighter under his punishment. In fact, he could not have told the score at any point of the game ; and, to judge by his face, was translated from the glare of that arena into a dark and splenetic world of his own.

When he wakened up, in the buzz and clack of tongues that followed the close of the game, Captain Lake glared round for a moment, like a man called up from sleep ; the noise rattled and roared in his ears, the talk sounded madly, and the faces of the people excited and menaced him undefinably, and he felt as if he was on the point of starting to his feet and stamping and shouting. The fact is, I suppose, he was confoundedly nervous, dyspeptic, or whatever else it might be, and the heat and glare were too much for him.

So, out he went into the chill, fresh night-air, and round the corner into the quaint main-street of Gylingden, and walked down it in the dark, nearly to the last house by the corner of the Redman's Dell road, and then back again, and so on, trying to tire himself, I think ; and every time he walked down the street, with his face toward London, his yellow eyes gleamed through the dark air, with the fixed gaze of a man looking out for the appearance of a vehicle. It, perhaps, indicated an anxiety and a mental look-out in that direction, for he really expected no such thing.

Then he dropped into the 'Brandon Arms,' and had a glass of brandy and water, and a newspaper, in the coffee-room ; and then he ordered a 'fly,' and drove in it to Lawyer Larkin's house —'The Lodge,' it was called—and entered Mr. Larkin's drawing-room very cheerfully.

'How quiet you are here,' said the captain. 'I have been awfully dissipated since I saw you.'

'In an innocent way, my dear Captain Lake, you mean, of course—in an innocent way.'

'Oh ! no ; billiards, I assure you. Do you play ?'

'Oh ! dear no—not that I see any essential harm in the game *as* a game, for those, I mean, who don't object to that sort of thing ; but for a resident here, putting aside other feelings—a resident holding a position—it would not do, I assure you. There are people there whom one could not associate with comfortably. I don't care, I hope, how poor a man may be, but do let him be a gentleman. I own to that prejudice. A man, my dear Captain Lake, whose father before him has been a gentleman (old Larkin, while in the flesh, was an organist, and kept a small day school at Dwiddleston, and his grandfather he did not care to enquire after), and who has had the education of one, does not feel himself at home, you know—I'm sure you have felt the same sort of thing yourself.'

'Oh ! of course ; and I had such a nice walk on the common first, and then a turn up and down before the 'Brandon Arms,' where at last I read a paper, and could not resist a glass of brandy and water, and, growing lazy, came home in a ' fly,' so I think I have had a very gay evening.

Larkin smiled benignantly, and would have said something no doubt worth hearing, but at that moment the door opened, and his old cook and elderly parlour-maid — no breath of scandal ever troubled the serene fair fame of his household, and everyone allowed that, in the prudential virtues, at least, he was nearly perfect—and Sleddon the groom, walked in, with those sad faces which, I suppose, were first learned in the belief that they were acceptable to their master.

' Oh !' said Mr. Larkin, in a low, reverential tone, and the smile vanished ; ' prayers !'

' Well, then, if you permit me, being a little tired, I'll go to my bed-room.'

With a grave and affectionate interest, Mr. Larkin looked in his face, and sighed a little and said :—

' Might I, perhaps, venture to beg, just this one night——'

That chastened and entreating look it was hard to resist. But somehow the whole thing seemed to Lake to say, ' Do allow me this once to prescribe ; do give your poor soul this one chance,' and Lake answered him superciliously and irreverently.

' No, thank you, no—any prayers I require I can manage for myself, thank you. Good-night.'

And he lighted a bed-room candle and left the room.

' What a beast that fellow is. I don't know why the d— I stay in his house.'

One reason was, perhaps, that it saved him nearly a guinea a day, and he may have had some other little reasons just then.

' Family prayers indeed ! and such a pair of women—witches, by Jove !—and that rascally groom, and a hypocritical attorney ! And the vulgar brute will be as rich as Crœsus, I dare say.'

Here soliloquised Stanley Lake in that gentleman's ordinary vein. His momentary disgust had restored him for a few seconds to his normal self. But certain anxieties of a rather ghastly kind, and speculations as to what might be going on in London just then, were round him again, like armed giants, in another moment, and the riches or hypocrisy of his host were no more to him than those of Overreach or Tartuffe.

CHAPTER XXI.

IN WHICH CAPTAIN LAKE VISITS HIS SISTER'S SICK-BED.

 SUSPECT there are very few mere hypocrites on earth. Of course, I do not reckon those who are under compulsion to affect purity of manners and a holy integrity of heart—and there are such—but those who volunteer an extraordinary profession of holiness, being all the while conscious villains. The Pharisees, even while devouring widows' houses, believed honestly in their own supreme righteousness.

I am afraid our friend Jos. Larkin wore a mask. I am sure he often wore it when he was quite alone. I don't know indeed, that he ever took it off. He was, perhaps, content to see it, even when he looked in the glass, and had not a very distinct idea what the underlying features might be. It answers with the world ; it almost answers with himself. Pity it won't do everywhere ! 'When Moses went to speak with God,' says the admirable Hall, 'he pulled off his veil. It was good reason he should present to God that face which he had made. There had been more need of his veil to hide the glorious face of God from him than to hide his from God. Hypocrites are contrary to Moses. He showed his worst to men, his best to God ; they show their best to men, their worst to God ; but God sees both their veil and their face, and I know not whether He more hates their veil of dissimulation or their face of wickedness.'

Captain Lake wanted rest—sleep—quiet thoughts at all events. When he was alone he was at once in a state of fever and gloom, and seemed always watching for something. His strange eyes glanced now this way, now that, with a fierce restlessness—now to the window—now to the door—and you would have said he was listening intently to some indistinct and too distant conversation affecting him vitally, there was such a look of fear and conjecture always in his face.

He bolted his door and unlocked his dressing case, and from a little silver box in that glittering repository he took, one after the other, two or three little wafers of a dark hue, and placed them successively on his tongue, and suffered them to melt, and so swallowed them. They were not liquorice. I am afraid Captain Lake dabbled a little in opium. He was not a great adept—yet, at least—like those gentlemen who can swallow five hundred drops of laudanum at a sitting. But he knew the virtues of the drug, and cultivated its acquaintance, and was oftener under its influence than perhaps any mortal, except him-self, suspected.

The greater part of mankind are, upon the whole, happier and more cheerful than they are always willing to allow. Nature subserves the majority. She smiled very brightly next morning. There was a twittering of small birds among the brown leaves and ivy, and a thousand other pleasant sounds and sights stirring in the sharp, sunny air. This sort of inflexible merry-making in nature seems marvellously selfish, in the eyes of anxious Captain Lake. Fear hath torment—and fear is the worst ingredient in mental pain. This is the reason why suspense is so intolerable, and the retrospect even of the worst less terrible.

Stanley Lake would have given more than he could well afford that it were that day week, and he no worse off. Why did time limp so tediously away with him, prolonging his anguish gratuitously? He felt truculently, and would have murdered that week, if he could, in the midst of its loitering sunshine and gaiety.

There was a strange pain at his heart, and the pain of intense and fruitless calculation in his brain; and, as the Mahometan prays towards Mecca, and the Jew towards Jerusalem, so Captain Lake's morning orisons, whatsoever they were, were offered at the window of his bed-room toward London, from whence he looked for his salvation, or it might be the other thing—with a dreadful yearning.

He hated the fresh glitter of that morning scene. Why should the world be cheerful? It was a repast spread of which he could not partake, and it spited him. Yes; it was selfish—and hating selfishness—he would have struck the sun out of the sky that morning with his walking-cane, if he could, and draped the world in black.

He saw from his window the good vicar walk smiling by, in white choker and seedy black, his little boy holding by his fingers, and capering and wheeling in front, and smiling up in his face. They were very busy talking.

Little 'Fairy' used to walk, when parochial visits were not very distant, with his 'Wapsie;' how that name came about no one remembered, but the vicar answered to it more cheerily than to any other. The little man was solitary, and these rambles were a delight. A beautiful smiling little fellow, very exacting of attention—troublesome, perhaps; he was so sociable, and needed sympathy and companionship, and repaid it with a boundless, sensitive *love*. The vicar told him the stories of David and Goliath, and Joseph and his brethren, and of the wondrous birth in Bethlehem of Judea, the star that led the Wise Men, and the celestial song heard by the shepherds keeping their flocks by night, and snatches of ' Pilgrim's Progress; and sometimes, when they made a feast and eat their pennyworth of cherries, sitting on the style, he treated him, I am afraid, to the profane histories of Jack the Giant-killer and the Yellow Dwarf; the vicar had theories about imagination, and fancied it was an important faculty, and that the Creator had not given children their unextinguishable love of stories to no purpose.

I don't envy the man who is superior to the society of children. What can he gain from children's talk? Is it witty, or wise, or learned? Be frank. Is it not, honestly, a mere noise and interruption—a musical cackling of geese, and silvery braying of tiny asses? Well, say I, out of my large acquaintance, there are not many men to whom I would go for wisdom; learning is better found in books, and, as for wit, is it always pleasant? The most companionable men are not always the greatest intellects. They laugh, and though they don't converse, they make a cheerful noise, and show a cheerful countenance.

There was not a great deal in Will Honeycomb, for instance; but our dear Mr. Spectator tells us somewhere that ' he laughed easily,' which I think quite accounts for his acceptance with the club. He was kindly and enjoying. What is it that makes your dog so charming a companion in your walks? Simply that he thoroughly likes you and enjoys himself. He appeals imperceptibly to your affections, which cannot be stirred—such is God's will—ever so lightly, without some little thrillings of happiness; and through the subtle absorbents of your sympathy he infuses into you something of his own hilarious and exulting spirit.

When Stanley Lake saw the vicar, the lines of his pale face contracted strangely, and his wild gaze followed him, and I don't think he breathed once until the thin smiling man in black, with the little gambolling bright boy holding by his hand, had passed by. He was thinking, you may be sure, of his Brother Mark.

When Lake had ended his toilet and stared in the glass, he still looked so haggard, that on greeting Mr. Larkin in the parlour, he thought it necessary to mention that he had taken cold in that confounded billiard-room last night, which spoiled his sleep, and made him awfully seedy that morning. Of course, his host was properly afflicted and sympathetic.

' By-the-bye, I had a letter this morning from that party —our common friend, Mr. W., you know,' said Larkin, gracefully.

' Well, what is he doing, and when does he come back? You mean Wylder, of course?'

' Yes; my good client, Mr. Mark Wylder. Permit me to assist you to some honey, you'll find it remarkably good, I venture to say; it comes from the gardens of Queen's Audley. The late marquis, you know, prided himself on his honey—and my friend, Thornbury, cousin to Sir Frederick Thornbury—I suppose you know him—an East Indian judge, you know—very

kindly left it at Dollington for me, on his way to the Earl of
Epsom's.'

'Thank you—delicious, I'm sure, it has been in such good
company.　　May I see Wylder's note—that is, if there's no
private business?'

'Oh, certainly.'

And, with Wylder's great red seal on the back of the envelope,
the letter ran thus :—

'DEAR LARKIN,—I write in haste to save post, to say I shall
be detained in town a few days longer than I thought.　　Don't
wait for me about the parchments ; I am satisfied.　　If anything
crosses your mind, a word with Mr. De C. at the Hall, will clear
all up.　　Have all ready to sign and seal when I come back—certainly, within a week.

　　　　　　　　　　　'Yours sincerely,
　　　　　　　　　　　　'M. WYLDER,
　　　　　　　　　　　　　　　'London.'

It was evidently written in great haste, with the broad-nibbed
pen he liked ; but notwithstanding the sort of swagger with
which the writing marched across the page, Lake might have
seen here and there a little quaver—indicative of something
different from haste—the vibrations of another sort of flurry.

'"Certainly within a week," he writes.　　Does he mean he'll
be here in a week or only to have the papers ready in a week?'
asked Lake.

'The question, certainly, does arise.　　It struck me on the
first perusal,' answered the attorney.　　'His address is rather a
wide one, too — London !　　Do you know his club, Captain
Lake?'

'The *Wanderers*.　　He has left the *United Service*.　　Nothing
for me, by-the-way?'

'No letter.　　No.'

'*Tant mieux*, I hate them,' said the captain.　　'I wonder how
my sister is this morning.'

'Would you like a messenger?　　I'll send down with pleasure
to enquire.'

'Thank you, no ; I'll walk down and see her.'

And Lake yawned at the window, and then took his hat and
stick and sauntered toward Gylingden.　　At the post-office window he tapped with the silver tip of his cane, and told Miss
Driver with a sleepy smile—

'I'm going down to Redman's Farm, and any letters for my
sister, Miss Lake, I may as well take with me.'

Everybody 'in business' in the town of Gylingden, by this
time, knew Captain Lake and his belongings—a most respectable party—a high man ; and, of course, there was no difficulty.

There was only one letter — the address was written—'Miss Lake, Redman's Farm, near Brandon Park, Gylingden,' in a stiff hand, rather slanting backwards.

Captain Lake put it in his paletot pocket, looked in her face gently, and smiled, and thanked her in his graceful way — and, in fact, left an enduring impression upon that impressible nature.

Turning up the dark road at Redman's Dell, the gallant captain passed the old mill, and, all being quiet up and down the road, he halted under the lordly shadow of a clump of chestnuts, and opened and read the letter he had just taken charge of. It contained only these words :—

'Wednesday.

'On Friday night, next, at half-past twelve.'

This he read twice or thrice, pausing between whiles. The envelope bore the London postmark. Then he took out his cigar case, selected a promising weed, and wrapping the laconic note prettily round one of his scented matches, lighted it, and the note flamed pale in the daylight, and dropped still blazing, at the root of the old tree he stood by, and sent up a little curl of blue smoke — an incense to the demon of the wood — and turned in a minute more into a black film, overrun by a hundred creeping sparkles ; and having completed his mysterious incremation, he, with his yellow eyes, made a stolen glance around, and lighting his cigar, glided gracefully up the steep road, under the solemn canopy of old timber, to the sound of the moaning stream below, and the rustle of withered leaves about him, toward Redman's Farm.

As he entered the flower-garden, the jaundiced face of old Tamar, with its thousand small wrinkles and its ominous gleam of suspicion, was looking out from the darkened porch. The white cap, kerchief, and drapery, courtesied to him as he drew near, and the dismal face changed not.

'Well, Tamar, how do you do ?—how are all ? Where is that girl Margery ?'

'In the kitchen, Master Stanley,' said she, courtesying again.

'Are you sure ?' said Captain Lake, peeping toward that apartment over the old woman's shoulder.

'Certain sure, Master Stanley.'

'Well, come up stairs to your mistress's room,' said Lake, mounting the stairs, with his hat in his hand, and on tip-toe, like a man approaching a sick chamber.

There was something I think grim and spectral in this ceremonious ascent to the empty chamber. Children had once occupied that silent floor for there was a little balustraded gate across the top of the staircase.

'I keep this closed,' said old Tamar, 'and forbid her to cross it, lest she should disturb the mistress. Heaven forgive me !'

'Very good,' he whispered, and he peeped over the banister, and then entered Rachel's silent room, darkened with closed shutters, the white curtains and white coverlet so like 'the dark chamber of white death.'

He had intended speaking to Tamar there, but changed his mind, or rather could not make up his mind ; and he loitered silently, and stood with the curtain in his gloved hand, looking upon the cold coverlet, as if Rachel lay dead there.

'That will do,' he said, awaking from his wandering thought. We'll go down now, Tamar.'

And in the same stealthy way, walking lightly and slowly, down the stairs they went, and Stanley entered the kitchen.

'How do you do, Margery? You'll be glad to hear your mistress is better. You must run down to the town, though, and buy some jelly, and you are to bring her back change of this.'

And he placed half-a-crown in her hand.

'Put on your bonnet and my old shawl, child ; and take the basket, and come back by the side door,' croaked old Tamar.

So the girl dried her hands—she was washing the teacups— and in a twinkling was equipped and on her way to Gylingden.

CHAPTER XXII.

IN WHICH CAPTAIN LAKE MEETS A FRIEND NEAR THE WHITE HOUSE.

LAKE had no very high opinion of men or women, gentle or simple.

'She listens, I dare say, the little spy,' said he.

'No, Master Stanley! She's a good little girl.'

'She quite believes her mistress is up stairs, eh?'

'Yes; the Lord forgive me—I'm deceiving her.'

He did not like the tone and look which accompanied this.

'Now, my good old Tamar, you really can't be such an idiot as to fancy there can be any imaginable wrong in keeping that prying little slut in ignorance of that which in no wise concerns her. This is a critical matter, do you see, and if it were known in this place that your young mistress had gone away as she has done—though quite innocently—upon my honour—I think it would blast her. You would not like, for a stupid crotchet, to ruin poor Radie, I fancy.'

'I'm doing just what you both bid me,' said the old woman.

'You sit up stairs chiefly?'

She nodded sadly.

'And keep the hall door shut and bolted?'

Again she nodded.

'I'm going up to the Hall, and I'll tell them she's much better, and that I've been in her room, and that, perhaps, she may go up to see them in the morning.'

Old Tamar shook her head and groaned.

'How long is all this to go on for, Master Stanley?'

'Why, d— you, Tamar, can't you listen?' he said, clutching her wrist in his lavender kid grasp rather roughly. 'How long —a very short time, I tell you. She'll be home immediately. I'll come to-morrow and tell you exactly—maybe to-morrow evening—will that do? And should they call, you must say the same; and if Miss Dorcas, Miss Brandon, you know—should wish to go up to see her, tell her she's asleep. Stop that hypocritical grimacing, will you. It is no part of your duty to tell the world what can't possibly concern them, and may bring your young mistress to—*perdition*. That does not strike me as any part of your religion.'

Tamar groaned again, and she said: 'I opened my Bible, Lord help me, three times to-day, Master Stanley, and could not go on. It's no use—I can't read it.'

'Time enough—I think you've read more than is good for you.

I think you are half mad, Tamar; but think what you may, it must be done. Have not you read of straining at gnats and swallowing camels? You used not, I've heard, to be always so scrupulous, old Tamar.'

There was a vile sarcasm in his tone and look.

' It is not for the child I nursed to say that,' said Tamar.

There were scandalous stories of wicked old Tiberius—bankrupt, dead, and buried—compromising the fame of Tamar—not always a spectacled and cadaverous student of Holy Writ. These, indeed, were even in Stanley's childhood old-world, hazy, traditions of the servants' hall. But boys hear often more than is good, and more than gospel, who live in such houses as old General Lake, the old millionaire widower, kept.

' I did not mean anything, upon my honour, Tamar, that could annoy you. I only meant you used not to be a fool, and pray don't begin now; for I assure you Radie and I would not ask it if it could be avoided. You have Miss Radie's secret in your hands, I don't think you'd like to injure her, and you used to be trustworthy. I don't think your Bible teaches you anywhere to hurt your neighbour and to break faith.'

' Don't speak of the Bible now; but you needn't fear me, Master Stanley,' answered the old woman, a little sternly. ' I don't know why she's gone, nor why it's a secret—I don't, and I'd rather not. Poor Miss Radie, she never heard anything but what was good from old Tamar, whatever I might ha' bin myself, miserable sinners are we all; and I'll do as you bid me, and I *have* done, Master Stanley, howsoever it troubles my mind;' and now old Tamar's words spoke—that's all.

' Old Tamar is a sensible creature, as she always was. I hope I did not vex you, Tamar. I did not mean, I assure you; but we get rough ways in the army, I'm afraid, and you won't mind me. You never *did* mind little Stannie when he was naughty, you know.'

There was here a little subsidence in his speech. He was thinking of giving her a crown, but there were several reasons against it, so that handsome coin remained in his purse.

' And I forgot to tell you, Tamar, I've a ring for you in town—a little souvenir; you'll think it pretty—a gold ring, with a stone in it — it belonged to poor dear Aunt Jemima, you remember. I left it behind; so stupid !'

So he shook hands with old Tamar, and patted her affectionately on the shoulder, and he said :—

' Keep the hall-door bolted. Make any excuse you like : only it would not do for anyone to open it, and run up to the room as they might, so don't forget to secure the door when I go. I think that is all. Ta-ta, dear Tamar. I'll see you in the morning.'

As he walked down the mill-road toward the town, he met Lord Chelford on his way to make enquiry about Rachel at

Redman's Farm ; and Lake, who, as we know, had just seen his sister, gave him all particulars.

Chelford, like the lawyer, had heard from Mark Wylder that morning—a few lines, postponing his return. He merely mentioned it, and made no comment ; but Lake perceived that he was annoyed at his unexplained absence.

Lake dined at Brandon that evening, and though looking ill, was very good company, and promised to bring an early report of Rachel's convalescence in the morning.

I have little to record of next day, except that Larkin received another London letter. Wylder plainly wrote in great haste, and merely said :—

' I shall have to wait a day or two longer than I yesterday .hought, to meet a fellow from whom I am to receive something of importance, rather, as I think, to me. Get the deeds ready, as I said in my last. If I am not in Gylingden by Monday, we must put off the wedding for a week later—there is no help for it. You need not talk of this. I write to Chelford to say the same.'

This note was as unceremonious, and still shorter. Lord Chelford would have written at once to remonstrate with Mark on the unseemliness of putting off his marriage so capriciously, or, at all events, so mysteriously—Miss Brandon not being considered, nor her friends consulted. But Mark had a decided objection to many letters : he had no fancy to be worried, when he had made up his mind, by prosy remonstrances ; and he shut out the whole tribe of letter-writers by simply omitting to give them his address.

His cool impertinence, and especially this cunning precaution, incensed old Lady Chelford. She would have liked to write him one of those terse, courteous, biting notes, for which she was famous ; and her fingers, morally, tingled to box his ears. But what was to be done with mere ' London ?' Wylder was hidden from mortal sight, like a heaven-protected hero in the ' Iliad,' and a cloud of invisibility girdled him.

Like most rustic communities, Gylingden and its neighbourhood were early in bed. Few lights burned after half-past ten, and the whole vicinity was deep in its slumbers before twelve o'clock.

At that dread hour, Captain Lake, about a mile on the Dollington, which was the old London road from Gylingden, was pacing backward and forward under the towering tiles of beech that overarch it at that point.

The ' White House' public, with a wide panel over its door, presenting, in tints subdued by time, a stage-coach and four horses in mid career, lay a few hundred yards nearer to Gylingden. Not a soul was stirring—not a sound but those, sad and soothing, of nature was to be heard.

Stanley Lake did not like waiting any more than did Louis

XIV. He was really a little tired of acting sentry, and was very peevish by the time the ring of wheels and horse-hoofs approaching from the London direction became audible. Even so, he had a longer wait than he expected, sounds are heard so far by night. At last, however, it drew nearer—nearer—quite close—and a sort of nondescript vehicle—one horsed—loomed in the dark, and he calls—

'Hallo! there—I say—a passenger for the "WhiteHouse?"'

At the same moment, a window of the cab—shall we call it—was let down, and a female voice—Rachel Lake's—called to the driver to stop.

Lake addressed the driver—

'You come from Johnson's Hotel—don't you—at Dollington?'

'Yes, Sir.'

'Well, I'll pay you half-fare to bring me there.'

'All right, Sir. But the 'oss, Sir, must 'av 'is oats fust.'

'Feed him here, then. They are all asleep in the "White House." I'll be with you in five minutes, and you shall have something for yourself when we get into Dollington.'

Stanley opened the door. She placed her hand on his, and stepped to the ground. It was very dark under those great trees. He held her hand a little harder than was his wont.

'All quite well, ever since. You are not very tired, are you? I'm afraid it will be necessary for you to walk to "Redman's Farm," dear Radie—but it is hardly a mile, I think—for, you see, the fellow must not know who you are ; and I must go back with him, for I have not been very well—indeed I've been, I may say, very ill—and I told that fellow, Larkin, who has his eyes about him, and would wonder what kept me out so late, that I would run down to some of the places near for a change, and sleep a night there ; and that's the reason, dear Radie, I can walk only a short way with you ; but you are not afraid to walk a part of the way home without me? You are so sensible, and you have been, really, so very kind, I assure you I appreciate it, Radie—I do, indeed ; and I'm very grateful—I am, upon my word.'

Rachel answered with a heavy sigh.

CHAPTER XXIII.

HOW RACHEL SLEPT THAT NIGHT IN REDMAN'S FARM.

'ALLOW me—pray do,' and he took her little bag from her hand. 'I hope you are not very tired, darling; you've been so very good; and you're not afraid—you know the place is so quiet—of the little walk by yourself. Take my arm; I'll go as far as I can, but it is very late you know—and you are sure you are not afraid?'

'I ought to be afraid of nothing now, Stanley, but I think I am afraid of everything.'

'Merely a little nervous—it's nothing—I've been wretchedly since, myself; but, I'm so glad you are home again; you shall have no more trouble, I assure you; and not a creature suspects you have been from home. Old Tamar has behaved admirably.'

Rachel sighed again and said—

'Yes—poor Tamar.'

'And now, dear, I'm afraid I must leave you—I'm very sorry; but you see how it is; keep to the shady side, close by the hedge, where the trees stop; but I'm certain you will meet no one. Tamar will tell you who has called—hardly anyone—I saw them myself every day at Brandon, and told them you were ill. You've been very kind, Radie; I assure you I'll never forget it. You'll find Tamar up and watching for you—I arranged all that; and I need not say you'll be very careful not to let that girl of yours hear anything. You'll be very quiet—she suspects nothing; and I assure you, so far as personal annoyance of any kind is concerned, you may be perfectly at ease. Good-night, Radie; God bless you, dear. I wish very much I could see you all the way, but there's a risk in it, you know. Good-night, dear Radie. By-the-bye, here's your bag; I'll take the rug, it's too heavy for you, and I may as well have it to Dollington.'

He kissed her cheek in his slight way, and left her, and was soon on his way to Dollington, where he slept that night — rather more comfortably than he had done since Rachel's departure.

Rachel walked on swiftly. Very tired, but not at all sleepy—on the contrary, excited and nervous, and rather relieved, notwithstanding that Stanley had left her to walk home alone.

It seemed to her that more than a month had passed since she saw the mill-road last. How much had happened! how awful was the change! Familiar objects glided past her, the same, yet the fashion of the countenance was altered ; there was something estranged and threatening.

The pretty parsonage was now close by : in the dews of night the spirit of peace and slumbers smiled over it ; but the sight of its steep roof and homely chimney-stacks smote with a shock at her brain and heart—a troubled moan escaped her. She looked up with the instinct of prayer, and clasped her hands on the handle of that little bag which had made the mysterious journey with her ; a load which no man could lift lay upon her heart.

Then she commenced her dark walk up the mill-road—her hands still clasped, her lips moving in broken appeals to Heaven. She looked neither to the right nor to the left, but passed on with inflexible gaze and hasty steps, like one who crosses a plank over some awful chasm.

In such darkness Redman's dell was a solemn, not to say an awful, spot ; and at any time, I think, Rachel, in a like solitude and darkness, would have been glad to see the red glimmer of old Tamar's candle proclaiming under the branches the neighbourhood of human life and sympathy.

The old woman, with her shawl over her head, sat listening for her young mistress's approach, on the little side bench in the trellised porch, and tottered hastily forth to meet her at the garden wicket, whispering forlorn welcomes, and thanksgivings, which Rachel answered only with a kiss.

Safe, safe at home ! Thank Heaven at least for that. Secluded once more—hidden in Redman's Dell ; but never again to be the same—the careless mind no more. The summer sunshine through the trees, the leafy songs of birds, obscured in the smoke and drowned in the discord of an untold and everlasting trouble.

The hall-door was now shut and bolted. Wise old Tamar had turned the key upon the sleeping girl. There was nothing to be feared from prying eyes and listening ears.

'You are cold, Miss Radie, and tired—poor thing ! I lit a bit of fire in your room, Miss ; would you like me to go up stairs with you, Miss ?'

'Come.'

And so up stairs they went ; and the young lady looked round with a strange anxiety, like a person seeking for something, and forgetting what ; and, sitting down, she leaned her head on her hand with a moan, the living picture of despair.

'You've a headache, Miss Radie ?' said the old woman, standing by her with that painful enquiry which sat naturally on her face.

'A heartache, Tamar.'

'Let me help you off with these things, Miss Radie, dear.'

The young lady did not seem to hear, but she allowed Tamar to remove her cloak and hat and handkerchief.

The old servant had placed the tea-things on the table, and what remained of that wine of which Stanley had partaken on the night from which the eclipse of Rachel's life dated. So, without troubling her with questions, she made tea, and then some negus, with careful and trembling hands.

'No,' said Rachel, a little pettishly, and put it aside.

'See now, Miss Radie, dear. You look awful sick and tired. You are tired to death and pale, and sorry, my dear child ; and to please old Tamar, you'll just drink this.'

'Thank you, Tamar, I believe you are right.'

The truth was she needed it ; and in the same dejected way she sipped it slowly ; and then there was a long silence—the silence of a fatigue, like that of fever, near which sleep refuses to come. But she sat in that waking lethargy in which are sluggish dreams of horror, and neither eyes nor ears for that which is before us.

When at last with another great sigh she lifted her head, her eyes rested on old Tamar's face, at the other side of the fire-place, with a dark, dull surprise and puzzle for a moment, as if she could not tell why she was there, or where the place was ; and then rising up, with piteous look in her old nurse's face, she said, 'Oh ! Tamar, Tamar. It is a dreadful world.'

'So it is, Miss Radie, answered the old woman, her glittering eyes returning her sad gaze wofully. 'Aye, so it is, sure !—and such it was and will be. For so the Scripture says—" Cursed is the ground for thy sake "—hard to the body—a vale of tears— dark to the spirit. But it is the hand of God that is upon you, and, like me, you will say at last, " It is good for me that I have been in trouble." Lie down, dear Miss Radie, and I'll read to you the blessed words of comfort that have been sealed for me ever since I saw you last. They have—but that's over.'

And she turned up her pallid, puckered face, and, with a trembling and knotted pair of hands uplifted, she muttered an awful thanksgiving.

Rachel said nothing, but her eyes rested on the floor, and, with the quiet obedience of her early childhood, she did as Tamar said. And the old woman assisted her to undress, and so she lay down with a sigh in her bed. And Tamar, her round spectacles by this time on her nose, sitting at the little table by her pillow, read, in a solemn and somewhat quavering voice, such comfortable passages as came first to memory.

Rachel cried quietly as she listened, and at last, worn out by many feverish nights, and the fatigues of her journey, she fell into a disturbed slumber, with many startings and sudden wak-ings, with cries and strange excitement.

Old Tamar would not leave her, but kept her seat in the high-backed arm-chair throughout the night, like a nurse—as indeed she was—in a sick chamber. And so that weary night limped tediously away, and morning dawned, and tipped the dis-coloured foliage of the glen with its glow, awaking the songs of all the birds, and dispersing the white mists of darkness. And Rachel with a start awoke, and sat up with a wild look and a cry—

'What is it?'

'Nothing, dear Miss Radie—only poor old Tamar.' And a new day had begun.

CHAPTER XXIV.

DORCAS BRANDON PAYS RACHEL A VISIT.

T was not very much past eleven that morning when the pony carriage from Brandon drew up before the little garden wicket of Redman's Farm.

The servant held the ponies' heads, and Miss Dorcas passed through the little garden, and met old Tamar in the porch.

'Better to-day, Tamar?' enquired this grand and beautiful young lady.

The sun glimmered through the boughs behind her; her face was in shade, and its delicate chiselling was brought out in soft reflected lights; and old Tamar looked on her in a sort of wonder, her beauty seemed so celestial and splendid.

Well, she *was* better, though she had had a bad night. She was up and dressed, and this moment coming down, and would be very happy to see Miss Brandon, if she would step into the drawing-room.

Miss Brandon took old Tamar's hand gently and pressed it. I suppose she was glad and took this way of showing it; and tall, beautiful, graceful, in rustling silks, she glided into the tiny drawing-room silently, and sate down softly by the window, looking out upon the flowers and the falling leaves, mottled in light and shadow.

We have been accustomed to see another girl—bright and fair-haired Rachel Lake—in the small rooms of Redman's Farm; but Dorcas only in rich and stately Brandon Hall—the beautiful 'genius loci' under lofty ceilings, curiously moulded in the first James's style—amid carved oak and richest draperies, tall china vases, paintings, and cold white statues; and somehow in this low-roofed room, so small and homely, she looks like a displaced divinity — an exile under Juno's jealousy from the cloudy splendours of Olympus—dazzlingly melancholy, and 'humano major' among the meannesses and trumperies of earth.

So there came a step and a little rustling of feminine draperies, the small door opened, and Rachel entered, with her hand extended, and a pale smile of welcome.

Women can hide their pain better than we men, and bear it better, too, except when *shame* drops fire into the dreadful chalice. But poor Rachel Lake had more than that stoical hypocrisy which enables the tortured spirits of her sex to lift a pale face through the flames and smile.

She was sanguine, she was genial and companionable, and her spirits rose at the sight of a friendly face. This transient spring and lighting up are beautiful—a glamour beguiling our senses. It wakens up the frozen spirit of enjoyment, and leads the sad faculties forth on a wild forgetful frolic.

'Rachel, dear, I'm so glad to see you,' said Dorcas, placing her arms gently about her neck, and kissing her twice or thrice. There was something of sweetness and fondness in her tones and manner, which was new to Rachel, and comforting, and she returned the greeting as kindly, and felt more like her former self. 'You have been more ill than I thought, darling, and you are still far from quite recovered.'

Rachel's pale and sharpened features and dilated eye struck her with a painful surprise.

'I shall soon be as well as I am ever likely to be—that is, quite well,' answered Rachel. 'You have been very kind. I've heard of your coming here, and sending, so often.'

They sat down side by side, and Dorcas held her hand.

'Maybe, Rachel dear, you would like to drive a little?'

'No, darling, not yet; it is very good of you.'

'You have been so ill, my poor Rachel.'

'Ill and troubled, dear—troubled in mind, and miserably nervous.'

Poor Rachel! her nature recoiled from deceit, and she told, at all events, as much of the truth as she dared.

Dorcas's large eyes rested upon her with a grave enquiry, and then Miss Brandon looked down in silence for a while on the carpet, and was thinking a little sternly, maybe, and with a look of pain, still holding Rachel's hand, she said, with a sad sort of reproach in her tone,

'Rachel, dear, you have not told my secret?'

'No, indeed, Dorcas—never, and never will; and I think, though I have learned to fear death, I would rather die than let Stanley even suspect it.'

She spoke with a sudden energy, which partook of fear and passion, and flushed her thin cheek, and made her languid eyes flash.

'Thank you, Rachel, my Cousin Rachel, my only friend. I ought not to have doubted you,' and she kissed her again.

Chelford had a note from Mr. Wylder this morning—another

note—his coming delayed, and something of his having to see some person who is abroad,' continued Dorcas, after a little pause. 'You have heard, of course, of Mr. Wylder's absence?'

'Yes, something—*everything*,' said Rachel, hurriedly, looking frowningly at a flower which she was twirling in her fingers.

'He chose an unlucky moment for his departure. I meant to speak to him and end all between us ; and I would now write, but there is no address to his letters. I think Lady Chelford and her son begin to think there is more in this oddly-timed journey of Mr. Wylder's than first appeared. When I came into the parlour this morning I knew they were speaking of it. If he does not return in a day or two, Chelford, I am sure, will speak to me, and then I shall tell him my resolution.'

'Yes,' said Rachel.

'I don't understand his absence. I think *they* are puzzled, too. Can you conjecture why he is gone?'

Rachel made no answer, but rose with a dreamy look, as if gazing at some distant object among the dark masses of forest trees, and stood before the window so looking across the tiny garden.

'I don't think, Rachel dear, you heard me?' said Dorcas.

'Can I conjecture why he is gone?' murmured Rachel, still gazing with a wild kind of apathy into distance. 'Can I? What can it now be to you or me—why? Yes, we sometimes conjecture right, and sometimes wrong ; there are many things best not conjectured about at all—some interesting, some abominable, some that pass all comprehension : I never mean to conjecture, if I can help it, again.'

And the wan oracle having spoken, she sate down in the same sort of abstraction again beside Dorcas, and she looked full in her cousin's eyes.

'I made you a voluntary promise, Dorcas, and now you will make me one. Of Mark Wylder I say this : his name has been for years hateful to me, and recently it has become frightful ; and you will promise me simply this, that you will never ask me to speak again about him. Be he near, or be he far, I regard his very name with horror.'

Dorcas returned her gaze with one of haughty amazement; and Rachel said,

'Well, Dorcas, you promise?'

'You speak truly, Rachel, you *have* a right to my promise : I give it.'

'Dorcas, you are changed ; have I lost your love for asking so poor a kindness?'

'I'm only disappointed, Rachel ; I thought you would have trusted me, as I did you.'

'It is an antipathy—an antipathy I cannot get over, dear Dorcas ; you may think it a madness, but don't blame me. Remember I am neither well nor happy, and forgive what you cannot like in me. I have very few to love me now, and I thought you might love me, as I have begun to love you. Oh ! Dorcas, darling, don't forsake me ; I am very lonely here, and my spirits are gone, and I never needed kindness so much before.'

And she threw her arms round her cousin's neck, and brave Rachel at last burst into tears.

Dorcas, in her strange way, was moved.

' I like you still, Rachel ; I'm sure I'll always like you. You resemble me, Rachel : you are fearless and inflexible and generous. That spirit belongs to the blood of our strange race ; all our women were so. Yes, Rachel, I do love you. I was wounded to find you had thoughts you would not trust to me ; but I have made the promise, and I'll keep it ; and I love you all the same.'

' Thank you, Dorcas, dear. I like to call you cousin—kindred is so pleasant. Thank you, from my heart, for your love ; you will never know, perhaps, how much it is to me.'

The young queen looked on her kindly, but sadly, through her large, strange eyes, clouded with a presage of futurity, and she kissed her again, and said—

' Rachel, dear, I have a plan for you and me : we shall be old maids, you and I, and live together like the ladies of Llangollen, careless and happy recluses. I'll let Brandon and abdicate. We will make a little tour together, when all this shall have blown over, in a few weeks, and choose our retreat ; and with the winter's snow we'll vanish from Brandon, and appear with the early flowers at our cottage among the beautiful woods and hills of Wales. Will you come, Rachel ?'

At sight of this castle or cottage in the air, Rachel lighted up. The little whim had something tranquillising and balmy. It was escape—flight from Gylingden—flight from Brandon—flight from Redman's Farm : they and all their hated associations would be far behind, and that awful page in her story, not torn out, indeed, but gummed down as it were, and no longer glaring and glowering in her eyes every moment of her waking life.

So she smiled upon the picture painted on the clouds ; it was the first thing that had interested her for days. It was a hope. She seized it; she clung to it. She knew, perhaps, it was the merest chimera ; but it rested and consoled her imagination, and opened, in the blackness of her sky, one small vista, through whose silvery edge the blue and stars of heaven were visible.

CHAPTER XXV.

CAPTAIN LAKE LOOKS IN AT NIGHTFALL.

N the queer little drawing-room of Redman's **Farm it** was twilight, so dense were the shadows **from the** great old chestnuts that surrounded it, **before the sun** was well beneath the horizon ; and you could, **from** its darkened window, see its red beams still tinting the high grounds of Willerston, visible through the stems of the old trees that were massed in the near foreground.

A figure which had lost its energy—a face stamped with the lines and pallor of a dejection almost guilty—with something of the fallen grace and beauty of poor Margaret, as we see her with her forehead leaning on her slender hand, by the stirless spinning-wheel—the image of a strange and ineffaceable sorrow, sat Rachel Lake.

Tamar might glide in and out ; her mistress did **not speak ;** the shadows deepened round her, but she did look up, nor call, in the old cheerful accents, for lights. No more roulades and ringing chords from the piano—no more clear spirited tones of the lady's voice sounded through the low ceilings of Redman's Farm, and thrilled with a haunting melody the deserted glen, wherein the birds had ended their vesper songs and gone to rest.

A step was heard at the threshold—it entered the hall ; the door of the little chamber opened, and Stanley Lake entered, saying in a doubtful, almost timid way—

'It is I, Radie, come to thank you, and just to ask you how you do, and to say I'll never forget your kindness ; upon my honour, I never can.'

Rachel shuddered as the door opened, and there was a ghastly sort of expectation in her look. Imperfectly as it was seen, he could understand it. She did not bid him welcome or even speak. There was a silence.

'Now, you're not angry with me, Radie dear ; I venture to say I suffer more than you : and how could I have anticipated the strange turn things have taken ? You know how it all came about, and you must see I'm not really to blame, at least in intention, for all this miserable trouble ; and even if I were, where's the good in angry feeling or reproaches now, don't you see, when I can't mend it ? Come, Radie, let by-gones be by-gones. There's a good girl ; won't you ?'

'Aye, by-gones are by-gones ; the past is, indeed, immutable, and the future is equally fixed, and more dreadful.'

'Come, Radie; a clever girl like you can make your own future.'

'And what do you want of me now?' she asked, with a fierce cold stare.

'But I did not say I wanted anything.'

'Of course you do, or I should not have seen you. Mark me though, I'll go no further in the long route of wickedness you seem to have marked out for me. I'm sacrificed, it is true, but I won't renew my hourly horrors, and live under the rule of your diabolical selfishness.'

'Say what you will, but keep your temper—will you?' he answered, more like his angry self. But he checked the rising devil within him, and changed his tone; he did not want to quarrel—quite the reverse.

'I don't know really, Radie, why you should talk as you do. I don't want you to do anything—upon my honour I don't—only just to exercise your common sense—and you have lots of sense, Radie. Don't you think people have eyes to see, and ears and tongues in this part of the world? Don't you know very well, in a small place like this, they are all alive with curiosity? and if you choose to make such a tragedy figure, and keep moping and crying, and all that sort of thing, and look so *funeste* and miserable, you'll be sure to fix attention and set the whole d—d place speculating and gossiping? and really, Radie, you're making mountains of mole-hills. It is because you live so solitary here, and it *is* such a gloomy out-o'-the-way spot—so awfully dark and damp, nobody *could* be well here, and you really must change. It is the very temple of blue-devilry, and I assure you if I lived as you do I'd cut my throat before a month —you *mustn't.* And old Tamar, you know, such a figure! The very priestess of despair. She gives me the horrors, I assure you, whenever I look at her; you must not keep her, she's of no earthly use, poor old thing; and, you know, Radie, we're not rich enough—you and I—to support other people. You must really place yourself more cheerfully, and I'll speak to Chelford about Tamar. There's a very nice place—an asylum, or something, for old women—near—(Dollington he was going to say, but the associations were not pleasant)—near some of those little towns close to this, and he's a visitor, or governor, or whatever they call it. It is really not fair to expect you or me to keep people like that.'

'She has not cost you much hitherto, Stanley, and she will give you very little trouble hereafter. I won't part with Tamar.'

'She has not cost me much?' said Lake, whose temper was not of a kind to pass by anything. 'No; of course, she has not. *I* can't afford a guinea. You're poor enough; but in proportion to my expenses—a woman, of course, can live on less than half what a man can—I'm a great deal poorer than you;

and I never said I gave her sixpence—did I? I have not got it to give, and I don't think she's fool enough to expect it ; and, to say the truth, I don't care. I only advise you. There are some cheerful little cottages near the green, in Gylingden, and I venture to think, this is one of the very gloomiest and most uncomfortable places you could have selected to live in.'

Rachel looked drearily toward the window and sighed—it was almost a groan.

'It was cheerful always till this frightful week changed everything. Oh! why, why, why did you ever come?' She threw back her pale face, biting her lip, and even in that deepening gloom her small pearly teeth glimmered white ; and then she burst into sobs and an agony of tears.

Captain Lake knew something of feminine paroxysms. Rachel was not given to hysterics. He knew this burst of anguish was unaffected. He was rather glad of it. When it was over he expected clearer weather and a calm. So he waited, saying now and then a soothing word or two.

'There—there—there, Radie—there's a good girl. Never mind—there—there.' And between whiles his mind, which, in truth, had a good deal upon it, would wander and pursue its dismal and perplexed explorations, to the unheard accompaniment of her sobs.

He went to the door, but it was not to call for water, or for old Tamar. On the contrary, it was to observe whether she or the girl was listening. But the house, though small, was built with thick partition walls, and sounds were well enclosed in the rooms to which they belonged.

With Rachel this weakness did not last long. It was a gust —violent—soon over ; and the ' o'er-charged' heart and brain were relieved. And she pushed open the window, and stood for a moment in the chill air, and sighed, and whispered a word or two over the closing flowers of her little garden toward the darkening glen, and with another great sigh closed the window, and returned.

'Can I do anything, Radie? You're better now. I knew you would be. Shall I get some water from your room?'

'No, Stanley ; no, thank you. I'm very well now,' she said, gently.

'Yes, I think so. I knew you'd be better.' And he patted her shoulder with his soft hand ; and then followed a short silence.

'I wish you were more pleasantly lodged, Radie ; but we can speak of that another time.'

'Yes—you're right. This place is dreadful, and its darkness dreadful ; but light is still more dreadful now, and I think I'll change; but, as you say, there is time enough to think of all that.'

'Quite so—time enough. By-the-bye, Radie, you mentioned our old servant, whom my father thought so highly of—Jim Dutton—the other evening. I've been thinking of him, do you know, and I should like to find him out. He was a very honest fellow, and attached, and a clever fellow, too, my father thought; and *he* was a good judge. Hadn't you a letter from his mother lately? You told me so, I think; and if it is not too much trouble, dear Radie, would you allow me to see it?'

Rachel opened her desk, and silently selected one of those clumsy and original missives, directed in a staggering, round hand, on paper oddly shaped and thick, such as mixes not naturally with the aristocratic fabric, on which crests and ciphers are impressed, and placed it in her brother's hand.

'But you can't read it without light,' said Rachel.

'No; but there's no hurry. Does she say where she is staying, or her son?'

'Both, I think,' answered Rachel, languidly; 'but he'll never make a servant for you—he's a rough creature, she says, and was a groom. You can't remember him, nor I either.'

'Perhaps—very likely;' and he put the letter in his pocket.

'I was thinking, Rachel, you could advise me, if you would, you are so clever, you know.'

'Advise!' said Rachel, softly; but with a wild and bitter rage ringing under it. 'I did advise when it was yet time to profit by advice. I bound you even by a promise to take it, but you know how it ended. You don't want my advice.'

'But really I do, Radie. I quite allow I was wrong—worse than wrong—but where is the use of attacking me now, when I'm in this dreadful fix? I took a wrong step; and what I now have to do is to guard myself, if possible, from what I'm threatened with.'

She fancied she saw his pale face grow more bloodless, even in the shadow where he sat.

'I know you too well, Stanley. You want *no* advice. You never took advice—you never will. Your desperate and ingrained perversity has ruined us both.'

'I wish you'd let me know my own mind. I say I do—(and he uttered an unpleasant exclamation). Do you think I'll leave matters to take their course, and sit down here to be destroyed? I'm no such idiot. I tell you I'll leave no stone unturned to save myself; and, in some measure, *you* too, Radie. You don't seem to comprehend the tremendous misfortune that menaces me—*us*—*you* and me.'

And he cursed Mark Wylder with a gasp of hatred not easily expressed.

She winced at the name, and brushed her hand to her ear.

'Don't—don't—*don't,*' she said, vehemently.

'Well, what the devil do you mean by refusing to help me,

even with a hint? I say—I *know*—all the odds are against us
It is sometimes a long game ; but unless I'm sharp, I can't escape what's coming. I *can't*—you can't—sooner or later. It is
in motion already—d— him—it's coming, and you expect me
to do everything alone.'

' I repeat it, Stanley,' said Rachel, with a fierce cynicism in
her low tones, ' you don't want advice ; you have formed your
plan, whatever it is, and that plan you will follow, and no other,
though men and angels were united to dissuade you.'

There was a pause here, and a silence for a good many
seconds.

' Well, perhaps, I *have* formed an outline of a plan, and it
strikes me as very well I have—for I don't think you are likely
to take that trouble. I only want to explain it, and get your advice, and any little assistance you can give me ; and surely that
is not unreasonable ? '

' I have learned one secret, and am exposed to one danger. I
have taken—to save you—it may be only a *respite*—one step, the
remembrance of which is insupportable. But I was passive.
I am fallen from light into darkness. There ends my share in
your confidence and your fortunes. I will know no more secrets
—no more disgrace ; do what you will, you shall never use me
again.'

' Suppose these heroics of yours, Miss Radie, should contribute
to bring about—to bring about the worst,' said Stanley, with a
sneer, through which his voice trembled.

' Let it come—my resolution is taken.'

Stanley walked to the window, and in his easy way, as he
would across a drawing-room to stand by a piano, and he looked
out upon the trees, whose tops stood motionless against the
darkened sky, like masses of ruins. Then he came back as
gently as he had gone, and stood beside his sister ; she could
not see his yellow eyes now as he stood with his back to the
window.

' Well, Radie, dear—you have put your hand to the plough,
and you sha'n't turn back now.'

' What ? '

' No—you sha'n't turn back now.'

' You seem, Sir, to fancy that I have no right to choose for
myself,' said Miss Rachel, spiritedly.

' Now, Radie, you must be reasonable—who have I to advise
with ? '

' Not me, Stanley—keep your plots and your secrets to yourself. In the guilty path you have opened for me one step more
I will never tread.'

' Excuse me, Radie, but you're talking like a fool.'

' I am not sorry you think so—you can't understand motives
higher than your own.'

'You'll see that you must, though. You'll see it in a little while. Self-preservation, dear Radie, is the first law of nature.'

'For yourself, Stanley; and for *me*, self-sacrifice,' she retorted, bitterly.

'Well, Radie, I may as well tell you *one* thing that I'm resolved to carry out,' said Lake, with a dreamy serenity, looking on the dark carpet.

'I'll hear no secret, Stanley.'

'It can't be long a secret, at least from you—you can't help knowing it,' he drawled gently. 'Do you recollect, Radie, what I said that morning when I first called here, and saw you?'

'Perhaps I do, but I don't know what you mean,' answered she.

'I said, Mark Wylder——'

'Don't name him,' she said, rising and approaching him swiftly.

'I said *he* should go abroad, and so he shall,' said Lake, in a very low tone, with a grim oath.

'Why do you talk that way? You terrify me,' said Rachel, with one hand raised toward his face with a gesture of horror and entreaty, and the other closed upon his wrist.

'I say he *shall*, Radie.'

'Has he lost his wits? I can't comprehend you—you frighten me, Stanley. You're talking wildly on purpose, I believe, to terrify me. You know the state I'm in—sleepless—half wild—all alone here. You're talking like a maniac. It's cruel—it's cowardly.'

'I mean to *do* it—you'll see.'

Suddenly she hurried by him, and in a moment was in the little kitchen, with its fire and candle burning cheerily. Stanley Lake was at her shoulder as she entered, and both were white with agitation.

Old Tamar rose up affrighted, her stiff arms raised, and uttered a blessing. She did not know what to make of it. Rachel sat down upon one of the kitchen chairs, scarce knowing what she did, and Stanley Lake halted near the threshold—gazing for a moment as wildly as she, with the ghost of his sly smile on his smooth, cadaverous face.

'What ails her—is she ill, Master Stanley?' asked the old woman, returning with her white eyes the young man's strange yellow glare.

'I—I don't know—maybe—give her some water,' said Lake.

'Glass of water—quick, child,' cried old Tamar to Margery.

'Put it on the table,' said Rachel, collected now, but pale and somewhat stern.

'And now, Stanley, dear,' said she, for just then she was past caring for the presence of the servants, 'I hope we understand one another—at least, that you do me. If not, it is not for want

of distinctness on my part ; and I think you had better leave me for the present, for, to say truth, I do not feel very well.'

'Good-night, Radie—good-night, old Tamar. I hope, Radie, you'll be better—every way—when next I see you. Good-night.'

He spoke in his usual clear low tones, and his queer ambiguous smile was there still ; and, hat in hand, with his cane in his fingers, he made another glance and a nod over his shoulder, at the threshold, and then glided forth into the little garden, and so to the mill-road, down which, at a swift pace, he walked towards the village.

———

CHAPTER XXVI.

CAPTAIN LAKE FOLLOWS TO LONDON.

WYLDER'S levanting in this way was singularly disconcerting. The time was growing short. He wrote with a stupid good-humour, and an insolent brevity which took no account of Miss Brandon's position, or that (though secondary in awkwardness) of her noble relatives. Lord Chelford plainly thought more than he cared to say ; and his mother, who never minced matters, said perhaps more than she quite thought.

Chelford was to give the beautiful heiress away. But the receiver of this rich and peerless gift—like some mysterious knight who, having carried all before him in the tourney, vanishes no one knows whither, when the prize is about to be bestowed, and whom the summons of the herald and the call of the trumpet follow in vain—had escaped them.

'Lake has gone up to town this morning—some business with his banker about his commission—and he says he will make Wylder out on his arrival, and write to me,' said Lord Chelford.

Old Lady Chelford glanced across her shoulder at Dorcas, who leaned back in a great chair by the window, listlessly turning over a book.

'She's a strange girl, she does not seem to feel her situation— a most painful and critical one. That low, coarse creature must be looked up somehow.'

'Lake knows where he is likely to be found, and will see him, I dare say, this evening—perhaps in time to write by to-night's post.'

So, in a quiet key, Miss Dorcas being at a distance, though in the same room, the dowager and her son discussed this unpleasant and very nervous topic.

That evening Captain Lake was in London, comfortably

quartered in a private hotel, in one of the streets off Piccadilly. He went to his club and dined better than he had done for many days. He really enjoyed his three little courses—his pint of claret, his cup of *café noir*, and his *chasse;* the great Babylon was his Jerusalem, and his spirit found rest there.

He was renovated and refreshed, his soul was strengthened, and his countenance waxed cheerful, and he began to feel like himself again, under the brown canopy of metropolitan smoke, and among the cabs and gaslights.

After dinner he got into a cab, and drove to Mark Wylder's club. Was he there?—No. Had he been there to-day?—No. Or within the last week?—No ; not for two months. He had left his address, and was in the country. The address to which his letters were forwarded was 'The Brandon Arms, Gylingden.'

So Captain Lake informed that functionary that his friend had come up to town, and asked him again whether he was quite certain that he had not called there, or sent for his letters.—No ; nothing of the sort. Then Captain Lake asked to see the billiard-marker, who was likely to know something about him. But he knew nothing. He certainly had not been at the 'Lark's Nest,' which was kept by the marker's venerable parent, and was a favourite haunt of the gay lieutenant.

Then our friend Stanley, having ruminated for a minute, pencilled a little note to Mark, telling him that he was staying at Muggeridge's Hotel, 7, Hanover Street, Piccadilly, and wished *most* particularly to see him for a few minutes ; and this he left with the hall-porter to give him should he call.

Then Lake got into his cab again, having learned that he had lodgings in St. James's Street when he did not stay at the club, and to these he drove. There he saw Mrs. M'Intyre, a Caledonian lady, at this hour somewhat mellow and talkative ; but she could say nothing to the purpose either. Mr. Wylder had not been there for nine weeks and three days ; and would owe her, on Saturday next, twenty-five guineas. So here, too, he left a little note to the same purpose ; and re-entering his cab, he drove a long way, and past St. Paul's, and came at last to a court, outside which he had to dismount from his vehicle, entering the grimy quadrangle through a narrow passage. He had been there that evening before, shortly after his arrival, with old Mother Dutton, as he called her, about her son, Jim.

Jim was in London, looking for a situation, all which pleased Captain Lake ; and he desired that she should send him to his hotel to see him in the morning.

But being in some matters of a nervous and impatient temperament, he had come again, as we see, hoping to find Jim there, and to anticipate his interview of the morning.

The windows, however, were dark, and a little research satisfied

Captain Lake that the colony was in bed. In fact, it was by this time half-past eleven o'clock, and working-people don't usually sit up to that hour. But our friend, Stanley Lake, was one of those persons who think that the course of the world's affairs should bend a good deal to their personal convenience, and he was not pleased with these unreasonable working-people who had gone to their beds, and brought him to this remote and grimy amphitheatre of black windows for nothing. So, wishing them the good-night they merited, he re-entered his cab, and drove rapidly back again towards the West-end.

This time he went to a somewhat mysterious and barricadoed place, where in a blaze of light, in various rooms, gentlemen in hats, and some in great coats, were playing roulette or hazard ; and I am sorry to say, that our friend, Captain Lake, played first at one and then at the other, with what success exactly I don't know. But I don't think it was very far from four o'clock in the morning when he let himself into his family hotel with that latch-key, the cock's tail of Micyllus, with which good-natured old Mrs. Muggeridge obliged the good-looking captain.

Captain Lake having given orders the evening before, that anyone who might call in the morning, and ask to see him, should be shown up to his bed-room *sans ceremonie*, was roused from deep slumber at a quarter past ten, by a knock at his door, and a waiter's voice.

'Who's that?' drawled Captain Lake, rising, pale and half awake, on his elbow, and not very clear where he was.

'The man, Sir, as you left a note for yesterday, which he de-sires to see you ?'

'Tell him to step in.'

So out went the waiter in pumps, and the sound of thick shoes was audible on the lobby, and a sturdier knock sounded on the door.

'Come in,' said the captain.

And Jim Dutton entered the room, and, closing the door, made, at the side of the bed, his reverence, consisting of a nod and a faint pluck at the lock of hair over his forehead.

Now Stanley Lake had, perhaps, expected to see some one else ; for though this was a very respectable-looking fellow for his walk in life, the gay young officer stared full at him, with a frightened and rather dreadful countenance, and actually sprung from his bed at the other side, with an ejaculation at once tragic and blasphemous.

The man plainly had not expected to produce any such result, and looked very queer. Perhaps he thought something had oc-curred to affect his personal appearance ; perhaps some doubt about the captain's state of health, and misgiving as to delirium tremens may have flickered over his brain.

They were staring at one another across the bed, the captain in his shirt.

At last the gallant officer seemed to discover things as **they** were, for he said—

'Jim Dutton, by Jove!'

The oath was not so innocent; but it was delivered quietly; and then the captain drew a long breath, and then, still staring at him, he laughed a ghastly little laugh, also quietly.

'And so it is you, Jim,' said the captain. 'And how do you do—quite well, Jim—and out of place? You've been hurt in the foot, eh? so old—your—Mrs. Dutton tells me, but that won't signify. I was dreaming when you came in; not quite awake yet, hardly; just wait a bit till I get my slippers on; and this—'

So into his red slippers he slid, and got his great shawl dressing-gown, such as fine gentlemen then wore, about his slender person, and knotted the silken cords with depending tassels, and greeted Jim Dutton again in very friendly fashion, enquiring very particularly how he had been ever since, and what his mother was doing; and I'm afraid not listening to Jim's answers as attentively as one might have expected.

Whatever may have been his intrinsic worth, Jim was not polished, and spoke, moreover, an uncouth dialect, which broke out now and then. But he was in a sort of way attached to the Lake family, the son of an hereditary tenant on that estate which had made itself wings, and flown away like the island of Laputa. It could not be said to be love; it was a sort of traditionary loyalty; a sentiment, however, not altogether unserviceable.

When they had talked together for a while, the captain said—

'The fact is, it is not quite on me you would have to attend; the situation, perhaps, is better. You have no objection to travel. You *have* been abroad, you know; and of course wages and all that will be in proportion.'

Well, Jim had not any objection to speak of.

'What's wanted is a trustworthy man, perfectly steady, you see, and a fellow who knows how to hold his tongue.'

The last condition, perhaps, struck the man as a little odd; he looked a little confusedly, and he conveyed that he would not like to be in anything that was not quite straight.

'Quite straight, Sir!' repeated Stanley Lake, looking round on him sternly; 'neither should I, I fancy. You are to suppose the case of a gentleman who is nursing his estate—you know what that means—and wants to travel, and keep quite quiet, and who requires a steady, trustworthy man to look after him, in such a way as I shall direct, with very little trouble and capital pay. I have a regard for you, Dutton; and seeing so good a situation was to be had, and thinking you the fittest man I know, I wished to serve you and my friend at the same time.'

Dutton became grateful and docile upon this.

'There are reasons, quite honourable I need not tell **you,** which make it necessary, James Dutton, that the whole of this affair should be kept perfectly to ourselves ; you are not to repeat one syllable I say to you to your mother, do you mind, or to any other person living. The gentleman is liberal, and if you can just hold your tongue, you will have little trouble in satisfying him upon all other points. But if you can't be quite silent, you had better, I frankly tell you, decline the situation, excellent in all respects as it is.'

'I'm a man, Sir, as can be close enough.'

'So much the better. You don't drink?'

Dutton coloured a little and coughed and said—

'No, Sir.'

'You have your papers ?'

'Yes, Sir.'

'We must be satisfied as to your sobriety, Dutton. Come back at half-past eleven and I'll see you, and bring your papers ; and, do you see, you are not to talk, you understand ; only you may say, if anyone presses, that I am thinking of hiring you to attend on a gentleman, whose name you don't yet know, who's going to travel. That's all.'

So Jim Dutton made his bow, and departed ; and Captain Lake continued to watch the door for some seconds after his departure, as if he could see his retreating figure through it. And, said he, with an oath, and his hand to his forehead, over his eyebrow—

'It *is* the most unaccountable thing in nature !'

Then, after a reverie of some seconds, the young gentleman applied himself energetically to his toilet ; and coming down to his sitting-room, he looked into his morning paper, and then into the street, and told the servant as he sate down to breakfast, that he expected a gentleman named Wylder to call that morning, and to be sure to show him up directly.

Captain Lake's few hours' sleep, contrary to popular ideas about gamesters' slumbers, had been the soundest and the most natural which he had enjoyed for a good many nights. He was refreshed. At Gylingden and Brandon he had been simulating Captain Stanley Lake—being, in truth, something quite different —with a vigilant histrionic effort which was awfully exhausting, and sometimes nearly intolerable. Here the captain was perceptibly stealing into his old ways and feelings. His spirit revived ; something like confidence in the future, and a possibility even of enjoying the present, was struggling visibly through the cold fog that environed him. Reason has, after all, so little to do with our moods. The weather, the scene, the stomach, how pleasantly they deal with facts—how they supersede philosophy, and even arithmetic, and teach us how much of life is intoxication and illusion.

Still there was the sword of Damocles over his pineal gland.

D— that sheer, cold blade ! D— him that forged it ! **Still** there was a great deal of holding in a horse-hair. Had not salmon, of I know not how many pounds' weight, been played and brought to land by that slender towage. There is the sword, a burnished piece of cutlery, weighing just so many pounds ; and the horsehair has sufficed for an hour, and why not for another —and so on ? Hang moping and nonsense ! Waiter, another pint of Chian ; and let the fun go forward.

So the literal waiter knocked at the door. 'A person wanted to see Captain Lake. No, it was not Mr. Wylder. It was the man who had been here in the morning—Dutton is his name.'

'And so it is really half-past eleven ?' said Lake, in a sleepy surprise. 'Let him come in.'

And so in comes Jim Dutton again, to hear particulars, and have, as he hopes, his engagement ratified.

CHAPTER XXVII.

LAWYER LARKIN'S MIND BEGINS TO WORK.

THAT morning Lake's first report upon his inquisition into the whereabouts of Mark Wylder — altogether disappointing and barren—reached Lord Chelford in a short letter ; and a similar one, only shorter, found Lawyer Larkin in his pleasant breakfast parlour.

Now this proceeding of Mr. Wylder's, at this particular time, struck the righteous attorney, and reasonably, as a very serious and unjustifiable step. There was, in fact, no way of accounting for it, that was altogether complimentary to his respected and nutritious client. Yes ; there was something every way *very* serious in the affair. It actually threatened the engagement which was so near its accomplishment. Some most powerful and mysterious cause must undoubtedly be in operation to induce so sharp a ' party,' so keen after this world's wealth, to risk so huge a prize. Whatever eminent qualities Mark Wylder might be deficient in, the attorney very well knew that cunning was not among the number.

'It is nothing of the nature of debt—plenty of money. It is nothing that money can buy off easily either, though he does not like parting with it. Ten—*twenty* to one—it is the old story— some unfortunate female connection—some ambiguous relation, involving a doubtful marriage.'

And Josiah Larkin turned up his small pink eyes, and shook his tall, bald head gently, and murmured, as he nodded it—

'The sins of his youth find him out ; the sins of his youth.'

And he sighed ; and his long palms were raised, and waved,
or rather paddled slowly to the rhythm of the sentiment.

If the butchers' boy then passing saw that gaunt and good attorney, standing thus in his bow-window, I am sure he thought
he was at his devotions and abated his whistling as he went by.

After this Mr. Larkin's ruminations darkened, and grew, perhaps, less distinct. He had no particular objection to a mystery.
In fact, he rather liked it, provided he was admitted to confidence. A mystery implied a difficulty of a delicate and formidable sort ; and such difficulties were not disadvantageous to a
clever and firm person, who might render himself very necessary
to an embarrassed principal with plenty of money.

Mr. Larkin had a way of gently compressing his under-lip
between his finger and thumb—a mild pinch, a reflective caress
—when contemplations of this nature occupied his brain. The
silver light of heaven faded from his long face, a deep shadow
of earth came thereon, and his small, dove-like eyes grew intense, hungry, and rat-like.

Oh ! Lawyer Larkin, your eyes, though very small, are very
sharp. They can read through the outer skin of ordinary men,
as through a parchment against the light, the inner writing, and
spell out its meanings. How is it that they fail to see quite
through one Jos. Larkin, a lawyer of Gylingden? The laywer
of Gylingden is somehow two opaque for them, I almost think.
Is he really too deep for you? Or is it that you don't care to
search him too narrowly, or have not time ? or as men in money
perplexities love not the scrutiny of their accounts or papers, you
don't care to tire your eyes over the documents in that neatly
japanned box, the respectable lawyer's conscience?

If you have puzzled yourself, you have also puzzled me. I
don't quite know what to make of you. I've sometimes thought
you were simply an impostor, and sometimes simply the dupe of
your own sorceries. The heart of man is deceitful above all
things and desperately wicked. Some men, with a piercing in-
sight into the evil of man's nature, have a blurred vision for their
own moralities. For them it is not easy to see where wisdom
ends and guile begins — what wiles are justified to honour,
and what partake of the genius of the robber, and where lie the
delicate boundaries between legitimate diplomacy and damnable
lying. I am not sure that Lawyer Larkin did not often think
himself very nearly what he wished the world to think him
—an 'eminent Christian.' What an awful abyss is self delusion.

Lawyer Larkin was, on the whole, I dare say, tolerably well
pleased with the position, as he would have said, of his spiritual
interest, and belonged to that complacent congregation who said,
' I am rich and have need of nothing ;' and who, no doubt, opened
their eyes wide enough, and misdoubted the astounding report

of their ears, when the Judge thundered, 'Thou art wretched and miserable, and poor and blind and naked.'

When Jos. Larkins had speculated thus, and built rich, but sombre, castles in the air, for some time longer, he said quietly to himself—

'Yes.'

And then he ordered his dog-cart, and drove off to Dollington, and put up at Johnson's Hotel, where Stanley Lake had slept on the night of his sister's return from London. The people there knew the lawyer very well; of course, they quite understood his position. Mr. Johnson, the proprietor, you may be sure, does not confound him with the great squires, the baronets, and feudal names of the county; but though he was by comparison easy in his company, with even a dash of familiarity, he still respected Mr. Larkin as a man with money, and a sort of influence, and in whose way, at election and other times, it might lie to do his house a good or an ill turn.

Mr. Larkin got into a little brown room, looking into the inn garden, and called for some luncheon, and pen and ink, and had out a sheaf of law papers he had brought with him, tied up in professional red tape; and asked the waiter, with a grand smile and recognition, how he did; and asked him next for his good friend, Mr. Johnson; and trusted that business was improving; and would be very happy to see him for two or three minutes, if he could spare time.

So, in due time, in came the corpulent proprietor, and Lawyer Larkin shook hands with him, and begged him to sit down, like a man who confers a distinction; and assured him that Lord Edward Buxleigh, whom he had recommended to stay at the house for the shooting, had been very well pleased with the accommodation—very highly so indeed—and his lordship had so expressed himself when they had last met at Sir Hugh Huxterley's, of Hatch Court.

The good lawyer liked illuminating his little narratives, compliments, and reminiscences with plenty of armorial bearings and heraldic figures, and played out his court-cards in easy and somewhat overpowering profusion.

Then he enquired after the two heifers that Mr. Johnson was so good as to feed for him on his little farm; and then he mentioned that his friend, Captain Lake, who was staying with him at his house at Gylingden, was also very well satisfied with his accommodation, when he, too, at Lawyer Larkin's recommendation, had put up for a night at Johnson's Hotel; and it was not every house which could satisfy London swells of Captain Lake's fashion and habits, he could tell him.

Then followed some conversation which, I dare say, interested the lawyer more than he quite showed in Mr. Johnson's company. For when that pleased and communicative host had withdrawn, Jos. Larkin made half-a-dozen little entries in his pocket-book, with 'Statement of Mr. William Johnson,' and the date of their conversation, at the head of the memorandum.

So the lawyer, having to run on as far as Charteris by the goods-train, upon business, walked down to the station, where, having half-an-hour to wait, he fell into talk with the station-master, whom he also knew, and afterwards with Tom Christmas, the porter; and in the waiting-room he made some equally business-like memoranda, being certain chips and splinters struck off the clumsy talk of these officials, and laid up in the lawyer's little private museum, for future illustration and analysis.

By the time his little book was again in the bottom of his pocket, the train had arrived, and doors swung open and clap' and people got in and out to the porter's accompaniment ('Dollington—Dollington—Dollington!' and Lawyer Larkin took his place, and glided away to Charteris, where he had a wait of two hours for the return train, and a good deal of barren talk with persons at the station, rewarded by one or two sentences worth noting, and accordingly duly entered in the same little pocket-book.

Thus was the good man's day consumed; and when he mounted his dog-cart, at Dollington, wrapped his rug about his legs, whip and reins in hand, and the ostler buckled the apron across, the sun was setting redly behind the hills; and the air was frosty, and the night dark, as he drew up before his own door-steps, near Gylingden. A dozen lines of one of these pages would suffice to contain the fruits of his day's work; and yet the lawyer was satisfied, and even pleased with it, and eat his late dinner very happily; and though dignified, of course, was more than usually mild and gracious with all his servants that evening, and 'expounded at family prayers' in a sense that was liberal and comforting; and went to bed after a calm and pleased review of his memoranda, and slept the sleep of the righteous.

CHAPTER XXVIII.

MARK WYLDER'S SUBMISSION.

EVERY day the position grew more critical and embarrassing. The day appointed for the nuptials was now
very near, and the bridegroom not only out of sight
but wholly untraceable. What was to be done?

A long letter from Stanley Lake told Lord Chelford, in detail,
all the measures adopted by that energetic young gentleman for
the discovery of the truant knight :—

'I have been at his club repeatedly, as also at his lodgings—
still *his*, though he has not appeared there since his arrival in
town. The billiard-marker at his club knows his haunts; and I
have taken the liberty to employ, through him, several persons
who are acquainted with his appearance, and, at my desire, frequent those places with a view to discovering him, and bringing
about an interview with me.

'He was seen, I have reason to believe, a day or two before
my arrival here, at a low place called the "Miller's Hall," in the
City, where members of the "Fancy" resort, at one of their
orgies, but not since. I have left notes for him wherever he is
likely to call, entreating an interview.

'On my arrival I was sanguine about finding him; but I regret to say my hopes have very much declined, and I begin to
think he must have changed his quarters. If you have heard
from him within the last few days, perhaps you will be so kind as
to send me the envelope of his letter, which, by its postmark, may
possibly throw some light or hint some theory as to his possible
movements. He is very clever; and having taken this plan of
concealing his residence, will conduct it skilfully. If the case
were mine I should be much tempted to speak with the detective
authorities, and try whether they might not give their assistance,
of course without *éclat*. But this is, I am aware, open to objection, and, in fact, would not be justifiable, except under the very
peculiar urgency of the case.

'Will you be so good as to say what you think upon this
point; also, to instruct me what you authorise me to say should
I be fortunate enough to meet him. At present I am hardly in
a position to say more than an acquaintance—never, I fear, very
cordial on his part—would allow; which, of course, could hardly
exceed a simple mention of your anxiety to be placed in communication with him.

'If I might venture to suggest, I really think a peremptory

alternative should be presented to him. Writing, however, in ignorance of what may since have passed at Brandon, I may be assuming a state of things which, possibly, no longer exists. Pray understand that in any way you please to employ me, I am entirely at your command. It is also possible, though I hardly hope it, that I may be able to communicate something definite by this evening's post.

'I do not offer any conjectures as to the cause of this very embarrassing procedure on his part; and indeed I find a great difficulty in rendering myself useful, with any likelihood of really succeeding, without at the same exposing myself to an imputation of impertinence. You will easily see how difficult is my position.

'Whatever may be the cause of Mark Wylder's present line of conduct, it appears to me that if he really did attend that meeting at the " Miller's Hall," there cannot be anything *very* serious weighing upon his spirits. My business will detain me here, I rather think, three days longer.'

By return of post Lord Chelford wrote to Stanley Lake :—

'I am so very much obliged to you for all the trouble you have taken. The measures which you have adopted are, I think, most judicious; and I should not wish, on consideration, to speak to any official person. I think it better to trust entirely to the means you have already employed. Like you, I do not desire to speculate as to the causes of Wylder's extraordinary conduct; but, all the circumstances considered, I cannot avoid concluding, as you do, that there must be some *very* serious reason for it. I enclose a note, which, perhaps, you will be so good as to give him, should you meet before you leave town.'

The note to Mark Wylder was in these terms :—

'DEAR WYLDER,—I had hoped to see you before now at Brandon. Your unexplained absence longer continued, you must see, will impose on me the necessity of offering an explanation to Miss Brandon's friends, of the relations, under these strange circumstances, in which you and she are to be assumed to stand. You have accounted in no way for your absence. You have not even suggested a postponement of the day fixed for the completion of your engagement to that young lady; and, as her guardian, I cannot avoid telling her, should I fail to hear explicitly from you within three days from this date, that she is at liberty to hold herself acquitted of her engagement to you. I do not represent to you how much reason everyone interested by relationship in that young lady has to feel offended at the disrespect with which you have treated her. Still hoping, however, that all may yet be explained,

'I remain, my dear Wylder, yours very truly,

'CHELFORD.'

Lord Chelford had not opened the subject to Dorcas. Neither had old Lady Chelford, although she harangued her son upon it as volubly and fiercely as if he had been Mark Wylder in person, whenever he and she were *tête-à-tête.* She was extremely provoked, too, at Dorcas's evident repose under this astounding treatment, and was enigmatically sarcastic upon her when they sat together in the drawing-room.

She and her son were, it seemed, not only to think and act, but to feel also, for this utterly immovable young lady ! The Brandons, in her young days, were not wanting in spirit. No ; they had many faults, but they were not sticks or stones. They were not to be taken up and laid down like wax dolls; they could act and speak. It would not have been safe to trample upon them ; and they were not less beautiful for being something more than pictures and statues.

This evening, in the drawing-room, there were two very pretty ormolu caskets upon the little marble table.

' A new present from Mark Wylder,' thought Lady Chelford, as these objects met her keen glance. ' The unceremonious bridegroom has, I suppose, found his way back with a peace-offering in his hand.' And she actually peered through her spectacles into the now darkened corners of the chamber, half expecting to discover the truant Wylder awaiting there the lecture she was well prepared to give him ; but the square form and black whiskers of the prodigal son were not discernible there.

' So, so, something new, and very elegant and pretty,' said the old lady aloud, holding her head high, and looking as if she were disposed to be propitiated. ' I think I can risk a conjecture. Mr. Wylder is about to reappear, and has despatched these heralds of his approach, no doubt suitably freighted, to plead for his reacceptance into favour. You have heard, then, from Mr. Wylder, my dear Dorcas ? '

' No, Lady Chelford,' said the young lady with a grave serenity, turning her head leisurely towards her.

' No ? Oh, then where is my son? He, perhaps, can explain ; and pray, my dear, what are these ? '

' These caskets contain the jewels which Mr. Wylder gave me about six weeks since. I had intended restoring them to him ; but as his return is delayed, I mean to place them in Chelford's hands ; because I have made up my mind, a week ago, to put an end to this odious engagement. It is all over.'

Lady Chelford stared at the audacious young lady with a look of incensed amazement for some seconds, unable to speak.

' Upon my word, young lady ! vastly fine and independent ! You *chasser* Mr. Wylder without one moment's notice, and without deigning to consult me, or any other person capable of advising you. You are about to commit as gross and indelicate

a breach of faith as I recollect anywhere to have heard of.
What will be thought?—what will the world say?—what will
your friends say? Will you be good enough to explain yourself?
I'll not undertake your excuses, I promise you.'

'Excuses! I don't think of excuses, Lady Chelford; no
person living has a right to demand one.'

'Very tragic, young lady, and quite charming!' sneered the
dowager angrily.

'Neither one nor the other, I venture to think; but quite true,
Lady Chelford,' answered Miss Brandon, haughtily.

'I don't believe you are serious, Dorcas,' said Lady Chelford,
more anxiously, and also more gently. 'I can't suppose it. I'm
an old woman, my dear, and I sha'n't trouble you very long. I
can have no object in misleading you, and you have never
experienced from me anything but kindness and affection. I
think you might trust me a little, Dorcas—but that, of course,
is for you, you are your own mistress now—but, at least, you
may reconsider the question you propose deciding in so extraordinary a way. I allow you might do much better than
Mark Wylder, but also worse. He has not a title, and his
estate is not enough to carry the point *à force d' argent;* I grant
all that. But *together* the estates are more than most titled
men possess; and the real point is the fatal slip in your poor
uncle's will, which makes it so highly important that you and
Mark should be united; bear that in mind, dear Dorcas. I
look for his return every day—every hour, indeed—and no doubt
his absence will turn out to have been unavoidable. You must
not act precipitately, and under the influence of mere pique.
His absence, I will lay my life, will be satisfactorily accounted
for; he has set his heart upon this marriage, and I really think
you will almost drive him mad if you act as you threaten.'

'You have, indeed, dear Lady Chelford, been always very
kind to me, and I do trust you,' replied this beautiful heiress, turning her large shadowy eyes upon the dowager, and speaking in
slow and silvery accents, somehow very melancholy. 'I dare
say it is very imprudent, and I don't deny that Mr. Wylder may
have reason to complain of me, and the world will not spare me
either; but I have quite made up my mind, and nothing can
ever change me; all is over between me and Mr. Wylder—quite
over—for ever.'

'Upon my life, young lady, this is being very sharp, indeed.
Mr. Wylder's business detains him a day or two longer than he
expected, and he is punished by a final dismissal!'

The old lady's thin cheeks were flushed, and her eyes shot a
reddish light, and altogether she made an angry sight. It was hardly
reasonable. She had been inveighing against Miss Brandon's
apathy under Wylder's disrespect, and now that the young lady
spoke and acted too, she was incensed. She had railed upon

Wylder, in no measured terms, herself, and even threatened, a
the proper measure, that very step which Dorcas had announced; and now she became all at once the apologist of this
insolent truant, and was ready to denounce her unreasonable
irritation.

'So far, dear Lady Chelford, from provoking me to this
decision, his absence is, I assure you, the sole reason of my
having delayed to inform him of it.'

'And I assure you, Miss Brandon, *I* sha'n't undertake to
deliver your monstrous message. He will probably be here to-
morrow. You have prepared an agreeable surprise for him.
You shall have the pleasure of administering it yourself, Miss
Brandon. For my part, I have done my duty, and here and
now renounce all responsibility in the future management of
your affairs.'

Saying which, she rose, in a stately and incensed way, and
looking with flashing eyes over Dorcas's head to a far corner of
the apartment, without another word she rustled slowly and
majestically from the drawing-room.

She was a good deal shocked, and her feelings quite changed,
however, when next morning the post brought a letter to
Chelford from Mark Wylder, bearing the Boulogne postmark.
It said—

'DEAR CHELFORD,
　　'Don't get riled; but the fact is I don't see my
way out of my present business'—this last word was substituted for another, crossed out, which looked like 'scrape')—'for
a couple of months, maybe. Therefore, you see, my liberty and
wishes being at present interfered with, it would be very hard
lines if poor Dorcas should be held to her bargain. Therefore,
I will say this—*she is quite free* for me. Only, of course, I don't
decline to fulfil my part whenever at liberty. In the meantime I
return the miniature, with her hair in it, which I constantly wore
about me since I got it. But I have no right to it any longer,
till I know her decision. Don't be too hard on me, dear
Chelford. It is a very old lark has got me into this present
vexation. In the meantime, I wish to make it quite clear what
I mean. Not being able by any endeavour'—(here a nautical
phrase scratched out, and 'endeavour' substituted)—'of mine to
be up to time, and as these are P.P. affairs, I must only forfeit.
I mean, I am at the lady's disposal, either to fulfil my engagement the earliest day I can, or to be turned adrift. That is all
I can say.

'In more trouble than you suppose, I remain, dear Chelford,
yours, whatever you may think, faithfully,
　　　　　　　　　　　　　　'MARK WYLDER.'

CHAPTER XXIX.

HOW MARK WYLDER'S DISAPPEARANCE AFFECTED HIS FRIENDS.

LADY CHELFORD'S wrath was now turned anew upon Wylder—and the inconvenience of having no visible object on which to expend it was once more painfully felt. Railing at Mark Wylder was, alas! but beating the air. The most crushing invective was—thanks to his adroit mystification—simply a soliloquy. Poor Lady Chelford, who loved to give the ingenious youngsters of both sexes, when occasion invited, a piece of her mind, was here—in the case of this vulgar and most provoking delinquent—absolutely tongue-tied! If it had been possible to tell Wylder what she thought of him it would, perhaps, have made her more tolerable than she was for some days after the arrival of that letter, to other members of the family.

The idea of holding Miss Brandon to this engagement, and proroguing her nuptials from day to day, to convenience the bridegroom—absent without explanation—was of course quite untenable. Fortunately, the marriage, considering the antiquity and the territorial position of the two families who were involved, was to have been a very quiet affair indeed — no festivities—no fire-works—nothing of the nature of a county gala—no glare or thunder—no concussion of society—a dignified but secluded marriage.

This divested the inevitable dissolution of these high relations of a great deal of its *éclat* and ridicule.

Of course there was abundance of talk. Scarce a man or woman in the shire but had a theory or a story—sometimes bearing hard on the lady, sometimes on the gentleman; still it was an abstract breach of promise, and would have much improved by some outward and visible sign of disruption and disappoint- ment. Some concrete pageantries to be abolished and removed ; flag-staffs, for instance, and banners, marquees, pyrotechnic machinery, and long tiers of rockets, festoons of evergreens, triumphal arches with appropriate mottoes, to come down and hide themselves away, would have been pleasant to the many who like a joke, and to the few, let us hope, who love a sneer.

But there were no such fopperies to hurry off the stage dis- concerted. In the autumnal sun, among the embrowned and thinning foliage of the noble trees, Brandon Hall looked solemn, sad and magnificent, as usual, with a sort of retrospective serenity, buried in old-world glories and sorrows, and heeding little the follies and scandals of the hour.

In the same way Miss Brandon, with Lord and Lady Chelford, was seen next Sunday, serene and unchanged, in the great carved oak Brandon pew, raised like a dais two feet at least above the level of mere Christians, who frequented the family chapel. There, among old Wylder and Brandon tombs—some painted stone effigies of the period of Elizabeth and the first James, and some much older—stone and marble knights praying on their backs with their spurs on, and said to have been removed nearly three hundred years ago from the Abbey of Naunton Friars, when that famous monastery began to lose its roof and turn into a picturesque ruin, and by-gone generations of Wylders and Brandons had offered up their conspicuous devotions, with—judging from their heathen lives—I fear no very remarkable efficacy.

Here then, next Sunday afternoon, when the good vicar, the Rev. William Wylder, at three o'clock, performed his holy office in reading-desk and pulpit, the good folk from Gylingden assembled in force, saw nothing noticeable in the demeanour or appearance of the great Brandon heiress. A goddess in her aerial place, haughty, beautiful, unconscious of human gaze, and seen as it were telescopically by mortals from below. No shadow of trouble on that calm marble beauty, no light of joy, but a serene superb indifference.

Of course there was some satire in Gylingden; but, in the main, it was a loyal town, and true to its princess. Mr. Wylder's settlements were not satisfactory, it was presumed, or the young lady could not bring herself to like him, or however it came to pass, one way or another, that sprig of willow inevitably to be mounted by hero or heroine upon such equivocal occasions was placed by the honest town by no means in her breast, but altogether in his button-hole.

Gradually, in a more authentic shape, information traceable to old Lady Chelford, through some of the old county families who visited at Brandon, made it known that Mr. Wylder's affairs were not at present by any means in so settled a state as was supposed; and that a long betrothal not being desirable on the whole, Miss Brandon's relatives thought it advisable that the engagement should terminate, and had so decided, Mr. Wylder having, very properly, placed himself absolutely in their hands.

As for Mark, it was presumed he had gone into voluntary banishment, and was making the grand tour in the spirit of that lackadaisical gentleman in the then fashionable song, who says:—

> From sport to sport they hurry me,
> To banish my regret,
> And if they win a smile from me,
> They think that I forget.

It was known to be quite final, and as the lady evinced no chagrin and affected no unusual spirits, but held, swanlike and majestic, the even tenor of her way, there was, on the whole, little doubt anywhere that the gentleman had received his *congé*, and was hiding his mortification and healing his wounds in Paris or Vienna, or some other suitable retreat.

But though the good folk of Gylingden, in general, cared very little how Mark Wylder might have disposed of himself, there was one inhabitant to whom his absence was fraught with very serious anxiety and inconvenience. This was his brother, William, the vicar.

Poor William, sound in morals, free from vice, no dandy, a quiet, bookish, self-denying mortal, was yet, when he took holy orders and quitted his chambers at Cambridge, as much in debt as many a scamp of his college. He had been, perhaps, a little foolish and fanciful in the article of books, and had committed a serious indiscretion in the matter of a carved oak bookcase ; and, worse still, he had published a slender volume of poems, and a bulkier tome of essays, scholastic and theologic, both which ventures, notwithstanding their merits, had turned out unhappily ; and worse still, he had lent that costly loan, his sign manual, on two or three occasions, to friends in need, and one way or another found that, on winding up and closing his Cambridge life, his assets fell short of his liabilities very seriously.

The entire amount it is true was not very great. A pupil or two, and a success with his work 'On the Character and Inaccuracies of Eusebius,' would make matters square in a little time. But his advertisements for a resident pupil had not been answered ; they had cost him something, and he had not any more spare bread just then to throw upon the waters. So the advertisements for the present were suspended ; and the publishers, somehow, did not take kindly to Eusebius, who was making the tour of that fastidious and hard-hearted fraternity.

He had staved off some of his troubles by a little loan from an insurance company, but the premium and the instalments were disproportioned to his revenue, and indeed very nearly frightful to contemplate. The Cambridge tradesmen were growing minatory ; and there was a stern person who held a renewal of one of his old paper subsidies to the necessities of his scampish friend Clarkson, who was plainly a difficult and awful character to deal with.

Dreadful as were the tradesmen's peremptory and wrathful letters, the promptitude and energy of this latter personage were such as to produce a sense of immediate danger so acute that the scared vicar opened his dismal case to his Brother Mark.

Mark, sorely against the grain, and with no good grace, at last consented to advance £300 in this dread emergency, and the vicar blessed his benefactor, and in his closet on his knees, shed tears of thankfulness over his deliverance, and the sky opened and the flowers looked bright, and life grew pleasant once more.

But the £300 were not yet in his pocket, and Mark had gone away ; and although of course the loan was sure to come, the delay—any delay in his situation—was critical and formidable. Here was another would-be correspondent of Mark's foiled for want of his address. Still he would not believe it possible that he could forget his promise, or shut up his bowels of mercy, or long delay the remittance which he knew to be so urgently needed.

In the meantime, however, a writ reached the hand of the poor Vicar of Naunton Friars, who wrote in eager and confused terror to a friend in the Middle Temple on the dread summons, and learned that he was now ' in court,' and must ' appear,' or suffer judgment by default.

The end was that he purchased a respite of three months, by adding thirty pounds to his debt, and so was thankful for another deliverance, and was confident of the promised subsidy within a week, or at all events a fortnight, or, at worst, three months was a long reprieve—and the subsidy must arrive before the emergency.

> In this there can be no dismay ;
> My ships come home a month before the day.

When the ' service' was over, the neighbourly little congregation, with a sprinkling of visitors to Gylingden, for sake of its healing waters, broke up, and loitered in the vicinity of the porch, to remark on the sermon or the weather, and ask one another how they did, and to see the Brandon family enter their carriage and the tall, powdered footman shut the door upon them, and mount behind, and move off at a brilliant pace, and with a glorious clangour and whirl of dust ; and, this incident over, they broke up gradually into little groups, in Sunday guise, and many colours, some for a ramble on the common, and some to tea, according to the primitive hours that ruled old Gylingden.

The vicar, and John Hughes, clerk and sexton, were last out ; and the reverend gentleman, thin and tall, in white necktie, and black, a little threadbare, stood on the steps of the porch, in a sad abstraction. The red autumnal sun nearing the edge of the distant hills,

> Looked through the horizontal misty air
> Shorn of its beams—

and lighted the thin and gentle features of the vicar with a melancholy radiance. The sound of the oak door closing heavily behind him and John Hughes, and the key revolving in the lock recalled him, and with a sigh and a smile, and a kindly nod to John, he looked up and round on the familiar and pretty scenery undecided. It was not quite time to go home ; his troubles were heavy upon him, too, just then ; they have their paroxysms like ague ; and the quiet of the road, and the sweet air and sunshine, tempted him to walk off the chill and fever of the fit.

As he passed the little cottage where old Widow Maddock lay sick, Rachael Lake emerged. He was not glad. He would rather have had his sad walk in his own shy company. But there she was—he could not pass her by ; so he stopped, and lifted his hat, and greeted her ; and then they shook hands. She was going his way. He looked wistfully on the little hatch of old Widow Maddock's cottage ; for he felt a pang of reproach at passing her door ; but there was no comfort then in his thoughts, only a sense of fear and hopeless fatigue.

'How is poor old Mrs. Maddock ?' he asked ; 'you have been visiting the sick and afflicted, and I was passing by ; but, indeed, if I were capable at this moment I should not fail to see her, poor creature.'

There was something apologetic and almost miserable in his look as he said this.

'She is not better ; but you have been very good to her, and she is very grateful ; and I am glad,' said Rachel, 'that I happened to light on you.'

And she paused. They were by this time walking side by side ; and she glanced at him enquiringly ; and he thought that the handsome girl looked rather thin and pale.

'You once said,' Miss Lake resumed, 'that sooner or later I should be taught the value of religion, and would learn to prize my great privileges ; and that for some spirits the only approach to the throne of mercy was through great tribulation. I have often thought since of those words, and they have begun, for me, to take the spirit of a prophecy—sometimes that is—but at others they sound differently—like a dreadful menace—as if my afflictions were only to bring me to the gate of life to find it shut.'

'Knock, and it shall be opened,' said the vicar ; but the comfort was sadly spoken, and he sighed.

'But is not there a time, Mr. Wylder, when He shall have shut to the door, and are there not some who, crying to him to open, shall yet remain for ever in outer darkness ?'

'I see, dear Miss Lake, that your mind is at work—it is a good influence—at work upon the great. theme which every mortal spirit ought to be employed upon.'

'My fears are at work ; my mind is altogether dark and turbid ; I am sometimes at the brink of despair.'

'Take comfort from those fears. There is hope in that despair ;' and he looked at her with great interest in his gentle eyes.

She looked at him, and then away toward the declining sun, and she said despairingly—

'I cannot comprehend you.'

'Come !' said he, 'Miss Lake, bethink you ; was there not a time—and no very distant one—when futurity caused you no anxiety, and when the subject which has grown so interesting, was altogether distasteful to you. The seed of the Word is received at length into good ground ; but a grain of wheat will bring forth no fruit unless it die first. The seed dies to outward sense, and despair follows ; but the principle of life is working in it, and it will surely grow, and bring forth fruit—thirty, sixty, an hundred-fold—be not dismayed. The body dies, and the Lord of life compares it to the death of the seed in the earth ; and then comes the palingenesis—the rising in glory. In like manner He compares the reception of the principle of eternal life into the soul to the dropping of a seed into the earth ; it follows the general law of mortality. It too dies—such a death as the children of heaven die here—only to germinate afresh with celestial power and beauty.'

Miss Lake's way lay by a footpath across a corner of the park to Redman's Dell. So they crossed the stile, and still conversing, followed the footpath under the hedgerow of the pretty field, and crossing another stile, entered the park.

CHAPTER XXX.

IN BRANDON PARK.

TO me, from association, no doubt, that park has always had a melancholy character. The ground undulates beautifully, and noble timber studs it in all varieties of grouping; and now, as when I had seen the ill-omened form of Uncle Lorne among its solitudes, the descending sun shone across it with a saddened glory, tipping with gold the blades of grass and the brown antlers of the distant deer.

Still pursuing her solemn and melancholy discourse, the young lady followed the path, accompanied by the vicar.

'True,' said the vicar, 'your mind is disturbed, but not by doubt. No; it is by *truth*.' He glanced aside at the tarn where I had seen the phantom, and by which their path now led them —'You remember Parnell's pretty image?

'So when a smooth expanse receives imprest
 Calm nature's image on its watery breast,
 Down bend the banks, the trees depending grow,
 And skies beneath with answering colours glow;
 But if a stone the gentle scene divide,
 Swift ruffling circles curl on every side,
 And glimmering fragments of a broken sun,
 Banks, trees, and skies, in thick disorder run.

But, as I said, it is not a doubt that agitates your mind—that is well represented by the "stone," that subsides and leaves the pool clear, it maybe, but stagnant as before. Oh, no; it is an angel who comes down and troubles the water.'

'What a heavenly evening!' said a low, sweet voice, but with something insidious in it, close at his shoulder.

With a start, Rachel glanced back, and saw the pale, peculiar face of her brother. His yellow eyes for a moment gleamed into hers, and then on the vicar, and, with his accustomed smile, he extended his hand.

'How do you do?—better, I hope, Radie? How are you, William?'

Rachel grew deadly pale, and then flushed, and then was pale again.

'I thought, Stanley, you were in London.'

'So I was; but I arrived here this morning; I'm staying for a few days at the Lodge—Larkin's house; you're going home, I suppose, Radie?'

'Yes—oh, yes—but I don't know that I'll go this way. You say you must return to Gylingden now, Mr. Wylder; I think I'll turn also, and go home that way.'

'Nothing would give me greater pleasure,' said the vicar, truly as well as kindly, for he had grown interested in their conversation; 'but I fear you are tired'—he looked very kindly on her pale face—'and you know it will cost you a walk of more than two miles.'

'I forgot—yes—I believe I *am* a *little* tired; I'm afraid I have led *you*, too, farther than you intended.' She fancied that her sudden change of plan on meeting her brother would appear odd.

'I'll see you a little bit on your way home, Radie,' said Stanley.

It was just what she wished to escape. She was more nervous, though not less courageous than formerly. But the old, fierce, defiant spirit awoke. Why should she fear Stanley, or what could it be to her whether he was beside her in her homeward walk?

So the vicar made his adieux there, and began, at a brisker pace, to retrace his steps toward Gylingden; and she and Stanley, side by side, walked on toward Redman's Dell.

'What a charming park! and what delightful air, Radie; and the weather so very delicious. They talk of Italian evenings; but there is a pleasant sharpness in English evenings quite peculiar. Is not there just a little suspicion of frost—don't you think so—not actually cold, but crisp and sharp—unspeakably exhilarating; now really, this evening is quite celestial.'

'I've just been listening to a good man's conversation, and I wish to reflect upon it,' said Rachel, very coldly.

'Quite so; that is, of course, when you are alone,' answered Stanley, serenely. 'William was always a very clever fellow to talk—very well read in theology—is not he?—yes, he does talk very sweetly and nobly on religion; it is a pity he is not quite straight, or at least more punctual, in his money affairs.'

'He is distressed for money? William Wylder is distressed for money! Do you mean *that?*' said Rachel, in a tone of sudden surprise and energy, almost horror, turning full upon him, and stopping short.

'Oh, dear! no—not the least distressed that I ever heard of,' laughed Stanley coldly—'only just a little bit roguish, maybe.'

'That's so like you, Stanley,' said the young lady, with a quiet scorn, resuming her onward walk.

'How very beautiful that clump of birch trees is, near the edge of the slope there; you really can't imagine, who are always here, how very intensely a person who has just escaped from London enjoys all this.'

'I don't think, Stanley,' said the young lady coldly, and looking straight before her as she walked, 'you ever cared for natural scenery—or liked the country—and yet you are here. I don't think you ever loved me, or cared whether I was alone or in company ; and yet seeing—for you *did* see it—that I would now rather be alone, you persist in walking with me, and talking of trees and air and celestial evenings, and thinking of something quite different. Had not you better turn back to Gylingden, or the Lodge, or wherever you mean to pass the evening, and leave me to my quiet walk and my solitude ?'

'In a few minutes, dear Radie—you are so odd. I really believe you think no one can enjoy a ramble like this but yourself.'

'Come, Stanley, what do you want ?' said his sister, stopping short, and speaking with the flush of irritation on her cheek— 'do you mean to walk to Redman's Dell, or have you anything unpleasant to say ?'

'Neither, I hope,' said the captain, with his sleepy smile, his yellow eyes resting on the innocent grass blades before him.

'I don't understand you, Stanley. I am always uncomfortable when you are near me. You stand there like an evil spirit, with some purpose which I cannot divine ; but you shall not ensnare me. Go your own way, why can't you ? Pursue your own plots —your wicked plots ; but let me rest. I *will* be released, Sir, from your presence.'

'Really this is very fine, Radie, considering how we are related ; I'm Mephistopheles, I suppose, and you Margaret, or some other simple heroine—rebuking the fiend in the majesty of your purity.'

And indeed in the reddish light, and in that lonely and solemn spot, the slim form of the captain, pale, sneering, with his wild eyes, confronting the beautiful light-haired girl, looked not quite unlike a type of the jaunty fiend he was pleased to suppose himself.

'I tell you, Stanley, I feel that you design employing me in some of your crooked plans. I have horrible reasons, as you know, for avoiding you, and so I will. I hope I may never desire to see you alone again, but if I do, it shall not be to receive, but to impose commands. You had better return to Gylingden, and leave me.'

'So I will, dear Radie, by-and-by,' said he, with his amused smile.

'That is, you *won't* until you have said what you meditate. Well, then, as it seems I must hear it, pray speak at once, standing where we are, and quickly, for the sun will soon go down, and one step more I will not walk with you.'

'Well, Radie, you are pleased to be whimsical ; and, to say truth, I *was* thinking of saying a word or two, just about an

idea that has been in my mind some time, and which you half divined—you are so clever—the first day I saw you at Redman's Farm. You know you fancied I was thinking of marrying.'

'I don't remember that I said so, but I thought it. You mentioned Caroline Beauchamp, but I don't see how your visit *here* could have been connected with that plan.'

'But don't you think, Radie, I should do well to marry, that is, assuming everything to be suitable?'

'Well, perhaps, for *yourself*, Stanley; but——'

'Yes, of course,' said Lake; 'but the unfortunate girl, you were going to say—thank you. She's, of course, very much to be pitied, and you have my leave to pity her as much as you please.'

'I do pity her,' said Rachel.

'Thank you, again,' said Stanley; 'but seriously, Radie, you can be, I think, very essentially of use to me in this affair, and you must not refuse.'

'Now, Stanley, I will cut this matter short. I can't serve you. I won't. I don't know the young lady, and I don't mean to make her acquaintance.'

'But I tell you that you *can* serve me,' retorted Stanley, with a savage glare, and features whitened with passion, 'and you *shall* serve me; and you *do* know the young lady intimately.'

'I say, Sir, I do *not*,' replied Rachel, haughtily and fiercely.

'She is Dorcas Brandon; you know *her*, I believe. I came down here to marry her. I had made up my mind when I saw you first and I'll carry my point; I always do. She does not like me, maybe; but she *shall*. I never yet resolved to make a woman like me, and failed. You need not look so pale; and put on that damned affected look of horror. I may be wild, and—and what you please, but I'm no worse than that brute, Mark Wylder, and you never turned up your eyes when he was her choice; and I knew things about him that ought to have damned him, and she's well rid of a branded rascal. And now, Rachel, you know her, and you must say a good word for me. I expect your influence, and if you don't use it, and effectually, it will be worse for you. You women understand one another, and how to get a fellow favourably into one another's thoughts. So, listen to me, this is a vital matter; indeed, it is, Radie. I have lost a lot of money, like a—fool, I suppose; well, it is gone, and this marriage is indispensable. I must go in for it, it is life or death; and if I fail through your unkindness (here he swore an impious oath) I'll end all with a pistol, and leave a letter to Chelford, disclosing everything concerning you, and me, and Mark Wylder.'

I think Rachel Lake was as near fainting as ever lady was, without actually swooning. It was well they had stopped just by the stem of a great ash tree, against which Rachel leaned for some seconds, with darkness before her eyes, and the roar of a whirlpool in her ears.

After a while, with two or three gasps, she came to herself. Lake had been railing on all this time, and his voice, which, in ill-temper, was singularly bleak and terrible, was again in her ears the moment she recovered her hearing.

'I do not care to quarrel ; there are many reasons why we should not,' Lake said in his peculiar tones. 'You have some of my secrets, and you must have more ; it can't be helped, and, I say, you *must.* I've been very foolish. I'll give up play. It has brought me to this. I've had to sell out. I've paid away all I could, and given bills for the rest ; but I can't possibly pay them, don't you see ; and if things go to the worst, I tell you I'll not stay. I don't want to make my bow just yet, and I've no wish to injure you ; but I'll do as I have said (he swore again), and Chelford shall have a distinct statement under my hand of everything that has happened. I don't suppose you wish to be accessory to all this, and therefore it behoves you, Rachel, to do what you can to prevent it. One woman can always influence another, and you are constantly with Dorcas. You'll do all you can ; I'm sure you will ; and you can do a great deal. I know it ; I'll do as much for you, Radie ! Anything you like.'

For the first time her brother stood before her in a really terrible shape ; she felt his villainy turning with a cowardly and merciless treason upon her forlorn self. Sacrificed for him, and that sacrifice used by him to torture, to extort, perhaps to ruin. She quailed for a minute in the presence of this gigantic depravity and cruelty. But Rachel was a brave lass, and rallied quickly.

'After all I have done and suffered !' said she, with a faint smile of unimaginable bitterness ; 'I did not think that human wickedness could produce such a brother as you are.'

'Well, it is no news what you think of me, and not much matter, either. I don't see that I am a worse brother than you are a sister.' Stanley Lake was speaking with a livid intensity. 'You see how I'm placed ; a ruined man, with a pistol to my head ; what you can do to save me may amount to nothing, but it may be everything, and you say you won't try ! Now I say you *shall*, and with every energy and faculty you possess, or else abide the consequences.'

'And I tell you, Sir,' replied Rachel, 'I know you ; you are capable of anything but of hurting yourself. I'll never be your slave ; though, if I pleased, I might make you mine. I scorn your threats—I defy you.'

Stanley Lake looked transported, and the yellow fires of his deep-set eyes glared on her, while his lips moved to speak, but not a word came, and it became a contortion ; he grasped the switch in his hand as if to strike her.

'Take care, Sir, Lord Chelford's coming,' said the young lady, haughtily, with a contracted glance of horror fixed on Lake.

Lake collected himself. He was a man who could do it pretty quickly ; but he had been violently agitated, and the traces of his fury could not disappear in a moment.

Lord Chelford was, indeed, approaching, only a few hundred yards away.

'Take my arm,' said Lake.

And Rachel mechanically, as story-tellers say, placed her slender gloved hand upon his arm—the miscreant arm that had been so nearly raised to strike her ; and they walked along, brother and sister, in the Sabbath sunset light, to meet him.

CHAPTER XXXI.

IN REDMAN'S DELL.

LORD CHELFORD raised his hat, smiling : ' I am so very glad I met you, I was beginning to feel so solitary !' he placed himself beside Miss Lake. ' I've had such a long walk across the park. How do you do, Lake? when did you come?'

And so on—Lake answering and looking wonderfully as usual.

I think Lord Chelford perceived there was something amiss between the young people, for his eye rested on Rachel with a momentary look of enquiry, unconscious, no doubt, and quickly averted, and he went on chatting pleasantly ; but he looked, once or twice, a little hard at Stanley Lake. I don't think he had an extraordinarily good opinion of that young gentleman. He seldom expressed an ill one of anybody, and then it was in very measured language. But though he never hinted at an un-favourable estimate of the captain, his intimacies with him were a little reserved ; and I think I have seen him, even when he smiled, look the least little bit in the world uncomfortable, as if he did not quite enter into the captain's pleasantries.

They had not walked together very far, when Stanley recol-lected that he must take his leave, and walk back to Gylingden ; and so the young lady and Lord Chelford were left to pursue their way towards Redman's Farm together.

It would have been a more unaccountable proceeding on the part of Stanley Lake, and a more romantic situation, if Rachel

and his lordship had not had before two or three little accidental rambles together in the grounds and gardens of
Brandon. There was nothing quite new in the situation, therefore ; and Rachel was for a moment indescribably relieved by
Stanley's departure.

The shock of her brief interview with her brother over, reflection assured her, knowing all she did, that Stanley's wooing
would prosper, and so this cause of quarrel had really nothing
in it ; no, nothing but a display of his temper and morals—not
very astonishing, after all—and, like an ugly picture or a dreadful dream, in no way to affect her after-life, except as an odious
remembrance.

Therefore, little by little, like a flower that has been bruised,
in the tranquillising influences about her, the young lady got up,
expanded, and grew like herself again—not like enough, indeed,
to say much, but to listen and follow his manly, refined, and
pleasant talk, every moment with a pang, that had yet something pleasurable in it, contrasting the quiet and chivalric tone
of her present companion, with the ferocious duplicity of the
sly, smooth terrorist who had just left her side.

It was rather a marked thing—as lean Mrs. Loyd, of Gylingden, who had two thin spinsters with pink noses under her
wing, remarked—this long walk of Lord Chelford and Miss Lake
in the park ; and she enjoined upon her girls the propriety of
being specially reserved in their intercourse with persons of
Lord Chelford's rank ; not that they were much troubled with
dangers from any such quarter. Miss Lake had, she supposed,
her own notions, and would act as she pleased ; but she owned
for her part she preferred the old fashion, and thought the men
did also ; and was sure, too, that young ladies lost nothing by a
little reserve and modesty.

Now something of this, no doubt, passed in the minds of
Lord Chelford and his pretty companion. But what was to be
done ? That perverse and utterly selfish brother, Stanley Lake,
had cnosen to take his leave. Lord Chelford could not desert
the young lady, and would it have been a very nice delicacy in
Miss Lake to make her courtesy in the middle of the park, and
protest against pursuing their walk together any further ?

Lord Chelford was a lively and agreeable companion ; but
there was something unusually gentle, almost resembling tenderness, in his manner. She was so different from her gay,
fiery self in this walk—so gentle ; so subdued—and he was more
interested by her, perhaps, than he had ever been before.

The sun just touched the verge of the wooded uplands, as the
young people began to descend the slope of Redman's Dell.

'How very short !' Lord Chelford paused, with a smile, at
these words. 'I was just going to say how short the days have
grown, as if it had all happened without notice, and contrary

to the almanac ; but really the sun sets cruelly early this evening, and I am so *very* sorry our little walk is so soon to end.'

There was not much in this little speech, but it was spoken in
a low, sweet voice ; and Rachel looked down on the ferns before her feet, as they walked on side by side, not with a smile,
but with a blush, and that beautiful look of gratification so becoming and indescribable. Happy that moment—that enchanted
moment of oblivion and illusion ! But the fitful evening breeze
came up through Redman's Dell, with a gentle sweep over the
autumnal foliage. Sudden as a sigh, and cold ; in her ear it
sounded like a whisper or a shudder, and she lifted up her eyes
and saw the darkening dell before her ; and with a pang, the
dreadful sense of reality returned. She stopped, with something
almost wild in her look. But with an effort she smiled, and said,
with a little shiver, ' The air has grown quite chill, and the sun
nearly set ; we loitered, Stanley and I, a great deal too long in
the park, but I am now at home, and I fear I have brought you
much too far out of your way already ; good-bye.' And she extended her hand.

' You must not dismiss your escort here. I must see you
through the enchanted dell—it is only a step—and then I shall
return with a good conscience, like a worthy knight, having
done my devoir honestly.'

She looked down the dell, with a dark and painful glance,
and then she said a few words of hesitating apology and
acquiescence, and in a few minutes more they parted at the
little wicket of Redman's Farm. They shook hands. He had
a few pleasant, lingering words to say. She paused as he spoke
at the other side of that little garden door. She seemed to
like those lingering sentences—and hung upon them—and even
smiled—but in her eyes there was a vague and melancholy
pleading—a wandering and unfathomable look that pained him.

They shook hands again—it was the third time—and then
she walked up the little gravel walk, hardly a dozen steps, and
disappeared within the door of Redman's Farm, without turning another parting look on Lord Chelford, who remained at
the little paling—expecting one, I think—to lift his hat and say
one more parting word.

She turned into the little drawing-room at the left, and, herself unseen, did take that last look, and saw him go up the road
again towards Brandon. The shadows and mists of Redman's
Dell anticipated night, and it was already deep twilight there.

On the table there lay a letter which Margery had brought
from the post-office. So Rachel lighted her candles and read it
with very little interest, for it concerned a world towards which
she had few yearnings. There was just one sentence which
startled her attention : it said, ' We shall soon be at Knowlton
—for Christmas, I suppose. It is growing too wintry for

mamma near the sea, though I like it better in a high wind than in a calm ; and a gale is such **fun**—such a romp. The Dulhamptons have arrived : the old Marchioness never appears till three o'clock, and only out in the carriage twice since they came. I can't say I very much admire Lady Constance, though she is to be Chelford's wife. She has fine eyes—and I think no other good point — much too dark for my taste — but they say clever ;' and not another word was there on this subject.

'Lady Constance! arranged, I suppose, by Lady Chelford—no great dot—and an unamiable family—an odious family—nothing to recommend her but her rank.'

So ruminated Rachel Lake as she looked out on her shadowy garden, and tapped a little feverish tattoo with her finger on the window pane ; and she meditated a great while, trying to bring back distinctly her recollection of Lady Constance, and also vaguely conjecturing who had arranged the marriage, and how it had come about.

'Chelford cannot like her. It is all Lady Chelford's doing. Can I have mistaken the name ?'

But no. Nothing could be more perfectly distinct than 'Chelford,' traced in her fair correspondent's very legible hand.

'He treats the young lady very coolly,' thought Rachel, forgetting, perhaps, that his special relations to Dorcas Brandon had compelled his stay in that part of the world.

Mingled with this criticism, was a feeling quite unavowed even to herself—a sore feeling that Lord Chelford had been—and this she never admitted to herself before—more particular —no, not exactly that — but more something or other—not exactly expressible in words, in his approaches to her, than was consistent with his situation. But then she had been very guarded; not stiff or prudish, indeed, but frank and cold enough with him, and that was comforting.

Still there was a sense of wonder — a great blank, and something of pain in the discovery—yes, pain—though she smiled a faint blushing smile—alone as she was ; and then came a deep sigh ; and then a sort of start.

'Rachel, Rachel, is it possible ?' murmured the young lady, with the same dubious smile, looking down upon the ground, and shaking her head. 'Yes, I do really think you had begun to like Lord Chelford— only *begun*, the least little insidious bit ; but thank you, wild Bessie Frankleyn, you have quite opened my eyes. Rachel, Rachel, girl ! what a fool you were near becoming !'

She looked like her old pleasant self during this little speech —arch and fresh, and still smiling—she looked up and sighed, and then her dark look returned, and she said dismally,

'What utter madness !'

And leaned for a while with her fingers upon the window

sash ; and when she turned to old Tamar, who brought in her tiny tea equipage, it seemed as if the shadow of the dell, into which she had been vacantly gazing, still rested on her face.

'Not here, Tamar ; I'll drink tea in my room ; and you must bring your tea-cup, too, and we'll take it together. I am—I think I am—a little nervous, darling, and you won't leave me?'

So they sat down together in her chamber. It was a cheery little bed-room, when the shutters were closed, and the fire burning brightly in the grate.

'My good Tamar will read her chapters aloud. I wish I could enjoy them like you. I can only wish. You must pray for me, Tamar. There is a dreadful image—and I sometimes think a dreadful being always near me. Though the words you read are sad and awful, they are also sweet, like funeral music a long way off, and they tranquillise me without making me better, as the harping of David did the troubled and forsaken King Saul.'

So the old nurse mounted her spectacles, glad of the invitation, and began to read. Her reading was very slow, and had other faults too, being in that sing-song style in which some people inexplicably like to read Holy Writ ; but it was reverent and distinct, and I have heard worse even in the reading desk.

'Stop,' said Rachel suddenly, as she reached about the middle of the chapter.

The old woman looked up, with her watery eyes wide open, and there was a short pause.

'I beg your pardon, dear Tamar, but you must first tell me that story you used to tell me long ago of Lady Ringdove, that lived in Epping Forest, to whom the ghost came and told something she was never to reveal, and who slowly died of the secret, growing all the time more and more like the spectre ; and besought the priest when she was dying, that he would have her laid in the abbey vault, with her mouth open, and her eyes and ears sealed, in token that her term of slavery was over, that her lips might now be open, and that her eyes were to see no more the dreadful sight, nor her ears to hear the frightful words that used to scare them in her life-time ; and then, you remember, whenever afterwards they opened the door of the vault, the wind entering in, made such moanings in her hollow mouth, and declared things so horrible that they built up the door of the vault, and entered it no more. Let me have the entire story, just as you used to tell it.'

So old Tamar, who knew it was no use disputing a fancy of her young mistress, although on Sunday night she would have preferred other talk, recounted her old tale of wonder.

'Yes, it is true—a true allegory, I mean, Tamar. Death will close the eyes and ears against the sights and sounds of earth ; but even the tomb secures no secrecy. The dead themselves declare their dreadful secrets, open-mouthed, to the winds. Oh, Tamar ! turn over the pages, and try to find some part which says where safety and peace may be found at any price ; for sometimes I think I am almost bereft of—reason.'

CHAPTER XXXII.

MR. LARKIN AND THE VICAR.

THE good vicar was not only dismayed but endangered by his brother's protracted absence. It was now the first week in November. Bleak and wintry that ungenial month set in at Gylingden ; and in accord with the tempestuous and dismal weather the fortunes of the Rev. William Wylder were darkened and agitated.

This morning a letter came at breakfast, by post, and when he had read it, the poor vicar grew a little white, and he folded it very quietly and put it in his waistcoat pocket, and patted little Fairy on the head. Little Fairy was asking him a question all this time, very vehemently, ' How long was Jack's sword that he killed the giants with ?' and several times to this distinct question he received only the unsatisfactory reply, ' Yes, my darling ;' and at last, when little Fairy mounted his knee, and hugging the abstracted vicar round the neck, urged his question with kisses and lamentations, the parson answered with a look of great perplexity, and only half recalled, said, ' Indeed, little man, I don't know. How long, you say, was Jack's sword? Well, I dare say it was as long as the umbrella.' He got up, with the same perplexed and absent look, as he said this, and threw an anxious glance about the room, as if looking for something he had mislaid.

' You are not going to write now, Willie, dear ?' expostulated his good little wife, ' you have not tasted your tea yet.'

' I have, indeed, dear ; haven't I ? Well, I will.'

And, standing, he drank nearly half the cup she had poured out for him, and set it down, and felt in his pocket, she thought, for his keys.

' Are you looking for anything, Willie, darling? Your keys are in my basket.'

' No, darling ; no, darling—nothing. I have everything I want. I think I must go to the Lodge and see Mr. Larkin, for a moment.'

' But you have eaten nothing,' remonstrated his partner ; ' you must not go until you have eaten something.'

'Time enough, darling; I can't wait—I sha'n't be away twenty minutes—time enough when I come back.'

'Have you heard anything of Mark, darling?' she enquired eagerly.

'Of Mark? Oh, no!—nothing of Mark.' And he added with a deep sigh, 'Oh, dear! I wonder he does not write—no, nothing of Mark.'

She followed him into the hall.

'Now, Willie darling, you must not go till you have had your breakfast—you will make yourself ill—indeed you will—do come back, just to please me, and eat a little first.'

'No, darling; no, my love—I can't, indeed. I'll be back immediately; but I must catch Mr. Larkin before he goes out. It is only a little matter—I want to ask his opinion—and—oh! here is my stick—and I'll return immediately.'

'And I'll go with you,' cried little Fairy.

'No, no, little man; I can't take you—no, it is business—stay with mamma, and I'll be back again in a few minutes.'

So, spite of Fairy's clamours and the remonstrances of his fond, clinging little wife, with a hurried kiss or two, away he went alone, at a very quick pace, through the high street of Gylingden, and was soon in the audience chamber of the serious, gentleman attorney.

The attorney rose with a gaunt and sad smile of welcome—begged Mr. Wylder, with a wave of his long hand, to be seated—and then seating himself and crossing one long thigh over the other, he threw his arm over the back of his chair, and leaning back with what he conceived to be a graceful and gentlemanly negligence—with his visitor full in the light of the window and his own countenance in shadow, the light coming from behind—a diplomatic arrangement which he affected—he fixed his small, pink eyes observantly upon him, and asked if he could do anything for Mr. William Wylder.

'Have you heard anything since, Mr. Larkin? Can you conjecture where his address may now be?' asked the vicar, a little abruptly.

'Oh! Mr. Mark Wylder, perhaps, you refer to?'

'Yes; my brother, Mark.'

Mr. Larkin smiled a sad and simple smile, and shook his head.

'No, indeed—not a word—it is very sad, and involves quite a world of trouble—and utterly inexplicable; for I need not tell you, in my position, it can't be pleasant to be denied all access to the client who has appointed me to act for him, nor conducive to the apprehension of his wishes upon many points, which I should much prefer not being left to my discretion. It is really, as I say, inexplicable, for Mr. Mark Wylder must thoroughly see all this: he is endowed with eminent talents for business, and must perfectly appreciate the embarrassment in which the mystery with which he surrounds the place of his abode must involve those whom he has appointed to conduct his business.'

'I have heard from him this morning,' resumed the lawyer; 'he was pleased to direct a power of attorney to me to receive his rents and sign receipts; and he proposes making Lord Viscount Chelford and Captain Lake trustees, to fund his money or otherwise invest it for his use, and'—

'Has he—I beg pardon—but did he mention a little matter in which I am deeply—indeed, vitally interested?' The vicar paused.

'I don't quite apprehend; perhaps if you were to frame your question a little differently, I might possibly—a—you were saying'—

'I mean a matter of very deep interest to me,' said the poor vicar, colouring a little, 'though no very considerable sum, viewed absolutely; but, under my unfortunate circumstances, of the most urgent importance—a loan of three hundred pounds—did he mention it?'

Again Mr. Larkin shook his head, with the same sad smile.

'But, though we do not know how to find him, he knows very well where to find us—and, as you are aware, we hear from him constantly—and no doubt he recollects his promise, and will transmit the necessary directions all in good time.'

'I earnestly hope he may,' and the poor cleric lifted up his eyes unconsciously and threw his hope into the form of a prayer. 'For, to speak frankly, Mr. Larkin, my circumstances are very pressing. I have just heard from Cambridge, and find that my good friend, Mr. Mountain, the bookseller, has been dead two months, and his wife—he was a widower when I knew him, but it would seem has married since—is his sole executrix, and has sold the business, and directed two gentlemen—attorneys—to call in all the debts due to him—peremptorily—and they say I must pay before the 15th; and I have, absolutely, but five pounds in the world, until March, when my half-year will be paid. And indeed, only that the tradespeople here are so very kind, we should often find it very difficult to manage.'

'Perhaps,' said Mr. Larkin, blandly, 'you would permit me to look at the letter you mention having received from the solicitors at Cambridge?'

'Oh, thank you, certainly; here it is,' said William Wylder, eagerly, and he gazed with his kind, truthful eyes upon the attorney's countenance as he glanced over it, trying to read something of futurity therein.

'Foukes and Mauley,' said Mr. Larkin. 'I have never had but one transaction with them; they are not always pleasant people to deal with. Mind, I don't say anything affecting their integrity—Heaven forbid; but they certainly did take rather what I would call a short turn with us on the occasion to which I refer. You must be cautious; indeed, my dear Sir, *very* cautious. The fifteenth—just ten clear days. Well, you know you have till then to look about you; and you know we may any day hear from your brother, directing the loan to be paid over to you. And now, my dear and reverend friend, you know me, I hope,' continued Mr. Larkin, very kindly, as he handed back the letter; 'and you won't attribute what I say to impertinent curiosity; but your brother's intended advance of three hundred pounds can hardly have had relation only to this trifling claim upon you. There are, no doubt—pardon me—several little matters to be arranged; and considerable circumspection will be needed, pending your brother's absence, in dealing with the persons who are in a position to press their claims unpleasantly. You must not trifle with these things. And let me recommend you seeing your legal adviser, whoever he is, immediately.'

'You mean,' said the vicar, who was by this time very much flushed, 'a gentleman of your profession, Mr. Larkin. Do you really think—well, it has frequently crossed my mind—but the expense, you know; and although my affairs are in a most unpleasant and complicated state, I am sure that everything would be perfectly smooth if only I had received the loan my kind brother intends, and which, to be sure, as you say, any day I may receive.'

'But, my dear Sir, do you really mean to say that you would pay claims from various quarters—how old is this, for instance? —without examination!'

The vicar looked very blank.

'I—this—well, this I certainly do owe; it has increased a little with interest, though good Mr. Mountain never charged more than six per cent. It was, I think, about fifteen pounds—books —I am ashamed to say how long ago; about a work which I began then, and laid aside—on Eusebius; but which is now complete, and will, I hope, eventually repay me.'

'Were you of age, my dear Sir, when he gave you these books on credit? Were you twenty-one years of age?'

'Oh! no; not twenty; but then I owe it, and I could not, as a Christian man, you know, evade my debts.'

'Of course; but you can't pay it at present, and it may be highly important to enable you to treat this as a debt of honour, you perceive. Suppose, my dear Sir, they should proceed to arrest you, or to sequestrate the revenue of your vicarage. Now, see, my dear Sir, I am, I humbly hope, a Christian man; but you will meet with men in every profession—and mine is no exception—disposed to extract the last farthing which the law by its extremest process will give them. And I really must tell you, frankly, that if you dream of escaping the most serious consequences, you must at once place yourself and your affairs in the hands of a competent man of business. It will probably be found that you do not in reality owe sixty pounds of every hundred claimed against you.'

'Oh, Mr. Larkin, if I could induce *you*.'

Mr. Larkin smiled a melancholy smile, and shook his head.

'My dear Sir, I only wish I could ; but my hands are so awfully full,' and he lifted them up and shook them, and shook his tall, bald head at the same time, and smiled a weary smile. 'Just look there,' and he waved his fingers in the direction of the Cyclopean wall of tin boxes, tier above tier, each bearing, in yellow italics, the name of some country gentleman, and two baronets among the number ; 'everyone of them laden with deeds and papers. You can't have a notion—no one has—what it is.'

'I see, indeed,' murmured the honest vicar, in a compassionating tone, and quite entering into the spirit of Mr. Larkin's mournful appeal, as if the being in large business was the most distressing situation in which an attorney could well find himself.

'It was very unreasonable of me to think of troubling you with my wretched affairs ; but really I do not know very well where to turn, or whom to speak to. Maybe, my dear Sir, you can think of some conscientious and Christian practitioner who is not so laden with other people's cares and troubles as you are. I am a very poor client, and indeed more trouble than I could possibly be gain to anyone. But there may be some one ; pray think ; ten days *is* so short a time, and I can do nothing.'

Mr. Larkin stood at the window ruminating, with his left hand in his breeches pocket, and his right, with finger and thumb pinching his under lip, after his wont, and the despairing accents of the poor vicar's last sentence still in his ear.

'Well,' he said hesitatingly, 'it is not easy, at a moment's notice, to point out a suitable solicitor ; there are many, of course, very desirable gentlemen, but I feel it, my dear Sir, a very serious responsibility naming one for so peculiar a matter. But you shall not, in the meantime, go to the wall for want of advice. Rely upon it, we'll do the best we can for you,' he continued, in a patronising way, with his chin raised, and extending his hand kindly to shake that of the parson. 'Yes, I certainly will—you must have advice. Can you give me two hours to-morrow evening—say to tea—if you will do me the honour. My friend, Captain Lake, dines at Brandon to-morrow. He's staying here with me, you are aware, on a visit ; but we shall be quite by ourselves, say at seven o'clock. Bring all your papers, and I'll get at the root of the business, and see, if possible, in each particular case, what line is best to be adopted.'

'How can I thank you, my dear Sir,' cried gentle William

Wylder, his countenance actually beaming with delight **and** gratitude—a brighter look than it had worn for many weeks.

'Oh, don't—*pray* don't mention it. I assure you, it is a happiness to me to be of any little use ; and, really, I don't see how you could possibly hold your own among the parties who are pressing you without professional advice.'

'I feel,' said the poor vicar, and his eyes filled as he smiled, and his lip quivered a little—'I feel as if my prayer for direction and deliverance were answered at last. Oh ! my dear Sir, I have suffered a great deal ; but something assures me I am rescued, and shall have a quiet mind once more—I am now in safe and able hands.' And he shook the safe and able, and rather large, hands of the amiable attorney in both his.

'You make too much of it, my dear Sir. I should at any time be most happy to advise you,' said Mr. Larkin, with a lofty and pleased benevolence, 'and with great pleasure, *provisionally*, until we can hit upon a satisfactory solicitor with a little more time at his disposal, I undertake the management of your case.'

'Thank Heaven !' again said the vicar, who had not let go his hands. 'And it is so delightful to have for my guide a Christian man, who, even were I so disposed, would not lend himself to an unworthy or questionable defence ; and although at this moment it is not in my power to reward your invaluable assistance——'

'Now really, my dear Sir, I must insist—no more of this, I beseech you. I do most earnestly insist that you promise me you will never mention the matter of professional remuneration more, until, at least, I press it, which, rely upon it, will not be for a good while.'

The attorney's smile plainly said, that his 'good while' meant in fact 'never.'

'This is, indeed, unimaginable kindness. How *have* I deserved so wonderful a blessing !'

'And I have no doubt,' said the attorney, fondling the vicar's arm in his large hand, 'that these claims will ultimately be reduced fully thirty per cent. I had once a good deal of professional experience in this sort of business ; and, oh ! my dear Sir, it is really *melancholy !* ' and up went his small pink eyes in a pure horror, and his hands were lifted at the same time ; 'but we will bring them to particulars ; and you may rely upon it, you will have a much longer time, at all events, than they are disposed to allow you

CHAPTER XXXIII.

THE LADIES ON GYLINGDEN HEATH.

UST at this moment they became aware of a timil little tapping which had been going on at the window during the latter part of this conference, and looking up, the attorney and the vicar saw 'little Fairy's' violet eyes peering under his light hair, with its mild, golden shadow, and the odd, sensitive smile, at once shy and arch ; his cheeks were wet with tears, and his pretty little nose red, though he was smiling ; and he drew his face aside among the jessamine, when he saw the gaunt attorney directing his patronising smile upon him.

'I beg pardon,' said the vicar, rising with a sudden smile, and going to the window. 'It is my little man. Fairy ! Fairy ! What has brought you here, my little man ?'

Fairy glanced, still smiling, but very shamefacedly at the grand attorney, and in his little fist he held a pair of rather seedy gloves to the window pane.

'So I did. I protest I forgot my gloves. Thank you, little man. Who is with you ? Oh ! I see. That is right.'

The maid ducked a short courtesy.

'Indeed, Sir, please, Master Fairy was raising the roof (a nursery phrase, which implied indescribable bellowing), and as naughty as could be, until missis allowed him to come after you.'

'Oh ! my little man, you must not do that. Ask nicely, you know ; always quietly, like a little gentleman.'

'But, oh ! Wapsie, your hands would be cold ;' and he held the gloves to him against the glass.

'Well, darling, thank you ; you are a kind little man, and I'll be with you in a moment,' said the vicar, smiling very lovingly on his naughty little man.

'Mr. Larkin,' said he, turning very gratefully to the attorney 'you can lay this Christian comfort to your kind heart, that you have made mine a hundredfold lighter since I entered this blessed room ; indeed, you have lifted a mountain from it by the timely proffer of your invaluable assistance.'

Again the attorney waved off, with a benignant and humble smile, rather oppressive to see, all idea of obligation, and accompanied his grateful client to the glass door of his little porch, where Fairy was already awaiting him with the gloves in his hand.

'I do believe,' said the good vicar, as he walked down what Mr. Larkin called 'the approach,' and looking up with irrepressible gratitude to the blue sky and the white clouds sailing over his head, 'if it be not presumption, I *must* believe that I have been directed hither—yes, darling, yes, my hands are warm' (this was addressed to little Fairy, who was clamouring for information on the point, and clinging to his arm as he capered by his side). 'What immense relief;' and he murmured another thanksgiving, and then quite hilariously—

'If little man would like to come with his Wapsie, we'll take such a nice little walk together, and we'll go and see poor Widow Maddock; and we'll buy three muffins on our way home, for a feast this evening; and we'll look at the pictures in the old French "Josephus;" and Mamma and I will tell stories; and I have a halfpenny to buy apples for little Fairy.'

The attorney stood at his window with a shadow on his face, and his small eyes a little contracted and snakelike, following the slim figure of the threadbare vicar and his golden-haired, dancing little comrade; and then he mounted a chair, and took down successively four of his japanned boxes; two of them, in yellow letters, bore respectively the label '*Brandon, No.* 1,' and '*No.* 2;' the other '*Wylder, No* 1,' and '*No.* 2.'

He opened the 'Wylder' box first, and glanced through a neat little 'statement of title,' prepared for counsel when draughting the deed of settlement for the marriage which was never to take place.

'The limitations, let me see, is not there something that one might be safe in advancing a trifle upon—eh?—h'm—yes.'

And, with his lip in his finger and thumb, he conned over those remainders and reversions with a skilled and rapid eye.

Rachel Lake was glad to see the slender and slightly-stooped figure of the vicar standing that morning—his bright little boy by the hand—in the wicket of the tiny flower-garden of Redman's Farm. She went out quickly to greet him. The sick man likes the sound of his kind doctor's step on the stairs; and, be his skill much or little, trusts in him, and will even joke a little asthmatic joke, and smile a feeble hectic smile about his ailments, when he is present.

So they fell into discourse among the autumnal flowers and withered leaves; and, as the day was still and genial, they remained standing in the garden; and away went busy little 'Fairy,' smiling and chatting with Margery, to see the hens and chickens in the yard.

The physician, after a while, finds the leading features of most cases pretty much alike. He knows when inflammation may be expected and fever will supervene; he is not surprised if the patient's mind wanders a little at times; expects the period of prostration and the return of appetite; and has his measures and his palliatives ready for each successive phase of sickness and recovery. In like manner, too, the good and skilful parson comes by experience to know the signs and stages of the moral ailments and recoveries which some of them know how so tenderly and so wisely to care for. They, too, have ready—having often proved their consolatory efficacy—their febrifuges and their tonics, culled from that tree of life whose 'leaves are for the healing of the nations.'

Poor Rachel's hours were dark, and life had grown in some sort terrible, and death seemed now so real and near—aye, quite a fact—and, somehow, not unfriendly. But, oh! the immense futurity beyond, that could not be shirked, to which she was certainly going.

Death, and sleep so welcome! But, oh! that stupendous LIFE EVERLASTING, now first unveiled. She could only close her eyes and wring her hands. Oh! for some friendly voice and hand to stay her through the Valley of the Shadow of Death!

They talked a long while—Rachel chiefly a listener, and often quietly weeping; and, at last, a very kindly parting, and a promise from the simple and gentle vicar that he would often look in at Redman's Farm.

She watched his retreating figure as he and little Fairy walked down the tenebrose road to Gylingden, following them with a dismal gaze, as a benighted and wounded wayfarer in that 'Valley' would the pale lamp's disappearing that had for a few minutes, in a friendly hand, shone over his dreadful darkness.

And when, in fitful reveries, fancy turned for a moment to an earthly past and future, all there was a blank—the past saddened, the future bleak. She did not know, or even suspect, that she had been living in an aerial castle, and worshipping an unreal image, until, on a sudden, all was revealed in that chance gleam of cruel lightning, the line in that letter, which she read so often, spelled over, and puzzled over so industriously, though it was clear enough. How noble, how good, how bright and true, was that hero of her unconscious romance.

Well, no one else suspected that incipient madness—that was something; and brave Rachel would quite master it. Happy she had discovered it so soon. Besides, it was, even if Chelford were at her feet, a wild impossibility now; and it was well, though despair were in the pang, that she had, at last, quite explained this to herself.

As Rachel stood in her little garden, on the spot where she had bidden farewell to the vicar, she was roused from her vague and dismal reverie by the sound of a carriage close at hand. She had just time to see that it was a brougham, and to recognise the Brandon liveries, when it drew up at the garden wicket, and Dorcas called to her from the open window.

'I'm come, Rachel, expressly to take you with me; and I won't be denied.'

'You are very good, Dorcas ; thank you, dear, very much ; but I am not very well, and a very dull companion to-day.'

'You think I am going to bore you with visits. No such thing, I assure you. I have taken a fancy to walk on the common, that is all—a kind of longing ; and you must come with me ; quite to ourselves, you and I. You won't refuse me, darling ; I know you'll come.'

Well, Rachel did go. And away they drove through the quiet town of Gylingden together, and through the short street on the right, and so upon the still quieter common.

This plain of green turf broke gradually into a heath ; and an irregular screen of timber and underwood divided the common of Gylingden in sylvan fashion from the moor. The wood passed, Dorcas stopped the carriage, and the two young ladies descended. It was a sunny day, and the air still ; and the open heath contrasted pleasantly with the sombre and confined scenery of Redman's Dell ; and altogether Rachel was glad now that she had made the effort, and come with her cousin.

'It was good of you to come, Rachel,' said Miss Brandon ; 'and you look tired ; but you sha'n't speak more than you like ; and I'll tell you all the news. Chelford is just returned from Brighton ; he arrived this morning ; and he and Lady Chelford will stay for the Hunt Ball. I made it a point. And he called at Hockley, on his way back, to see Sir Julius. Do you know him ?'

'Sir Julius Hockley ? No—I've heard of him only.'

'Well, they say he is wasting his property very fast ; and I think him every way very nearly a fool ; but Chelford wanted to see him about Mr. Wylder. Mark Wylder, you know, of course, has turned up again in England. His letter to Chelford, six weeks ago, was from Boulogne ; but his last was from Brighton ; and Sir Julius Hockley witnessed—I think they call it—that letter of attorney which Mark sent about a week since to Mr. Larkin ; and Chelford, who is most anxious to trace Mark Wylder, having to surrender—I think they call it—a "trust" is not it—or something—I really don't understand these things —to him, and not being able to find out his address, Mr. Larkin wrote to Sir Julius, whom Chelford did not find at home, to ask him for a description of Mark, to ascertain whether he had disguised himself ; and Sir Julius wrote to Chelford such an absurd description of poor Mark, in doggrel rhyme—so like—his odd walk, his great whiskers, and everything. Chelford does not like personalities, but he could not help laughing. Are you ill, darling ?'

Though she was walking on beside her companion, Rachel looked on the point of fainting.

'My darling, you must sit down ; you do look very ill. I

forgot my promise about Mark Wylder. How stupid I have been ! and perhaps I have distressed you.'

' No, Dorcas, I am pretty well; but I have been ill, and I am a little tired ; and, Dorcas, I don't deny it, I *am* amazed, you tell me such things. That letter of attorney, or whatever it is, must not be acted upon. It is incredible. It is all horrible wickedness. Mark Wylder's fate is dreadful, and Stanley is the mover of all this. Oh ! Dorcas, darling, I wish I could tell you everything. Some day I may be—I am sick and terrified.'

They had sat down, by this time, side by side, on the crisp bank. Each lady looked down, the one in suffering, the other in thought.

' You are better, darling ; are not you better?' said Dorcas, laying her hand on Rachel's, and looking on her with a melancholy gaze.

' Yes, dear, better—very well'—answered Rachel, looking up but without an answering glance at her cousin.

' You blame your brother, Rachel, in this affair.'

' Did I ? Well—maybe—yes, he *is* to blame—the miserable man—whom I hate to think of, and yet am always thinking of—Stanley well knows is not in a state to do it.'

' Don't you think, Rachel, remembering what I have confided to you, that you might be franker with me in this?'

' Oh, Dorcas ! don't misunderstand me. If the secret were all my own—Heaven knows, hateful as it is, how boldly I would risk all, and throw myself on your fidelity or your mercy—I know not how you might view it ; but it is different, Dorcas, at least for the present. You know me—you know how I hate secrets ; but this *is* not mine—only in part—that is, I dare not tell it—but may be soon free—and to us all, dear Dorcas, a woful, *woful* day will it be.'

' I made you a promise, Rachel,' said her beautiful cousin, gravely, and a little coldly and sadly, too ; ' I will never break it again—it was thoughtless. Let us each try to forget that there is anything hidden between us.'

' If ever the time comes, dear Dorcas, when I may tell it to you, I don't know whether you will bless or hate me for having kept it so well ; at all events, I think you'll pity me, and at last understand your miserable cousin.'

' I said before, Rachel, that I liked you. You are one of us, Rachel. You are beautiful, wayward, and daring, and one way or another, misfortune always waylays us ; and *I* have, I know it, calamity before me. Death comes to other women in its accustomed way ; but we have a double death. There is not a beautiful portrait in Brandon that has not a sad and true story. Early death of the frail and fair tenement of clay—but a still earlier death of happiness. Come, Rachel, shall we escape from the spell and the destiny into solitude? What do you think of my old plan of the valleys and lakes of Wales? a pretty foreign tongue spoken round us, and no one but ourselves to commune with, and books, and music. It is not, Radie, altogether jest. I sometimes yearn for it, as they say foreign girls do for convent life.'

'Poor Dorcas,' said Rachel, very softly, fixing her eyes upon her with a look of inexpressible sadness and pity.

'Rachel,' said Dorcas, 'I am a changeable being—violent. self-willed. My fate may be quite a different one from that which *I* suppose or *you* imagine. I may yet have to retract *my* secret.'

'Oh! would it were so—would to Heaven it were so.'

'Suppose, Rachel, that I had been deceiving you—perhaps deceiving myself—time will show.'

There was a wild smile on beautiful Dorcas's face as she said this, which faded soon into the proud serenity that was its usual character.

'Oh! Dorcas, if your good angel is near, listen to his warnings.'

'We have no good angels, my poor Rachel: what modern necromancers, conversing with tables, call "mocking spirits," have always usurped their place with us : singing in our drowsy ears, like Ariel—visiting our reveries like angels of light—being really our evil genii—ah, yes!'

'Dorcas, dear,' said Rachel, after both had been silent for a time, speaking suddenly, and with a look of pale and keen entreaty—'Beware of Stanley—oh! beware, beware. I think I am beginning to grow afraid of him myself.'

Dorcas was not given to sighing—but she sighed—gazing sadly across the wide, bleak moor, with her proud, apathetic look, which seemed passively to defy futurity—and then, for awhile, they were silent.

She turned, and caressingly smoothed the golden tresses over Rachel's frank, white forehead, and kissed them as she did so.

'You are better, darling; you are rested?' she said.

'Yes, dear Dorcas,' and she kissed the slender hand that smoothed her hair.

Each understood that the conversation on that theme was ended, and somehow each was relieved.

CHAPTER XXXIV.

SIR JULIUS HOCKLEY'S LETTER.

JOS. LARKIN mentioned in his conversation with the vicar, just related, that he had received a power of attorney from Mark Wylder. Connected with this document there came to light a circumstance so very odd, that the reader must at once be apprised of it.

This legal instrument was attested by two witnesses, and bore date about a week before the interview, just related, between the vicar and Mr. Larkin. Here, then, was a fact established. Mark Wylder had returned from Boulogne, for the power of attorney had been executed at Brighton. Who were the witnesses? One was Thomas Tupton, of the Travellers' Hotel, Brighton.

This Thomas Tupton was something of a sporting celebrity, and a likely man enough to be of Mark's acquaintance.

The other witness was Sir Julius Hockley, of Hockley, an unexceptionable evidence, though a good deal on the turf.

Now our friend Jos. Larkin had something of the Red Indian's faculty for tracking his game, by hardly perceptible signs and tokens, through the wilderness; and this mystery of Mark Wylder's flight and seclusion was the present object of his keen and patient pursuit.

On receipt of the ' instrument,' therefore, he wrote by return of post, ' presenting his respectful compliments to Sir Julius Hockley, and deeply regretting that, as solicitor of the Wylder family, and the *gentleman (sic)* empowered to act under the letter of attorney, it was imperative upon him to trouble him (Sir Julius H.) with a few interrogatories, which he trusted he would have no difficulty in answering.'

The first was, whether he had been acquainted with Mr. Mark Wylder's personal appearance before seeing him sign, so as to be able to identify him. The second was, whether he (Mr. M. W.) was accompanied, at the time of executing the instrument, by any friend ; and if so, what were the name and address of such friend. And the third was, whether he could communicate any information whatsoever respecting Mr. M. W.'s present place of abode?

The same queries were put in a somewhat haughty and peremptory way to the sporting hotel-keeper, who answered that Mr. Mark Wylder had been staying for a week at his house, about five months ago ; and that he had seen him twice—once 'backing' Jonathan, when he beat the great American billiard-player ; and another time, when he lent him his copy of 'Bell's Life,' in the coffee-room ; and thus he was enabled to identify him. For the rest he could say nothing.

Sir Julius's reply was of the hoity-toity and rollicking sort, bordering in parts very nearly on nonsense, and generally impertinent. It reached Mr. Larkin as he sat at breakfast with his friend, Stanley Lake.

'Pray read your letters, and don't mind me, I entreat. Perhaps you will allow me to look at the "Times ;" and I'll trouble you for the sardines.'

The postmark 'Hockley,' stared the lawyer in the face ; and, longing to break the seal, he availed himself of the captain's permission. So Lake opened the 'Times ;' and, as he studied its columns, I think he stole a glance or two over its margin at the attorney, now deep in the letter of Sir Julius Hockley.

He (Sir J. H.) 'presented his respects to Mr. Lark*ens*, or Lark*ins*, or Lark*me*, or Lark*us*—Sir J. H. is not able to read *which* or *what ;* but he is happy to observe, at all events, that, end how he may, the gentleman begins with a "lark !" which Sir J. H. always does, when he can.   Not being able to discover his terminal syllable, he will take the liberty of styling him by his sprightly beginning, and calling him shortly "Lark." As Sir J. never objected to a lark, the gentleman so designated introduces himself with a strong prejudice, in Sir J.'s mind, in his favour—so much so, that by way of a lark, Sir J. will answer Lark's questions, which are not, he thinks, very impertinent. The wildest of all Lark's questions refers to Wylder's place of abode, which Sir J. was never wild enough to think of asking after, and does not know ; and so little was he acquainted with the gentleman, that he forgot he was an evangelist doing good under the style and title of Mark.   Lark may, therefore, tell Mark, if he sees him, or his friends—Matthew, Luke, and John—that Sir Julius saw Mark only on two successive days, at the cricket-match, played between Paul's Eleven—the coincidence is remarkable—and the Ishmaelites (these, I am bound to observe, were literally the designations of the opposing sides) ; and that he had the honour of being presented to Mark—saint or sinner, as he may be—on the ground, by his, Sir J. H.'s, friend, Captain Stanley Lake, of the Guards.'

Here was an astounding fact. Stanley Lake had been in Mark Wylder's company only ten days ago, when that great match was played at Brighton !   What a deep gentleman was that Stanley Lake, who sat at the other end of the table with the 'Times' before him.   What a varnished rascal—what a matchless liar !

He had returned to Gylingden, direct, in all likelihood, from his conferences with Mark Wylder, to tell all concerned that **it** was vain endeavouring to trace him, and still offering his disinterested services in the pursuit.

No matter! We must take things coolly and cautiously. All this chicanery will yet break down, and the conspiracy, be it what it may, will be thoroughly exposed. Mystery is the shadow of guilt ; and, most assuredly, thought Mr. Larkin, there is some *infernal* secret, *well worth knowing*, at the bottom of all this. You little think I have you here ! and he slid Sir Julius Hockley's piece of rubbishy banter into his waistcoat pocket, and then opened and glanced at half-a-dozen other letters, in a cool, quick official way, endorsing a little note on the back of each with his gold, patent pencil. All Mr. Jos. Larkin's 'properties' were handsome and imposing, and he never played with children without producing his gold repeater, and making it strike, and exhibiting its wonders for their amusement, and the edification of the adults, whose presence, of course, he forgot.

' Paul's Eleven have challenged the Gipsies,' said Lake, languidly lifting his eyes from the paper. ' By-the-bye, are you anything of a cricketer ? And they are to play at Hockley, Sir Julius Hockley's ground. You know Sir Julius, don't you ?'

' Very slightly. I may say I *have* that honour, but we have never been thrown together ; a mere—a—the slightest thing in the world.'

' Not schoolfellows——you are not an Eton man, eh ?' said Lake.

' Oh no ! My dear father' (the organist) 'would not send a boy of his to what he called an idle school. But my acquaintance with Sir Julius was a trifling matter. Hockley is a very pretty place, is not it ?'

' A sweet place. A great match was played between those fellows at Brighton : Paul's Eleven beat fifteen of the Ishmaelites, about a fortnight since ; but they have no chance with the Gipsies. It will be quite a hollow thing — a one-innings affair.'

' Have you ever seen Paul's Eleven play ?' asked the lawyer, carelessly taking up the newspaper which Lake had laid down.

' I saw them play that match at Brighton, I mentioned just now, a few days ago.'

' Ah ! did you ?'

' Did not you *know* I was there?' said Lake, in rather a changed tone. Larkin looked up, and Lake laughed in his face quietly the most impertinent laugh he had ever seen or heard, with his yellow eyes fixed on the lawyer's pink little optics. ' I was there, and Hockley was there, and Mark Wylder was there— was not he ?' and Lake stared and laughed, and the attorney stared ; and Lake added, ' What a d—d cunning fellow you are ; ha, ha, ha !'

Larkin was not easily put out, but he *was* disconcerted now; and his cheeks and forehead grew suddenly pink, and he coughed a little, and tried to throw a look of mild surprise into his face.

'Why, you have this moment had a letter from Hockley. Don't you think I knew his hand and the post-mark, and your look said quite plainly, "Here's news of my friend Stanley Lake and Mark Wylder. I had an uncle in the Foreign Office, and they said he would have been quite a distinguished diplomatist if he had lived ; and I was said to have a good deal of his talent ; and I really think I have brought my little evidences very prettily together, and jumped to a right conclusion—eh ?'

A flicker of that sinister shadow I have sometimes mentioned crossed Larkin's face, and contracted his eyes, as he said, a little sternly—

'I have nothing on earth to conceal, Sir ; I never had. All *my* conduct has been as open as the light ; there's not a letter, Sir, I ever write or receive, that might not, so far as *I* am concerned, with my good will, lie open on that table for every visitor that comes in to read ;—open as the day, Sir :' and the attorney waved his hand grandly.

'Hear, hear, hear,' said Lake, languidly, and tapping a little applause on the table, while he watched the solicitor's rhetoric with his sly, disconcerting smile.

'It was but conscientious, Captain Lake, that I should make particular enquiry respecting the genuineness of a legal instrument conferring such very considerable powers. How, on earth, Sir, could I have the slightest suspicion that *you* had seen my client, Mr. Wylder, considering the tenor of your letters and conversation ? And I venture to say, Captain Lake, that Lord Chelford will be just as much surprised as I, when he hears it.'

Jos. Larkin, Esq., delivered this peroration from a moral elevation, all the loftier that he had a peer of the realm on his side. But peers did not in the least overawe Stanley Lake, who had been all his days familiar with those idols ; and the moral altitudes of the attorney amused him vastly.

'But he'll *not* hear it ; *I* won't tell him, and you sha'n't ; because I don't think it would be prudent of us—do you ?—to quarrel with Mark Wylder, and he does not wish our meeting known. It is nothing on earth to me ; on the contrary, it rather places me in an awkward position keeping other people's secrets.'

The attorney made one of his slight, gentlemanlike bows, and threw back his head with a lofty and reserved look.

'I don't know, Captain Lake, that I would be quite justified in withholding the substance of Sir Julius Hockley's letter from Lord Chelford, consulted, as I have had the honour to be, by that nobleman. I shall, however, turn it over in my mind.'

'Don't the least mind me. In fact, I would rather tell it than

not. And I can explain to Chelford why *I* could not mention
the circumstance. Wylder, in fact, tied me down by a promise,
and he'll be devilish angry with you; but, it seems, you don't
very much mind that.'

He knew that Mr. Larkin *did* very much mind it; and the
quick glance of the attorney could read nothing whatever in the
captain's pallid face and downcast eyes, smiling on the points
of his varnished boots.

'Of course, you know, Captain Lake, in alluding to the possibility of my making any communication to Lord Chelford, I
limit myself strictly to the letter of Sir Julius Hockley, and do
not, by any means, my dear Captain Lake, include the conversation which has just occurred, and the communication which you
have volunteered to make me.'

'Oh! quite so,' said the captain, looking up suddenly, as was
his way, with a momentary glare, like a man newly-waked from
a narcotic doze.

CHAPTER XXXV.

THE HUNT BALL.

BY this time your humble servant, the chronicler of these
Gylingden annals, had taken his leave of magnificent
old Brandon, and of its strangely interesting young
mistress, and was carrying away with him, as he flew
along the London rails, the broken imagery of that grand and
shivered dream. He was destined, however, before very long,
to revisit these scenes; and in the meantime heard, in rude outline, the tenor of what was happening — the minute incidents
and colouring of which were afterwards faithfully communicated.

I can, therefore, without break or blur, continue my description; and to say truth, at this distance of time, I have some
difficulty—so well acquainted was I with the actors and the
scenery—in determining, without consulting my diary, what por-
tions of the narrative I relate from hearsay, and what as a spectator. But that I am so far from understanding myself, I should
often be amazed at the sayings and doings of other people. As
it is, I behold in myself an abyss, I gaze down and listen, and
discover neither light nor harmony, but thunderings and light-
nings, and voices and laughter, and a medley that dismays me.
There rage the elements which God only can control. Forgive
us our trespasses; lead us not into temptation; deliver us from
the Evil One! How helpless and appalled we shut our eyes over
that awful chasm.

I have long ceased, then, to wonder why any living soul does anything that is incongruous and unanticipated. And therefore I cannot say how Miss Brandon persuaded her handsome Cousin Rachel to go with her party, under the wing of Old Lady Chelford, to the Hunt Ball of Gylingden. And knowing now all that then hung heavy at the heart of the fair tenant of Redman's Farm, I should, indeed, wonder inexpressibly, were it not, as I have just said, that I have long ceased to wonder at any vagaries of myself or my fellow creatures.

The Hunt Ball is the great annual event of Gylingden. The critical process of 'coming out' is here consummated by the young ladies of that town and vicinage. It is looked back upon for one-half of the year, and forward to for the other. People date by it. The battle of Inkerman was fought immediately before the Hunt Ball. It was so many weeks after the Hunt Ball that the Czar Nicholas died. The Carnival of Venice was nothing like so grand an event. Its solemn and universal importance in Gylingden and the country round, gave me, I fancied, some notion of what the feast of unleavened bread must have been to the Hebrews and Jerusalem.

The connubial capabilities of Gylingden are positively wretched. When I knew it, there were but three single men, according even to the modest measure of Gylingden housekeeping, capable of supporting wives, and these were difficult to please, set a high price on themselves—looked the country round at long ranges, and were only wistfully and meekly glanced after by the frugal vestals of Gylingden, as they strutted round the corners, or smoked the pipe of apathy at the reading-room windows.

Old Major Jackson kept the young ladies in practice between whiles, with his barren gallantries and graces, and was, just so far, better than nothing. But, as it had been for years well ascertained that he either could not or would not afford to marry, and that his love passages, like the passages in Gothic piles that 'lead to nothing,' were not designed to terminate advantageously, he had long ceased to excite, even in that desolate region, the smallest interest.

Think, then, what it was, when Mr. Pummice, of Copal and Pummice, the splendid house-painters at Dollington, arrived with his artists and charwomen to give the Assembly Room its annual touching-up and bedizenment, preparatory to the Hunt Ball. The Gylingden young ladies used to peep in, and from the lobby observe the wenches dry-rubbing and waxing the floor, and the great Mr. Pummice, with his myrmidons, in aprons and paper caps, retouching the gilding.

It was a tremendous crisis for honest Mrs. Page, the confectioner, over the way, who, in legal phrase, had 'the carriage' of the supper and refreshments, though largely assisted by Mr. Battersby, of Dollington. During the few days' agony of preparation that immediately preceded this notable orgie, the good lady's countenance bespoke the magnitude of her cares. Though the weather was usually cold, I don't think she ever was cool during that period—I am sure she never slept—I don't think she ate—and I am afraid her religious exercises were neglected.

Equally distracting, emaciating, and godless, was the condition to which the mere advent of this festival reduced worthy Miss Williams, the dressmaker, who had more white muslin and young ladies on her hands than she and her choir of needle-women knew what to do with. During this tremendous period Miss Williams hardly resembled herself—her eyes dilated, her lips were pale, and her brow corrugated with deep and inflexible lines of fear and perplexity. She lived on bad tea—sat up all night—and every now and then burst into helpless floods of tears. But somehow, generally things came pretty right in the end. One way or another, the gay belles and elderly spinsters, and fat village chaperones, were invested in suitable costume by the appointed hour, and in a few weeks Miss Williams' mind recovered its wonted tone, and her countenance its natural expression.

The great night had now arrived. Gylingden was quite in an uproar. Rural families of eminence came in. Some in old-fashioned coaches ; others, the wealthier, more in London style. The stables of the ' Brandon Arms,' of the ' George Inn,' of the ' Silver Lion,' even of the ' White House,' though a good way off, and generally every vacant standing for horses in or about the town were crowded ; and the places of entertainment we have named, and minor houses of refection, were vocal with the talk of flunkeys, patrician with powdered heads, and splendent in variegated liveries.

The front of the Town Hall resounded with the ring of horse-hoofs, the crack of whips, the bawling of coachmen, the clank of carriage steps and clang of coach doors. A promiscuous mob of the plebs and profanum vulgus of Gylingden beset the door, to see the ladies — the slim and the young in white muslins and artificial flowers, and their stout guardian angels, of maturer years, in satins and velvets, and jewels—some real, and some, just as good, of paste. In the cloak-room such a fuss, unfurling of fans, and last looks and hurried adjustments.

When the Crutchleighs, of Clay Manor, a good, old, formal family, were mounting the stairs in solemn procession—they were always among the early arrivals—they heard a piano and a tenor performing in the supper-room.

Now, old Lady Chelford chose to patronise Mr. Page, the Dollington professor, and partly, I fancy, to show that she could turn things topsy-turvy in this town of Gylingden, had made a point, with the rulers of the feast, that her client should sing half-a-dozen songs in the supper-room before dancing commenced.

Mrs. Crutchleigh stayed her step upon the stairs abruptly, and turned, with a look of fierce surprise upon her lean, white-headed lord, arresting thereby the upward march of Corfe Crutchleigh, Esq., the hope of his house, who was pulling on his gloves, with his eldest spinster sister on his lank arm.

'There appears to be a concert going on ; we came here to a ball. Had you not better enquire, Mr. Crutchleigh ; it would seem we have made a mistake ?'

Mrs. Crutchleigh was sensitive about the dignity of the family of Clay Manor ; and her cheeks flushed above the rouge, and her eyes flashed severely.

'That's singing—particularly *loud singing.* Either we have mistaken the night, or somebody has taken upon him to upset all the arrangements. You'll be good enough to enquire whether there will be dancing to-night ; I and Anastasia will remain in the cloak-room ; and we'll all leave if you please, Mr. Crutchleigh, if this goes on.'

The fact is, Mrs. Crutchleigh had got an inkling of this performance, and had affected to believe it impossible ; and, detesting old Lady Chelford for sundry slights and small impertinences, and envying Brandon and its belongings, was resolved not to be put down by presumption in that quarter.

Old Lady Chelford sat in an arm-chair in the supper-room, where a considerable audience was collected. She had a splendid shawl or two about her, and a certain air of demi-toilette, which gave the Gylingden people to understand that her ladyship did not look on this gala in the light of a real ball, but only as a sort of rustic imitation—curious, possibly amusing, and, like other rural sports, deserving of encouragement, for the sake of the people who made innocent holiday there.

Mr. Page, the performer, was a plump young man, with black whiskers, and his hair in oily ringlets, such as may be seen in the model wigs presented on smiling, waxen dandies, in Mr. Rose's front window at Dollington. He bowed and smiled in the most unexceptionable of white chokers and the dapperest of dress coats, and drew off the whitest imaginable pair of kid gloves, when he sat down to the piano, subsiding in a sort of bow upon the music-stool, and striking those few, brisk and noisy chords with which such artists proclaim silence and reassure themselves.

Stanley Lake, that eminent London swell, had attached himself as gentleman-in-waiting to Lady Chelford's household, and was perpetually gliding with little messages between her ladyship and the dapper vocalist of Dollington, who varied his programme and submitted to an occasional *encore* on the private order thus communicated.

'I told you Chelford would be here,' said Miss Brandon to Rachel, in a low tone, glancing at the young peer.

'I thought he had returned to Brighton. I fancied he might be—you know the Dulhamptons are at Brighton; and Lady Constance, of course, has a claim on his time and thoughts.'

Rachel smiled as she spoke, and was adjusting her bouquet, as Dorcas made answer—

'Lady Constance, my dear Radie! That, you know, was never more than a mere whisper; it was only Lady Chelford and the marchioness who talked it over—they would have liked it very well. But Chelford won't be managed or scolded into anything of the kind; and will choose, I think, for himself, and I fancy not altogether according to their ideas, when the time comes. And I assure you, dear Radie, there is not the least truth in that story about Lady Constance.'

Why should Dorcas be so earnest to convince her handsome cousin that there was nothing in this rumour? Rachel made no remark, and there was a little silence.

'I'm so glad I succeeded in bringing you here,' said Dorcas; 'Chelford made such a point of it; and he thinks you are losing your spirits among the great trees and shadows of Redman's Dell; and he made it quite a little cousinly duty that I should succeed.'

At this moment Mr. Page interposed with the energetic prelude of his concluding ditty. It was one of Tom Moore's melodies.

Rachel leaned back, and seemed to enjoy it very much. But when it was over, I think she would have found it difficult to say what the song was about.

Mr. Page had now completed his programme, and warned by the disrespectful violins from the gallery of the ball-room, whence a considerable caterwauling was already announcing the approach of the dance, he made his farewell flourish, and bow and, smiling, withdrew.

CHAPTER XXXVI.

THE BALL ROOM.

ACHEL LAKE, standing by the piano, turned over the leaves of the volume of 'Moore's Melodies,' from which the artist in black whiskers and white waistcoat had just entertained his noble patroness and his audience.

Everyone has experienced, I suppose for a few wonderful moments, now and then, a glow of seemingly causeless happiness, in which the earth and its people are glorified—peace and sunlight rest on everything—the spirit of music and love is in the air, and the heart itself sings for joy. In the light of this celestial illusion she stood now by the piano, turning over the pages of poor Tom Moore, as I have said, when a low pleasant voice near her said—

' I was so glad to see that Dorcas had prevailed, and that you were here. We both agreed that you are too much a recluse in that Der Frieschutz Glen—at least, for your friends' pleasure ; and owe it to us all to appear now and then in this upper world.'

' Excelsior, Miss Lake,' interposed dapper little Mr. Buttle, with a smirk ; ' I think this little bit of music—it was got up, you know, by that old quiz, Dowager Lady Chelford—was really not so bad—a rather good idea, after all, Miss Lake. Don't you ? '

Poor Mr. Buttle did not know Lord Chelford, and thus shooting his ' arrow o'er the house,' he ' hurt his brother.' Chelford turned away, and bowed and smiled to one or two friends at the other side of the room.

' Yes, the music was very pretty, and some of the songs were quite charmingly sung. I agree with you—we are very much obliged to Lady Chelford—that is her son, Lord Chelford.'

' Oh ! ' said Buttle, whose smirk vanished on the instant in a very red and dismal vacancy, ' I—I'm afraid he'll think me shockingly rude.' And in a minute more Buttle was gone.

Miss Lake again looked down upon the page, and as she did so, Lord Chelford turned and said—

' You are a worshipper of Tom Moore, Miss Lake ? '

' An admirer, perhaps—certainly no worshipper. Yet, I can't say. Perhaps I do worship ; but if so, it is a worship strangely mixed with contempt.' And she laughed a little. ' A kind of adoring which I fancy belongs properly to the lords of creation, and which we of the weaker sex have no right to practise.'

'Miss Lake is pleased to be ironical to-night,' he said, with a smile.

'Am I ? I dare say. All women are. Irony is the weapon of cowardice, and cowardice the vice of weakness. Yet I think I was naturally bold and true. I hate cowardice and deception even in myself—I hate perfidy—I hate *fraud.*'

She tapped a little emphasis upon the floor with her white satin shoe, and her eyes flashed with a dark and angry meaning among the crowd at the other end of the room, as if for a second or two following an object to whom in some way the statement applied.

The strange bitterness of her tone, though it was low enough, and something wild, suffering, and revengeful in her look, though but momentary, and hardly definable, did not escape Lord Chelford, and he followed unconsciously the direction of her glance ; but there was nothing there to guide him to a conclusion, and the good people who formed that polite and animated mob were in his eyes, one and all, quite below the level of tragedy, or even of melodrame.

'And yet, Miss Lake, we are all more or less cowards or deceivers—at least, to the extent of suppression. Who would speak the whole truth, or like to hear it ?—not I, I know.'

'Nor I,' she said, quietly.

'And I do think, if people had no reserves, they would be very uninteresting,' he added.

She was looking, with a strange light upon her face—a smile, perhaps—upon the open pages of 'Moore's Melodies' as he spoke.

'I like a little puzzle and mystery—they surround our future and our past ; and the present would be insipid, I think, without them. Now, I can't tell, Miss Lake, as you look on Tom Moore there, and I try to read your smile, whether you happen at this particular moment to adore or despise him.'

'Moore's is a daring morality—what do you think, for instance, of these lines ? ' she said, touching the verse with her bouquet.

Lord Chelford read—

> ' I ask not, I know not, if guilt's in thy heart :
> I but know that I love thee, whatever thou art.'

He laughed.

'Very passionate, but hardly respectable. I once knew,' he continued a little more gravely, 'a marriage made upon that principle, and not very audaciously either, which turned out very unhappily.'

'So I should conjecture,' she said, rising from her chair, rather drearily and abstractedly, 'and there is good old Lady Sarah. I must go and ask her how she does.' She paused for a moment, holding her bouquet drooping towards the floor, and looking with her clouded eyes down—down—through it ; and then she looked up suddenly, with an odd, fierce smile, and she said bitterly enough—'and yet, if I were a man, and capable of loving, I could love no other way ; because I suppose love to be a madness, and the sublimest and the most despicable of states. And I admire Moore for that flash of the fallen angelic—it is the sentiment of a hero and a madman—too base and too *noble* for this cool, wise world.'

She was already moving away, nebulous in hovering folds of snowy muslin. And she floated down like a cloud upon the ottoman, beside old Lady Sarah, and smiled and leaned towards her, and talked in her sweet, low, distinct accents. And Lord Chelford followed her, with a sad sort of smile, admiring her greatly.

Of course, *non cuivis contigit*, it was not every man's privilege to dance with the splendid Lady of Brandon. It was only the demigods who ventured within the circle. Her kinsman, Lord Chelford, did so ; and now handsome Sir Harry Bracton, six feet high, so broad-shouldered and slim-waisted, his fine but not very wise face irradiated with indefatigable smiles, stood and conversed with her, with that jaunty swagger of his—his weight now on this side, now on that, squaring his elbows like a crack whip with four-in-hand, and wagging his perfumed tresses—boisterous, rollicking, beaming with immeasurable self-complacency.

Stanley Lake left old Lady Chelford's side, and glided to that of Dorcas Brandon.

'Will you dance this set—are you engaged, Miss Brandon ?' he said, in low eager tones.

'Yes, to both questions,' answered she, with the faintest gleam of the conventional smile, and looking now gravely again at her bouquet.

'Well, the next possibly, I hope ?'

'I never do that,' said the apathetic beauty, serenely.

Stanley looked as if he did not quite understand, and there was a little silence.

'I mean, I never engage myself beyond one dance. I hope you do not think it rude—but I never do.'

'Miss Brandon can make what laws she pleases for all here, and for some of us everywhere,' he replied, with a mortified smile and a bow.

At that moment Sir Harry Bracton arrived to claim her, and Miss Kybes—elderly and sentimental, and in no great request—timidly said, in a gobbling, confidential whisper—

'What a handsome couple they do make ! Does not it quite realise your conception, Captain Lake, of young Lochinvar, you know, and his fair Helen—

So stately his form and so lovely her face—

You remember—

'That never a hall such a galliard did grace.

Is not it?'

'So it is, really; it did not strike me. And that "one cup of wine"—you recollect—which the hero drank; and, I dare say it made young Lochinvar a little noisy and swaggering, when he proposed "treading the measure"—is not that the phrase? Yes, really; it is a very pretty poetical parallel.'

And Miss Kybes was pleased to think that Captain Lake would be sure to report her elegant little compliment in the proper quarters, and that her incense had not missed fire.

When Miss Brandon returned, Lake was unfortunately on duty beside old Lady Chelford, whom it was important to propitiate, and who was in the middle of a story—an extraordinary favour from her ladyship; and he had the vexation to see Lord Chelford palpably engaging Miss Brandon for the next dance.

When she returned, she was a little tired, and doubtful whether she would dance any more—certainly not the next dance. So he resolved to lie in wait, and anticipate any new suitor who might appear.

His eyes, however, happened to wander, in an unlucky moment, to old Lady Chelford, who instantaneously signalled to him with her fan.

'— the woman,' mentally exclaimed Lake, telegraphing, at the same time, with a bow and a smile of deferential alacrity, and making his way through the crowd as deftly as he could; what a —— fool I was to go near her.'

So the captain had to assist at the dowager lady's supper; and not only so, but in some sort at her digestion also, which she chose should take place for some ten minutes in the chair that she occupied at the supper table.

When he escaped, Miss Brandon *was* engaged once more—and to Sir Harry Bracton, for a second time.

And moreover, when he again essayed his suit, the young lady had peremptorily made up her mind to dance no more that night.

'How *can* Dorcas endure that man,' thought Rachel, as she saw Sir Harry lead her to her seat, after a second dance. 'Handsome, but so noisy and foolish, and wicked; and is not he vulgar, too?'

But Dorcas was not demonstrative. Her likings and dislikings were always more or less enigmatical. Still Rachel Lake fancied that she detected signs, not only of tolerance, but of positive liking, in her haughty cousin's demeanour, and wondered, after all, whether Dorcas was beginning to like Sir Harry Bracton. Dorcas had always puzzled her—not, indeed, so much latterly—but this night the mystery began to darken once more.

Twice, for a moment, their eyes met; but only for a moment. Rachel knew that a tragedy might be—at that instant, and under the influence of that very spectacle—gathering its thunders silently in another part of the room, where she saw Stanley's pale, peculiar face; and although he appeared in nowise occupied by what was passing between Dorcas Brandon and Sir Harry, she perfectly well knew that nothing of it escaped him.

The sight of that pale face was a cold pang at her heart—a face prophetic of evil, at sight of which the dark curtain which hid futurity seemed to sway and tremble, as if a hand from behind was on the point of drawing it. Rachel sighed profoundly, and her eyes looked sadly through her bouquet on the floor.

'I'm very glad you came, Radie,' said a sweet voice, which somehow made her shiver, close to her ear. 'This kind of thing will do you good; and you really wanted a little fillip. Shall I take you to the supper-room?'

'No, Stanley, thank you; I prefer remaining.'

'Have you observed how Dorcas has treated me this evening?'

'No, Stanley; nothing unusual, is there?' answered Rachel, glancing uneasily round, lest they should be overheard.

'Well, I think she has been more than usually repulsive—quite marked; I almost fancy these Gylingden people, dull as they are, must observe it. I have a notion I sha'n't trouble Gylingden or her after to-morrow.'

Rachel glanced quickly at him. He was deadly pale, with his faint unpleasant smile; and he returned her glance for a second wildly, and then dropped his eyes to the ground.

'I told you,' he resumed again, after a short pause, and commencing with a gentle laugh, 'that she liked that fellow, Bracton.'

'You did say something, I think, of that, some time since,' said Rachel; 'but really——'

'But really, Radie, dear, you can't need any confirmation more than this evening affords. We both know Dorcas very well; she is not like other girls. She does not encourage fellows as they do; but if she did not like Bracton very well indeed, she would send him about his business. She has danced with him twice, on the contrary, and has suffered his agreeable conversation all the evening; and that from Dorcas Brandon means, you know, everything.'

'I don't know that it means anything. I don't see why it should; but I am very certain,' said Rachel, who, in the midst of this crowded, gossiping ball-room, was talking much more freely to Stanley, and also, strange to say, in more sisterly fashion, than she would have done in the little parlour of Redman's Farm; 'I am very certain, Stanley, that if this supposed preference leads you to abandon your wild pursuit of Dorcas, it will prevent more ruin than, perhaps, either of us anticipates; and, Stanley,' she added in a whisper, looking full in his eyes, which were raised for a moment to hers, 'it is hardly credible that you dare still to persist in so desperate and cruel a project.'

'Thank you,' said Stanley quietly, but the yellow lights glared fiercely from their sockets, and were then lowered instantly to the floor.

'She has been very rude to me to-night; and you have not been, or tried to be, of any earthly use to me; and I will take a decided course. I perfectly know what I'm about. You don't seem to be dancing. *I* have not either; we have both got something more serious, I fancy, to think of.'

And Stanley Lake glided slowly away, and was lost in the crowd. He went into the supper-room, and had a glass of seltzer water and sherry. He loitered at the table. His ruminations were dreary, I fancy, and his temper by no means pleasant; and it needed a good deal of that artificial command of countenance which he cultivated, to prevent his betraying something of the latter, when Sir Harry Bracton, talking loud and volubly as usual, swaggered into the supper-room, with Dorcas Brandon on his arm.

CHAPTER XXXVII.

THE SUPPER-ROOM.

IT was rather trying, in this state of things, to receive from the triumphant baronet, with only a parenthetical 'Dear Lake, I beg your pardon,' a rough knock on the elbow of the hand that held his glass, and to be then summarily hustled out of his place. It was no mitigation of the rudeness, in Lake's estimate, that Sir Harry was so engrossed and elated as to seem hardly conscious of any existence but Miss Brandon's and his own.

Lake was subject to transient paroxysms of exasperation; but even in these he knew how to command himself pretty well before witnesses. His smile grew a little stranger, and his face a degree whiter, as he set down his glass, quietly glided a little away, and brushed off with his handkerchief the aspersion which his coat had suffered.

In a few minutes more Miss Brandon had left the supper-room leaning upon Lord Chelford's arm; and Sir Harry remained, with a glass of pink champagne, such as young fellows drink with a faith and comfort so wonderful, at balls and *fêtes champêtres.*

Sir Harry Bracton was already ' chaffing a bit,' as he expressed it, with the young lady who assisted in dispensing the good things across the supper-table, and was just calling up her blushes by a pretty parallel between her eyes and the sparkling quality of his glass, and telling her her mamma must have been sweetly pretty.

Now, Sir Harry's rudeness to Lake had not been, I am afraid, altogether accidental. The baronet was sudden and vehement in his affairs of the heart ; but curable on short absences, and easily transferable. He had been vehemently enamoured of the heiress of Brandon a year ago and more ; but during an absence Mark Wylder's suit grew up and prospered, and Sir Harry Bracton acquiesced ; and, to say truth, the matter troubled his manly breast but little.

He had hardly expected to see her here in this rollicking, rustic gathering. She was, he thought, even more lovely than he remembered her. Beauty sometimes seen again does excel our recollections of it. Wylder had gone off the scene, as Mr. Carlyle says, into infinite space. Who could tell exactly the cause of his dismissal, and why the young lady had asserted her capricious resolve to be free ?

There were pleasant theories adaptable to the circumstances ; and Sir Harry cherished an agreeable opinion of himself ; and so, all things favouring, the old flame blazed up wildly, and the young gentleman was more in love then, and for some weeks after the ball, than perhaps he had ever been before.

Now some men—and Sir Harry was of them—are churlish and ferocious over their loves, as certain brutes are over their victuals. In one of these tender paroxysms, when in the presence of his Dulcinea, the young baronet was always hot, short, and saucy with his own sex ; and when his jealousy was ever so little touched, positively impertinent.

He perceived what other people did not, that Miss Brandon's eye once on that evening rested for a moment on Captain Lake with a peculiar expression of interest. This look was but once and momentary ; but the young gentleman resented it, and brooded over it, every now and then, when the pale face of the captain crossed his eye ; and two or three times, when the beautiful young lady's attention seemed unaccountably to wander from his agreeable conversation, he thought he detected her haughty eye moving in the same direction. So he looked that way too ; and although he could see nothing noticeable in Stanley's demeanour, he could have felt it in his heart to box his ears.

Therefore, I don't think he was quite so careful as he might have been to spare Lake that jolt upon the elbow, which coming from a rival in a moment of public triumph was not altogether easy to bear like a Christian.

'Some grapes, please,' said Lake, to the young lady behind the table.

'Oh, *uncle!* Is that you, Lake?—beg pardon; but you *are* so like my poor dear uncle, Langton. I wish you'd let me adopt you for an uncle. He was such a pretty fellow, with his fat white cheeks and long nose, and he looked half asleep. Do, pray, Uncle Lake; I should like it so,' and the baronet, who was, I am afraid, what some people would term, perhaps, vulgar, winked over his glass at the blooming confectioner, who turned away and tittered over her shoulder at the handsome baronet's charming banter.

The girl having turned away to titter, forgot Lake's grapes; so he helped himself, and leaning against the table, looked superciliously upon Sir Harry, who was not to be deterred by the drowsy gaze of contempt with which the captain retorted his angry 'chaff.'

'Poor uncle died of love, or chicken pox, or something, at forty. You're not ailing, Nunkie, are you? You do look wofully sick though; too bad to lose a second uncle at the same early age. You're near forty, eh, Nunkie? and such a pretty fellow! You'll take care of me in your will, Nunkie, won't you? Come, what will you leave me; not much tin, I'm afraid.'

'No, not much tin,' answered Lake; 'but I'll leave you what you want more, my sense and decency, with a request that you will use them for my sake.'

'You're a devilish witty fellow, Lake; take care your wit don't get you into trouble,' said the baronet, chuckling and growing angrier, for he saw the Hebe laughing; and not being a ready man, though given to banter, he sometimes descended to menace in his jocularity.

'I was just thinking your dulness might do the same for you,' drawled Lake.

'When do you mean to pay Dawlings that bet on the Derby?' demanded Sir Harry, his face very red, and only the ghost of his smile grinning there. 'I think you'd better; of course it is quite easy.'

The baronet was smiling his best, with a very red face, and that unpleasant uncertainty in his contracted eyes which accompanies suppressed rage.

'As easy as that,' said Lake, chucking a little bunch of grapes full into Sir Harry Bracton's handsome face.

Lake recoiled a step; his face blanched as white as the cloth; his left arm lifted, and his right hand grasping the haft of a table-knife.

There was just a second in which the athletic baronet stood, as it were breathless and incredulous, and then his Herculean fist whirled in the air with a most unseemly oath: the girl screamed, and a crash of glass and crockery, whisked away by their coats, resounded on the ground.

A chair between Lake and Sir Harry impeded the baronet's stride, and his uplifted arm was caught by a gentleman in moustache, who held so fast that there was no chance of shaking it loose.

'D— it, Bracton ; d— you, what the devil—don't be a—fool,' and other soothing expressions escaped this peacemaker, as he clung fast to the young baronet's arm.

'The people—hang it !—you'll have all the people about you. Quiet—quiet—can't you, I say. Settle it quietly. Here I am.'

'Well, let me go ; that will do,' said he, glowering furiously at Lake, who confronted him, in the same attitude, a couple of yards away. 'You'll hear,' and he turned away.

'I am at the "Brandon Arms" till to-morrow,' said Lake, with white lips, very quietly, to the gentleman in moustaches, who bowed slightly, and walked out of the room with Sir Harry.

Lake poured out some sherry in a tumbler, and drank it off. He was a little bit stunned, I think, in his new situation.

Except for the waiters, and the actors in it, it so happened that the supper-room was empty during this sudden fracas. Lake stared at the frightened girl, in his fierce abstraction. Then, with his wild gaze, he followed the line of his adversary's retreat, and shook his ears slightly, like a man at whose hair a wasp has buzzed.

'Thank you,' said he to the maid, suddenly recollecting himself, with a sort of smile ; 'that will do. What confounded nonsense ! He'll be quite cool again in five minutes. Never mind.'

And Lake pulled on his white glove, glancing down the file of silent waiters—some looking frightened, and some reserved—in white ties and waistcoats, and he glided out of the room—his mind somewhere else—like a somnambulist.

It was not perfectly clear to the gentlemen and ladies in charge of the ices, chickens, and champagne, between which of the three swells who had just left the room the quarrel was—it had come so suddenly, and was over so quickly, like a clap of thunder. Some had not seen any, and others only a bit of it, being busy with plates and ice-tubs ; and the few who had seen it all did not clearly comprehend it— only it was certain that the row had originated in jealousy about Miss Jones, the pretty apprentice, who was judiciously withdrawn forthwith by Mrs. Page, the properest of confectioners.

CHAPTER XXXVIII.

AFTER THE BALL.

LAKE glided from the feast with a sense of a tremendous liability upon him. There was no retreat. The morning—yes, the morning—what then? Should he live to see the evening? Sir Harry Bracton was the crack shot of Swivel's gallery. He could hit a walking-cane at fifteen yards, at the word. There he was, talking to old Lady Chelford. Very well; and there was that fellow with the twisted moustache — plainly an officer and a gentleman — twisting the end of one of them, and thinking profoundly, with his back to the wall, evidently considering his coming diplomacy with Lake's 'friend.' Aye, by-the-bye, and Lake's eye wandered in bewilderment among village dons and elderly country gentlemen, in search of that inestimable treasure.

These thoughts went whisking and whirling round in Captain Lake's brain, to the roar and clatter of the Joinville Polka, to which fifty pair of dancing feet were hopping and skimming over the floor.

'Monstrous hot, Sir—hey? ha, ha, by Jove!' said Major Jackson, who had just returned from the supper-room, where he had heard several narratives of the occurrence. 'Don't think I was so hot since the ball at Government House, by Jove, Sir, in 1828—awful summer that!'

The major was jerking his handkerchief under his florid nose and chin, by way of ventilation; and eyeing the young man shrewdly the while, to read what he might of the story in his face.

'Been in Calcutta, Lake?'

'No; very hot, indeed. Could I say just a word with you—this way a little. So glad I met you.' And they edged into a little nook of the lobby, where they had a few minutes' confidential talk, during which the major looked grave and consequential, and carried his head high, nodding now and then with military decision.

Major Jackson whispered an abrupt word or two in his ear, and threw back his head, eyeing Lake with grave and sly defiance. Then came another whisper and a wink; and the major shook his hand, briefly but hard, and the gentlemen parted.

Lake strolled into the ball-room, and on to the upper end, where the 'best' people are, and suddenly he was in Miss Brandon's presence.

'I've been very presumptuous, I fear, to-night, Miss **Brandon**,' he said, in his peculiar low tones. 'I've been very importunate —I prized the honour I sought so very much, I forgot how little I deserved it. And I do not think it likely you'll see me for a good while—possibly for a very long time. I've therefore ventured to come, merely to say good-bye—only that, just—good-bye. And—and to beg that flower'—and he plucked it resolutely from her bouquet—'which I will keep while I live. Good-bye, Miss Brandon.'

And Captain Stanley Lake, that pale apparition, was gone.

I do not know at all how Miss Brandon felt at this instant; for I never could quite understand that strange lady. But I believe she looked a little pale as she gravely adjusted the flowers so audaciously violated by the touch of the cool young gentleman.

I can't say whether Miss Brandon deigned to follow him with her dark, dreamy gaze. I rather think not. And three minutes afterwards he had left the Town Hall.

The Brandon party did not stay very late. And they dropped Rachel at her little dwelling. How very silent Dorcas was, thought Rachel, as they drove from Gylingden. Perhaps others were thinking the same of Rachel.

Next morning, at half-past seven o'clock, a dozen or so of rustics, under command of Major Jackson, arrived at the back entrance of Brandon Hall, bearing Stanley Lake upon a shutter, with glassy eyes, that did not seem to see, sunken face, and a very blue tinge about his mouth.

The major fussed into the house, and saw and talked with Larcom, who was solemn and bland upon the subject, and went out, first, to make personal inspection of the captain, who seemed to him to be dying. He was shot somewhere in the shoulder or breast—they could not see exactly where, nor disturb him as he lay. A good deal of blood had flowed from him, upon the arm and side of one of the men who supported his head.

Lake said nothing—he only whispered rather indistinctly one word, 'water'—and was not able to lift his head when it came ; and when they poured it into and over his lips, he sighed and closed his eyes.

'It is not a bad sign, bleeding so freely, but he looks devilish shaky, you see. I've seen lots of our fellows hit, you know, and I don't like his looks—poor fellow. You'd better see Lord Chelford this minute. He could not stand being brought all the way to the town. I'll run down and send up the doctor, and he'll take him on if he can bear it.'

Major Jackson did not run. Though I have seen with an astonishment that has never subsided, fellows just as old and as fat, and braced up, besides, in the inflexibilities of regimentals,

keeping up at double quick, at the heads of their companies, for
a good quarter of a mile, before the colonel on horseback mercifully called a halt.

He walked at his best pace, however, and indeed was confoundedly uneasy about his own personal liabilities.

The major surprised Doctor Buddle shaving. He popped in
unceremoniously. The fat little doctor received him in drawers
and a very tight web worsted shirt, standing by the window, at
which dangled a small looking-glass.

'By George, Sir, they've been at mischief,' burst forth the
major ; and the doctor, razor in hand, listened with wide open
eyes and half his face lathered, to the story. Before it was
over the doctor shaved the unshorn side, and (the major still in
the room) completed his toilet in hot haste.

Honest Major Jackson was very uncomfortable. Of course,
Buddle could not give any sort of opinion upon a case which he
had not seen ; but it described uglily, and the major consulted
in broken hints, with an uneasy wink or two, about a flight to
Boulogne.

'Well, it will be no harm to be ready ; but take no step till I
come back,' said the doctor, who had stuffed a great roll of lint
and plaister, and some other medicinals, into one pocket, and
his leather case of instruments, forceps, probe, scissors, and all
the other steel and silver horrors, into the other ; so he strutted
forth in his great coat, unnaturally broad about the hips ; and
the major, 'devilish uncomfortable,' accompanied him at a
smart pace to the great gate of Brandon. He did not care to
enter, feeling a little guilty, although he explained on the way
all about the matter. How devilish stiff Bracton's man was
about it. And, by Jove, Sir ! you know, what was to be said ?
for Lake, like a fool, chucked a lot of grapes in his face—for
nothing, by George !'

The doctor, short and broad, was now stumping up the
straight avenue, under the noble trees that roofed it over, and
Major Jackson sauntered about in the vicinity of the gate,
more interested in Lake's safety than he would have believed
possible a day or two before.

Lord Chelford being an early man, was, notwithstanding
the ball of the preceding night, dressing, when St. Ange, his
Swiss servant, knocked at his door with a dozen pockethand-
kerchiefs, a bottle of eau-de-cologne, and some other properties
of his metier.

St. Ange could not wait until he had laid them down, but
broke out with—

'Oh, mi Lor !—qu'est-il arrivé?—le pauvre capitaine ! il est tué
—il se meurt—he dies—d'un coup de pistolet. He comes de se
battre from beating himself in duel — il a été atteint dans la
poitrine—le pauvre gentil-homme ! of a blow of the pistol.'

And so on, the young nobleman gathering the facts as best he might.

'Is Larcom there?'

'In the gallery, mi lor.'

'Ask him to come in.'

So Monsieur Larcom entered, and bowed ominously.

'You've seen him, Larcom. Is he very much hurt?'

'He appears, my lord, to me, I regret to say, almost a-dying like.'

'Very weak? Does he speak to you?'

'Not a word, my lord. Since he got a little water he's quite quiet.'

'Poor fellow. Where have you put him?'

'In the housekeeper's lobby, my lord. I rather think he's a-dying. He looks uncommon bad, and I and Mrs. Esterbroke, the housekeeper, my lord, thought you would not like he should die out of doors.'

'Has she got your mistress's directions?'

'Miss Brandon is not called up, my lord, and Mrs. Esterbroke is unwillin' to halarm her; so she thought it better I should come for orders to your lordship; which she thinks also the poor young gentleman is certainly a-dying.'

'Is there any vacant bed-room near where you have placed him? What does Mrs. —— the housekeeper, say?'

'She thinks, my lord, the room hopposit, where Mr. Sledd. the architeck, slep, when 'ere, would answer very nice. It is roomy and hairy, and no steps. Majòr Jackson, who is gone to the town to fetch the doctor, my lord, says Mr. Lake won't a-bear carriage; and so the room on the level, my lord, would, perhaps, be more convenient.'

'Certainly; tell her so. I will speak to Miss Brandon when she comes down. How soon will the doctor be here?'

'From a quarter to half an hour, my lord.'

'Then tell the housekeeper to arrange as she proposes, and don't remove his clothes until the doctor comes. Everyone must assist. I know, St. Ange, you'll like to assist.'

So Larcom withdrew ceremoniously, and Lord Chelford hastened his toilet, and was down stairs, and in the room assigned by the housekeeper to the ill-starred Captain Lake, before Doctor Buddle had arrived.

It had already the dismal character of a sick chamber. Its light was darkened; its talk was in whispers; and its to-ings and fro-ings on tip-toe. An obsolete chambermaid had been already installed as nurse. Little Mrs. Esterbroke, the housekeeper, was fussing hither and thither about the room noiselessly.

So this gay, astute man of fashion had fallen into the dungeon of sudden darkness, and the custody of old women; and lay

helpless in the stocks, awaiting the judgment of Buddle.
Ridiculous little pudgy Buddle—how awful on a sudden are
you grown—the interpreter of death in this very case. '*My*
case,' thought that seemingly listless figure on the bed ; '*my*
case—I suppose it *is* fatal—I am to go out of this room in a
long cloth-covered box. I am going to try, alone and for ever,
the value of those theories of futurity and the unseen which I
have quietly scouted all my days. Oh, that the prophet Buddle
were here, to end my tremendous suspense, and to announce a
reprieve from Heaven.'

While the wounded captain lay on the bed, with his clothes
on, and the coverlet over him, and that clay-coloured apathetic
face, with closed eyes, upon the pillow, without sigh or motion,
not a whispered word escaped him ; but his brain was appalled,
and his heart died within him in the unspeakable horror of
death.

Lord Chelford, too, having looked on Lake with silent, but
awful misgivings, longed for the arrival of the doctor ; and was
listening and silent when Buddle's short step and short respiration were heard in the passage. So Larcom came to the door
to announce the doctor in a whisper, and Buddle fussed into
the room, and made his bow to Lord Chelford, and his brief
compliments and condolences.

' Not asleep?' he enquired, standing by the bed.

The captain's lips moved a disclaimer, I suppose, but no
sound came.

So the doctor threw open the window-shutters, and clipped
Stanley Lake's exquisite coat ruthlessly through with his scissors,
and having cleared the room of all useless hands, he made his
examination.

It was a long visit. Buddle in the hall afterwards declined
breakfast—he had a board to attend. He told Lord Chelford
that the case was ' a very nasty one.'

In fact, the chances were against the captain, and he, Buddle,
would wish a consultation with a London surgeon—whoever
Lord Chelford had most confidence in—Sir Francis Seddley,
he thought, would be very desirable—but, of course, it was for
the family to decide. If the messenger caught the quarter to
eleven up train at Dollington, he would be in London at six,
and could return with the doctor by the down mail train, and
so reach Dollington at ten minutes past four next morning,
which would answer, as he would not operate sooner.

As the doctor toddled towards Gylingden, with sympathetic
Major Jackson by his side, before they entered the town they
were passed by one of the Brandon men riding at a hard canter
for Dollington.

' London?' shouted the doctor, as the man touched his hat
in passing.

'Yes, Sir.'

'Glad o' that,' said the major, looking after him.

'So am I,' said the learned Buddle. 'I don't see how we're to get the bullet out of him, without mischief. Poor devil, I'm afraid he'll do no good.'

The ladies that morning had tea in their rooms. It was near twelve o'clock when Lord Chelford saw Miss Brandon. She was in the conservatory amongst her flowers, and on seeing him stepped into the drawing-room.

'I hope, Dorcas, you are not angry with me. I've been, I'm afraid, very impertinent; but I was called on to decide for you, in your absence, and they all thought poor Lake could not be moved on to Gylingden without danger.'

'You did quite rightly, Chelford, and I thank you,' said Miss Brandon, coldly; and she seated herself, and continued—

'Pray, what does the doctor really say?'

'He speaks very seriously.'

'Does he think there is danger?'

'Very great danger.'

Miss Brandon looked down, and then, with a pale gaze suddenly in Chelford's face—

'He thinks he may die?' said she.

'Yes,' said Lord Chelford, in a very low tone, returning her gaze solemnly.

'And nobody to advise but that village doctor, Buddle—that's hardly credible, I think.'

'Pardon me. At his suggestion I have sent for Sir Francis Seddley, from town, and I hope he may arrive early to-morrow morning.'

'Why, Stanley Lake may die to-day.'

'He does not apprehend that. But it is necessary to remove the bullet, and the operation will be critical, and it is for that specially that Sir Francis is coming down.'

'It is to take place to-morrow, and he'll die in that operation. You know he'll die,' said Dorcas, pale and fierce.

'I assure you, Dorcas, I have been perfectly frank. He looks upon poor Lake as in very great danger—but that is all.'

'What brutes you men are!' said Dorcas, with a wild scorn in her look and accent, and her cheeks flushed with passion. 'You knew quite well last night there was to be this wicked duel in the morning—and you—a magistrate—a lord-lieutenant —what are you?—you connived at this bloody conspiracy—and *he*—your own cousin, Chelford—your cousin!'

Chelford looked at her, very much amazed.

'Yes; you are worse than Sir Harry Bracton—for you're no fool; and worse than that wicked old man, Major Jackson— who shall never enter these doors again—for he was employed —trusted in their brutal plans; but you had no excuse and every opportunity—and you have allowed your Cousin Stanley to be murdered.'

'You do me great injustice, Dorcas. I did not know, or even suspect that a hostile meeting between poor Lake and Bracton was thought of. I merely heard that there had been some trifling altercation in the supper-room; and when, intending to make peace between them, I alluded to it, just before we left, and Bracton said it was really nothing—quite blown over—and that he could not recollect what either had said. I was entirely deceived—you know I speak truth—quite deceived. They think it fair, you know, to dupe other people in such affairs; and I will also say,' he continued, a little haughtily, 'that you might have spared your censure until at least you had heard what I had to say.'

'I do believe you, Chelford; you are not vexed with me. Won't you shake hands?'

He took her hand with a smile.

'And now,' said she, 'Chelford, ought not we to send for poor Rachel: her only brother? Is not it sad?'

'Certainly; shall I ask my mother, or will you write?'

'I will write,' she said.

CHAPTER XXXIX.

IN WHICH MISS RACHEL LAKE COMES TO BRANDON, AND DOCTOR BUDDLE CALLS AGAIN.

IN about an hour afterwards, Rachel Lake arrived in the carriage which had been despatched for her with Dorcas's note.

She was a good deal muffled up, and looked very pale, and asked whether Miss Brandon was in her room, whither she glided rapidly up stairs. It was a sort of boudoir or dressing-room, with a few pretty old portraits and miniatures, and a number of Louis Quatorze looking-glasses hung round, and such pretty quaint cabriole gilt and pale green furniture.

Dorcas met her at the door, and they kissed silently.

'How is he, Dorcas?'

'Very ill, dear, I'm afraid—sit down, darling.'

Rachel was relieved, for in her panic she almost feared to ask if he were living.

'Is there immediate danger?'

'The doctor says not, but he is very much alarmed for to-morrow.'

'Oh! Dorcas, darling, he'll die; I know it. Oh! merciful Heaven! how tremendous.'

'You will not be so frightened in a little time. You have only just heard it, Rachel dearest, and you are startled. I was so myself.'

'I'd like to see him, Dorcas.'

'Sit here a little and rest, dear. The doctor will make his visit immediately, and then we can ask him. He's a good-natured little creature—poor old Buddle—and I am certain if it can safely be, he won't prevent it.'

'Where is he, darling—where is Stanley?'

So Dorcas described as well as she could.

'Oh, poor Stanley. Oh, Stanley — poor Stanley,' gasped Rachel, with white lips. 'You have no idea, Dorcas—no one can—how terrific it is. Oh, poor Stanley—poor Stanley.'

'Drink this water, darling ; you must not be so excited.'

'Dorcas, say what the doctor may, see him I must.'

'There is time to think of that, darling.'

'Has he spoken to anyone?'

'Very little, I believe. He whispers a few words now and then—that is all.'

'Nothing to Chelford—nothing particular, I mean?'

'No—nothing—at least that I have heard of.'

'Did he wish to see no one?'

'No one, dear.'

'Not poor William Wylder?'

'No, dear. I don't suppose he cares more for a clergyman than for any other man ; none of his family ever did, when they came to lie on a bed of sickness, or of death either.'

'No, no,' said Rachel, wildly ; 'I did not mean to pray. I was not thinking of that ; but William Wylder was different ; and he did not mention *me* either?'

Dorcas shook her head.

'I knew it,' continued Rachel, with a kind of shudder. 'And tell me, Dorcas, does he know that he is in danger—such imminent danger?'

'That I cannot say, Rachel, dear. I don't believe doctors like to tell their patients so.'

There was a silence of some minutes, and Rachel, clasping her hands in an agony, said—

'Oh, yes—he's gone—he's certainly gone ; and I remain alone under that dreadful burden.'

'Please, Miss Brandon, the doctor's down stairs with Captain Lake,' said the maid, opening the door.

'Is Lord Chelford with him?'

'Yes, Miss, please.'

'Then tell him I will be so obliged if he will come here for a moment, when the doctor is gone ; and ask the doctor now, from me, how he thinks Captain Lake.'

In a little while the maid returned. Captain Lake was not

so low, and rather better than this morning, the doctor said ; and Rachel raised her eyes, and whispered an agitated thanksgiving. 'Was Lord Chelford coming ?'

'His lordship had left the room when she returned, and Mr. Larcom said he was with Lawyer Larkin in the library.'

'Mr. Larkin can wait. Tell Lord Chelford I wish very much to see him here.'

So away went the maid again. A message in that great house was a journey ; and there was a little space before they heard a knock at the door of Dorcas's pretty room, and Lord Chelford, duly invited, came in.

Lord Chelford was surprised to see Rachel, and held her hand, while he congratulated her on the more favourable opinion of the physician this afternoon ; and then he gave them, as fully and exactly as he could, all the lights emitted by Dr. Buddle, and endeavoured to give his narrative as cheerful and confident an air as he could. Then, at length, he recollected that Mr. Larkin was waiting in the study.

'I quite forgot Mr. Larkin,' said he ; 'I left him in the library, and I am so very glad we have had a pleasanter report upon poor Lake this evening ; and I am sure we shall all feel more comfortable on seeing Sir Francis Seddley. He *is* such an admirable surgeon ; and I feel sure he'll strike out something for our poor patient. I've known him hit upon such original expedients, and make such wonderful successes.'

So with a kind smile he left the room.

Then there was a long pause.

'Does he really think that Stanley will recover ?' said Rachel.

'I don't know ; I suppose he hopes it. I don't know, Rachel, what to think of anyone or anything. What wild beasts they are. How "swift to shed blood," as poor William Wylder said last Sunday. Have you any idea what they quarrelled about ?'

'None in the world. It was that odious Sir Harry Bracton —was not it ?'

'Why so odious, Rachel ? How can you tell which was in the wrong ? I only know he seems to be a better marksman than your poor brother.'

Rachel looked at her with something of haughty and surprised displeasure, but said nothing.

'You look at me, Radie, as if I were a monster—or *monstress*, I should say—whereas I am only a Brandon. Don't you remember how our great ancestor, who fought for the House of York, changed suddenly to Lancaster, and how Sir Richard left the King and took part with Cromwell, not for any particular advantage, I believe, or for any particular reason even, but for wickedness and wounded pride, perhaps.'

'I don't quite see your meaning, Dorcas. I can't understand how *your* pride has been hurt ; but if Stanley had any, I can well imagine what torture it must have endured; wretched, wicked, punished fool!'

'You suspect what they fought about, Radie!'

Rachel made no answer.

'You do, Radie, and why do you dissemble with me?'

'I don't dissemble; I don't care to speak; but if you will have me say so, I *do* suspect—I think it must have originated in jealousy of you.'

'You look, Radie, as if you thought I had managed it — whereas I really did not care.'

'I do not understand you, Dorcas; but you appear to me very cruel, and you smile, as I say so.'

'I smile, because I sometimes think so myself.'

With a fixed and wrathful stare Rachel returned the enigmatical gaze of her beautiful cousin.

'If Stanley dies, Dorcas, Sir Harry Bracton shall hear of it. I'll lose my life, but he shall pay the forfeit of his crime.'

So saying, Rachel left the room, and gliding through passages, and down stairs, she knocked at Stanley's door. The old woman opened it.

'Ah, Dorothy! I'm so glad to see *you* here!' and she put a present in her hard, crumpled hand.

So, noiselessly, Rachel Lake, without more parley, stepped into the room, and closed the door. She was alone with Stanley. With a beating heart, and a kind of chill stealing over her, by her brother's bed.

The room was not so dark that she could not see distinctly enough.

There lay her brother, such as he was—still her brother, on the bleak, neutral ground between life and death. His features, peaked and earthy, and that look, so new and peculiar, which does not savour of life upon them. He did not move, but his strange eyes gazed cold and earnest from their deep sockets upon her face in awful silence. Perhaps he thought he saw a phantom.

'Are you better, dear?' whispered Rachel.

His lips stirred and his throat, but he did not speak until a second effort brought utterance, and he murmured,

'Is that you, Radie?'

'Yes, dear. Are you better?'

'*No.* I'm shot. I shall die to-night. Is it night yet?'

'Don't despair, Stanley, dear. The great London doctor, Sir Francis Seddley, will be with you early in the morning, and Chelford has great confidence in him. I'm sure he will relieve you.'

'This is Brandon?' murmured Lake.

'Yes, dear.'

She thought he was going to say more, but he remained silent, and she recollected that he ought not to speak, and also that she had that to say which must be said.

Sharp, dark, and strange lay that familiar face upon the white pillow. The faintest indication of something like a peevish sneer ; it might be only the lines of pain and fatigue ; still it had that unpleasant character remaining fixed on its features.

' Oh, Stanley ! you say you think you are dying. Won't you send for William Wylder and Chelford, and tell all you know of Mark ? '

She saw he was about to say something, and she leaned her head near his lips, and she heard him whisper,—

' It won't serve Mark.'

' I'm thinking of *you*, Stanley—I'm thinking of you.'

To which he said either ' Yes ' or ' So.' She could not distinguish.

' I view it now quite differently. You said, you know, in the park, you would tell Chelford ; and I resisted, I believe, but I don't now. I had *rather* you did. Yes, Stanley, I conjure you to tell it all.'

The cold lips, with a livid halo round them, murmured, ' Thank you.'

It was a sneer, very shocking just then, perhaps ; but unquestionably a sneer.

' Poor Stanley ! ' she murmured, with a kind of agony, looking down upon that changed face. ' One word more, Stanley. Remember, it's I, the only one on earth who stands near you in kindred, your sister, Stanley, who implores of you to take this step before it is too late ; at least, to consider.'

He said something. She thought it was ' I'll think ;' and then he closed his eyes. It was the only motion she had observed, his face lay just as it had done on the pillow. He had not stirred all the time she was there ; and now that his eyelids closed, it seemed to say, our interview is over—the curtain has dropped ; and so understanding it, with that one awful look that may be the last, she glided from the bed-side, told old Dorothy that he seemed disposed to sleep, and left the room.

There is something awful always in the spectacle of such a sick-bed as that beside which Rachel had just stood. But not quite so dreadful is the sight as are the imaginings and the despair of absence. So reassuring is the familiar spectacle of life, even in its subsidence, so long as bodily torture and mental aberration are absent.

In the meanwhile, on his return to the library, Lord Chelford found his dowager mother in high chat with the attorney, whom she afterwards pronounced ' a very gentlemanlike man for his line of life.'

The conversation, indeed, was chiefly that of Lady Chelford, the exemplary attorney contributing, for the most part, a polite

acquiescence, and those reflections which most appositely
pointed the moral of her ladyship's tale, which concerned altogether the vagaries of Mark Wylder—a subject which piqued her
curiosity and irritated her passions.

It was a great day for Jos. Larkin ; for by the time Lord
Chelford returned the old lady had asked him to stay for dinner,
which he did, notwithstanding his morning dress, to his great
inward satisfaction, because he could henceforward mention,
' the other day, when I dined at Brandon,' or 'old Lady Chelford assured me, when last I dined at Brandon ;' and he could
more intimately speak of ' our friends at Brandon,' and ' the
Brandon people,' and, in short, this dinner was very serviceable
to the excellent attorney.

It was not very amusing this interchange of thought and
feeling between Larkin and the dowager, upon a theme already
so well ventilated as Mark Wylder's absconding, and therefore
I let it pass.

After dinner, when the dowager's place knew her no more,
Lord Chelford resumed his talk with Larkin.

' I am quite confirmed in the view I took at first,' he said.
' Wylder has no claim upon me. There are others on whom
much more naturally the care of his money would devolve, and
I think that my undertaking the office he proposes, under his
present strange circumstances, might appear like an acquiescence
in the extraordinary course he has taken, and a sanction
generally of his conduct, which I certainly can't approve. So,
Mr. Larkin, I have quite made up my mind. I have no business
to undertake this trust, simple as it is.'

' I have only, my lord, to bow to your lordship's decision ; at
the same time I cannot but feel, my lord, how peculiar and painful is the position in which it places me. There are rents to be
received by me, and sums handed over, to a considerable—I
may say, indeed, a very large amount : and my friend Lake—
Captain Lake—now, unhappily, in so very precarious a state,
appears to dislike the office, also, and to anticipate annoyance,
in the event of his consenting to act. Altogether, your lordship
will perceive that the situation is one of considerable, indeed
very great embarrassment, as respects me. There is, however,
one satisfactory circumstance disclosed in his last letter. His
return, he says, cannot be delayed beyond a very few months,
perhaps *weeks;* and he states, in his own rough way, that he will
then explain the motives of his conduct to the entire satisfaction
of all those who are cognizant of the measures which he has
adopted—no more claret, thanks—no more—a delicious wine—
and he adds, it will then be quite understood that he has acted
neither from caprice, nor from any motive other than self-preservation. I assure you, my lord, that is the identical phrase he
employs—self-preservation. I all along suspected, or, rather, I

mean, supposed, that Mr. Wylder had been placed in this matter under coercion—a—a threat.'

'A little more wine?' asked Lord Chelford, after another interval.

'No—no more, I thank you. Your lordship's very good, and the wine, I may say, excellent—delicious claret; indeed, quite so—ninety shillings a dozen, I should venture to say, and hardly to be had at that figure; but it grows late, I rather think, and the trustees of our little Wesleyan chapel—we've got a little into debt in that quarter, I am sorry to say—and I promised to advise with them this evening at nine o'clock. They have called me to counsel more than once, poor fellows; and so, with your lordship's permission, I'll withdraw.'

Lord Chelford walked with him to the steps. It was a beautiful night—very little moon, but that and the stars wonderfully clear and bright, and all things looking so soft and airy.

'Try one of these,' said the peer, presenting his cigar case.

Larkin, with a glow of satisfaction, took one of these noble cigars, and rolled it in his fingers, and smelt it.

'Fragrant—wonderfully fragrant!' he observed, meekly, with a connoisseur's shake of the head.

The night was altogether so charming that Lord Chelford was tempted. So he took his cap, and lighted his cigar, too, and strolled a little way with the attorney.

He walked under the solemn trees—the same under whose airy groyning Wylder and Lake had walked away together on that noteworthy night on which Mark had last turned his back upon the grand old gables and twisted chimneys of Brandon Hall.

This way was rather a round, it must be confessed, to the Lodge—Jos. Larkin's peaceful retreat. But a stroll with a lord was worth more than that sacrifice, and every incident which helped to make a colourable case of confidential relations at Brandon—a point in which the good attorney had been rather weak hitherto—was justly prized by that virtuous man.

If the trustees, Smith the pork-butcher, old Captain Snoggles, the Town Clerk, and the rest, had to wait some twenty minutes in the drawing-room at the Lodge, so much the better. An apology was, perhaps, the best and most modest shape into which he could throw the advertisement of his dinner at Brandon—his confidential talk with the proud old dowager, and his after-dinner ramble with that rising young peer, Lord Chelford. It would lead him gracefully into detail, and altogether the idea, the situation, the scene and prospect, were so soothing and charming, that the good attorney felt a silent exaltation as he listened to Lord Chelford's two or three delighted sentences upon the illimitable wonders and mysteries glimmering in the heavens above them.

The cigar was delicious, the air balmy and pleasant, his digestion happy, the society unexceptionably aristocratic—a step had just been gained, and his consideration in the town and the country round improved, by the occurrences of the evening, and his whole system, in consequence, in a state so serene, sweet and satisfactory, that I really believe there was genuine moisture in his pink, dove-like eyes, as he lifted them to the heavens, and murmured, 'Beautiful, beautiful!' And he mistook his sensations for a holy rapture and silent worship.

Cigars, like other pleasures, are transitory. Lord Chelford threw away his stump, tendered his case again to Mr. Larkin, and then took his leave, walking slowly homewards.

CHAPTER XL.

THE ATTORNEY'S ADVENTURES ON THE WAY HOME.

MR. JOS. LARKIN was now moving alone, under the gigantic limbs of the Brandon trees. He knew the path, as he had boasted to Lord Chelford, from his boyhood; and, as he pursued his way, his mind got upon the accustomed groove, and amused itself with speculations respecting the vagaries of Mark Wylder.

'I wonder what his lordship thinks. He was very close—very,' ruminated Larkin; 'no distinct ideas about it possibly; and did not seem to wish to lead me to the subject. Can he *know* anything? Eh, can he possibly? Those high fellows are very knowing often—so much on the turf, and all that; very sharp and very deep.'

He was thinking of a certain noble lord in difficulties, who had hit a client of his rather hard, and whose affairs did not reflect much credit upon their noble conductor.

'Aye, I dare say, deep enough, and intimate with the Lakes. He expects to be home in two months' time. *He's* a deep fellow too; he does not like to let people know what he's about. I should not be surprised if he came to-morrow. Lake and Lord Chelford may both know more than they say. Why should they both object merely to receive and fund his money? They think he wants to get them into a fix—hey? If I'm to conduct his business, I ought to know it; if he keeps a secret from me, affecting all his business relations, like this, and driving him about the world like an absconding bankrupt, how can I advise him?'

All this drifted slowly through his mind, and each suggestion had its collateral speculations; and so it carried him pleasantly a good way on his walk, and he was now in the shadow of the dense copsewood that mantles the deep ravine which debouches into Redman's Dell.

The road was hardly two yards wide, and the wood walled it in, and overhung it occasionally in thick, irregular masses. As the attorney marched leisurely onward, he saw, or fancied that he saw, now and then, in uncertain glimpses, something white in motion among the trees beside him.

At first he did not mind ; but it continued, and grew gradually unpleasant. It might be a goat, a white goat ; but no, it was too tall for that. Had he seen it at all ? Aye ! there it was, no mistake now. A poacher, maybe ? But their poachers were not of the dangerous sort, and there had not been a robber about Gylingden within the memory of man. Besides, why on earth should either show himself in that absurd way ?

He stopped—he listened—he stared suspiciously into the profound darkness. Then he thought he heard a rustling of the leaves near him, and he hallooed, 'Who's there?' But no answer came.

So, taking heart of grace, he marched on, still zealously peering among the trees, until, coming to an opening in the pathway, he more distinctly saw a tall, white figure, standing in an ape-like attitude, with its arms extended, grasping two boughs, and stooping, as if peeping cautiously, as he approached.

The good attorney drew up and stared at this gray phantasm, saying to himself, 'Yes,' in a sort of quiet hiss.

He stopped in a horror, and as he gazed, the figure suddenly drew back and disappeared.

'Very pleasant this !' said the attorney, after a pause, recovering a little. 'What on earth can it be ?'

Jos. Larkin could not tell which way it had gone. He had already passed the midway point, where this dark path begins to descend through the ravine into Redman's Dell. He did not like going forward—but to turn back might bring him again beside the mysterious figure. And though he was not, of course, afraid of ghosts, nor in this part of the world, of robbers, yet somehow he did not know what to make of this gigantic gray monkey.

So, not caring to stay longer, and seeing nothing to be gained by turning back, the attorney buttoned the top button of his coat, and holding his head very erect, and placing as much as he could of the path between himself and the side where the figure had disappeared, marched on steadily. It was too dark, and the way not quite regular enough, to render any greater speed practicable.

From the thicket, as he proceeded, he heard a voice—he had often shot woodcocks in that cover—calling in a tone that sounded in his ears like banter, ' Mark—Mark—Mark—Mark.'

He stopped, holding his breath, and the sound ceased.

'Well, this certainly is not usual,' murmured Mr. Larkin, who was a little more perturbed than perhaps he quite cared to acknowledge even to himself. 'Some fellow perhaps watching for a friend—or tricks, maybe.'

Then the attorney, trying his supercilious smile in the dark, listened again for a good while, but nothing was heard except those whisperings of the wind which poets speak of. He looked before him with his eyebrows screwed, in a vain effort to pierce the darkness, and the same behind him ; and then after another pause, he began uncomfortably to move down the path once more.

In a short time the same voice, with the same uncertain echo among the trees, cried faintly, 'Mark—Mark,' and then a pause ; then again, 'Mark—Mark—Mark,' and then it grew more distant, and sounded among the trees and reverberations of the glen like laughter.

'Mark—ha—ha—hark—ha—ha—ha—hark—Mark—Mark—ha—ha—hark !'

'Who's there ?' cried the attorney, in a tone rather ferocious from fright, and stamping on the path. But his summons and the provocation died away together in the profoundest silence.

Mr. Jos. Larkin did not repeat his challenge. This cry of 'Mark !' was beginning to connect itself uncomfortably in his mind with his speculations about his wealthy client, which in that solitude and darkness began to seem not so entirely pure and disinterested as he was in the habit of regarding them, and a sort of wood-demon, such as a queer little schoolfellow used long ago to read a tale about in an old German story-book, was now dogging his darksome steps, and hanging upon his flank with a vindictive design.

Jos. Larkin was not given to fancy, nor troubled with superstition. His religion was of a comfortable, punctual, business-like cast, which according with his genius—denied him, indeed, some things for which, in truth, he had no taste—but in no respect interfered with his main mission upon earth, which was getting money. He had found no difficulty hitherto in serving God and Mammon. The joint business prospered. Let us suppose it was one of those falterings of faith, which try the best men, that just now made him feel a little queer, and gave his thoughts about Mark Wylder, now grown habitual, that new and ghastly complexion which made the situation so unpleasant.

He wished himself more than once well out of this confounded pass, and listened nervously for a good while, and stared once more, half-frightened, in various directions, into the darkness.

If I thought there could be anything the least wrong or reprehensible—we are all fallible—in my allowing my mind to turn so much upon my client, I can certainly say I should be very far from allowing it—I shall certainly consider it—and I may promise myself to decide in a Christian spirit, and if there be a doubt, to give it against myself.'

This resolution, which was, he trusted, that of a righteous man, was, I am afraid, the effect rather of fright than reflection, and employed in that sense somewhat in the manner of an exorcism—whispered rather to the ghost than to his conscience.

I am sure Larkin did not himself suppose this. On the contrary, he really believed, I am convinced, that he scouted the ghost, and had merely volunteered this salutary self-examination as an exercise of conscience. He could not, however, have doubted that he was very nervous—and that he would have been glad of the companionship even of one of the Gylingden shopkeepers, through this infested bit of wood.

Having again addressed himself to his journey, he was now approaching that part of the path where the trees recede a little, leaving a considerable space unoccupied at either side of his line of march. Here there was faint moonlight and starlight, very welcome ; but a little in advance of him, where the copsewood closed in again, just above those stone steps which Lake and his sister Rachel had mounted together upon the night of the memorable rendezvous, he fancied that he again saw the gray figure cowering among the foremost stems of the wood.

It was a great shock. He stopped short—and as he stared upon the object, he felt that electric chill and rising of the hair which accompany supernatural panic.

As he gazed, however, it was gone. Yes. At all events, he could see it no more. Had he seen it there at all? He was in such an odd state he could not quite trust himself. He looked back hesitatingly. But he remembered how very long and dark the path that way was, and how unpleasant his adventures there had been. And although there was a chance that the gray monkey was lurking somewhere near the path, still there was now but a short space between him and the broad carriage track down Redman's Dell, and once upon that he considered himself almost in the street of Gylingden.

So he made up his mind, and marched resolutely onward, and had nearly reached that point at which the converging screen of thicket again overshadows the pathway, when close at his side he saw the tall, white figure push itself forward among the branches, and in a startling under-tone of enquiry, like a conspirator challenging his brother, a voice—the same which he had so often heard during this walk—cried over his shoulder,

' Mark *Wylder !* '

Larkin sprung back a pace or two, turning his face full upon the challenger, who in his turn was perhaps affrighted, for the same voice uttered a sort of strangled shriek, and he heard the branches crack and rustle as he pushed his sudden retreat through them—leaving the attorney more horrified than ever.

No other sound but the melancholy soughing of the night-breeze, and the hoarse murmur of the stream rising from the stony channel of Redman's Dell, were now, or during the remainder of his walk through these haunted grounds, again audible.

So, with rapid strides passing the dim gables of Redman's Farm, he at length found himself, with a sense of indescribable relief, upon the Gylingden road, and could see the twinkling lights in the windows of the main street.

CHAPTER XLI.

IN WHICH SIR FRANCIS SEDDLEY MANIPULATES.

AT about two o'clock Buddle was called up, and spirited away to Brandon in a dog-cart. A hæmorrhage, perhaps, a sudden shivering, and inflammation—a sinking, maybe, or delirium—some awful change, probably—for Buddle did not return.

Old Major Jackson heard of it, in his early walk, at Buddle's door. He had begun to grow more hopeful. But hearing this he walked home, and replaced the dress-coat and silk stockings he had ventured to remove, promptly in his valise, which he buckled down and locked—swallowed with agitated voracity some fragments of breakfast—got on his easy boots and gaiters —brushed his best hat, and locked it into its leather case—placed his rug, great-coat, and umbrella, and a rough walking-stick for service, and a gold-tipped, exquisite cane, for duty on promenades of fashion, neatly on top of his valise, and with his old white hat and shooting-coat on, looking and whistling as much as possible as usual, he popped carelessly into John Hobbs's stable, where he was glad to see three horses standing, and he mentally chose the black cob for his flight to Dollington.

'A bloodthirsty rascal that Bracton,' muttered the major. The expenses were likely to be awful, and some allowance was to be made for his state of mind.

He was under Doctor Buddle's porch, and made a flimsy rattle with his thin brass knocker. 'Maybe he has returned?' He did not believe it, though.

Major Jackson was very nervous, indeed. The up trains from Dollington were 'few and far between,' and that *diddled* Crutchleigh would be down on him the moment the breath was out of poor Lake. 'It was plain yesterday at the sessions that infernal woman (his wife) had been at him. She hates Bracton like poison, because he likes the Brandon people ; and, by Jove, he'll have up every soul concerned. The Devil and his wife I call them. If poor Lake goes off anywhere between eleven and four o'clock, I'm nabbed, by George!'

The door was opened. The doctor peeped out of his parlour.

'Well?' enquired the major, confoundedly frightened.

'Pretty well, thank ye, but awfully fagged—up all night, and no use.'

'But how *is* he?' asked the major, with a dreadful qualm of dismay.

'Same as yesterday—no change—only a little bleeding last night—not arterial; venous you know—only venous.'

The major thought he spoke of the goddess, and though he did not well comprehend, said he was 'glad of it.'

'Think he'll do then?'

'He may—very unlikely though. A nasty case, as you can imagine.'

'He'll certainly not go, poor fellow, before four o'clock P.M. I dare say—eh?'

The major's soul was at the Dollington station, and was regulating poor Lake's departure by 'Bradshaw's Guide.'

'Who knows? We expect Sir Francis this morning. Glad to have a share of the responsibility off my shoulders, I can tell you. Come in and have a chop, will you?'

'No, thank you, I've had my breakfast.'

'You have, have you? Well, I haven't,' cried the doctor, with an agreeable chuckle, shaking the major's hand, and disappearing again into his parlour.

I found in my lodgings in London, on my return from Doncaster, some two months later, a copy of the county paper of this date, with a cross scrawled beside the piece of intelligence which follows. I knew that tremulous cross. It was traced by the hand of poor old Miss Kybes—with her many faults always kind to me. It bore the Brandon postmark, and altogether had the impress of authenticity. It said:—

'We have much pleasure in stating that the severe injury sustained four days since by Captain Stanley Lake, at the time a visitor at the Lodge, the picturesque residence of Josiah Larkin, Esq., in the vicinity of Gylingden, is not likely to prove so difficult of treatment or so imminently dangerous as was at first apprehended. The gallant gentleman was removed from the scene of his misadventure to Brandon Hall, close to which the accident occurred, and at which mansion his noble relatives, Lord Chelford and the Dowager Lady Chelford, are at present staying on a visit. Sir Francis Seddley came down express from London, and assisted by our skilful county practitioner, Humphrey Buddle, Esq., M.D. of Gylingden, operated most successfully on Saturday last, and we are happy to say the gallant patient has since been going on as favourably as could

possibly have been anticipated. Sir Francis Seddley returned
to London on Sunday afternoon.'

Within a week after the operation, Buddle began to talk so
confidently about his patient, that the funereal cloud that overhung Brandon had almost totally disappeared, and Major Jackson had quite unpacked his portmanteau.

About a week after the 'accident' there came one of Mr. Mark
Wylder's strange letters to Mr. Jos. Larkin. This time it was
from Marseilles, and bore date the 27th November. It was
much the longest he had yet received, and was in the nature of
a despatch, rather than of those short notes in which he had
hitherto, for the most part, communicated.

Like the rest of his letters it was odd, but written, as it seemed
in better spirits.

'DEAR LARKIN,—You will be surprised to find me in this
port, but I think my secret cruise is nearly over now, and you
will say the plan was a master-stroke, and well executed by a
poor devil, with nobody to advise him. I am coiling such a web
round them, and making it fast, as you may see a spider, first to
this point and then to the other, that I won't leave my persecutors
one solitary chance of escape. I'll draw it quietly round and round
—closer and closer—till they can neither blow nor budge, and
then up to the yardarm they go, with what breath is left in them.
You don't know yet *how* I am dodging, or why my measures are
taken ; but I'll shorten your long face a good inch with a genuine broad grin when you learn how it all was. I may see you
to tell the story in four weeks' time ; but keep this close. Don't
mention where I write from, nor even so much as my name. I
have reasons for everything, which you may guess, I dare say,
being a sharp chap ; and it is not for nothing, be very sure, that
I am running this queer rig, masquerading, hiding, and dodging,
like a runaway forger, which is not pleasant anyway, and if you
doubt it, only try ; but needs must when the old boy drives. He
is a clever fellow, no doubt, but has been sometimes out-witted
before now. You must arrange about Chelford and Lake. I
don't know where Lake is staying. I don't suppose at Brandon ;
but he won't stay in the country nor spend his money to please
you or I. Therefore you must have him at your house—be sure
—and I will square it with you ; I think three pounds a week
ought to do it very handsome. Don't be a muff and give him
expensive wines—a pint of sherry is plenty between you ; and
when he dines at his club half-a-pint does him. *I* know ; but if
he costs you more, I hereby promise to pay it. Won't that do?
Well, about Chelford : I have been thinking he takes airs, and
maybe he is on his high-horse about that awkward business
about Miss Brandon. But there is no reason why Captain Lake
should object. He has only to hand you a receipt in my name
for the amount of cheques you may give him, and to lodge a

portion of it where I told him, and the rest to buy Consols ; and I suppose he will expect payment for his no-trouble. Every fellow, particularly these gentlemanlike fellows, they have a pluck at you when they can. If he is at that, give him at the rate of a hundred a-year, or a hundred and fifty if you think he won't do for less ; though 100*l.* ought to be a good deal to Lake ; and tell him I have a promise of the adjutancy of the county militia, if he likes that ; and I am sure of a seat in Parliament either for the county or for Dollington, as you know, and can do better for him then ; and I rely on you, one way or another, to make him undertake it. And now for myself : I think my vexation is very near ended. I have not fired a gun yet, and they little think what a raking broadside I'll give them. Any of the county people you meet, tell them I'm making a little excursion on the Continent ; and if they go to particularise, you may say the places I have been at. Don't let anyone know more. I wish there was any way of stopping that old she '—(it looked like dragon or devil—but was traced over with a cloud of flourishes, and only ' Lady Chelford's mouth' was left untouched). ' Don't expect to hear from me so long a yarn for some time again ; and don't write. I don't stay long anywhere, and don't carry my own name—and never ask for letters at the post. I've a good glass, and can see pretty far, and make a fair guess enough what's going on aboard the enemy.

' I remain always,
' Dear Larkin,
' Ever yours truly,
' MARK WYLDER.'

' He hardly trusts Lake more than he does me, I presume,' murmured Mr. Larkin, elevating his tall bald head with an offended and supercilious air ; and letting the thin, open letter fall, or rather throwing it with a slight whisk upon the table.

' No, I take leave to think he certainly does *not.* Lake has got private directions about the disposition of a portion of the money. Of course, if there are persons to be dealt with who are not pleasantly approachable by respectable professional people —in fact it would not suit me. It is really rather a compliment, and relieves me of the unpleasant necessity of saying— no.'

Yet Mr. Larkin was very sore, and curious, and in a measure, hated both Lake and Wylder for their secret confidences, and was more than ever resolved to get at the heart of Mark's mystery.

CHAPTER XLII.

A PARAGRAPH IN THE COUNTY PAPER.

HE nature of his injury considered, Captain Lake recovered with wonderful regularity and rapidity. In four weeks he was out, rather pale and languid, but still able to walk without difficulty, leaning on a stick, for ten or fifteen minutes at a time. In another fortnight he had made another great advance, had thrown away his crutch handled stick, and recovered flesh and vigour. In a fortnight more he had grown quite like himself again ; and in a very few weeks more, I read in the same county paper, transmitted to me by the same fair hands, but this time not with a cross, but three distinct notes of admiration standing tremulously at the margin of the paragraph, the following to me for a time incredible, and very nearly to this day amazing, announcement :—

'MARRIAGE IN HIGH LIFE.

'The auspicious event so interesting to our county, which we have this day to announce, though for some time upon the *tapis*, has been attended with as little publicity as possible. The contemplated union between Captain Stanley Lake, late of the Guards, sole surviving son of the late General Williams Stanley Stanley Lake, of Plasrhwyn, and the beautiful and accomplished Miss Brandon, of Brandon Hall, in this county, was celebrated in the ancestral chapel of Brandon, situated within the manorial boundaries, in the immediate vicinity of the town of Gylingden, on yesterday. Although the marriage was understood to be strictly private—none but the immediate relations of the bride and bridegroom being present — the bells of Gylingden rang out merry peals throughout the day, and the town was tastefully decorated with flags, and brilliantly illuminated at night.

'A deputation of the tenantry of the Gylingden and the Longmoor estates, together with those of the Brandon estate, went in procession to Brandon Hall in the afternoon, and read a well-conceived and affectionate address, which was responded to in appropriate terms by Captain Lake, who received them, with his beautiful bride at his side, in the great gallery—perhaps the noblest apartment in that noble ancestral mansion. The tenantry were afterwards handsomely entertained under the immediate direction of Josiah Larkin, Esq., of the Lodge, the respected manager of the Brandon estates, at the "Brandon

Arms," in the town of Gylingden. It is understood that the great territorial influence of the Brandon family will obtain a considerable accession in the estates of the bridegroom in the south of England.'

There was some more which I need not copy, being very like what we usually see on such occasions.

I read this piece of intelligence half a dozen times over during breakfast. 'How that beautiful girl has thrown herself away!' I thought. 'Surely the Chelfords, who have an influence there, ought to have exerted it to prevent her doing anything so mad. His estates in the south of England, indeed! Why, he can't have £300 a year clear from that little property in Devon. He *is* such a liar; and so absurd, as if he could succeed in deceiving anyone upon the subject.

So I read the paragraph over again, and laid down the paper, simply saying, 'Well, certainly, that *is* disgusting!'

I had heard of his duel. It was also said that it had in some way had reference to Miss Brandon. But this was the only rumoured incident which would at all have prepared one for the occurrence. I tried to recollect anything particular in his manner—there was nothing; and she positively seemed to dislike him. I had been utterly mystified, and so, I presume, had all the other lookers-on.

Well! after all, 'twas no particular business of mine.

At the club, I saw it in the 'Morning Post;' and an hour after, old Joe Gabloss, that prosy Argus who knows everything, recounted the details with patient precision, and in legal phrase, 'put in' letters from two or three country houses proving his statement.

So there was no doubting it longer: and Captain Stanley Lake, late of Her Majesty's — Regiment of Guards, idler, scamp, coxcomb, and the beautiful Dorcas Brandon, heiress of Brandon, were man and wife.

I wrote to my fair friend, Miss Kybes, and had an answer confirming, if that were needed, the public announcement, and mentioning enigmatically, that it had caused 'a great deal of conversation.'

The posture of affairs in the small world of Gylingden, except in the matter of the alliance just referred to, was not much changed.

Since the voluminous despatch from Marseilles, promising his return so soon, not a line had been received from Mark Wylder. He might arrive any day or night. He might possibly have received some unexpected check—if not checkmate, in that dark and deep game on which he seemed to have staked so awfully. Mr. Jos. Larkin sometimes thought one thing, sometimes another.

In the meantime, Captain Lake accepted the trust. Larkin at

times thought there was a constant and secret correspondence going on between him and Mark Wylder, and that he was his agent in adjusting some complicated and villainous piece of diplomacy by means of the fund — secret-service money — which Mark had placed at his disposal.

He, Mr. Larkin, was treated like a child in this matter, and his advice never so much as asked, nor his professional honour accredited by the smallest act of confidence.

Sometimes his supicions took a different turn, and he thought that Lake might be one of those ' persecutors' of whom Mark spoke with such mysterious hatred ; and that the topic of their correspondence was, perhaps, some compromise, the subject or the terms of which would not bear the light.

Lake certainly made two visits to London, one of them of a week's duration. The attorney being a sharp, long-headed fellow, who knew very well what business was, knew perfectly well, too, that two or three short letters might have settled any legitimate business which his gallant friend had in the capital.

But Lake was now married, and under the incantation whistled over him by the toothless Archdeacon of Mundlebury, had sprung up into a county magnate, and was worth cultivating, and to be treated tenderly.

So the attorney's business was to smile and watch—to watch, and of course, to pray as heretofore—but specially to watch. He himself hardly knew all that was passing in his own brain. There are operations of physical nature which go on actively without your being aware of them ; and the moral respiration, circulation, insensible perspiration, and all the rest of that peculiar moral system which exhibited its type in Jos. Larkin, proceeded automatically in the immortal structure of that gentleman.

Being very gentlemanlike in externals, with a certain grace, amounting very nearly to elegance, and having applied himself diligently to please the county people, that proud fraternity, remembering his father's estates, condoned his poverty, and took Captain Lake by the hand, and lifted him into their superb, though not very entertaining order.

There were solemn festivities at Brandon, and festive solemnities at the principal county houses in return. Though not much of a sportsman, Lake lent himself handsomely to all the sporting proceedings of the county, and subscribed in a way worthy of the old renown of Brandon Hall to all sorts of charities and galas. So he was getting on very pleasantly with his new neighbours, and was likely to stand very fairly in that dull, but not unfriendly society

About three weeks after this great county marriage, there arrived, this time from Frankfort, a sharp letter, addressed to Jos. Larkin, Esq. It said :—

'MY DEAR SIR,—I think I have reason to complain. I have just seen by accident the announcement of the marriage at Brandon. I think as my friend, and a friend to the Brandon family, you ought to have done something to delay, if you could not stop it. Of course, you had the settlements, and devil's in it if you could not have beat about a while—it was not so quick with me—and not doubled the point in a single tack; and you know the beggar has next to nothing. Any way, it was your duty to have printed some notice that the thing was thought of. If you had put it, like a bit of news, in " Galignani," I would have seen it, and known what to do. Well, that ship's blew up. But I won't let all go. The cur will begin to try for the county or for Dollington. You must quietly stop that, mind; and if he persists, just you put an advertisement in " Galignani," saying *Mr. Smith will take notice, that the other party is desirous to purchase, and becoming very pressing.* Just you hoist that signal, and *somebody* will bear down, and blaze into him at all hazards —you'll see how. Things have not gone quite smooth with me since; but it won't be long till I run up my flag again, and take the command. Be perfectly civil with Stanley Lake till I come on board—that is indispensable; and keep this letter as close from every eye as sealed orders. You may want a trifle to balk S. L.'s electioneering, and there's an order on Lake for 200*l.* Don't trifle about the county and borough. He must have no footing in either till I return.

> 'Yours, dear Larkin,
> > 'Very truly
> '(but look after my business better),
> > > 'M. WYLDER.'

The order on Lake, a little note, was enclosed :—

'DEAR LAKE,—I wish you joy, and all the good wishes going, as I could not make the prize myself.

'Be so good to hand my lawyer, Mr. Jos. Larkin, of the Lodge, Gylingden, 200*l.* sterling, on my account.

> 'Yours, dear Lake,
> > 'Very faithfully,
> > > 'M. WYLDER.
> 200*l.*)
'23rd Feb., &c. &c.'

When Jos. Larkin presented this little order, it was in the handsome square room in which Captain Lake transacted business—a lofty apartment, wainscoted in carved oak, and with a great stone mantelpiece, with the Wylder arms, projecting in bold relief, in the centre, and a florid scroll, with ' 𝕽𝕰𝕾𝖀𝕽𝕲𝕬𝕸,' standing forth as sharp as the day it was chiselled nearly three hundred years before.

There was some other business—Brandon business—to be talked over first; and that exhausted, Mr. Larkin sat as usual, with one long thigh crossed upon the other—his arm thrown over the back of his chair, and his tall, bald head a little back, and his small mild eyes twinkling through their pink lids on the enigmatical captain, who had entered upon the march of ambition in a spirit so audacious and conquering.

'I had a line from Mr. Mark Wylder yesterday afternoon, as usual without any address but the postmark;' and good Mr. Larkin laughed a mild, little patient laugh, and lifted his open hand, and shook his head. ' It really is growing too absurd—a mere order upon you to hand me 200*l.* How I'm to dispose of it, I have not the faintest notion.'

And he laughed again; at the same time he gracefully poked the little note, between two fingers, to Captain Lake, who glanced full on him, for a second, as he took it.

'And how is Mark?' enquired Lake, with his odd, sly smile, as he scrawled a little endorsement on the order. ' Does he say anything?'

' No; absolutely nothing—he's a very strange client!' said Larkin, laughing again. ' There can be no objection, of course, to your reading it; and he thinks — he thinks — he'll be here soon again—oh, here it is.'

Mr. Larkin had been fumbling, first in his deep waistcoat, and then in his breast-pocket, as if for the letter, which was locked fast into the iron safe, with Chubb's patent lock, in his office at the Lodge. But it would not have done to have kept a secret from Captain Lake, of Brandon; and therefore his not seeing the note was a mere accident.

' Oh! no—stupid!—that's Mullett and Hock's. I have not got it with me; but it does not signify, for there's nothing in it. I hope I shall soon be favoured with his directions as to what to do with the money.'

' He's an odd fellow; and I don't know how he feels towards me; but on my part there is no feeling, I do assure you, but the natural desire to live on the friendly terms which our ties of family and our position in the county'—

Stanley Lake was writing the cheque for 200*l.* meanwhile, and handed it to Larkin; and as that gentleman penned a receipt, the captain continued—his eyes lowered to the little vellum-bound book in which he was now making an entry:—

' You have handed me a large sum, Mr. Larkin—3,276*l.* 11*s.* 4*d.* I undertook this, you know, on the understanding that it was not to go on very long; and I find my own business pretty nearly as much as I can manage. Is Wylder at all definite as to when we may expect his return?'

' Oh, dear no—quite as usual—he expects to be here soon; but that is all. I so wish I had brought his note with me; but I'm positive that is all.'

So, this little matter settled, the lawyer took his leave.

CHAPTER XLIII.

AN EVIL EYE LOOKS ON THE VICAR.

THERE were influences of a wholly unsuspected kind already gathering round the poor vicar, William Wylder ; as worlds first begin in thinnest vapour, and whirl themselves in time into consistency and form, so do these dark machinations, which at times gather round unsuspecting mortals as points of revolution, begin nebulously and intangibly, and grow in volume and in density, till a colossal system, with its inexorable tendencies and forces, crushes into eternal darkness the centre it has enveloped.

Thou shalt not covet ; thou shalt not cast an eye of desire ; out of the heart proceed *murders ;*—these dreadful realities shape themselves from so filmy a medium as thought !

Ever since his conference with the vicar, good Mr. Larkin had been dimly thinking of a thing. The good attorney's weakness was money. It was a speck at first ; a metaphysical microscope of no conceivable power could have developed its exact shape and colour—a mere speck, floating, as it were, in a transparent kyst, in his soul—a mere germ—by-and-by to be an impish embryo, and ripe for action. When lust hath conceived it bringeth forth sin, and sin when it is finished bringeth forth death.

The vicar's troubles grew and gathered, as such troubles will ; and the attorney gave him his advice ; and the business of the Rev. William Wylder gradually came to occupy a good deal of his time. Here was a new reason for wishing to know really how Mark Wylder stood. William had undoubtedly the reversion of the estate ; but the attorney suspected sometimes—just from a faint phrase which had once escaped Stanley Lake—as the likeliest solution, that Mark Wylder had made a left-handed marriage somehow and somewhere, and that a subterranean wife and family would emerge at an unlucky moment, and squat upon that remainder, and defy the world to disturb them. This gave to his plans and dealings in relation to the vicar a character of irresolution and caprice foreign to his character, which was grim and decided enough when his data were clear, and his object in sight.

William Wylder, meanwhile, was troubled, and his mind clouded by more sorrows than one.

Poor William Wylder had those special troubles which haunt nervous temperaments and speculative minds, when under the solemn influence of religion. What the great Luther called,

without describing them, his 'tribulations'— those dreadful
doubts and apathies which at times menace and darken the
radiant fabric of faith, and fill the soul with nameless horrors.
The worst of these is, that unlike other troubles, they are not
always safely to be communicated to those who love us best.
These terrors and dubitations are infectious.   Other spiritual
troubles, too, there are ; and I suppose our good vicar was not
exempt from them any more than other Christians.

The best man, the simplest man that ever lived, has his reserves.   The conscious frailty of mortality owes that sad reverence to itself, and to the esteem of others.   You can't be too
frank and humble when you have wronged your neighbour ; but
keep your offences against God to yourself, and let your battle
with your own heart be waged under the eye of Him alone.
The frankness of the sentimental Jean Jacques Rousseau, and
of my coarse friend, Mark Wylder, is but a damnable form of
vicious egotism.   A miserable sinner have I been, my friend,
but details profit neither thee nor me.   The inner man had best
be known only to himself and his Maker.   I like that good and
simple Welsh parson, of Beaumaris, near two hundred years
ago, who with a sad sort of humour, placed for motto under his
portrait, done in stained glass, *nunc primum transparui.*

But the spiritual tribulation which came and went was probably connected with the dreadful and incessant horrors of his
money trouble.   The gigantic Brocken spectre projected from
himself upon the wide horizon of his futurity.

The poor vicar !   He felt his powers forsaking him.   Hope,
the life of action, was gone.   Despair is fatalism, and can't help
itself.   The inevitable mountain was always on his shoulders.
He could not rise—he could not stir.   He could scarcely turn
his head and look up beseechingly from the corners of his eyes.

Why is that fellow so supine?   Why is his work so ill done,
when he ought most to exert himself?   He disgusts the world
with his hang-dog looks.   Alas ! with the need for action, the
power of action is gone.   Despair—distraction—the Furies sit
with him.   Stunned, stupid, and wild—always agitated—it is
not easy to compose his sermons as finely as heretofore.   He is
always jotting down little sums in addition and subtraction.
The cares of the world—the miseries of what the world calls
'difficulties' and a 'struggle'—these were for the poor vicar ;
—the worst torture, for aught we know, which an average soul
out of hell can endure.   Other sorrows bear healing on their
wings ;—this one is the Promethean vulture.   It is a falling into
the hands of men, not of God.   The worst is, that its tendencies
are so godless.   It makes men bitter ; its promptings are blasphemous.   Wherefore, He who knew all things, in describing
the thorns which choke the word, places the *cares* of this world
first, and *after* them the deceitfulness of riches and the lusts of

other things. So if money is a root of evil, the want of it, with debt, is root, and stem, and branches.

But all human pain has its intervals of relief. The pain is suspended, and the system recruits itself to endure the coming paroxysm. An hour of illusion—an hour of sleep—an hour's respite of any sort, to six hours of pain—and so the soul, in anguish, finds strength for its long labour, abridged by neither death nor madness.

The vicar, with his little boy, Fairy, by the hand, used twice, at least, in the week to make, sometimes an hour's, sometimes only half an hour's, visit at Redman's Farm. Poor Rachel Lake made old Tamar sit at her worsteds in the window of the little drawing-room while these conversations proceeded. The young lady was so intelligent that William Wylder was obliged to exert himself in controversy with her eloquent despair; and this combat with the doubts and terrors of a mind of much more than ordinary vigour and resource, though altogether feminine, compelled him to bestir himself, and so, for the time, found him entire occupation; and thus memory and forecast, and suspense, were superseded, for the moment, by absorbing mental action.

Rachel's position had not been altered by her brother's marriage. Dorcas had urged her earnestly to give up Redman's Farm, and take up her abode permanently at Brandon. This kindness, however, she declined. She was grateful, but no, nothing could move her. The truth was, she recoiled from it with a species of horror.

The marriage had been, after all, as great a surprise to Rachel as to any of the Gylingden gossips. Dorcas,. knowing how Rachel thought upon it, had grown reserved and impenetrable upon the subject; indeed, at one time, I think, she had half made up her mind to fight the old battle over again and resolutely exercise this fatal passion. She had certainly mystified Rachel, perhaps was mystifying herself.

Rachel grew more sad and strange than ever after this marriage. I think that Stanley was right, and that living in that solitary and darksome dell helped to make her hypochondriac.

One evening Stanley Lake stood at her door.

'I was just thinking, dear Radie,' he said in his sweet low tones, which to her ear always bore a suspicion of mockery in them, 'how pretty you contrive to make this bright little garden at all times of the year—you have such lots of those evergreens, and ivy, and those odd flowers.'

'They call them *immortelles* in France,' said Rachel, in a cold strange tone, 'and make chaplets of them to lay upon the coffin-lids and the graves.'

'Ah, yes, to be sure, I have seen them there and in Père la Chaise—so they do; they have them in all the cemetries—I forgot that. How cheerful; how very sensible. **Don't you** think it would be a good plan to stick up a death's-head and cross-bones here and there, and to split up old coffin-lids for your setting-sticks, and get old Mowlders, the sexton, to bury your roots, and cover them in with a "dust to dust," and so forth, and plant a yew tree in the middle, and stick those bits of painted board, that look so woefully like gravestones, all round it, and then let old Tamar prowl about for a ghost? I assure you, Radie, I think you, all to nothing, the perversest fool I ever encountered or heard of in the course of my life.'

'Well, Stanley, suppose you do, I'll not dispute it. Perhaps you are right,' said Rachel, still standing at the door of her little porch.

'Perhaps,' he repeated with a sneer; 'I venture to say, *most positively*, I can't conceive any sane reason for your refusing Dorcas's entreaty to live with us at Brandon, and leave this triste, and unwholesome, and everyway objectionable place.'

'She was very kind, but I can't do it.'

'Yes, you can't do it, simply because it would be precisely the most sensible, prudent, and comfortable arrangement you could possibly make; you *won't* do it—but you can and will practise all the airs and fooleries of a bad melodrama. You have succeeded already in filling Dorcas's mind with surmise and speculation, and do you think the Gylingden people are either blind or dumb? You are taking, I've told you again and again, the very way to excite attention and gossip. What good can it possibly do you? You'll not believe until it happens, and when it does, you'd give your eyes you could undo it. It is so like you.'

'I have said how very kind I thought it of Dorcas to propose it. I can't explain to her all my reasons for declining; and to you I need not. But I cannot overcome my repugnance—and I won't try.'

'I wonder,' said Stanley, with a sly look of enquiry, 'that you who read the Bible—and a very good book it is, no doubt —and believe in all sorts of things—'

'That will do, Stanley. I'm not so weak as you suppose.'

'You know, Radie, I'm a Sadducee, and that sort of thing does not trouble me the least in the world. It is a little cold here. May we go into the drawing-room? You can't think how I hate this—house. We are always unpleasant in it.'

This auspicious remark he made taking off his hat, and placing it and his cane on her work-table.

But this was not a tempestuous conference by any means. I don't know precisely what they talked about. I think it was probably the pros and cons of that migration to Brandon, against which Rachel had pronounced so firmly.

'I can't do it, Stanley. My motives are unintelligible to you,

I know, and you think me obstinate and stupid ; but, be I what I may, my objections are insurmountable. And does it not strike you that my staying here, on the contrary, would—would tend to prevent the kind of conversation you speak of?'

'Not the least, dear Radie—that is, I mean, it could have no possible effect, unless the circumstances were first supposed, and then it could be of no appreciable use. And your way of life and your looks—for both are changed—are likely, in a little prating village, where every human being is watched and discussed incessantly, to excite conjecture ; that is all, and that is *every thing.*'

It had grown dark while Stanley sat in the little drawing-room, and Rachel stood on her doorstep, and saw his figure glide away slowly into the thin mist and shadow, and turn upward to return to Brandon, by that narrow ravine where they had held rendezvous with Mark Wylder, on that ill-omened night when trouble began for all.

To Rachel's eyes, that disappearing form looked like the moping spirit of guilt and regret, haunting the scene of the irrevocable.

When Stanley took his leave after one of these visits—stolen visits, somehow, they always seemed to her—the solitary mistress of Redman's Farm invariably experienced the nervous reaction which follows the artificial calm of suppressed excitement. Something of panic or horror, relieved sometimes by a gush of tears —sometimes more slowly and painfully subsiding without that hysterical escape.

She went in and shut the door, and called Tamar. But Tamar was out of the way. She hated that little drawing-room in her present mood—its associations were odious and even ghastly ; so she sat herself down by the kitchen fire, and placed her pretty feet—cold now — upon the high steel fender, and extended her cold hands towards the embers, leaning back in her rude chair.

And so she got the girl to light candles, and asked her a great many questions, and obliged her, in fact, to speak constantly though she seemed to listen but little. And when at last the girl herself, growing interested in her own narrative about a kidnapper, grew voluble and animated, and looked round upon the young lady at the crisis of the tale, she was surprised to remark, on a sudden, that she was gazing vacantly into the bars ; and when Margery, struck by her fixed and melancholy countenance, stopped in the midst of a sentence, the young lady turned and gazed on her wistfully, with large eyes and pale face, and sighed heavily.

CHAPTER XLIV.

IN WHICH OLD TAMAR LIFTS UP HER VOICE IN PROPHECY.

ERTAINLY Stanley Lake was right about Redman's Dell. Once the sun had gone down behind the distant hills, it was the darkest, the most silent, and the most solitary of nooks.

It was not, indeed, quite dark yet. The upper sky had still a faint gray twilight halo, and the stars looked wan and faint. But the narrow walk that turned from Redman's Dell was always dark in Stanley's memory; and Sadducees, although they believe neither in the resurrection nor the judgment, are no more proof than other men against the resurrections of memory and the penalties of association and of fear.

Captain Lake had many things to think of. Some pleasant enough as he measured pleasure, others troublesome. But as he mounted the stone steps that conducted the passenger up the steep acclivity to the upper level of the dark and narrow walk he was pursuing, one black sorrow met him and blotted out all the rest.

Captain Lake knew very well and gracefully practised the art of not seeing inconvenient acquaintances in the street. But here in this narrow way there met him full a hated shadow whom he would fain have 'cut,' by looking to right or left, or up or down, but which was not to be evaded—would not only have his salutation but his arm, and walked—a horror of great darkness, by his side—through this solitude.

Committed to a dreadful game, in which the stakes had come to exceed anything his wildest fears could have anticipated, from which he could not, according to his own canons, by any imaginable means recede—*here* was the spot where the dreadful battle had been joined, and his covenant with futurity sealed.

The young captain stood for a moment still on reaching the upper platform. A tiny brook that makes its way among briars and shingle to the more considerable mill-stream of Redman's Dell, sent up a hoarse babbling from the darkness beneath. Why exactly he halted there he could not have said. He glanced over his shoulder down the steps he had just scaled. Had there been light his pale face would have shown just then a malign anxiety, such as the face of an ill-conditioned man might wear, who apprehends danger of treading on a snake.

He walked on, however, without quickening his pace, waving very slightly from side to side his ebony walking-cane—thin as a pencil—as if it were a wand to beckon away the unseen things

that haunt the darkness; and now he came upon the wider
plateau, from which, the close copse receding, admitted something more of the light, faint as it was, that lingered in the
heavens.

A tall gray stone stands in the centre of this space. There
had once been a boundary and a stile there. Stanley knew it
very well, and was not startled as the attorney was the other
night when he saw it. As he approached this, some one said
close in his ear,

'I beg your pardon, Master Stanley.'

He cowered down with a spring, as I can fancy a man duck-
ing under a round-shot, and glanced speechlessly, and still in
his attitude of recoil, upon the speaker.

'It's only me, Master Stanley—your poor old Tamar. Don't
be afraid, dear.'

'I'm *not* afraid—woman. Tamar to be sure—why, of course,
I know you; but what the devil brings you here?' he said.

Tamar was dressed just as she used to be when sitting in the
open air at her knitting, except that over her shoulders she had
a thin gray shawl. On her head was the same close linen nightcap, borderless and skull-like, and she laid her shrivelled, freckled
hand upon his arm, and looking with an earnest and fearful
gaze in his face she said—

'It has been on my mind this many a day to speak to you,
Master Stanley; but whenever I meant to, summat came over
me, and I couldn't.'

'Well, well, well,' said Lake, uneasily; 'I mean to call to-
morrow, or next day, or some day soon, at Redman's Farm. I'll
hear it then; this is no place, you know, Tamar, to talk in;
besides I'm pressed for time, and can't stay now to listen.'

'There's no place like this, Master Stanley; it's so awful
secret,' she said, with her hand still upon his arm.

'Secret! Why one place is as well as another; and what
the devil have I to do with secrets? I tell you, Tamar, I'm in
haste and can't stay. I *won't* stay. There!'

'Master Stanley, for the love of Heaven—you know what I'm
going to speak of; my old bones have carried me here—'tis years
since I walked so far. I'd walk till I dropped to reach you—but
I'd say what's on my mind, 'tis like a message from heaven—
and I *must* speak—aye, dear, I must.'

'But I say I can't stay. Who made you a prophet? You
used not to be a fool, Tamar; when I tell you I can't, that's
enough.'

Tamar did not move her fingers from the sleeve of his coat,
on which they rested, and that thin pressure mysteriously detained him.

'See, Master Stanley, if I don't say it to *you*, I must to another,' she said.

'You mean to threaten me, woman,' said he with a pale, malevolent look.

'I'm threatening nothing but the wrath of God, who hears us.'

'Unless you mean to do me an injury, Tamar, I don't know what else you mean,' he answered, in a changed tone.

'Old Tamar will soon be in her coffin, and this night far in the past, like many another, and 'twill be everything to you, one day, for weal or woe, to hearken to her words *now*, Master Stanley.'

'Why, Tamar, haven't I told you I'm ready to listen to you. I'll go and see you—upon my honour I will—to-morrow, or next day, at the Dell ; what's the good of stopping me here ?'

'Because, Master Stanley, something told me 'tis the best place ; we're quiet, and you're more like to weigh my words here—and you'll be alone for a while after you leave me, and can ponder my advice as you walk home by the path.'

'Well, whatever it is, I suppose it won't take very long to say —let us walk on to the stone there, and then I'll stop and hear it—but you must not keep me all night,' he said, very peevishly.

It was only twenty steps further on, and the woods receded round it, so as to leave an irregular amphitheatre of some sixty yards across ; and Captain Lake, glancing from the corners of his eyes, this way and that, without raising or turning his face, stopped listlessly at the time-worn white stone, and turning to the old crone, who was by his side, he said,

'Well, then, you have your way ; but speak low, please, if you have anything unpleasant to say.'

Tamar laid her hand upon his arm again ; and the old woman's face afforded Stanley Lake no clue to the coming theme. Its expression was quite as usual — not actually discontent or peevishness, but crimped and puckered all over with unchanging lines of anxiety and suffering. Neither was there any flurry in her manner—her bony arm and discoloured hand, once her fingers lay upon his sleeve, did not move—only she looked very earnestly in his face as she spoke.

'You'll not be angry, Master Stanley, dear ? though if you be, I can't help it, for I must speak. I've heard it all—I heard you and Miss Radie speak on the night you first came to see her, after your sickness ; and I heard you speak again, by my room door, only a week before your marriage, when you thought I was asleep. So I've heard it all—and though I mayn't understand all the ins and outs on't, I know it well in the main Oh, Master Stanley, Master Stanley ! How can you go on with it ?'

'Come, Tamar, what do you want of me ? What do you mean ? What the d— is it all about ?'

'Oh ! well you know, Master Stanley, what it's about.'

'Well, there *is* something unpleasant, and I suppose you have heard a smattering of it in your muddled way ; but it is quite plain you don't in the least understand it, when you fancy I can do anything to serve anyone in the smallest degree connected with that disagreeable business—or that I am personally in the least to blame in it ; and I can't conceive what business you had listening at the keyhole to your mistress and me, nor why I am wasting my time talking to an old woman about my affairs, which she can neither understand nor take part in.'

'Master Stanley, it won't do. I heard it—I could not help hearing. I little thought you had any such matter to speak— and you spoke so sudden like, I could not help it. You were angry, and raised your voice. What could old Tamar do ? I heard it all before I knew where I was.'

'I really think, Tamar, you've taken leave of your wits—you are quite in the clouds. Come, Tamar, tell me, once for all— only drop your voice a little, if you please—what the plague has got into your old head. Come, I say, what is it ?'

He stooped and leaned his ear to Tamar ; and when she had done, he laughed. The laugh, though low, sounded wild and hollow in that dark solitude.

'Really, dear Tamar, you must excuse my laughing. You dear old witch, how the plague could you take any such frightful nonsense into your head ? I do assure you, upon my honour, I never heard of so ridiculous a blunder. Only that I know you are really fond of us, I should never speak to you again. I forgive you. But listen no more to other people's conversation. I could tell you how it really stands now, only I have not time ; but you'll take my word of honour for it, you have made the most absurd mistake that ever an old fool tumbled into. No, Tamar, I can't stay any longer now ; but I'll tell you the whole truth when next I go down to Redman's Farm. In the meantime, you must not plague poor Miss Radie with your nonsense. She has too much already to trouble her, though of quite another sort. Good-night, foolish old Tamar.'

'Oh, Master Stanley, it will take a deal to shake my mind ; and if it be so, as I say, what's to be done next—what's to be done—oh, what *is* to be done ?'

'I say good-night, old Tamar ; and hold your tongue, do you see ?'

'Oh, Master Stanley, Master Stanley ! my poor child—my child that I nursed !—anything would be better than this. Sooner or later judgment will overtake you, so sure as you persist in it. I heard what Miss Radie said ; and is not it true—is not it cruel —is not it frightful to go on ?'

'You don't seem to be aware, my good Tamar, that you have been talking slander all this while, and might be sent to gaol for it. There, I'm not angry—only you're a fool. Good-night.'

He shook her hand, and jerked it from him with suppressed fury, passing on with a quickened pace. And as he glided through the dark, towards splendid old Brandon, he ground his teeth, and uttered two or three sentences which no respectable publisher would like to print.

CHAPTER XLV.

DEEP AND SHALLOW.

AWYER LARKIN'S mind was working more diligently than anyone suspected upon this puzzle of Mark Wylder. The investigation was a sort of scientific recreation to him, and something more. His sure instinct told him it was a secret well worth mastering.

He had a growing belief that Lake, and perhaps he *only*—except Wylder himself—knew the meaning of all this mysterious marching and counter-marching. Of course, all sorts of theories were floating in his mind ; but there was none that would quite fit all the circumstances. The attorney, had he asked himself the question, what was his object in these inquisitions, would have answered—' I am doing what few other men would. I am, Heaven knows, giving to this affair of my absent client's, gratuitously, as much thought and vigilance as ever I did to any case in which I was duly remunerated. This is self-sacrificing and noble, and just the conscientious conduct I should expect from myself.'

But there was also this consideration, which you failed to define.

' Yes ; my respected client, Mr. Mark Wylder, is suffering under some acute pressure, applied perhaps by my friend Captain Lake. Why should not I share in the profit—if such there be—by getting my hand too upon the instrument of compression? It is worth trying. Let us try.'

The Reverend William Wylder was often at the Lodge now. Larkin had struck out a masterly plan. The vicar's reversion, a very chimerical contingency, he would by no means consent to sell. His little man—little Fairy—oh ! no, he could not. The attorney only touched on this, remarking in a friendly way—

' But then, you know, it is so mere a shadow.'

This indeed, poor William knew very well. But though he spoke quite meekly, the attorney looked rather black, and his converse grew somewhat dry and short.

This sinister change was sudden, and immediately followed the suggestion about the reversion ; and the poor vicar was a

little puzzled, and began to consider whether he had said anything *gauche* or offensive—'it would be so very painful to appear
ungrateful.'

The attorney had the statement of title in one hand, and leaning back in his chair, read it demurely in silence, with the
other tapping the seal-end of his gold pencil-case between his
lips.

'Yes,' said Mr. Larkin, mildly, 'it *is* so *very* shadowy—and that
feeling, too, in the way. I suppose we had better, perhaps, put
it aside, and maybe something else may turn up.' And the attorney rose grandly to replace the statement of title in its tin
box, intimating thereby that the audience was ended.

But the poor vicar was in rather urgent circumstances just
then, and his troubles had closed in recently with a noiseless,
but tremendous contraction, like that iron shroud in Mr. Mud-
ford's fine tale ; and to have gone away into outer darkness, with
no project on the stocks, and the attorney's countenance averted,
would have been simply despair.

'To speak frankly,' said the poor vicar, with that hectic in his
cheek that came with agitation, 'I never fancied that my rever-
sionary interest could be saleable.'

'Neither is it, in all probability,' answered the attorney. 'As
you are so seriously pressed, and your brother's return delayed,
it merely crossed my mind as a thing worth trying.'

'It was very kind and thoughtful ; but that feeling—the—my
poor little man ! However, I may be only nervous and foolish,
and I think I'll speak to Lord Chelford about it.'

The attorney looked down, and took his nether lip gently between his finger and thumb. I rather think he had no particular wish to take Lord Chelford into council.

'I think before troubling his lordship upon the subject—if, indeed, on reflection, you should not think it would be a little odd
to trouble him at all in reference to it—I had better look a
little more carefully into the papers, and see whether anything
in that direction is really practicable at all.'

'Do you think, Mr. Larkin, you can write that strong letter to
stay proceedings which you intended yesterday ?'

The attorney shook his head, and said, with a sad sort of dryness—'I can't see my way to it.'

The vicar's heart sank with a flutter, and then swelled, and
sank another bit, and his forehead flushed.

There was a silence.

'You see, Mr. Wylder, I relied, in fact, altogether upon this a
—arrangement ; and I don't see that any thing is likely to come
of it.'

The attorney spoke in the same dry and reserved way, and
there was a shadow on his long face.

'I have forfeited his good-will somehow—he has ceased to

take any interest in my wretched affairs ; I am abandoned, and must be ruined.'

These dreadful thoughts filled in another silence ; and then the vicar said—

'I am afraid I have, quite unintentionally, offended you, Mr. Larkin—perhaps in my ignorance of business ; and I feel that I should be quite ruined if I were to forfeit your good offices ; and, pray tell me, if I have said anything I ought not.'

'Oh, no—nothing, I assure you,' replied Mr. Larkin, with a lofty and gentle dryness. 'Only, I think, I have, perhaps, a little mistaken the relation in which I stood, and fancied, wrongly, it was in the light somewhat of a friend as well as of a professional adviser ; and I thought, perhaps, I had rather more of your confidence than I had any right to, and did not at first see the necessity of calling in Lord Chelford, whose experience of business is necessarily very limited, to direct you. You remember, my dear Mr. Wylder, that I did not at all invite these relations ; and I don't think you will charge me with want of zeal in your business.'

'Oh ! my dear Mr. Larkin, my dear Sir, you have been my preserver, my benefactor — in fact, under Heaven, very nearly my last and only hope.'

'Well, I *had* hoped I was not remiss or wanting in diligence.'

And Mr. Larkin took his seat in his most gentlemanlike fashion, crossing his long legs, and throwing his tall head back, raising his eyebrows, and letting his mouth languidly drop a little open.

'My idea was, that Lord Chelford would see more clearly what was best for little Fairy. I am so very slow and so silly about business, and you so much my friend—I have found you so— —that you might think only of me.'

'I should, of course, consider the little boy,' said Mr. Larkin, condescendingly ; 'a most interesting child. I'm very fond of children myself, and should, of course, put the entire case—as respected him as well as yourself—to the best of my humble powers before you. Is there any thing else just now you think of, for time presses, and really we have ground to apprehend something unpleasant *to-morrow.* You ought not, my dear Sir —pray permit me to say—you really ought *not* to have allowed it to come to this.'

The poor vicar sighed profoundly, and shook his head, a contrite man. They both forgot that it was arithmetically impossible for him to have prevented it, unless he had got some money.

'Perhaps,' said the vicar, brightening up suddenly, and looking in the attorney's eyes for answer, 'Perhaps something might be done with the reversion, as a security, to borrow a sufficient sum, without selling.'

The attorney shook his high head, and whiskers gray and

foxy, and meditated with the seal of his pencil case between his lips.

'I don't see it,' said he, with another shake of that long head.

'I don't know that any lender, in fact, would entertain such a security. If you wish it I will write to Burlington, Smith, and Company, about it—they are largely in policies and *post-obits*.'

'It is very sad—very sad, indeed. I wish so much, my dear Sir, I could be of use to you ; but you know the fact is, we solicitors seldom have the command of our own money ; always in advance—always drained to the uttermost shilling, and I am myself in the predicament you will see there.'

And he threw a little note from the Dollington Bank to Jos. Larkin, Esq., The Lodge, Gylingden, announcing the fact that he had overdrawn his account certain pounds, shillings, and pence, and inviting him forthwith to restore the balance.

The vicar read it with a vague comprehension, and in his cold fingers shook the hand of his fellow sufferer. Less than fifty pounds would not do ! Oh, where was he to turn? It was *quite* hopeless, and poor Larkin pressed too !

Now, there was this consolation in 'poor Larkin's case,' that although he was quite run aground, and a defaulter in the Dollington Bank to the extent of 7*l.* 12*s.* 4*d.*, yet in that similar institution, which flourished at Naunton, only nine miles away, there stood to his name the satisfactory credit of 564*l.* 11*s.* 7*d.* One advantage which the good attorney derived from his double account with the rival institutions was, that whenever convenient he could throw one of these certificates of destitution and impotence sadly under the eyes of a client in want of money like poor Will Wylder.

The attorney had no pleasure in doing people ill turns. But he had come to hear the distresses of his clients as tranquilly as doctors do the pangs of their patients. As he stood meditating near his window, he saw the poor vicar, with slow limbs and downcast countenance, walk under his laburnums and laurustinuses towards his little gate, and suddenly stop and turn round, and make about a dozen quick steps, like a man who has found a bright idea, towards the house, and then come to a thoughtful halt, and so turn and recommence his slow march of despair homeward.

At five o'clock—it was dark now—there was a tread on the door-steps, and a double tattoo at the tiny knocker. It was the 'lawyer.'

Mr. Larkin entered the vicar's study, where he was supposed to be busy about his sermon.

'My dear Sir ; thinking about you—and I have just heard from an old humble friend, who wants high interest, and of course is content to take security somewhat personal in its nature. I have written already. He's in the hands of Burlington, Smith, and Company. I have got exactly 55*l.* since I saw you, which makes me all right at Dollington ; and here's my check for 50*l.* which you can send—or perhaps *I* had better send by this night's post—to those Cambridge people. It settles *that ;* and you give me a line on this stamp, acknowledging the 50*l.* on account of money to be raised on your reversion. So that's off your mind, my dear Sir.'

'Oh, Mr. Larkin—my—my—you don't know, Sir, what you have done for me—the agony—oh, thank God ! what a friend is raised up.'

And he clasped and wrung the long hands of the attorney, and I really think there was a little moisture in that gentleman's pink eyes for a moment or two.

When he was gone the vicar returned from the door-step, radiant—not to the study but to the parlour.

'Oh, Willie, darling, you look so happy—you were uneasy this evening,' said his little ugly wife, with a beautiful smile, jumping up and clasping him.

'Yes, darling, I was—*very* uneasy ; but thank God, it is over.'

And they cried and smiled together in that delightful embrace, while all the time little Fairy, with a paper cap on his head, was telling them half-a-dozen things together, and pulling Wapsie by the skirts.

Then he was lifted up and kissed, and smiled on by that sunshine only remembered in the sad old days — parental love. And there was high festival kept in the parlour that night. I am told six crumpets, and a new egg apiece besides at tea, to make merry with, and stories and little songs for Fairy. Willie was in his old college spirits. It was quite delightful ; and little Fairy was up a great deal too late ; and the vicar and his wife had quite a cheery chat over the fire, and he and she both agreed he would make a handsome sum by Eusebius.

Thus, if there are afflictions, there are also comforts : great consolations, great chastisements. There is a comforter, and there is a chastener. Every man must taste of death : every man must taste of life. It shall not be all bitter nor all sweet for any. It shall be life. The unseen ministers of a stupendous equity have their eyes and their hands about every man's portion ; 'as it is written, he that had gathered much had nothing over ; and he that had gathered little had no lack.'

It is the same earth for all ; the same earth for the dead, great and small ; dust to dust. The same earth for the living. 'Thorns, also, and thistles shall it bring forth,' and God provides the flowers too.

CHAPTER XLVI.

DEBATE AND INTERRUPTION.

RACHEL beheld the things which were coming to pass like an awful dream. She had begun to think, and not without evidence, that Dorcas, for some cause or caprice, had ceased to think of Stanley as she once did. And the announcement, without preparation or apparent courtship, that her brother had actually won this great and beautiful heiress, and that, just emerged from the shades of death, he, a half-ruined scapegrace, was about to take his place among the magnates of the county, and, no doubt, to enter himself for the bold and splendid game of ambition, the stakes of which were now in his hand, towered before her like an incredible and disastrous illusion of magic.

Stanley's uneasiness lest Rachel's conduct should compromise them increased. He grew more nervous about the relations between him and Mark Wylder, in proportion as the world grew more splendid and prosperous for him.

Where is the woman who will patiently acquiesce in the reserve of her husband who shares his confidence with another? How often had Stanley Lake sworn to her there was no secret; that he knew nothing of Mark Wylder beyond the charge of his money, and making a small payment to an old Mrs. Dutton, in London, by his direction, and that beyond this, he was as absolutely in the dark as she or Chelford.

What, then, did Rachel mean by all that escaped her, when he was in danger?

'How the — could he tell? He really believed she was a little—*ever* so little—crazed. He supposed she, like Dorcas, fancied he knew everything about Wylder. She was constantly hinting something of the kind; and begging of him to make a disclosure — disclosure of what? It was enough to drive one mad, and would make a capital farce. Rachel has a ridiculous way of talking like an oracle, and treating as settled fact every absurdity she fancies. She is very charming and clever, of course, so long as she speaks of the kind of thing she understands. But when she tries to talk of serious business—poor Radie! she certainly does talk such nonsense! She can't reason; she runs away with things. It *is* the most tiresome thing you can conceive.'

'But you have not said, Stanley, that she does not suspect the truth.'

'Of course, I say it; I *have* said it. I swear 't, if you like.

I've said plainly, and I'm ready to swear it. Upon my honour
and soul I know no more of his movements, plans, or motives,
than you do. If you reflect you must see it. We were never good
friends, Mark and I. It was no fault of mine, but I never liked
him ; and he, consequently, I suppose, never liked me. There
was no intimacy or confidence between us. I was the last man
on earth he would have consulted with. Even Larkin, his own
lawyer, is in the dark. Rachel knows all this. I have told her
fifty times over, and she seems to give way at the moment. Indeed the thing is too plain to be resisted. But as I said, poor
Radie, she can't reason ; and by the time I see her next, her old
fancy possesses her. I can't help it ; because with more reluctance than I can tell, I at length consent, at Larkin's *entreaty*,
I may say, to bank and fund his money.'

But Dorcas's mind retained its first impression. Sometimes
his plausibilities, his vehemence, and his vows disturbed it for
a time ; but there it remained like the picture of a camera
obscura, into which a momentary light has been admitted, unseen for a second, but the images return with the darkness, and
group themselves in their old colours and places again. Whatever it was Rachel probably knew it. There was a painful confidence between them ; and there was growing in Dorcas's mind
a feeling towards Rachel which her pride forbade her to define.

She did not like Stanley's stealthy visits to Redman's Farm ;
she did not like his moods or looks after those visits, of which
he thought she knew nothing. She did not know whether to be
pleased or sorry that Rachel had refused to reside at Brandon ;
neither did she like the stern gloom that overcast Rachel's
countenance when Stanley was in the room, nor those occasional
walks together, up and down the short yew walk, in which Lake
looked so cold and angry, and Rachel so earnest. What was
this secret ? How dared her husband mask from her what he
confided to another ? How dared Rachel confer with him—influence him, perhaps, under her very eye, walking before the
windows of Brandon—that Brandon which was *hers*, and to
which she had taken Stanley, passing her gate a poor and tired
wayfarer of the world, and made him — *what ?* Oh, mad
caprice ! Oh, fit retribution !

A wild voice was talking this way, to-and-fro, and up and
down, in the chambers of memory. But she would not let
it speak from her proud lips. She smiled, and to outward
seeming, was the same ; but Rachel felt that the fashion of her
countenance towards her was changed.

Since her marriage she had not hinted to Rachel the subject
of their old conversations : burning beneath her feeling about it
was now a deep-rooted anger and jealousy. Still she was
Stanley's sister, and to be treated accordingly. The whole
household greeted her with proper respect, and Dorcas met her

graciously, and with all the externals of kindness. The change was so little, that I do not think any but she and Rachel saw it ; and yet it was immense.

There was a dark room, a sort of ante-room, to the library, with only two tall and narrow windows, and hung with old Dutch tapestries, representing the battles and sieges of men in peri-wigs, pikemen, dragoons in buff coats, and musketeers with matchlocks—all the grim faces of soldiers, generals, drummers, and the rest, grown pale and dusky by time, like armies of ghosts.

Rachel had come one morning to see Dorcas, and, awaiting her appearance, sat down in this room. The door of the library opened, and she was a little surprised to see Stanley enter.

' Why, Stanley, they told me you were gone to Naunton.'

' Oh ! did they ? Well, you see, I'm here, Radie.'

Somehow he was not very well pleased to see her.

' I think you'll find Dorcas in the drawing-room, or else in the conservatory,' he added.

' I am glad, Stanley, I happened to meet you. Something *must* be done in the matter I spoke of immediately. Have you considered it ? '

' Most carefully,' said Stanley, quietly.

' But you have done nothing.'

' It is not a thing to be done in a moment.'

' You can, if you please, do a great deal in a moment.'

' Certainly ; but I may repent it afterwards.'

' Stanley, you may regret postponing it, much more.'

' You have no idea, Rachel, how very tiresome you've grown.'

' Yes, Stanley, I can quite understand it. It would have been better for you, perhaps for myself, I had died long ago.'

' Well, that is another thing ; but in the meantime, I assure you, Rachel, you are disposed to be very impertinent.'

' Very impertinent ; yes, indeed, Stanley, and so I shall con-tinue to be until——'

' Pray how does it concern you ? I say it is no business on earth of yours.'

Stanley Lake was growing angry.

' Yes, Stanley, it *does* concern me.'

' That is false.'

' True, *true*, Sir. Oh, Stanley, it is a load upon my conscience —a mountain—a mountain between me and my hopes. I can't endure the misery to which you would consign me ; you *shall* do it—immediately, too' (she stamped wildly as she said it), ' and if you hesitate, Stanley, I shall be compelled to speak, though the thought of it makes me almost mad with terror.'

' What is he to do, Rachel ? ' said Dorcas, standing near the door.

It was a very awkward pause. The splendid young bride was

the only person on the stage who looked very much as usual.
Stanley turned his pale glare of fury from Rachel to Dorcas,
and Dorcas said again,

'What is it, Rachel, darling?'

Rachel, with a bright blush on her cheeks, stepped quickly up
to her, put her arms about her neck and kissed her, and over
her shoulder she cried to her brother—

'Tell her, Stanley.'

And so she quickly left the room and was gone.

'Well, Dorkie, love, what's the matter?' said Stanley sharply,
at last breaking the silence.

'I really don't know—you, perhaps, can tell,' answered she
coldly.

'You have frightened Rachel out of the room, for one thing,'
answered he with a sneer.

'I simply asked her what she urged you to do—I think I have
a claim to know. It is strange so reasonable a question from a
wife should scare your sister from the room.'

'I don't quite see that—for my part, I don't think *anything*
strange in a woman. Rachel has been talking the rankest nonsense, in the most unreasonable temper conceivable; and
because she can't persuade me to accept her views of what is
Christian and sensible, she threatens to go mad—I think that is
her phrase.'

'I don't think Rachel is a fool,' said Dorcas, quietly, her eye
still upon Stanley.

'Neither do I—when she pleases to exert her good sense—
but she *can*, when she pleases, both talk and act like a fool.'

'And pray, what does she want you to do, Stanley?'

'The merest nonsense.'

'But what is it?'

'I really can hardly undertake to say I very well understand
it myself, and I have half-a-dozen letters to write; and really if
I were to stay here and try to explain, I very much doubt whether
I could. Why don't you ask *her*? If she has any clear ideas
on the subject I don't see why she should not tell you. For my
part, I doubt if she understands herself—*I* certainly don't.'

Dorcas smiled bitterly.

'Mystery already—mystery from the first. *I* am to know
nothing of your secrets. You confer and consult in my house—
you debate and decide upon matters most nearly concerning, for
aught I know, my interests and my happiness—certainly deeply
affecting you, and therefore which I have a *right* to know; and
my entering the room is the signal for silence—a guilty silence
—for departure and for equivocation. Stanley, you are isolating
me. Beware—I may entrench myself in that isolation. You
are choosing your confidant, and excluding me; rest assured
you shall have no confidence of mine while you do so.'

Stanley Lake looked at her with a gaze at once peevish and inquisitive.

' You take a wonderfully serious view of Rachel's nonsense.'

' I do.'

' Certainly, you women have a marvellous talent for making mountains of molehills—you and Radie are adepts in the art. Never was a poor devil so lectured about nothing as I between you. Come now, Dorkie, be a good girl—you must not look so vexed.'

' I'm not vexed.'

' What then ? '

' I'm only *thinking*.'

She said this with the same bitter smile. Stanley Lake looked for a moment disposed to break into one of his furies, but instead he only laughed his unpleasant laugh.

' Well, I'm thinking too, and I find it quite possible to be vexed at the same time. I assure you, Dorcas, I really am busy ; and it is too bad to have one's time wasted in solemn lectures about stuff and nonsense. Do make Rachel explain herself, if she can—*I* have no objection, I assure you ; but I must be permitted to decline undertaking to interpret that oracle.' And so saying, Stanley Lake glided into the library and shut the door with an angry clap.

Dorcas did not deign to look after him. She had heard his farewell address, looking from the window at the towering and sombre clumps of her ancestral trees—pale, proud, with perhaps a peculiar gleam of resentment—or malignity—in her exquisite features.

So she stood, looking forth on her noble possessions—on terraces—' long rows of urns '—noble timber—all seen in slanting sunlight and long shadows—and seeing nothing but the great word FOOL ! in letters of flame in the air before her.

CHAPTER XLVII.

A THREATENING NOTICE.

STANLEY LAKE was not a man to let the grass grow under his feet when an object was to be gained. It was with a sure prescience that Mark Wylder's letter had inferred that Stanley Lake would aspire to the representation either of the county or of the borough of Dollington. His mind was already full of these projects.

Electioneering sehemes are conducted, particularly at their initiation, like conspiracies—in fact, they *are* conspiracies, and therefore there was nothing remarkable in the intense caution with which Stanley Lake set about his. He was not yet 'feeling his way.' He was only preparing to feel his way.

All the data, except the muster-roll of electors, were *in nubibus* —who would retire—who would step forward, as yet altogether in the region of conjecture. There are men to whom the business of elections—a life of secrecy, excitement, speculation, and combat —has all but irresistible charms ; and Tom Wealdon, the Town Clerk, was such a spirit.

A bold, frank, good-humoured fellow—he played at elections as he would at cricket. Every faculty of eye, hand, and thought —his whole heart and soul in the game. But no ill-will—no malevolence in victory—no sourness in defeat. A successful *coup* made Tom Wealdon split with laughing. A ridiculous failure amused him nearly as much. He celebrated his last great defeat with a pic-nic in the romantic scenery of Nolton, where he and his comrades in disaster had a roaring evening, and no end of 'chaff.' When he and Jos. Larkin carried the last close contest at Dollington, by a majority of two, he kicked the crown out of the grave attorney's chimney-pot, and flung his own wide-awake into the river. He did not show much ; his official station precluded prominence. He kept in the background, and did his spiriting gently. But Tom Wealdon, it was known—as things *are* known without evidence—was at the bottom of all the clever dodges, and long-headed manœuvres. When, therefore, Mr. Larkin heard from the portly and veracious Mr. Larcom, who was on very happy relations with the proprietor of the Lodge, that Tom Wealdon had been twice quietly to Brandon to lunch, and had talked an hour alone with the captain in the library each time ; and that they seemed very 'hernest like, and stopped of talking directly he (Mr. Larcom) entered the room with the post-bag'—the attorney knew very well what was in the wind.

Now, it was not quite clear what was right—by which the good attorney meant prudent—under the circumstances. He was in confidential—which meant lucrative—relations with Mark Wylder. Ditto, ditto with Captain Lake, of Brandon. He did not wish to lose either. Was it possible to hold to both, or must he cleave only to one and despise the other?

Wylder might return any day, and Tom Wealdon would probably be one of the first men whom he would see. He must 'hang out the signal' in 'Galignani.' Lake could never suspect its meaning, even were he to see it. There was but one risk in it, which was in the coarse perfidy of Mark Wylder himself, who would desire no better fun, in some of his moods, than boasting to Lake of the whole arrangement in Jos. Larkin's presence.

However, on the whole, it was best to obey Mark Wylder's orders, and accordingly 'Galignani' said : '*Mr. Smith will take notice that the other party is desirous to purchase, and becoming very pressing.*'

In the meantime Lake was pushing his popularity among the gentry with remarkable industry, and with tolerable success. Wealdon's two little visits explained perfectly the active urbanities of Captain Stanley Lake.

About three weeks after the appearance of the advertisement in 'Galignani,' one of Mark Wylder's letters reached Larkin. It was dated from Geneva (!) and said :—

'DEAR LARKIN,— I saw my friend *Smith* here in the café, who has kept a bright look out, I dare say ; and tells me that Captain Stanley Lake is thinking of standing either for the county or for Dollington. I will thank you to apprise him that I mean to take my choice first ; and please hand him the enclosed notice open as you get it ; and, if you please, to let him run his eye also over this note to you, as I have my own reasons for wishing him to know that you have seen it.

'This is all I will probably trouble you about elections for some months to come, or, at least, weeks. It being time enough when I go back, and no squalls a-head just now at home, though foreign politics look muggy enough.

' I have nothing particular at present about tenants or timber, except the three acres of oak behind Farmer Tanby's — have it took down. Thomas Jones and me went over it last September, and it ought to bring near 3,000*l.* I must have a good handful of money by May next.

'   Yours, my dear Larkin,
'   Very truly,
'   MARK WYLDER.'

Folded in this was a thin slip of foreign paper, on which were traced these lines :—

'*Private.*

'DEAR LARKIN,—Don't funk the interview with the beast Lake—a hyæna has no pluck in him. When he reads what I send him by your hand, he'll be as mild as you please. Parkes must act for me as usual—no bluster about giving up. Lake's afraid of yours,

'M. W.'

Within was what he called his '*notice*' to Stanley Lake, and it was thus conceived :—

'*Private.*

'DEAR LAKE—I understand you are trying to make all safe for next election in Dollington or the county. Now, understand at once, that *I won't permit that.* There is not a country gentleman on the grand jury who is not your superior ; and there is no extremity I will not make you feel—and you know what I mean—if you dare despise this first and not unfriendly warning.

'Yours truly,
'MARK WYLDER.'

Now there certainly was need of Wylder's assurance that nothing unpleasant should happen to the conscious bearer of such a message to an officer and a gentleman. Jos. Larkin did not like it. Still there was a confidence in his own conciliatory manners and exquisite tact. Something, too, might be learned by noting Lake's looks, demeanour, and language under this direct communication from the man to whom his relations were so mysterious.

Larkin looked at his watch ; it was about the hour when he was likely to find Lake in his study. The attorney withdrew the little private enclosure, and slipt it, with a brief endorsement, into the neat sheaf of Wylder's letters, all similarly noted, and so locked it up in the iron safe. He intended being perfectly ingenuous with Lake, and showing him that he had 'no secrets—no concealments—all open as the day'—by producing the letter in which the 'notice' was enclosed, and submitting it for Captain Lake's perusal.

When Lawyer Larkin reached the dim chamber, with the Dutch tapestries, where he had for a little while to await Captain Lake's leisure, he began to anticipate the scene now so immediately impending more uncomfortably than before. The 'notice' was, indeed, so outrageous in its spirit, and so intolerable in its language, that, knowing something of Stanley's wild and truculent temper, he began to feel a little nervous about the explosion he was about to provoke.

The Brandon connection, one way or other, was worth to the

attorney in hard cash between five and six hundred a-year. In influence, and what is termed 'position,' it was, of course, worth a great deal more. It would be a very serious blow to lose this. He did not, he hoped, care for money more than a good man ought ; but such a loss, he would say, he could not afford.

Precisely the same, however, was to be said of his connection with Mark Wylder ; and in fact, of late years, Mr. Jos. Larkin, of the Lodge, had begun to put by money so fast that he was growing rapidly to be a very considerable man indeed. 'Everything,' as he said, 'was doing very nicely ;' and it would be a deplorable thing to mar, by any untoward act, this pilgrim's quiet and prosperous progress.

In this stage of his reverie he was interrupted by a tall, powdered footman, in the Brandon livery, who came respectfully to announce that his master desired to see Mr. Larkin.

Larkin's soul sneered at this piece of state. Why could he not put his head in at the door and call him ? But still I think it impressed him, and that, diplomatically, Captain Lake was in the right to environ himself with the ceremonial of a lord of Brandon.

'Well, Larkin, how d'ye do ? Anything about Raikes's lease?' said the great Captain Lake, rising from behind his desk, with his accustomed smile, and extending his gentlemanlike hand.

'No, Sir—nothing, Captain Lake. He has not come, and I don't think we should show any anxiety about it,' replied the attorney, taking the captain's thin hand rather deferentially. 'I've had—a—such a letter from my—my client, Mr. Mark Wylder. He writes in a violent passion, and I'm really placed in a most disagreeable position.'

'Won't you sit down ?'

'A—thanks—a—well I thought, on the whole, having received the letter and the enclosure, which I must say very much surprises me—very much *indeed*.' And Larkin looked reprovingly on an imaginary Mark Wylder, and shook his head a good deal.

'He has not appointed another man of business ?'

'Oh, dear, no,' said Larkin, quickly, with a faint, supercilious smile. 'No, nothing of that kind. The thing—in fact, there has been some gossiping fellow. Do you happen to know a person at all versed in Gylingden matters—or, perhaps, a member of your club—named Smith ?'

'Smith ? I don't, I think, recollect any particular Smith, just at this moment. And what is Smith doing or saying ?'

'Why, he has been talking over election matters. It seems Wylder—Mr. Wylder—has met him in Geneva, from whence he dates ; and he says — he says — oh, here's the letter, and you'll see it all there.'

He handed it to Lake, and kept his eye on him while he read

it. When he saw that Lake, who bit his lip during the perusal, had come to the end, by his glancing up again at the date, Larkin murmured—

'Something, you see, has gone wrong with him. I can't account for the temper otherwise—so violent.

'Quite so,' said Lake, quietly; 'and where is the notice he speaks of here?'

'Why, really, Captain Lake, I did not very well know, it *is such* a production— I could not say whether you would wish it presented; and in any case you will do me the justice to understand that I, for my part—I really don't know how to speak of it.'

'Quite so,' repeated Lake, softly, taking the thin, neatly folded piece of paper which Larkin, with a sad inclination of his body, handed to him.

Lake, under the 'lawyer's' small, vigilant eyes, quietly read Mark Wylder's awful threatenings through, twice over, and Larkin was not quite sure whether there was any change of countenance to speak of as he did so.

'This is dated the 29th,' said Lake, in the same quiet tone; 'perhaps you will be so good as to write a line across it, stating the date of your handing it to me.'

'I—of course—I can see no objection. I may mention, I suppose, that I do se at your request.'

And Larkin made a neat little endorsement to that effect, and he felt relieved. The hyæna certainly was not showing fight.

'And now, Mr. Larkin, you'll admit, I think, that I've exhibited no ill-temper, much less violence, under the provocation of that note.'

'Certainly; none whatever, Captain Lake.'

'And you will therefore perceive that whatever I now say, speaking in cool blood, I am not likely to recede from.'

Lawyer Larkin bowed.

'And may I particularly ask that you will so attend to what I am about to say, as to be able to make a note of it for Mr. Wylder's consideration?'

'Certainly, if you desire; but I wish to say that in this particular matter I beg it may be clearly understood that Mr. Wylder is in no respect more my client than you, Captain Lake, and that I merely act as a most reluctant messenger in the matter.'

'Just so,' said Captain Lake.

'Now, as to my thinking of representing either county or borough,' he resumed, after a little pause, holding Mark Wylder's 'notice' between his finger and thumb, and glancing at it from time to time, as a speaker might at his notes, 'I am just as well qualified as he in every respect; and if it lies between him and me, I will undoubtedly offer myself, and accompany my address with the publication of this precious document which he calls his notice—the composition, in all respects, of a ruffian—and which will inspire every gentleman who reads it with disgust, abhorrence, and contempt. His threat I don't understand. I despise his machinations. I defy him utterly ; and the time is coming when, in spite of his manœuvring, I'll drive him into a corner and pin him to the wall. He very well knows that flitting and skulking from place to place, like an escaped convict, he is safe in writing what insults he pleases through the post. I can't tell how or where to find him. He is not only no gentleman, but no man—a coward as well as a ruffian. But his game of hide-and-seek cannot go on for ever ; and when next I can lay my hand upon him, I'll make him eat that paper on his knees, and place my heel upon his neck.'

The peroration of this peculiar invective was emphasised by an oath, at which the half-dozen short grizzled hairs that surmounted the top of Mr. Jos. Larkin's shining bald head no doubt stood up in silent appeal.

The attorney was standing during this sample of Lake's parliamentary rhetoric a little flushed, for he did not know the moment when a blue flicker from the rhetorical thunder-storm might splinter his own bald head, and for ever end his connection with Brandon.

There was a silence, during which pale Captain Lake locked up Mark Wylder's warning, and the attorney twice cleared his voice.

'I need hardly say, Captain Lake, how I feel in this business. I——'

'Quite so,' said the captain, in his soft low tones. 'I assure you I altogether acquit you of sympathy with any thing so utterly ruffianly,' and he took the hand of the relieved attorney with a friendly condescension. 'The only compensation I exact for your involuntary part in the matter is that you distinctly convey the tenor of my language to Mr. Wylder, on the first occasion on which he affords you an opportunity of communicating with him. And as to my ever again acting as his trustee ;—though, yes, I forgot'—he made a sudden pause, and was lost for a minute in annoyed reflection—'yes, I must for a while. It can't last very long ; he *must* return soon, and I can't well refuse to act until at least some other arrangement is made. There are quite other persons and I can't allow them to starve.'

So saying, he rose, with his peculiar smile, and extended his hand to signify that the conference was at an end.

'And I suppose,' he said, 'we are to regard this little conversation, for the present, as confidential ?'

'Certainly, Captain Lake, and permit me to say that I fully appreciate the just and liberal construction which you have

placed upon my conduct—a construction which a party less
candid and honourably-minded than yourself might have failed
to favour me with.'

And with this pretty speech Larkin took his hat, and gracefully withdrew.

CHAPTER XLVIII.

IN WHICH I GO TO BRANDON, AND SEE AN OLD ACQUAINT-
ANCE IN THE TAPESTRY ROOM.

O my surprise, a large letter, bearing the Gylingden postmark, and with a seal as large as a florin, showing,
had I examined the heraldry, the Brandon arms with
the Lake bearings quartered thereon, and proving to
be a very earnest invitation from Stanley Lake, found me in
London just about this time.

I paused, I was doubtful about accepting it, for the business
of the season was just about to commence in earnest, and the
country had not yet assumed its charms. But I now know very
well that from the first it was quite settled that down I should
go. I was too curious to see the bride in her new relations, and
to observe something of the conjugal adminstration of Lake, to
allow anything seriously to stand in the way of my proposed
trip.

There was a postscript to Lake's letter which might have
opened my eyes as to the motives of this pressing invitation,
which I pleased myself by thinking, though penned by Captain
Lake, came in reality from his beautiful young bride.

This small appendix was thus conceived :—

' P.S.—Tom Wealdon, as usual, deep in elections, under the
rose, begs you kindly to bring down whatever you think to be
the best book or books on the subject, and he will remit to your
bookseller. Order them in his name, but bring them down with
you.'

So I was a second time going down to Brandon as honorary
counsel, without knowing it. My invitations, I fear, were obtained, if not under false pretences, at least upon false estimates,
and the laity rated my legal lore too highly.

I reached Brandon rather late. The bride had retired for the
night. I had a very late dinner—in fact a supper—in the parlour. Lake sat with me chatting, rather cleverly, not pleasantly.
Wealdon was at Brandon about sessions business, and as usual

full of election stratagems and calculations. Stanley volunteered to assure me he had not the faintest idea of looking for a constituency. I really believe—and at this distance of time I may use strong language in a historical sense—that Captain Lake was the greatest liar I ever encountered with. He seemed to do it without a purpose—by instinct, or on principle—and would contradict himself solemnly twice or thrice in a week, without seeming to perceive it. I dare say he lied always, and about everything. But it was in matters of some moment that one perceived it.

What object could he gain, for instance, by the fib he had just told me? On second thoughts this night he coolly apprised me that he *had* some idea of sounding the electors. So, my meal ended, we went into the tapestry room where, the night being sharp, a pleasant bit of fire burned in the grate, and Wealdon greeted me.

My journey, though by rail, and as easy as that of the Persian gentleman who skimmed the air, seated on a piece of carpet, predisposed me to sleep. Such volumes of fine and various country air, and such an eight hours' procession of all sorts of natural pictures are not traversed without effect. Sitting in my well-stuffed chair, my elbows on the cushioned arms, the conversation of Lake and the Town Clerk now and then grew faint, and their faces faded away, and little 'fyttes' and fragments of those light and pleasant dreams, like fairy tales, which visit such stolen naps, superseded with their picturesque and musical illusions the realities and recollections of life.

Once or twice a nod a little too deep or sudden called me up. But Lake was busy about the Dollington constituency, and the Town Clerk's bluff face was serious and thoughtful. It was the old question about Rogers, the brewer, and whether Lord Adleston and Sir William could not get him; or else it had gone on to the great railway contractor, Dobbs, and the question how many votes his influence was really worth; and, somehow, I never got very far into the pros and cons of these discussions, which soon subsided into the fairy tale I have mentioned, and that sweet perpendicular sleep—all the sweeter, like everything else, for being contraband and irregular.

For one bout—I fancy a good deal longer than the others— my nap was much sounder than before, and I opened my eyes at last with the shudder and half horror that accompany an awakening from a general chill—a dismal and frightened sensation.

I was facing a door about twenty feet distant, which exactly as I opened my eyes, turned slowly on its hinges, and the figure of Uncle Lorne, in his loose flannel habiliments, ineffaceably traced upon my memory, like every other detail of that ill-omened apparition, glided into the room, and crossing the thick carpet with long, soft steps, passed near me, looking upon me with a malign sort of curiosity for some two or three seconds, and sat down by the declining fire, with a side-long glance still fixed upon me.

I continued gazing on this figure with a dreadful incredulity, and the indistinct feeling that it must be an illusion—and that if I could only wake up completely, it would vanish.

The fascination was disturbed by a noise at the other end of the room, and I saw Lake standing close to him, and looking both angry and frightened. Tom Wealdon looking odd, too, was close at his elbow, and had his hand on Lake's arm, like a man who would prevent violence. I do not know in the least what had passed before, but Lake said—

'How the devil did he come in?'

'Hush!' was all that Tom Wealdon said, looking at the gaunt spectre with less of fear than inquisitiveness.

'What are you doing here, Sir?' demanded Lake, in his most unpleasant tones.

'Prophesying,' answered the phantom.

'You had better write your prophecies in your room, Sir—had not you?—and give them to the Archbishop of Canterbury to proclaim, when they are finished; we are busy here just now, and don't require revelations, if you please.'

The old man lifted up his long lean finger, and turned on him with a smile which I hate even to remember.

'Let him alone,' whispered the Town Clerk, in a significant whisper, 'don't cross him, and he'll not stay long.'

'*You're* here, a scribe,' murmured Uncle Lorne, looking upon Tom Wealdon.

'Aye, Sir, a scribe and a Pharisee, a Sadducee and a publican, and a priest, and a Levite,' said the functionary, with a wink at Lake. 'Thomas Wealdon, Sir; happy to see you, Sir, so well and strong, and likely to enlighten the religious world for many a day to come. It's a long time, Sir, since I had the honour of seeing you; and I'm always, of course, at your command.'

'Pshaw!' said Lake, angrily.

The Town Clerk pressed his arm with a significant side nod and a wink, which seemed to say, 'I understand him; can't you let me manage him?'

The old man did not seem to hear what they said; but his tall figure rose up, and he extended the fingers of his left hand close to the candle for a few seconds, and then held them up to his eyes, gazing on his finger-tips, with a horrified sort of scrutiny, as if he saw signs and portents gathered there, like Thomas Aquinas' angels at the needles' points, and then the same cadaverous grin broke out over his features.

'Mark Wylder is in an evil plight,' said he.

'Is he?' said Lake, with a sly scoff, though he seemed to me a good deal scared. 'We hear no complaints, however, and fancy he must be tolerably comfortable notwithstanding.'

'You know where he is,' said Uncle Lorne.

'Aye, in Italy; everyone knows that,' answered Lake.

'In Italy,' said the old man, reflectively, as if trying to gather up his ideas, 'Italy. Oh! yes, Vallombrosa—aye, Italy, I know it well.'

'So do we, Sir; thank you for the information,' said Lake, who nevertheless appeared strangely uneasy.

'He has had a great tour to make. It is nearly accomplished now; when it is done, he will be like me, *humano major*. He has seen the places which you are yet to see.'

'Nothing I should like better; particularly Italy,' said Lake.

'Yes,' said Uncle Lorne, lifting up slowly a different finger at each name in his catalogue. 'First, Lucus Mortis; then Terra Tenebrosa; next, Tartarus; after that, Terra Oblivionis; then Herebus; then Barathrum; then Gehenna, and then Stagium Ignis.'

'Of course,' acquiesced Lake, with an ugly sneer, and a mock bow.

'And to think that all the white citizens were once men and women!' murmured Uncle Lorne, with a scowl.

'Quite so,' whispered Lake.

'I know where he is,' resumed the old man, with his finger on his long chin, and looking down upon the carpet.

'It would be very convenient if you would favour us with his address,' said Stanley, with a gracious sneer.

'I know what became of him,' continued the oracle.

'You are more in his confidence than we are,' said Lake.

'Don't be frightened—but he's alive; I think they'll make him mad. It is a frightful plight. Two angels buried him alive in Vallombrosa by night; I saw it, standing among the lotus and hemlock. A negro came to me, a black clergyman with white eyes, and remained beside me; and the angels imprisoned Mark; they put him on duty forty days and forty nights, with his ear to the river listening for voices; and when it was over we blessed them; and the clergyman walked with me a long while, to-and-fro, to-and-fro upon the earth, telling me the wonders of the abyss.'

'And is it from the abyss, Sir, he writes his letters?' enquired the Town Clerk, with a wink at Lake.

'Yes, yes, very diligent; it behoves him; and his hair is always standing straight on his head for fear. But he'll be sent up again, at last, a thousand, a hundred, ten and one, black marble steps, and then it will be the other one's turn. So it was prophesied by the black magician.'

'I thought, Sir, you mentioned just now he was a clergyman,' suggested Mr. Wealdon, who evidently enjoyed this wonderful yarn.

'Clergyman and magician both, and the chief of the lying prophets with thick lips. He'll come here some night and see you,' said Uncle Lorne, looking with a cadaverous apathy on Lake, who was gazing at him in return, with a sinister smile.

'Maybe it was a vision, Sir,' suggested the Town Clerk.

'Yes, Sir ; a vision, maybe,' echoed the cavernous tones of the old man ; 'but in the flesh or out of the flesh, I saw it.'

'You have had revelations, Sir, I've heard,' said Stanley's mocking voice.

'Many,' said the seer ; 'but a prophet is never honoured. We live in solitude and privations—the world hates us—they stone us—they cut us asunder, even when we are dead. Feel me—I'm cold and white all over—I died too soon—I'd have had wings now only for that pistol. I'm as white as Gehazi, except on my head, when that blood comes.'

Saying which, he rose abruptly, and with long jerking steps limped to the door, at which, I saw, in the shade, the face of a dark-featured man, looking gloomily in.

When he reached the door Uncle Lorne suddenly stopped and faced us, with a countenance of wrath and fear, and threw up his arms in an attitude of denunciation, but said nothing. I thought for a moment the gigantic spectre was about to rush upon us in an access of frenzy ; but whatever the impulse, it subsided—or was diverted by some new idea ; his countenance changed, and he beckoned as if to some one in the corner of the room behind us, and smiled his dreadful smile, and so left the apartment.

'That d—d old madman is madder than ever,' said Lake, in his fellest tones, looking steadfastly with his peculiar gaze upon the closed door. 'Jermyn is with him, but he'll burn the house or murder some one yet. It's all d—d nonsense keeping him here —did you see him at the door ?—he was on the point of assailing some of us. He ought to be in a madhouse.'

'He used to be very quiet,' said the Town Clerk, who knew all about him.

'Oh ! very quiet—yes, of course, very quiet, and quite harmless to people who don't live in the house with him, and see him but once in half-a-dozen years ; but you can't persuade me it is quite so pleasant for those who happen to live under the same roof, and are liable to be intruded upon as we have been to-night every hour of their existence.'

'Well, certainly it is not pleasant, especially for ladies,' admitted the Town Clerk.

'No, not pleasant—and I've quite made up my mind it sha'n't go on. It is too absurd, really, that such a monstrous thing should be enforced ; I'll get a private Act, next Session, and regulate those absurd conditions in the will. The old fellow ought to be under restraint; and I rather think it would be better for himself that he were.'

' Who is he?' I asked, speaking for the first time.

' I thought you had seen him before now,' said Lake.

' So I have, but quite alone, and without ever learning who he was,' I answered.

' Oh! He is the gentleman, Julius, for whom in the will, under which we take, those very odd provisions are made—such as I believe no one but a Wylder or a Brandon would have dreamed of. It is an odd state of things to hold one's estate under condition of letting a madman wander about your house and place, making everybody in it uncomfortable and insecure, and exposing him to the imminent risk of making away with himself, either by accident or design. I happen to know what Mark Wylder would have done—for he spoke very fiercely on the subject—perhaps he consulted you?'

' No.'

' No? well, he intended locking him quietly into the suite of three apartments, you know, at the far end of the old gallery, and giving him full command of the mulberry garden by the little private stair, and putting a good iron door to it; so that " my beloved brother, Julius, at present afflicted in mind " (Lake quoted the words of the will, with an unpleasant sneer), should have had his apartments and his pleasure grounds quite to himself.'

' And would that arrangement of Mr. Wylder's have satisfied the conditions of the will?' said the Town Clerk.

' I rather think, with proper precautions, it would. Mark Wylder was very shrewd, and would not have run himself into a fix,' answered Lake. ' I don't know any man shrewder; he is, certainly.'

And Lake looked at us, as he added these last words, in turn, with a quick, suspicious glance, as if he had said something rash, and doubted whether we had observed it.

After a little more talk, Lake and the Town Clerk resumed their electioneering conference, and the lists of electors were passed under their scrutiny, name by name, like slides under the miscroscope.

There is a great deal in nature, physical and moral, that had as well not be ascertained. It is better to take things on trust, with something of distance and indistinctness. What we gain in knowledge by scrutiny is sometimes paid for in a ghastly sort of disgust. It is marvellous in a small constituency of 300 average souls, what a queer moral result one of these business-like and narrow investigations which precede an election will furnish. How you find them rated and classified—what odd notes you make to them in the margin; and after the trenchant and rapid vivisection, what sinister scars and seams remain, and how gaunt and repulsive old acquaintances stand up from it.

The Town Clerk knew the constituency of Dollington at his fingers' ends ; and Stanley Lake quietly enjoyed, as certain minds will, the nefarious and shabby metamorphosis which every now and then some familiar and respectable burgess underwent, in the spell of half-a-dozen dry sentences whispered in his ear ; and all this minute information is trustworthy and quite without malice.

I went to my bed-room, and secured the door, lest Uncle Lorne, or Julius, should make me another midnight visit. So that mystery was cleared up. Neither ghost nor spectral illusion, but flesh and blood—though in my mind there has always been a horror of a madman akin to the ghostly or demoniac.

I do not know how late Tom Wealdon and Stanley Lake sat up over their lists ; but I dare say they were in no hurry to leave them, for a dissolution was just then expected, and no time was to be lost.

When I saw Tom Wealdon alone next day in the street of Gylingden, he walked a little way with me, and, said Tom, with a grave wink—

' Don't let the captain up there be hard on the poor old gentleman. He's quite harmless—he would not hurt a fly. I know all about him ; for Jack Ford and I spent five weeks in the Hall, about twelve years ago, when the family were away and thought the keeper was not kind to him. He's quite gentle, and sometimes he'd make you die o' laughing. He fancies, you know, he's a prophet ; and says he's that old Sir Lorne Brandon that shot himself in his bed-room. Well, he is a rum one ; and we used to draw him out—poor Jack and me. I never laughed so much, I don't think, in the same time, before or since. But he's as innocent as a child—and you know them directions in the will is very strong ; and they say Jos. Larkin does not like the captain a bit too well—and he has the will off, every word of it ; and I think, if Captain Lake does not take care, he may get into trouble ; and maybe it would not be amiss if you gave him a hint.'

Tom Wealdon, indeed, was a good-natured fellow : and if he had had his way, I think the world would have gone smoothly enough with most people.

CHAPTER XLIX.

LARCOM, THE BUTLER, VISITS THE ATTORNEY.

OW I may as well mention here an occurrence which, seeming very insignificant, has yet a bearing upon the current of this tale, and it is this. About four days after the receipt of the despatches to which the conference of Captain Lake and the attorney referred, there came a letter from the same prolific correspondent, dated 20th March, from Genoa, which altogether puzzled Mr. Larkin. It commenced thus :—

'Genoa : 20th March.

'DEAR LARKIN,—I hope you did the three commissions all right. Wealdon won't refuse, I reckon—but don't let Lake guess what the 150*l*. is for. Pay Martin for the job when finished ; it is under 60*l*. mind ; and get it looked at first.'

There was a great deal more, but these were the passages which perplexed Larkin. He unlocked the iron safe, and took out the sheaf of Wylder's letters, and conned the last one over very carefully.

'Why,' said he, holding the text before his eyes in one hand and with the fingers of the other touching the top of his bald forehead, 'Tom Wealdon is not once mentioned in this, nor in any of them ; and this palpably refers to some direction. And 150*l*.?—no such sum has been mentioned. And what is this job of Martin's ? Is it Martin of the China Kilns, or Martin of the bank ? That, too, plainly refers to a former letter—not a word of the sort. This is very odd indeed.'

Larkin's finger-tips descended over his eyebrow, and scratched in a miniature way there for a few seconds, and then his large long hand descended further to his chin, and his under-lip was, as usual in deep thought, fondled and pinched between his finger and thumb.

'There has plainly been a letter lost, manifestly. I never knew anything wrong in this Gylingden office. Driver has been always correct ; but it is hard to know any man for certain in this world. I don't think the captain would venture anything so awfully hazardous. I really can't suspect so monstrous a thing ; but, *unquestionably*, a letter *has* been lost—and who's to *take* it ?'

Larkin made a fuller endorsement than usual on this particular letter, and ruminated over the correspondence a good while, with his lip between his finger and thumb, and a shadow on his face, before he replaced it in its iron drawer.

'It is not a thing to be passed over,' murmured the attorney, who had come to a decision as to the first step to be taken, and he thought with a qualm of the effect of one of Wylder's confidential notes getting into Captain Lake's hands.

While he was buttoning his walking boots, with his foot on the chair before the fire, a tap at his study door surprised him. A hurried glance on the table satisfying him that no secret paper or despatch lay there, he called—

'Come in.'

And Mr. Larcom, the grave butler of Brandon, wearing outside his portly person a black garment then known as a 'zephyr,' a white choker, and black trousers, and well polished, but rather splay shoes, and, on the whole, his fat and serious aspect considered, being capable of being mistaken for a church dignitary, or at least for an eminent undertaker, entered the room with a solemn and gentlemanlike reverence.

'Oh, Mr. Larcom! a message, or business?' said Mr. Larkin, urbanely.

'Not a message, Sir; only an enquiry about them few shares,' answered Mr. Larcom, with another serene reverence, and remaining standing, hat in hand, at the door.

'Oh, yes; and how do you do, Mr. Larcom? Quite well, I trust. Yes—about the Naunton Junction. Well, I'm happy to tell you—but pray take a chair—that I have succeeded, and the directors have allotted you five shares; and it's your own fault if you don't make two ten-and-six a share. The Chowsleys are up to six and a-half, I see here,' and he pointed to the 'Times.'

Mr. Larcom's fat face smiled, in spite of his endeavour to keep it under. It was part of his business to look always grave, and he coughed, and recovered his gravity.

'I'm very thankful, Sir,' said Mr. Larcom, 'very.'

'But do sit down, Mr. Larcom—pray do,' said the attorney, who was very gracious to Larcom. 'You'll get the scrip, you know, on executing, but the shares are allotted. They sent the notice for you here. And—and how are the family at Brandon —all well, I trust?'

Mr. Larcom blew his nose.

'All, Sir, well.'

'And—and let me give you a glass of sherry, Mr. Larcom, after your walk. I can't compete with the *Brandon* sherry, Mr. Larcom. Wonderful fine wine that!—but still I'm told this is not a *bad* wine notwithstanding.'

Larcom received it with grave gratitude, and sipped it, and spoke respectfully of it.

'And—and any news in that quarter of Mr. Mark Wylder— —any—any *surmise?* I—you know—I'm interested for all parties.'

'Well, Sir, of Mr. Wylder, I can't say as I know no more than he's been a subjek of much unpleasant feelin', which I should say there has been a great deal of angry talk since I last saw you, Sir, between Miss Lake and the capting.'

'Ah, yes, you mentioned something of the kind; and your own impression, that Captain Lake, which I trust may turn out to be so, knows where Mr. Mark Wylder is at present staying.'

'I much misdoubt, Sir, it won't turn out to be no good story for no one,' said Mr. Larcom, in a low and sad tone, and with a long shake of his head.

'No good story—hey? How do you mean, Larcom?'

'Well, Sir, I know you won't mention me, Mr. Larkin.'

'Certainly not—go on.'

'When people gets hot a-talking they won't mind a body comin' in; and that's how the capting and Miss Rachel Lake they carried on their dispute like, though me coming into the room.'

'Just so; and what do you found your opinion about Mr. Mark Wylder on?'

'Well, Sir, I could not hear more than a word now and a sentince again; and pickin' what meaning I could out of what Miss Lake said, and the capting could not deny, I do suspeck, Sir, most serious, as how they have put Mr. Mark Wylder into a mad-house; and that's how I think it's gone with him; an' you'll never see him out again if the capting has his will.'

'Do you mean to say you actually think he's shut up in a mad-house at this moment?' demanded the attorney; his little pink eyes opened quite round, and his lank cheeks and tall forehead flushed, at the rush of wild ideas that whirred round him, like a covey of birds at the startling suggestion.

The butler nodded gloomily. Larkin continued to stare on him in silence, with his round eyes, for some seconds after.

'In a *mad*-house! Pooh, pooh! incredible! Pooh! impossible—*quite* impossible. Did either Miss Lake or the captain use the word mad-house?'

'Well, no.'

'Or any other word—lunatic asylum, or a—bedlam, or—or *any* other word meaning the same thing?'

'Well, I can't say, Sir, as I remember; but I rayther think not. I only know for certain, I took it so; and I do believe as how Mr. Mark Wylder is confined in a mad-house, and the captain knows all about it, and won't do nothing to get him out.'

'H'm—very odd—very strange; but it is only from the general tenor of what passed, by a sort of guess work, you have arrived at that conclusion?'

Larcom assented.

'Well, Mr. Larcom, I think you have been led into an erroneous conclusion. Indeed, I may mention I have reason to think so—in fact, to *know* that such is the case. What you mention to me, you know, as a friend of the family, and holding, as I do, a confidential position—in fact, a *very* confidential one —alike in relation to Mr. Wylder and to the family of Brandon Hall, is of course sacred ; and anything that comes from you, Mr. Larcom, is never heard in connection with your name beyond these walls. And let me add, it strikes me as highly important, both in the interests of the leading individuals in this unpleasant business, and also as pertaining to your own comfort and security, that you should carefully avoid communicating what you have just mentioned to any other party. You understand ?'

Larcom did understand perfectly, and so this little visit ended.

Mr. Larkin took a turn or two up and down the room thinking. He stopped, with his finger tips to his eyebrow, and thought more. Then he took another turn, and stopped again, and threw back his head, and gazed for a while on the ceiling, and then he stood for a time at the window, with his lip between his finger and thumb.

No, it was a mistake ; it could not be. It was Mark Wylder's penmanship—he could swear to it. There was no trace of madness in his letters, nor of restraint. It was not possible even that he was wandering from place to place under the coercion of a couple of keepers. No ; Wylder was an energetic and somewhat violent person, with high animal courage, and would be sure to blow up and break through any such machination. No, no; with Mark Wylder it was quite out of the question—altogether visionary and impracticable. Persons like Larcom do make such absurd blunders, and so misapprehend the conversation of educated people.

Nothwithstanding all which, there remained in his mind an image of Mark Wylder, in the straw and darkness of a solitary continental mad-house—squalid, neglected, and becoming gradually that which he was said to be. And he always shaped him somehow after the outlines of a grizzly print he remembered in his boyish days, of a maniac chained in a Sicilian cell, grovelling under the lash of a half-seen gaoler, and with his teeth buried in his own arm.

Quite impossible ! Mark Wylder was the last man in the world to submit to physical coercion. The idea, besides, could not be reconciled with the facts of the case. It was all a blundering chimera.

Mr. Larkin walked down direct to Gylingden, and paid a rather awful visit to Mr. Driver, of the post-office. A foreign letter, addressed to him, had most positively been lost. He had called to mention the circumstance, lest Mr. Driver should be taken by surprise by official investigation. Was it possible that the letter had been sent by mistake to Brandon—to Captain Lake ? Lake and Larkin, you know, might be mistaken. At all events, it would be well to make your clerks recollect themselves. (Mr. Larkin knew that Driver's 'clerks' were his daughters.) It is not easy to meet with a young fellow that is quite honest. But if they knew that they would be subjected to a sifting examination on oath, on the arrival of the commissioner, they might possibly prefer finding the letter, in which case there would be no more about it. Mr. Driver knew him (Mr. Larkin), and he might tell his young men if they got the letter for him they should hear no more of it.

The people of Gylingden knew very well that, when the rat-like glitter twinkled in Mr. Larkin's eyes, and the shadow came over his long face, there was mischief brewing.

CHAPTER L.

NEW LIGHTS.

A FEW days later 'Jos. Larkin, Esq., The Lodge, Gylingden,' received from London a printed form, duly filled in, and with the official signature attached, informing him that enquiry having been instituted in consequence of his letter, no result had been obtained.

The hiatus in his correspondence caused Mr. Larkin extreme uneasiness. He had a profound distrust of Captain Lake. In fact, he thought him capable of everything. And if there should turn out to be anything not quite straight going on at the post-office of Gylingden—hitherto an unimpeached institution—he had no doubt whatsoever that that dark and sinuous spirit was at the bottom of it.

Still it was too prodigious, and too hazardous to be probable; but the captain had no sort of principle, and a desperately strong head. There was not, indeed, when they met yesterday, the least change or consciousness in the captain's manner. That, in another man, would have indicated something; but Stanley Lake was so deep — such a mask — in him it meant nothing.

Mr. Larkin's next step was to apply for a commissioner to come down and investigate. But before he had time to take this step, an occurrence took place to arrest his proceedings. It was the receipt of a foreign letter, of which the following is an exact copy :—

'VENICE: March 28.

'DEAR LARKIN,—I read a rumour of a dissolution during the recess. Keep a bright look out. Here's three things for you :—

' 1. Try and get Tom Wealdon. He is a *sina que non.* [Mark's Latin was sailor-like.]

' 2. Cash the enclosed order for 150*l.* more, for *the same stake.*

' 3. Tell Martin the tiles I saw in August last will answer for the cow-house ; and let him put them down at once.

'In haste,
'Yours truly,
'M. WYLDER.'

Enclosed was an order on Lake for 150*l.*

When Larkin got this he was in his study.

'Why—why—this—*positively* this is the letter. *How's* this ?' And Mr. Larkin looked as much scared and astonished as if a spirit rose up before him.

'*This* is the letter—aye, this *is* the letter.'

He repeated this from time to time as he turned it over and looked at the postmark, and back again at the letter, and looked up at the date, and down at the signature, and read the note through.

'Yes, this is it—here it is—this is it. There's no doubt what-ever—this is the letter referred to in the last—Wealdon, Martin, and the 150*l.*'

And the attorney took out his keys, looking pale and stern, like a man about to open the door upon a horror, and unlocked his safe, and took out the oft-consulted and familiar series—letters tied up and bearing the label, ' Mark Wylder, Esq.'

'Aye, here it is, Genoa, 20th, and this, Venice, 28th. Yes, the postmarks correspond ; yet the letter from Genoa, dated 20th, refers back to the letter from Venice, written eight days later ! the— Well—I can't comprehend—how in the name of—how in the name——'

He placed the two letters on his desk, and read them over, and up and down, and pondered darkly over them.

'It is Mark Wylder's writing—I'll swear to it. What on earth *can* he mean? He can't possibly want to confuse us upon dates, as well as places, because that would simply render his letters, for purposes of business, nugatory, and there are many things he wishes attended to.'

Jos. Larkin rose from his desk, ruminating, and went to the window, and placed the letter against the pane. I don't think he had any definite motive in doing this, but something struck him that he had not remarked before.

There was something different in the quality of the ink that wrote the number of the date, 28th, from that used in the rest of the letter.

'What can that mean?' muttered Larkin, with a sort of gasp at his discovery; and shading his eyes with his hand, he scru-tinised the numerals—' 28th,' again ;—' a totally different ink !

He took the previous letter, frowned on it fiercely from his rat-like eyes, and then with an ejaculation, as like an oath as so good a man could utter, he exclaimed,

' I have it !'

Then came a pause, and he said—

' Both alike !—blanks left when the letters were written, and the dates filled in afterward—*not* the same hand I *think*—no, *not* the same—*positively* a different hand.'

Then Jos. Larkin examined these mysterious epistles once more.

' There may be something in what Larcom said—a very great deal, possibly. If he was shut up somewhere they could make him write a set of these letters off at a sitting, and send them from place to place to be posted, to make us think he was travelling, and prevent our finding where they keep him. Here it is plain there was a slip in posting the wrong one first.'

Trepanned, kidnapped, hid away in the crypts of some remote mad-house—reduced to submission by privation and misery—a case as desperate as that of a prisoner in the Inquisition. What could be the motive for this elaborate and hideous fraud? Would it not be a more convenient course, as well as more merciful to put him to death? The crime would hardly be greater. Why should he be retained in that ghastly existence?

Well, if Stanley Lake were at the bottom of this horrid conspiracy, *he* certainly had a motive in clearing the field of his rival. And then—for the attorney had all the family settlements present to his mind—there was this clear motive for prolonging his life, that by the slip in the will under which Dorcas Brandon inherited, the bulk of her estate would terminate with the life of Mark Wylder ; and this other motive too existed for retaining him in the house of bondage, that by preventing his marriage, and his having a family to succeed him, the reversion of his brother William was reduced to a certainty, and would become a magnificent investment for Stanley Lake whenever he might choose to purchase. Upon that purchase, however, the good attorney had cast his eye. He thought he now began to discern the outlines of a gigantic and symmetrical villainy emerging through the fog. If this theory were right, William Wylder's reversion was certain to take effect ; and it was exasperating that the native craft and daring of this inexperienced captain should forestall so accomplished a man of business as Jos. Larkin.

The attorney began to hate Stanley Lake as none but a man of that stamp can hate the person who mars a scheme of aggrandisement. But what was he to do exactly? If the captain had his eye on the reversion, it would require nice navigation to carry his plan successfully through.

On the other hand, it was quite possible that Wylder was a

free agent, and yet, for purposes of secrecy, employing another person to post his letters at various continental towns; and this blunder might just as well have happened in this case, as in any other that supposed the same machinery.

On the whole, then, it was a difficult question. But there were Larcom's conclusions about the mad-house to throw into the balance. And though, as respected Mark Wylder, they were grisly, the attorney would not have been sorry to be quite sure that they were sound. What he most needed were ascertained data. With these his opportunities were immense.

Mr. Larkin eyed the Wylder correspondence now with a sort of reverence that was new to him. There was something supernatural and talismanic in the mystery. The sheaf of letters lay before him on the table, like Cornelius Agrippa's 'bloody book' —a thing to conjure with. What prodigies might it not accomplish for its happy possessor, if only he could read it aright, and command the spirits which its spells might call up before him? Yes, it was a stupendous secret. Who knew to what it might conduct? There was a shade of guilt in his tamperings with it, akin to the black art, which he felt without acknowledging. This little parcel of letters was, in its evil way, a holy thing. While it lay on the table, the room became the holy of holies in his dark religion; and the lank attorney, with tall bald head, shaded face, and hungry dangerous eyes, a priest or a magician.

The attorney quietly bolted his study door, and stood erect, with his hands in his pockets, looking sternly down on the letters. Then he took a little gazetteer off a tiny shelf near the bell-rope, where was a railway guide, an English dictionary, a French ditto, and a Bible, and with his sharp penknife he deftly sliced from its place in the work of reference the folded map of Europe.

It was destined to illustrate the correspondence, and Larkin sat down before it and surveyed, with a solemn stare, the wide scene of Mark Wylder's operations, as a general would the theatre of his rival's strategy.

Referring to the letters as he proceeded, with a sharp pen in red ink, he made his natty little note upon each town or capital in succession, from which Wylder had dated a despatch. Boulogne, for instance, a neat little red cross over the town, and beneath, '12th October, 1854;' Brighton, ditto, '20th October, 1854;' Paris, ditto, '17th November, 1854;' Marseilles, ditto, 26th November, 1854;' Frankfurt, ditto, '22nd February, 1855;' Geneva, ditto, '10th March, 1855;' Genoa, ditto, '20th March, 1855;' Venice, ditto, '28th March, 1855.'

I may here mention that in the preceding notation I have marked the days and months exactly, but the years fancifully.

I don't think that Mr. Larkin had read the 'Wandering Jew.'

He had no great taste for works of fancy. If he had he might have been reminded, as he looked down upon the wild field of tactics just noted by his pen, of that globe similarly starred all over with little red crosses, which M. Rodin was wont to consult.

Now he was going into this business as he did into others, methodically. He, therefore, read what his gazetteer had to say about these towns and cities, standing, for better light, at the window. But though, the type being small, his eyes were more pink than before, he was nothing wiser, the information being of that niggardly historical and statistical kind which availed nothing in his present scrutiny. He would get Murray's hand-books, and all sorts of works—he was determined to read it up. He was going into this as into a great speculative case, in which he had a heavy stake, with all his activity, craft, and unscrupulousness. It might be the making of him.

His treasure—his oracle—his book of power, the labelled parcel of Wylder's letters, with the annotated map folded beside them—he replaced in their red-taped ligature in his iron safe, and with Chubb's key in his pocket, took his hat and cane—the day was fine—and walked forth for Brandon and the captain's study.

A pleasant day, a light air, a frosty sun. On the green the vicar, with his pretty boy by the hand, passed him, not a hundred yards off, like a ship at sea. There was a waving of hands, and smiles, and a shouted 'beautiful day.'

'What a position that poor fellow has got himself into!' good Mr. Larkin thought, with a shrug of compassion, to himself. 'That reversion! Why it's nothing—I really don't know why I think about it at all. If it were offered me this moment, positively I would not have it. Anything certain—*any* thing would be better.'

Little Fairy grew grave, in spite of the attorney's smiles, whenever he saw him. He was now saying—as holding his 'Wapsie's' hand, he capered round in front, looking up in his face—

'Why has Mr. Larkin no teeth when he laughs? Is he ever angry when he laughs—is he, Wapsie—oh, Wapsie, *is* he? Would you let him whip me, if I was naughty? I don't like him. Why does mamma say he is a good man, Wapsie?'

'Because, little man, he *is* a good man,' said the vicar, re-called by the impiety of the question. 'The best friend that Wapsie ever met with in his life.'

'But you would not give me to him, Wapsie?'

'Give you, darling! no—to no one but to God, my little man; for richer, for poorer, you're my own—your Wapsie's little man.'

And he lifted him up, and carried him in his arms against his loving heart, and the water stood in his eyes, as he laughed fondly into that pretty face.

But ' little man ' by this time was struggling to get down and give chase to a crow grubbing near them for dainties, with a muddy beak, and ' Wapsie's ' eyes followed, smiling, the wild vagaries of his little Fairy.

In the mean time Mr. Larkin had got among the noble trees of Brandon, and was approaching the lordly front of the Hall. His mind was busy. He had not very much fact to go upon. His theories were built chiefly of vapour, and every changing light or breath, therefore, altered their colouring and outlines.

' Maybe Mark Wylder is mad, and wandering in charge of a keeper ; maybe he is in some mad doctor's house, and *not* mad ; maybe in England, and there writes these letters which are sent from one continental town to another to be posted, and thus the appearance of locomotion is kept up. Perhaps he has been in- veigled into the hands of ruffians, and is living as it were under the vault of an Inquisition, and compelled to write what ever his gaolers dictate. Maybe he writes not under physical but moral coercion. Be the fact how it may, those Lakes, brother and sister, have a guilty knowledge of the affair.

' I will be firm—it is my duty to clear this matter up, if I can —we must do as we would be done by.'

CHAPTER LI.

A FRACAS IN THE LIBRARY.

IT was still early in the day. Larcom received him gravely in the hall. Captain Lake was at home, as usual, up to one o'clock in the library—the most diligent administrator that Brandon had perhaps ever known.

'Well, Larkin—letters, letters perpetually, you see. Quite well, I hope? Won't you sit down—no bad news? You look rather melancholy. Your other client is not ill—nothing sad about Mark Wylder, I hope?'

'No—nothing sad, Captain Lake—nothing—but a good deal that is strange.'

'Oh, is there?' said Lake, in his soft tones, leaning forward in his easy chair, and looking on the shining points of his boots.

'I have found out a thing, Captain Lake, which will no doubt interest *you* as much as it does me. It will lead, I think, to a much more exact *guess* about Mr. Mark Wylder.'

There was a sturdy emphasis in the attorney's speech which was far from usual, and indicated something.

'Oh! you have? May one hear it?' said Lake, in the same silken tone, and looking down, as before, on his boots.

'I've discovered something about his letters, said the attorney, and paused.

'Satisfactory, I hope?' said Lake as before.

'Foul play, Sir.'

'Foul play—is there? What is he doing now?' said Lake in the same languid way, his elbows on the arms of his chair, stooping forward, and looking serenely on the floor, like a man who is tired of his work, and enjoys his respite.

'Why, Captain Lake, the matter is this—it amounts, in fact, to *fraud.* It is plain that the letters are written in batches—several at a time—and committed to some one to carry from town to town, and post, *having previously filled in dates* to make them *correspond* with the exact period of posting them.'

The attorney's searching gaze was fixed on the captain, as he said this, with all the significance consistent with civility; but he could not observe the slightest indication of change. I dare say the captain felt his gaze upon him, and he undoubtedly heard his emphasis, but he plainly did not take either to himself.

'Indeed! that is very odd,' said Captain Lake.

'Very odd;' echoed the attorney.

It struck Mr. Larkin that his gallant friend was a little overacting, and showing perhaps less interest in the discovery than was strictly natural.

'But how can you show it?' said Lake with a slight yawn. 'Wylder *is* such a fellow. I don't the least pretend to understand him. It may be a freak of his.'

'I don't think, Captain Lake, that is exactly a possible solution here. I don't think, Sir, he would write two letters, one referring back to the other, at the same time, and post and date the latter more than a week *before* the other.'

'Oh!' said Lake, quietly, for the first time exhibiting a slight change of countenance, and looking peevish and excited; yes, that certainly does look very oddly.'

'And I think, Captain Lake, it behoves us to leave no stone unturned to sift this matter to the bottom.'

'With what particular purpose, I don't quite see,' said Lake. 'Don't you think possibly Mark Wylder might think us very impertinent?'

'I think, Captain Lake, on the contrary, we might be doing that gentleman the only service he is capable of receiving, and I know we should be doing something toward tracing and exposing the machinations of a conspiracy.'

'A conspiracy! I did not quite see your meaning. Then, you really think there is a conspiracy—formed *by* him or *against* him, which?'

'*Against* him, Captain Lake. Did the same idea never strike you?'

'Not, I think, that I can recollect.'

'In none of your conversations upon the subject with—with members of your family?' continued the attorney with a grave significance.

'I say, Sir, I don't recollect,' said Lake, glaring for an instant in his face very savagely. 'And it seems to me, that sitting here, you fancy yourself examining some vagrant or poacher at Gylingden sessions. And pray, Sir, have you no evidence in the letters you speak of but the insertion of dates, and the posting them in inverse order, to lead you to that strong conclusion?'

'None, as supplied by the letters themselves,' answered Larkin, a little doggedly, 'and I venture to think that is rather strong.'

'Quite so, to a mind like yours,' said Lake, with a faint gleam of his unpleasant smile thrown upon the floor, 'but other men don't see it; and I hope, at all events, there's a likelihood that Mark Wylder will soon return and look after his own business— I'm quite tired of it, and of' (he was going to say *you*)—'of everything connected with it.'

'This delay is attended with more serious mischief. The vicar, his brother, had a promise of money from him, and is disappointed—in very great embarrassments; and, in fact, were it not for some temporary assistance, which I may mention—al-

though I don't speak of such things—I afforded him myself, he
must have been ruined.'

'It is very sad,' said Lake ; 'but he ought not to have married
without an income.'

'Very true, Captain Lake—there's no defending that—it was
wrong, but the retribution is terrible,' and the righteous man
shook his tall head.

'Don't you think he might take steps to relieve himself considerably ?'

'I don't see it, Captain Lake,' said the attorney, sadly and
drily.

'Well, you know best ; but are not there resources ?'

'I don't see, Captain Lake, what you point at.'

'I'll give him something for his reversion, if he chooses, and
make him comfortable for his life.'

The attorney somehow, didn't seem to take kindly to this
proposition. We know he had imagined for himself some little
flirtation on this behalf, and cherished a secret *tendre* for the
same reversion. Perhaps he had other plans, too. At all
events it flashed the same suspicion of Lake upon his mind
again ; and he said—

'I don't know, Sir, that the Reverend Mr. Wylder would entertain anything in the nature of a sale of his reversion. I rather
think the contrary. I don't think his friends would advise it.'

'And why not ? It was never more than a contingency ; and
now they say Mark Wylder is married, and has children ; they
tell me he was seen at Ancona ?' said Lake tranquilly.

'*They* tell you ! who are *they* ?' said the attorney, and his dove's
eyes were gone again, and the rat's eyes unequivocally looking
out of the small pink lids.

'They—they,' repeated Captain Lake. 'Why, of course, Sir,
I use the word in its usual sense—that is, there was a rumour
when I was last in town, and I really forget who told me. Some
one, two, or three, perhaps.'

'Do you think it's true, Sir ?' persisted Mr. Larkin.

'No, Sir, I don't,' said Captain Lake, fixing his eyes for a moment with a frank stare on the attorney's face ; 'but it is quite
possible it *may* be true.'

'If it *is*, you know, Sir,' said Jos. Larkin, 'the reversion would
be a bad purchase at a halfpenny. I don't believe it either, Sir,'
resumed the attorney, after a little interval ; 'and I could not
advise the party you named, Sir, to sell his remainder for a song.'

'You'll advise as you please, Sir, and no doubt not without
sufficient reason,' retorted Captain Lake.

There was a suspicion of a sneer—not in his countenance, not
in his tone, not necessarily in his words—but somehow a suspicion, which stung the attorney like a certainty, and a pinkish
flush tinged his forehead.

Perhaps Mr. Larkin had not yet formed any distinct plans, and was really in considerable dubitation. But as we know, perceiving that the situation of affairs, like all uncertain conjunctures, offered manifestly an opportunity for speculation, he was, perhaps, desirous, like our old friend, Sindbad, of that gleam of light which might show him the gold and precious stones with which the floor of the catacomb was strewn.

'You see, Captain Lake, to speak quite frankly—there's nothing like being perfectly frank and open—although you have not treated me with confidence, which, of course, was not called for in this particular instance—I may as well say, in passing, that I have no doubt on my mind you know a great deal more than you care to tell about the fate of Mr. Mark Wylder. I look upon it, Sir, that that party has been made away with.'

'Old villain!' exclaimed Lake, starting up, with a sudden access of energy, and his face looked whiter still than usual—perhaps it was only the light.

'It won't do, Sir,' said Larkin, with a sinister quietude. 'I say there's been *foul play.* I think, Sir, you've got him into some foreign mad-house, or place of confinement, and I won't stop till it's sifted to the bottom. It is my duty, Sir.'

Captain Lake's slender hand sprang on the attorney's collar, coat and waistcoat together, and his knuckles, hard and sharp, were screwed against Mr. Larkin's jaw-bone, as he shook him, and his face was like a drift of snow, with two yellow fires glaring in it.

It was ferine and spectral, and so tremendously violent, that the long attorney, expecting nothing of the sort, was thrown out of his balance against the chimneypiece.

'You d—d old miscreant! I'll pitch you out of the window.'

'I—I say, let go. You're mad, Sir,' said the attorney, disengaging himself with a sudden and violent effort, and standing, with the back of a tall chair grasped in both hands, and the seat interposed between himself and Captain Lake. He was twisting his neck uncomfortably in his shirt collar, and for some seconds was more agitated, in a different way, than his patron was.

The fact was, that Mr. Larkin had a little mistaken his man. He had never happened before to see him in one of his violent moods, and fancied that his apathetic manner indicated a person more easily bullied. There was something, too, in the tone and look of Captain Lake which went a good way to confound and perplex his suspicions, and he half fancied that the masterstroke he had hazarded was a rank and irreparable blunder. Something of this, I am sure, appeared in his countenance, and Captain Lake looked av fully savage, and each gentleman stared the other full in the face, with more frankness than became two such diplomatists.

'Allow me to speak a word, Captain Lake.'

'You d—d old miscreant!' repeated the candescent captain.

'Allow me to say, you misapprehend.'

'You infernal old cur!'

'I mean no imputation upon *you*, Sir. I thought you might have committed a mistake—any man may; perhaps you have. I have acted, Captain Lake, with fidelity in all respects to you, and to every client for whom I've been concerned. Mr. Wylder is my client, and I was bound to say I was not satisfied about his present position, which seems to me unaccountable, except on the supposition that he is under restraint of some sort. I never said you were to blame; but you may be in error respecting Mr. Wylder. You may have taken steps, Captain Lake, under a mistake. I never went further than that. On reflection, you'll say so. I didn't upon my honour.'

'Then you did not mean to insult me, Sir,' said Lake.

'Upon my honour, and conscience, and soul, Captain Lake,' said the attorney, stringing together, in his vindication, all the articles he was assumed most to respect, 'I am perfectly frank, I do assure you. I never supposed for an instant more than I say. I could not imagine—I am amazed you have so taken it.'

'But you think I exercise some control or coercion over my cousin, Mr. Mark Wylder. He's not a man, I can tell you, wherever he is, to be bullied, no more than I am. I don't correspond with him. I have nothing to do with him or his affairs; I wash my hands of him.'

Captain Lake turned and walked quickly to the door, but came back as suddenly.

'Shake hands, Sir. We'll forget it. I accept what you say; but don't talk that way to me again. I can't imagine what the devil put such stuff in your head. I don't care twopence. No one's to blame but Wylder himself. I say I don't care a farthing. Upon my honour, I quite see—I now acquit you. You could not mean what you seemed to say; and I can't understand how a sensible man like you, knowing Mark Wylder, and knowing me, Sir, could use such—such *ambiguous* language. I have no more influence with him, and can no more affect his doings, or what you call his *fate*—and, to say the truth, care about them no more than the child unborn. He's his own master, of course. What the devil can you have been dreaming of. I don't even get a letter from him. He's *nothing* to me.'

'You have misunderstood me; but that's over, Sir. I may have spoken with warmth, fearing that you might be acting under some cruel misapprehension—that's all; and you don't think worse of me, I'm very sure, Captain Lake, for a little indiscreet zeal on behalf of a gentleman who has treated me with such unlimited confidence as Mr. Wylder. I'd do the same for you, Sir; it's my character.'

The two gentlemen, you perceive, though still agitated, were becoming reasonable, and more or less complimentary and conciliatory ; and the masks which an electric gust had displaced for a moment, revealing gross and somewhat repulsive features, were being readjusted, while each looked over his shoulder.

I am sorry to say that when that good man, Mr. Larkin, left his presence, Captain Lake indulged in a perfectly blasphemous monologue. His fury was excited to a pitch that was very nearly ungovernable ; and after it had exhibited itself in the way I have said, Captain Lake opened a little despatch-box, and took therefrom a foreign letter, but three days received. He read it through : his ill-omened smile expanded to a grin that was undisguisedly diabolical. With a scissors he clipt his own name where it occurred from the thin sheet, and then, in red ink and Roman capitals, he scrawled a line or two across the interior of the letter, enclosed it in an envelope, directed it, and then rang the bell.

He ordered the tax-cart and two horses to drive tandem. The captain was rather a good whip, and he drove at a great pace to Dollington, took the train on to Charteris, there posted his letter, and so returned ; his temper continuing savage all that evening, and in a modified degree in the same state for several days after.

CHAPTER LII.

AN OLD FRIEND LOOKS INTO THE GARDEN AT REDMAN'S FARM.

LADY CHELFORD, with one of those sudden changes of front which occur in female strategy, on hearing that Stanley Lake was actually accepted by Dorcas, had assailed both him and his sister, whom heretofore she had a good deal petted and distinguished, with a fury that was startling. As respects Rachel, we know how unjust was the attack.

And when the dowager opened her fire on Rachel, the young lady replied with a spirit and dignity to which she was not at all accustomed.

So soon as Dorcas obtained a hearing, which was not for sometime—for she, 'as a miserable and ridiculous victim and idiot,' was nearly as deep in disgrace as those ' shameless harpies the Lakes '—she told the whole truth as respected all parties with her superb and tranquil frankness.

Lady Chelford ordered her horses, and was about to leave Brandon next morning. But rheumatism arrested her indignant flight ; and during her week's confinement to her room, her son contrived so that she consented to stay for ' the odious ceremony,' and was even sourly civil to Miss Lake, who received her advances quite as coldly as they were made.

To Miss Lake, Lord Chelford, though not in set terms, yet in many pleasant ways, apologised for his mother's impertinence. Dorcas had told *him* also the story of Rachel's decided opposition to the marriage.

He was so particularly respectful to her—he showed her by the very form into which he shaped his good wishes that he knew how frankly she had opposed the marriage—how true she had been to her friend Dorcas—and she understood him and was grateful.

In fact, Lord Chelford, whatever might be his opinion of the motives of Captain Lake and the prudence of Dorcas, was clearly disposed to make the best of the inevitable, and to stamp the new Brandon alliance with what ever respectability his frank recognition could give it.

Old Lady Chelford's bitter and ominous acquiescence also came, and the presence of mother and son at the solemnity averted the family scandal which the old lady's first access of frenzy threatened.

This duty discharged, she insisted, in the interest of her

rheumatism, upon change of air; and on arriving at **Duxley,** was quite surprised to find Lady Dulhampton and her daughters there upon a similar quest.

About the matrimonial likelihoods of gentlemen with titles and estates Fame, that most tuft-hunting of divinities, is always distending her cheeks, and blowing the very finest flourishes her old trumpet affords.

Lord Chelford was not long away when the story of Lady Constance was again alive and vocal. It reached old Jackson through his sister, who was married to the brother of the Marquis of Dulhampton's solicitor. It reached Lake from Tom Twitters, of his club, who kept the Brandon Captain *au courant* of the town-talk; and it came to Dorcas in a more authentic fashion, though mysteriously, and rather in the guise of a conundrum than of a distinct bit of family intelligence, from no less a person than the old Dowager Lady Chelford herself.

Stanley Lake, who had begun to entertain hopes for Rachel in that direction, went down to Redman's Farm, and, after his bleak and bitter fashion, rated the young lady for having perversely neglected her opportunities and repulsed that most desirable *parti*. In this he was intensely in earnest, for the connection would have done wonders for Captain Lake in the county.

Rachel met this coarse attack with quiet contempt; told him that Lord Chelford had, she supposed, no idea of marrying out of his own rank; and further, that he, Captain Lake, must perfectly comprehend, if he could not appreciate, the reasons which would for ever bar any such relation.

But Rachel, though she treated the subject serenely in this interview, was sadder and more forlorn than ever, and lay awake at night, and, perhaps, if we knew all, shed some secret tears; and then with time came healing of these sorrows.

It was a fallacy, a mere chimera, that was gone; an impracticability too. She had smiled at it as such when Dorcas used to hint at it; but are there no castles in the clouds which we like to inhabit, although we know them altogether air-built, and whose evaporation desolates us?

Rachel's talks with the vicar were frequent; and poor little Mrs. William Wylder, who knew not the reason of his visits, fell slowly, and to the good man's entire bewilderment, into a chronic jealousy. It expressed itself enigmatically; it was circumlocutory, sad, and mysterious.

'Little Fairy was so pleased with his visit to Redman's Farm to-day. He told me all about it; did not you, little man? But still you love poor old mamma best of all; you would not like to have a new mamma. Ah, no; you'd rather have your poor old, ugly Mussie. I wish I was handsome, my little man, and clever; but wishing is vain.'

'Ah! Willie, there was a time when you could not see how ugly and dull your poor foolish little wife was; but it could not last for ever. How did it happen—oh, how?—you such a scholar so clever, so handsome, my beautiful Willie—how did you ever look down on poor wretched me?'

'I think it will be fine, Willie, and Miss Lake will expect you at Redman's Farm; and little Fairy will go too; yes, you'd like to go, and mamma will stay at home, and try to be useful in her poor miserable way,' and so on.

The vicar, thinking of other things, never seeing the reproachful irony in all this, would take it quite literally, assent sadly, and with little Fairy by the hand, set forth for Redman's Farm; and the good little body, to the amazement of her two maids, would be heard passionately weeping in the parlour in her forsaken state.

At last there came a great upbraiding, a great *éclaircissement*, and laughter, and crying, and hugging; and the poor little woman, quite relieved, went off immediately, in her gratitude, to Rachel, and paid her quite an affectionate little visit.

Jealousy is very unreasonable. But have we no compensation in this, that the love which begets it is often as unreasonable? Look in the glass, and then into your own heart, and ask your conscience, next, 'Am I really quite a hero, or altogether so lovely, as I am beloved?' Keep the answer to yourself, but be tender with the vehement follies of your jealous wife. Poor mortals! It is but a short time we have to love, and be jealous, and love again.

One night, after a long talk in the morning with good William Wylder, and great dejection following, all on a sudden. Rachel sat up in her bed, and in a pleasant voice, and looking more like herself than she had for many months, she said—

'I think I have found the true way out of my troubles, Tamar. At every sacrifice to be quite honest; and to that, Tamar, I have made up my mind at last, thank God. Come, Tamar, and kiss me, for I am free once more.'

So that night passed peacefully.

Rachel—a changed Rachel still—though more like her early self, was now in the tiny garden of Redman's Farm. The early spring was already showing its bright green through the brown of winter, and sun and shower alternating, and the gay gossiping of sweet birds among the branches, were calling the young creation from its slumbers. The air was so sharp, so clear, so sunny, the mysterious sense of coming life so invigorating, and the sounds and aspect of nature so rejoicing, that Rachel with her gauntlets on, her white basket of flower seeds, her trowel, and all her garden implements beside her, felt her own spring of life return, and rejoiced in the glad hour that shone round her.

Lifting up her eyes, she saw Lord Chelford looking over the little gate.

'What a charming day,' said he, with his pleasant smile, raising his hat, 'and how very pleasant to see you at your pretty industry again.'

As Rachel came forward in her faded gardening costume, an old silk shawl about her shoulders, and hoodwise over her head, somehow very becoming, there was a blush—he could not help seeing it—on her young face, and for a moment her fine eyes dropped, and she looked up, smiling a more thoughtful and a sadder smile than in old days. The picture of that smile so gay and fearless, and yet so feminine, rose up beside the sadder smile that greeted him now, and he thought of Ondine without and Ondine with a soul.

'I am afraid I am a very impertinent—at least a very inquisitive—wayfarer ; but I could not pass by without a word, even at the risk of interrupting you. And the truth is, I believe, if it had not been for that chance of seeing and interrupting you, I should not have passed through Redman's Dell to-day.'

He laughed a little as he said this ; and held her hands some seconds longer than is strictly usual in such a greeting.

'You are staying at Brandon?' said Rachel, not knowing exactly what to say.

'Yes ; Dorcas, who is always very good to me, made me promise to come whenever I was at Drackley. I arrived yesterday, and they tell me you stay so much at home, that possibly you might not appear in the upper world for two or three days ; so I had not patience, you see.'

It was now Rachel's turn to laugh a musical little roulade ; but somehow her talk was neither so gay, nor so voluble, as it used to be. She liked to listen ; she would not for the world their little conversation ended before its time ; but there was an unwonted difficulty in finding anything to say.

'It is quite true ; I am more a stay-at-home than I used to be. I believe we learn to prize home more the longer we live.'

'What a wise old lady ! I did not think of that ; I have only learned that whatever is most prized is hardest to find.'

'And spring is come again,' continued Rachel, passing by this little speech, 'and my labours recommence. And though the day is longer, there is more to do in it, you see.'

'I don't wonder at your being a stay-at-home, for, to my eyes, it is the prettiest spot of earth in all the world ; and if you find it half as hard to leave it as I do, your staying here is quite accounted for.'

This little speech, also, Rachel understood quite well, though she went on as if she did not.

'And this little garden costs, I assure you, a great deal of wise thought. In sowing my annuals I have so much to forecast and arrange ; suitability of climate, for we have sun and shade here, succession of bloom and contrast of colour, and ever so many other important things.'

' I can quite imagine it, though it did not strike me before,' he said, looking on her with a smile of pleasant and peculiar interest, which somehow gave a reality to this playful talk. ' It is quite true ; and I should not have thought of it—it is very pretty,' and he laughed a gentle little laugh, glancing over the tiny garden.

' But, after all, there is no picture of flowers, or still life, or even of landscape, that will interest long. You must be very solitary here at times—that is, you must have a great deal more resource than I, or, indeed, almost anyone I know, or this solitude must at times be oppressive. I hope so, at least, for that would force you to appear among us sometimes.'

' No, I am not lonely—that is, not lonelier than is good for me. I have such a treasure of an old nurse—poor old Tamar— who tells me stories, and reads to me, and listens to my follies and temper, and sometimes says very wise things, too ; and the good vicar comes often—this is one of his days—with his beautiful little boy, and talks so well, and answers my follies and explains all my perplexities, and is really a great help and comfort.'

' Yes,' said Lord Chelford, with the same pleasant smile, ' he told me so ; and seems so pleased to have met with so clever a pupil. Are you coming to Brandon this evening ? Lake asked William Wylder, perhaps he will be with us. I do hope you will come. Dorcas says there is no use in writing ; but that you know you are always welcome. May I say you'll come ?'

Rachel smiled sadly on the snow-drops at her feet, and shook her head a little.

' No, I must stay at home this evening—I mean I have not spirits to go to Brandon. Thank Dorcas very much from me— that is, if you really mean that she asked me.'

' I am so sorry—I am so disappointed,' said Lord Chelford, looking gravely and enquiringly at her. He began, I think, to fancy some estrangement there. ' But perhaps to-morrow — perhaps even to-day—you may relent, you know. Don't say it is impossible.'

Rachel smiled on the ground, as before ; and then, with a little sigh and a shake of her head, said—

' No.'

' Well, I must tell Dorcas she was right—you are very inexorable and cruel.'

' I am very cruel to keep you here so long—and I, too, am forgetting the vicar, who will be here immediately, and I must meet him in a costume less like the Woman of Endor.'

Lord Chelford, leaning on the little wicket, put his arm over and she gave him her hand again.

'Good-bye,' said Rachel.

'Well, I suppose I, too, must say good-bye ; and I'll say a great deal more,' said he, in a peculiar, odd tone, that was very firm, and yet indescribably tender. And he held her slender hand, from which she had drawn the gauntlet, in his. 'Yes, Rachel, I will—I'll say everything. We are old friends now—you'll forgive me calling you Rachel—it may be perhaps the last time.'

Rachel was standing there with such a beautiful blush, and downcast eyes, and her hand in his.

'I liked you always, Rachel, from the first moment I saw you —I liked you better and better—indescribably—indeed, I do ; and I've grown to like you so, that if I lose you, I think I shall never be the same again.'

There was a very little pause, the blush was deeper, her eyes lower still.

'I admire you, Rachel—I like your character—I have grown to love you with all my heart and mind—quite desperately, I think. I know there are things against me—there are better-looking fellows than I—and—and a great many things—and I know very well that you will judge for yourself—quite differently from other girls ; and I can't say with what fear and hope I await what you may say ; but this you may be sure of, you will never find anyone to love you better, Rachel—I think so well —and—and now—that is all. Do you think you could *ever* like me ? '

But Rachel's hand, on a sudden, with a slight quiver, was drawn from his.

'Lord Chelford, I can't describe how grateful I am, and how astonished, but it could never be—no—never.'

'Rachel, perhaps you mean my mother — I have told her everything—she will receive you with all the respect you so well deserve ; and with all her faults, she loves me, and will love you still more.'

'No, Lord Chelford, no.' She was pale now, and looking very sadly in his eyes. 'It is not that, but only that you must never, never speak of it again.'

'Oh ! Rachel, darling, you must not say that—I love you so —so *desperately*, you don't know.'

'I can say nothing else, Lord Chelford. My mind is quite made up—I am inexpressibly grateful—you will never know how grateful— but except as a friend—and won't you still be my friend ?— I never can regard you.'

Rachel was so pale that her very lips were white as she spoke this in a melancholy but very firm way.

'Oh, Rachel, it is a great blow—maybe if you thought it over ! —I'll wait any time.'

'No, Lord Chelford, I'm quite unworthy of your preference ;

out time cannot change me—and I am speaking, not from impulse, but conviction. This is our secret—yours and mine—and we'll forget it ; and I could not bear to lose your friendship—you'll be my friend still—won't you ? Good-bye.'

' God bless you, Rachel !' And he hurriedly kissed the hand she had placed in his, and without a word more, or looking back, he walked swiftly down the wooded road towards Gylingden.

So, then, it had come and gone—gone for ever.

' Margery, bring the basket in ; I think a shower is coming.'

And she picked up her trowel and other implements, and placed them in the porch, and glanced up towards the clouds, as if she saw them, and had nothing to think of but her gardening and the weather, and as if her heart was not breaking.

CHAPTER LIII.

THE VICAR'S COMPLICATIONS, WHICH LIVELY PEOPLE HAD BETTER NOT READ.

WILLIAM WYLDER'S reversion was very tempting. But Lawyer Larkin knew the value of the precious metals, and waited for more data. The more he thought over his foreign correspondence, and his interview with Lake, the more steadily returned upon his mind the old conviction that the gallant captain was deep in the secret, whatever it might be.

Whatever his motive—and he always had a distinct motive, though sometimes not easily discoverable—he was a good deal addicted now to commenting, in his confidential talk, with religious gossips and others, upon the awful state of the poor vicar's affairs, his inconceivable prodigality, the unaccountable sums he had made away with, and his own anxiety to hand over the direction of such a hopeless complication of debt, and abdicate in favour of any competent skipper the command of the water-logged and foundering ship.

' Why, his Brother Mark could get him cleverly out of it—could not he ?' wheezed the pork-butcher.

' More serious than you suppose,' answered Larkin, with a shake of his head.

' It can't go beyond five hundred, or say nine hundred—eh, at the outside ?'

' Nine *hundred* — say double as many *thousand*, and I'm afraid you'll be nearer the mark. You'll not mention, of course, and I'm only feeling my way just now, and speaking conjecturally altogether; but I'm afraid it is enormous. I need not remind you not to mention.'

I cannot, of course, say how Mr. Larkin's conjectures reached so prodigious an elevation, but I can now comprehend why it was desirable that this surprising estimate of the vicar's liabilities should prevail. Mr. Jos. Larkin had a weakness for enveloping much of what he said and wrote in an honourable mystery. He liked writing *private* or *confidential* at top of his notes, without apparent right or even reason to impose either privacy or confidence upon the persons to whom he wrote. There was, in fact, often in the good attorney's mode of transacting business just a *soupçon* or flavour of an *arrière pensée* of a remote and unseen plan, which was a little unsatisfactory.

Now, with the vicar he was imperative that the matter of the reversion should be strictly confidential—altogether 'sacred,' in fact.

'You see, the fact is, my dear Mr. Wylder, I never meddle in speculative things. It is not a class of business that I like or would touch with one of my fingers, so to speak,' and he shook his head gently; 'and I may say, if I were supposed to be ever so slightly engaged in these risky things, it would be the *ruin* of me. I don't like, however, sending you into the jaws of the City sharks—I use the term, my dear Mr. Wylder, advisedly—and I make a solitary exception in your case; but the fact is, if I thought you would mention the matter, I could not touch it even for you. There's Captain Lake, of Brandon, for instance --I should not be surprised if I lost the Brandon business the day after the matter reached his ears. All men are not like you and me, my dear Mr. Wylder. The sad experience of my profession has taught me that a suspicious man of the world, without religion, my dear Mr. Wylder,' and he lifted his pink eyes, and shook his long head and long hands in unison—'without religion —will imagine anything. They can't understand us.'

Now, the fifty pounds which good Mr. Larkin had procured for the improvident vicar, bore interest, I am almost ashamed to say, at thirty per cent. per annum, and ten per cent. more the first year. But you are to remember that the security was altogether speculative; and Mr. Larkin, of course, made the best terms he could.

	£	s.	d.
Annual premium on a policy for £100 [double insurance being insisted upon by lender, to cover contingent expenses, and life not insurable, a delicacy of the lungs being admitted, on the ordinary scale] . . .	10	0	0
Annuity payable to lender, clear of premium, the security being unsatisfactory	7	10	0
	£17	10	0

Ten pounds of which (the premium), together with four pounds ten shillings for expenses, &c. were payable in advance. So that thirty-two pounds, out of his borrowed fifty, were forfeit for these items within a year and a month. In the meantime the fifty pounds had gone, as we know, direct to Cambridge ; and he was called upon to pay forthwith ten pounds for premium, and four pounds ten shillings for 'expenses.' *Quod impossibile.*

The attorney had nothing for it but to try to induce the lender to let him have another fifty pounds, pending the investigation of title—another fifty, of which he was to get, in fact, eighteen pounds. Somehow, the racking off of this bitter vintage from one vessel into another did not seem to improve its quality. On the contrary, things were growing decidedly more awful.

Now, there came from Messrs. Burlington and Smith a peremptory demand for the fourteen pounds ten shillings, and an equally summary one for twenty-eight pounds fourteen shillings and eight pence, their costs in this matter.

When the poor vicar received this latter blow, he laid the palm of his hand on the top of his head, as if to prevent his brain from boiling over. Twenty-eight pounds fourteen shillings and eight pence ! *Quod impossibile* again.

When he saw Larkin, that conscientious guardian of his client's interests scrutinised the bill of costs very jealously, and struck out between four and five pounds. He explained to the vicar the folly of borrowing insignificant and insufficient sums —the trouble, and consequently the cost, of which were just as great as of an adequate one. He was determined, if he could, to pull him through this. But he must raise a sufficient sum, for the expense of going into title would be something ; and he would write sharply to Burlington, Smith, and Co., and had no doubt the costs would be settled for twenty-three pounds. And Mr. Jos. Larkin's opinion upon the matter was worthy of respect, inasmuch as he was himself, under the rose, the ' Co.' of that firm, and ministered its capital.

'The fact is you must, my dear Mr. Wylder, make an effort. ˉt won't do peddling and tinkering in such a case You will be in a worse position than ever, unless you boldly raise a thousand pounds—if I can manage such a transaction upon a security of the kind. Consolidate all your liabilities, and keep a sum in hand. You are well connected — powerful relatives — your brother has Huxton, four hundred a year, whenever old—the—the present incumbent goes—and there are other things beside —but you must not allow yourself to be ruined through timidity ; and if you go to the wall without an effort, and allow yourself to be slurred in public, what becomes of your chance of preferment?'

And now 'title' went up to Burlington, Smith, and Co. to examine and approve ; and from that firm, I am sorry to say, a bill of costs was coming, when deeds were prepared and all done, exceeding three hundred and fifty pounds ; and there was a little reminder from good Jos. Larkin for two hundred and fifty pounds more. This, of course, was to await Mr. Wylder's perfect convenience. The vicar knew *him*—*he* never pressed any man. Then there would be insurances in proportion ; and interest, as we see, was not trifling. And altogether, I am afraid, our friend the vicar was being extricated in a rather embarrassing fashion.

Now, I have known cases in which good-natured debauchees have interested themselves charitably in the difficulties of forlorn families ; and I think *I* knew, almost before they suspected it, that their generous interference was altogether due to one fine pair of eyes, and a pretty *tournure*, in the distressed family circle. Under a like half-delusion, Mr. Jos. Larkin, in the guise of charity, was prosecuting his designs upon the vicar's reversion, and often most cruelly and most artfully, when he frankly fancied his conduct most praiseworthy.

And really I do not myself know, that, considering poor William's liabilities and his means, and how many chances there were against that reversion ever becoming a fact, that I would not myself have advised his selling it, if a reasonable price were obtainable.

'All this power will I give thee,' said the Devil, 'and the glory of them ; for that is delivered unto me, and to whomsoever I will I give it.' The world belongs to the rascals. It is like 'the turf,' where, everyone admits, an honest man can hardly hold his own. Jos. Larkin looked down on the seedy and distracted vicar from an immense moral elevation. He heard him talk of religion with disgust. He owed him costs, and, beside, costs also to Burlington, Smith, and Co. Was there not Talkative in 'Pilgrim's Progress?' I believe there are few things more provoking than that a man who owes you money, and can't pay the interest, should pretend to religion to your face, except, perhaps, his giving sixpence in charity.

The attorney was prosperous. He accounted for it by his attributes, and the blessing that waits on industry and integrity. He did not see that luck and selfishness had anything to do with it. No man ever failed but through his own fault—none ever succeeded but by his deservings. The attorney was in a position to lecture the Rev. Mr. Wylder. In his presence, religion, in the vicar's mouth, was an impertinence.

The vicar, on the other hand, was all that we know. Perhaps, in comparison, his trial is, in some sort, a blessing ; and that there is no greater snare than the state of the man with whom all goes smoothly, and who mistakes his circumstances for his virtues.

The poor vicar and his little following were got pretty well into the Furcæ Caudinæ. Mr. Jos. Larkin, if he did not march him out, to do him justice, had had no hand in primarily bringing him there. There was no reason, however, why the respectable lawyer should not make whatever was to be fairly made of the situation. The best thing for both was, perhaps, that the one should sell and the other buy the reversion. Larkin had no apprehensions about the nature of the dealing. He was furnished with an excellent character—his cheques were always honoured—his 'tots' always unexceptionable—his vouchers never anything but exact. He had twice been publicly complimented in this sense, when managing Lord Hedgerow's estate. No man had, I believe, a higher reputation in his walk—few men were more formidable. I think it was Lawyer Larkin's private canon, in his dealings with men, that everything was moral that was not contrary to an Act of Parliament.

CHAPTER LIV.

BRANDON CHAPEL ON SUNDAY.

FOR a month and three days Mr. Jos. Larkin was left to ruminate without any new light upon the dusky landscape now constantly before his eyes. At the end of that time a foreign letter came for him to the Lodge. It was not addressed in Mark Wylder's hand—not the least like it. Mark's was a bold, free hand, and if there was nothing particularly elegant, neither was there anything that could be called vulgar in it. But this was a decidedly villainous scrawl—in fact it was written as a self-educated butcher might pen a bill. There was nothing impressed on the wafer, but a poke of something like the ferrule of a stick.

The interior corresponded with the address, and the lines slanted confoundedly. It was, however, on the whole, better spelled and expressed than the penmanship would have led one to expect. It said—

'MISTER LARKINS,—Respeckted Sir, I write you, Sir, to let you know has how there is no more Chance you shud ear of poor Mr. Mark Wylder—of hose orrible Death I make bold to acquainte you by this writing—which is Secret has yet from all—he bing Hid, and made away with in the dark. It is only Right is family shud know all, and his sad ending—wich I

will tell before you, Sir, in full, accorden to my Best guess, as bin the family Lawyer (and, Sir, you will find it usful to Tell this in secret to Capten Lake, of Brandon Hall — But not on No account to any other). It is orrible, Sir, to think a young gentleman, with everything the world can give, shud be made away with so crewel in the dark. Though you do not rekelect me, Sir, I know you well, Mr. Larkins, haven seen you hoffen when a boy. I wud not wish, Sir, no noise made till I cum—which I am returning hoame, and will then travel to Gylingden strateways to see you.   Sir, your obedient servant,
                                        'JAMES DUTTON.'

This epistle disturbed Mr. Jos. Larkin profoundly. He could recollect no such name as James Dutton. He did not know whether to believe this letter or not. He could not decide what present use to make of it, nor whether to mention it to Captain Lake, nor, if he did so, how it was best to open the matter.

Captain Lake, he was confident, knew James Dutton—why, otherwise, should that person have desired his intelligence communicated to him. At least it proved that Dutton assumed the captain to be specially interested in what concerned Mark Wylder's fate ; and in so far it confirmed his suspicions of Lake. Was it better to wait until he had seen Dutton, and heard his story, before hinting at his intelligence and his name—or was it wiser to do that at once, and watch its effect upon the gallant captain narrowly, and trust to inspiration and the moment for striking out the right course.

If this letter was true there was not a moment to be lost in bringing the purchase of the vicar's reversion to a point. The possibilities were positively dazzling. They were worth risking something. I am not sure that Mr. Larkin's hand did not shake a little as he took the statement of title again out of the Wylder tin box No. 2.

Now, under the pressure of this enquiry, a thing struck Mr. Larkin, strangely enough, which he had quite overlooked before. There were certain phrases in the will of the late Mr. Wylder, which limited a large portion of the great estate in strict settlement. Of course an attorney's opinion upon a question of real property is not conclusive. Still they can't help knowing something of the barrister's special province ; and these words were very distinct—in fact, they stunted down the vicar's reversion in the greater part of the property to a strict life estate.

Long did the attorney pore over his copy of the will, with his finger and thumb closed on his under lip. The language was quite explicit—there was no way out of it. It was strictly a life estate. How could he have overlooked that? His boy, indeed, would take an estate tail—and could disentail whenever—if ever —he came of age. But that was in the clouds. Mackleston-on-

the-Moor, however, and the Great Barnford estate, were unaffected by these limitations ; and the rental which he now carefully consulted, told him these jointly were in round numbers
worth 2,300*l.* a year, and improvable.

This letter of Dutton's, to be sure, may turn out to be all a lie
or a blunder. But it may prove to be strictly true ; and in that
case it will be *every* thing that the deeds should be executed and
the purchase completed before the arrival of this person, and the
public notification of Mark Wylder's death.

'What a world it is, to be sure !' thought Mr. Larkin, as he
shook his long head over Dutton's letter. 'How smoothly and
simply everything would go, if only men would stick to truth !
Here's this letter—how much time and trouble it costs me—how
much opportunity possibly sacrificed, simply by reason of the
incurable mendacity of men.' And he knocked the back of his
finger bitterly on the open page.

Another thought now struck him for the first time. Was there
no mode of 'hedging,' so that whether Mark Wylder were living
or dead the attorney should stand to win ?

Down came the Brandon boxes. The prudent attorney turned
the key in the door, and forth came the voluminous marriage
settlement of Stanley Williams Lake, of Slobberligh, in the
county of Devon, late captain, &c., &c. of the second part, and
Dorcas Adderley Brandon, of Brandon Hall, in the county of
&c., &c. of the second part, and so forth. And as he read this
pleasant composition through, he two or three times murmured
approvingly, 'Yes—yes—yes.' His recollection had served him
quite rightly. There was the Five Oaks estate, specially exclu-
ded from settlement, worth 1,400*l.* a year ; but it was conditioned
that the said Stanley Williams Lake was not to deal with the
said lands, except with the consent in writing of the said Dorcas,
&c., who was to be a consenting party to the deed.

If there was really something 'unsound in the state of Lake's
relations,' and that he could be got to consider Lawyer Larkin
as a friend worth keeping, that estate might be had a bargain—
yes, a *great* bargain.

Larkin walked off to Brandon, but there he learned that Captain *Brandon* Lake as he now chose to call himself, had gone
that morning to London.

'Business, I venture to say, and he went into that electioneering without ever mentioning it either.'

So thought Larkin, and he did not like this. It looked ominous, and like an incipient sliding away of the Brandon business,
Well, no matter, all things worked together for good. It was
probably well that he should not be too much shackled with considerations of that particular kind in the important negotiation
about Five Oaks.

That night he posted a note to Burlington, Smith, and Co.,

and by Saturday night's post there came down to the sheriff an execution for 123*l.* and some odd shillings, upon a judgment on a warrant to confess, at the suit of that firm, for costs and money advanced, against the poor vicar, who never dreamed, as he conned over his next day's sermon with his solitary candle, that the blow had virtually descended, and that his homely furniture, the silver spoons his wife had brought him, and the two shelves half full of old books which he had brought her, and all the rest of their little frugal trumpery, together with his own thin person, had passed into the hands of Messrs. Burlington, Smith, and Co.

The vicar on his way to the chapel passed Mr. Jos. Larkin on the green—not near enough to speak—only to smile and wave his hand kindly, and look after the good attorney with one of those yearning grateful looks, which cling to straws upon the drowning stream of life.

The sweet chapel bell was just ceasing to toll as Mr. Jos Larkin stalked under the antique ribbed arches of the little aisle Slim and tall, he glided, a chastened dignity in his long upturned countenance, and a faint halo of saint-hood round his tall bald head. Having whispered his orisons into his well-brushed hat and taken his seat, his dove-like eyes rested for a moment upon the Brandon seat.

There was but one figure in it—slender, light-haired, with his yellow moustache and pale face, grown of late a little fatter. Captain Brandon Lake was a very punctual church-goer since the idea of trying the county at the next election had entered his mind. Dorcas was not very well. Lord Chelford had taken his departure, and your humble servant, who pens these pages, had gone for a few days to Malwich. There was no guest just then at Brandon, and the captain sat alone on that devotional dais, the elevated floor of the great oaken Brandon seat.

There were old Brandon and Wylder monuments built up against the walls. Figures cut in stone, and painted and gilded in tarnished splendour, according to the gorgeous barbarism of Elizabeth's and the first James's age ; tablets in brass, marble-pillared monuments, and a couple of life-sized knights, armed *cap-à-pie,* on their backs in the aisle.

There is a stained window in the east which connoisseurs in that branch of mediæval art admire. There is another very fine one over the Brandon pew—a freak, perhaps, of some of those old Brandons or Wylders, who had a strange spirit of cynicism mingling in their profligacy and violence.

Reader, you have looked on Hans Holbein's ' Dance of Death,' that grim, phantasmal pageant, symbolic as a dream of Pharaoh ; and perhaps you bear in mind that design called ' The Elector,' in which the Prince, emerging from his palace gate, with a cloud of courtiers behind, is met by a poor woman, her little child by the hand, appealing to his compassion, despising whom, he turns away with a serene disdain. Beneath, in black letter, is inscribed the text—'*Princeps induetur mœrore et quiescere faciam superbiam potentium*'—and gigantic Death lays his fingers on the great man's ermine tippet.

It is a copy of this, which, in very splendid colouring, fills the window that lights the Brandon state seat in the chapel. The gules and gold were reflected on the young man's head, and with a vain augury, the attorney read again the solemn words from Holy Writ, '*Princeps induetur mœrore.*' The golden glare rested like a glory on his head; but there was also a gorgeous stain of blood that bathed his ear and temple. His head was busy enough at that moment, though it was quite still, and his sly eyes rested on his Prayer-book; for Sparks, the millionaire clothier, who had purchased Beverley, and was a potent voice in the Dollington Bank, and whose politics were doubtful, and relations amphibious, was sitting in the pew nearly opposite, and showed his red, fat face and white whiskers over the oak wainscoting.

Jos. Larkin, like the rest of the congregation, was by this time praying, his elbows on the edge of the pew, his hands clasped, his thumbs under his chin, and his long face and pink eyes raised heavenward, with now and then a gentle downward dropping of the latter. He was thinking of Captain Lake, who was opposite, and, like him, praying.

He was thinking how aristocratic he looked and how well, in externals, he became the Brandon seat; and there were one or two trifles in the captain's attitude and costume of which the attorney, who, as we know, was not only good, but elegant, made a note. He respected his audacity and his mystery, and he wondered intensely what was going on in that small skull under the light and glossy hair, and anxiously guessed how vitally it might possibly affect him, and wondered what his schemes were after the election—*quiescere faciam superbiam potentium;* and more darkly about his relations with Mark Wylder—*Princeps induetur mœrore.*

His eye was on the window now and then it dropped, with a vague presage, upon the sleek head of the daring and enigmatical captain, reading the Litany, from 'battle, murder, and sudden death, good Lord deliver us,' and he almost fancied he saw a yellow skull over his shoulder glowering cynically on the Prayer-book. So the good attorney prayed on, to the edification of all who saw, and mothers in the neighbouring seats were specially careful to prevent their children from whispering or fidgeting.

When the service was over Captain Lake went across to Mr. Sparks, and asked him to come to Brandon to lunch. But the clothier could not, and his brougham whirled him away to Naunton Friars. So Stanley Lake walked up the little aisle to-

ward the communion table, thinking, and took hold of the railing
that surrounded the brass monument of Sir William de Braundon,
and seemed to gaze intently on the effigy, but was really thinking profoundly of other matters, and once or twice his sly side-
long glance stole ominously to Jos. Larkin, who was talking at
the church door with the good vicar.

In fact, he was then and there fully apprising him of his awful
situation; and poor William Wylder looking straight at him,
with white face and damp forehead, was listening stunned, and
hardly understanding a word he said, and only the dreadful
questions rising to his mouth, 'Can *anything* be done? Will
the people come *to-day?*'

Mr. Larkin explained the constitutional respect for the Sabbath.

'It would be better, Sir—the publicity of an arrest' (it was a
hard word to utter) 'in the town would be very painful—it would
be better, I think, that I should walk over to the prison—it is only
six miles—and see the authorities there, and give myself up.'

And his lip quivered; he was thinking of the leave-taking—of
poor Dolly and little Fairy.

'I've a great objection to speak of business to-day,' said Mr.
Larkin, holily; 'but I may mention that Burlington and Smith
have written very sternly; and the fact is, my dear Sir, we must
look the thing straight in the face; they are determined to go
through with it; and you know my opinion all along about the
fallacy—you *must* excuse me, seeing all the trouble it has involved you in—the infatuation of hesitating about the sale of that
miserable reversion, which they could have disposed of on fair
terms. In fact, Sir, they look upon it that you don't want to pay
them, and, of course, they are very angry.'

'I'm sure I was wrong. I'm such a fool!'

'I must only go to the Sheriff the first thing in the morning,
and beg of him to hold over that thing, you know, until I have
heard from Burlington and Smith; and I suppose I may say to
them that you see the necessity of disposing of the reversion,
and agree to sell it if it be not too late.'

The vicar assented; indeed, he had grown, under this urgent
pressure, as nervously anxious to sell as he had been to retain it.

'And they can't come *to-day?*'

'Certainly not.'

And poor William Wylder breathed again in the delightful
sense of even momentary escape, and felt he could have em-
braced his preserver.

'I'll be very happy to see you to-morrow, if you can conven-
iently look in—say at twelve, or half-past, to report progress.'

So that was arranged; and again in the illusive sense of deliverance, the poor vicar's hopes brightened and expanded.
Hitherto his escapes had not led to safety, and he was only
raised from the pit to be sold to the Ishmaelites.

CHAPTER LV.

THE CAPTAIN AND THE ATTORNEY CONVERSE AMONG THE TOMBS.

 CANNOT tell whether that slender, silken machinator, Captain Lake, loitered in the chapel for the purpose of talking to or avoiding Jos. Larkin, who was standing at the doorway, in sad but gracious converse with the vicar.

He was certainly observing him from among the tombs in his sly way. And the attorney, who had a way, like him, of noting things without appearing to see them, was conscious of it, and was perhaps decided by this trifle to accost the gallant captain.

So he glided up the short aisle with a sad religious smile, suited to the place, and inclined his lank back and his tall bald head toward the captain in ceremonious greeting as he approached.

' How d'ye do, Larkin? The fog makes one cough a little this evening.'

Larkin's answer, thanks, and enquiries, came gravely in return. And with the same sad smile he looked round on the figures, some marble, some painted stone, of departed Brandons and Wylders, with garrulous epitaphs, who surrounded them in various costumes, quite a family group, in which the attorney was gratified to mingle.

' *Ancestry*, Captain Lake—*your* ancestry—noble assemblage —monuments and timber. Timber like the Brandon oaks, and monuments like these—these are things which, whatever else he may acquire, the *novus homo*, Captain Brandon Lake—the *parvenu*—can never command.'

Mr. Jos. Larkin had a smattering of school Latin, and knew half-a-dozen French words, which he took out on occasion.

' Certainly our good people do occupy some space here ; more regular attendants in church, than, I fear, they formerly were ; and their virtues more remarked, perhaps, than before the stonecutter was instructed to publish them with his chisel,' answered Lake, with one of his quiet sneers.

' Beautiful chapel this, Captain Lake—beautiful chapel, Sir,' said the attorney, again looking round with a dreary smile of admiration. But though his accents were engaging and he smiled—of course, a Sabbath-day smile—yet Captain Lake perceived that it was not the dove's but the rat's eyes that were doing duty under that tall bald brow.

' Solemn thoughts, Sir—solemn thoughts, Captain Lake—

silent mentors, eloquent monitors!' And he waved his long lank hand toward the monumental groups.

'Yes,' said Lake, in the same mocking tone, that was low and sweet, and easily mistaken for something more amiable. 'You and they go capitally together—so solemn, and eloquent, and godly—capital fellows! *I*'m not half good enough for such company—and the place is growing rather cold—is not it?'

'A great many Wylders, Sir—a great many *Wylders*.' And the attorney dropped his voice, and paused at this emphasis, pointing a long finger toward the surrounding effigies.

Captain Lake, after his custom, glared a single full look upon the attorney, sudden as the flash of a pair of guns from their embrasures in the dark; and he said quietly, with a wave of his cane in the same direction—

'Yes, a precious lot of Wylders.'

'Is there a *Wylder* vault here, Captain Brandon Lake?'

'Hanged if I know!—what the devil's that to you or me, Sir?' answered the captain, with a peevish sullenness.

'I was thinking, Captain Lake, whether in the event of its turning out that Mr. Mark Wylder was *dead*, it would be thought proper to lay his body here?'

'Dead, Sir!—and what the plague puts that in your head? You are corresponding with him—aren't you?'

'I'll tell you exactly how that is, Captain Lake. May I take the liberty to ask you for one moment to look up?'

As between these two gentlemen, this, it must be allowed, was an impertinent request. But Captain Lake did look up, and there was something extraordinarily unpleasant in his yellow eyes, as he fixed them upon the contracted pupils of the attorney, who, nothing daunted, went on—

'Pray, excuse me—thank you, Captain Lake—they say one is better heard when looked at than when not seen; and I wish to speak rather low, for reasons.'

Each looked the other in the eyes, with that uncertain and sinister gaze which has a character both of fear and menace.

'I have received those letters, Captain Lake, of which I spoke to you when I last had the honour of seeing you, as furnishing, in certain circumstances connected with them, grave matter of suspicion, since when I have *not* received one with Mr. Wylder's signature. But I *have* received, only the other day, a letter from a new correspondent—a person signing himself James Dutton—announcing his belief that Mr. Mark Wylder is dead —*is dead*—and has been made away with by foul means; and I have arranged, immediately on his arrival, at his desire, to meet him professionally, and to hear the entire narrative, both of what he knows and of what he suspects.'

As Jos. Larkin delivered this with stern features and emphasis, the captain's countenance underwent such a change as convinced the attorney that some indescribable evil had befallen Mark Wylder, and that Captain Brandon Lake had a guilty knowledge thereof. With this conviction came a sense of superiority and a pleasant confidence in his position, which betrayed itself in a slight frown and a pallid smile, as he looked steadily in the young man's face, with his small, crafty, hungry eyes.

Lake knew that his face had betrayed him. He had felt the livid change of colour, and that twitching at his mouth and cheek which he could not control. The mean, tyrannical, triumphant gaze of the attorney was upon him, and his own countenance was his accuser.

Lake ground his teeth, and returned Jos. Larkin's intimidating smirk with a look of fury, which—for he now believed he held the winning cards—did not appal him.

Lake cleared his throat twice, but did not find his voice, and turned away and read half through the epitaph on Lady Mary Brandon, which is a pious and somewhat puritanical composition. I hope it did him good.

'You know, Sir,' said Captain Lake, but a little huskily, turning about and smiling at last, 'that Mark Wylder is nothing to me. We don't correspond : we have not corresponded. I know —upon my honour and soul, Sir—nothing on earth about him— what he's doing, where he is, or what's become of him. But I can't hear a man of business like you assert, upon what he conceives to be reliable information—situated as the Brandon title is—depending, I mean, in some measure, upon his life— that Mark Wylder is no more, without being a good deal shocked.'

'I quite understand, Sir—quite, Captain Lake. It is very serious, Sir, very ; but I can't believe it has gone that length, quite. I shall know more, of course, when I've seen James Dutton. I can't think, I mean, he's been made away with in that sense ; nor how that could benefit anyone ; and I'd much rather, Captain Lake, move in this matter—since move I must —in your interest—I mean, as your friend and man of business —than in any way, Captain Lake, that might possibly involve you in trouble.'

'You *are* my man of business—aren't you? and have no grounds for ill-will—eh ?' said the captain, drily.

'No ill-will certainly—quite the reverse. Thank Heaven, I think I may truly say, I bear ill-will to no man living ; and wish you, Captain Lake, nothing but good, Sir—nothing but good.'

'Except a hasty word or two, I know no reason you should *not*,' said the captain, in the same tone.

'Quite so. But, Captain Brandon Lake, there is nothing like being completely above-board — it has been my rule

through life; and I will say—it would not be frank and candid to say anything else—that I have of late been anything
but satisfied with the position which, ostensibly your professional
adviser and confidential man of business, I have occupied.
Have I been consulted?—I put it to you; have I been trusted?
Has there been any real confidence, Captain Lake, upon your
part? You have certainly had relations with Mr. Mark Wylder
—correspondence, for anything I know. You have entertained
the project of purchasing the Reverend William Wylder's reversion; and you have gone into electioneering business, and
formed connections of that sort, without once doing me the
honour to confer with me on the subject. Now, the plain question is, do you wish to retain my services?'

'Certainly,' said Captain Lake, biting his lip, with a sinister
little frown.

'Then, Captain Lake, upon the same principle, and speaking
quite above-board, you must dismiss at once from your mind
the idea that you *can* do so upon the terms you have of late
seen fit to impose. I am speaking frankly when I say there
must be a total change. I must *be* in reality what I am held
out to the world as being—your trusted, and responsible, and
sole adviser. I don't aspire to the position—I am willing at
this moment to retire from it; but I never yet knew a divided
direction come to good. It is an office of great responsibility,
and I for one will not consent to touch it on any other conditions
than those I have taken the liberty to mention.'

'These are easily complied with—in fact I undertake to show
you they have never been disturbed,' answered Lake, rather
sullenly. 'So that being understood—eh?—I suppose we have
nothing particular to add?'

And Captain Lake extended his gloved hand to take leave.

But the attorney looked down and then up, with a shadow on
his face, and his lip in his finger and thumb, and he said—

'That's all very well, and a *sine qua non*, so far as it
goes! but, my dear Captain Lake, let us be plain. You
must see, my dear Sir, with such rumours, possibly about
to get afloat, and such persons about to appear, as this
James Dutton, that matters are really growing critical, and
there's no lack of able solicitors who would on speculation,
undertake a suit upon less evidence, perhaps, than may be forth-
coming, to upset your title, under the will, through Mrs. Dorcas
Brandon Lake—your joint title—in favour of the reversioner.'

Lake only bit his lip and shook his head. The attorney
knew, however, that the danger was quite appreciated, and went
on—

'You will, therefore, want a competent man—who has the
papers at his fingers' ends, and knows how to deal ably—*ably*,
Sir, with a fellow of James Dutton's stamp—at your elbow.

The fact is, to carry you safely through you will need pretty nearly the undivided attention of a well-qualified, able, and confidential practitioner ; and I need not say, such a man is not to be had for nothing.'

Lake nodded a seeming assent, which seemed to say, 'I have found it so.'

'Now, my dear Captain Lake, I just mention this—I put it before you—that is, because you know the county is not to be contested for nothing—and you'll want a very serious sum of money for the purpose, and possibly a petition—and I can, one way or another, make up, with an effort, about £15,000*l*. Now it strikes me that it would be a wise thing for you—the wisest thing, perhaps, my dear Captain Lake, you ever did—to place me in the same boat with yourself.'

'I don't exactly see.'

'I'll make it quite clear.' The attorney's tall forehead had a little pink flush over it at this moment, and he was looking down a little and poking the base of Sir William de Braundon's monument with the point of his umbrella. 'I wish, Captain Lake, to be perfectly frank, and, as I said, above-board. You'll want the money, and you must make up your mind to sell Five Oaks.'

Captain Lake shifted his foot, as if he had found it on a sudden on a hot flag.

'Sell Five Oaks—that's fourteen hundred a year,' said he.

'Hardly so much, but nearly, perhaps.'

'Forty-three thousand pounds were offered for it. Old Chudworth offered that about ten years ago.'

'Of course, Captain Lake, if you are looking for a fancy price from me I must abandon the idea. I was merely supposing a dealing between friends, and in that sense I ventured to name the extreme limit to which I could go. Little more than five per cent. for my money, if I insure—and possibly to defend an action before I've been six months in possession. I think my offer will strike you as a *great* one, considering the posture of affairs. Indeed, I apprehend, my friends will hardly think me justified in offering so much.'

The sexton was walking back and forward near the door, making the best clatter he decently could, and wondering the Captain and Lawyer Larkin could find no better place to talk in than the church.

'In a moment—in a moment,' said the lawyer, signalling to him to be quiet, as loftily as if chapel, hall, and sexton were his private property.

It was one of those moments into which a good deal of talk is fitted, and which seem somewhat of the longest to those who await its expiration.

The chapel was growing dark, and its stone and marble company of bygone Wylders and Brandons were losing themselves in shadow. Part of the periwig and cheek of Sir Marcus Brandon still glimmered whitish, as at a little distance did also the dim marble face and arm of the young Countess of Lydingworth, mourning these hundred and thirty years over her dead baby. Sir William Wylder, in ruff, rosettes, and full dress of James I.'s fashion, on his back, defunct, with children in cloaks kneeling at head and foot, was hardly distinguishable ; and the dusky crimson and tarnished gold had gone out of view till morning. The learned Archbishop Brandon, a cadet, who filled the see of York in his day, and was the only unexceptionably godly personage of that long line, was praying, as usual, at his desk—perhaps to the saints and Virgin, for I believe he was before the Reformation—in beard and skull-cap, as was evident from the black profile of head and uplifted hands, against the dim sky seen through the chapel window. A dusky glow from the west still faintly showed Hans Holbein's proud 'Elector,' in the Brandon window, fading, with Death himself, and the dread inscription, 'Princeps induetur mœrore,' into utter darkness.

The ice once broken, Jos. Larkin urged his point with all sorts of arguments, always placing the proposed transaction in the most plausible lights and attitudes, and handling his subject in round and flowing sentences. This master of persuasion was not aware that Captain Lake was arguing the question for himself, on totally different grounds, and that it was fixed in his mind pretty much in these terms :—

'That old villain wants an exorbitant bribe—is he worth it ?'

He knew what the lawyer thought he did *not* know—that Five Oaks was held by the lawyers to be possibly *without* those unfortunate limitations which affected all the rest of the estate. It was only a moot-point ; but the doubt had led Mr. Jos. Larkin to the selection.

'I'll look in upon you between eight and nine in the morning, and I'll say yes or no then,' said the captain, as they parted under the old stone porch, the attorney with a graceful inclination, a sad smile, and a wave of his hand—the captain with his hands in the pockets of his loose coat, and a sidelong glance from his yellow eyes.

The sky, as he looked toward Brandon, was draped in black cloud, intensely black, meeting a black horizon—except for one little rent of deep crimson which showed westward behind those antique gables and lordly trees, like a lake of blood.

CHAPTER LVI.

THE BRANDON CONSERVATORY.

APTAIN LAKE did look in at the Lodge in the morning, and remained an hour in conference with Mr. Jos. Larkin. I suppose everything went off pleasantly. For although Stanley Lake looked very pale and vicious as he walked down to the iron gate of the Lodge among the evergreens and bass-mats, the good attorney's countenance shone with a serene and heavenly light, so pure and bright, indeed, that I almost wonder his dazzled servants, sitting along the wall while he read and expounded that morning, did not respectfully petition that a veil, after the manner of Moses, might be suspended over the seraphic effulgence.

Somehow his 'Times' did not interest him at breakfast; these parliamentary wrangles, commercial speculations, and foreign disputes, are they not, after all, but melancholy and dreary records of the merest worldliness ; and are there not moments when they become almost insipid ? Jos. Larkin tossed the paper upon the sofa. French politics, relations with Russia, commercial treaties, party combinations, how men *can* so wrap themselves up in these things !

And he smiled ineffable pity over the crumpled newspaper— on the poor souls in that sort of worldly limbo. In which frame of mind he took from his coat pocket a copy of Captain Lake's marriage settlement, and read over again a covenant on the captain's part that, with respect to this particular estate of Five Oaks, he would do no act, and execute no agreement, deed, or other instrument whatsoever, in any wise affecting the same, without the consent in writing of the said Dorcas Brandon ; and a second covenant binding him and the trustees of the settlement against executing any deed, &c., without a similar consent ; and especially directing, that in the event of alienating the estate, the said Dorcas must be made an assenting party to the deed.

He folded the deed, and replaced it in his pocket with a peaceful smile and closed eyes, murmuring—

' I'm much mistaken if the gray mare's the better horse in that stud.'

He laughed gently, thinking of the captain's formidable and unscrupulous nature, exhibitions of which he could not fail to remember.

' No, no, Miss Dorkie won't give us much trouble.'

He used to call her 'Miss Dorkie,' playfully to his clerks. It gave him consideration, he fancied. And now with this Five

Oaks to begin with—£1,400 a year—a great capability, immensely improvable, he would stake half he's worth on making it more than £2,000 within five years ; and with other things at his back, an able man like him might before long look as high as she. And visions of the grand jury rose dim and splendid—an heiress and a seat for the county ; perhaps he and Lake might go in together, though he'd rather be associated with the Hon. James Cluttworth, or young Lord Griddlestone. Lake, you see, wanted weight, and, nothwithstanding his connections, was, it could not be denied, a new man in the county.

So Wylder, Lake, and Jos. Larkin had each projected for himself, pretty much the same career ; and probably each saw glimmering in the horizon the golden round of a coronet. And I suppose other modest men are not always proof against similar flatteries of imagination.

Jos. Larkin had also the vicar's business and reversion to attend to. The Rev. William Wylder had a letter containing three lines from him at eight o'clock, to which he sent an answer, whereupon the solicitor despatched a special messenger, one of his clerks to Dollington, with a letter to the sheriff's deputy, from whom he received duly a reply, which necessitated a second letter with a formal undertaking, to which came another reply ; whereupon he wrote to Burlington, Smith, and Co., acquainting them respectfully, in diplomatic fashion, with the attitude which affairs had assumed.

With this went a private and confidential, non-official, note to Smith, desiring him to answer stiffly and press for an immediate settlement, and to charge costs fairly, as Mr. William Wylder would have ample funds to liquidate them. Smith knew what *fairly* meant, and his entries went down accordingly. By the same post went up to the same firm a proposition—an afterthought—sanctioned by a second miniature correspondence with his client, now sailing before the wind, to guarantee them against loss consequent against staying the execution in the sheriff's hands for a fortnight, which, if they agreed to, they were further requested to send a draft of the proposed undertaking by return, at foot of which, in pencil, he wrote, ' N.B.—*Yes.*'

This arrangement necessitated his providing himself with a guarantee from the vicar ; and so the little account as between the vicar and Jos. Larkin, solicitor, and the vicar and Messrs. Burlington, Smith, and Co., solicitors, grew up and expanded with a tropical luxuriance.

About the same time—while Mr. Jos. Larkin, I mean, was thinking over Miss Dorkie's share in the deed, with a complacent sort of interest, anticipating a struggle, but sure of victory—that beautiful young lady was walking slowly from flower to flower, in the splendid conservatory which projects southward from the house, and rears itself in glacial arches high over the short sward and flowery patterns of the outer garden of Brandon. The unspeakable sadness of wounded pride was on her beautiful features, and there was a fondness in the gesture with which she laid her fingers on these exotics and stooped over them, which gave to her solitude a sentiment of the pathetic.

From the high glass doorway, communicating with the drawing-rooms, at the far end, among towering ranks of rare and gorgeous flowers, over the encaustic tiles, and through this atmosphere of perfume, did Captain Stanley Lake, in his shooting coat, glide, smiling, toward his beautiful young wife.

She heard the door close, and looking half over her shoulder, in a low tone indicating surprise, she merely said :

'Oh !' receiving him with a proud sad look.

'Yes, Dorkie, I'm here at last. I've been for some weeks so insufferably busy,' and he laid his white hand lightly over his eyes, as if they and the brain within were alike weary.

'How charming this place is—the temple of Flora, and you the divinity !'

And he kissed her cheek.

'I'm now emancipated for, I hope, a week or two. I've been so stupid and inattentive. I'm sure, Dorkie, you must think me a brute. I've been shut up so in the library, and keeping such tiresome company—you've no idea ; but I think you'll say it was time well spent, at least I'm sure you'll approve the result ; and now that I have collected the facts, and can show you, darling, exactly what the chances are, you must consent to hear the long story, and when you have heard, give me your advice.'

Dorcas smiled, and only plucked a little flowery tendril from a plant that hung in a natural festoon above her.

'I assure you, darling, I am serious ; you must not look so incredulous ; and it is the more provoking, because I love you so. I think I have a right to your advice, Dorkie.'

'Why don't you ask Rachel, she's cleverer than I, and you are more in the habit of consulting her ?'

'Now, Dorkie is going to talk her wicked nonsense over again, as if I had never answered it. What about Radie ? I do assure you, so far from taking her advice, and thinking her an oracle, as you suppose, I believe her in some respects very little removed from a fool.'

'I think her very clever, on the contrary,' said Dorcas, enigmatically.

'Well, she is clever in some respects ; she is gay, at least she used to be, before she fell into that transcendental parson's hands—I mean poor dear William Wylder ; and she can be amusing, and talks very well, but she has no sense—she is utterly Quixotic—she is no more capable of advising than a child.'

'I should not have fancied that, although you say so, Stanley.' she answered carelessly, adding a geranium to her bouquet.

'You are thinking, I know, because you have seen us once or twice talking together——'

Stanley paused, not knowing exactly how to construct the remainder of his sentence.

Dorcas added another blossom.

'I think that blue improves it wonderfully. Don't you?'

'The blue? Oh yes, certainly.'

'And now that little star of yellow will make it perfect,' said Dorcas.

'Yes—yellow—quite perfect,' said Stanley. 'But when you saw Rachel and me talking together, or rather Rachel talking to me, I do assure you, Dorcas, upon my sacred honour, one half of what she said I do not to this moment comprehend, and the whole was based on the most preposterous blunder; and I will tell you in a little time everything about it. I would this moment —I'd be delighted—only just until I have got a letter which I expect—a letter, I assure you, nothing more—and until I have got it, it would be simply to waste your time and patience to weary you with any such—any such.'

'*Secret*,' said Dorcas.

'*Secret*, then, if you will have it so,' retorted Stanley, suddenly, with one of those glares that lasted for just one fell moment; but he instantly recovered himself. '*Secret*—yes—but no secret in the evil sense—a secret only awaiting the evidence which I daily expect, and then to be stated fully and frankly to you, my only darling, and as completely blown to the winds.'

Dorcas looked in his strange face with her proud, sad gaze, like one guessing at a funereal allegory.

He kissed her cheek again, placing one arm round her slender waist, and with his other hand taking hers.

'Yes, Dorcas, my beloved, my only darling, you will yet know all it has cost me to retain from you even this folly; and when you have heard all—which upon my soul and honour, you shall the moment I am enabled to *prove* all—you will thank me for having braved your momentary displeasure, to spare you a great deal of useless and miserable suspense. I trust you, Dorcas, in everything implicitly. Why won't you credit what I say?'

'I don't urge you—I never have—to reveal that which you describe so strangely as a concealment, yet no secret; as an absurdity, and yet fraught with miserable suspense.'

'Ah, Dorcas, why will you misconstrue me? Why will you not believe me? I long to tell you this, which, after all, *is* an *utter* absurdity, a thousand times more than you can desire to hear it; but my doing so now, unfortified by the evidence I shall have in a very few days, would be attended with a danger which you will then understand. Won't you trust me?'

'And now for my advice,' said Dorcas, smiling down in her mysterious way upon a crimson exotic near her feet.

'Yes, darling, thank you. In sober earnest, your advice,' answered Lake; 'and you must advise me. Several of our neighbours—the Hillyards, the Ledwiches, the Wyndermeres, and ever so many more—have spoken to me very strongly about contesting the county, on the old Whig principles, at the election which is now imminent. There is not a man with a chance of acceptance to come forward, if I refuse. Now, you know what even moderate success in the House, when family and property go together, may accomplish. There are the Dodminsters. Do you think they would ever have got their title by any other means? There are the Forresters——'

'I know it all, Stanley; and at once I say, go on. I thought you must have formed some political project, Mr. Wealdon has been with you so often; but you tell me nothing, Stanley.'

'Not, darling, till I know it myself. This plan, for instance, until you spoke this moment, was but a question, and one which I could not submit until I had seen Wealdon, and heard how matters stood, and what chances of success I should really have. So, darling, you have it all; and I am so glad you advise me to go on. It is five-and-thirty years since anyone connected with Brandon came forward. But it will cost a great deal of money, Dorkie.'

'Yes, I know. I've always heard it cost my uncle and Sir William Camden fifteen thousand pounds.'

'Yes, it will be expensive, Wealdon thinks—*very*, this time. The other side will spend a great deal of money. It often struck me as a great mistake, that, where there is a good income, and a position to be maintained, there is not a little put by every year to meet cases like this—what they call a reserve fund in trading companies.'

'I do not think there is much money. *You* know, Stanley.'

'Whatever there is, is under settlement, and we cannot apply it, Dorkie. The only thing to be done, it strikes me, is to sell a part of Five Oaks.'

'I'll not sell any property, Stanley.'

'And what *do* you propose, then?'

'I don't know. I don't understand these things. But there are ways of getting money by mortgages and loans, and paying them off, without losing the property.'

'I've the greatest possible objection to raising money in that way. It is, in fact, the first step towards ruin; and nobody has ever done it who has not regretted that he did not sell instead.'

'I won't sell Five Oaks, Stanley,' said the young lady, seriously.

'I only said a part,' replied Stanley.

'I won't sell at all.'

'Oh? And *I* won't mortgage,' said Stanley. 'Then the thing can't go on?'

' I can't help it.'

' But I'm resolved it *shall*,' answered Stanley.

' I tell you, Stanley, plainly, I will not sell. The Brandon estate shall not be diminished in my time.'

' Why, you perverse idiot, don't you perceive you impair the estate as much by mortgaging as by selling, with ten times the ultimate danger. I tell you *I* won't mortgage, and *you shall sell.*'

' This, Sir, is the first time I have been spoken to in such terms.'

' And why do you contradict and thwart me upon business of which I know something and you nothing? What object on earth can I have in impairing the estate? I've as deep an interest in it as you. It is perfectly plain we should sell; and I am determined we shall. Come now, Dorcas—I'm sorry—I'm such a brute, you know, when I'm vexed. You mustn't be angry; and if you'll be a good girl, and trust me in matters of business——'

' Stanley, I tell you plainly once more, I never will consent to sell one acre of the Brandon estates.'

' Then we'll see what I can do without you, Dorkie,' he said in a pleasant, musing way.

He was now looking down, with his sly, malign smile; and Dorcas could almost fancy two yellow lights reflected upon the floor.

' I shall protect the property of my family, Sir, from your folly or your machinations; and I shall write to Chelford, as my trustee, to come here to advise me.'

' And I snap my fingers at you both, and meet you with *defiance;*' and Stanley's singular eyes glared upon her for a few seconds.

Dorcas turned in her grand way, and walked slowly toward the door.

' Stay a moment, I'm going,' said Stanley, overtaking and confronting her near the door. ' I've only one word. I don't think you quite know me. It will be an evil day for you, Dorkie, when you quarrel with me.'

He looked steadily on her, smiling for a second or two more, and then glided from the conservatory.

It was the first time Dorcas had seen Stanley Lake's features in that translated state which indicated the action of his evil nature, and the apparition haunted her for many a day and night.

CHAPTER LVII.

CONCERNING A NEW DANGER WHICH THREATENED CAPTAIN STANLEY LAKE.

THE ambitious captain walked out, sniffing, white, and incensed. There was an air of immovable resolution in the few words which Dorcas had spoken which rather took him by surprise. The captain was a terrorist. He acted instinctively on the theory that any good that was to be got from human beings was to be extracted from their fears. He had so operated on Mark Wylder; and so sought to coerce his sister Rachel. He had hopes, too, of ultimately catching the good attorney napping, and leading him too, bound and docile, into his ergastulum, although he was himself just now in jeopardy from that quarter. James Dutton, too. Sooner or later he would get Master Jim into a fix, and hold him also spell-bound in the same sort of nightmare.

It was not from malice. The worthy attorney had much more of that leaven than he. Stanley Lake did not care to smash any man, except such as stood in his way. He had a mercantile genius, and never exercised his craft, violence and ferocity, on men or objects, when no advantage was obtainable by so doing. When, however, fortune so placed them that one or other must go to the wall, Captain Stanley Lake was awfully unscrupulous. But, having disabled, and struck him down, and won the stakes, he would have given what remained of him his cold, white hand to shake, or sipped claret with him at his own table, and told him stories, and entertained him with sly, sarcastic sallies, and thought how he could make use of him in an amicable way.

But Stanley Lake's cold, commercial genius, his craft and egotism, were frustrated occasionally by his temper, which, I am afraid, with all its external varnish, was of the sort which is styled diabolical. People said also, what is true of most terrorists, that he was himself quite capable of being frightened; and also, that he lied with too fertile an audacity: and, like a man with too many bills afloat, forgot his endorsements occasionally, and did not recognise his own acceptances when presented after an interval. Such were some of this dangerous fellow's weak points. But on the whole it was by no means a safe thing to cross his path; and few who did so came off altogether scathless.

He pursued his way with a vague feeling of danger and rage, having encountered an opposition of so much more alarming a character than he had anticipated, and found his wife not only competent *ferre aspectum* to endure his maniacal glare and scowl, but serenely to defy his violence and his wrath. He had abundance of matter for thought and perturbation, and felt himself, when the images of Larcom, Larkin, and Jim Dutton crossed the retina of his memory, some thrill of the fear which 'hath torment'—the fear of a terrible coercion which he liked so well to practise in the case of others.

In this mood he paced, without minding in what direction he went, under those great rows of timber which over-arch the pathway leading toward Redman's Dell—the path that he and Mark Wylder had trod in that misty moonlight walk on which I had seen them set out together.

Before he had walked five minutes in this direction, he was encountered by a little girl in a cloak, who stopped and dropped a courtesy. The captain stopped also, and looked at her with a stare which, I suppose, had something forbidding in it, for the child was frightened. But the wild and menacing look was unconscious, and only the reflection of the dark speculations and passions which were tumbling and breaking in his soul.

'Well, child,' said he, gently, 'I think I know your face, but I forget your name.'

'Little Margery, please Sir, from Miss Lake at Redman's Farm,' she replied with a courtesy.

'Oh! to be sure, yes. And how is Miss Rachel?'

'Very bad with a headache, please, Sir.'

'Is she at home?'

'Yes, Sir, please.'

'Any message?'

'Yes, Sir, please—a note for you, Sir;' and she produced a note, rather, indeed, a letter.

'She desired me, Sir, please, to give it into your own hand, if I could, and not to leave it, please, Sir, unless you were at home when I reached.'

He read the direction, and dropped it unopened into the pocket of his shooting coat. The peevish glance with which he eyed it betrayed a presentiment of something unpleasant.

'Any answer required?'

'No, Sir, please—only to leave it.'

'And Miss Lake is quite well?'

'No, Sir, please—a bad headache to-day.'

'Oh! I'm very sorry, indeed. Tell her so. She is at home, is she?'

'Yes, Sir.'

'Very well; that's all. Say I am very sorry to hear she is suffering; and if I can find time, I hope to see her to-day; and remember to say I have not read her letter, but if I find it requires an answer, it shall have one.'

He looked round like a man newly awakened, and up among the great boughs and interlacing foliage of the noble trees, and the child made him two courtesies, and departed towards Redman's Farm.

Lake sauntered back slowly toward the Hall. On his way, a rustic seat under the shadow invited him, and he sat down, drawing Rachel's letter from his pocket.

What a genius they have for teasing ! How women do contrive to waste our time and patience over nonsense ! How ingeniously perverse their whimsies are ! I do believe Beelzebub employs them still, as he did in Eden, for the special plague of us, poor devils. Here's a lecture or an exhortation from Miss Radie, and a quantity of infinitely absurd advice, all which I am to read and inwardly digest, and discuss with her whenever she pleases. I've a great mind to burn it quietly.'

But he applied his match, instead, to his cigar ; and having got it well lighted, he leaned back, and broke the seal, and read this letter, which, I suspect, notwithstanding his preliminary thoughts, he fancied might contain matter of more practical import :—

'I write to you, my beloved and only brother, Stanley, in an altered state of mind, and with clearer views of duty than, I think, I have ever had before.'

'Just as I conjectured,' muttered Stanley, with a bitter smile, as he shook the ashes off the top of his cigar—'a woman's homily.'

He read on, and a livid frown gradually contracted his forehead as he did so.

'I do not know, Stanley, what your feelings may be. Mine have been the same ever since that night in which I was taken into a confidence so dreadful. The circumstances are fearful ; but far more dreadful to me, the mystery in which I have lived ever since. I sometimes think I have only myself to blame. But you know, my poor brother, why I consented, and with what agony. Ever since, I have lived in terror, and worse, in degradation. I did not know, until it was too late, how great was my guilt. Heaven knows, when I consented to that journey, I did not comprehend its full purpose, though I knew enough to have warned me of my danger, and undertook it in great fear and anguish of mind. I can never cease to mourn over my madness. Oh ! Stanley, you do not know what it is to feel, as I do, the shame and treachery of my situation ; to try to answer the smiles of those who, at least, once loved me, and to take their hands ; to kiss Dorcas and good Dolly ; and feel that all the time I am a vile impostor, stained incredibly, from whom, if they knew me, they would turn in horror and disgust. Now, Stanley, I can bear anything but this baseness—anything but the life-long practice of perfidy—that, I will not and cannot endure. *Dorcas must know the truth.* That there is a secret jealously guarded from her, she does know—no woman could fail to perceive that ; and there are few, Stanley, who would not prefer the certainty of the worst, to the anguish of such relations of mystery and reserve with a *husband.* She is clever, she is generous, and has many noble qualities. She will see what is right, and do it. Me she may hate, and must despise ; but that were to me more endurable than friendship gained on false pretences. I repeat, therefore, Stanley, that *Dorcas must know the whole truth.* Do not suppose, my poor brother, that I write from impulse—I have deeply thought on the subject.'

'*Deeply,*' repeated Stanley, with a sneer.

'And the more I reflect, the more am I convinced—if *you* will not tell her, Stanley, that *I* must. But it will be wiser and better, terrible as it may be, that the revelation should come from *you,* whom she has made her husband. The dreadful confidence would be more terrible from any other. Be courageous then, Stanley ; you will be happier when you have disclosed the truth, and released, at all events, one of your victims.

'Your sorrowful and only sister,

'RACHEL.'

On finishing the letter, Stanley rose quickly to his feet. He had become gradually so absorbed in reading it, that he laid his cigar unconsciously beside him, and suffered it to go out. With downcast look, and an angry contortion, he tore the sheets of note-paper across, and was on the point of reducing them to a thousand little snow flakes, and giving them to the wind, when, on second thoughts, he crumpled them together, and thrust them into his breast pocket.

His excitement was too intense for foul terms, or even blasphemy. With the edge of his nether lip nipped in his teeth, and his clenched hands in his pockets, he walked through the forest trees to the park, and in his solitudes hurried onward as if his life depended on his speed. Gradually he recovered his self-possession. He sat down under the shade of a knot of beech trees, overlooking that ill-omened tarn, which we have often mentioned, upon a lichen-stained rock, his chin resting on his clenched hand, his elbow on his knee, and the heel of his other foot stamping out bits of the short, green sod.

'That d—d girl deserves to be shot for her treachery,' was the first sentence that broke from his white lips.

It certainly was an amazing outrage upon his self-esteem, that the secret which was the weapon of terror by which he meant to rule his sister Rachel, should, by her slender hand, be taken so easily from his grasp, and lifted to crush him.

The captain's plans were not working by any means so smoothly as he had expected. That sudden stab from Jos. Lar-

kin, whom he always despised, and now hated—whom he believed to be a fifth-rate, pluckless rogue, without audacity, without invention ; whom he was on the point of tripping up, that
he should have turned short and garotted the gallant captain,
was a provoking turn of fortune.

That when a dire necessity subjugated his will, his contempt,
his rage, and he inwardly decided that the attorney's extortion
must be submitted to, his wife—whom he never made any account of in the transaction, whom he reckoned carelessly on
turning about as he pleased, by a few compliments and cajoleries
—should have started up, cold and inflexible as marble, in his
path, to forbid the payment of the black mail, and expose him
to the unascertained and formidable consequences of Dutton's
story, and the disappointed attorney's vengeance—was another
stroke of luck which took him altogether by surprise.

And to crown all, Miss Radie had grown tired of keeping her
own secret, and must needs bring to light the buried disgraces
which all concerned were equally interested in hiding away for
ever.

Stanley Lake's position, if all were known, was at this moment
formidable enough. But he had been fifty times over, during his
brief career, in scrapes of a very menacing kind ; once or twice,
indeed, of the most alarming nature. His temper, his craft, his
impetus, were always driving him into projects and situations
more or less critical. Sometimes he won, sometimes he failed ;
but his audacious energy hitherto had extricated him. The
difficulties of his present situation were, however, appalling, and
almost daunted his semi-diabolical energies.

From Rachel to Dorcas, from Dorcas to the attorney, and
from him to Dutton, and back again, he rambled in the infernal
litany he muttered over the inauspicious tarn, among the enclos-
ing banks and undulations, and solitary and lonely woods.

'Lake Avernus,' said a hollow voice behind him, and a long
grisly hand was laid on his shoulder.

A cold breath of horror crept from his brain to his heel, as
he turned about and saw the large, blanched features and glassy
eyes of Uncle Lorne bent over him.

'Oh, Lake Avernus, is it?' said Lake, with an angry sneer,
and raising his hat with a mock reverence.

'Ay ! it is the window of hell, and the spirits in prison come
up to see the light of it. Did you see him looking up?' said
Uncle Lorne, with his pallid smile.

'Oh ! of course—Napoleon Bonaparte leaning on old Dr.
Simcock's arm,' answered Lake.

It was odd, in the sort of ghastly banter in which he played
off this old man, how much hatred was perceptible.

'No—not he. It is Mark Wylder,' said Uncle Lorne ; 'his
face comes up like a white fish within a fathom of the top—it

makes me laugh. That's the way they keep holiday. **Can you** tell by the sky when it is holiday in hell? *I* can.'

And he laughed, and rubbed his long fingers together softly.

'Look! ha! ha!—Look! ha! ha! ha!—*Look!*' he resumed pointing with his cadaverous forefinger towards the middle of the pool.

'I told you this morning it was a holiday,' and he laughed very quietly to himself.

'Look how his nostrils go like a fish's gills. It is a funny way for a gentleman, and *he's* a gentleman. Every fool knows the Wylders are gentlemen—all gentlemen in misfortune. He has a brother that is walking about in his coffin. Mark has no coffin; it is all marble steps; and a wicked seraph received him, and blessed him till his hair stood up. Let me whisper you.'

'No, not just at this moment, please,' said Lake, drawing away, disgusted, from the maniacal leer and titter of the gigantic old man.

'Aye, aye—another time—some night there's aurora borealis in the sky. You know this goes under ground all the way to Vallambrosa?'

'Thank you; I was not aware: that's very convenient. Had you not better go down and speak to your friend in the water?'

'Young man, I bless you for remembering,' said Uncle Lorne, solemnly. 'What was Mark Wylder's religion, that I may speak to him comfortably?'

'An Anabaptist, I conjecture, from his present situation,' replied Lake.

'No, that's in the lake of fire, where the wicked seraphim and cherubim baptise, and anabaptise, and hold them under, with a great stone laid across their breasts. I only know two of their clergy—the African viçar, quite a gentleman, and speaks through his nose; and the archbishop with wings; his face is so burnt, he's all eyes and mouth, and on one hand has only one finger, and he tickles me with it till I almost give up the ghost. The ghost of Miss Baily is a lie, he said, by my soul; and he likes you—he loves you. Shall I write it all in a book, and give it you? I meet Mark Wylder in three places sometimes. Don't move, till I go down; he's as easily frightened as a fish.'

And Uncle Lorne crept down the bank, tacking, and dodging, and all the time laughing softly to himself; and sometimes winking with a horrid, wily grimace at Stanley, who fervently wished him at the bottom of the tarn.

'I say,' said Stanley, addressing the keeper, whom by a beck he had brought to his side, 'you don't allow him, surely, to go alone now?'

'No, Sir—since your order, Sir,' said the stern, reserved official.

'Nor to come into any place but this—the park, I mean?'

'No, Sir.'

'And do you mind, try and get him home always before night-fall. It is easy to frighten him. Find out what frightens him, and do it or say it. It is dangerous, don't you see? and he might break his d—d neck any time among those rocks and gullies, or get away altogether from you in the dark.'

So the keeper, at the water's brink, joined Uncle Lorne, who was talking, after his fashion, into the dark pool. And Stanley Lake—a general in difficulties—retraced his steps toward the park gate through which he had come, ruminating on his situation and resources.

CHAPTER LVIII.

MISS RACHEL LAKE BECOMES VIOLENT.

S O soon as the letter which had so surprised and incensed Stanley Lake was despatched, and beyond recall, Rachel, who had been indescribably agitated before, grew all at once calm. She knew that she had done right. She was glad the die was cast, and that it was out of her power to retract.

She kneeled at her bedside, and wept and prayed, and then went down and talked with old Tamar, who was knitting in the shade by the porch.

Then the young lady put on her bonnet and cloak, and walked down to Gylingden, with an anxious, but still a lighter heart, to see her friend, Dolly Wylder.

Dolly received her in a glad sort of fuss.

'I'm so glad to see you, Miss Lake.'

'Call me Rachel; and won't you let me call you Dolly?'

'Well, Rachel, dear,' replied Dolly, laughing, 'I'm delighted you're come; I have such good news—but I can't tell it till I think for a minute—I must begin at the beginning.'

'Anywhere, everywhere, only if it is good news, let me hear it at once. I'll be sure to understand.'

'Well, Miss—I mean Rachel, dear—you know—I may tell you now—the vicar—my dear Willie—he and I—we've been in great trouble—oh, such trouble—Heaven *only* knows——' and she dried her eyes quickly—'money, my dear——' and she smiled with a bewildered shrug—'some debts at Cambridge—no fault of his—you can't imagine what a saving darling he is—but these were a few old things that mounted up with interest, my dear—you understand—and law costs—oh, you can't think—and indeed, dear Miss—well, *Rachel*—I forgot—I sometimes thought we must be quite ruined.'

'Oh, Dolly, dear,' said Rachel, very pale, 'I feared it. I thought you might be troubled about money. I was not sure, but I was afraid ; and, to say truth, it was partly to try your friendship with a question on that very point that I came here, and not indeed, Dolly, dear, from impertinent curiosity, but in the hope that maybe you might allow me to be of some use.'

'How wonderfully good you are ! How friends are raised up !' and with a smile that shone like an April sun through her tears, she stood on tiptoe, and kissed the tall young lady, who—not smiling, but with a pale and very troubled face—bowed down and returned her kiss.

'You know, dear, before he went, Mark promised to lend dear Willie a large sum of money. Well, he went away in such a hurry, that he never thought of it; and though he constantly wrote to Mr. Larkin—you have no idea, my dear Miss Lake, what a blessed angel that man is—oh ! *such* a friend as has been raised up to us in that holy and wise man, words cannot express ; but what was I saying ?—oh, yes—Mark, you know—it was very kind, but he has so many things on his mind it quite escaped him — and he keeps, you know, wandering about on the Continent, and never gives his address ; so he, can't, you see, be written to; and the delay — but, Rachel, darling, are you ill ?'

She rang the bell, and opened the window, and got some water.

'My darling, you walked too fast here. You were very near fainting.'

'No, dear—nothing—I am quite well now—go on.'

But she did not go on immediately, for Rachel was trembling in a kind of shivering fit, which did not pass away till after poor Dolly, who had no other stimulant at command, made her drink a cup of very hot milk.

'Thank you, darling. You are too good to me, Dolly. Oh ! Dolly, you are too good to me.'

Rachel's eyes were looking into hers with a careworn, en-treating gaze, and her cold hand was pressed on the back of Dolly's.

Nearly ten minutes passed before the talk was renewed.

'Well, now, what do you think—that good man, Mr. Larkin, just as things were at the worst, found a way to make every-thing—oh, blessed mercy !—the hand of Heaven, my dear—quite right again—and we'll be so happy. Like a bird I could sing, and fly almost—a foolish old thing—ha ! ha ! ha !—such an old goose !' and she wiped her eyes again.

'Hush ! is that Fairy ? Oh, no, it is only Anne singing. Little man has not been well yesterday and to-day. He won't eat, and looks pale, but he slept very well, my darling man ; and Doctor Buddle—I met him this morning—so kindly took him into his room, and examined him, and says it may be nothing at all, please Heaven,' and she sighed, smiling still.

' Dear little Fairy—where is he?' asked Rachel, her sad eyes looking toward the door.

' In the study with his Wapsie. Mrs. Woolaston, she is such a kind soul, lent him such a beautiful old picture book — "Woodward's Eccentricities" it is called—and he's quite happy —little Fairy, on his little stool at the window.'

' No headache or fever?' asked Miss Lake cheerfully, though, she knew not why, there seemed something ominous in this little ailment.

' None at all ; oh, none, thank you ; none in the world. I'd be so frightened if there was. But, thank Heaven, Doctor Buddle says there's nothing to make us at all uneasy. My blessed little man ! And he has his canary in the cage in the window, and his kitten to play with in the study. He's quite happy.'

' Please Heaven, he'll be quite well to-morrow—the darling little man,' said Rachel, all the more fondly for that vague omen that seemed to say, ' He's gone.'

' Here's Mr. Larkin !' cried Dolly, jumping up, and smiling and nodding at the window to that long and natty apparition, who glided to the hall-door with a sad smile, raising his well-brushed hat as he passed, and with one grim glance beyond Mrs. Wylder, for his sharp eye half detected another presence in the room.

He was followed not accompanied—for Mr. Larkin knew what a gentleman he was—by a young and bilious clerk, with black hair and a melancholy countenance, and by old Buggs— his conducting man—always grinning, whose red face glared in the little garden like a great bunch of hollyhocks. He was sober as a judge all the morning, and proceeded strictly on the principle of business first, and pleasure afterward. But his orgies, when off duty, were such as to cause the good attorney, when complaints reached him, to shake his head, and sigh profoundly, and sometimes to lift up his mild eyes and long hands ; and, indeed, so scandalous an appendage was Buggs, that if he had been less useful, I believe the pure attorney, who, in the uncomfortable words of John Bunyan, ' had found a cleaner road to hell,' would have cashiered him long ago.

' There is that awful Mr. Buggs,' said Dolly, with a look of honest alarm. ' I often wonder so Christian a man as Mr. Larkin can countenance him. He is hardly ever without a black eye. He has been three nights together without once putting off his clothes—think of that ; and, my dear, on Friday week he fell through the window of the Fancy Emporium, at two o'clock in the morning ; and Doctor Buddle says if the cut on his jaw had been half an inch lower, he would have cut some artery, and lost his life—wretched man !'

'They have come about law business, Dolly!' enquired the young lady, who had a profound, instinctive dread of Mr. Larkin.

'Yes, my dear; a most important windfall. Only for Mr. Larkin, it never could have been accomplished, and, indeed, I don't think it would ever have been thought of.'

'I hope he has some one to advise him,' said Miss Lake, anxiously. 'I—I think Mr. Larkin a very cunning person; and you know your husband does not understand business.'

'Is it Mr. Larkin, my dear? Mr. Larkin! Why, my dear, if you knew him as we do, you'd trust your life in his hands.'

'But there are people who know him still better; and I think they fancy he is a very crafty man. I do not like him myself, and Dorcas Brandon dislikes him too; and, though I don't think we could either give a reason—I don't know, Dolly, but I should not like to trust him.'

'But, my dear, he is an excellent man, and such a friend, and he has managed all this most troublesome business so delightfully. It is what they call a reversion.'

'William Wylder is not selling his reversion?' said Rachel, fixing a wild and startled look on her companion.

'Yes, reversion, I am sure, is the name. And why not, dear? It is most unlikely we should ever get a farthing of it any other way, and it will give us enough to make us quite happy.'

'But, my darling, don't you know the reversion under the will is a great *fortune?* He must not think of it;' and up started Rachel, and before Dolly could interpose or remonstrate, she had crossed the little hall, and entered the homely study, where the gentlemen were conferring.

William Wylder was sitting at his desk, and a large sheet of law scrivenery, on thick paper, with a stamp in the corner, was before him. The bald head of the attorney, as he leaned over him, and indicated an imaginary line with his gold pencil-case, was presented toward Miss Lake as she entered.

The attorney had just said '*there*, please,' in reply to the vicar's question, 'Where do I write my name?' and red Buggs, grinning with his mouth open, like an over-heated dog, and the sad and bilious young gentleman, stood by to witness the execution of the cleric's autograph.

Tall Jos. Larkin looked up, smiling with his mouth also a little open, as was his wont when he was particularly affable. But the rat's eyes were looking at her with a hungry suspicion, and smiled not.

'William Wylder, I am so glad I'm in time,' said Rachel, rustling across the room.

'*There*,' said the attorney, very peremptorily, and making a little furrow in the thick paper with the seal end of his pencil.

'Stop, William Wylder, don't sign ; I've a word to say — you *must* pause.'

'If it affects our business, Miss Lake, I do request that you address yourself to me ; if not, may I beg, Miss Lake, that you will defer it for a moment.'

'William Wylder, lay down that pen ; as you love your little boy, lay it *down*, and hear me,' continued Miss Lake.

The vicar looked at her with his eyes wide open, puzzled, like a man who is not quite sure whether he may not be doing something wrong.

'I—really, Miss Lake—pardon me, but this is very irregular, and, in fact, unprecedented !' said Jos. Larkin. 'I think—I suppose, you can hardly be aware, Ma'am, that I am here as the Rev. Mr. Wylder's confidential solicitor, acting solely for him, in a matter of a strictly private nature.'

The attorney stood erect, a little flushed, with that peculiar contraction, mean and dangerous, in his eyes.

'Of course, Mr. Wylder, if you. Sir, desire me to leave, I shall instantaneously do so ; and, indeed, unless you proceed to sign, I had better go, as my time is generally, I may say, a little pressed upon, and I have, in fact, some business elsewhere to attend to.'

'What *is* this law-paper ?' demanded Rachel, laying the tips of her slender fingers upon it.

'Am I to conclude that you withdraw from your engagement ?' asked Mr. Larkin. 'I had better, then, communicate with Burlington and Smith by this post ; as also with the sheriff, who has been very kind.'

'Oh, no ! — oh, no, Mr. Larkin ! — pray, I'm quite ready to sign.'

'Now, William Wylder, you *sha'n't* sign until you tell me whether this is a sale of your reversion.'

The young lady had her white hand firmly pressed upon the spot where he was to sign, and the ring that glittered on her finger looked like a talisman interposing between the poor vicar and the momentous act he was meditating.

'I think, Miss Lake, it is pretty plain you are not acting for yourself here—you have bent sent, Ma'am,' said the attorney, looking very vicious, and speaking a little huskily and hurriedly ; 'I quite conceive by whom.'

'I don't know what you mean, Sir,' replied Miss Lake, with grave disdain.

'You have been commissioned, Ma'am, I venture to think, to come here to watch the interests of another party.'

'I say, Sir, I don't in the least comprehend you.'

'I think it is pretty obvious, Ma'am—Miss Lake, I beg pardon —you have had some conversation with your *brother*,' answered the attorney, with a significant sneer.

'I don't know what you mean, Sir, I repeat. I've just heard, in the other room, from your wife, William Wylder, that you were about selling your reversion in the estates, and I want to know whether that is so ; for if it be, it is the act of a madman, and I'll prevent it, if I possibly can.'

'Upon my word ! possibly'—said the vicar, his eyes very wide open, and looking with a hesitating gaze from Rachel to the attorney—'there may be something in it which neither you nor I know ; does it not strike you—had we not better consider ?'

'Consider *what*, Sir ?' said the attorney, with a snap, and losing his temper somewhat. 'It is simply, Sir, that this young lady represents Captain Lake, who wishes to get the reversion for himself.'

'That is utterly false, Sir !' said Miss Lake, flashing and blushing with indignation. 'You, William, are a *gentleman;* and such inconceivable meanness cannot enter *your* mind.'

The attorney, with what he meant to be a polished sarcasm, bowed and smiled toward Miss Lake.

Pale little Fairy, sitting before his 'picture-book,' was watching the scene with round eyes and round mouth, and that mixture of interest, awe, and distress, with which children witness the uncomprehended excitement and collision of their elders.

'My dear Miss Lake, I respect and esteem you ; you quite mistake, I am persuaded, my good friend Mr. Larkin ; and, indeed, I don't quite comprehend ; but if it were so, and that your brother really wished—do you think he does, Mr. Larkin ?—to buy the reversion, he might think it more valuable, perhaps.'

'I can say with certainty, Sir, that from that quarter you would get nothing like what you have agreed to take ; and I must say, once for all, Sir, that — quite setting aside every consideration of honour and of conscience, and of the highly prejudicial ,position in which you would place me as a man of business, by taking the very *short turn* which this young lady, Miss Lake, suggests—your letters amount to an equitable agreement to sell, which, on petition, the court would compel you to do.'

'So you see, my dear Miss Lake, there is no more to be said,' said the vicar, with a careworn smile, looking upon Rachel's handsome face.

'Now, now, we are all friends, aren't we ?' said poor Dolly, who could not make anything of the debate, and was staring, with open mouth, from one speaker to another. 'We are all agreed, are not we ? You are all so good, and fond of Willie, that you are actually ready almost to quarrel for him. But her little laugh produced no echo, except a very joyless and flushed effort from the attorney, as he looked up from consulting his watch.

'Eleven minutes past three,' said he, 'and I've a meeting at my house at half-past : so, unless you complete that instrument *now,* I regret to say I must take it back unfinished, and the result may be to defeat the arrangement altogether, and if the consequences should prove serious, I, at least, am not to blame.'

'Don't sign, I entreat, I *implore* of you. William Wylder, you *shan't.*'

'But, my dear Miss Lake, we have considered everything, and Mr. Larkin and I agree that my circumstances are such as to make it inevitable.'

'Really, this is child's play ; *there,* if you please,' said the attorney, once more.

Rachel Lake, during the discussion, had removed her hand. The faintly-traced line on which the vicar was to sign was now fairly presented to him.

'Just in your usual way,' murmured Mr. Larkin.

So the vicar's pen was applied, but before he had time to trace the first letter of his name, Rachel Lake resolutely snatched the thick, bluish sheet of scrivenery, with its handsome margins, and red ink lines, from before him, and tore it across and across, with the quickness of terror, and in fewer seconds than one could fancy, it lay about the floor and grate in pieces little bigger than dominoes.

The attorney made a hungry snatch at the paper, over William Wylder's shoulder, nearly bearing that gentleman down on his face, but his clutch fell short.

'Hallo ! Miss Lake, Ma'am—the paper !'

But wild words were of no avail. The whole party, except Rachel, were aghast. The attorney's small eye glanced over the ground and hearthstone, where the bits were strewn, like

> Ladies' smocks, all silver white,
> That paint the meadows with delight.

He had nothing for it but to submit to fortune with his best air. He stood erect ; a slanting beam from the window glimmered on his tall, bald head, and his face was black and menacing as the summit of a thunder-crowned peak.

'You are not aware, Miss Lake, of the nature of your act, and of the consequences to which you have exposed yourself, Madam. But that is a view of the occurrence in which, except as a matter of deep regret, I cannot be supposed to be immediately inter-ested. I will mention, however, that your interference, your *vio-lent* interference, Madam, may be attended with most serious consequences to my reverend client, for which, of course, you constituted yourself fully responsible, when you entered on the course of unauthorised interference, which has resulted in destroying the articles of agreement, prepared with great care and labour, for his protection ; and retarding the transmission of the document, by at least four-and-twenty hours, to London. You may, Madam, I regret to observe, have ruined my client.'

'Saved him, I hope.'

'And run yourself, Madam, into a *very* serious scrape.'

'Upon that point you have said quite enough, Sir. Dolly, William, don't look so frightened ; you'll both live to thank me for this.'

All this time little Fairy, unheeded, was bawling in great anguish of soul, clinging to Rachel's dress, and crying—' Oh ! he'll hurt her—he'll hurt her—he'll hurt her. Don't let him—don't let him. Wapsie, don't let him. Oh ! the frightle man !—don't let him—he'll hurt her—the frightle man !' And little man's cheeks were drenched in tears, and his wee feet danced in an agony of terror on the floor, as, bawling, he tried to pull his friend Rachel into a corner.

'Nonsense, little man,' cried his father, with quick reproof, on hearing this sacrilegious uproar. 'Mr. Larkin never hurt anyone ; tut, tut ; sit down, and look at your book.'

But Rachel, with a smile of love and gratification, lifted the little man up in her arms, and kissed him ; and his thin, little legs were clasped about·her waist, and his arms round her neck, and he kissed her with his wet face, devouringly, blubbering 'the frightle man—you doatie !—the frightle man !'

'Then, Mr. Wylder, I shall have the document prepared again from the draft. You'll see to that, Mr. Buggs, please ; and perhaps it will be better that you should look in at the Lodge.'

When he mentioned the Lodge, it was in so lofty a way that a stranger would have supposed it something very handsome indeed, and one of the sights of the county.

'Say, about nine o'clock to-morrow morning. Farewell, Mr. Wylder, farewell. I regret the enhanced expense—I regret the delay—I regret the risk—I regret, in fact, the whole scene. Farewell, Mrs. Wylder.' And with a silent bow to Rachel—perfectly polished, perfectly terrible—he withdrew, followed by the sallow clerk, and by that radiant scamp, old Buggs, who made them several obeisances at the door.

'Oh, dear Miss Lake—Rachel, *i* mean—Rachel, dear, I hope it won't be all off. Oh, you don't know—Heaven only knows—the danger we are in. Oh, Rachel, dear, if this is broken off, I don't know what is to become of us—I don't know.'

Dolly spoke quite wildly, with her hands on Rachel's shoulders. It was the first time she had broken down, the first time, at least, the vicar had seen her anything but cheery, and his head sank, and it seemed as if his last light had gone out, and he was quite benighted.

'Do you think,' said he, 'there is much danger of that ? Do you really think so ?'

'Now, don't blame me,' said Miss Lake, 'and don't be frightened till you have heard me. Let us sit down here—we shan't be interrupted—and just answer your wretched friend, Rachel, two or three questions, and hear what she has to say.'

Rachel was flushed and excited, and sat with the little boy still in her arms.

So, in reply to her questions, the vicar told her frankly how he stood; and Rachel said—'Well, you must not think of selling your reversion. Oh! think of your little boy—think of Dolly—if *you* were taken away from her.'

'But,' said Dolly, 'Mr. Larkin heard from Captain Lake that Mark is privately married, and actually has, he says, a large family; and he, you know, has letters from him, and Mr. Larkin thinks, knows more than anyone else about him; and if that were so, none of us would ever inherit the property. So'—

'*Do* they say that Mark is married? Nothing can be more *false*. I *know* it is altogether a falsehood. He neither is nor ever will be married. If my brother *dared* say that in my presence, I would make him confess, before you, that he *knows* it cannot be. Oh! my poor little Fairy—my poor Dolly—my poor good friend, William! What shall I say? I am in great distraction of mind.' And she hugged and kissed the pale little boy, she herself paler.

'Listen to me, good and kind as you are. You are never to call me your friend, mind that. I am a most unhappy creature forced by circumstances to be your enemy, for a time—not always. You have no conception *how*, and may never even suspect. Don't ask me, but listen.'

Wonder stricken and pained was the countenance with which the vicar gazed upon her, and Dolly looked both frightened and perplexed.

'I have a little more than three hundred a-year. There is a little annuity charged on Sir Hugh Landon's estate, and his solicitor has written, offering me six hundred pounds for it. I will write to-night accepting that offer, and you shall have the money to pay those debts which have been pressing so miserably upon you. *Don't* thank—not a word—but listen. I would so like, Dolly, to come and live with you. We could unite our incomes. I need only bring poor old Tamar with me, and I can give up Redman's Farm in September next. I should be so much happier; and I think my income and yours joined would enable us to live without any danger of getting into debt. Will you agree to this, Dolly, dear; and promise me, William Wylder, that you will think no more of selling that reversion, which may be the splendid provision of your dear little boy. Don't thank me—don't say anything now; and oh! don't reject my poor entreaty. Your refusal would almost make me mad. I would try, Dolly, to be of use. I think I could. Only try me.'

She fancied she saw in Dolly's face, under all her gratitude, some perplexity and hesitation, and feared to accept a decision then. So she hurried away, with a hasty and kind good-bye.

A fortnight before, I think, during Dolly's jealous fit, this magnificent offer of Rachel's would, notwithstanding the dreadful necessities of the case, have been coldly received by the poor little woman. But that delusion was quite cured now—no reserve, or doubt, or coldness left behind. And Dolly and the vicar felt that Rachel's noble proposal was the making of them.

CHAPTER LIX.

AN ENEMY IN REDMAN'S DELL.

JOS. LARKIN grew more and more uncomfortable about the unexpected interposition of Rachel Lake as the day wore on. He felt, with an unerring intuition, that the young lady both despised and suspected him. He also knew that she was impetuous and clever, and he feared from that small white hand a fatal mischief—he could not tell exactly how—to his plans.

Jim Dutton's letter had somehow an air of sobriety and earnestness, which made way with his convictions. His doubts and suspicions had subsided, and he now believed, with a profound moral certainty, that Mark Wylder was actually dead, within the precincts of a mad-house or of some lawless place of detention abroad. What was that to the purpose? Dutton might arrive at any moment. Low fellows are always talking; and the story might get abroad before the assignment of the vicar's interest.. Of course there was something speculative in the whole transaction, but he had made his book well, and by his 'arrangement' with Captain Lake, whichever way the truth lay, he stood to win. So the attorney had no notion of allowing this highly satisfactory arithmetic to be thrown into confusion by the fillip of a small gloved finger.

On the whole he was not altogether sorry for the delay. Everything worked together he knew. One or two covenants and modifications in the articles had struck him as desirable, on reading the instrument over with William Wylder. He also thought a larger consideration should be stated and acknowledged as paid, say 22,000*l.* The vicar would really receive just 2,200*l.* 'Costs' would do something to reduce the balance, for Jos. Larkin was one of those oxen who, when treading out corn, decline to be muzzled. The remainder was—the vicar would clearly understand—one of those ridiculous pedantries of law, upon which our system of crotchets and fictions insisted. And William Wylder, whose character, simply and sensitively honourable, Mr. Larkin appreciated, was to write to Burlington and Smith a letter, for the satisfaction of their speculative and nervous client, pledging his honour, as a gentleman, and his conscience, as a Christian, that in the event of the sale being completed, he would never do, countenance, or permit, any act or proceeding, whatsoever, tending on any ground to impeach or invalidate the transaction.

'I've no objection—have I ?—to write such a letter,' asked the vicar of his adviser.

'Why, I suppose you have no intention of trying to defeat your own act, and that is all the letter would go to. I look on it as wholly unimportant, and it is really not a point worth standing upon for a second.'

So that also was agreed to.

Now while the improved 'instrument' was in preparation, the attorney strolled down in the evening to look after his clerical client, and keep him 'straight' for the meeting at which he was to sign the articles next day.

It was by the drowsy faded light of a late summer's evening that he arrived at the quaint little parsonage. He maintained his character as 'a nice spoken gentleman,' by enquiring of the maid who opened the door how the little boy was. 'Not so well—gone to bed—but would be better, everyone was sure, in the morning.' So he went in and saw the vicar, who had just returned with Dolly from a little ramble. Everything promised fairly—the quiet mind was returning—the good time coming— all the pleasanter for the storms and snows of the night that was over.

'Well, my good invaluable friend, you will be glad—you will rejoice with us, I know, to learn that, after all, the sale of our reversion is unnecessary.'

The attorney allowed his client to shake him by both hands, and he smiled a sinister congratulation as well as he could, grinning in reply to the vicar's pleasant smile as cheerfully as was feasible, and wofully puzzled in the meantime. Had James Dutton arrived and announced the death of Mark—no ; it could hardly be *that*—decency had not yet quite taken leave of the earth ; and stupid as the vicar was, he would hardly announce the death of his brother to a Christian gentleman in a fashion so outrageous. Had Lord Chelford been invoked, and answered satisfactorily? Or Dorcas—or had Lake, the diabolical sneak, interposed with his long purse, and a plausible hypocrisy of kindness, to spoil Larkin's plans? All these fanciful queries flitted through his brain as the vicar's hands shook both his, and he laboured hard to maintain the cheerful grin with which he received the news, and his guileful rapacious little eyes searched narrowly the countenance of his client.

So after a while, Dolly assisting, and sometimes both talking together, the story was told, Rachel blessed and panegyrised, and the attorney's congratulations challenged and yielded once more. But there was something not altogether joyous in Jos. Larkin's countenance, which struck the vicar, and he said—

'You don't see any objection?' and paused.

'Objection? Why, *objection*, my dear Sir, is a strong word; but I fear I do see a difficulty—in fact, several difficulties. Perhaps you would take a little turn on the green—I must call for a moment at the reading-room—and I'll explain. You'll forgive me, I hope, Mrs. Wylder,' he added, with a playful condescension, 'for running away with your husband, but only for a few minutes—ha, ha!'

The shadow was upon Jos. Larkin's face, and he was plainly meditating a little uncomfortably, as they approached the quiet green of Gylingden.

'What a charming evening,' said the vicar, making an effort at cheerfulness.

'Delicious evening—yes,' said the attorney, throwing back his long head, and letting his mouth drop. But though his face was turned up towards the sky, there was a contraction and a darkness upon it, not altogether heavenly.

'The offer,' said the attorney, beginning rather abruptly, 'is no doubt a handsome offer at the first glance, and it may be well meant. But the fact is, my dear Mr. Wylder, six hundred pounds would leave little more than a hundred remaining after Burlington and Smith have had their costs. You have no idea of the expense and trouble of title, and the inevitable costliness, my dear Sir, of all conveyancing operations. The deeds, I have little doubt, in consequence of the letter you directed me to write, have been prepared—that is, in draft, of course—and then, my dear Sir, I need not remind you, that there remain the costs to me—those, of course, await your entire convenience—but still it would not be either for your or my advantage that they should be forgotten in the general adjustment of your affairs, which I understand you to propose.'

The vicar's countenance fell. In fact, it is idle to say that, being unaccustomed to the grand scale on which law costs present themselves on occasion, he was unspeakably shocked and he grew very pale and silent on hearing these impressive sentences.

'And as to Miss Lake's residing with you—I speak now, you will understand, in the strictest confidence, because the subject is a painful one; as to her residing with you, as she proposes, Miss Lake is well aware that I am cognizant of circumstances which render any such arrangement absolutely impracticable. I need not, my dear Sir, be more particular—at present, at least. In a little time you will probably be made acquainted with them, by the inevitable disclosures of time, which, as the wise man says, "discovers all things."'

'But—but what'—stammered the pale vicar, altogether shocked and giddy.

'You will not press me, my dear Sir; you'll understand that, just now, I really *cannot* satisfy any particular enquiry. Miss Lake has spoken, in charity I *will* hope and trust, without thought. But I am much mistaken, or she will herself, on half-an-hour's calm consideration, see the moral impossibilities which interpose between her, to me, most amazing plan and its realisation.'

There was a little pause here, during which the tread of their feet on the soft grass alone was audible.

'You will quite understand,' resumed the attorney, 'the degree of confidence with which I make this communication; and you will please, specially not to mention it to any person whatsoever. I do not except, in fact, *any*. You will find, on consideration, that Miss Lake will not press her residence upon you. No; I've no doubt Miss Lake is a very intelligent person, and, when not excited, will see it clearly.'

The attorney's manner had something of that reserve, and grim sort of dryness, which supervened whenever he fancied a friend or client on whom he had formed designs was becoming impracticable. Nothing affected him so much as that kind of unkindness.

Jos. Larkin took his leave a little abruptly. He did not condescend to ask the vicar whether he still entertained Miss Lake's proposal. He had not naturally a pleasant temper—somewhat short, dark, and dangerous, but by no means noisy. This temper, an intense reluctance ever to say 'thank you,' and a profound and quiet egotism, were the ingredients of that ' pride' on which—a little inconsistently, perhaps, in so eminent a Christian—he piqued himself. It must be admitted, however, that his pride was not of that stamp which would prevent him from listening to other men's private talk, or reading their letters, if anything were to be got by it; or from prosecuting his small spites with a patient and virulent industry; or from stripping a man of his possessions, and transferring them to himself by processes from which most men would shrink.

'Well,' thought the vicar, 'that munificent offer is unavailing, it seems. The sum insufficient, great as it is; and other difficulties in the way.'

He was walking homewards, slowly and dejectedly; and was now beginning to feel alarm lest the purchase of the reversion should fail. The agreement was to have gone up to London by this day's mail, and now could not reach till the day after to-morrow—four-and-twenty hours later than was promised. The attorney had told him it was a 'touch-and-go affair,' and the whole thing might be off in a moment ; and if it *should* miscarry what inevitable ruin yawned before him ? Oh, the fatigue of these monotonous agitations—this never-ending suspense ! Oh, the yearning unimaginable for quiet and rest ! How awfully he comprehended the reasonableness of the thanksgiving which he had read that day in the churchyard—' We give .Thee hearty thanks for that it hath pleased Thee to deliver this our brother out of the miseries of this sinful world.'

With the attorney it was different. Making the most of his height, which he fancied added much to the aristocratic effect of his presence, with his head thrown back, and swinging his walking cane easily between his finger and thumb by his side, he strode languidly through the main street of Gylingden, in the happy belief that he was making a sensation among the denizens of the town.

And so he moved on to the mill-road, on which he entered, and was soon deep in the shadows of Redman's Dell.

He opened the tiny garden-gate of Redman's Farm, looking about him with a supercilious benevolence, like a man conscious of bestowing a distinction. He was inwardly sensible of a sort of condescension in entering so diminutive and homely a place —a kind of half amusing disproportion between Jos. Larkin, Esq., of the Lodge, worth, already, £27,000, and on the high road to greatness, and the trumpery little place in which he found himself.

Old Tamar was sitting in the porch, with her closed Bible upon her knees ; there was no longer light to read by. She rose up, like the ' grim, white woman who haunts yon wood,' before him.

Her young lady had walked up to Brandon, taking the little girl with her, and she supposed would be back again early.

Mr. Larkin eyed her for a second to ascertain whether she was telling lies. He always thought everyone might be lying. It was his primary impression here. But there was a recluse and unearthly character in the face of the crone which satisfied him that she would never think of fencing with such weapons with him.

Very good. Mr. Larkin would take a short walk, and as his business was pressing, he would take the liberty of looking in again in about half-an-hour, if she thought her mistress would be at home then.

So, although the weird white woman who leered after him so strangely as he walked with his most lordly air out of the little garden, and down the darkening road towards Gylingden, could not say, he resolved to make trial again.

In the meantime Rachel had arrived at Brandon Hall. Dorcas —whom, if the truth were spoken, she would rather not have met—encountered her on the steps. She was going out for a lonely, twilight walk upon the terrace, where many a beautiful Brandon of other days, the sunshine of whose smile glimmered only on the canvas that hung upon those ancestral walls, and whose sorrows were hid in the grave and forgotten by the world, had walked in other days, in the pride of beauty, or in the sadness of desertion.

Dorcas paused upon the door-steps, and received her sister-in-law upon that elevation.

' Have you really come all this way, Rachel, to see *me* this evening?' she said, and something of sarcasm thrilled in the cold, musical tones.

' No, Dorcas,' said Rachel, taking her proffered hand in the spirit in which it was given, and with the air rather of a defiance than of a greeting ; ' I came to see my brother.'

' You are frank, at all events, Rachel, and truth is better than courtesy ; but you forget that your brother could not have returned so soon.'

' Returned?' said Rachel ; ' I did not know he had left home.'

' It's strange he should not have consulted you. I, of course, knew nothing of it until he had been more than an hour upon his journey.'

Rachel Lake made no answer but a little laugh.

' He'll return to-morrow ; and perhaps your meeting may still be in time. I was thinking of a few minutes' walk upon the terrace, but you are fatigued : you had better come in and rest.'

' No, Dorcas, I won't go in.'

' But, Rachel, you are tired ; you must come in with me, and drink tea, and then you can go home in the brougham,' said Dorcas, more kindly.

' No, Dorcas, no ; I will not drink tea nor go in ; but I *am* tired, and as you are so kind, I will accept your offer of the carriage.'

Larcom had, that moment, appeared in the vestibule, and received the order.

' I'll sit in the porch, if you will allow me, Dorcas ; you must not lose your walk.'

' Then you won't come into the house, you won't drink tea with me, and you won't join me in my little walk ; and why not any of these?'

Dorcas smiled coldly, and continued,

' Well, I shall hear the carriage coming to the door, and I'll return and bid you good-night. It is plain, Rachel, you do not like my company.'

' True, Dorcas, I do *not* like your company. You are unjust ; you have no confidence in me ; you prejudge me without proof; and you have quite ceased to love me. Why should I like your company?'

Dorcas smiled a proud and rather sad smile at this sudden

change from the conventional to the passionate ; and the **direct** and fiery charge of her kinswoman was unanswered.

She stood meditating for a minute.

'You think I no longer love you, Rachel, as I did. Perhaps young ladies' friendships are never very enduring ; but, if it be so, the fault is not mine.'

'No, Dorcas, the fault is not yours, nor mine. The fault is in circumstances. The time is coming, Dorcas, when you will know all, and, maybe, judge me mercifully. In the meantime, Dorcas, *you* cannot like *my* company, because you do not like me ; and I do not like yours, just because, in spite of all, I do love you still ; and in yours I only see the image of a lost friend. You may be restored to me soon—maybe *never*—but till then, I have lost you.'

'Well,' said Dorcas, 'it may be there is a wild kind of truth in what you say, Rachel, and—no matter—*time*, as you say, and *light*—I don't understand you, Rachel ; but there is this in you that resembles me—we both hate hypocrisy, and we are both, in our own ways, proud. I'll come back, when I hear the carriage, and see you for a moment, as you won't stay, or come with me, and bid you good-bye.'

So Dorcas went her way ; and alone, on the terrace, looking over the stone balustrade—over the rich and sombre landscape, dim and vaporous in the twilight—she still saw the pale face of Rachel—paler than she liked to see it. Was she ill ?—and she thought how lonely she would be if Rachel were to die—how lonely she was now. There was a sting of compunction—a yearning—and then started a few bitter and solitary tears.

In one of the great stone vases, that are ranged along the terrace, there flourished a beautiful and rare rose. I forget its name. Some of my readers will remember. It is first to bloom —first to wither. Its fragrant petals were now strewn upon the terrace underneath. One blossom only remained untarnished, and Dorcas plucked it, and with it in her fingers, she returned to the porch where Rachel remained.

'You see, I have come back a little before my time,' said Dorcas. 'I have just been looking at the plant you used to admire so much, and the leaves are shed already, and it reminded me of our friendship, Radie ; but I am sure you are right ; it will all bloom again, after the winter, you know, and I thought I would come back, and say *that*, and give you this relic of the bloom that is gone—the last token,' and she kissed Rachel, as she placed it in her fingers, 'a token of remembrance and of hope.'

'I will keep it, Dorkie. It was kind of you,' and their eyes met regretfully.

'And—and, I think, I do trust you, Radie,' said the heiress of Brandon ; 'and I hope you will try to like me on till—till spring comes, you know. And, I wish,' she sighed softly, 'I wish we were as we used to be. I am not very happy; and—here's the carriage.'

And it drew up close to the steps, and Rachel entered; and her little handmaid got up in the seat behind; and Dorcas and Rachel kissed their hands, and smiled, and away the carriage glided; and Dorcas, standing on the steps, looked after it very sadly. And when it disappeared, she sighed again heavily, still looking in its track; and I think she said 'Darling!'

CHAPTER LX.

RACHEL LAKE BEFORE THE ACCUSER.

TWILIGHT was darker in Redman's Dell than anywhere else. But dark as it was, there was still light enough to enable Rachel, as she hurried across the little garden, on her return from Brandon, to see a long white face, and some dim outline of the figure to which it belonged, looking out upon her from the window of her little drawing-room.

But no, it could not be; who was there to call at so odd an hour? She must have left something—a bag, or a white basket upon the window-sash. She was almost startled, however, as she approached the porch, to see it nod, and a hand dimly waved in token of greeting.

Tamar was in the kitchen. Could it be Stanley! But faint as the outline was she saw, she fancied that it was a taller person than he. She felt a sort of alarm, in which there was some little mixture of the superstitious, and she pushed open the door, not entering the room, but staring in toward the window, where against the dim, external light, she clearly saw, without recognising it, a tall figure, greeting her with mop and moe.

'Who is that?' cried Miss Lake, a little sharply.

'It is I, Miss Lake, Mr. Josiah Larkin, of the Lodge,' said that gentleman, with what he meant to be an air of dignified firmness, and looking very like a tall constable in possession; 'I have taken the liberty of presenting myself, although, I fear, at a somewhat unseasonable hour, but in reference to a little business, which, unfortunately, will not, I think, bear to be deferred.'

'No bad news, Mr. Larkin, I hope—nothing has happened. The Wylders are all well, I hope?'

'Quite well, so far as I am aware,' answered the attorney, with a grim politeness; 'perfectly. Nothing has occurred, as yet at least, affecting the interests of that family; but something is—I will not say threatened—but I may say mooted, which, were any attempt seriously made to carry it into execution, would, I regret to say, involve very serious consequences to a party whom for, I may say, many reasons, I should regret being called upon to affect unpleasantly.'

'And pray, Mr. Larkin, can I be of any use?'

'*Every* use, Miss Lake, and it is precisely for that reason that I have taken the liberty of waiting upon you, at what, I am well aware, is a somewhat unusual hour.'

'Perhaps, Mr. Larkin, you would be so good as to call in the morning—any hour you appoint will answer me,' said the young lady, a little stiffly. She was still standing at the door, with her hand upon the brass handle.

'Pardon me, Miss Lake, the business to which I refer is really urgent.'

'*Very* urgent, Sir, if it cannot wait till to-morrow morning.'

'Very true, quite true, very urgent indeed,' replied the attorney, calmly; 'I presume, Miss Lake, I may take a chair?'

'Certainly, Sir, if you insist on my listening to-night, which I should certainly decline if I had the power.'

'Thank you, Miss Lake.' And the attorney took a chair, crossing one leg over the other, and throwing his head back as he reclined in it with his long arm over the back—the 'express image,' as he fancied, of a polished gentleman, conducting a diplomatic interview with a clever and high-bred lady.

'Then it is plain, Sir, I *must* hear you to-night,' said Miss Lake, haughtily.

'Not that, exactly, Miss Lake, but only that *I* must *speak* to-night—in fact, I have no choice. The subject of our conference really is, as you will find, an urgent one, and to-morrow morning, which we should each equally prefer, would be possibly too late —too late, at least, to obviate a very painful situation.'

'You will make it, I am sure, as short as you can, Sir,' said the young lady, in the same tone.

'Exactly my wish, Miss Lake,' replied Mr. Jos. Larkin. 'Bring candles, Margery.'

And so the little drawing-room was illuminated; and the bald head of the tall attorney, and the gloss on his easy, black frock-coat, and his gold watch-chain, and the long and large gloved hand, depending near the carpet, with the glove of the other in it. And Mr. Jos. Larkin rose with a negligent and lordly case, and placed a chair for Miss Lake, so that the light might fall full upon her features, in accordance with his usual diplomatic arrangement, which he fancied, complacently, no one had ever detected; he himself. resuming his easy *pose* upon his chair, with his back, as much as was practicable, presented to the candles, and the long, bony fingers of the arm which rested on the table, negligently shading his observing little eyes, and screening off the side light from his expressive features.

These arrangements, however, were disconcerted by Miss Lake's sitting down at the other side of the table, and quietly requesting Mr. Larkin to open his case.

'Why, really, it is hardly a five minutes' matter, Miss Lake. It refers to the vicar, the Rev. William Wylder, and his respectable family, and a proposition which he, as my client, mentioned to me this evening. He stated that you had offered to advance a sum of 600*l.* for the liquidation of his liabilities. It will, perhaps, conduce to clearness to dispose of this part of the matter firs:. May I therefore ask, at this stage, whether the Rev. William Wylder rightly conceived you, when he so stated your meaning to me?'

'Yes, certainly, I am most anxious to assist them with that little sum, which I have now an opportunity of procuring.'

'A—exactly—yes—well, Miss Lake, that is, of course, very kind of you—very kind, indeed, and creditable to your feelings ; but, as Mr. William Wylder's solicitor, and as I have already demonstrated to him, I must now inform you, that the sum of six hundred pounds would be absolutely *useless* in his position. No party, Miss Lake, in his position, ever quite apprehends, even if he could bring himself fully to state, the aggregate amount of his liabilities. I may state, however, to you, without betraying confidence, that ten times that sum would not avail to extricate him, even temporarily, from his difficulties. He sees the thing himself now ; but drowning men will grasp, we know, at straws. However, he *does* see the futility of this ; and, thanking you most earnestly, he, through me, begs most gratefully to decline it. In fact, my dear Miss Lake—it is awful to contemplate—he has been in the hands of sharks, harpies, my dear Madam ; but I'll beat about for the money, in the way of loan, if possible, and, one way or another, I am resolved, if the thing's to be done, to get him straight.'

There was here a little pause, and Mr. Larkin, finding that Miss Lake had nothing to say, simply added—

'And so, for these reasons, and with these views, my dear Miss Lake, we beg, most respectfully, and I will say gratefully, to decline the proffered advance, which, I will say, at the same time, does honour to your feelings.'

'I am sorry,' said Miss Lake, 'you have had so much trouble in explaining so simple a matter. I will call early to-morrow, and see Mr. Wylder.'

'Pardon me,' said the attorney, 'I have to address myself next to the second portion of your offer, as stated to me by Mr. W. Wylder, that which contemplates a residence in his house, and in the respectable bosom, I may say, of that, in many respects, unblemished family.'

Miss Lake stared with a look of fierce enquiry at the attorney.

'The fact is, Miss Lake, that that is an arrangement which

under existing circumstances I could not think of advising. I think, on reflection, you will see, that Mr. Wylder—the Reverend William Wylder and his lady—could not for one moment seriously entertain it, and that I, who am bound to do the best I can for them, could not dream of advising it.'

'I fancy it is a matter of total indifference, Sir, what you may and what you may not advise in a matter quite beyond your province—I don't in the least understand, or desire to understand you—and thinking your manner impertinent and offensive, I beg that you will now be so good as to leave my house.'

Miss Rachel was very angry—although nothing but her bright colour and the vexed flash of her eye showed it.

'I were most unfortunate—most unfortunate indeed, Miss Lake, if my manner could in the least justify the strong and undue language in which you have been pleased to characterise it. But I do not resent—it is not my way—"beareth all things," Miss Lake, "beareth all things"—I hope I try to practise the precept; but the fact of being misunderstood shall not deter me from the discharge of a simple duty.'

'If it is part of your duty, Sir, to make yourself intelligible, may I beg that you will do it without further delay.'

'My principal object in calling here was to inform you, Miss Lake, that you must quite abandon the idea of residing in the vicar's house, as you proposed, unless you wish me to state explicitly to him and to Mrs. Wylder the insurmountable objections which exist to any such arrangement. Such a task, Miss Lake, would be most painful to me. I hesitate to discuss the question even with you; and if you give me your word of honour that you quite abandon that idea, I shall on the instant take my leave, and certainly, for the present, trouble you no further upon a most painful subject.'

'And now, Sir, as I have no intention whatever of tolerating your incomprehensibly impertinent interference, and don't understand your meaning in the slightest degree, and do not intend to withdraw the offer I have made to good Mrs. Wylder, you will I hope perceive the uselessness of prolonging your visit, and be so good as to leave me in unmolested possession of my poor residence.'

'If I wished to do you an injury, Miss Lake, I should take you at your word. I don't—I wish to spare you. Your countenance, Miss Lake—you must pardon my frankness, it is my way—*your countenance* tells only too plainly that you now comprehend my allusion.'

There was a confidence and significance in the attorney's air and accent, and a peculiar look of latent ferocity in his evil countenance, which gradually excited her fears, and fascinated her gaze.

'Now, Miss Lake, we are sitting here in the presence of Him

who is the searcher of hearts, and before whom nothing is secret —your eye is upon mine and mine on yours—and I ask you, *do you remember the night of the 29th of September last?*'

That mean, pale, taunting face ! the dreadful accents that vibrated within her ! How could that ill-omened man have divined her connection with the incidents—the unknown incidents—of that direful night? The lean figure in the black frock-coat, and black silk waistcoat, with that great gleaming watch-chain, the long, shabby, withered face, and flushed, bald forehead ; and those paltry little eyes, in their pink setting, that nevertheless fascinated her like the gaze of a serpent. How had that horrible figure come there—why was this meeting—whence his knowledge? An evil spirit incarnate he seemed to her. She blanched before it—every vestige of colour fled from her features —she stared—she gaped at him with a strange look of imbecility —and the long face seemed to enjoy and protract its triumph.

Without removing his gaze he was fumbling in his pocket for his note-book, which he displayed with a faint smile, grim and pallid.

' I see you *do* remember that night—*as well you may*, Miss Lake,' he ejaculated, in formidable tones, and with a shake of his bald head.

' Now, Miss Lake, you see this book. It contains, Madam, the skeleton of a case. The bones and joints, Ma'am, of a case. I have it here, noted and prepared. There is not a fact in it without a note of the name and address of the witness who can prove it—the *witness*—observe me.'

Then there was a pause of a few seconds, during which he still kept her under his steady gaze.

' On that night, Miss Lake, the 29th September, you drove in Mr. Mark Wylder's tax-cart to the Dollington station, where, notwithstanding your veil, and your caution, you were *seen* and *recognised*. The same occurred at Charteris. You accompanied Mr. Mark Wylder in his midnight flight to London, Miss Lake. Of your stay in London I say nothing. In was protracted to the 2nd October, when you arrived in the down train at Dollington at twelve o'clock at night, and took a cab to the "White House," where you were met by a gentleman answering the description of your brother, Captain Lake. Now, Miss Lake, I have stated no particulars, but do you think that knowing all this, and knowing the *fraud* by which your absence was covered, and perfectly understanding, as every man conversant with this sinful world must do, the full significance of all this, I could dream of permitting you, Miss Lake, to become domesticated as an inmate in the family of a pure-minded, though simple and unfortunate clergyman?'

' It may become my duty,' he resumed, ' to prosecute a searching enquiry, Madam, into the circumstances of Mr. Mark

Wylder's disappearance. If you have the slightest regard for
your own honour, you will not precipitate that measure, Miss Lake ;
and so sure as you persist in your unwarrantable design of
residing in that unsuspecting family, I will publish what I shall
then feel called upon by my position to make known ; for I will
be no party to seeing an innocent family compromised by admit-
ting an inmate of whose real character they have not the faintest
suspicion, and I shall at once set in motion a public enquiry into
the circumstances of Mr. Mark Wylder's disappearance.'

Looking straight in his face, with the same expression of help-
lessness, she uttered at last a horrible cry of anguish that almost
thrilled that callous Christian.

' I think I'm going mad ! '

And she continued staring at him all the time.

' Pray compose yourself, Miss Lake—there's no need to agitate yourself—nothing of all this need occur if you do not force
it upon me—*nothing*. I beg you'll collect yourself—shall I call
for water, Miss Lake ? '

The fact is the attorney began to apprehend hysterics, or
something even worse, and was himself rather frightened. But
Rachel was never long overwhelmed by any shock—fear was
not for her—her brave spirit stood her in stead ; and nothing
rallied her so surely as the sense that an attempt was being made
to intimidate her.

' What have I heard—what have I endured ? Listen to me,
you cowardly libeller. It is true that I was at Dollington, and
at Charteris, on the night you name. Also true that I went to
London. Your hideous slander is garnished with two or three
bits of truth, but only the more villainous for that. All that
you have dared to insinuate is utterly false. Before Him who
judges all, and knows all things—*utterly* and *damnably* false ! '

The attorney made a bow—it was his best. He did not imitate a gentleman happily, and was never so vulgar as when he
was finest.

One word of her wild protest he did not believe. His bow
was of that grave but mocking sort which was meant to convey
it. Perhaps if he had accepted what she said it might have led
him to new and sounder conclusions. Here was light, but it
glared and flashed in vain for him.

Miss Lake was naturally perfectly frank. Pity it was she had
ever had a secret to keep ! These frank people are a sore puzzle
to gentlemen of Lawyer Larkin's quaint and sagacious turn of
mind. They can't believe that anybody ever speaks quite the
truth : when they hear it—they don't recognise it, and they wonder what the speaker is driving at. The best method of hiding
your opinion or your motives from such men, is to tell it to them.
They are owls. Their vision is formed for darkness, and light
blinds them.

Rachel Lake rang her bell sharply, and old Tamar appeared. 'Show Mr.—Mr.—; show him to the door,' said Miss Lake.

The attorney rose, made another bow, and threw back his head, and moved in a way that was oppressively gentlemanlike to the door, and speedily vanished at the little wicket. Old Tamar holding her candle to lighten his path, as she stood, white and cadaverous, in the porch.

'She's a little bit noisy to-night,' thought the attorney, as he descended the road to Gylingden ; 'but she'll be precious sober by to-morrow morning—and I venture to say we shall hear nothing more of that scheme of hers. A reputable inmate, truly, and a pleasant *éclaircissement* (this was one of his French words, and pronounced by him with his usual accuracy, precisely as it is spelt)—a pleasant *éclaircissement*—whenever that London excursion and its creditable circumstances come to light.'

CHAPTER LXI.

IN WHICH DAME DUTTON IS VISITED.

DULY next morning the rosy-fingered Aurora drew the gold and crimson curtains of the east, and the splendid Apollo, stepping forth from his chamber, took the reins of his unrivalled team, and driving four-in-hand through the sky, like a great swell as he is, took small note of the staring hucksters and publicans by the road-side, and sublimely overlooked the footsore and ragged pedestrians that crawl below his level. It was, in fact, one of those brisk and bright mornings which proclaim a universal cheerfulness, and mock the miseries of those dismal wayfarers of life, to whom returning light is a renewal of sorrow, who, bowing toward the earth, resume their despairing march, and limp and groan under heavy burdens, until darkness, welcome, comes again, and their eyelids drop, and they lie down with their loads on, looking up a silent supplication, and wishing that death would touch their eyelids in their sleep, and their journey end where they lie.

Captain Lake was in London this morning. We know he came about electioneering matters ; but he had not yet seen Leverett. Perhaps on second thoughts he rightly judged that Leverett knew no more than he did of the matter. It depended on the issue of the great debate that was drawing nigh. The Minister himself could not tell whether the dissolution was at hand ; and could no more postpone it, when the time came, than he could adjourn an eclipse.

Notwithstanding the late whist party of the previous night, the gallant captain made a very early toilet. With his little bag in his hand, he went down stairs, thinking unpleasantly, I believe, and jumped into the Hansom that awaited him at the door, telling the man to go to the —— station. They had hardly turned the corner, however, when he popped his head forward and changed the direction.

He looked at his watch. He had quite time to make his visit, and save the down-train after.

He did not know the City well. Many men who lived two hundred miles away, and made a flying visit only once in three years, knew it a great deal better than the London-bred rake who had lived in the West-end all his days.

Captain Lake looked peevish and dangerous, as he always did, when he was anxious. In fact he did not know what the next ten minutes might bring him. He was thinking what had best be done in any and every contingency. Was he still abroad, or had he arrived? was he in Shive's Court, or, cursed luck! had he crossed him yesterday by the down-train, and was he by this time closeted with Larkin in the Lodge? Lake, so to speak, stood at his wicket, and that accomplished bowler, Fortune, ball in hand, at the other end; will it be swift round-hand, or a slow twister, or a shooter, or a lob? Eye and hand, foot and bat, he must stand tense, yet flexible, lithe and swift as lightning, ready for everything—cut, block, slip, or hit to leg. It was not altogether pleasant. The stakes were enormous! and the suspense by no means conducive to temper.

Lake fancied that the man was driving wrong, once or twice, and was on the point of cursing him to that effect, from the window. But at last, with an anxious throb at his heart, he recognised the dingy archway, and the cracked brown marble tablet over the keystone, and he recognised Shive's Court.

So forth jumped the captain, so far relieved, and glided into the dim quadrangle, with its square of smoky sky overhead; and the prattle of children playing on the flags, and the scrape of a violin from a window, were in his ears, but as it were unheard. He was looking up at a window, with a couple of sooty scarlet geraniums in it. This was the court where Dame Dutton dwelt. He glided up her narrow stair and let himself in by the latch; and with his cane made a smacking like a harlequin's sword upon the old woman's deal table, crying: 'Mrs. Dutton; Mrs. Dutton. Is Mrs. Dutton at home?'

The old lady, who was a laundress, entered, in a short blue cotton wrapper, wiping the suds from her shrunken but sinewy arms with her apron, and on seeing the captain, her countenance, which was threatening, became very reverential indeed.

'How d'ye do, Mrs. Dutton' Quite well. Have you heard lately from Jim?'

' No.'

' You'll see him soon, however, and give him this note, d'ye
see, and tell him I was here, asking about you and him, and
very well, and glad if I can serve him again ? don't forget that,
very glad. Where will you keep that note ? Oh ! your tea-
caddy, not a bad safe ; and see, give him this, it's ten pounds.
You won't forget ; and you want a new gown, Mrs. Dutton. I'd
choose it myself, only I'm such a bad judge ; but you'll choose
it for me, won't you ? and let me see it on you when next I
come,' and with a courtesy and a great beaming smile on her
hot face, she accepted the five-pound note, which he placed in
her hand.

In another moment the captain was gone. He had just time
to swallow a cup of coffee at the ' Terminus Hotel,' and was
gliding away towards the distant walls of Brandon Hall.

He had a coupé all to himself. But he did not care for the
prospect. He saw Lawyer Larkin, as it were, reflected in the
plate-glass, with his hollow smile and hungry eyes before him,
knowing more than he should do, paying him compliments, and
plotting his ruin.

' Everything would have been quite smooth only for that d——
fellow. The Devil fixed him precisely there for the express
purpose of fleecing and watching, and threatening him —perhaps worse. He hated that sly, double-dealing reptile of prey
—the arachnida of social nature — the spiders with which also
naturalists place the scorpions. I dare say Mr. Larkin would
have had as little difficulty in referring the gallant captain to
the same family.

While Stanley Lake is thus scanning the shabby, but dangerous image of the attorney in the magic mirror before him, that
eminent limb of the law was not inactive in the quiet town of
Gylingden. Under ordinary circumstances his ' pride ' would
have condemned the vicar to a direful term of suspense, and
he certainly would not have knocked at the door of the pretty
little gabled house at the Dollington end of the town for many
days to come. The vicar would have had to seek out the
attorney, to lie in wait for and to woo him.

But Jos. Larkin's pride, like all his other passions—except
his weakness for the precious metals—was under proper regula-
tion. Jim Dutton might arrive at any moment, and it would
not do to risk his publishing the melancholy intelligence of
Mark Wylder's death before the transfer of the vicar's reversion ; and to prevent that risk the utmost promptitude was indispensable.

At nine o'clock, therefore, he presented himself, attended by
his legal henchmen as before.

' Another man might not have come here, Mr. Wylder, until
his presence had been specially invited, after the—the——'

when he came to define the offence it was not very easy to do
so, inasmuch as it consisted in the vicar's having unconsciously
very nearly escaped from his fangs ; 'but let that pass.   I have
had, I grieve to say, by this morning's post a most serious letter
from London ;' the attorney shook his head, while searching
his pocket. 'I'll read just a passage or two if you'll permit me ;
it comes from Burlington and Smith.   I protest I have forgot it
at home ; however, I may mention, that in consequence of the
letter you authorised me to write, and guaranteed by your bond,
on which they have entered judgment, they have gone to the
entire expense of drawing the deeds, and investigating title, and
they say that the purchaser will positively be off, unless the
articles are in their office by twelve o'clock to-morrow ; and, I
grieve to say, they add, that in the event of the thing falling
through, they will issue execution for the amount of their costs,
which, as I anticipated, a good deal exceeds four hundred
pounds.   I have, therefore, my dear Mr. Wylder, casting aside
all unpleasant feeling, called to entreat you to end and deter-
mine any hesitation you may have felt, and to execute without
one moment's delay the articles which are prepared, and which
must be in the post-office within half an hour.'

Then Mr. Jos. Larkin entered pointedly and briefly into Miss
Lake's offer, which he characterised as 'wholly nugatory, illusory, and chimerical ;' told him he had spoken on the subject,
yesterday evening, to the young lady, who now saw plainly that
there really was nothing in it, and that she was not in a position
to carry out that part of her proposition, which contemplated a
residence in the vicar's family.

This portion of his discourse he dismissed rather slightly and
mysteriously ; but he contrived to leave upon the vicar's mind a
very painful and awful sort of uncertainty respecting the young
lady of whom he spoke.

Then he became eloquent on the madness of further in-
decision in a state of things so fearfully menacing, freely ad-
mitting that it would have been incomparably better for the
vicar never to have moved in the matter, than, having put his
hand to the plough, to look back as he had been doing. If he
declined his advice, there was no more to be said, but to bow his
head to the storm, and that ponderous execution would descend
in wreck and desolation.

So the vicar, very much flushed, in panic and perplexity, and
trusting wildly to his protesting lawyer's guidance, submitted.
Buggs and the bilious youngster entered with the deed, and the
articles were duly executed, and the vicar signed also a receipt
for the fanciful part of the consideration, and upon it and the
deed he endorsed a solemn promise, in the terms I have mentioned before, that he would never take any step to question, set
aside, or disturb the purchase, or any matter connected therewith.

Then the attorney, now in his turn flushed and very much elated, congratulated the poor vicar on his emancipation from his difficulties ; and 'now that it was all done and over, told him, what he had never told him before, that, considering the nature of the purchase, he had got a *splendid* price for it.'

The good man had also his agreement from Lake to sell Five Oaks.

The position of the good attorney, therefore, in a commercial point of view, was eminently healthy and convenient. For less than half the value of Five Oaks alone, he was getting that estate, and a vastly greater one beside, to be succeeded to on Mark Wylder's death.

No wonder, then, that the good attorney was more than usually bland and happy that day. He saw the pork-butcher in his back-parlour, and had a few words to say about the chapel-trust, and his looks and talk were quite edifying. He met two little children in the street, and stopped and smiled as he stooped down to pat them on the heads, and ask them whose children they were, and gave one of them a halfpenny. And he sat afterwards, for nearly ten minutes, with lean old Mrs. Mullock, in her little shop, where toffey, toys, and penny books for young people were sold, together with baskets, tea-cups, straw-mats, and other adult ware ; and he was so friendly and talked so beautifully, and although, as he admitted in his lofty way, 'there might be differences in fortune and position,' yet were we not all members of one body ? And he talked upon this theme till the good lady, marvelling how so great a man could be so humble, was called to the receipt of custom, on the subject of 'paradise' and 'lemon-drops,' and the heavenly-minded attorney, with a celestial condescension, recognised his two little acquaintances of the street, and actually adding another halfpenny to his bounty—escaped, with a hasty farewell and a smile, to the street, as eager to evade the thanks of the little people, and the admiration of Mrs. Mullock.

It is not to be supposed, that having got one momentous matter well off his mind, the good attorney was to be long rid of anxieties. The human mind is fertile in that sort of growth. As well might the gentleman who shaves suppose, as his fingers glide, after the operation, over the polished surface of his chin— *factus ad unguem*—that he may fling his brush and strop into the fire, and bury his razor certain fathoms in the earth. No ! One crop of cares will always succeed another—not very oppressive, nor in any wise grand, perhaps—worries, simply, no more ; but needing a modicum of lather, the looking-glass, the strop, the diligent razor, delicate manipulation, and stealing a portion of our precious time every day we live ; and this must go on so long as the state of man is imperfect, and plenty of possible evil in futurity.

The attorney must run up to London for a day or two. What if that mysterious, and almost illegible brute, James Dutton, should arrive while he was away. Very unpleasant, possibly! For the attorney intended to keep that gentleman very quiet. Sufficient time must be allowed to intervene to disconnect the purchase of the vicar's remainder from the news of Mark Wylder's demise. A year and a-half, maybe, or possibly a year might do. For if the good attorney was cautious, he was also greedy, and would take possession as early as was safe. Therefore arrangements were carefully adjusted to detain that important person, in the event of his arriving; and a note, in the good attorney's hand, inviting him to remain at the Lodge till his return, and particularly requesting that 'he would kindly abstain from mentioning to *anyone*, during his absence, any matter he might intend to communicate to him in his professional capacity or otherwise.'

This, of course, was a little critical, and made his to-morrow's journey to London a rather anxious prospect.

In the meantime our friend, Captain Lake, arrived in a hired fly, with his light baggage, at the door of stately Brandon. So soon as the dust and ashes of railway travel were removed, the pale captain, in changed attire, snowy cambric, and with perfumed hair and handkerchief, presented himself before Dorcas.

'Now, Dorkie, darling, your poor soldier has come back, resolved to turn over a new leaf, and never more to reserve another semblance of a secret from you,' said he, so soon as his first greeting was over. 'I long to have a good talk with you, Dorkie. I have no one on earth to confide in but you. I think,' he said, with a little sigh, 'I would never have been so reserved with you, darling, if I had had anything pleasant to confide; but all I have to say is triste and tiresome—only a story of difficulties and petty vexations. I want to talk to you, Dorkie. Where shall it be?'

They were in the great drawing-room, where I had first seen Dorcas Brandon and Rachel Lake, on the evening on which my acquaintance with the princely Hall was renewed, after an interval of so many years.

'This room, Stanley, dear?'

'Yes, this room will answer very well,' he said, looking round. 'We can't be overhead, it is so large. Very well, darling, listen.'

CHAPTER LXII.

THE CAPTAIN EXPLAINS WHY MARK WYLDER ABSCONDED.

'HOW delicious these violets are!' said Stanley, lean‧ing for a moment over the fragrant purple dome that crowned a china stand on the marble table they were passing. 'You love flowers, Dorkie. Every perfect woman is, I think, a sister of Flora's. You are looking pale—you have not been ill? No! I'm very glad you say so. Sit down for a moment and listen, darling. And first I'll tell you, upon my honour, what Rachel has been worrying me about.'

Dorcas sate beside him on the sofa, and he placed his slender arm affectionately round her waist.

'You must know, Dorkie, that before his sudden departure, Mark Wylder promised to lend William, his brother, a sum sufficient to relieve him of all his pressing debts.'

'Debts! I never knew before that he had any,' exclaimed Dorcas. 'Poor William! I am so sorry.'

'Well, he has, like other fellows, only he can't get away as easily, and he has been very much pressed since Mark went, for he has not yet lent him a guinea, and in fact Rachel says she thinks he is in danger of being regularly sold out. She does not say she knows it, but only that she suspects they are in a great fix about money.'

'Well, you must know that *I* was the sole cause of Mark Wylder's leaving the country.'

'*You*, Stanley!'

'Yes, *I*, Dorkie. I believe I thought I was doing a duty; but really I was nearly mad with *jealousy*, and simply doing my utmost to drive a rival from *your* presence. And yet, without hope for myself, *desperately* in love.'

Dorcas looked down and smiled oddly; it was a sad and bitter smile, and seemed to ask whither has that desperate love, in so short a time, flown?

'I know I was right. He was a stained man, and was liable at any moment to be branded. It was villainous in him to seek to marry you. I told him at last that, unless he withdrew, your friends should know all. I expected he would show fight, and that a meeting would follow; and I really did not much care whether I were killed or not. But he went, on the contrary, rather quietly, threatening to pay me off, however, though he did not say how. He's a cunning dog, and not very soft-hearted; and

has no more conscience than that,' and he touched his finger to
the cold summit of a marble bust.

'He is palpably machinating something to my destruction
with an influential attorney on whom I keep a watch, and he
has got some fellow named Dutton into the conspiracy; and
not knowing how they mean to act, and only knowing how
utterly wicked, cunning, and bloody-minded he is, and that he
hates me as he probably never hated anyone before, I must be
prepared to meet him, and, if possible, to blow up that Satanic
cabal, which without *money* I can't. It was partly a mystification about the election; of course, it will be expensive, but
nothing like the other. Are you ill, Dorkie?'

He might well ask, for she appeared on the point of fainting.

Dorcas had read and heard stories of men seemingly no worse
than their neighbours—nay, highly esteemed, and praised, and
liked—who yet were haunted by evil men, who encountered
them in lonely places, or by night, and controlled them by the
knowledge of some dreadful crime. Was Stanley—her husband
—whose character she had begun to discern, whose habitual
mystery was, somehow, tinged in her mind with a shade of
horror, one of this two-faced, diabolical order of heroes?

Why should he dread this cabal, as he called it, even though
directed by the malignant energy of the absent and shadowy
Mark Wylder? What could all the world do to harm him in
free England, if he were innocent, if he were what he seemed—
no worse than his social peers?

Why should it be necessary to buy off the conspirators whom
a guiltless man would defy and punish?

The doubt did not come in these defined shapes. As a halo
surrounds a saint, a shadow rose suddenly, and enveloped pale,
scented, smiling Stanley, with the yellow eyes. He stood in the
centre of a dreadful medium, through which she saw him, ambiguous and awful; and she sickened.

'Are you ill, Dorkie, darling?' said the apparition in accents
of tenderness. 'Yes, you *are* ill.'

And he hastily threw open the window, close to which they
were sitting, and she quickly revived in the cooling air.

She saw his yellow eyes fixed upon her features, and his face
wearing an odd expression—was it interest, or tenderness, or
only scrutiny; to her there seemed a light of insincerity and
cruelty in its pallor.

'You are better, darling; thank Heaven, you are better.'

'Yes—yes—a great deal better; it is passing away.'

Her colour was returning, and with a shivering sigh, she
said—

'Oh! Stanley, you must speak truth; I am your wife. Do
they know anything very bad—are you in their power?'

'Why, my dearest, what on earth could put such a wild fancy

in your head?' said Lake, with a strange laugh, and, as she fancied, growing still paler. 'Do you suppose I am a highwayman in disguise, or a murderer, like—what's his name—Eugene Aram? I must have expressed myself very ill, if I suggested anything so tragical. I protest before Heaven, my darling, there is not one word or act of mine I need fear to submit to any court of justice or of honour on earth.'

He took her hand, and kissed it affectionately, and still fondling it gently between his, he resumed—

'I don't mean to say, of course, that I have always been better than other young fellows; I've been foolish, and wild, and—and—I've done wrong things, occasionally—as all young men will; but for high crimes and misdemeanors, or for melodramatic situations, I never had the slightest taste. There's no man on earth who can tell anything of me, or put me under any sort of pressure, thank Heaven; and simply because I have never in the course of my life done a single act unworthy of a gentleman, or in the most trifling way compromised myself. I swear it, my darling, upon my honour and soul, and I will swear it in any terms — the most awful that can be prescribed — in order totally and for ever to remove from your mind so amazing a fancy.'

And with a little laugh, and still holding her hand, he passed his arm round her waist, and kissed her affectionately.

'But you are perfectly right, Dorkie, in supposing that I *am* under very considerable apprehension from their machinations. Though they cannot slur our fair fame, it is quite possible they may very seriously affect our property. Mr. Larkin is in possession of all the family papers. I don't like it, but it is too late now. The estates have been back and forward so often between the Brandons and Wylders, I always fancy there may be a screw loose, or a frangible link somewhere, and he's deeply interested for Mark Wylder.'

'You are better, darling; I think you are better,' he said, looking in her face, after a little pause.

'Yes, dear Stanley, much better; but why should you suppose any plot against our title?'

'Mark Wylder is in constant correspondence with that fellow Larkin. I wish we were quietly rid of him, he is such an unscrupulous dog. I assure you, I doubt very much if the deeds are safe in his possession; at all events, he ought to choose between us and Mark Wylder. It is monstrous his being solicitor for both. The Wylders and Brandons have always been contesting the right to these estates, and the same thing may arise again any day.'

'But tell me, Stanley, how do you want to apply money? What particular good can it do us in this unpleasant uncertainty?'

'Well, Dorkie, believe me I have a sure instinct in matters of this kind. Larkin is plotting treason against us. Wylder is inciting him, and will reap the benefit of it. Larkin hesitates to strike, but that won't last long. In the meantime, he has made a distinct offer to buy Five Oaks. His doing so places him in the same interest with us ; and, although he does not offer its full value, still I should sleep sounder if it were concluded ; and the fact is, I don't think we are safe until that sale *is* concluded.'

Dorcas looked for a moment earnestly in his face, and then down, in thought.

'Now, Dorkie, I have told you all. Who is to advise you, if not your husband ? Trust my sure conviction, and promise me, Dorcas, that you will not hesitate to join me in averting, by a sacrifice we shall hardly feel, a really stupendous blow.'

He kissed her hand, and then her lips, and he said—

'You *will*, Dorkie, I *know* you will. Give me your promise.'

'Stanley, tell me once more, are you really quite frank when you tell me that you apprehend no personal injury from these people—apart, I mean, from the possibility of Mr. Larkin's conspiring to impeach our rights in favour of Mr. Wylder ?'

'Personal injury ? None in life, my darling.'

'And there is really no secret—nothing—*tell* your wife—nothing you fear coming to light ?'

'I swear again, nothing. *Won't* you believe me, darling ?'

'Then, if it be so, Stanley, I think we should hesitate long before selling any part of the estate, upon a mere conjecture of danger. You or I may over-estimate that danger, being so nearly affected by it. We must take advice ; and first, we must consult Chelford. Remember, Stanley, how long the estate has been preserved. Whatever may have been their crimes and follies, those who have gone before us never impaired the Brandon estate ; and, without full consideration, without urgent cause, I, Stanley, will not begin.'

'Why, it is only Five Oaks, and we shall have the money, you forget,' said Stanley.

'Five Oaks is an estate in itself ; and the idea of dismembering the Brandon inheritance seems to me like taking a plank from a ship—all will go down when that is done.'

'But you *can't* dismember it ; it is only a life estate.'

'Well, perhaps so ; but Chelford told me that one of the London people said he thought Five Oaks belonged to me absolutely.'

'In that case the inheritance *is* dismembered already.'

'I will have no share in selling the old estate, or any part of it, to strangers, Stanley, except in a case of necessity ; and we must do nothing precipitately ; and I must insist, Stanley, on consulting Chelford before taking any step. He will view the question more calmly than you or I can ; and we owe him that respect, Stanley, he has been so very kind to us.'

'Chelford is the very last man whom I would think of consulting,' answered Stanley, with his malign and peevish look.

'And why?' asked Dorcas.

'Because he is quite sure to advise against it,' answered Stanley, sharply. 'He is one of those Quixotic fellows who get on very well in fair weather, while living with a duke or duchess, but are sure to run you into mischief when they come to the inns and highways of common life. I know perfectly, he would protest against a compromise. Discharge Larkin—fight him—and see us valiantly stript of our property by some cursed law-quibble ; and think we ought to be much more comfortable so, than in this house, on the terms of a compromise with a traitor like Larkin. But *I* don't think so, nor any man of sense, nor anyone but a hairbrained, conceited knight-errant.'

'I think Chelford one of the most sensible as well as honourable men I know ; and I will take no step in selling a part of our estate to that odious Mr. Larkin, without consulting him, and at least hearing what he thinks of it.'

Stanley's eyes were cast down—and he was nipping the struggling hairs of his light moustache between his lips—but he made no answer. Only suddenly he looked up, and said quietly,

'Very well. Good-bye for a little, Dorkie,' and he leaned over her and kissed her cheek, and then passed into the hall, where he took his hat and cane.

Larcom presented him with a note, in a sealed envelope. As he took it from the salver he recognised Larkin's very clear and large hand. I suspect that grave Mr. Larcom had been making his observations and conjectures thereupon.

The captain took it with a little nod, and a peevish side-glance. It said—

'MY DEAR CAPTAIN BRANDON LAKE,—Imperative business calls me to London by the early train to-morrow. Will you therefore favour me, if convenient, *by the bearer*, with the small note of consent, which must accompany the articles agreeing to sell.

'I remain, &c. &c. &c.'

Larkin's groom was waiting for an answer.

'Tell him I shall propably see Mr. Larkin myself,' said the captain, snappishly ; and so he walked down to pretty little Gylingden.

On the steps of the reading-room stood old Tom Ruddle, who acted as marker in the billiard-room, treasurer, and book-keeper beside, and swept out the premises every morning, and went to and fro at the proper hours, between that literary and sporting institution and the post-office; and who, though seldom sober, was always well instructed in the news of the town.

'How do you do, old Ruddle—quite well?' asked the captain with a smile. 'Who have you got in the rooms?'

Well, Jos. Larkin was not there. Indeed he seldom showed in those premises, which he considered decidedly low, dropping in only now and then, like the great county gentlemen, on sessions days, to glance at the papers, and gossip on their own high affairs.

But Ruddle had seen Mr. Jos. Larkin on the green, not five minutes since, and thither the gallant captain bent his steps.

CHAPTER LXIII.

THE ACE OF HEARTS.

SO you are going to London—*to-morrow*, is not it?' said Captain Lake, when on the green of Gylingden where visitors were promenading, and the militia bands playing lusty polkas, he met Mr. Jos. Larkin, in lavender trousers and kid gloves, new hat, metropolitan black frock-coat, and shining French boots—the most elegant as well as the most Christian of provincial attorneys.

'Ah, yes—I think—should my engagements permit—of starting early to-morrow. The fact is, Captain Lake, our poor friend the vicar, you know, the Rev. William Wylder, has pressing occasion for some money, and I can't leave him absolutely in the hands of Burlington and Smith.'

'No, of course—quite so,' said Lake, with that sly smile which made every fellow on whom it lighted somehow fancy that the captain had divined his secret. 'Very honest fellows, with good looking after—eh?'

The attorney laughed a little awkwardly, with his pretty pink blush over his long face.

'Well, I'm far from saying that, but it is their business, you know, to take care of *their* client; and it would not do to give them the handling of *mine*. Can I do anything, Captain Lake, for you while in town?'

'Nothing on earth, thank you very much. But I am thinking of doing something for you. You've interested yourself a great deal about Mark Wylder's movements.'

'Not more than my duty clearly imposed.'

'Yes; but notwithstanding it will operate, I'm afraid, as you will presently see, rather to his prejudice. For to prevent your conjectural interference from doing him a more serious mischief,

I will now, and here, if you please, divulge the true and only cause of his absconding. It is fair to mention, however, that your knowing it will make you fully as odious to him as I am—and that, I assure you, is very odious indeed. There were four witnesses beside myself—Lieutenant-Colonel Jermyn, Sir James Carter, Lord George Vanbrugh, and Ned Clinton.'

'*Witnesses!* Captain Lake. Do you allude to a legal matter?' enquired Larkin, with his look of insinuating concern and enquiry.

'Quite the contrary—a very lawless matter, indeed. These four gentlemen, beside myself, were present at the occurrence. But perhaps you've heard of it?' said the captain, 'though that's not likely.'

'Not that I recollect, Captain Lake,' answered Jos. Larkin.

'Well, it is not a thing you'd forget easily—and indeed it was a very well kept secret, as well as an ugly one,' and Lake smiled in his sly quizzical way.

'And *where*, Captain Lake, did it occur, may I enquire?' said Larkin, with his charming insinuation.

'You may, and you shall hear—in fact, I'll tell you the whole thing. It was at Gray's Club, in Pall Mall. The whist party were old Jermyn, Carter, Vanbrugh, and Wylder. Clinton and I were at piquet, and were disturbed by a precious row the old boys kicked up. Jermyn and Carter were charging Mark Wylder, in so many words, with not playing fairly—there was an ace of hearts on the table played by him, and before three minutes they brought it home—and in fact it was quite clear that poor dear Mark had helped himself to it in quite an irregular way.'

'Oh, dear, Captain Lake, oh, dear, how shocking—how inexpressibly shocking! Is not it *melancholy?*' said Larkin, in his finest and most pathetic horror.

'Yes; but don't cry till I've done,' said Lake, tranquilly. 'Mark tried to bully, but the cool old heads were too much for him, and he threw himself at last entirely on our mercy—and very abject he became, poor thing.'

'How well the mountains look! I am afraid we shall have rain to-morrow.'

Larkin uttered a short groan.

'So they sent him into the small card-room, next that we were playing in. I think we were about the last in the club—it was past three o'clock—and so the old boys deliberated on their sentence. To bring the matter before the committee were utter ruin to Mark, and they let him off, on these conditions—he was to retire forthwith from the club; he was never to play any game of cards again; and, lastly, he was never more to address any one of the gentlemen who were present at his detection. Poor dear devil!—how he did jump at the conditions;—and provided they were each and all strictly observed, it was intimated that the occurrence should be kept secret. Well, you know, that was letting poor old Mark off in a coach; and I do assure you, though we had never liked one another, I really was very glad they did not move his expulsion—which would have involved his quitting the service—and I positively don't know how he could have lived if that had occurred.'

'I do solemnly assure you, Captain Lake, what you have told me has beyond expression amazed, and I will say, horrified me,' said the attorney, with a slow and melancholy vehemence. 'Better men might have suspected something of it—I do solemnly pledge my honour that nothing of the kind so much as crossed my mind—not naturally suspicious, I believe, but all the more shocked, Captain Lake, on that account.'

'He was poor then, you see, and a few pounds were everything to him, and the temptation immense; but clumsy fellows ought not to try that sort of thing. There's the highway—Mark would have made a capital garrotter.'

The attorney groaned, and turned up his eyes. The band was playing 'Pop goes the weasel,' and old Jackson, very well dressed and buckled up, with a splendid smile upon his waggish, military countenance, cried, as he passed, with a wave of his hand, 'How do, Lake—how do, Mr. Larkin—beautiful day!'

'I've no wish to injure Mark; but it is better that you should know at once, than go about poking everywhere for information.'

'I do assure you——'

'And having really no wish to hurt him,' pursued the captain, 'and also making it, as I do, a point that you shall repeat this conversation as little as possible, I don't choose to appear singular, as your sole informant, and I've given you here a line to Sir James Carter—he's member, you know, for Huddlesbury. I mention, that Mark, having broken his promise, and played for heavy stakes, too, both on board his ship, and at Plymouth and Naples, which I happen to know; and also by accosting me, whom, as one of the gentlemen agreeing to impose these conditions, he was never to address, I felt myself at liberty to mention it to you, holding the relation you do to me as well as to him, in consequence of the desirableness of placing you in possession of the true cause of his absconding, which was simply my telling him that I would not permit him, slurred as he was, to marry a lady who was totally ignorant of his actual position; and, in fact, that unless he withdrew, I must acquaint the young lady's guardian of the circumstances.'

There was quite enough probability in this story to warrant Jos. Larkin in turning up his eyes and groaning. But in the intervals, his shrewd eyes searched the face of the captain, not knowing whether to believe one syllable of what he related.

I may as well mention here, that the attorney did present the note to Sir J. Carter with which Captain Lake had furnished him ; indeed, he never lost an opportunity of making the acquaintance of a person of rank ; and that the worthy baronet, so appealed to, and being a blunt sort of fellow, and an old acquaintance of Stanley's, did, in a short and testy sort of way, corroborate Captain Lake's story, having previously conditioned that he was not to be referred to as the authority from whom Mr. Larkin had learned it.

The attorney and Captain Brandon Lake were now walking side by side over the more sequestered part of the green.

'And so,' said the captain, coming to a stand-still, ' I'll bid you good-bye, Larkin ; what stay, I forgot to ask, do you make in town ?'

'Only a day or two.'

'You'll not wait for the division on Trawler's motion ?'

'Oh, dear, no. I calculate I'll be here again, certainly, in three days' time. And, I suppose, Captain Lake, you received my note ?'

'You mean just now ? Oh, yes ; of course it is all right ; but one day is as good as another ; and you have got my agreement signed.'

'Pardon me, Captain Brandon Lake ; the fact is, one day, in this case, does *not* answer as well as another, for I must have drafts of the deeds prepared by my conveyancer in town, and the note is indispensable. Perhaps, if there is any difficulty, you will be so good as to say so, and I shall then be in a position to consider the case in its new aspect.'

'What the devil difficulty *can* there be, Sir ? I can't see it, any more than what *hurry* can possibly exist about it,' said Lake, stung with a momentary fury. It seemed as though everyone was conspiring to perplex and torment him ; and he, like the poor vicar, though for very different reasons, had grown intensely anxious to sell. He had grown to dread the attorney, since the arrival of Dutton's letter. He suspected that his journey to London had for its object a meeting with that person. He could not tell what might be going on in the dark. But the possibility of such a conjunction might well dismay him.

On the other hand, the more Mr. Larkin relied upon the truth of Dutton's letter, the cooler he became respecting the purchase of Five Oaks. It was, of course, a very good thing ; but not his first object. The vicar's reversion in that case was everything, and of it he was now sure.

'There is no difficulty about the note, Sir ; it contains but four lines, and I've given you the form. No difficulty can exist but in the one quarter ; and the fact is,' he added, steadily, ' unless I have that note before I leave to-morrow-morning, I'll assume that you wish to be off, Captain Lake, and I will adapt myself to circumstances.'

'You may have it *now*,' said the captain, with a fierce carelessness. 'D—d nonsense ! Who could have fancied any such stupid hurry ? Send in the morning, and you shall have it.' And the captain rather savagely turned away, skirting the crowd who hovered about the band, in his leisurely and now solitary ramble.

The captain was sullen that evening at home. He was very uncomfortable. His heart was failing him for the things that were coming to pass. One of his maniacal tempers, which had often before thrown him, as it were, 'off the rails,' was at the bottom of his immediate troubles. This proneness to sudden accesses of violence and fury was the compensation which abated the effect of his ordinary craft and self-command.

He had done all he could to obviate the consequences of his folly in this case. He hoped the attorney might not succeed in discovering Jim Dutton's whereabouts. At all events, he had been beforehand, and taken measures to quiet that person's dangerous resentment. But it was momentous in the critical state of things to give this dangerous attorney a handsome share in his stake—to place him, as he had himself said, 'in the same boat,' and enlist all his unscrupulous astuteness in maintaining his title : and if he went to London disappointed, and that things turned out unluckily about Dutton, it might be a very awful business indeed.

Dinner had been a very dull *tête-à-tête.* Dorcas sat stately and sad—looking from the window toward the distant sunset horizon, piled in dusky gold and crimson clouds, against the faded, green sky—a glory that is always melancholy and dreamy. Stanley sipped his claret, his eyes upon the cloth. He raised them and looked out, too ; and the ruddy light tinted his pale features.

A gleam of good humour seemed to come with it, and he said, ' I was just thinking, Dorkie, that for you and me, *alone,* these great rooms are a little dreary. Suppose we have tea in the tapestry room.'

'The Dutch room, Stanley—I think so—I should like it very well. So, I am certain, would Rachel. I've written to her to come. I hope she will. I expect her at nine. The brougham will be with her. She wrote such an odd note to-day, addressed to you ; but *I opened it.* Here it is.'

She did not watch his countenance, or look in his direction, as he read it. She addressed herself, on the contrary, altogether to her Liliputian white lap-dog, Snow, and played with his silken ears ; and chatted with him as ladies will.

A sealed envelope broken. That scoundrel, Larcom, knew perfectly it was meant for *me.* He was on the point of speaking his mind, which would hardly have been pleasant to hear, upon this piece of detective impertinence of his wife's. He could have smashed all the glass upon the table. But he looked serene, and leaned back with the corner of Rachel's note between two fingers. It was a case in which he clearly saw he must command himself.

CHAPTER LXIV.

IN THE DUTCH ROOM.

IS heart misgave him. He felt that a crisis was coming; and he read—

'I cannot tell you, my poor brother, how miserable I am. I have just learned that a very dangerous person has discovered more about that dreadful evening than we believed known to anybody in Gylingden. I am subjected to the most agonising suspicions and *insults*. Would to Heaven I were dead! But living, I cannot endure my present state of mind longer. To-morrow morning I will see Dorcas—poor Dorcas!—and tell her all. I am weary of urging you, *in vain*, to do so. It would have been much better. But although, after that interview, I shall, perhaps, never see her more, I shall yet be happier, and, I think, relieved from suspense, and the torments of mystery. So will she. At all events, it is her *right* to know all—and she shall.

'YOUR OUTCAST AND MISERABLE SISTER.'

On Stanley's lips his serene, unpleasant smile was gleaming, as he closed the note carelessly. He intended to speak, but his voice caught. He cleared it, and sipped a little claret.

'For a clever girl she certainly does write the most wonderful rubbish. Such an effusion! And she sends it tossing about, from hand to hand, among the servants. I've anticipated her, however, Dorkie.' And he took her hand and kissed it. 'She does not know I've told you *all* myself.'

Stanley went to the library, and Dorcas to the conservatory, neither very happy, each haunted by an evil augury, and a sense of coming danger. The deepening shadow warned Dorcas that it was time to repair to the Dutch room, where she found lights and tea prepared.

In a few minutes more the library door opened and Stanley Lake peeped in.

'Radie not come yet?' said he entering. 'We certainly are

much pleasanter in this room, Dorkie, more, in proportion, than we two should have been in the drawing-room.'

He seated himself beside her, drawing his chair very close to hers, and taking her hand in his. He was more affectionate this evening than usual. What did it portend? she thought. She had already begun to acquiesce in Rachel's estimate of Stanley, and to fancy that whatever he did it was with an un-acknowledged purpose.

'Does little Dorkie love me?' said Lake, in a sweet undertone.

There was reproach, but love too, in the deep soft glance she threw upon him.

'You must promise me not to be frightened at what I am going to tell you,' said Lake.

She heard him with sudden panic, and a sense of cold stole over her. He looked like a ghost—quite white—smiling. She knew something was coming—the secret she had invoked so long—and she was appalled.

'Don't be frightened, darling. It is necessary to tell you; but it is really not much when you hear me out. You'll say so when you have quite heard me. So you won't be frightened?'

She was gazing straight into his wild yellow eyes, fascinated, with a look of expecting terror.

'You are nervous, darling,' he continued, laying his hand on hers. 'Shall we put it off for a little? You are frightened.'

'Not much frightened, Stanley,' she whispered.

'Well, we had better wait. I see, Dorcas, you *are* frightened and nervous. Don't keep looking at me; look at something else, can't you? You make yourself nervous that way. I promise, upon my honour, I'll not say a word about it till you bid me.'

'I know, Stanley—I know.'

'Then, why won't you look down, or look up, or look any way you please, only don't stare at me so.'

'Yes—oh, yes,' and she shut her eyes.

'I'm sorry I began,' he said, pettishly. 'You'll make a fuss. You've made yourself quite nervous; and I'll wait a little.'

'Oh! no, Stanley, *now*—for Heaven's sake, *now*. I was only a little startled; but I am quite well again. Is it anything about marriage? Oh, Stanley, in mercy, tell me *was* there any other engagement?'

'Nothing, darling—nothing on earth of the sort;' and he spoke with an icy little laugh. 'Your poor soldier is altogether yours, Dorkie,' and he kissed her cheek.

'Thank God for that!' said Dorcas, hardly above her breath.

'What I have to say is quite different, and really nothing that need affect you; but Rachel has made such a row about it. Fifty fellows, I know, are in much worse fixes; and though it is not of so much consequence, still I think I should not have told you ; only, without knowing it, you were thwarting me, and help-ing to get me into a serious difficulty by your obstinacy—or what you will—about Five Oaks.'

Somehow trifling as the matter was, Stanley seemed to grow more and more unwilling to disclose it, and rather shrank from it now.

'Now, Dorcas, mind, there must be no trifling. You must not treat me as Rachel has. If you can't keep a secret—for it *is* a secret—say so. Shall I tell you ?'

'Yes, Stanley—yes. I'm your wife.'

'Well, Dorcas, I told you something of it ; but only a part, and some circumstances I *did* intentionally colour a little ; but I could not help it, unless I had told everything ; and no matter what you or Rachel may say, it was kinder to withhold it as long as I could.'

He glanced at the door, and spoke in a lower tone.

And so, with his eyes lowered to the table at which he sat, glancing ever and anon sideways at the door, and tracing little figures with the tip of his finger upon the shining rosewood, he went on murmuring his strange and hateful story in the ear of his wife.

It was not until he had spoken some three or four minutes that Dorcas suddenly uttered a wild scream, and started to her feet. And Stanley also rose precipitately, and caught her in his arms, for she was falling.

As he supported her in her chair, the library door opened, and the sinister face of Uncle Lorne looked in, and returned the captain's stare with one just as fixed and horrified.

'Hush !' whispered Uncle Lorne, and he limped softly into the room, and stopped about three yards away, ' she is not dead, but sleepeth.'

'Hallo ! Larcom,' shouted Lake.

'I tell you she's dreaming the same dream that I dreamt in the middle of the night.'

'Hallo ! Larcom.'

'Mark's on leave to-night, in uniform ; his face is flattened against the window. This is his lady, you know.'

'Hallo ! D— you—are you there ?' shouted the captain, very angry.

'I saw Mark following you like an ape, on all-fours ; such nice white teeth ! grinning at your heels. But he can't bite yet —ha, ha, ha ! Poor Mark !'

'Will you be so good, Sir, as to touch the bell ?' said Lake, changing his tone.

He was afraid to remove his arm from Dorcas, and he was splashing water from a glass upon her face and forehead.

'No—no. No bell yet—time enough—ding, dong. You say, dead and gone.'

Captain Lake cursed him and his absent keeper between his teeth ; still in a rather flurried way, prosecuting his conjugal attentions.

'There was no bell for poor Mark ; and he's always listening, and stares so. A cat may look, you know.'

'Can't you touch the bell, Sir ? What are you standing there for ?' snarled Lake, with a glare at the old man. He looked as if he could have murdered him.

'Standing between the living and the dead !'

'Here, Reuben, here ; where the devil have you been—take him away. He has terrified her. By —— he ought to be shot.'

The keeper silently slid his arm into Uncle Lorne's, and, un-resisting, the old man talking to himself the while, drew him from the room.

Larcom, about to announce Miss Lake, and closely followed by that young lady, passed the grim old phantom on the lobby.

'Be quick, you are wanted there,' said the attendant as he passed.

Dorcas, pale as marble, sighing deeply again and again, her rich black hair drenched in water, which trickled over her cheeks, like the tears and moisture of agony, was recovering. There was water spilt on the table, and the fragments of a broken glass upon the floor.

The moment Rachel saw her, she divined what had happened, and, gliding over, she placed her arm round her.

'You're better, darling. Open the window, Stanley. Send her maid.'

'Aye, send her maid,' cried Captain Lake to Larcom. 'This is your d—d work. A nice mess you have made of it among you.'

'Are you better, Dorcas ?' said Rachel.

'Yes—much better. I'm glad, darling, I understand you now. Radie, kiss me.'

Next morning, before early family prayers, while Mr. Jos. Larkin was locking the despatch box which was to accompany him to London, Mr. Larcom arrived at the Lodge.

He had a note for Mr. Larkin's hand, which he must himself deliver ; and so he was shown into that gentleman's official cabinet, and received with the usual lofty kindness.

'Well, Mr. Larcom, pray sit down. And can I do anything for you, Mr. Larcom ?' said the good attorney, waving his long hand toward a vacant chair.

'A note, Sir.'

'Oh, yes ; very well.' And the tall attorney rose, and, facing the rural prospect at his window, with his back to Mr. Larcom, he read, with a faint smile, the few lines, in a delicate hand, consenting to the sale of Five Oaks.

He had to look for a time at the distant prospect to allow his smile to subside, and to permit the conscious triumph which he knew beamed through his features to discharge itself and evaporate in the light and air before turning to Mr. Larcom, which he did with an air of sudden recollection.

'Ah—all right, I was forgetting ; I must give you a line.'

So he did, and hid away the note in his despatch-box, and said—

The family all quite well, I hope?' whereat Larcom shook his head.

'My mistress'—he always called her so, and Lake the capting—'has been takin' on hoffle, last night, whatever come betwixt 'em. She was fainted outright in her chair in the Dutch room ; and he said it was the old gentleman—Old Flannels, we calls him, for shortness—but lor' bless you, she's too used to him to be frightened, and that's only a make-belief; and Miss Dipples, her maid, she says as how she was worse up stairs, and she's made up again with Miss Lake, which *she* was very glad, no doubt, of the making friends, I do suppose ; but it's a bin a bad row, and I suspeck amost he's used vilins.'

'Compulsion, I suppose ; you mean constraint?' suggested Larkin, very curious.

'Well, that may be, Sir, but I amost suspeck she's been hurted somehow. She got them crying fits up stairs, you know ; and the capting, he's hoffle bad-tempered this morning, and he never looked near her once, after his sister came ; and he left them together, talking and crying, and he locked hisself into the library, like one as knowed he'd done something to be ashamed on, half the night.'

'It's not happy, Larcom, I'm much afraid ; it's *not* happy,' and the attorney rose, shaking his tall bald head, and his hands in his pockets, and looked down in meditation.

'In the Dutch room, after tea, I suppose?' said the attorney.

'Before tea, Sir, just as Miss Lake harrived in the brougham.'

And so on. But there was no more to be learned, and Mr. Larcom returned and attended the captain very reverentially at his solitary breakfast.

Mr. Jos. Larkin was away for London. And a very serene companion he was, if not very brilliant. Everything was going perfectly smoothly with him. A celestial gratitude glowed and expanded within his breast. His angling had been prosperous hitherto, but just now he had made a miraculous draught, and his nets and his heart were bursting. Delightful sentiment, the gratitude of a righteous man ; a man who knows that his heart is not set upon the things of the world ; who has, like King Solomon, made wisdom his first object, and who finds riches added thereto !

There was no shadow of self-reproach to slur the sunny landscape. He had made a splendid purchase from Captain Lake it was true. He drew his despatch-box nearer to him affection-ately, as he thought on the precious records it contained. But who in this wide-awake world was better able to take care of himself than the gallant captain? If it were not the best thing for the captain, surely it would not have been done. Whom have I defrauded? My hands are clean! He had made a still better purchase from the vicar; but what would have become of the vicar if he had not been raised up to purchase? And was it not speculative, and was it not possible that he should lose all that money, and was it not, on the whole, the wisest thing that the vicar, under his difficulties, could have been advised to do?

So reasoned the good attorney, as with a languid smile and a sigh of content, his long hand laid across the cover of the des-patch-box by his side, he looked forth through the plate-glass window upon the sunny fields and hedgerows that glided by him, and felt the blessed assurance, 'look, whatsoever he doeth it shall prosper,' mingling in the hum of surrounding nature. And as his eyes rested on the flying diorama of trees, and farmsteads, and standing crops, and he felt already the pride of a great landed proprietor, his long fingers fiddled pleasantly with the rough tooling of his morocco leather box; and thinking of the signed articles within, it seemed as though an angelic hand had placed them there while he slept, so wondrous was it all; and he fancied under the red tape a label traced in the neatest scrivenery, with a pencil of light, containing such gratifying testimonials to his deserts, 'as well done good and faithful ser-vant,' 'the saints shall inherit the earth,' and so following; and he sighed again in the delicious luxury of having secured both heaven and mammon. And in this happy state, and volunteer-ing all manner of courtesies, opening and shutting windows lending his railway guide and his newspapers whenever he had an opportunity, he at length reached the great London terminus, and was rattling over the metropolitan pavement, with his hand on his despatch-box, to his cheap hotel near the Strand.

CHAPTER LXV.

I REVISIT BRANDON HALL.

RACHEL LAKE was courageous and energetic ; and, when once she had taken a clear view of her duty, wonderfully persistent and impracticable. Her dreadful interview with Jos. Larkin was always in her mind The bleached face, so meek, so cruel, of that shabby spectre, in the small, low parlour of Redman's Farm, was always before her. There he had spoken the sentences which made the earth tremble, and showed her distinctly the cracking line beneath her feet, which would gape at his word into the fathomless chasm that was to swallow her. But, come what might, she would not abandon the vicar and his little boy, and good Dolly, to the arts of that abominable magician.

The more she thought, the clearer was her conviction. She had no one to consult with ; she knew the risk of exasperating that tall man of God, who lived at the Lodge. But, determined to brave all, she went down to see Dolly and the vicar at home.

Poor Dolly was tired ; she had been sitting up all night with sick little Fairy. He was better to-day ; but last night he had frightened them so, poor little man ! he began to rave about eleven o'clock ; and more or less his little mind continued wandering until near six, when he fell into a sound sleep, and seemed better for it ; and it was such a blessing there certainly was neither scarlatina nor small-pox, both which enemies had appeared on the northern frontier of Gylingden, and were picking down their two or three cases each in that quarter.

So Rachel first made her visit to little man, sitting up in his bed, very pale and thin, and looking at her, not with his pretty smile, but a languid, earnest wonder, and not speaking. How quickly and strikingly sickness tells upon children. Little man's frugal store of toys, chiefly the gifts of pleasant Rachel, wild beasts, Noah and his sons, and part of a regiment of foot soldiers, with the usual return of broken legs and missing arms, stood peacefully mingled upon the board across his bed which served as a platform.

But little man was leaning back ; his fingers once so busy, lay motionless on the coverlet, and his tired eyes rested on the toys with a joyless, earnest apathy.

'Didn't play with them a minute,' said the maid.

'I'll bring him a new box. I'm going into the town ; won't

that be pretty?' said Rachel, parting his golden locks over the young forehead, and kissing him ; and she took his little hand in hers—it was hot and dry.

'He looks better—a little better, don't you think ; just a little better?' whispered his mamma, looking, as all the rest were, on that wan, sad little face.

But he really looked worse.

'Well, he can't look better, you know, dear, till there's a decided change. What does Doctor Buddle say?'

'He saw him yesterday morning. He thinks it's all from his stomach, and he's feverish ; no meat. Indeed he won't eat anything, and you see the light hurts his eyes.'

There was only a chink of the shutter open.

'But it is always so when he is ever so little ill, my precious little man ; and I *know* if he thought it anything the *least* serious, Doctor Buddle would have looked in before now, he's so very kind.'

'I wish my darling could get a little sleep. He's very tired, nurse,' said Rachel.

'Yes'm, very tired'm ; would he like his precious head lower a bit? No ; very well, darling, we'll leave it so.'

'Dolly, darling, you and nurse must be so tired sitting up. I have a little wine at Redman's Farm. I got it, you remember, more than a year ago, when Stanley said he was coming to pay me a visit. I never take any, and a little would be so good for you and poor nurse. I'll send some to you.'

So coming down stairs Rachel said, 'Is the vicar at home?' Yes, he was in the study, and there they found him brushing his seedy hat, and making ready for his country calls in the neighbourhood of the town. The hour was dull without little Fairy ; but he would soon be up and out again, and he would steal up now and see him. He could not go out without his little farewell at the bed-side, and he would bring him in some pretty flowers.

'You've seen little Fairy !' asked the good vicar, with a very anxious smile, 'and you think him better, dear Miss Lake, don't you?'

'Why, I can't say that, because you know, so soon as he's better, he'll be quite well ; they make their recoveries all in a moment.'

'But he does not look worse?' said the vicar, lifting his eyes eagerly from his boot, which he was buttoning on the chair.

'Well, he *does* look more *tired*, but that must be till his recovery begins, which will be, please Heaven, immediately.'

'Oh, yes, my little man has had two or three attacks *much* more serious than this, and always shook them off so easily, I was reminding Dolly, always, and good Doctor Buddle assures us it is none of those horrid complaints.'

And so they talked over the case of the little man, who with Noah and his sons, and the battered soldiers and animals before him, was fighting, though they only dimly knew it, silently in his little bed, the great battle of life or death.

'Mr. Larkin came to me the evening before last,' said Rachel, '*and told me* that the little sum I mentioned — now don't say a word till you have heard me — was not sufficient; so I want to tell you what I have quite resolved on. I have been long intending some time or other to change my place of residence, perhaps I shall go to Switzerland, and I have made up my mind to sell my rent-charge on the Dulchester estate. It will produce, Mr. Young says, a very large sum, and I wish to lend it to you, either *all* or as much as will make you *quite* comfortable—you must not refuse. I had intended leaving it to my dear little man up stairs; and you must promise me solemnly that you will not listen to the advice of that bad, cruel man, Mr. Larkin.'

'My dear Miss Lake, you misunderstood him. But what can I say — how can I thank you?' said the vicar, clasping her hand.

'A wicked and merciless man, I say,' repeated Miss Lake. 'From my observation of him, I am certain of two things—I am sure that he has some reason for thinking that your brother, Mark Wylder, is dead ; and secondly, that he is himself deeply interested in the purchase of your reversion. I feel a little ill : Dolly, open the window.'

There was a silence for a little while, and Rachel resumed :—

'Now, William Wylder, I am convinced, that you and your wife (and she kissed Dolly), and your dear little boy, are marked out for plunder — the objects of a conspiracy ; and I'll lose my life, but I'll prevent it.'

'Now, maybe, Willie, upon my word, perhaps, she's quite right ; for, you know, if poor Mark *is* dead, *then* would not *he* have the estate *now;* is not that it, Miss Lake, and—and, you know, that would be dreadful, to sell it all for next to nothing, is not that what you mean, Miss Lake—Rachel dear, I mean.'

'Yes, Dolly, stripping yourselves of a splendid inheritance, and robbing your poor little boy. I protest, in the name of Heaven, against it, and you have no excuse now, William, with my offer before you ; and, Dolly, it will be inexcusable *wickedness* in you, if you allow it.'

'Now, Willie dear, do you hear that — do you hear what she says?'

'But, Dolly darling—dear Miss Lake, there is no reason whatever to suppose that poor Mark is dead,' said the vicar, very pale.

'I tell you again, I am convinced the attorney *believes* it. He did not say so, indeed ; but, cunning as he is, I think I've quite seen through his plot; and even in what he said to me, there was something that half betrayed him every moment. And. Dolly, if you allow this sale, you deserve the ruin you are inviting, and the remorse that will follow you to your grave.'

'Do you hear that, Willie?' said Dolly, with her hand on his arm.

'But, dear, it is too late—I *have* signed this—this instrument —and it is too late. I hope—God help me—I have not done wrong. Indeed, whatever happens, dear Miss Lake, may Heaven for ever bless you. But respecting good Mr. Larkin, you are, indeed, in error; I am sure you have quite misunderstood him. You don't know how kind—how *disinterestedly* good he has been; and *now*, my dear Miss Lake, it is too late—*quite* too late.'

'No; it is *not* too late. Such wickedness as that cannot be lawful—I won't believe the law allows it,' cried Rachel Lake. 'It is all a fraud—even if you have signed—all a fraud. You must procure able advice at once. Your enemy is that dreadful Mr. Larkin. Write to some good attorney in London. I'll pay everything.'

'But, dear Miss Lake, I can't,' said the vicar, dejectedly; 'I am bound in honour and conscience not to disturb it—I have written to Messrs. Burlington and Smith to that effect. I assure you, dear Miss Lake, we have not acted inconsiderately— nothing has been done without careful and deep consideration.'

'You *must* employ an able attorney immediately. You have been duped. Your little boy must not be ruined.'

'But—but I do assure you, I have so pledged myself by the letter I have mentioned, that I *could* not—no, it is *quite impossible*,' he added, as he recollected the strong and pointed terms in which he had pledged his honour and conscience to the London firm, to guarantee them against any such disturbance as Miss Lake was urging him to attempt.

'I am going into the town, Dolly, and so are you,' said Rachel, after a little pause. 'Let us go together.'

And to this Dolly readily assented; and the vicar, evidently much troubled in mind, having run up to the nursery to see his little man, the two ladies set out together. Rachel saw that she had made an impression upon Dolly, and was resolved to carry her point. So, in earnest terms, again she conjured her, at least, to lay the whole matter before some friend on whom she could rely; and Dolly, alarmed and eager, quite agreed with Rachel, that the sale must be stopped, and she would do whatever dear Rachel bid her.

'But do you think Mr. Larkin really supposes that poor Mark is dead?'

'I do, dear—I suspect he knows it.'

'And what makes you think that, Rachel, darling?'

'I can't define—I've no proofs to give you. One knows things, sometimes. I perceived it—and I think I can't be mistaken ; and now I've said all, and pray ask me no more upon that point.'

Rachel spoke with a hurried and fierce impatience, that rather startled her companion.

It is wonderful that she showed her state of mind so little. There was, indeed, something feverish, and at times even fierce, in her looks and words. But few would have guessed her agony, as she pleaded with the vicar and his wife ; or the awful sense of impending consequences that closed over her like the shadow of night, the moment the excitement of her pleading was over —'Rachel, are you mad ?——Fly, fly, fly !' was always sounding in her ears. The little street of Gylingden, through which they were passing, looked strange and dream-like. And as she listened to Mrs. Crinkle's babble over the counter, and chose his toys for poor little 'Fairy,' she felt like one trifling on the way to execution.

But her warnings and entreaties, I have said, were not quite thrown away ; for, although the vicar was inflexible, she had prevailed with his wife, who, at parting, again promised Rachel, that if she could do it, the sale should be stopped.

When I returned to Brandon, a few mornings later, Captain Lake received me joyfully at his solitary breakfast. He was in an intense electioneering excitement. The evening papers for the day before lay on the breakfast table.

'A move of some sort suspected—the opposition prints all hinting at tricks and ambuscades. They are whipping their men up awfully. Old Wattles, not half-recovered, went by the early train yesterday, Wealdon tells me. It will probably kill him. Stower went up the day before. Lee says he saw him at Charteris. He never speaks—only a vote—and a fellow that never appears till the minute.'

'Brittle, the member for Stoney-Muckford, was in the next carriage to me yesterday ; and he's a slow coach, too,' I threw in. 'It does look as if the division was nearer than they pretend.'

'Just so. I heard from Gybes last evening—what a hand that fellow writes—only a dozen words—" Look out for squalls," and " keep your men in hand." I've sent for Wealdon. I wish the morning papers were come. I'm a quarter past eleven— what are you ? The post's in at Dollington fifty minutes before we get our letters here. D—d nonsense—it's all that heavy 'bus of Driver's—I'll change that. They leave London at five, and get to Dollington at half-past ten, and Driver never has them in sooner than twenty minutes past eleven ! D—d humbug ! I'd undertake to take a dog-cart over the ground in twenty minutes.'

'Is Larkin here ?' I asked.

'Oh, no—run up to town. I'm so glad he's away—the clumsiest dog in England—nothing clever—no invention—only a bully—the people hate him. Wealdon's my man. I wish he'd give up that town-clerkship — it can't be worth much, and it's in his way—I'd make it up to him somehow. Will you just look at that—it's the 'Globe'—only six lines, and tell me what *you* make of it?'

'It does look like it, certainly.'

'Wealdon and I have jotted down a few names here,' said Lake, sliding a list of names before me ; 'you know some of them, I think—rather a strong committee ; don't you think so? Those fellows with the red cross before have promised.'

'Yes ; it's very strong—capital !' I said, crunching my toast. 'Is it thought the writs will follow the dissolution unusually quickly?'

'They must, unless they want a very late session. But it is quite possible the government may win — a week ago they reckoned upon eleven.'

And as we were talking the post arrived.

'Here they are !' cried Lake, and grasping the first morning paper he could seize on, he tore it open with a greater display of energy than I had seen that languid gentleman exhibit on any former occasion.

CHAPTER LXVI.

LADY MACBETH.

'HERE it is,' said the captain. 'Beaten'—then came an oath—'three votes—how the devil was that?—there it is, by Jove—no mistake—majority against ministers, three! Is that the "Times?" What does *it* say?'

'A long leader—no resignation—immediate dissolution. That is what I collect from it.'

'How on earth could they have miscalculated so! Swivell, I see, voted in the majority; that's very odd; and, by Jove, there's Surplice, too, and he's good for seven votes. Why his own paper was backing the ministers! What a fellow that is! That accounts for it all. A difference of fourteen votes.'

And thus we went on, discussing this unexpected turn of luck, and reading to one another snatches of the leading articles in different interests upon the subject.

Then Lake, recollecting his letters, opened a large-sealed envelope, with S. C. G. in the corner.

'This is from Gybes—let us see. Oh! *before* the division. "It looks a little fishy," he says—well, so it does—"We may take the division to-night. Should it prove adverse, you are to expect an immediate dissolution; this *on the best authority*. I write to mention this, as I may be too much hurried to-morrow."'

We were discussing this note when Wealdon arrived.

'Well, captain; great news, Sir. The best thing, I take it, could have happened ministers, ha, ha, ha! A rotten house—down with it—blow it up—three votes only—but as good as three hundred for the purpose—of the three hundred, grant but three, you know—of course, they don't think of resigning.'

'Oh, dear, no—an immediate dissolution. Read that,' said Lake, tossing Gybes' note to him.

'Ho, then, we'll have the writs down hot and heavy. We must be sharp. The sheriff's all right; that's a point. You must not lose an hour in getting your committee together, and printing your address.'

'Who's on the other side?'

'You'll have Jennings, of course; but they are talking of four different men, already, to take Sir Harry Twisden's place. *He'll* resign; that's past a doubt now. He has his retiring address written; Lord Edward Mordun read it; and he told FitzStephen on Sunday, after church, that he'd never sit again.'

'Here, by Jove, is a letter from Mowbray,' said Lake, opening
it. 'All about his brother George. Hears I'm up for the
county. Lord George ready to join and go halves. What shall
I say?'

'Could not have a better man. Tell him you desire no better,
and will bring it at once before your committee; and let him
know the moment they meet; and tell him *I* say he knows
Wealdon pretty well—he may look on it as settled. That will
be a spoke in Sir Harry's wheel.'

'Sir Harry who?' said Lake.

'Bracton. I think it's only to spoil your game, you see,' answered Wealdon.

'Abundance of malice; but I don't think he's countenanced?'

'He'll try to get the start of you; and if he does, one or
other must go to the wall; for Lord George is too strong to be
shook out. Do *you* get forward at once; that's your plan,
captain.'

Then the captain recurred to his letters, which were a larger
pack than usual this morning, chatting all the time with Wealdon
and me on the tremendous topic, and tossing aside every letter
that did not bear on the coming struggle.

'Who can this be?' said Lake, looking at the address of one
of these. 'Very like my hand,' and he examined the seal. It
was only a large wafer-stamp, so he broke it open, and drew out
a shabby, very ill-written scroll. He turned suddenly away,
talking the while, but with his eyes upon the note, and then he
folded, or rather crumpled it up, and stuffed it into his pocket,
and continued his talk; but it was now plain to me there was
something more on his mind, and he was thinking of the shabby
letter he had just received.

But, no matter; the election was the pressing topic, and Lake
was soon engaged in it again.

There was now a grand *coup* under discussion—the forestall-
ing of all the horses and vehicles along the line of railway, and
in all the principal posting establishments throughout the
county.

'They'll want to keep it open for a bid from the other side.
It is a heavy item any way; and if you want to engage them
now, you'll have to give double what they got last time.'

But Lake was not to be daunted. He wanted the seat, and
would stick at nothing to secure it; and so, Wealdon got instructions, in his own phrase, to go the whole animal.

As I could be of no possible use in local details, I left the
council of war sitting, intending a stroll in the grounds.

In the hall, I met the mistress of the house, looking very
handsome, but with a certain witch-like beauty, very pale, something a little haggard in her great, dark eyes, and a strange,
listening look. Was it watchfulness? was it suspicion? She

was dressed gravely but richly, and received me kindly—and, strange to say, with a smile that, yet, was not joyful.

'I hope she is happy. Lake is such a beast; I hope he does not bully her.'

In truth, there were in her exquisite features the traces of that mysterious misery and fear which seemed to fall wherever Stanley Lake's ill-omened confidences were given.

I walked down one of the long alleys, with tall, close hedges of beech, as impenetrable as cloister walls to sight, and watched the tench basking and flickering in the clear pond, and the dazzling swans sailing majestically along.

What a strange passion is ambition, I thought. Is it really the passion of great minds, or of little. Here is Lake, with a noble old place, inexhaustible in variety; with a beautiful, and I was by this time satisfied, a very singular and interesting woman for his wife, who must have married him for love, pure and simple; a handsome fortune; the power to bring his friends —those whom he liked, or who amused him—about him, and to indulge luxuriously every reasonable fancy, willing to forsake all, and follow the beck of that phantom. Had he knowledge, public talents, training? Nothing of the sort. Had he patriotism, any one noble motive or fine instinct to prompt him to public life? The mere suggestion was a sneer. It seemed to me, simply, that Stanley Lake was a lively, amusing, and even intelligent man, without any internal resource; vacant, peevish, with an unmeaning passion for corruption and intrigue, and the sort of egotism which craves distinction. So I supposed.

Yet, with all its weakness, there was a dangerous force in the character which, on the whole, inspired an odd mixture of fear and contempt. I was bitten, however, already, by the interest of the coming contest. It is very hard to escape that subtle and intoxicating poison. I wondered what figure Stanley would make as a hustings orator, and what impression in his canvass. The latter, I was pretty confident about. Altogether, curiosity, if no deeper sentiment, was highly piqued; and I was glad I happened to drop in at the moment of action, and wished to see the play out.

At the door of her boudoir, Rachel Lake met Dorcas.

'I am so glad, Radie, dear, you are come. You must take off your things, and stay. You must not leave me to-night. We'll send home for whatever you want; and you won't leave me, Radie, I'm certain.'

'I'll stay, dear, as you wish it,' said Rachel, kissing her.

'Did you see Stanley? I have not seen him to-day,' said Dorcas.

'No, dear; I peeped into the library, but he was not there; and there are two men writing in the Dutch room, very busily,'

'It must be about the election,'

'What election, dear?' asked Rachel.

'There is going to be an election for the county, and—only think—he intends coming forward. I sometimes think he is mad, Radie.'

'I could not have supposed such a thing. If I were he, I think I should fly to the antipodes. I should change my name, sear my features with vitriol, and learn another language. I should obliterate my past self altogether; but men are so different, so audacious—some men, at least—and Stanley, ever since his ill-omened arrival at Redman's Farm, last autumn, has amazed and terrified me.'

'I think, Radie, we have both courage—*you* have certainly; you have shown it, darling, and you must cease to blame yourself; I think you a *heroine*, Radie; but you know *I* see with the wild eyes of the Brandons.'

'I am grateful, Dorcas, that you don't hate me. Most women I am sure would abhor me—yes, Dorcas—*abhor* me.'

'You and I against the world, Radie!' said Dorcas, with a wild smile and a dark admiration in her look, and kissing Rachel again. 'I used to think myself brave; it belongs to women of our blood; but this is no common strain upon courage, Radie. I've grown to fear Stanley somehow like a ghost; I fear it is even worse than he says,' and she looked with a horrible enquiry into Rachel's eyes.

'So do *I*, Dorcas,' said Rachel, in a firm low whisper, returning her look as darkly.

'What's done cannot be undone,' said Rachel, sadly, after a little pause, unconsciously quoting from a terrible soliloquy of Shakespeare. 'I know what you mean, Radie; and you warned me, with a strange second-sight, before the evil was known to either of us. It was an irrevocable step, and I took it, not seeing all that has happened, it is true; but forewarned. And this I will say, Radie, if I *had* known the worst, I think even that would not have deterred me. It was madness—it *is* madness, for I love him still. Rachel, though I know him and his wickedness, and am filled with horror—I love him desperately.'

'I am very glad,' said Rachel, 'that you do know everything. It is so great a relief to have companionship. I often thought I must go mad in my solitude.'

'Poor Rachel! I think you wonderful—I think you a heroine—I do, Radie; you and I are made for one another—the same blood—something of the same wild nature; I can admire you, and understand you, and will always love you.'

'I've been with William Wylder and Dolly. That wicked attorney, Mr. Larkin, is resolved on robbing them. I wish they had anyone able to advise them. Stanley I am sure could save them; but he does not choose to do it. He was always so angry when I urged him to help them, that I knew it would be useless asking him ; I don't think he knows what **Mr. Larkin** has been doing ; but, Dorcas, I am afraid the very same thought has been in his mind.'

' I hope not, Radie,' and Dorcas sighed deeply.   ' Everything is so wonderful and awful in the light that has come.'

That morning, poor William Wylder had received a letter from Jos. Larkin, Esq., mentioning that he had found Messrs. Burlington and Smith anything but satisfied with him — the vicar.   What exactly he had done to disoblige them he could not bring to mind.   But Jos. Larkin told him that he had done all in his power ' to satisfy them of the *bonâ fide* character' of his reverend client's dealings from the first.   But ' they still express themselves dissatisfied upon the point, and appear to suspect a disposition to shilly-shally.'   I have said ' all I could to disabuse them of the unpleasant prejudice ; but I think I should hardly be doing my duty if I were not to warn you that you will do wisely to exhibit no hesitation in the arrangements by which your agreement is to be carried out, and that in the event of your showing the slightest disposition to qualify the spirit of your strong note to them, or in anywise disappointing their client, you must be prepared, from what I know of the firm, for very sharp practice indeed.'

What could they do to him, or why should they hurt him, or what had he done to excite either the suspicion or the temper of the firm ?   They expected their client, the purchaser, in a day or two.   He was already grumbling at the price, and certainly would stand no trifling.   Neither would Messrs. Burlington and Smith, who, he must admit, had gone to very great expense in investigating title, preparing deeds, &c., and who were noted as a very expensive house.   He was aware that they were in a position to issue an execution on the guarantee for the entire amount of their costs ; but he thought so extreme a measure would hardly be contemplated, notwithstanding their threats, unless the purchaser were to withdraw or the vendor to exhibit symptoms of—he would not repeat their phrase—irresolution in his dealing.   He had, however, placed the vicar's letter in their hands, and had accompanied it with his own testimony to the honour and character of the Rev. William Wylder, which he was happy to say seemed to have considerable weight with Messrs. Burlington and Smith.   There was also this passage . ' Feeling acutely the anxiety into which the withdrawal of the purchaser must throw you—though I trust nothing of that sort may occur—I told them that rather than have you thrown upon your beam-ends by such an occurrence, I would myself step in and purchase on the terms agreed on.   This will, I trust, quiet them on the subject of their costs, and also prevent any low *dodging* on the part of the purchaser.'

This letter would almost seem to have been written with a

supernatural knowledge of what was passing in Gylingden, and was certainly well contrived to prevent the vicar from wavering.

But all this time the ladies are conversing in Dorcas's boudoir.

'This election frightens me, Radie—everything frightens me now—but this is *so* audacious. If there be powers either in heaven or hell, it seems like a defiance and an invocation. I am glad you are here, Radie—I have grown so nervous—so superstitious, I believe ; watching always for signs and omens. Oh, darling, the world's ghastly for me now.'

'I wish, Dorcas, we were away—as you used to say—in some wild and solitary retreat, living together—two recluses—but all that is visionary—quite visionary now.'

Dorcas sighed.

'You know, Rachel, the world must not see this—we will carry our heads high. Wicked men, and brave and suffering women—that is the history of our family—and men and women always quite unlike the rest of the world—unlike the human race ; and somehow they interest me unspeakably. I wish I knew more about those proud, forlorn beauties, whose portraits are fading on the walls. Their spirit, I am sure, is in us, Rachel ; and their pictures and traditions have always supported me. When I was a little thing, I used to look at them with a feeling of melancholy and mystery. They were in my eyes, reserved prophetesses, who could speak, if they would, of my own future.'

'A poor support, Dorcas—a broken reed. I wish we could find another—the true one, in the present, and in the coming time.'

·Dorcas smiled faintly, and I think there was a little gleam of a ghastly satire in it. I am afraid that part of her education which deals with futurity had been neglected.

'I am more likely to turn into a Lady Macbeth than a *dévote,*' said she, coldly, with the same painful smile. 'I found myself last night sitting up in my bed, talking in the dark about it.'

There was a silence for a time, and Rachel said,—

'It is growing late, Dorcas.'

'But you must not go, Rachel—you *must* stay and keep me company—you must, *indeed,* Radie,' said Dorcas.

'So I will,' she answered ; 'but I must send a line to old Tamar ; and I promised Dolly to go down to her to-night, if that darling little boy should be worse—I am very unhappy about him.'

'And is he in danger, the handsome little fellow ?' said Dorcas.

'Very great danger, I fear,' said Rachel. 'Doctor Buddle has been very kind—but he is, I am afraid, more desponding than poor William or Dolly imagines—Heaven help them !'

'But children recover wonderfully. What is his ailment ?'

'Gastric fever, the doctor says. I had a foreboding of evil the moment I saw him—before the poor little man was put to his bed.'

Dorcas rang the bell.

'Now, Radie, if you wish to write, sit down here—or if you prefer a message, Thomas can take one very accurately ; and he shall call at the vicar's, and see Dolly, and bring us word how the dear little boy is. And don't fancy, darling, I have forgotten what you said to me about duty—though I would call it differently—only I feel so wild, I can think of nothing clearly yet. But I am making up my mind to a great and bold step, and when I am better able, I will talk it over with you—my only friend, Rachel.'

And she kissed her.

CHAPTER LXVII.

MR. LARKIN IS VIS-A-VIS WITH A CONCEALED COMPANION.

THE time had now arrived when our friend Jos. Larkin was to refresh the village of Gylingden with his presence. He had pushed matters forward with wonderful despatch. The deeds, with their blue and silver stamps, were handsomely engrossed—having been approved in draft by Crompton S. Kewes, the eminent Queen's Counsel, on a case furnished by Jos. Larkin, Esq., The Lodge, Brandon Manor, Gylingden, on behalf of his client, the Reverend William Wylder ; and in like manner on behalf of Stanley Williams Brandon Lake, of Brandon Hall, in the county of ——, Esq.

In neither draft did Jos. Larkin figure as the purchaser by name. He did not care for advice on any difficulty depending on his special relations to the vendors in both these cases. He wished, as was his custom, everything above-board, and such 'an opinion' as might be published by either client in the 'Times' next day if he pleased it. Besides these matters of Wylder and of Lake, he had also a clause to insert in a private Act, on behalf of the trustees of the Baptist Chapel, at Naunton Friars ; a short deed to be consulted upon on behalf of his client, Pudder Swynfen, Esq., of Swynfen Grange, in the same county ; and a deed to be executed at Shillingsworth, which he would take *en route* for Gylingden, stopping there for that night, and going on by next morning's train.

Those little trips to town paid very fairly.

In this particular case his entire expenses reached exactly £5 3s., and what do you suppose was the good man's profit upon that small item ? Precisely £62 7s. ! The process is simple.

Jos. Larkin made his own handsome estimate of his expenses, and the value of his time to and from London, and then he charged this in its entirety—shall we say integrity—to each client separately. In this little excursion he was concerned for no less than *five.*

His expenses, I say, reached exactly £5 3*s.* But he had a right to go to Dondale's if he pleased, instead of that cheap hostelery near Covent Garden. He had a right to a handsome lunch and a handsome dinner, instead of that economical fusion of both meals into one, at a cheap eating-house, in an out-of-the-way quarter. He had a right to his pint of high-priced wine, and to accomplish his wanderings in a cab, instead of, as the Italians say, 'partly on foot, and partly walking.' Therefore, and on this principle, Mr. Jos. Larkin had 'no difficulty' in acting. His savings, if the good man chose to practise self-denial, were his own—and it was a sort of problem while he stayed, and interested him curiously—keeping down his bill in matters which he would not have dreamed of denying himself at home.

The only client among his wealthy supporters, who ever went in a grudging spirit into one of these little bills of Jos. Larkin's, was old Sir Mulgrave Bracton—the defunct parent of the Sir Harry, with whom we are acquainted.

'Don't you think, Mr. Larkin, you could perhaps reduce *this,* just a little?'

'Ah, the expenses?'

'Well, yes.'

Mr. Jos. Larkin smiled—the smile said plainly, 'what would he have me live upon, and where?' We do meet persons of this sort, who would fain 'fill our bellies with the husks' that swine digest; what of that—we must remember who we are—*gentlemen* —and answer this sort of shabbiness, and every other endurable annoyance, as Lord Chesterfield did—with a bow and a smile.

'I think so,' said the baronet, in a bluff, firm way.

'Well, the fact is, when I represent a client, Sir Mulgrave Bracton, of a certain rank and position, I make it a principle— and, as a man of business, I find it tells—to present myself in a style that is suitably handsome.'

'Oh! an expensive house—*where* was this, now?'

'Oh, Sir Mulgrave, pray don't think of it—I'm only too happy —pray, draw your pen across the entire thing.'

'I think so,' said the baronet unexpectedly. 'Don't you think if we said a pound a-day, and your travelling expenses?'

'Certainly—*any*thing—what*ever* you please, Sir.'

And the attorney waved his long hand a little, and smiled almost compassionately; and the little alteration was made, and henceforward he spoke of Sir Mulgrave as not quite a pleasant man to deal with in money matters; and his confidential friends knew that in a transaction in which he had paid money out of his own pocket for Sir Mulgrave he had never got back more than seven and sixpence in the pound ; and, what made it worse, it was a matter connected with the death of poor Lady Bracton ! And he never lost an opportunity of conveying his opinion of Sir Mulgrave, sometimes in distinct and confidential sentences, and sometimes only by a sad shake of his head, or by awfully declining to speak upon the subject.

In the present instance Jos. Larkin was returning in a heavenly frame of mind to the Lodge, Brandon Manor, Gylingden. Whenever he was away he interpolated ' Brandon Manor,' and stuck it on his valise and hat-case ; and liked to call aloud to the porters tumbling among the luggage—' Jos. Larkin, Esquire, *Brandon Manor, if* you please ;' and to see the people read the inscription in the hall of his dingy hostelry. Well might the good man glow with a happy consciousness of a blessing. In small things as in great he was prosperous.

This little excursion to London would cost him, as I said, exactly £5 3s. It might have cost him £13 10s. and at that sum his expenses figured in his ledger ; and as he had five clients on this occasion, the total reached £67 10s., leaving a clear profit, as I have mentioned, of £62 7s. on this item.

But what was this little tip from fortune, compared with the splendid pieces of scrivenery in his despatch box. The white parchment—the blue and silver stamps in the corner—the German text and flourishes at the top, and those broad, horizontal lines of recital, ' habendum,' and so forth—marshalled like an army in procession behind his march of triumph into Five Oaks, to take the place of its deposed prince ? From the captain's deed to the vicar's his mind glanced fondly.

He would yet stand the highest man in his county. He had found time for a visit to the King-at-Arms and the Heralds' Office. He would have his pictures and his pedigree. His grandmother had been a Howard. Her branch, indeed, was a little under a cloud, keeping a small provision-shop in the town of Dwiddleston. But this circumstance need not be in prominence. She was a Howard—*that* was the fact he relied on—no mortal could gainsay it ; and he would be, first, J. Howard Larkin, then Howard Larkin, simply ; then Howard Larkin Howard, and the Five Gaks' Howards would come to be very great people indeed. And the Brandons had intermarried with other Howards, and Five Oaks would naturally, therefore, go to Howards ; and so he and his, with clever management, would be anything but *novi homtnes* in the county.

' He shall be like a tree planted by the water-side, that will bring forth his fruit in due season. His leaf also shall not wither. So thought this good man complacently. He liked these fine consolations of the Jewish dispensation—actual milk and honey, and a land of promise on which he could set his foot. Jos. Larkin, Esq., was as punctual as the clock at the terminus. He did not come a minute too soon or too late, but precisely at the moment which enabled him, without fuss, and without a tiresome wait, to proceed to the details of ticket, luggage, selection of place, and ultimate ascension thereto.

So now having taken all measures, gliding among the portmanteaus, hand-barrows, and porters, and the clangorous bell ringing, he mounted, lithe and lank, into his place.

There was a pleasant evening light still, and the gas-lamps made a purplish glow against it. The little butter-cooler of a glass lamp glimmered from the roof. Mr. Larkin established himself, and adjusted his rug and mufflers about him, for, not withstanding the season, there had been some cold, rainy weather, and the evening was sharp ; and he set his two newspapers, his shilling book, and other triumphs of cheap literature in sundry shapes, in the vacant seat at his left hand, and made everything handsome about him. He glanced to the other end of the carriage, where sat his solitary fellow-passenger. This gentleman was simply a mass of cloaks and capes, culminating in a queer battered felt hat ; his shoulders were nestled into the corner, and his face buried among his loose mufflers. They sat at corners diagonally opposed, and were, therefore, as far apart as was practicable—an arrangement, not sociable, to be sure, but on the whole, very comfortable, and which neither seemed disposed to disturb.

Mr. Larkin had a word to say to the porter from the window, and bought one more newspaper ; and then looked out on the lamplit platform, and saw the officials loitering off to the clang of the carriage doors ; then came the whistle, and then the clank and jerk of the start. And so the brick walls and lamps began to glide backward, and the train was off.

Jos. Larkin tried his newspaper, and read for ten minutes, or so, pretty diligently ; and then looked for a while from the window, upon receding hedgerows and farmsteads, and the level and spacious landscape ; and then he leaned back luxuriously, his newspaper listlessly on his knees, and began to read, instead, at his ease, the shapeless, wrapt-up figure diagonally opposite.

The quietude of the gentleman in the far corner was quite singular. He produced neither tract, nor newspaper, nor volume— not even a pocket-book or a letter. He brought forth no cigarcase, with the stereotyped, 'Have you any objection to my smoking a cigar?' He did not even change his attitude ever so little. A burly roll of cloaks, rugs, capes, and loose wrappers, placed in the corner, and *tanquam cadaver*, passive and motionless.

I have sometimes in my travels lighted on a strangely shaped mountain, whose huge curves, and sombre colouring have interested me indefinably. In the rude mass at the far angle, Mr. Jos. Larkin, I fancy, found some such subject of contemplation. And the more he looked, the more he felt disposed to look.

As they got on there was more night fog, and the little lamp at top shone through a halo. The fellow-passenger at the opposite angle lay back, all cloaks and mufflers, with nothing distinct emerging but the felt hat at top, and the tip—it was only the tip now—of the shining shoe on the floor.

The gentleman was absolutely motionless and silent. And Mr. Larkin, though his mind was pretty universally of the inquisitive order, began in this particular case to feel a special curiosity. It was partly the monotony and their occupying the carriage all to themselves—as the two uncommunicative seamen did the Eddystone Lighthouse—but there was, beside, an indistinct feeling, that, in spite of all these wrappers and swathings, he knew the outlines of that figure ; and yet the likeness must have been of the rudest possible sort.

He could not say that he recognised anything distinctly—only he fancied that some one he knew was sitting there, unrevealed, inside that mass of clothing. And he felt, moreover, as if he ought to be able to guess who he was.

CHAPTER LXVIII.

THE COMPANION DISCLOSES HIMSELF.

BUT this sort of musing and wonderment leads to nothing ; and Mr. Jos. Larkin being an active-minded man, and practical withal, in a little while shook it off, and from his breast-pocket took a tiny treasure of a pocket-book, in which were some bank-notes, precious memoranda in pencil, and half-a-dozen notes and letters, bearing upon cases and negotiations on which, at this juncture, he was working.

Into these he got, and now and then brought out a letter bearing on some point of speculation, and read it through, and then closed his eyes for three minutes at a time, and thought. But he had not his tin boxes there ; and, with a man of his stamp, speculation, which goes upon guess as to dates and quantities, which are all ascertainable by reference to black and white, soon loses its interest. And the evidence in his pocket being pretty soon exhausted, he glanced again at his companion over the way.

He had not moved all this while. He had a high stand-up collar to the cape he wore, which covered his cheeks and nose and outside was loosely swathed a large, cream-coloured, cash-mere handkerchief. The battered felt hat covered his forehead and eyebrows, and left, in fact, but a narrow streak of separation between.

Through this, however, for the first time, Jos. Larkin now saw the glitter of a pair of eyes gazing at him, he fancied. At all events there was the glitter, and the gentleman was awake.

Jos. returned the gentleman's gaze. It was his lofty aristocratic stare; and he expected to see the glittering lights that peeped through the dark chink between brim and collar shut up under its rebuke. But nothing of the kind took place, and the ocular exercises of the attorney were totally ineffectual.

If the fellow knew that his fixed stare was observed through his narrow embrasure—and Larkin thought he could hardly be insensible to the reproof of his return fire—he must be a par-ticularly impertinent person. It would be ridiculous, however, to continue a contest of this kind; so the attorney lowered the window and looked out. Then he pulled it up, and took to his newspaper again, and read the police cases, and a very curious letter from a poor-house doctor, describing a boy who was quite blind in daylight, but could see very fairly by gas or candle light, and then he lighted upon a very odd story, and said to be under-going special sifting at the hands of Sir Samuel Squailes, of a policeman on a certain beat, in Fleet Street, not far from Temple Bar, who every night saw, at or about the same hour, a certain suspicious-looking figure walk along the flag-way and enter a passage. Night after night he pursued this figure, but always lost it in the same passage. On the last occasion, however, he succeeded in keeping him in view, and came up with him in a court, when he was rewarded with a sight of such a face as caused him to fall to the ground in a fit. This was the Clamp-court ghost, and I believe he was left in that debatable state, and never after either exploded or confirmed.

So having ended all these studies, the attorney lifted up his eyes again, as he lowered his newspaper, and beheld the same glittering gaze fixed upon him through the same horizontal cranny.

He fancied the eyes were laughing. He could not be sure, of course, but at all events the persistent stare was extremely, and perhaps determinedly, impertinent. Forgetting the constitutional canon through which breathes the genuine spirit of British liberty, he felt for a moment that he was such a king as that cat had no business to look at; and he might, perhaps, have politely intimated something of the kind, had not the enveloped offender made a slight and lazy turn which, burying his chin still deeper in his breast, altogether concealed his eyes, and so closed the offensive scrutiny.

In making this change in his position, slight as it was, the gentleman in the superfluous clothing reminded Mr. Jos. Larkin very sharply for an instant of—*some*body. There was the rub ; who could it be ?

The figure was once more a mere mountain of rug. What was the peculiarity in that slight movement—something in the knee ? something in the elbow ? something in the general character ?

Why had he not spoken to him ? The opportunity, for the present, was past. But he was now sure that his fellow-traveller was an acquaintance, who had probably recognised him. Larkin —except when making a mysterious trip at election times, or in an emergency, in a critical case—was a frank, and as he believed could be a fascinating *compagnon de voyage,* such and so great was his urbanity on a journey. He rather liked talking with people ; he sometimes heard things not wholly valueless, and once or twice had gathered hints in this way, which saved him trouble, or money, which is much the same thing. Therefore upon principle he was not averse from that direst of bores, railway conversation.

And now they slackened speed, with a long, piercing whistle, and came to a standstill at ' East Had*don*' (with a jerk upon the last syllable), ' East Had*don,* East Had*don,*' as the herald of the station declared, and Lawyer Larkin sat straight up, very alert, with a budding smile, ready to blow out into a charming radiance the moment his fellow-traveller rose perpendicular, as was to be expected, and peeped from his window.

But he seemed to know intuitively that Larkin intended telling him, *apropos* of the station, that story of the Haddon property, and Sir James Wotton's will, which as told by the good attorney and jumbled by the clatter, was perhaps a little dreary. At all events he did not stir, and carefully abstained from wakening, and in a few seconds more they were again in motion.

They were now approaching Shillingsworth, where the attorney was to get out, and put up for the night, having a deed with him to be executed in that town, and so sweetening his journey with this small incident of profit.

Now, therefore, looking at his watch, and consulting his time table, he got his slim valise from under on top of the seat before him, together with his hat-case, despatch-box, stick, and umbrella, and brushed off with his handkerchief some of the gritty railway dust that lay drifted in exterior folds and hollows of his coat, rebuttoned that garment with precision, arranged his shirt-collar, stuffed his muffler into his coat-pocket, and made generally that rude sacrifice to the graces with which natty men precede their exit from the dust and ashes of this sort of sepulture.

At this moment he had just eight minutes more to go, and the glitter of the pair of eyes, staring between the muffler and the rim of the hat, met his view once more.

Mr. Larkin's cigar-case was open in his hand in a moment, and with such a smile as a genteel perfumer offers his wares with, he presented it toward the gentleman who was built up in the stack of garments.

He merely shook his head with the slightest imaginable nod and a wave of a pudgy hand in a soiled dog-skin glove, which emerged for a second from under a cape, in token that he gratefully declined the favour.

Mr. Larkin smiled and shrugged regretfully, and replaced the case in his coat pocket. Hardly five minutes remained now. Larkin glanced round for a topic.

'My journey is over for the present, Sir, and perhaps you would find these little things entertaining.'

And he tendered with the same smile 'Punch,' the 'Penny Gleaner,' and 'Gray's Magazine,' a religious serial. They were, however, similarly declined in pantomime.

'He's not particularly polite, whoever he is,' thought Mr. Larkin, with a sniff. However, he tried the effect of a direct observation. So getting one seat nearer, he said :—

'Wonderful place Shillingsworth, Sir ; one does not really, until one has visited it two or three times over, at all comprehend its wealth and importance ; and how justly high it deserves to hold its head amongst the provincial emporia of our productive industry.'

The shapeless traveller in the corner touched his ear with his pudgy dogskin fingers, and shook his hand and head a little, in token either that he was deaf, or the noise such as to prevent his hearing, and in the next moment the glittering eyes closed, and the pantomimist appeared to be asleep.

And now, again, the train subsided to a stand-still, and Shillingsworth resounded through the night air, and Larkin scrambled forward to the window, by which sat the enveloped gentleman, and called the porter, and, with many unheeded apologies, pulled out his various properties, close by the knees of the tranquil traveller. So, Mr. Larkin was on the platform, and his belongings stowed away against the wall of the station-house.

He made an enquiry of the guard, with whom he was acquainted, about his companion ; but the guard knew nothing of the 'party,' neither did the porter, to whom the guard put a similar question.

So, as Larkin walked down the platform, the whistle sounded and the train glided forward, and as it passed him, the gentleman in the cloak and queer hat was looking out. A lamp shone full on him. Mr. Larkin's heart stood still for a moment, and then bounded up as if it would choke him.

'It's him, by — !' and Mr. Larkin, forgetting syntax, and propriety, and religion, all together, and making a frantic race to keep up with the train, shouted—

'Stop it, stop it—hollo !—stop—stop—ho, stop !'

But he pleaded with the winds ; and before he had reached the end of the platform, the carriage windows were flying by him with the speed of wheel-spokes, and the end of the coupé, with its red lantern, sailed away through the cutting.

'Forgot summat, Sir,' said the porter, touching his hat.

'Yes—signal—stop him, can you?'

The porter only scratched his head, under his cap, and smiled sheepishly after the train. Jos. Larkin knew, the next moment, he had talked nonsense.

'I—I—yes—I have—have you an engine here :—express—I'll pay anything.'

But, no, there was 'no engine—not nearer than the junction, and she might not be spared.'

'How far is the junction?'

'Nineteen and a-half.'

'Nineteen miles ! They'll never bring me there, by horse, under two hours, they are so cursed tedious. Why have not you a spare engine at a place like this ? Shillingsworth ! Nice management ! Are you certain ? Where's the station-master?'

All this time he kept staring after the faint pulsations on the air that indicated the flight of the engine.

But it would not do. The train—the image upon earth of the irrevocable, the irretrievable—was gone, neither to be overtaken nor recalled. The telegraph was not then, as now, whispering secrets all over England, at the rate of two hundred miles a second, and five shillings per twenty words. Larkin would have given large money for an engine, to get up with the train that was now some five miles on its route, at treble, quadruple, the common cost of such a magical appliance ; but all was vain. He could only look and mutter after it wildly. Vain to conjecture for what station that traveller in the battered hat was bound ! Idle speculation ! Mere distraction !

Only that Mr. Larkin was altogether the man he was, I think he would have cursed freely.

CHAPTER LXIX.

OF A SPECTRE WHOM OLD TAMAR SAW.

LITTLE FAIRY, all this while, continued, in our Church language, 'sick and weak.' The vicar was very sorry, but not afraid. His little man was so bright and merry, that he seemed to him the very spirit of life. He could not dream of his dying. It was sad, to be sure, the little man so many days in his bed, too languid to care for toy or story, quite silent, except when, in the night time, those weird monologues began which showed that the fever had reached his brain. The tones of his pleasant little voice, in those sad flights of memory and fancy, busy with familiar scenes and occupations, sounded wild and plaintive in his ear. And when 'Wapsie' was mentioned, sometimes the vicar's eyes filled, but he smiled through this with a kind of gladness at the child's affection. ' It will soon be over, my darling ! You will be walking with Wapsie in a week again.' The sun could. as soon cease from shining as little Fairy from living. The thought he would not allow near him.

Doctor Buddle had been six miles away that evening with a patient, and looked in at the vicar's long after the candles were lighted.

He was not satisfied with little Fairy—not at all satisfied. He put his hand under the clothes and felt his thin, slender limbs—thinner than ever now. Dry and very hot they were—and little man babbling his nonsense about little boys, and his ' Wapsie,' and toys, and birds, and the mill-stream, and the church-yard—of which, with so strange a fatality, children, not in romance only, but reality, so often prattle in their feverish wanderings.

He felt his pulse. He questioned his mamma, and cross-examined the nurse, and looked grave and very much annoyed ; and then bethought him of something to be tried ; and having given his directions to the maid, he went home in haste, and returned in half an hour with the something in a phial—a few drops in water, and little man sat up, leaning on his Wapsie's arm, and 'took it very good,' his nurse said, approvingly ; and he looked at them all wonderingly, for two or three moments, and so tired ; and they laid him down again, and then his spoken dreams began once more.

Doctor Buddle was dark and short in his answers to voluble little Mrs. Wylder—though, of course, quite respectful—and the vicar saw him down the narrow stairs, and they turned into the study for a moment, and, said Buddle, in an under tone—

He s very ill—I can say nothing else.'

And there was a pause.

The little colour he had receded from the vicar's face, for the looks and tones of good-natured Buddle were not to be mistaken. He was reading little Fairy's death warrant.

'I see, doctor—I see; you think he'll die,' said the vicar, staring at him. 'Oh doctor, my little Fairy!'

The doctor knew something of the poor vicar's troubles—of course in a village most things of the kind *are* known—and often, in his brisk, rough way, he thought as, with a nod and a word, he passed the lank cleric, under the trees or across the common, with his bright, prattling, sunny-haired little boy by the hand—or encountered them telling stories on the stile, near the castle meadow—what a gleam of sunshine was always dancing about his path, in that smiling, wayward, loving little fellow—and now a long Icelandic winter was coming, and his path was to know that light no more.

'With children, you know, I—I always say there's a chance—but you are right to look the thing in the face—and I'll be here the first call in the morning; and you know where to find me, in the meantime;' and the doctor shook hands very hard with the vicar at the hall-door, and made his way homeward—the vicar's eyes following him till he was out of sight.

Then William Wylder shut the hall-door, and turned about.

Little Fairy's drum was hanging from a peg on the hat-stand —the drum that was to sound no more in the garden, or up and down the hall, with the bright-haired little drummer's song. There would be no more interruption now—the vicar would write his sermons undisturbed; no more consolations claimed—no more broken toys to be mended—some of the innocent little rubbish lay in the study. It should never move from that—nor his drum—nor that little hat and cape, hanging on their peg, with the tiny boots underneath.

No more prattling at unseasonable times—no more crying—no more singing—no more laughing; all these interruptions were quiet now, and altogether gone—'Little man! little Fairy! Oh, was it possible!' But memory would call up the vicar from his half-written sermon. He would miss his troublesome little man, when the sun shone out that he used to welcome—when the birds hopped on the window-stone, to find the crumbs that little man used to strew there; and when his own little canary—'Birdie' he used to call him—would sing and twitter in his cage —and the time came to walk out on his lonely visits.

He must walk alone by the shop-doors—where the little man was so admired—and up the mill-road, and in the castle meadow and over the stile where they used to sit.

Poor Dolly! Her Willie would not tell her yet. He kneeled down in the study—'Little man's' top, and some cut paper nondescripts, were lying where he had left them, at his elbow—and he tried to pray, and then he remembered that his darling ought to know that he was going into the presence of his Maker.

Yes, he would tell poor Dolly first, and then his little man. He would repeat his hymn with him, and pray—and so he went up the nursery stairs.

Poor Dolly, very tired, had gone to lie down for a little. He would not disturb her—no, let her enjoy for an hour more her happy illusion.

When he went into the nursery little Fairy was sitting up, taking his medicine ; the nurse's arm round his thin shoulders. He sat down beside him, weeping gently, his thin face turned a little away, and his hand on the coverlet.

Little man looked wonderingly from his tired eyes on Wapsie, and his thin fingers crept on his hand, and Wapsie turned about, drying his eyes, and said—

'Little man ! my darling !'

'He's like himself, Sir, while he's sitting up—his little head quite right again.'

'My head's quite right, Wapsie,' the little man whispered, sadly.

'Thank God, my darling !' said the vicar. The tears were running down his cheeks while he parted little Fairy's golden hair with his fingers.

'When I am quite well again,' whispered the little man, 'won't you bring me to the castle meadow, where the wee river is, and we'll float races with daisies and buttercups—the way you did on my birthday.'

'They say that little mannikin——' suddenly the vicar stopped. 'They say that little mannikin won't get well.'

'And am I always to be sick, here in my little bed, Wapsie?' whispered little Fairy, in his dreamy, earnest way, that was new to him.

'No, darling ; not always sick : you'll be happier than ever—but not here ; little man will be taken by his Saviour, that loves him best of all—and he'll be in heaven—and only have a short time to wait, and maybe his poor Wapsie will come to him, please God, and his darling mamma—and we'll all be happy together, for ever, and never be sick or sorry any more, my treasure—my little Fairy—my darling.'

And little man looked on him with his tired eyes, not quite understanding what it meant, nor why Wapsie was crying ; and the nurse said—

'He'd like to be dozin', Sir, he's so tired, please.' So down the poor little fellow lay, his 'Wapsie' praying by his bedside.

When, in a little time, poor Dolly returned, her Willie took her round the waist, as on the day when she accepted him, and led her tenderly into the other room, and told her all, and they hugged and wept together.

'Oh, Dolly, Dolly!'

'Oh, Willie, darling! Oh, Willie, our precious treasure—our only one.'

And so they walked up and down that room, his arm round her waist, and in that sorrowful embrace, murmuring amid their sobs to one another, their thoughts and remembrances of 'little man.' How soon the treasure grows a retrospect!

Then Dolly bethought her of her promise to Rachel.

She made me promise to send for her if he was worse—she loved him so—everyone loved him—they could not help—oh, Willie! our bright darling.'

'I think, Dolly, we could not live here. I'd like to go on some mission, and maybe come back in a great many years—maybe, Dolly, when we are old. I'd like to see the place again—and—and the walks—but not, I think, for a long time. He was such a darling.'

Perhaps the vicar was thinking of the church-yard, and how he would like, when his time came, to lie beside the golden-haired little comrade of his walks. So Dolly despatched the messenger with a lantern, and thus it was there came a knocking at the door of Redman's Farm at that unseasonable hour. For some time old Tamar heard the clatter in her sleep, disturbing and mingling with her dreams. But in a while she wakened quite, and heard the double knocks one after another in quick succession; and huddling on her clothes, and muttering to herself all the way, she got into the hall, and standing a couple of yards away from the door, answered in shrill and querulous tones, and questioning the messenger in the same breath.

How could she tell what it might or might not portend? Her alarms quickly subsided, however, for she knew the voice well.

So the story was soon told. Poor little Fairy; it was doubtful if he was to see another morning; and the maid being wanted at home, old Tamar undertook the message to Brandon Hall, where her young mistress was, and sallied forth in her cloak and bonnet, under the haunted trees of Redman's Dell.

Tamar had passed the age of ghostly terrors. There are a certain sober literality and materialism in old age which abate the illusions of the supernatural as effectually as those of love; and Tamar, though not without awe, for darkness and solitude, even were there no associations of a fearful kind in the locality, are suggestive and dismal to the last.

Her route lay, as by this time my reader is well aware, by that narrow defile reached from Redman's Farm by a pathway which scales a flight of rude steps, the same which Stanley Lake and his sister had mounted on the night of Mark Wylder's disappearance.

Tamar knew the path very well. It was on the uppei level of it that she had held that conference with Stanley Lake, which obviously referred to that young gentleman's treatment of the vanished Mark. As she came to this platform, round which the trees receded a little so as to admit the moonlight, the old woman was tired.

She would have gladly chosen another spot to rest in, but fatigue was imperious ; and she sat down under the gray stone which stood perpendicularly there, on what had once been the step of a stile, leaning against the rude column behind her.

As she sat here she heard the clank of a step approaching measuredly from the Brandon side. It was twelve o'clock now ; the chimes from the Gylingden church-tower had proclaimed that in the distance some minutes before. The honest Gylingden folk seldom heard the tower chimes tell eleven, and gentle and simple had, of course, been long in their beds.

The old woman had a secret hatred of this place, and the un-expected sounds made her hold her breath. She peeped round the stone, in whose shadow she was sitting. The steps were not those of a man walking briskly with a purpose : they were the desultory strides of a stroller lounging out an hour's watch. The steps approached. The figure was visible—that of a short broadish man, with a mass of cloaks, rugs, and mufflers across his arm.

Carrying them with a sort of swagger, he came slowly up to the part of the pathway opposite to the pillar, where he dropped those draperies in a heap upon the grass ; and availing himself of the clear moonlight, he stopped nearly confronting her.

It was the face of Mark Wylder—she knew it well—but grown fat and broader, and there was—but this she could not see dis-tinctly—a purplish scar across his eyebrow and cheek. She quivered with terror lest he should have seen her, and might be meditating some mischief. But she was seated close to the ground, several yards away, and in the sharp shadow of the old block of stone.

He consulted his watch, and she sat fixed and powerless as a portion of the block on which she leaned, staring up at this, to her, terrific apparition. Mark Wylder's return boded, she be-lieved, something tremendous.

She saw the glimmer of the gold watch, and, distinctly, the great black whiskers, and the face pallid in the moonlight. She was afraid for a minute, during which he loitered there, that he was going to seat himself upon the cloaks which he had just thrown upon the ground, and felt that she could not possibly escape detection for many seconds more. But she was relieved ; for, after a short pause, leaving these still upon the ground, he turned, and walked slowly, like a policeman on his beat, toward Brandon.

With a gasp she began to recover herself; but she felt too faint and ill to get up and commence a retreat towards Redman's Farm. Besides, she was sure he would return—she could not tell how soon—and although the clump of alders hid her from view, she could not tell but that the next moment would disclose his figure retracing his leisurely steps, and ready to pursue and overtake, if by a precipitate movement she had betrayed her presence.

In due time the same figure, passing at the same rate, did emerge again, and approached just as before, only this time he was carelessly examining some small but clumsy steel instrument which glittered occasionally in the light. From Tamar's description of it, I conclude it was a revolver.

He passed the pile of cloaks but a few steps, and again turned toward Brandon. So soon as he was once more concealed by the screen of underwood, old Tamar, now sufficiently recovered, crept hurriedly away in the opposite direction, half dead with terror, until she had descended the steps, and was buried once more in friendly darkness.

Old Tamar did not stop at Redman's Farm; she passed it and the mills, and never stopped till she reached the Vicarage. In the hall, she felt for a moment quite overpowered, and sitting in one of the old chairs that did duty there, she uttered a deep groan, and looked with such a gaze in the face of the maid who had admitted her, that she thought the old woman was dying.

Sick rooms, even when, palpably, doctors, nurses, friends, have all ceased to hope, are not to those who stand in the *very* nearest and most tender relations to the patient, altogether chambers of despair. There are those who hover about the bed and note every gleam and glow of subsiding life, and will read in sunset something of the colours of the dawn, and cling wildly to these hallucinations of love; and no one has the heart to tear them from them.

Just now, Dolly fancied that 'little man was better—the darling! the treasure! oh, precious little man! He was coming back!'

So, she ran down with this light of hope in her face, and saw old Tamar in the hall, and gave her a glass of the wine which Rachel had provided, and the old woman's spirit came again.

'She was glad—yes, very glad. She was thankful to hear the dear child was better.' But there was a weight upon her soul, and a dreadful horror on her countenance still.

'Will you please, Ma'am, write a little note—my old hand shakes so, she could hardly read my writing—to my mistress—Miss Radie, Ma'am. I see pen and ink on the table there. I was not able to go up to the Hall, Ma'am, with the message. There's something on the road I could not pass.'

'Something! What was it?' said Dolly, staring with round

eyes in the old woman's woeful face, her curiosity aroused for a moment.

'Something, Ma'am—a person—I can't exactly tell—above the steps, in the Blackberry path. It would cost my young mistress her life. For Heaven's sake, Ma'am, write, and promise, if you send for her, she shall get the note.'

So, Dolly made the promise, and bringing old Tamar with her into the study, penned these odd lines from her dictation, merely adjusting the grammar.

'MISS RADIE, DEAR,—If coming down to-night from Brandon, this is to tell you, it is as much as your life is worth to pass the Blackberry walk above the steps. My old eyes have seen him there, walking back and forward, lying at catch for some one, this night—the great enemy of man ; you can suppose in what shape.

'Your dutiful and loving servant,

'TAMAR.'

So, old Tamar, after a little, took her departure ; and it needed a great effort to enable her to take the turn up the dark and lonely mill-road, leading to Redman's Farm ; so much did she dread the possibility of again encountering the person she had just described.

CHAPTER LXX.

THE MEETING IN THE LONG POND ALLEY.

I SUPPOSE there were few waking heads at this hour in all the wide parish of Gylingden, though many a usually idle one was now busy enough about the great political struggle which was to muster its native forces, both in borough and county, and agitate these rural regions with the roar and commotion of civil strife.

But generals must sleep like other men ; and even Tom Wealdon was snoring in the fairy land of dreams.

The night was very still—a sharp night, with a thin moon, like a scimitar, hanging bright in the sky, and a myriad of intense stars blinking in the heavens, above the steep roofs and spiral chimneys of Brandon Hall, and the ancient trees that surrounded it.

It was late in the night, as we know. The family, according to their custom, had sought their slumbers early ; and the great old house was perfectly still.

One pair, at least, of eyes, however, were wide open ; one head busy ; and one person still in his daily costume. This was Mr. Larcom—the grave *major domo*, the bland and attached butler. He was not busy about his plate, nor balancing the cellar book, nor even perusing his Bible.

He was seated in that small room or closet which he had, years ago, appropriated as his private apartment. It is opposite the housekeeper's room—a sequestered, philosophic retreat. He dressed in it, read his newspaper there, and there saw his select acquaintance. His wardrobe stood there. The iron safe in which he kept his keys, filled one of its nooks. He had his two or three shelves of books in the recess ; not that he disturbed them much, but they were a grave and gentlemanlike property, and he liked them for their binding, and the impression they produced on his visitors. There was a meditative fragrance of cigars about him, and two or three Havannah stumps under the grate.

The fact is, he was engaged over a letter, the writing of which, considering how accomplished a gentleman he was, he had found rather laborious and tedious. The penmanship was, I am afraid, clumsy, and the spelling here and there, irregular. It was finished however, and he was now reading it over with care.

It was thus expressed :—

'RESPECTET SIR,—In accordens with your disier, i av took my pen to say a fue words. There has cum a leter for a sertun persen this morning, with a Lundun posmark, and i do not now hand nor sele, but bad writting, which i have not seen wot contanes, but I may, for as you told me offen, you are anceus for welfare of our famly, as i now to be no more than trewth, so I am anceus to ascest you Sir, wich my conseynce is satesfid, but leter as trubeled a sertun persen oufull, hoo i new was engry, and look oufull put about, wich do not offen apen, and you may sewer there is sumthing in wind, he is alday so oufull peefish, you will not thing worse of me speeken plane as yo disier, there beeing a deel to regret for frends of the old famly i feer in a sertun resent marrege, if I shud lern be chance contense of letter i will sewer rite you.—i Remane your humbel servant,

'JOHN LARCOM.'

Just as grave Mr. Larcom had ended the perusal of this bulletin, he heard a light step on the stair, at the end of the passage, which made his manly heart jump unpleasantly within his fat ribs. He thrust the unfolded letter roughly into the very depths of his breeches pocket, and blew out both candles ; and then listened, as still as a mouse.

What frightened him was the certainty that the step, which he well knew, was Stanley Lake's. And Stanley being a wide-awake and violent person, and his measures sharp and reckless, Mr. Larcom cherished a nervous respect for him.

He listened ; the captain's step came lightly to the foot of the stairs, and paused. Mr. Larcom prepared to be fast asleep in the chair, in the event of the captain's making a sudden advance, and entering his sanctum. But this movement was not executed.

There was a small door at the foot of the stairs. It shut with a spring lock, of which Captain Lake had a latch-key. Mr. Larcom accidentally had another—a cylindrical bit of steel, with a hinge in the end of it, and a few queer wards.

Now, of this little door he heard the two iron bolts stealthily drawn, and then the handle of the spring-lock turned, and the door cautiously opened, and as gently closed.

Mr. Larcom's fears now naturally subsided, and curiosity as naturally supervened. He drew near his window ; and it was well he had extinguished his lights, for as he did so, Captain Lake's light figure, in a gray paletot and cloth cap, glided by like a spirit in the faint moonlight.

This phenomenon excited the profoundest interest in the corresponding friend of the family, who, fumbling his letter between his finger and thumb in his breeches' pocket, standing on tip-toe, with mouth agape, and his head against the shutter, followed the receding figure with a greedy stare.

Mr. Larcom had no theory whatsoever to account for this procedure on the part of his master. It must be something very extraordinary, and well worth investigating—of course, for the benefit of the family—which could have evoked the apparition which had just crossed his window. With his eyes close to the window pane, he saw his master glide swiftly along the short terrace which covers this side of the house, and disappear down the steps, like a spectre sinking into the earth.

It is a meeting, thought Mr. Larcom, taking courage, for he already felt something of the confidence and superiority of possessing a secret ; and as quickly as might be, the trustworthy man, with his latch-key in his pocket, softly opened the portal through which the object of his anxiety had just emerged, closed the door behind him, and stood listening intently in the recess of the entrance, where he heard the now more careless step of the captain, treading, as he thought, the broad yew-walk, which turns at a right angle at the foot of the terrace step. The black yew hedge was a perfect screen.

Here was obviously presented a chance of obtaining the command of a secret of greater or less importance. It was a considerable stake to play for, and well worth a trifling risk.

He did not hesitate to follow—but with the soft tread of a polite butler, doing his offices over the thick carpet of a drawing-room—and it was in his mind—'Suppose he does discover me, what then ? *I*'m as much surprised as he ! Thomas Brewen, the footman, who is under notice to leave, has twice, to the captain's knowledge, played me the same trick, and stole out through the gunroom window at night, and denied it afterwards ; so I sat up to detect him, and hearing the door open, and a step, I pursued, and find I've made a mistake ; and beg pardon with proper humility—supposing the master is on the same errand—what can he say? It will bring me a present, and a hint to say nothing of my having seen him in the yew-walk at this hour.'

Of course he did not run through all this rigmarole in detail ; but the situation, the excuse, and the result, were present to his mind, and filled him with a comfortable assurance.

Therefore, with decision and caution, he followed Captain Lake's march, and reaching the yew-walk, he saw the slim figure in the cap and paletot turn the corner, and enter the broad walk between the two wall-like beech hedges, which led direct to the first artificial pond—a long, narrow parallelogram, round which the broad walk passed in two straight lines, fenced with the towering beech hedges, shorn as smooth as the walls of a nunnery.

When the butler reached the point at which Captain Lake had turned, he found himself all at once within fifty steps of that eccentric gentleman, who was talking, but in so low a tone, that not even the sound of the voices reached him, with a rather short, broad-shouldered person, buttoned up in a surtout, and wearing a queer, Germanesque, felt hat, battered and crushed a good deal.

Mr. Larcom held his breath. He was profoundly interested. After a while, with an oath, he exclaimed—

'That's *him!*'

Then, after another pause, he gasped another oath :—

'It *is* him !'

The square-built man in the surtout had a great pair of black whiskers ; and as he stood opposite Lake, conversing, with, now and again, an earnest gesture, he showed a profile which Mr. Larcom knew very well ; and now they turned and walked slowly side by side along the broad walk by that perpendicular wall of crisp brown leaves, he recognised also a certain hitch in his shoulder, which made him swear and asseverate again.

He would have given something to hear what was passing. He thought uneasily whether there might not be a side-path or orifice anywhere through which he might creep so as to get to the other side of the hedge and listen. But there was no way, and he must rest content with such report as his eyes might furnish.

'They're not quarrelling no ways,' murmured he.

And, indeed, they walked together, stopping now and again, as it seemed, very amicably. Captain Lake seemed to have most to say.

'He's awful cowed, he is ; I never did think to see Mr. Wylder so affeard of Lake ; he *is* affeard ; yes, he is—*that* he is.

And indeed there was an indescribable air of subservience in the demeanour of the square-built gentleman very different from what Mark Wylder once showed.

He saw the captain take from the pocket of his paletot a square box or packet, it might be jewels or only papers, and hand them to his companion, who popped them into his left-hand surtout pocket, and kept his hand there as if the freightage were specially valuable.

Then they talked earnestly a little longer, standing together by the pond ; and then, side-by-side, they paced down the broad walk by its edge. It was a long walk. Honest Larcom would have followed if there had been any sort of cover to hide his advance ; but there being nothing of the kind he was fain to abide at his corner. Thence he beheld them come at last slowly to a stand-still, talk evidently a little more, and finally they shook hands—an indefinable something still of superiority in Lake's air—and parted.

The captain was now all at once walking at a swift pace, alone, towards Larcom's post of observation, and his secret confederate nearly as rapidly in an opposite direction. It would not do for the butler to be taken or even seen by Lake, nor yet to be left at the outside of the door and barred out. So the captain had hardly commenced his homeward walk, when Larcom, though no great runner, threw himself into an agitated amble, and reached and entered the little door just in time to escape observation. He had not been two minutes in his apartment again when he once more beheld the figure of his master cross the window, and heard the small door softly opened and closed, and the bolts slowly and cautiously drawn again into their places. Then there was a pause. Lake was listening to ascertain whether anyone was stirring, and being satisfied, reascended the stairs, leaving the stout and courteous butler ample matter for romantic speculation.

It was now the butler's turn to listen, which he did at the halfopened door of his room. When he was quite assured that all was quiet, he shut and bolted his door, closed the windowshutters, and relighted his pair of wax candles.

Mr. Larcom was a good deal excited. He had seen strange things that night. He was a good deal blown and heated by his run, and a little wild and scared at the closeness of the captain's unconscious pursuit. His head beside was full of amazing conjectures. After a while he took his crumpled letter from his pocket, unfolded and smoothed it, and wrote upon a blank halfpage—

'RESPECTED SIR,—Since the above i ave a much to tel mos surprisen, the gentleman you wer anceous of tiding mister M. W. is cum privet, and him and master met tonite nere 2 in morning, in the long pond allee, so is near home then we suposed, no more at present Sir from your

'humbel servent JOHN
'LARCOM.

'i shall go to dolington day arter to-morrow by eleven o'clock trane if you ere gong, Sir.'

When the attorney returned, between eleven and twelve o'clock next morning, this letter awaited him. It did not, of course, surprise him, but it conclusively corroborated all his inferences.

Here had been Mark Wylder. He had stopped at Dollington, as the attorney suspected he would, and he had kept tryst, in the Brandon grounds, with sly Captain Lake, whose relations with him it became now more difficult than ever clearly to comprehend.

Wylder was plainly under no physical coercion. He had come and gone unattended. For one reason or other he was, at least, as strongly interested as Lake in maintaining secrecy.

That Mark Wylder was living was the grand fact with which he had just then to do. How near he had been to purchasing the vicar's reversion ! The engrossed deeds lay in the black box there. And yet it might be all true about Mark's secret marriage. At that moment there might be a whole rosary of sons, small and great, to intercept the inheritance ; and the Reverend William Wylder might have no more chance of the estates than he had of the crown.

What a deliverance for the good attorney. His money was quite safe. The excellent man's religion was, we know, a little Jewish, and rested upon temporal rewards and comforts. He thought, I am sure, that a competent staff of angels were placed specially in charge of the interests of Jos. Larkin, Esq., who attended so many services and sermons on Sundays, and led a life of such ascetic propriety. He felt quite grateful to them, in his priggish way—their management in this matter had been so eminently satisfactory. He regretted that he had not an opportunity of telling them so personally. I don't say that he would have expressed it in these literal terms ; but it was fixed in his mind that the carriage of his business was supernaturally arranged. Perhaps he was right, and he was at once elated and purified, and his looks and manner that afternoon were more than usually meek and celestial.

CHAPTER LXXI.

SIR HARRY BRACTON'S INVASION OF GYLINGDEN.

JIM DUTTON had not turned up since, and his letter was one of those mares' nests of which gentlemen in Mr. Larkin's line of business have so large an experience. Of Mark Wylder not a trace was discoverable. His enquiries on this point were, of course, conducted with caution and remoteness. Gylingden, however, was one of those places which, if it knows anything, is sure to find a way of telling it, and the attorney was soon satisfied that Mark's secret visit had been conducted with sufficient caution to baffle the eyes and ears of the good folk of the town.

Well, one thing was plain. The purchase of the reversion was to wait, and fraudulent as was the price at which he had proposed to buy it, he was now resolved to get it for less than half that sum, and he wrote a short note to the vicar, which he forthwith despatched.

In the meantime there was not a moment to be lost in clenching the purchase of Five Oaks. And Mr. Jos. Larkin, with one of his 'young men' with him in the tax-cart, reached Brandon Hall in a marvellously short time after his arrival at home.

Jos. Larkin, his clerk, and the despatch-box, had a short wait in the Dutch room, before his admission to the library, where an animated debate was audible. The tremendous contest impending over the county was, of course, the theme. In the Dutch room, where they waited, there was a large table, with a pyramid of blank envelopes in the middle, and ever so many cubic feet of canvassing circulars, six chairs, and pens and ink. The clerks were in the housekeeper's room at that moment, partaking of refreshment. There was a gig in the court-yard, with a groom at the horse's head, and Larkin, as he drew up, saw a chaise driving round to the stable yard. People of all sorts were coming and going, and Brandon Hall was already growing like an inn.

'How d'ye do, dear Larkin?' said Captain Brandon Stanley Lake, the hero of all this debate and commotion, smiling his customary sly greeting, and extending his slim hand across the arm of his chair—'I'm so sorry you were away—this thing has come, after all, so suddenly—we are getting on famously though —but I'm awfully fagged.' And, indeed, he looked pale and tired, though smiling. 'I've a lot of fellows with me; they've just run in to luncheon; won't you take something?'

But Jos. Larkin, smiling after his sort, excused himself. He was glad they had a moment to themselves. He had brought the money, which he knew would be acceptable at such a moment, and he thought it would be desirable to sign and seal forthwith, to which the captain, a little anxiously, agreed. So he got in one of the clerks who were directing the canvassing circulars, and gave him the draft, approved by his counsel, to read aloud, while he followed with his eye upon the engrossed deed.

The attorney told down the money in bank bills. He fancied that exception might be taken to his cheque for so large a sum, and was eager to avoid delay, and came from London so provided.

The captain was not sorry, for in truth he was in rather imminent jeopardy just then. He had spoken truth, strangely enough, when he mentioned his gambling debts as an incentive to his marriage with the heiress of Brandon, in that Sunday walk with Rachel in the park ; and hardly ten minutes had passed when Melton Hervey, trustiest of aide-de-camps, was on his way to Dollington to make a large lodgment to the captain's credit in the county bank, and to procure a letter of credit for a stupendous sum in favour of Messrs. Hiram and Jacobs, transmitted under cover to Captain Lake's town solicitor. The captain had signed, sealed, and delivered, murmuring that formula about hand and seal, and act and deed, and Dorcas glided in like a ghost, and merely whispering an enquiry to Lake, did likewise, the clerk deferentially putting the query, ' this is your hand and seal, &c. ?' and Jos. Larkin drawing a step or two backward.

Of course the lady saw that lank and sinister man of God quite distinctly, but she did not choose to do so, and Larkin, with a grand sort of prescience, forésaw a county feud between the Houses of Five Oaks and Brandon, and now the lady had vanished. The money, carefully counted, was rolled in Lake's pocket-book, and the bright new deed which made Jos. Larkin, of the Lodge, Esq., master of Five Oaks, was safely locked into the box, under his long arm, and the attorney vanished, bowing very much, and concealing his elation under a solemn sort of *nonchalance.*

The note, which by this time the vicar had received, though short, was, on the whole, tremendous. It said :—

' (Private.)

' REV. AND DEAR SIR,—I have this moment arrived from London, where I deeply regret to state the negotiation on which we both relied to carry you comfortably over your present difficulties has fallen through, in consequence of what I cannot but regard as the inexcusable caprice of the intending purchaser. He declines stating any reason for his withdrawal. I fear that the articles were so artfully framed by his solicitors, in one particular which it never entered into my mind to refer to anything like trick or design, that we shall find it impossible to compel him to carry out what, in the strongest terms, I have represented to Messrs. Burlington and Smith as a bargain irrevocably concluded in point of honour and morality. The refusal of their own client to make the proposed investment has alarmed those gentlemen, I regret to add, for the safety of their costs, which, as I before apprised you, are, though I cannot say excessive, certainly *very heavy;* and I fear we must be prepared for extreme measures upon their part. I have carefully reconsidered the very handsome proposal which Miss Lake was so good as to submit ; but the result is that, partly on technical, and partly on other grounds, I continue of the clear opinion that the idea is absolutely impracticable, and must be peremptorily laid aside in attempting to arrive at an estimate of any resources which you may be conscious of commanding. If, under these deplorably untoward circumstances, you still think I can be of any use to you, may I beg that you will not hesitate to say how.

' I remain, my dear and reverend Sir, with profound regrets and sympathy, yours very sincerely,

'JOS. H. LARKIN.'

He had already imported the H. which was to germinate, in a little while, into Howard.

When Jos. Larkin wanted to get a man's property a bargain —and he had made two or three excellent hits, though, comparatively, on a very small scale—he liked so to contrive matters as to bring his client to his knees, begging him to purchase on the terms he wished ; and then Jos. Larkin came forward, in the interests of humanity, and unable to resist the importunities of ' a party whom he respected,' he did ' what, at the time, appeared a very risky thing, although it has turned out tolerably safe in the long run.'

The screw was now twisted pretty well home upon the poor vicar, who, if he had any sense at all, would, remembering Larkin's expressions only a week before, suggest his buying, and so, the correspondence would disclose, in a manner most honourable to the attorney, the history of the purchase.

But the clouds had begun to break, and the sky to clear, over the good vicar, just at the point where they had been darkest and most menacing.

Little Fairy, after all, was better. Good-natured Buddle had been there at nine, quite amazed at his being so well, still reserved and cautious, and afraid of raising hopes. But when he came back, at eleven, and had completed his examination, he told them, frankly, that there was a decided change ; in fact, that the little man, with, of course, great care, might do very well, and *ought* to recover, if nothing went wrong.

Honest Buddle was delighted. He chuckled over the little man's bed. He could not suppress his grins. He was a miracle of a child! a prodigy! By George, it was the most extraordinary case he had ever met with! It was all that bottle, and that miraculous child; they seemed made for one another. From two o'clock, last night, the action of his skin has commenced, and never ceased since. When he was here last night, the little fellow's pulse was a hundred and forty-four, and now down to ninety-seven.

The doctor grew jocular; and who can resist a doctor's jokes, when they garnish such tidings as he was telling. Was ever so pleasant a doctor! Laughter through tears greeted these pleasantries; and oh, such transports of gratitude broke forth when he was gone!

It was well for Driver, the postmaster, and his daughters, that all the circulars made up that day in Brandon Hall were not des-patched through the Gylingden post-office. It was amazing how so many voters could find room in one county. Next day, it was resolved, the captain's personal canvass was to commence. The invaluable Wealdon had run through the list of his to-morrow's visits, and given him an inkling of the idiosyncrasies, the feuds, and the likings of each elector in the catalogue. 'Busy times, Sir!' Tom Wealdon used to remark, with a chuckle, from time to time, in the thick of the fuss and conspiration which was the breath of his nostrils; and, doubtless, so they are, and were, and ever will be, until the time-honoured machinery of our elec-tion system has been overhauled, and adapted to the civilisation of these days.

Captain Brandon Lake was as much as possible at head quarters in these critical times; and, suddenly, Mr. Crump, the baker, and John Thomas, of the delft, ironmongery, sponge, and umbrella shop, at the corner of Church Street, in Gylingden, were announced by the fatigued servant. They bowed, and stood, grinning, near the door; and the urbane and cordial captain, with all a candidate's good fellowship, shook them both by the hands, and heard their story; and an exciting one it was.

Sir Harry Bracton had actually invaded the town of Gyling-den. There was a rabble of the raff of Queen's Bracton along with him. He, with two or three young swells by him, had made a speech, from his barouche, outside the 'Silver Lion,' near the green; and he was now haranguing from the steps of the Court House. They had a couple of flags, and some music. It was 'a regular, planned thing;' for the Queen's Bracton people had been dropping in an hour before. The shop-keepers were shutting their windows. Sir Harry was 'chaffing the capting,' and hitting him very hard 'for a hupstart'—and, in fact, Crump was more particular in reporting the worthy baronet's language than was absolutely necessary. And it was thought that Sir Harry was going to canvass the town.

The captain was very much obliged, indeed, and begged they would go into the parlour, and take luncheon ; and, forthwith, Wealdon took the command. The gamekeepers, the fifty hay-makers in the great meadow, they were to enter the town from the top of Church Street, where they were to gather all the boys and blackguards they could. The men from the gas-works, the masons, and blacksmiths, were to be marched in by Luke Sam-ways. Tom Wealdon would, himself, in passing, give the men at the coal-works a hint. Sir Harry's invasion was the most audacious thing on record ; and it was incumbent on Gylingden to make his defeat memorably disgraceful and disastrous.

His barouche was to be smashed, and burnt on the green ; his white topcoat and hat were to clothe the effigy, which was to swing over the bonfire. The captured Bracton banners were to hang in the coffee-room of the 'Silver Lion,' to inspire the roughs. What was to become of the human portion of the hostile pageant, Tom, being an official person, did not choose to hint.

All these, and fifty minor measures, were ordered by the fertile Wealdon in a minute, and suitable messengers on the wing to see after them. The captain, accompanied by Mr. Jekyl, myself, and a couple of the grave scriveners from the next room, were to go by the back approach and Redman's Dell to the Assembly Rooms, which Crump and Thomas, already on their way in the fly, undertook to have open for their reception, and furnished with some serious politicians from the vicinity. From the windows, the captain, thus supported, was to make his maiden speech, one point in which Tom Wealdon insisted upon, and that was an injunction to the 'men of Gylingden' on no account to break the peace. 'Take care to say it, and we'll have it well reported in the "Chronicle," and our lads won't mind it, nor hear it neither, for that matter.'

So, there was mounting in hot haste in the courtyard of old Brandon, and a rather ponderous selection of walking-sticks by the politicians—of whom I was one—intended for the windows of the assembly room.

Lake rode ; Tom Wealdon, myself, and two scriveners, squeezed into the dog-cart, which was driven by Jekyl, and away we went. It was a pleasant drive, under the noble old trees. But we were in no mood for the picturesque. A few minutes brought us into the Blackberry hollow, which debouches into Redman's Dell.

Here, the road being both steep and rugged, our speed abated. The precipitous banks shut out the sunlight, except at noon, and the road through this defile, overhung by towering trees and rocks, was even now in solemn shadow. The cart-road leading down to Redman's Dell, and passing the mills near Redman's Farm, diverges from the footpath with which we are so well acquainted, near that perpendicular block of stone which stands a little above the steps which the footpath here descends.

––––––––

CHAPTER LXXII.

MARK WYLDER'S HAND.

JUST at the darkest point of the road, a little above the rude column which I have mentioned, Lake's horse, a young one, shied, stopped short, recoiling on its haunches, and snorted fiercely into the air. At the same time, the two dogs which had accompanied us began to bark furiously beneath in the ravine.

The tall form of Uncle Lorne was leaning against a tree at the edge of the ravine, with his left hand extended towards us, and his right pointing down the precipice. Perhaps it was this odd apparition that startled Lake's horse.

'I told you he was coming up—lend him a hand,' yelled Uncle Lorne, in great excitement.

No one at such a moment minded his maunderings : but many people afterwards thought that the crazed old man, in one of his night-rambles, had seen that which, till now, no one had imagined ; and that Captain Lake himself, whose dislike of him was hardly disguised, suspected him, at times of that alarming knowledge.

Lake plunged the spurs into his beast, which reared so straight that she toppled backward toward the edge of the ravine.

' Strike her on the head ; jump off,' shouted Wealdon.

But he did neither.

' D— it ! put her head down ; lean forward,' bellowed Wealdon again.

But it would not do. With a crash among briars, and a heavy thump from beneath that shook the earth, the mare and her rider went over. A shout of horror broke from us all ; and Jekyl, watching the catastrophe, was very near pulling our horse over the edge, and launching us all together, like the captain, into the defile.

In a moment more we were all on the ground, and scrambling down the side of the ravine, among rocks, boughs, brambles, and ferns, in the deep shadows of the gorge, the dogs still yelling furiously from below.

' Here he is,' cried Jekyl. ' How are you, Lake ? Much hurt, old boy ? By Jove, he's killed, I think.'

Lake groaned.

He lay about twelve feet below the edge. The mare, now lying near the bottom of the gorge, had, I believe, fallen upon him, and then tumbled over.

Strange to say, Lake was conscious, and in a few seconds, he said, in reply to the horrified questions of his friend—

' I'm *all* smashed. Don't move me ; ' and, in a minute more — ' Don't mind that d—d brute ; she's killed. Let her lie.'

It appeared very odd, but so it was, he appeared eager upon this point, and, faint as he was, almost savage.

' Tell them to let her lie there.'

Wealdon and I, however, scrambled down the bank. He was right. The mare lay stone dead, on her side, at the bottom. He lifted her head, by the ear, and let it fall back.

In the meantime the dogs continued their unaccountable yelling close by.

' What the devil's that ? ' said Wealdon.

Something like a stunted, blackened branch was sticking out of the peat, ending in a set of short, thickish twigs. This is what it seemed. The dogs were barking at it. It was, really, a human hand and arm, disclosed by the slipping of the bank, undermined by the brook, which was swollen by the recent rains.

The dogs were sniffing and yelping about it.

' It's a hand ! ' cried Wealdon, with an oath.

' A hand ? ' I echoed.

We were both peering at it, having drawn near, stooping and hesitating as men do in a curious horror.

It was, indeed, a human hand and arm, disclosed from about the elbow, enveloped in a discoloured coat-sleeve, which fell back from the limb, and the fingers, like it black, were extended in the air. Nothing more of the body to which it belonged, except the point of a knee, in stained and muddy trousers, protruding from the peat, was visible.

It must have lain there a considerable time, for, notwithstanding the antiseptic properties of that sort of soil, mixed with the decayed bark and fibre of trees, a portion of the flesh of the hand was decomposed, and the naked bone disclosed. On the little finger something glimmered dully.

In this livid hand, rising from the earth, there was a character both of menace and appeal ; and on the finger, as I afterwards saw at the inquest, glimmered the talismanic legend ' Resurgam —I will rise again ! ' It was the corpse of Mark Wylder, which had lain buried here undiscovered for many months. A horrible odour loaded the air. Perhaps it was this smell of carrion, from which horses sometimes recoil with a special terror, that caused the swerving and rearing which had ended so fatally. At that moment we heard a voice calling, and raising our eyes, saw Uncle Lorne looking down from the rock with an agitated scowl.

'I've done with him now—*emeritus*—he touches me, no more. Take him by the hand, merciful lads, or they'll draw him down again.'

And with these words Uncle Lorne receded, and I saw him no more.

As yet we had no suspicion whose was the body thus unexpectedly discovered.

We beat off the dogs, and on returning to Lake, found Jekyl trying to raise him a little against a tree. We were not far from Redman's Farm, and it was agreed, on hasty consultation, that our best course would be to carry Lake thither at once by the footpath, and that one of us—Wealdon undertook this—should drive the carriage on, and apprising Rachel on the way of the accident which had happened, and that her brother was on his way thither, should drive on to Buddle's house, sending assistance to us from the town.

It was plain that Stanley Lake's canvass was pretty well over. There was not one of us who looked at him that did not feel convinced that he was mortally hurt. I don't think he believed so himself then; but we could not move him from the place where he lay without inflicting so much pain, that we were obliged to wait for assistance.

'D— the dogs, what are they barking for?' said Lake, faintly. He seemed distressed by the noise.

'There's a dead body partly disclosed down there—some one murdered and buried; but one of Mr. Juke's young men is keeping them off.'

Lake made an effort to raise himself, but with a grin and a suppressed moan he abandoned it.

'Is there no doctor—I'm very much hurt?' said Lake, faintly, after a minute's silence.

We told him that Buddle had been sent for; and that we only awaited help to get him down to Redman's Farm.

When Rachel heard the clang of hoofs and the rattle of the tax-cart driving down the mill-road, at a pace so unusual, a vague augury of evil smote her. She was standing in the porch of her tiny house, and old Tamar was sitting knitting on the bench close by.

'Tamar, they are galloping down the road, I think—what can it mean?' exclaimed the young lady, scared she could not tell why; and old Tamar stood up, and shaded her eyes with her shrunken hand.

Tom Wealdon pulled up at the little wicket. He was pale. He had lost his hat, too, among the thickets, and could not take time to recover it. Altogether he looked wild.

He put his hand to where his hat should have been in token of salutation, and said he—

'I beg pardon, Miss Lake, Ma am, but I'm sorry to say your brother the captain's badly hurt, and maybe you could have a shakedown in the parlour ready for him by the time I come back with the doctor, Ma'am?'

Rachel, she did not know how, was close by the wheel of the vehicle by this time.

'Is it Sir Harry Bracton? He's in the town, I know. Is Stanley shot?'

'Not shot; only thrown, Miss, into the Dell; his mare shied at a dead body that's there. You'd better stay where you are, Miss; but if you could send up some water, I think he'd like it. Going for the doctor, Ma'am; good-bye, Miss Lake.'

And away went Wealdon, wild, pale, and hatless, like a man pursued by robbers.

'Oh! Tamar, he's killed— Stanley's killed— I'm sure he's killed, and all's discovered'—and Rachel ran wildly up the hill a few steps, but stopped and returned as swiftly.

'Thank God, Miss,' said old Tamar, lifting up her trembling fingers and white eyes to Heaven. 'Better dead, Miss, than living on in sin and sorrow, better discovered than hid by daily falsehood and cruelty. Old Tamar's tired of life; she's willing to go, and wishin' for death this many a day. Oh! Master Stanley, my child!'

Rachel went into the parlour and kneeled down, with white upturned face and clasped hands. But she could not pray. She could only look her wild supplication;—deliverance—an issue out of the terrors that beset her; and 'oh! poor miserable lost Stanley!' It was just a look and an inarticulate cry for mercy.

An hour after Captain Stanley Brandon Lake, whose 'election address' was figuring that evening in the 'Dollington Courier,' and in the 'County Chronicle,' lay with his clothes still on, in the little drawing-room of Redman's Farm, his injuries ascertained, his thigh broken near the hip, and his spine fractured. No hope —no possibility of a physical reascension, this time.

Meanwhile, in the Blackberry Dell, Doctor Buddle was assisting at a different sort of inquisition. The two policemen who constituted the civil force of Gylingden, two justices of the peace, the doctor, and a crowd of amateurs, among whom I rank myself, were grouped in the dismal gorge, a little to windward of the dead body, which fate had brought to light, while three men were now employed in cautiously disinterring it.

When the operation was completed, there remained no doubt whatever on my mind: discoloured and disfigured as were both clothes and body, I was sure that the dead man was no other than Mark Wylder. When the clay with which is was clotted was a little removed, it became indubitable. The great whiskers ; the teeth so white and even ; and oddly enough, one black lock of hair which he wore twisted in a formal curl flat on his forehead, remained undisturbed in its position, as it was fixed there at his last toilet for Brandon Hall.

In the rude and shallow grave in which he lay, his purse was found, and some loose silver mixed in the mould. The left hand, on which was the ring of 'the Persian magician,' was bare ; the right gloved, with the glove of the other hand clutched firmly in it.

The body was got up in a sheet to a sort of spring cart which awaited it, and so conveyed to the 'Silver Lion,' in Gylingden, where it was placed in a disused coach-house to await the inquest. There the examination was continued, and his watch (the chain broken) found in his waistcoat pocket. In his coat-pocket were found (of course, in no very presentable condition) his cigar-case, his initials stamped on it, for Mark had, in his day, a keen sense of property ; his handkerchief, also marked ; a pocket-book with some entries nearly effaced ; and a letter unopened, and sealed with Lord Chelford's seal. The writing was nearly washed away, but the letters ' lwich,' or ' twich,' were still legible near the corner, and it turned out to be a letter to Dulwich, which Mark Wylder had undertaken to put in the Gylingden post-office, on the last night on which he appeared at Brandon.

The whole town was in a ferment that night. Great debate and conjecture in the reading-room, and even on the benches of the billiard-room. The 'Silver Lion' did a great business that night. Mine host might have turned a good round sum only by showing the body, were it not that Edwards, the chief police-man, had the keys of the coach-house. Much to-ing and fro-ing there was between the town and Redman's Farm, the respectable inhabitants all sending or going up to enquire how the captain was doing. At last Doctor Buddle officially interfered. The constant bustle was injurious to his patient. An hourly bulletin up to twelve o'clock should be in the hall of the 'Brandon Arms ;' and Redman's Dell grew quiet once more.

When William Wylder heard the news, he fainted ; not al-together through horror or grief, though he felt both ; but the change in his circumstances was so amazing and momentous. It was a strange shock—immense relief—immense horror—quite overwhelming.

Mark had done some good-natured things for him in a small five-pound way ; he had promised him that loan, too, which would have lifted him out of his Slough of Despond, and he clung with an affectionate gratitude to these exhibitions of brotherly love. Besides, he had accustomed himself—the organ of veneration standing prominent on the top of the vicar's head —to regard Mark in the light of a great practical genius—' natus rebus agendis ;' he knew men so thoroughly—he understood the

world so marvellously ! The vicar was not in the least surprised
when Mark came in for a fortune. He had always predicted
that Mark must become *very* rich, and that nothing but in-
dolence could prevent his ultimately becoming a very great man.
The sudden and total disappearance of so colossal an object was
itself amazing.

There was another person very strongly, though differently, affected by the news. Under pretext of business at Naunton, Jos.
Larkin had driven off early to Five Oaks, to make inspection of
his purchase. He dined like a king in disguise, at the humble
little hostelry of Naunton Friars, and returned in the twilight to
the Lodge, which he would make the dower-house of Five Oaks,
with the Howard shield over the door. He was gracious to his
domestics, but the distance was increased : he was nearer to the
clouds, and they looked smaller.

'Well, Mrs. Smithers,' said he, encouragingly, his long feet on
the fender, for the evening was sharp, and Mrs. S. knew that he
liked a bit of fire at his tea—'any letters—any calls—any news
stirring?'

'No letters, nor calls, Sir, please, except the butcher's book.
I s'pose, Sir, you were viewing the body?'

'What body?'

'Mr. Wylder's, please, Sir.'

'The vicar!' exclaimed Mr. Larkin, his smile of condescension suddenly vanishing.

'No, Sir ; Mr. *Mark* Wylder, please ; the gentleman, Sir, as
was to 'av married Miss Brandon.'

'What the devil do you mean, woman?' ejaculated the attorney, his back to the fire, standing erect, and a black shadow
over his amazed and offended countenance.

'The devil,' in such a mouth, was so appalling and so amazing, that the worthy woman gazed, thunder-struck, upon him for
a moment.

'Beg your pardon, Sir ; but his body's bin found, Sir.'

'You mean Mr. *Mark?*'

'Yes, please, Sir ; in a hole near the mill road—it's up in the
"Silver Lion" now, Sir.'

'It must be the vicar's—it *must*,' said Jos. Larkin, getting his
hat on, sternly, and thinking how likely he was to throw himself
into the mill race, and impossible it was that Mark, whom he
and Larcom had both seen alive and well last night—the latter,
indeed, *this morning*—could possibly be the man. And thus
comforting himself, he met old Major Jackson on the green, and
that gentleman's statement ended with the words : 'and in an
advanced stage of decomposition.'

'That settles the matter,' said Larkin, breathing again, and
with a toss of his head, and almost a smile of disdain : 'for I
saw Mr. Mark Wylder late last night at Shillingsworth.'

Leaving Major Jackson in considerable surprise, Mr. Larkin walked off to Edwards' dwelling, at the top of Church Street, and found that active policeman at home. In his cool, grand, official way, Mr. Larkin requested Mr. Edwards to accompany him to the 'Silver Lion,' where in the same calm and commanding way, he desired him to attend him to view the corpse. In virtue of his relation to Mark Wylder, and of his position as sole resident and legal practitioner, he was obeyed.

The odious spectacle occupied him for some minutes. He did not speak while they remained in the room. On coming out there was a black cloud upon the attorney's features, and he said, sulkily, to Edwards, who had turned the key in the lock, and now touched his hat as he listened,

'Yes, there is a resemblance, but it is all a mistake. I travelled as far as Shillingsworth last night with Mr. Mark Wylder : he was perfectly well. This can't be he.'

But there was a terrible impression on Mr. Jos. Larkin's mind that this certainly *was* he, and with a sulky nod to the policeman, he walked darkly down to the vicar's house. The vicar had been sent for to Naunton to pray with a dying person ; and Mr. Larkin, disappointed, left a note to state that in writing that morning, as he had done, in reference to the purchase of the reversion, through Messrs. Burlington and Smith, he had simply expressed his own surmises as to the probable withdrawal of the intending purchaser, but had received no formal, nor, indeed, *any* authentic information, from either the party or the solicitors referred to, to that effect. That he mentioned this lest misapprehension should arise, but not as attaching any importance to the supposed discovery which seemed to imply Mr. Mark Wylder's death. That gentleman, on the contrary, he had seen alive and well at Shillingsworth on the night previous ; and he had been seen in conference with Captain Lake at a subsequent hour, at Brandon.

From all this the reader may suppose that Mr. Jos. Larkin was not quite in a comfortable state, and he resolved to get the deeds, and go down again to the vicar's, and persuade him to execute them. He could make William Wylder, of course, do whatever he pleased.

There were a good many drunken fellows about the town, but there was an end of election demonstrations in the Brandon interest. Captain Lake was not going in for that race ; he would be on another errand by the time the writ came down.

CHAPTER LXXIII.

THE MASK FALLS.

HERE was a 'stop press' that evening in the county paper—'We have just learned that a body has been disinterred, early this afternoon, under very strange circumstances, in the neighbourhood of Gylingden; and if the surmises which are afloat prove well-founded, the discovery will set at rest the speculations which have been busy respecting the whereabouts of a certain gentleman of large property and ancient lineage, who, some time since, mysteriously disappeared, and will, no doubt, throw this county into a state of very unusual excitement. We can state, upon authority, that the coroner will hold his inquest on the body, to-morrow at twelve o'clock, in the town of Gylingden.

There was also an allusion to Captain Lake's accident—with the expression of a hope that it would 'prove but a trifling one,' and an assurance 'that his canvass would not be prevented by it—although for a few days it might not be a personal one. But his friends might rely on seeing him at the hustings, and hearing him too, when the proper time arrived.'

It was quite well known, however, in Gylingden, by this time, that Captain Lake was not to see the hustings — that his spine was smashed—that he was lying on an extemporised bed, still in his clothes, in the little parlour of Redman's Farm—cursing the dead mare in gasps—railing at everybody—shuddering whenever they attempted to remove his clothes—hoping, in broken sentences, that his people would give Bracton and—good licking. Bracton's outrage was the cause of the entire thing—and so help him Heaven, so soon as he should be on his legs again, he would make him feel it, one way or other.

Buddle thought he was in so highly excited a state, that his brain must have sustained some injury also.

He asked Buddle about ten o'clock (having waked up from a sort of stupor)—'what about Jim Dutton?' and then, whether there was not some talk about a body they had found, and what it was. So Buddle told him all that was yet known, and he listened very attentively.

'But Larkin has been corresponding with Mark Wylder up to a very late day, and if this body has been so long buried, how the devil can it be he? And if it be as bodies usually are after such a time, how can anybody pretend to identify it? And I happen to know that Mark Wylder is living,' he added, suddenly.

The doctor told him not to tire himself talking, and offered, if he wished to make a statement before a magistrate, to arrange that one should attend and receive it.

'I rather dislike it, because Mark wants to keep it quiet ; but if, on public grounds, it is desirable, I will make it, of course. You'll use your discretion in mentioning the subject.'

So the captain was now prepared to acknowledge the secret meeting of the night before, and to corroborate the testimony of his attorney and his butler.

Stanley Lake had now no idea that his injuries were dangerous. He said he had a bad bruise under his ribs, and a sprained wrist, and was a little bit shaken ; and he talked of his electioneering as only suspended for a day or two.

Buddle, however, thought the case so imminent, that on his way to the 'Brandon Arms,' meeting Larkin, going, attended by his clerk, again to the vicar's house, he stopped him for a moment, and told him what had passed, adding, that Lake was so frightfully injured, that he might begin to sink at any moment, and that by next evening, at all events, he might not be in a condition to make a deposition.

'It is odd enough—very odd,' said Larkin. 'It was only an hour since, in conversation with our policeman, Edwards, that I mentioned the fact of my having myself travelled from London to Shillingsworth last night with Mr. Mark Wylder, who went on by train in this direction, I presume, to meet our unfortunate friend, Captain Lake, by appointment. Thomas Sleddon, of Wadding Hall—at this moment in the "Brandon Arms"—is just the man ; if you mention it to him, he'll go up with you to Redman's Farm, and take the deposition. Let it be a *deposition,* do you mind ; a statement is mere hearsay.'

Comforted somewhat, reassured in a certain way, and in strong hopes that, at all events, such a muddle would be established as to bewilder the jury, Mr. Jos. Larkin, with still an awful foreboding weighing at his heart, knocked at the vicar's door, and was shown into the study. A solitary candle being placed, to make things bright and pleasant for the visitor, who did not look so himself, the vicar, very pale, and appearing to have grown even thinner since he last saw him, entered, and shook his hand with an anxious attempt at a smile, which faded almost instantly.

'I am so delighted that you have come. I have passed a day of such dreadful agitation. Poor Mark !'

'There is no doubt, Sir, whatsoever that he is perfectly well. Three different persons — unexceptionable witnesses — can depose to having seen him last night, and he had a long conference with Captain Lake, who is by this time making his deposition. It is with respect to the other little matter—the execution of the deed of conveyance to Messrs. Burlington and

Smith's clients. You know my feeling about the note I wrote this morning a little—I will not say incautiously, because with a client of your known character and honour, no idea of the sort can find place—but I will say thoughtlessly. If there be any hanging back, or appearance of it, it may call down unpleasant —indeed, to be quite frank, ruinous—consequences, which, I think, in the interest of your family, you would hardly be justified in invoking upon the mere speculation of your respected brother's death.'

There was a sound of voices at the door. 'Do come in— pray do,' was heard in Dolly's voice. 'Won't you excuse me, but pray do. Willie, darling, don't you wish him to come in?'

'Most particularly. Do *beg* of him, in my name—and I know Mr. Larkin would wish it so much.'

And so Lord Chelford, with a look which, at another time, would have been an amused one, quite conscious of the oddity of his introduction, came in and slightly saluted Mr. Larkin, who was for a few seconds pretty obviously confounded, and with a pink flush all over his bald forehead, tried to smile, while his hungry little eyes searched the viscount with fear and suspicion.

Larkin's tone was now much moderated. Any sort of dealing was good enough for the simple vicar ; but here was the quiet, sagacious peer, who had shown himself, on two remarkable committees, so quick and able a man of business, and the picture of the vicar's situation, and of the powers and terrors of Messrs. Burlington and Smith, were to be drawn with an exacter pencil, and far more delicate colouring.

Lord Chelford listened so quietly that the tall attorney felt he was making way with him, and concluded his persuasion by appealing to him for an opinion.

'That is precisely as I said. I knew my friend, Mr. Larkin, would be only too glad of an opinion in this difficulty from you,' threw in the vicar.

The opinion came—very clear, very quiet, very unpleasant— dead against Mr. Larkin's view, and concluding with the remark that he thought there was more in the affair than had yet come to light.

'I don't see exactly how, my lord,' said Mr. Larkin, a little loftily, and redder than usual.

'Nor do I, Mr. Larkin, at present ; but the sum offered is much too small, and the amount of costs and other drawbacks utterly monstrous, and the result is, after deducting all these claims, including your costs, Mr. Larkin——'

Here Mr. Larkin threw up his chin a little, smiling, and waving his long hand, and saying, 'Oh ! as to *mine*,' in a way that plainly expressed, 'They are merely put down for form's sake. It is playing at costs. You know Jos. Larkin—he never so much as dreamed of looking for them.'

'There remain hardly nine hundred and fifty pounds applicable to the payment of the Reverend Mr. Wylder's debts—a sum which would have been ample, before this extraordinary negotiation was commenced, to have extricated him from all his pressing difficulties, and which I would have been only too happy at being permitted to advance, and which, and a great deal more, Miss Lake, whose conduct has been more than kind —quite noble—wished to place in your client's hands.'

'*That*,' said the attorney, flushing a little, 'I believe to have been technically impossible; and it was accompanied by a proposition which was on other grounds untenable.'

'You mean Miss Lake's proposed residence here—an arrangement, it appears to me, every way most desirable.'

'I objected to it on, I will say, *moral* grounds, my lord. It is painful to me to disclose what I know, but that young lady accompanied Mr. Mark Wylder, my lord, in his midnight flight from Dollington, and remained in London, under, I presume, his protection for some time.'

'That statement, Sir, is, I happen to *know*, utterly contrary to fact. The young lady you mention never even saw Mr. Mark Wylder, since she took leave of him in the drawing-room at Brandon; and I state this not in vindication of her, but to lend weight to the caution I give you against ever again presuming to connect her name with your surmises.'

The peer's countenance was so inexpressibly stern, and his eyes poured such a stream of fire upon the attorney, that he shrank a little, and looked down upon his great fingers which were drumming, let us hope, some sacred music upon the table.

'I am truly rejoiced, my lord, to hear you say so. Except to the young party herself, and in this presence, I have never mentioned it; and I can show you the evidence on which my conclusions rested.'

'Thank you—no Sir; my evidence is conclusive.'

I don't know what Mr. Larkin would have thought of it; it was simply Rachel's letter to her friend Dolly Wylder on the subject of the attorney's conference with her at Redman's Farm. It was a frank and passionate denial of the slander, breathing undefinably, but irresistibly, the spirit of truth.

'Then am I to understand, in conclusion,' said the attorney, 'that defying all consequences, the Rev. Mr. Wylder refuses to execute the deed of sale?'

'Certainly,' said Lord Chelford, taking this reply upon himself.

'You know, my dear Mr. Wylder, I told you from the first that Messrs. Burlington and Smith were, in fact, a very sharp house ; and I fear they will execute any powers they possess in the most summary manner.' The attorney's eye was upon the vicar as he spoke, but Lord Chelford answered.

'The powers you speak of are quite without parallel in a negotiation to purchase ; and in the event of their hazarding such a measure, the Rev. Mr. Wylder will apply to a court of equity to arrest their proceedings. My own solicitor is retained in the case.'

'Mr. Larkin's countenance darkened and lengthened visibly, and his eyes assumed their most unpleasant expression, and there was a little pause, during which, forgetting his lofty ways, he bit his thumb-nail rather viciously.

'Then I am to understand, my lord, that I am superseded in the management of this case?' said the attorney at last, in a measured way, which seemed to say, 'you had better think twice on this point.'

'Certainly, Mr. Larkin,' said the viscount.

'I'm not the least surprised, knowing, I am sorry to say, a good deal of the ways of the world, and expecting very little gratitude, for either good will or services.' This was accompanied with a melancholy sneer directed full upon the poor vicar, who did not half understand the situation, and looked rather guilty and frightened. 'The Rev. Mr. Wylder very well knows with what reluctance I touched the case—a nasty case ; and I must be permitted to add, that I am very happy to be quite rid of it, and only regret the manner in which my wish has been anticipated, a discourtesy which I attribute, however, to female influence.'

The concluding sentence was spoken with a vile sneer and a measured emphasis directed at Lord Chelford, who coloured with a sudden access of indignation, and stood stern and menacing, as the attorney, with a general bow to the company, and a lofty *nonchalance*, made his exit from the apartment.

Captain Lake was sinking very fast next morning. He made a statement to Chelford, who was a magistrate for the county, I suppose to assist the coroner's inquest. He said that on the night of Mark Wylder's last visit to Brandon, he had accompanied him from the Hall ; that Mark had seen some one in the neighbourhood of Gylingden, a person pretending to be his wife, or some near relative of hers, as well as he, Captain Lake, could understand, and was resolved to go to London privately, and have the matter arranged there. He waited near the 'White House,' while he, Stanley Lake, went to Gylingden and got his tax-cart at his desire. He could give particulars as to that. Captain Lake overtook him, and he got in and was driven to Dollington, where he took the up-train. That some weeks afterwards he saw him at Brighton ; and the night before last, by appointment, in the grounds of Brandon ; and that he understood Larkin had some lights to throw upon the same subject.

The jury were not sworn until two o'clock. The circumstances of the discovery of the body were soon established. But the question which next arose was very perplexed—was the body that of Mr. Mark Wylder? There could be no doubt as to a general resemblance ; but, though marvellously preserved, in its then state, certainty was hardly attainable. But there was a perfectly satisfactory identification of the dress and properties of the corpse as those of Mr. Mark Wylder. On the other hand there was the testimony of Lord Chelford, who put Captain Lake's deposition in evidence, as also the testimony of Larkin, and the equally precise evidence of Larcom, the butler.

The proceedings had reached this point when an occurrence took place which startled Lord Chelford, Larkin, Larcom, and every one in the room who was familiar with Mark Wylder's appearance.

A man pushed his way to the front of the crowd, and for a moment it seemed that Mark Wylder stood living before them.

'Who are you?' said Lord Chelford.

'Jim Dutton, Sir ; I come by reason of what I read in the "Chronicle" over night, about Mr. Mark Wylder being found.'

'Do you know anything of him?' asked the coroner.

'Nowt,' answered the man bluffly, 'only I writ to Mr. Larkin, there, as I wanted to see him. I remember him well when I was a boy. I seed him in the train from Lunnon t'other night ; and he seed me on the Shillingsworth platform, and I think he took me for some one else. I was comin' down to see the Captain at Brandon—and seed him the same night.'

'Why have you come here?' asked the coroner.

'Thinkin' I might be mistook,' answered the man. 'I *was* twice here in England, and three times abroad.'

'For whom?'

'Mr. Mark Wylder,' answered he.

'It is a wonderful likeness,' said Lord Chelford.

Larkin stared at him with his worst expression ; and Larcom, I think, thought he was the devil.

I was as much surprised as any for a few seconds. But there were points of difference—Jim Dutton was rather a taller and every way a larger man than Mark Wylder. His face, too, was broader and coarser, but in features and limbs the relative proportions were wonderfully preserved. It was such an exaggerated portrait as a rustic genius might have executed upon a sign-board. He had the same black, curly hair, and thick, black whiskers : and the style of his dress being the same, helped the illusion. In fact, it was a rough, but powerful likeness — startling at the moment—unexceptionable at a little distance—but which failed on a nearer and exacter examination

There was, beside, a scar, which, however, was not a very glaring inconsistency, although it was plainly of a much older standing than the date of Mark's disappearance. All that could be got from Jim Dutton was that 'he thought he might be mistook,' and so attended. But respecting Mr. Mark Wylder he could say 'nowt.' He knew 'nowt.'

Lord Chelford was called away at this moment by an urgent note. It was to request his immediate attendance at Redman's Farm, to see Captain Lake, who was in a most alarming state. The hand was Dorcas's—and Lord Chelford jumped into the little pony carriage which awaited him at the door of the ' Silver Lion.'

When he reached Redman's Farm, Captain Lake could not exert himself sufficiently to speak for nearly half-an-hour. At the end of that time he was admitted into the tiny drawing-room in which the captain lay. He was speaking with difficulty.

' Did you see Buddle, just now ? '

' No, not since morning.'

' He seems to have changed—bad opinion—unless he has a *law* object — those d — d doctors — never can know. Dorcas thinks—I'll do no good. Don't you think—he may have an object—and not believe I'm in much danger ? You don't ? '

Lake's hand, with which he clutched and pulled Chelford's, was trembling.

' You must reflect, my dear Lake, how very severe are the injuries you have sustained. You certainly *are* in danger—*great* danger.'

Lake became indescribably agitated, and uttered some words, not often on his lips, that sounded like desperate words of supplication. Not that seaworthy faith which floats the spirit through the storm, but fragments of its long-buried wreck rolled up from the depths and flung madly on the howling shore.

' I'd like to see Rachel,' at last he said, holding Chelford's hand in both his, very hard. ' She's clever — and I don't think she gives me up yet, no—a drink !—and they think I'm more hurt than I really am—Buddle, you know—only an apothecary —village ; ' and he groaned.

His old friend, Sir Francis Seddley, summoned by the telegraph, was now gliding from London along the rails for Dollington station ; but another—a pale courier — on the sightless coursers of the air, was speeding with a different message to Captain Stanley Lake, in the small and sombre drawing-room in Redman's Dell.

I had promised Chelford to run up to Redman's Farm, and let him know if the jury arrived at a verdict during his absence. They did so ; finding that the body was that of Marcus Wylder, Esquire, of Raddiston, and 'that he had come by his death in consequence of two wounds inflicted with a sharp instrument, in the region of the heart, by some person or persons unknown, at a period of four weeks since or upwards.'

Chelford was engaged in the sick room, as I understood, in conference with the patient. It was well to have heard, without procrastination, what he had to say ; for next morning, at a little past four o'clock, he died.

A nurse who had been called in from the county infirmary, said he made a very happy ending. He mumbled to himself, in his drowsy state, as she was quite sure, in prayer ; and he made a very pretty corpse when he was laid out, and his golden hair looked so nice, and he was all so slim and shapely.

Rachel and Dorcas were sitting in the room with him—not expecting the catastrophe then. Both tired ; both silent ; the nurse dozing a little in her chair, near the bed's head ; and Lake said, in his clear, low tone, on a sudden, just as he spoke when perfectly well—

'Quite a mistake, upon my honour.'

As a clear-voiced sentence sometimes speaks out in sleep, followed by silence, so no more was heard after this—no more for ever. The nurse was the first to perceive 'the change.'

'There's a change, Ma'am'—and there was a pause. 'I'm afraid, Ma'am, he's gone,' said the nurse.

Both ladies, in an instant, were at the bedside, looking at the peaked and white countenance, which was all they were ever again to see of Stanley ; the yellow eyes and open mouth.

Rachel's agony broke forth in a loud, wild cry. All was forgotten and forgiven in that tremendous moment.

'Oh ! Stanley, Stanley !—brother, brother, oh, brother !'

There was the unchanged face, gaping its awful farewell of earth. All over !—never to stir more.

'Is he dead?' said Dorcas, with the peculiar sternness of agony.

There could be no doubt. It was a sight too familiar to deceive the nurse.

And Dorcas closed those strange, wild eyes that had so fatally fascinated her, and then she trembled, without speaking or shedding a tear. Her looks alarmed the nurse, who, with Rachel's help, persuaded her to leave the room. And then came one of those wild scenes which close such tragedies—paroxysms of despair and frantic love, over that worthless young man who lay dead below stairs ; such as strike us sometimes with a desolate scepticism, and make us fancy that all affection is illusion, and perishable with the deceits and vanities of earth.

CHAPTER LXXIV.

WE TAKE LEAVE OF OUR FRIENDS.

THE story which, in his last interview with Lord Chelford, Stanley Lake had related, was, probably, as near the truth as he was capable of telling.

On the night when Mark Wylder had left Brandon in his company they had some angry talk ; Lake's object being to induce Mark to abandon his engagement with Dorcas Brandon. He told Stanley that he would not give up Dorcas, but that he, Lake, must fight him, and go to Boulogne for the purpose, and they should arrange matters so that one or other *must* fall. Lake laughed quietly at the proposition, and Mark retorted by telling him he would so insult him, if he declined, as to compel a meeting. When they reached that lonely path near the flight of stone steps, Stanley distinctly threatened his companion with a disclosure of the scandalous incident in the card-room of the club, which he afterwards related, substantially as it had happened, to Jos. Larkin. When he took this decisive step, Lake's nerves were strung, I dare say, to a high pitch of excitement. Mark Wylder, he knew, carried pistols, and, all things considered, he thought it just possible he might use them. He did not, but he struck Lake with the back of his hand in the face, and Lake, who walked by his side, with his fingers on the handle of a dagger in his coat pocket, instantly retorted with a stab, which he repeated as Mark fell.

He solemnly averred that he never meant to have used the dagger, except to defend his life. That he struck in a state of utter confusion, and when he saw Mark dead, with his feet on the path, and his head lying over the edge, he would have given a limb almost to bring him back. The terror of discovery and ruin instantly supervened.

He propped the body against the bank, and tried to stanch the bleeding. But there could be no doubt that he was actually dead. He got the body easily down the nearly precipitous declivity. Lake was naturally by no means wanting in resource, and a certain sort of coolness, which supervened when the momentary distraction was over.

He knew it would not do to leave the body so, among the rocks and brambles. He recollected that only fifty yards back they had passed a spade and pick, lying, with some other tools, by the side of the path, near that bit of old wall which was being removed. Like a man doing things in a dream, without thought or trouble, only waiting and listening for a moment before he disturbed them, he took away the implements which he required ; and when about to descend, a sort of panic and insurmountable disgust seized him ; and in a state of supernatural dismay, he felt for a while disposed to kill himself. In that state it was he reached Redman's Farm, and his interview with Rachel occurred. It was the accidental disclosure of the blood, in which his shirt sleeve was soaked, that first opened Rachel's eyes to the frightful truth.

After her first shock, all her terrors were concentrated on the one point—Stanley's imminent danger. He must be saved. She made him return ; she even accompanied him as far as the top of the rude flight of steps I have mentioned so often, and there awaited his return—the condition imposed by his cowardice—and made more dreadful by the circumstance that they had heard retreating footsteps along the walk, and Stanley saw the tall figure of Uncle Julius or Lorne, as he called himself, turning the far corner.

There was a long wait here, lest he should return ; but he did not appear, and Stanley — though I now believe observed by this strange being—executed his horrible task, replaced the implements, and returned to Rachel, and with her to Redman's Farm ; where—his cool cunning once more ascendant—he penned those forgeries, closing them with Mark Wylder's seal, which he compelled his sister — quite unconscious of all but that their despatch by post, at the periods pencilled upon them, was essential to her wretched brother's escape. It was the success of this, his first stratagem, which suggested that long series of frauds which, with the aid of Jim Dutton, selected for his striking points of resemblance to Mark Wylder, had been carried on for so long with such consummate art in a different field.

It was Lake's ungoverned fury, when Larkin discovered the mistake in posting the letters in wrong succession, which so nearly exploded his ingenious system. He wrote in terms which roused Jim Dutton's wrath. Jim had been spinning theories about the reasons of his mysterious, though very agreeable occupation, and announced them broadly in his letter to Larkin. But he had cooled by the time he reached London, and the letter from Lake, received at his mother's and appointing the meeting at Brandon, quieted that mutiny.

I never heard that Jim gave any member of the family the least trouble afterward. He handed to Lord Chelford a parcel of those clever and elaborate forgeries, with which Lake had last furnished him, with a pencilled note on each, directing the date and town at which it was to be despatched. Years after, when Jim was emigrating, I believe Lord Chelford gave him a handsome present.

Lord Chelford was advised by the friend whom he consulted

that he need not make those painful particulars public, affecting only a dead man, and leading to no result.

Lake admitted that Rachel had posted the letters in London, believing them to be genuine, for he pretended that they were Wylder's. It is easy to look grave over poor Rachel's slight, and partly unconscious, share in the business of the tragedy. But what girl of energy and strong affections would have had the melancholy courage to surrender her brother to public justice under the circumstances? Lord Chelford, who knew all, says that she 'acted nobly.'

'Now, Joseph, being a just man, was minded to put her away privily.' The *law* being what? That she was to be publicly stigmatised and punished. His *justice* being what? Simply that he would have her to be neither—but screened and parted 'with privily.' Let the Pharisees who would have *summum jus* against their neighbours, rememember that God regards the tender and compassionate, who forbears, on occasion, to put the law in motion, as the *just* man.

The good vicar is a great territorial magnate now; but his pleasures and all his ways are still simple. He never would enter Brandon as its master, and never will, during Dorcas Brandon's lifetime. And although with her friend, Rachel Lake, she lives abroad, chiefly in Italy and Switzerland, Brandon Hall, by the command of its proprietor, lies always at her disposal.

I don't know whether Rachel Lake will ever marry. The tragic shadow of her life has not chilled Lord Chelford's strong affection. Neither does the world know or suspect anything of the matter. Old Tamar died three years since, and lies in the pretty little churchyard of Gylingden. And Mark's death is, by this time, a nearly forgotten mystery.

Jos. Larkins's speculations have not turned out luckily. The trustees of Wylder, a minor, tried, as they were advised they must, his title to Five Oaks, by ejectment. A point had been overlooked—as sometimes happens—and Jos. Larkin was found to have taken but an estate for the life of Mark Wylder, which terminated at his decease. The point was carried on to the House of Lords, but the decision of 'the court below' was ultimately affirmed.

The flexible and angry Jos. Larkin then sought to recoup himself out of the assets of the deceased captain; but here he failed. In his cleverness—lest the inadequate purchase-money should upset his bargain—he omitted the usual covenant guaranteeing the vendor's title to sell the fee-simple, and recited, moreover, that, grave doubts existing on the point, it was agreed that the sum paid should not exceed twelve years' purchase. Jos. then could only go upon the point that it was known to Lake at the period of the sale that Mark Wylder was dead. Unluckily, however, for Jos.'s case, one of his clever letters, written during the negotiation, turned up, and was put in evidence, in which he pressed Captain Lake with the fact, that he, the purchaser, was actually in possession of information to the effect that Mark was dead, and that he was, therefore, buying under a liability of having his title litigated, with a doubtful result, the moment he should enter into possession. This shut up the admirable man, who next tried a rather bold measure, directed against the Reverend William Wylder. A bill was filed by Messrs. Burlington and Smith, to compel him to execute a conveyance to their client—on the terms of the agreement. The step was evidently taken on the calculation that he would strike, and offer a handsome compromise; but Lord Chelford was at his elbow—the suit was resisted. Messrs. Burlington and Smith did not care to run the awful risk which Mr. Larkin, behind the scenes, invited them to accept for his sake. There was first a faltering; then a bold renunciation and exposure of Mr. Jos. Larkin by the firm, who, though rather lamely, exonerated themselves as having been quite taken in by the Gylingden attorney.

Mr. Jos. Larkin had a holy reliance upon his religious reputation, which had always stood him in stead. But a worldly Judge will sometimes disappoint the expectations of the Christian suitor; and the language of the Court, in commenting upon Mr. Jos. Larkin, was, I am sorry to say, in the highest degree offensive—'flagitious,' 'fraudulent,' and kindred epithets, were launched against that tall, bald head, in a storm that darkened the air and obliterated the halo that usually encircled it. He was dismissed, in a tempest, with costs. He vanished from court, like an evil spirit, into the torture-chamber of taxation.

The whole structure of rapine and duplicity had fallen through with a dismal crash. Shrewd fellows wondered, as they always do, when a rash game breaks down, at the infatuation of the performer. But the cup of his tribulation was not yet quite full. Jos. Larkin's name was ultimately struck from the roll of solicitors and attorneys, and there were minute and merciless essays in the papers, surrounding his disgrace with a dreadful glare. People say he has not enough left to go on with. He had lodgings somewhere near Richmond, as Howard Larkin, Esq., and is still a religious character. I am told that he shifts his place of residence about once in six months, and that he has never paid one shilling of rent for any, and has sometimes positively received money for vacating his abode. So substantially valuable is a thorough acquaintance with the capabilities of the law. I saw honest Tom Wealdon about a fortnight ago—grown stouter and somewhat more phlegmatic by time, but still the same in good nature and inquisitiveness. From him I learned that Jos. Larkin is likely to figure once more in the courts about some very ugly defalcations in the cash of the Penningstal Mining Company, and that this time the persecutions of that eminent Christian are likely to take a different turn, and, as Tom said, with a gloomy shrewdness, to end in 'ten years penal.'

Some summers ago, I was, for a few days, in the wondrous city of Venice. Everyone knows something of the enchantment of the Italian moon, the expanse of dark and flashing blue, and the phantasmal city, rising like a beautiful spirit from the waters. Gliding near the Lido—where so many rings of Doges lie lost beneath the waves—I heard the pleasant sound of female voices upon the water—and then, with a sudden glory, rose a sad, wild hymn, like the musical wail of the forsaken sea :—

> The spouseless Adriatic mourns her lord.

The song ceased. The gondola which bore the musicians floated by—a slender hand over the gunwale trailed its fingers in the water. Unseen I saw. Rachel and Dorcas, beautiful in the sad moonlight, passed so near we could have spoken—passed me like spirits—never more, it may be, to cross my sight in life.

THE END

A CATALOGUE OF SELECTED DOVER BOOKS
IN ALL FIELDS OF INTEREST

A CATALOGUE OF SELECTED DOVER
BOOKS IN ALL FIELDS OF INTEREST

CELESTIAL OBJECTS FOR COMMON TELESCOPES, T. W. Webb. The most used book in amateur astronomy: inestimable aid for locating and identifying nearly 4,000 celestial objects. Edited, updated by Margaret W. Mayall. 77 illustrations. Total of 645pp. 5⅜ x 8½.

20917-2, 20918-0 Pa., Two-vol. set $8.00

HISTORICAL STUDIES IN THE LANGUAGE OF CHEMISTRY, M. P. Crosland. The important part language has played in the development of chemistry from the symbolism of alchemy to the adoption of systematic nomenclature in 1892. ". . . wholeheartedly recommended,"—Science. 15 illustrations. 416pp. of text. 5⅝ x 8¼.

63702-6 Pa. $6.00

BURNHAM'S CELESTIAL HANDBOOK, Robert Burnham, Jr. Thorough, readable guide to the stars beyond our solar system. Exhaustive treatment, fully illustrated. Breakdown is alphabetical by constellation: Andromeda to Cetus in Vol. 1; Chamaeleon to Orion in Vol. 2; and Pavo to Vulpecula in Vol. 3. Hundreds of illustrations. Total of about 2000pp. 6⅛ x 9¼.

23567-X, 23568-8, 23673-0 Pa., Three-vol. set $26.85

THEORY OF WING SECTIONS: INCLUDING A SUMMARY OF AIR-FOIL DATA, Ira H. Abbott and A. E. von Doenhoff. Concise compilation of subatomic aerodynamic characteristics of modern NASA wing sections, plus description of theory. 350pp. of tables. 693pp. 5⅜ x 8½.

60586-8 Pa. $6.50

DE RE METALLICA, Georgius Agricola. Translated by Herbert C. Hoover and Lou H. Hoover. The famous Hoover translation of greatest treatise on technological chemistry, engineering, geology, mining of early modern times (1556). All 289 original woodcuts. 638pp. 6¾ x 11.

60006-8 Clothbd. $17.50

THE ORIGIN OF CONTINENTS AND OCEANS, Alfred Wegener. One of the most influential, most controversial books in science, the classic statement for continental drift. Full 1966 translation of Wegener's final (1929) version. 64 illustrations. 246pp. 5⅜ x 8½. 61708-4 Pa. $3.00

THE PRINCIPLES OF PSYCHOLOGY, William James. Famous long course complete, unabridged. Stream of thought, time perception, memory, experimental methods; great work decades ahead of its time. Still valid, useful; read in many classes. 94 figures. Total of 1391pp. 5⅜ x 8½.

20381-6, 20382-4 Pa., Two-vol. set $13.00

THE SENSE OF BEAUTY, George Santayana. Masterfully written discussion of nature of beauty, materials of beauty, form, expression; art, literature, social sciences all involved. 168pp. 5⅜ x 8½. 20238-0 Pa. $2.50

ON THE IMPROVEMENT OF THE UNDERSTANDING, Benedict Spinoza. Also contains *Ethics, Correspondence,* all in excellent R. Elwes translation. Basic works on entry to philosophy, pantheism, exchange of ideas with great contemporaries. 402pp. 5⅜ x 8½. 20250-X Pa. $3.75

THE TRAGIC SENSE OF LIFE, Miguel de Unamuno. Acknowledged masterpiece of existential literature, one of most important books of 20th century. Introduction by Madariaga. 367pp. 5⅜ x 8½.
20257-7 Pa. $3.50

THE GUIDE FOR THE PERPLEXED, Moses Maimonides. Great classic of medieval Judaism attempts to reconcile revealed religion (Pentateuch, commentaries) with Aristotelian philosophy. Important historically, still relevant in problems. Unabridged Friedlander translation. Total of 473pp. 5⅜ x 8½. 20351-4 Pa. $5.00

THE I CHING (THE BOOK OF CHANGES), translated by James Legge. Complete translation of basic text plus appendices by Confucius, and Chinese commentary of most penetrating divination manual ever prepared. Indispensable to study of early Oriental civilizations, to modern inquiring reader. 448pp. 5⅜ x 8½. 21062-6 Pa. $4.00

THE EGYPTIAN BOOK OF THE DEAD, E. A. Wallis Budge. Complete reproduction of Ani's papyrus, finest ever found. Full hieroglyphic text, interlinear transliteration, word for word translation, smooth translation. Basic work, for Egyptology, for modern study of psychic matters. Total of 533pp. 6½ x 9¼. (Available in U.S. only) 21866-X Pa. $4.95

THE GODS OF THE EGYPTIANS, E. A. Wallis Budge. Never excelled for richness, fullness: all gods, goddesses, demons, mythical figures of Ancient Egypt; their legends, rites, incarnations, variations, powers, etc. Many hieroglyphic texts cited. Over 225 illustrations, plus 6 color plates. Total of 988pp. 6⅛ x 9¼. (Available in U.S. only)
22055-9, 22056-7 Pa., Two-vol. set $12.00

THE ENGLISH AND SCOTTISH POPULAR BALLADS, Francis J. Child. Monumental, still unsuperseded; all known variants of Child ballads, commentary on origins, literary references, Continental parallels, other features. Added: papers by G. L. Kittredge, W. M. Hart. Total of 2761pp. 6½ x 9¼.
21409-5, 21410-9, 21411-7, 21412-5, 21413-3 Pa., Five-vol. set $37.50

CORAL GARDENS AND THEIR MAGIC, Bronsilaw Malinowski. Classic study of the methods of tilling the soil and of agricultural rites in the Trobriand Islands of Melanesia. Author is one of the most important figures in the field of modern social anthropology. 143 illustrations. Indexes. Total of 911pp. of text. 5⅝ x 8¼. (Available in U.S. only)
23597-1 Pa. $12.95

THE PHILOSOPHY OF HISTORY, Georg W. Hegel. Great classic of Western thought develops concept that history is not chance but a rational process, the evolution of freedom. 457pp. 5⅜ x 8½. 20112-0 Pa. $4.50

LANGUAGE, TRUTH AND LOGIC, Alfred J. Ayer. Famous, clear introduction to Vienna, Cambridge schools of Logical Positivism. Role of philosophy, elimination of metaphysics, nature of analysis, etc. 160pp. 5⅜ x 8½. (Available in U.S. only) 20010-8 Pa. $1.75

A PREFACE TO LOGIC, Morris R. Cohen. Great City College teacher in renowned, easily followed exposition of formal logic, probability, values, logic and world order and similar topics; no previous background needed. 209pp. 5⅜ x 8½. 23517-3 Pa. $3.50

REASON AND NATURE, Morris R. Cohen. Brilliant analysis of reason and its multitudinous ramifications by charismatic teacher. Interdisciplinary, synthesizing work widely praised when it first appeared in 1931. Second (1953) edition. Indexes. 496pp. 5⅜ x 8½. 23633-1 Pa. $6.00

AN ESSAY CONCERNING HUMAN UNDERSTANDING, John Locke. The only complete edition of enormously important classic, with authoritative editorial material by A. C. Fraser. Total of 1176pp. 5⅜ x 8½. 20530-4, 20531-2 Pa., Two-vol. set $14.00

HANDBOOK OF MATHEMATICAL FUNCTIONS WITH FORMULAS, GRAPHS, AND MATHEMATICAL TABLES, edited by Milton Abramowitz and Irene A. Stegun. Vast compendium: 29 sets of tables, some to as high as 20 places. 1,046pp. 8 x 10½. 61272-4 Pa. $12.50

MATHEMATICS FOR THE PHYSICAL SCIENCES, Herbert S. Wilf. Highly acclaimed work offers clear presentations of vector spaces and matrices, orthogonal functions, roots of polynomial equations, conformal mapping, calculus of variations, etc. Knowledge of theory of functions of real and complex variables is assumed. Exercises and solutions. Index. 284pp. 5⅝ x 8¼. 63635-6 Pa. $4.50

THE PRINCIPLE OF RELATIVITY, Albert Einstein et al. Eleven most important original papers on special and general theories. Seven by Einstein, two by Lorentz, one each by Minkowski and Weyl. All translated, unabridged. 216pp. 5⅜ x 8½. 60081-5 Pa. $3.00

THERMODYNAMICS, Enrico Fermi. A classic of modern science. Clear, organized treatment of systems, first and second laws, entropy, thermodynamic potentials, gaseous reactions, dilute solutions, entropy constant. No math beyond calculus required. Problems. 160pp. 5⅜ x 8½. 60361-X Pa. $2.75

ELEMENTARY MECHANICS OF FLUIDS, Hunter Rouse. Classic undergraduate text widely considered to be far better than many later books. Ranges from fluid velocity and acceleration to role of compressibility in fluid motion. Numerous examples, questions, problems. 224 illustrations. 376pp. 5⅝ x 8¼. 63699-2 Pa. $5.00

THE COMPLETE BOOK OF DOLL MAKING AND COLLECTING, Catherine Christopher. Instructions, patterns for dozens of dolls, from rag doll on up to elaborate, historically accurate figures. Mould faces, sew clothing, make doll houses, etc. Also collecting information. Many illustrations. 288pp. 6 x 9. 22066-4 Pa. $4.00

THE DAGUERREOTYPE IN AMERICA, Beaumont Newhall. Wonderful portraits, 1850's townscapes, landscapes; full text plus 104 photographs. The basic book. Enlarged 1976 edition. 272pp. 8¼ x 11¼. 23322-7 Pa. $6.00

CRAFTSMAN HOMES, Gustav Stickley. 296 architectural drawings, floor plans, and photographs illustrate 40 different kinds of "Mission-style" homes from The Craftsman (1901-16), voice of American style of simplicity and organic harmony. Thorough coverage of Craftsman idea in text and picture, now collector's item. 224pp. 8⅛ x 11. 23791-5 Pa. $6.00

PEWTER-WORKING: INSTRUCTIONS AND PROJECTS, Burl N. Osborn. & Gordon O. Wilber. Introduction to pewter-working for amateur craftsman. History and characteristics of pewter; tools, materials, step-by-step instructions. Photos, line drawings, diagrams. Total of 160pp. 7⅞ x 10¾. 23786-9 Pa. $3.50

THE GREAT CHICAGO FIRE, edited by David Lowe. 10 dramatic, eyewitness accounts of the 1871 disaster, including one of the aftermath and rebuilding, plus 70 contemporary photographs and illustrations of the ruins—courthouse, Palmer House, Great Central Depot, etc. Introduction by David Lowe. 87pp. 8¼ x 11. 23771-0 Pa. $4.00

SILHOUETTES: A PICTORIAL ARCHIVE OF VARIED ILLUSTRATIONS, edited by Carol Belanger Grafton. Over 600 silhouettes from the 18th to 20th centuries include profiles and full figures of men and women, children, birds and animals, groups and scenes, nature, ships, an alphabet. Dozens of uses for commercial artists and craftspeople. 144pp. 8⅜ x 11¼. 23781-8 Pa. $4.00

ANIMALS: 1,419 COPYRIGHT-FREE ILLUSTRATIONS OF MAMMALS, BIRDS, FISH, INSECTS, ETC., edited by Jim Harter. Clear wood engravings present, in extremely lifelike poses, over 1,000 species of animals. One of the most extensive copyright-free pictorial sourcebooks of its kind. Captions. Index. 284pp. 9 x 12. 23766-4 Pa. $7.50

INDIAN DESIGNS FROM ANCIENT ECUADOR, Frederick W. Shaffer. 282 original designs by pre-Columbian Indians of Ecuador (500-1500 A.D.). Designs include people, mammals, birds, reptiles, fish, plants, heads, geometric designs. Use as is or alter for advertising, textiles, leathercraft, etc. Introduction. 95pp. 8¾ x 11¼. 23764-8 Pa. $3.50

SZIGETI ON THE VIOLIN, Joseph Szigeti. Genial, loosely structured tour by premier violinist, featuring a pleasant mixture of reminiscenes, insights into great music and musicians, innumerable tips for practicing violinists. 385 musical passages. 256pp. 5⅝ x 8¼. 23763-X Pa. $3.50

TONE POEMS, SERIES II: TILL EULENSPIEGELS LUSTIGE STREICHE, ALSO SPRACH ZARATHUSTRA, AND EIN HELDEN-LEBEN, Richard Strauss. Three important orchestral works, including very popular *Till Eulenspiegel's Marry Pranks,* reproduced in full score from original editions. Study score. 315pp. 9⅜ x 12¼. (Available in U.S. only)
23755-9 Pa. $7.50

TONE POEMS, SERIES I: DON JUAN, TOD UND VERKLARUNG AND DON QUIXOTE, Richard Strauss. Three of the most often performed and recorded works in entire orchestral repertoire, reproduced in full score from original editions. Study score. 286pp. 9⅜ x 12¼. (Available in U.S. only)
23754-0 Pa. $7.50

11 LATE STRING QUARTETS, Franz Joseph Haydn. The form which Haydn defined and "brought to perfection." *(Grove's).* 11 string quartets in complete score, his last and his best. The first in a projected series of the complete Haydn string quartets. Reliable modern Eulenberg edition, otherwise difficult to obtain. 320pp. 8⅜ x 11¼. (Available in U.S. only)
23753-2 Pa. $6.95

FOURTH, FIFTH AND SIXTH SYMPHONIES IN FULL SCORE, Peter Ilyitch Tchaikovsky. Complete orchestral scores of Symphony No. 4 in F Minor, Op. 36; Symphony No. 5 in E Minor, Op. 64; Symphony No. 6 in B Minor, "Pathetique," Op. 74. Bretikopf & Hartel eds. Study score. 480pp. 9⅜ x 12¼.
23861-X Pa. $10.95

THE MARRIAGE OF FIGARO: COMPLETE SCORE, Wolfgang A. Mozart. Finest comic opera ever written. Full score, not to be confused with piano renderings. Peters edition. Study score. 448pp. 9⅜ x 12¼. (Available in U.S. only)
23751-6 Pa. $11.95

"IMAGE" ON THE ART AND EVOLUTION OF THE FILM, edited by Marshall Deutelbaum. Pioneering book brings together for first time 38 groundbreaking articles on early silent films from *Image* and 263 illustrations newly shot from rare prints in the collection of the International Museum of Photography. A landmark work. Index. 256pp. 8¼ x 11.
23777-X Pa. $8.95

AROUND-THE-WORLD COOKY BOOK, Lois Lintner Sumption and Marguerite Lintner Ashbrook. 373 cooky and frosting recipes from 28 countries (America, Austria, China, Russia, Italy, etc.) include Viennese kisses, rice wafers, London strips, lady fingers, hony, sugar spice, maple cookies, etc. Clear instructions. All tested. 38 drawings. 182pp. 5⅜ x 8.
23802-4 Pa. $2.50

THE ART NOUVEAU STYLE, edited by Roberta Waddell. 579 rare photographs, not available elsewhere, of works in jewelry, metalwork, glass, ceramics, textiles, architecture and furniture by 175 artists—Mucha, Seguy, Lalique, Tiffany, Gaudin, Hohlwein, Saarinen, and many others. 288pp. 8⅜ x 11¼.
23515-7 Pa. $6.95

THE AMERICAN SENATOR, Anthony Trollope. Little known, long un-available Trollope novel on a grand scale. Here are humorous comment on American vs. English culture, and stunning portrayal of a heroine/villainess. Superb evocation of Victorian village life. 561pp. 5⅜ x 8½.
23801-6 Pa. $6.00

WAS IT MURDER? James Hilton. The author of *Lost Horizon* and *Good-bye, Mr. Chips* wrote one detective novel (under a pen-name) which was quickly forgotten and virtually lost, even at the height of Hilton's fame. This edition brings it back—a finely crafted public school puzzle resplendent with Hilton's stylish atmosphere. A thoroughly English thriller by the creator of Shangri-la. 252pp. 5⅜ x 8. (Available in U.S. only)
23774-5 Pa. $3.00

CENTRAL PARK: A PHOTOGRAPHIC GUIDE, Victor Laredo and Henry Hope Reed. 121 superb photographs show dramatic views of Central Park: Bethesda Fountain, Cleopatra's Needle, Sheep Meadow, the Blockhouse, plus people engaged in many park activities: ice skating, bike riding, etc. Captions by former Curator of Central Park, Henry Hope Reed, provide historical view, changes, etc. Also photos of N.Y. landmarks on park's periphery. 96pp. 8½ x 11.
23750-8 Pa. $4.50

NANTUCKET IN THE NINETEENTH CENTURY, Clay Lancaster. 180 rare photographs, stereographs, maps, drawings and floor plans recreate unique American island society. Authentic scenes of shipwreck, light-houses, streets, homes are arranged in geographic sequence to provide walking-tour guide to old Nantucket existing today. Introduction, captions. 160pp. 8⅞ x 11¾.
23747-8 Pa. $6.95

STONE AND MAN: A PHOTOGRAPHIC EXPLORATION, Andreas Feininger. 106 photographs by *Life* photographer Feininger portray man's deep passion for stone through the ages. Stonehenge-like megaliths, fortified towns, sculpted marble and crumbling tenements show textures, beauties, fascination. 128pp. 9¼ x 10¾.
23756-7 Pa. $5.95

CIRCLES, A MATHEMATICAL VIEW, D. Pedoe. Fundamental aspects of college geometry, non-Euclidean geometry, and other branches of mathematics: representing circle by point. Poincare model, isoperimetric property, etc. Stimulating recreational reading. 66 figures. 96pp. 5⅝ x 8¼.
63698-4 Pa. $2.75

THE DISCOVERY OF NEPTUNE, Morton Grosser. Dramatic scientific history of the investigations leading up to the actual discovery of the eighth planet of our solar system. Lucid, well-researched book by well-known historian of science. 172pp. 5⅜ x 8½.
23726-5 Pa. $3.00

THE DEVIL'S DICTIONARY. Ambrose Bierce. Barbed, bitter, brilliant witticisms in the form of a dictionary. Best, most ferocious satire America has produced. 145pp. 5⅜ x 8½.
20487-1 Pa. $1.75

HISTORY OF BACTERIOLOGY, William Bulloch. The only comprehensive history of bacteriology from the beginnings through the 19th century. Special emphasis is given to biography-Leeuwenhoek, etc. Brief accounts of 350 bacteriologists form a separate section. No clearer, fuller study, suitable to scientists and general readers, has yet been written. 52 illustrations. 448pp. 5⅝ x 8¼.   23761-3 Pa. $6.50

THE COMPLETE NONSENSE OF EDWARD LEAR, Edward Lear. All nonsense limericks, zany alphabets, Owl and Pussycat, songs, nonsense botany, etc., illustrated by Lear. Total of 321pp. 5⅜ x 8½. (Available in U.S. only)   20167-8 Pa. $3.00

INGENIOUS MATHEMATICAL PROBLEMS AND METHODS, Louis A. Graham. Sophisticated material from Graham *Dial*, applied and pure; stresses solution methods. Logic, number theory, networks, inversions, etc. 237pp. 5⅜ x 8½.   20545-2 Pa. $3.50

BEST MATHEMATICAL PUZZLES OF SAM LOYD, edited by Martin Gardner. Bizarre, original, whimsical puzzles by America's greatest puzzler. From fabulously rare *Cyclopedia*, including famous 14-15 puzzles, the Horse of a Different Color, 115 more. Elementary math. 150 illustrations. 167pp. 5⅜ x 8½.   20498-7 Pa. $2.50

THE BASIS OF COMBINATION IN CHESS, J. du Mont. Easy-to-follow, instructive book on elements of combination play, with chapters on each piece and every powerful combination team—two knights, bishop and knight, rook and bishop, etc. 250 diagrams. 218pp. 5⅜ x 8½. (Available in U.S. only)   23644-7 Pa. $3.50

MODERN CHESS STRATEGY, Ludek Pachman. The use of the queen, the active king, exchanges, pawn play, the center, weak squares, etc. Section on rook alone worth price of the book. Stress on the moderns. Often considered the most important book on strategy. 314pp. 5⅜ x 8½.   20290-9 Pa. $3.50

LASKER'S MANUAL OF CHESS, Dr. Emanuel Lasker. Great world champion offers very thorough coverage of all aspects of chess. Combinations, position play, openings, end game, aesthetics of chess, philosophy of struggle, much more. Filled with analyzed games. 390pp. 5⅜ x 8½.   20640-8 Pa. $4.00

500 MASTER GAMES OF CHESS, S. Tartakower, J. du Mont. Vast collection of great chess games from 1798-1938, with much material nowhere else readily available. Fully annotated, arranged by opening for easier study. 664pp. 5⅜ x 8½.   23208-5 Pa. $6.00

A GUIDE TO CHESS ENDINGS, Dr. Max Euwe, David Hooper. One of the finest modern works on chess endings. Thorough analysis of the most frequently encountered endings by former world champion. 331 examples, each with diagram. 248pp. 5⅜ x 8½.   23332-4 Pa. $3.50

SECOND PIATIGORSKY CUP, edited by Isaac Kashdan. One of the greatest tournament books ever produced in the English language. All 90 games of the 1966 tournament, annotated by players, most annotated by both players. Features Petrosian, Spassky, Fischer, Larsen, six others. 228pp. 5⅜ x 8½. 23572-6 Pa. $3.50

ENCYCLOPEDIA OF CARD TRICKS, revised and edited by Jean Hugard. How to perform over 600 card tricks, devised by the world's greatest magicians: impromptus, spelling tricks, key cards, using special packs, much, much more. Additional chapter on card technique. 66 illustrations. 402pp. 5⅜ x 8½. (Available in U.S. only) 21252-1 Pa. $3.95

MAGIC: STAGE ILLUSIONS, SPECIAL EFFECTS AND TRICK PHO-TOGRAPHY, Albert A. Hopkins, Henry R. Evans. One of the great classics; fullest, most authorative explanation of vanishing lady, levitations, scores of other great stage effects. Also small magic, automata, stunts. 446 illustrations. 556pp. 5⅜ x 8½. 23344-8 Pa. $5.00

THE SECRETS OF HOUDINI, J. C. Cannell. Classic study of Houdini's incredible magic, exposing closely-kept professional secrets and revealing, in general terms, the whole art of stage magic. 67 illustrations. 279pp. 5⅜ x 8½. 22913-0 Pa. $3.00

HOFFMANN'S MODERN MAGIC, Professor Hoffmann. One of the best, and best-known, magicians' manuals of the past century. Hundreds of tricks from card tricks and simple sleight of hand to elaborate illusions involving construction of complicated machinery. 332 illustrations. 563pp. 5⅜ x 8½. 23623-4 Pa. $6.00

MADAME PRUNIER'S FISH COOKERY BOOK, Mme. S. B. Prunier. More than 1000 recipes from world famous Prunier's of Paris and London, specially adapted here for American kitchen. Grilled tournedos with anchovy butter, Lobster a la Bordelaise, Prunier's prized desserts, more. Glossary. 340pp. 5⅜ x 8½. (Available in U.S. only) 22679-4 Pa. $3.00

FRENCH COUNTRY COOKING FOR AMERICANS, Louis Diat. 500 easy-to-make, authentic provincial recipes compiled by former head chef at New York's Fitz-Carlton Hotel: onion soup, lamb stew, potato pie, more. 309pp. 5⅜ x 8½. 23665-X Pa. $3.95

SAUCES, FRENCH AND FAMOUS, Louis Diat. Complete book gives over 200 specific recipes: bechamel, Bordelaise, hollandaise, Cumberland, apricot, etc. Author was one of this century's finest chefs, originator of vichyssoise and many other dishes. Index. 156pp. 5⅜ x 8. 23663-3 Pa. $2.50

TOLL HOUSE TRIED AND TRUE RECIPES, Ruth Graves Wakefield. Authentic recipes from the famous Mass. restaurant: popovers, veal and ham loaf, Toll House baked beans, chocolate cake crumb pudding, much more. Many helpful hints. Nearly 700 recipes. Index. 376pp. 5⅜ x 8½. 23560-2 Pa. $4.00

"OSCAR" OF THE WALDORF'S COOKBOOK, Oscar Tschirky. Famous American chef reveals 3455 recipes that made Waldorf great; cream of French, German, American cooking, in all categories. Full instructions, easy home use. 1896 edition. 907pp. 6⅝ x 9⅜.   20790-0 Clothbd. $15.00

COOKING WITH BEER, Carole Fahy. Beer has as superb an effect on food as wine, and at fraction of cost. Over 250 recipes for appetizers, soups, main dishes, desserts, breads, etc. Index. 144pp. 5⅜ x 8½. (Available in U.S. only)   23661-7 Pa. $2.50

STEWS AND RAGOUTS, Kay Shaw Nelson. This international cookbook offers wide range of 108 recipes perfect for everyday, special occasions, meals-in-themselves, main dishes. Economical, nutritious, easy-to-prepare: goulash, Irish stew, boeuf bourguignon, etc. Index. 134pp. 5⅜ x 8½.   23662-5 Pa. $2.50

DELICIOUS MAIN COURSE DISHES, Marian Tracy. Main courses are the most important part of any meal. These 200 nutritious, economical recipes from around the world make every meal a delight. "I . . . have found it so useful in my own household,"—*N.Y. Times.* Index. 219pp. 5⅜ x 8½.   23664-1 Pa. $3.00

FIVE ACRES AND INDEPENDENCE, Maurice G. Kains. Great back-to-the-land classic explains basics of self-sufficient farming: economics, plants, crops, animals, orchards, soils, land selection, host of other necessary things. Do not confuse with skimpy faddist literature; Kains was one of America's greatest agriculturalists. 95 illustrations. 397pp. 5⅜ x 8½.   20974-1 Pa. $3.50

A PRACTICAL GUIDE FOR THE BEGINNING FARMER, Herbert Jacobs. Basic, extremely useful first book for anyone thinking about moving to the country and starting a farm. Simpler than Kains, with greater emphasis on country living in general. 246pp. 5⅜ x 8½.

23675-7 Pa. $3.50

HARDY BULBS, Louise Beebe Wilder. Fullest, most thorough book on plants grown from bulbs, corms, rhizomes and tubers. 40 genera and 335 species covered: selecting, cultivating, naturalizing; name, origins, blooming season, when to plant, special requirements. 127 illustrations. 432pp. 5⅜ x 8½.   23102-X Pa. $4.50

A GARDEN OF PLEASANT FLOWERS (PARADISI IN SOLE: PARADISUS TERRESTRIS), John Parkinson. Complete, unabridged reprint of first (1629) edition of earliest great English book on gardens and gardening. More than 1000 plants & flowers of Elizabethan, Jacobean garden fully described, most with woodcut illustrations. Botanically very reliable, a "speaking garden" of exceeding charm. 812 illustrations. 628pp. 8½ x 12¼.   23392-8 Clothbd. $25.00

MUSHROOMS, EDIBLE AND OTHERWISE, Miron E. Hard. Profusely illustrated, very useful guide to over 500 species of mushrooms growing in the Midwest and East. Nomenclature updated to 1976. 505 illustrations. 628pp. 6½ x 9¼. 23309-X Pa. $7.95

AN ILLUSTRATED FLORA OF THE NORTHERN UNITED STATES AND CANADA, Nathaniel L. Britton, Addison Brown. Encyclopedic work covers 4666 species, ferns on up. Everything. Full botanical information, illustration for each. This earlier edition is preferred by many to more recent revisions. 1913 edition. Over 4000 illustrations, total of 2087pp. 6⅛ x 9¼. 22642-5, 22643-3, 22644-1 Pa., Three-vol. set $24.00

MANUAL OF THE GRASSES OF THE UNITED STATES, A. S. Hitchcock, U.S. Dept. of Agriculture. The basic study of American grasses, both indigenous and escapes, cultivated and wild. Over 1400 species. Full descriptions, information. Over 1100 maps, illustrations. Total of 1051pp. 5⅜ x 8½. 22717-0, 22718-9 Pa., Two-vol. set $12.00

THE CACTACEAE,, Nathaniel L. Britton, John N. Rose. Exhaustive, definitive. Every cactus in the world. Full botanical descriptions. Thorough statement of nomenclatures, habitat, detailed finding keys. The one book needed by every cactus enthusiast. Over 1275 illustrations. Total of 1080pp. 8 x 10¼. 21191-6, 21192-4 Clothbd., Two-vol. set $35.00

AMERICAN MEDICINAL PLANTS, Charles F. Millspaugh. Full descriptions, 180 plants covered: history; physical description; methods of preparation with all chemical constituents extracted; all claimed curative or adverse effects. 180 full-page plates. Classification table. 804pp. 6½ x 9¼. 23034-1 Pa. $10.00

A MODERN HERBAL, Margaret Grieve. Much the fullest, most exact, most useful compilation of herbal material. Gigantic alphabetical encyclopedia, from aconite to zedoary, gives botanical information, medical properties, folklore, economic uses, and much else. Indispensable to serious reader. 161 illustrations. 888pp. 6½ x 9¼. (Available in U.S. only) 22798-7, 22799-5 Pa., Two-vol. set $11.00

THE HERBAL or GENERAL HISTORY OF PLANTS, John Gerard. The 1633 edition revised and enlarged by Thomas Johnson. Containing almost 2850 plant descriptions and 2705 superb illustrations, Gerard's *Herbal* is a monumental work, the book all modern English herbals are derived from, the one herbal every serious enthusiast should have in its entirety. Original editions are worth perhaps $750. 1678pp. 8½ x 12¼. 23147-X Clothbd. $50.00

MANUAL OF THE TREES OF NORTH AMERICA, Charles S. Sargent. The basic survey of every native tree and tree-like shrub, 717 species in all. Extremely full descriptions, information on habitat, growth, locales, economics, etc. Necessary to every serious tree lover. Over 100 finding keys. 783 illustrations. Total of 986pp. 5⅜ x 8½. 20277-1, 20278-X Pa., Two-vol. set $10.00

AMERICAN BIRD ENGRAVINGS, Alexander Wilson et al. All 76 plates. from Wilson's *American Ornithology* (1808-14), most important ornithological work before Audubon, plus 27 plates from the supplement (1825-33) by Charles Bonaparte. Over 250 birds portrayed. 8 plates also reproduced in full color. 111pp. 9⅜ x 12½.   23195-X Pa. $6.00

CRUICKSHANK'S PHOTOGRAPHS OF BIRDS OF AMERICA, Allan D. Cruickshank. Great ornithologist, photographer presents 177 closeups, groupings, panoramas, flightings, etc., of about 150 different birds. Expanded *Wings in the Wilderness*. Introduction by Helen G. Cruickshank. 191pp. 8¼ x 11.   23497-5 Pa. $6.00

AMERICAN WILDLIFE AND PLANTS, A. C. Martin, et al. Describes food habits of more than 1000 species of mammals, birds, fish. Special treatment of important food plants. Over 300 illustrations. 500pp. 5⅜ x 8½.
20793-5 Pa. $4.95

THE PEOPLE CALLED SHAKERS, Edward D. Andrews. Lifetime of research, definitive study of Shakers: origins, beliefs, practices, dances, social organization, furniture and crafts, impact on 19th-century USA, present heritage. Indispensable to student of American history, collector. 33 illustrations. 351pp. 5⅜ x 8½.   21081-2 Pa. $4.00

OLD NEW YORK IN EARLY PHOTOGRAPHS, Mary Black. New York City as it was in 1853-1901, through 196 wonderful photographs from N.-Y. Historical Society. Great Blizzard, Lincoln's funeral procession, great buildings. 228pp. 9 x 12.   22907-6 Pa. $7.95

MR. LINCOLN'S CAMERA MAN: MATHEW BRADY, Roy Meredith. Over 300 Brady photos reproduced directly from original negatives, photos. Jackson, Webster, Grant, Lee, Carnegie, Barnum; Lincoln; Battle Smoke, Death of Rebel Sniper, Atlanta Just After Capture. Lively commentary. 368pp. 8⅜ x 11¼.   23021-X Pa. $6.95

TRAVELS OF WILLIAM BARTRAM, William Bartram. From 1773-8, Bartram explored Northern Florida, Georgia, Carolinas, and reported on wild life, plants, Indians, early settlers. Basic account for period, entertaining reading. Edited by Mark Van Doren. 13 illustrations. 141pp. 5⅜ x 8½.   20013-2 Pa. $4.50

THE GENTLEMAN AND CABINET MAKER'S DIRECTOR, Thomas Chippendale. Full reprint, 1762 style book, most influential of all time; chairs, tables, sofas, mirrors, cabinets, etc. 200 plates, plus 24 photographs of surviving pieces. 249pp. 9⅞ x 12¾.   21601-2 Pa. $6.50

AMERICAN CARRIAGES, SLEIGHS, SULKIES AND CARTS, edited by Don H. Berkebile. 168 Victorian illustrations from catalogues, trade journals, fully captioned. Useful for artists. Author is Assoc. Curator, Div. of Transportation of Smithsonian Institution. 168pp. 8½ x 9½.
23328-6 Pa. $5.00

YUCATAN BEFORE AND AFTER THE CONQUEST, Diego de Landa. First English translation of basic book in Maya studies, the only significant account of Yucatan written in the early post-Conquest era. Translated by distinguished Maya scholar William Gates. Appendices, introduction, 4 maps and over 120 illustrations added by translator. 162pp. 5⅜ x 8½.
23622-6 Pa. $3.00

THE MALAY ARCHIPELAGO, Alfred R. Wallace. Spirited travel account by one of founders of modern biology. Touches on zoology, botany, ethnography, geography, and geology. 62 illustrations, maps. 515pp. 5⅜ x 8½.
20187-2 Pa. $6.95

THE DISCOVERY OF THE TOMB OF TUTANKHAMEN, Howard Carter, A. C. Mace. Accompany Carter in the thrill of discovery, as ruined passage suddenly reveals unique, untouched, fabulously rich tomb. Fascinating account, with 106 illustrations. New introduction by J. M. White. Total of 382pp. 5⅜ x 8½. (Available in U.S. only) 23500-9 Pa. $4.00

THE WORLD'S GREATEST SPEECHES, edited by Lewis Copeland and Lawrence W. Lamm. Vast collection of 278 speeches from Greeks up to present. Powerful and effective models; unique look at history. Revised to 1970. Indices. 842pp. 5⅜ x 8½. 20468-5 Pa. $6.95

THE 100 GREATEST ADVERTISEMENTS, Julian Watkins. The priceless ingredient; His master's voice; 99 44/100% pure; over 100 others. How they were written, their impact, etc. Remarkable record. 130 illustrations. 233pp. 7⅞ x 10 3/5. 20540-1 Pa. $5.00

CRUICKSHANK PRINTS FOR HAND COLORING, George Cruickshank. 18 illustrations, one side of a page, on fine-quality paper suitable for watercolors. Caricatures of people in society (c. 1820) full of trenchant wit. Very large format. 32pp. 11 x 16. 23684-6 Pa. $4.50

THIRTY-TWO COLOR POSTCARDS OF TWENTIETH-CENTURY AMERICAN ART, Whitney Museum of American Art. Reproduced in full color in postcard form are 31 art works and one shot of the museum. Calder, Hopper, Rauschenberg, others. Detachable. 16pp. 8¼ x 11.
23629-3 Pa. $2.50

MUSIC OF THE SPHERES: THE MATERIAL UNIVERSE FROM ATOM TO QUASAR SIMPLY EXPLAINED, Guy Murchie. Planets, stars, geology, atoms, radiation, relativity, quantum theory, light, antimatter, similar topics. 319 figures. 664pp. 5⅜ x 8½.
21809-0, 21810-4 Pa., Two-vol. set $10.00

EINSTEIN'S THEORY OF RELATIVITY, Max Born. Finest semi-technical account; covers Einstein, Lorentz, Minkowski, and others, with much detail, much explanation of ideas and math not readily available elsewhere on this level. For student, non-specialist. 376pp. 5⅜ x 8½.
60769-0 Pa. $4.00

THE STANDARD BOOK OF QUILT MAKING AND COLLECTING, Marguerite Ickis. Full information, full-sized patterns for making 46 traditional quilts, also 150 other patterns. Quilted cloths, lame, satin quilts, etc. 483 illustrations. 273pp. 6⅞ x 9⅝. 20582-7 Pa. $3.95

ENCYCLOPEDIA OF VICTORIAN NEEDLEWORK, S. Caulfield, Blanche Saward. Simply inexhaustible gigantic alphabetical coverage of every traditional needlecraft—stitches, materials, methods, tools, types of work; definitions, many projects to be made. 1200 illustrations; double-columned text. 697pp. 8⅛ x 11. 22800-2, 22801-0 Pa., Two-vol. set $12.00

MECHANICK EXERCISES ON THE WHOLE ART OF PRINTING, Joseph Moxon. First complete book (1683-4) ever written about typography, a compendium of everything known about printing at the latter part of 17th century. Reprint of 2nd (1962) Oxford Univ. Press edition. 74 illustrations. Total of 550pp. 6⅛ x 9¼. 23617-X Pa. $7.95

PAPERMAKING, Dard Hunter. Definitive book on the subject by the foremost authority in the field. Chapters dealing with every aspect of history of craft in every part of the world. Over 320 illustrations. 2nd, revised and enlarged (1947) edition. 672pp. 5⅜ x 8½. 23619-6 Pa. $7.95

THE ART DECO STYLE, edited by Theodore Menten. Furniture, jewelry, metalwork, ceramics, fabrics, lighting fixtures, interior decors, exteriors, graphics from pure French sources. Best sampling around. Over 400 photographs. 183pp. 8⅜ x 11¼. 22824-X Pa. $5.00

Prices subject to change without notice.